AMY'S BiG BROTHER

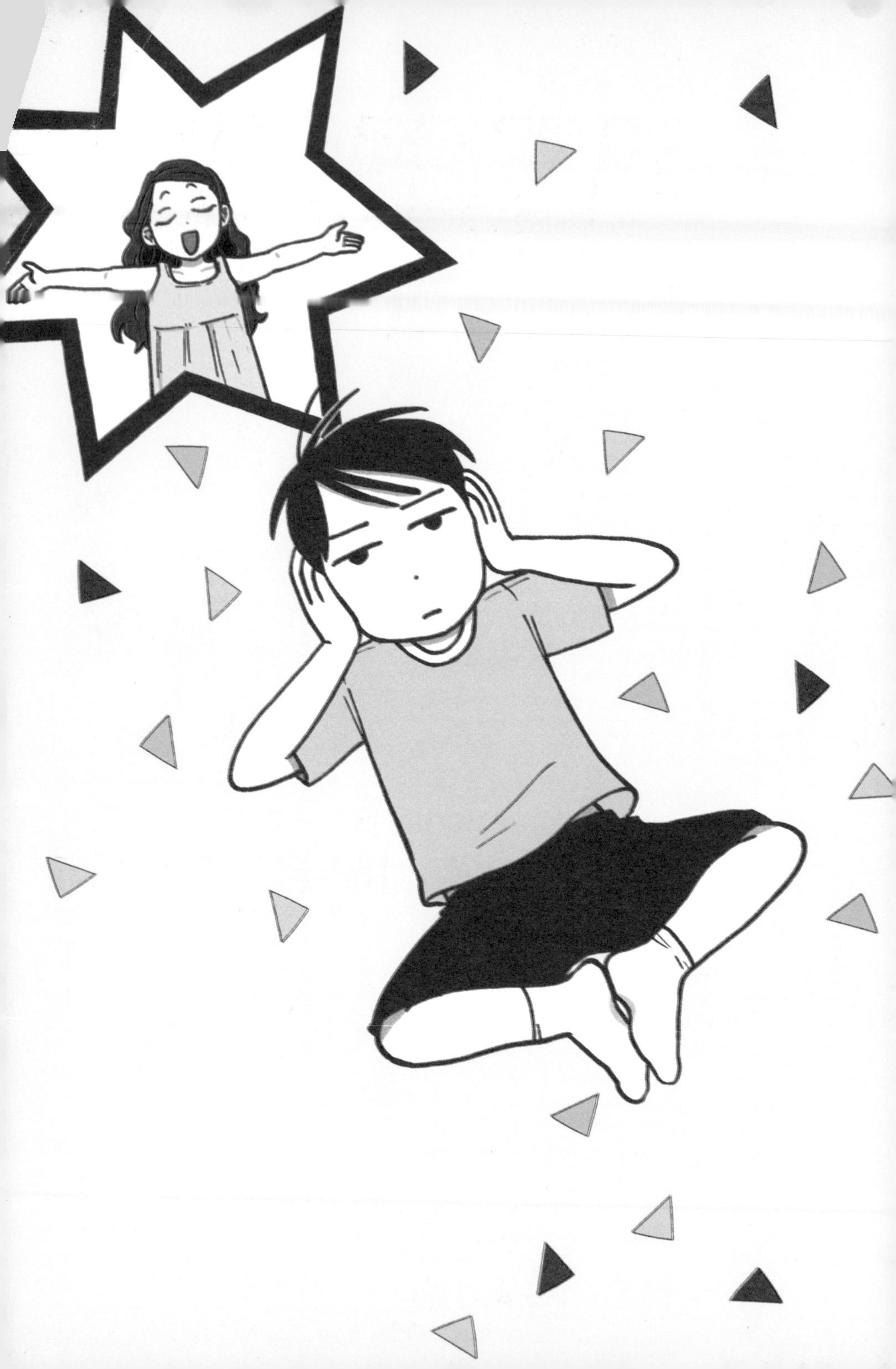

AMY'S BiG BROTHER

Story & art by
BonHyung Jeong

New York

AMY'S BIG BROTHER

BONHYUNG JEONG

JY
150 West 30th Street, 19th Floor
New York, NY 10001

Visit us at jyforkids.com
facebook.com/jyforkids • twitter.com/jyforkids
jyforkids.tumblr.com • instagram.com/jyforkids

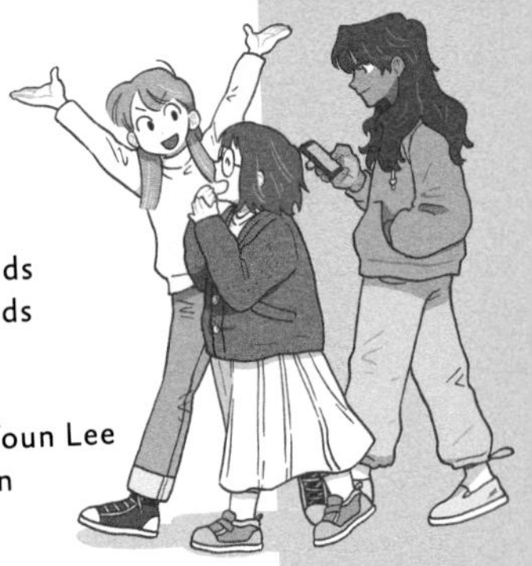

First JY Edition: December 2023
Edited by Yen Press Editorial: Won Young Seo, JuYoun Lee
Designed by Yen Press Design: Wendy Chan

JY is an imprint of Yen Press, LLC.
The JY name and logo are trademarks of Yen Press, LLC.

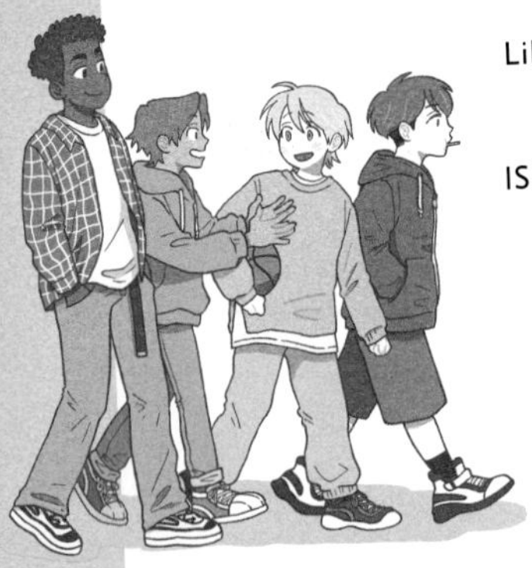

Library of Congress Control Number:
2023946105

ISBNs: 978-1-9753-5110-6 (hardcover)
978-1-9753-5109-0 (paperback)
978-1-9753-5111-3 (ebook)

1 3 5 7 9 10 8 6 4 2

WOR

Printed in the
United States of America

Table of Contents

Chapter 1

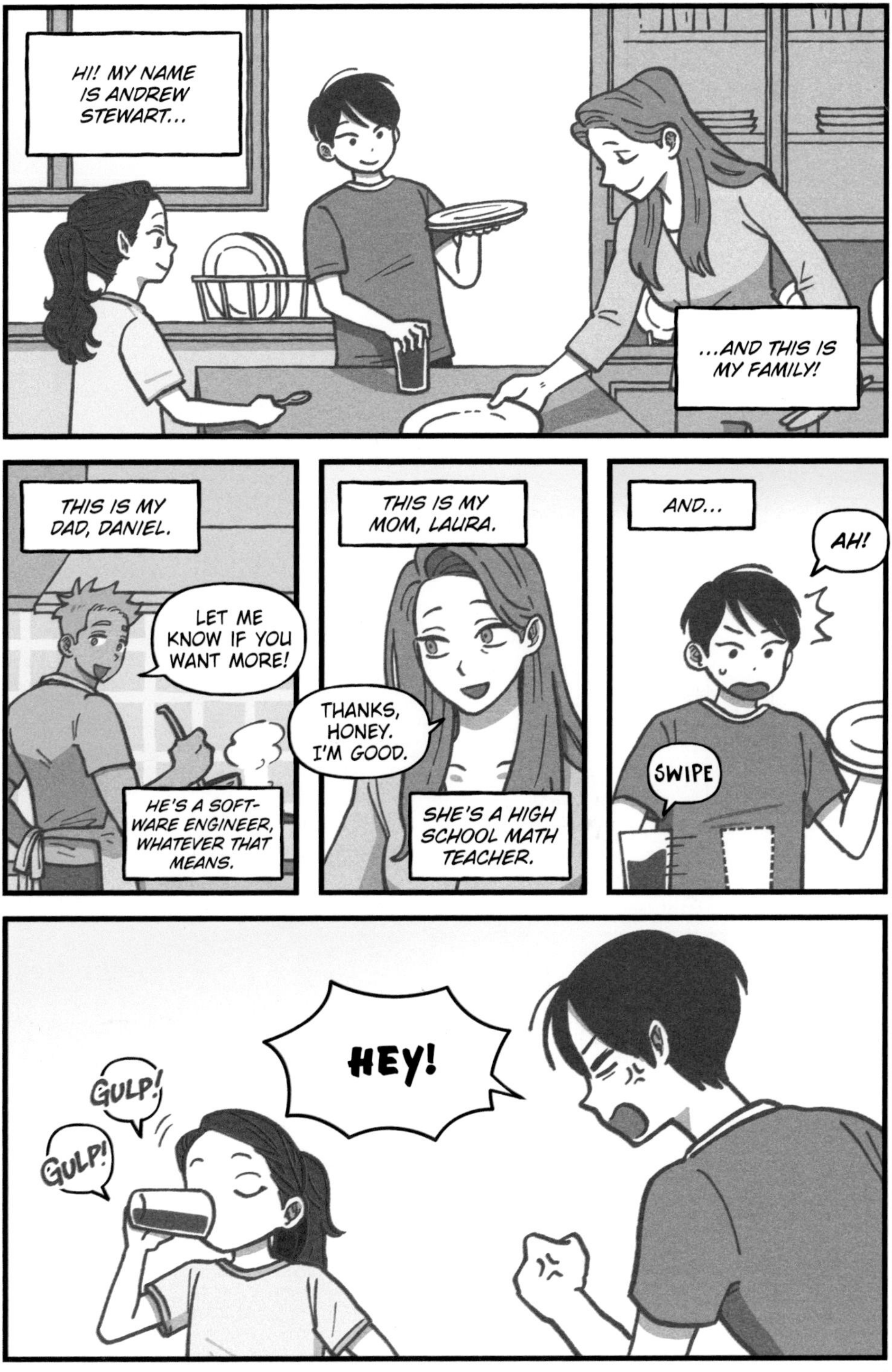
HI! MY NAME IS ANDREW STEWART...
...AND THIS IS MY FAMILY!
THIS IS MY DAD, DANIEL.
LET ME KNOW IF YOU WANT MORE!
HE'S A SOFT-WARE ENGINEER, WHATEVER THAT MEANS.
THIS IS MY MOM, LAURA.
THANKS, HONEY. I'M GOOD.
SHE'S A HIGH SCHOOL MATH TEACHER.
AND...
AH!
SWIPE
GULP!
GULP!
HEY!

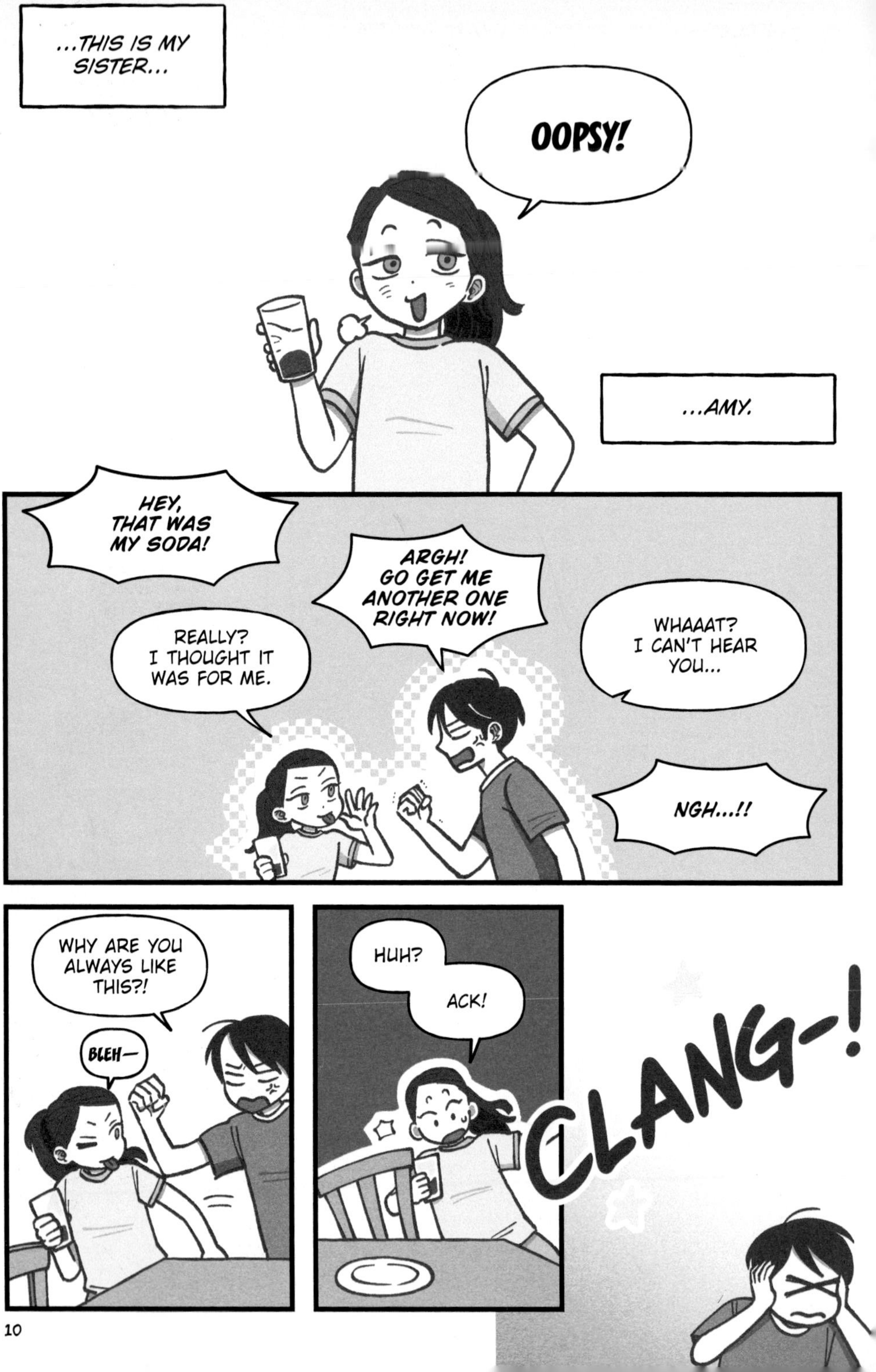
...THIS IS MY SISTER...
OOPSY!
...AMY.
HEY, THAT WAS MY SODA!
ARGH! GO GET ME ANOTHER ONE RIGHT NOW!
REALLY? I THOUGHT IT WAS FOR ME.
WHAAAT? I CAN'T HEAR YOU...
NGH...!!
WHY ARE YOU ALWAYS LIKE THIS?!
BLEH—
HUH?
ACK!
CLANG-!

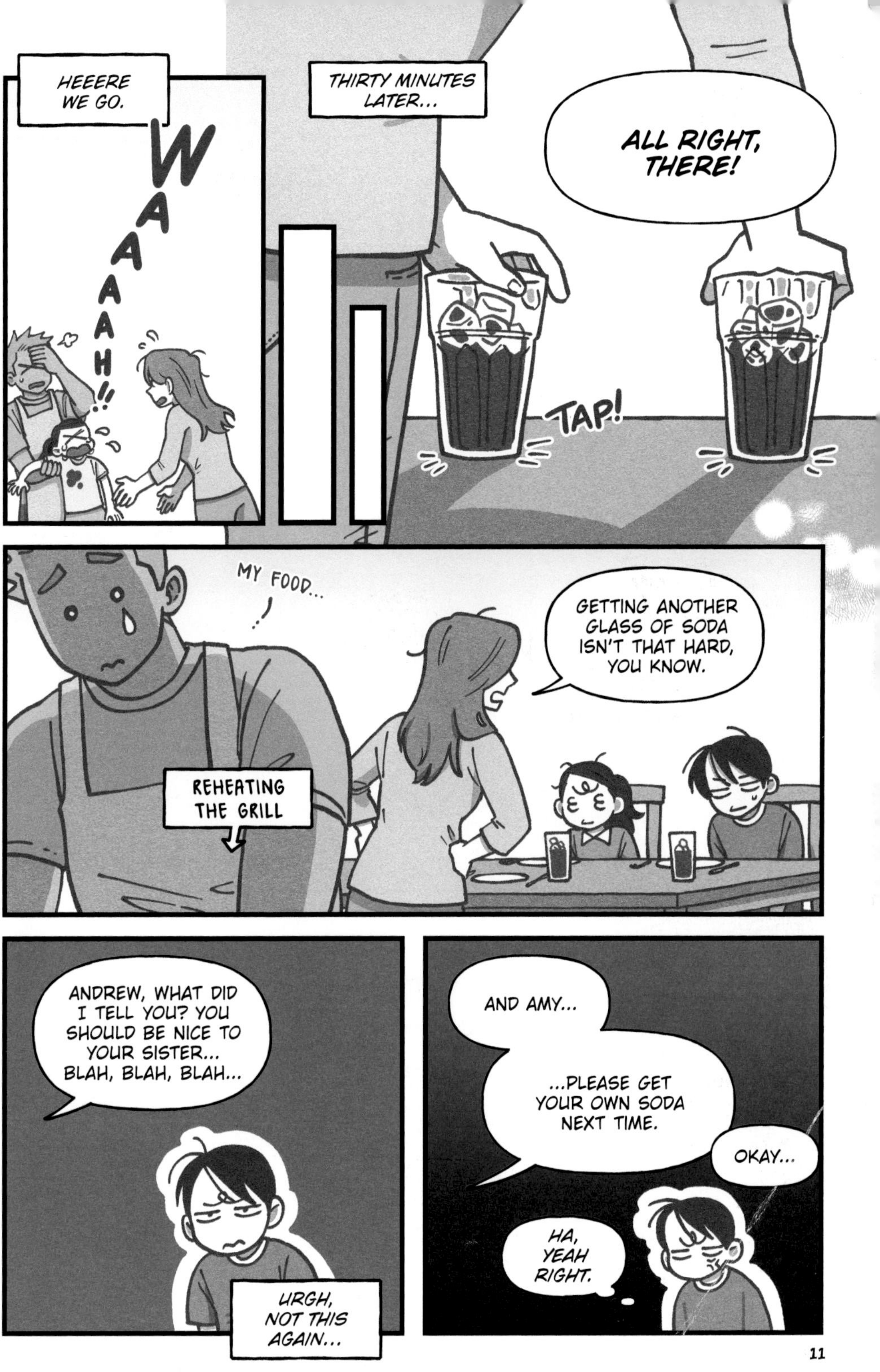
HEEERE WE GO.
WAAAAAH!!
THIRTY MINUTES LATER...
ALL RIGHT, THERE!
TAP!
MY FOOD...
GETTING ANOTHER GLASS OF SODA ISN'T THAT HARD, YOU KNOW.
REHEATING THE GRILL
ANDREW, WHAT DID I TELL YOU? YOU SHOULD BE NICE TO YOUR SISTER... BLAH, BLAH, BLAH...
URGH, NOT THIS AGAIN...
AND AMY...
...PLEASE GET YOUR OWN SODA NEXT TIME.
OKAY...
HA, YEAH RIGHT.

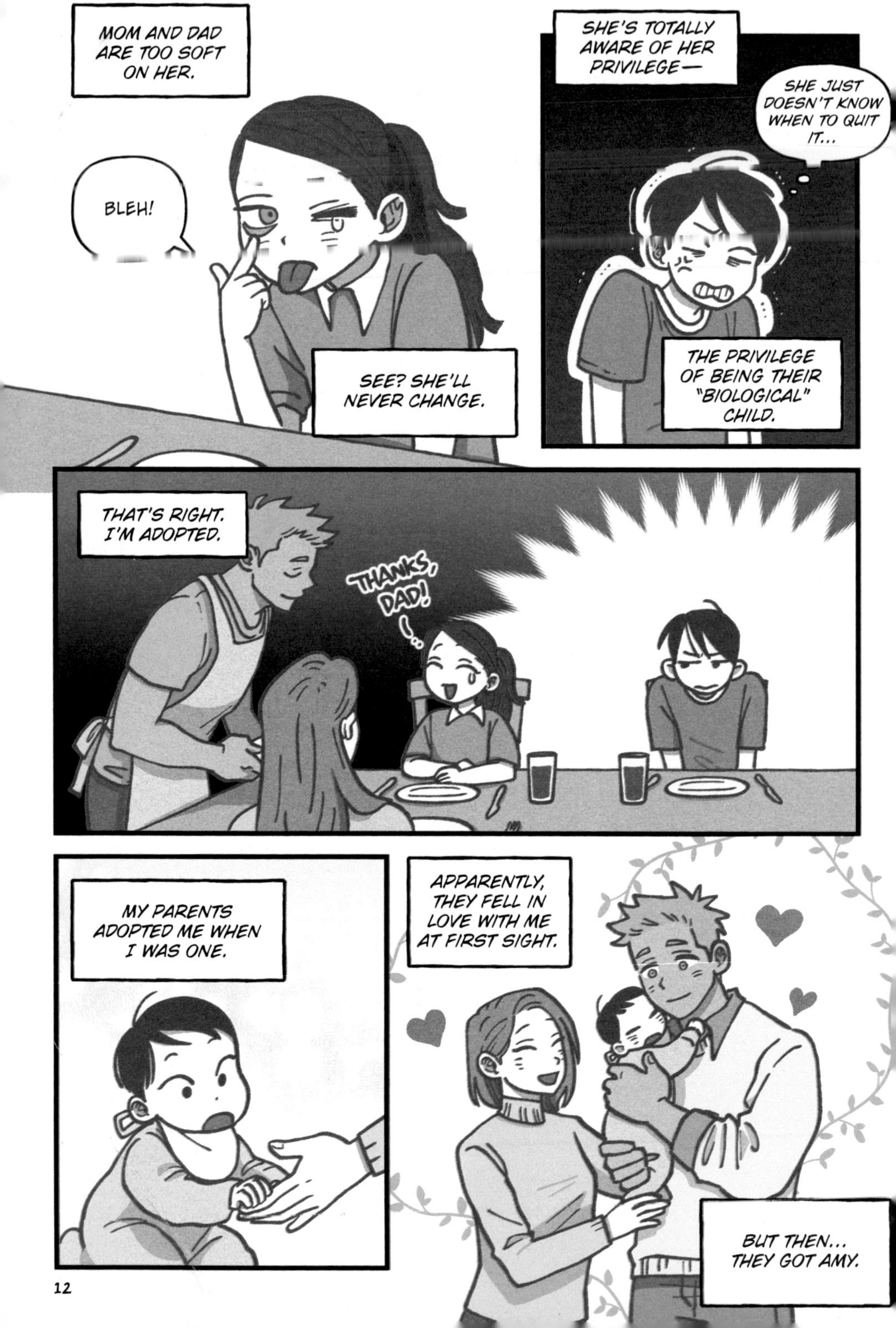
MOM AND DAD ARE TOO SOFT ON HER.
BLEH!
SEE? SHE'LL NEVER CHANGE.
SHE'S TOTALLY AWARE OF HER PRIVILEGE—
SHE JUST DOESN'T KNOW WHEN TO QUIT IT...
THE PRIVILEGE OF BEING THEIR "BIOLOGICAL" CHILD.
THAT'S RIGHT. I'M ADOPTED.
THANKS, DAD!
MY PARENTS ADOPTED ME WHEN I WAS ONE.
APPARENTLY, THEY FELL IN LOVE WITH ME AT FIRST SIGHT.
BUT THEN... THEY GOT AMY.

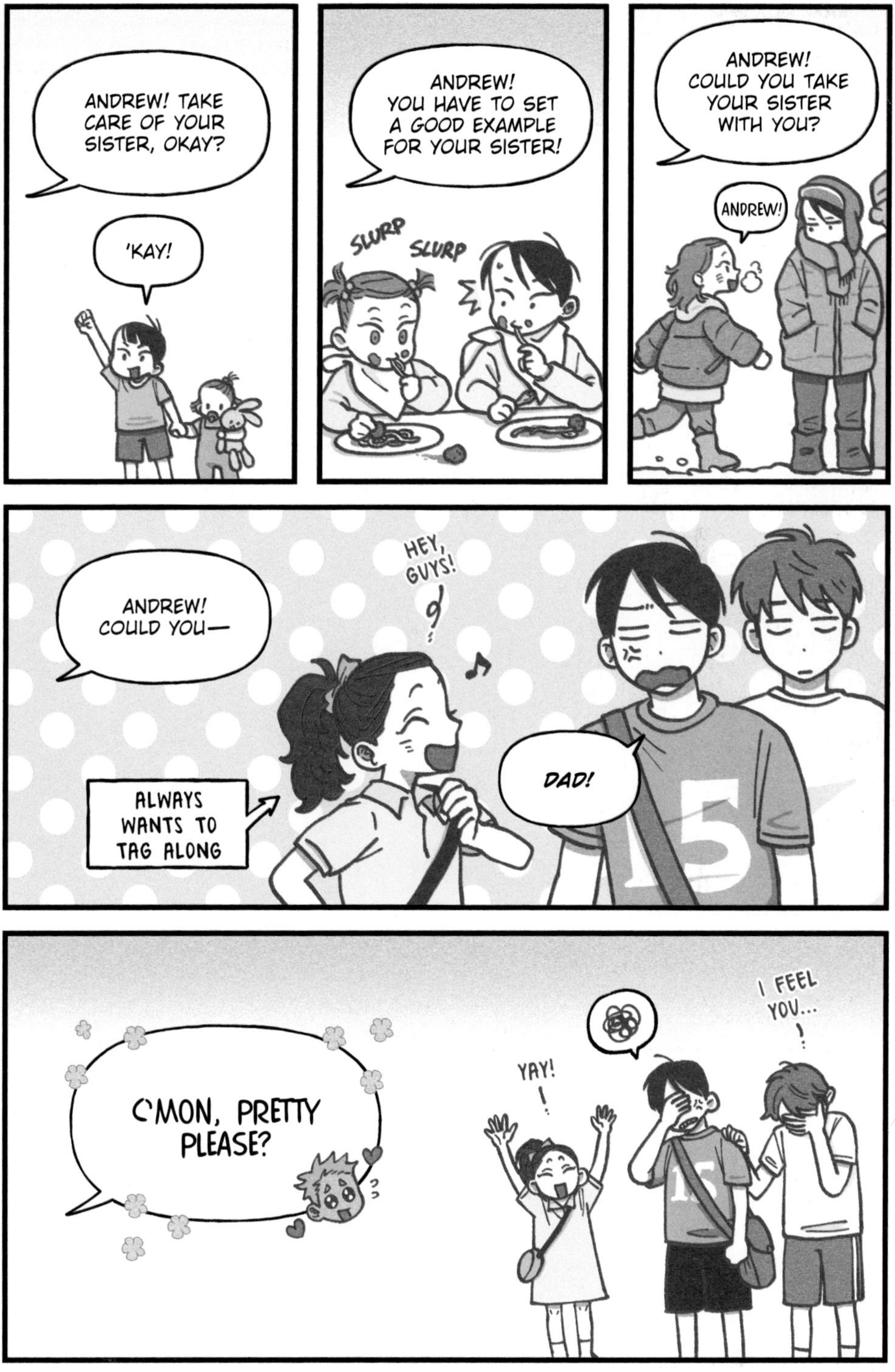
ANDREW! TAKE CARE OF YOUR SISTER, OKAY?
'KAY!
ANDREW! YOU HAVE TO SET A GOOD EXAMPLE FOR YOUR SISTER!
SLURP
SLURP
ANDREW! COULD YOU TAKE YOUR SISTER WITH YOU?
ANDREW!
ANDREW! COULD YOU—
HEY, GUYS!
ALWAYS WANTS TO TAG ALONG
DAD!
C'MON, PRETTY PLEASE?
YAY!
I FEEL YOU...

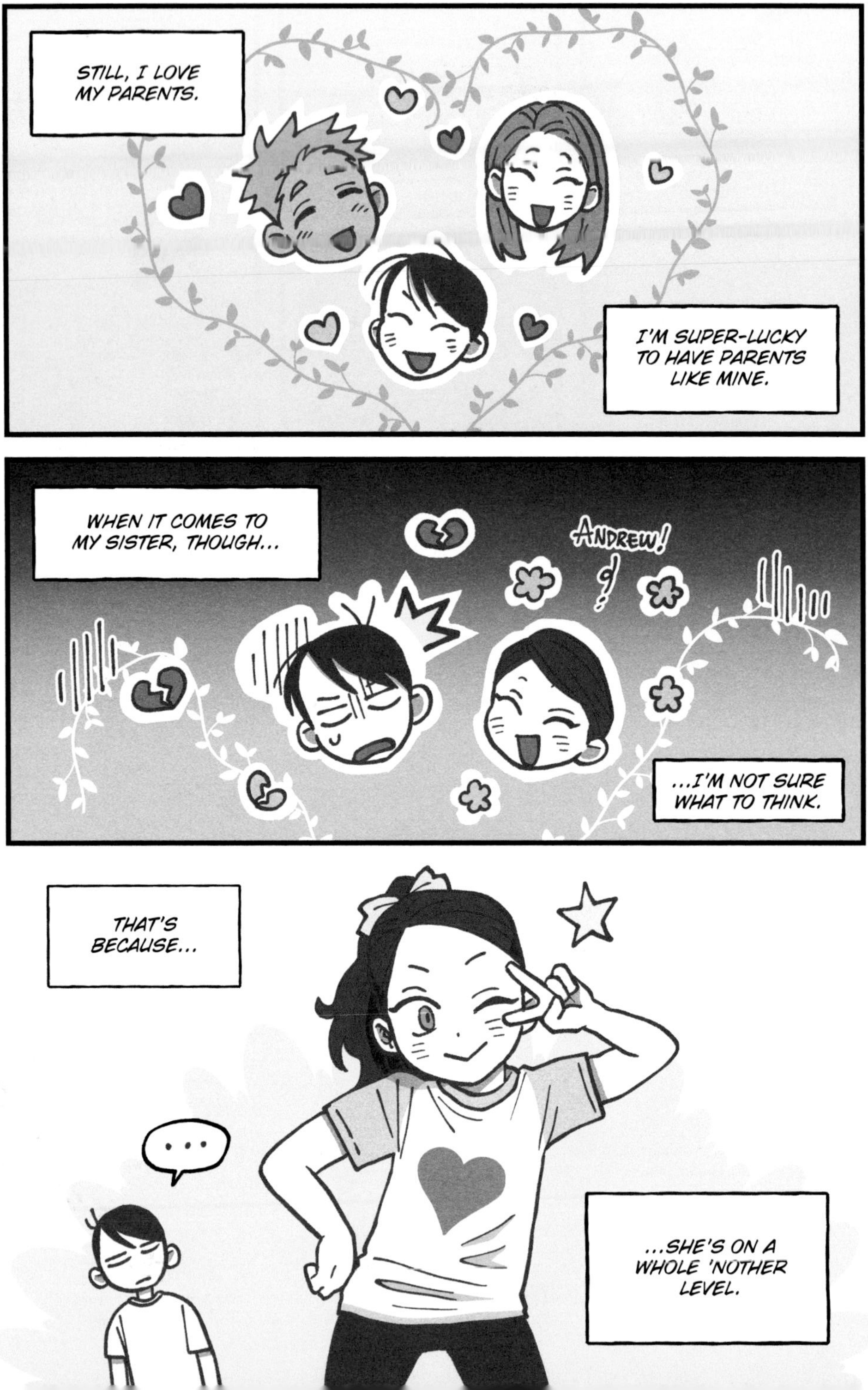
STILL, I LOVE MY PARENTS.
I'M SUPER-LUCKY TO HAVE PARENTS LIKE MINE.
WHEN IT COMES TO MY SISTER, THOUGH...
ANDREW!
...I'M NOT SURE WHAT TO THINK.
THAT'S BECAUSE...
...
...SHE'S ON A WHOLE 'NOTHER LEVEL.

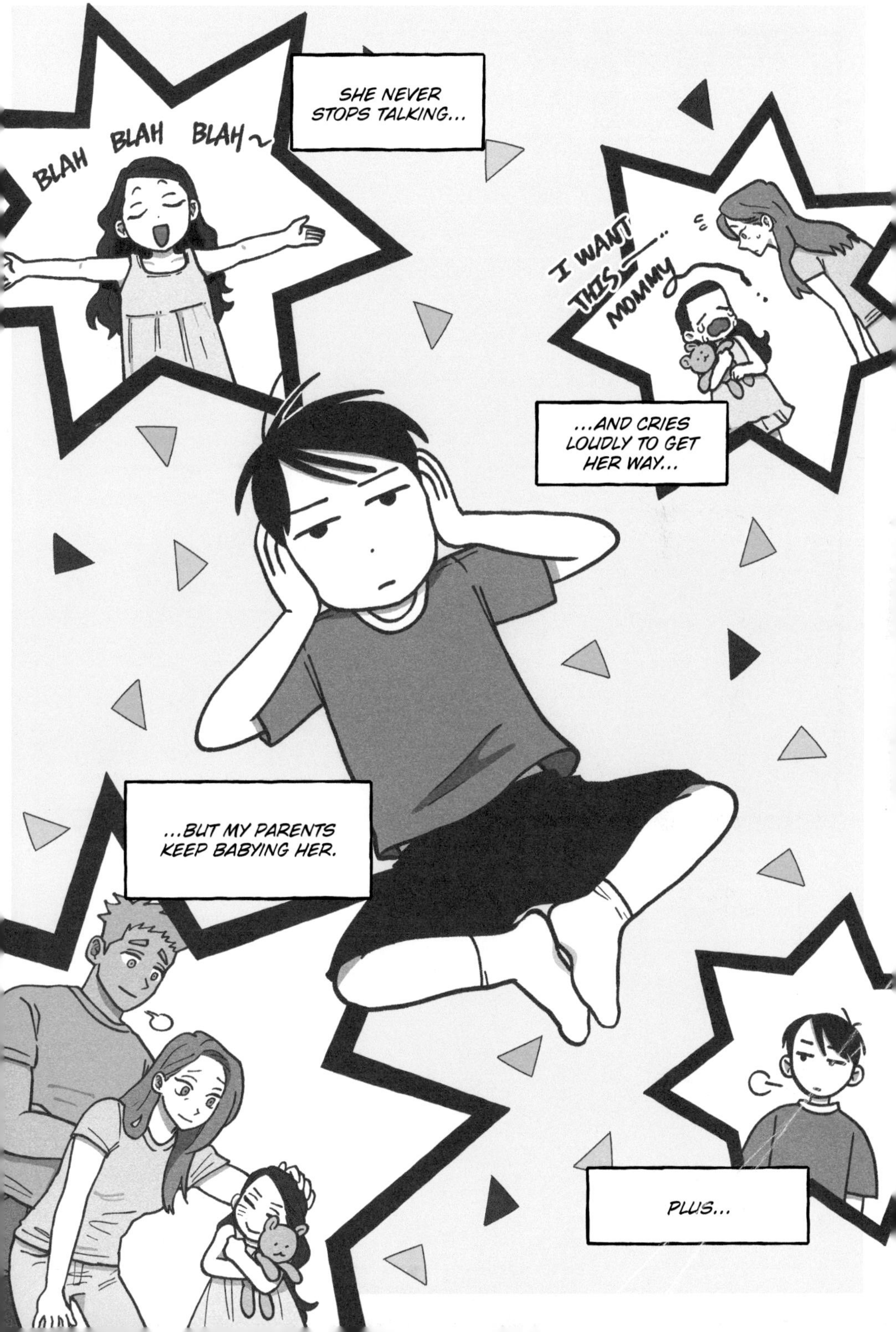
SHE NEVER STOPS TALKING...
BLAH BLAH BLAH~
I WANT THIS MOMMY
...AND CRIES LOUDLY TO GET HER WAY...
...BUT MY PARENTS KEEP BABYING HER.
PLUS...

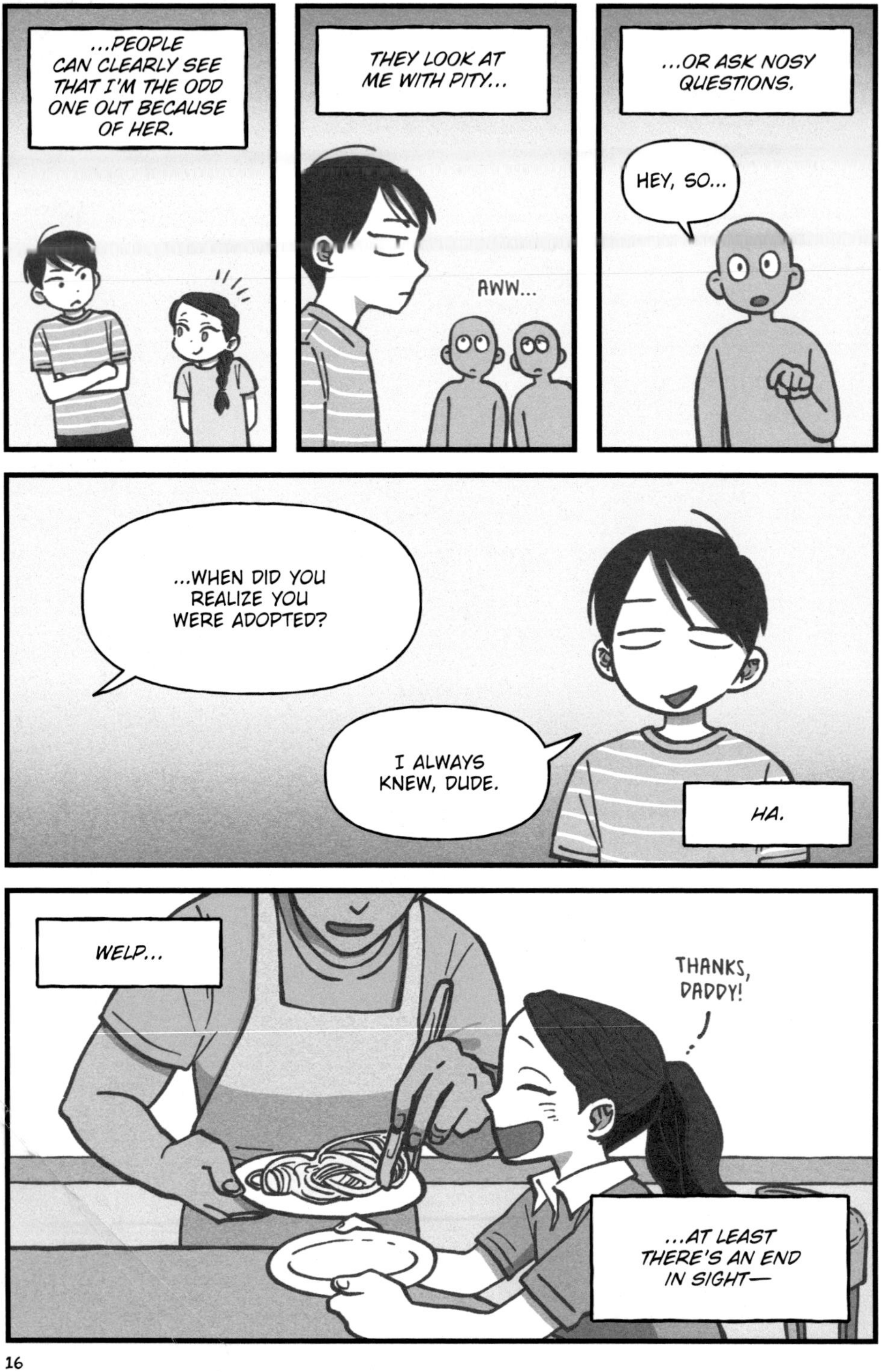
...PEOPLE CAN CLEARLY SEE THAT I'M THE ODD ONE OUT BECAUSE OF HER.
THEY LOOK AT ME WITH PITY...
AWW...
...OR ASK NOSY QUESTIONS.
HEY, SO...
...WHEN DID YOU REALIZE YOU WERE ADOPTED?
I ALWAYS KNEW, DUDE.
HA.
WELP...
THANKS, DADDY!
...AT LEAST THERE'S AN END IN SIGHT—

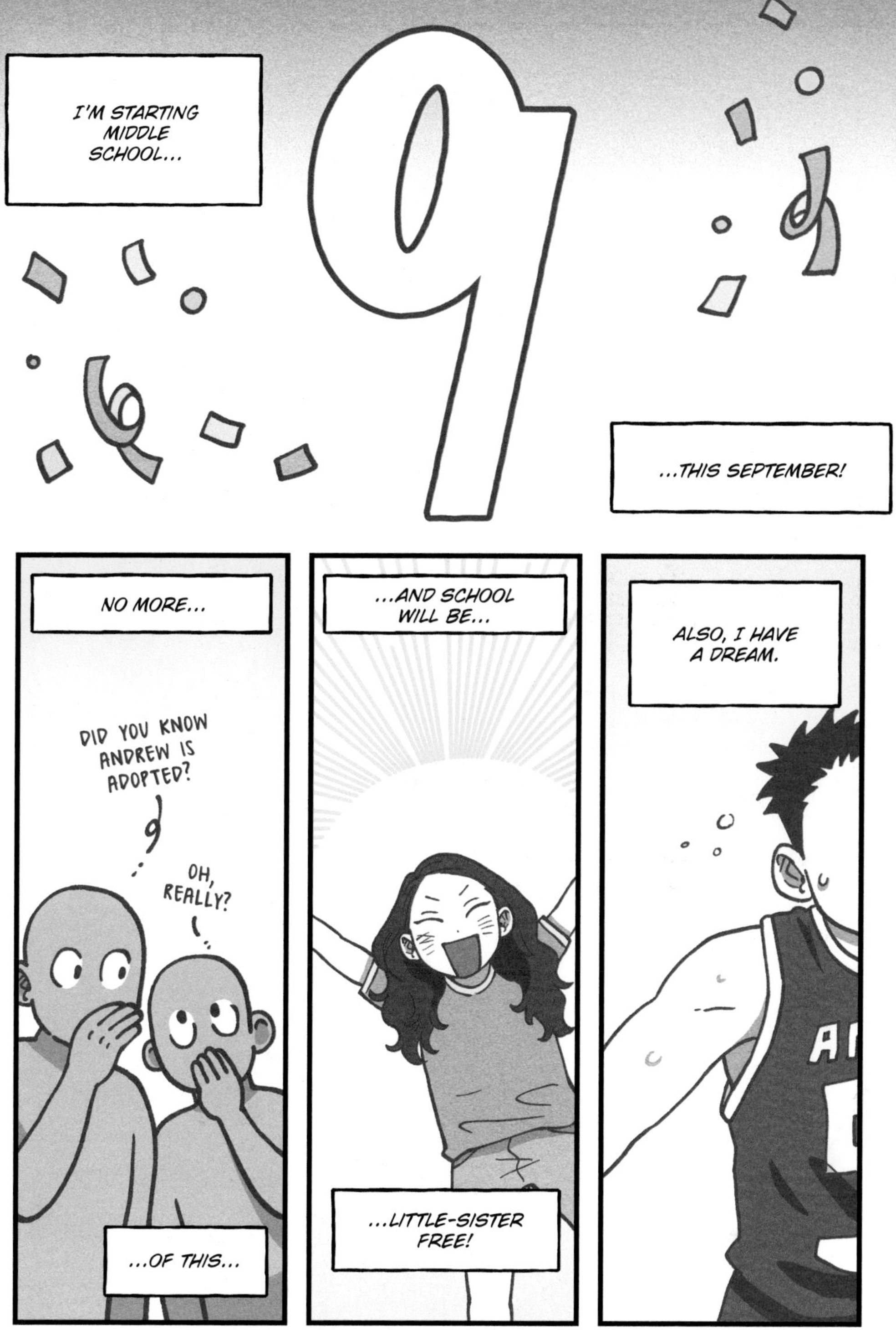

I'M STARTING MIDDLE SCHOOL...
9
...THIS SEPTEMBER!
NO MORE...
DID YOU KNOW ANDREW IS ADOPTED?
OH, REALLY?
...OF THIS...
...AND SCHOOL WILL BE...
...LITTLE-SISTER FREE!
ALSO, I HAVE A DREAM.

I WANT TO BE A STAR BASKETBALL PLAYER ONE DAY...

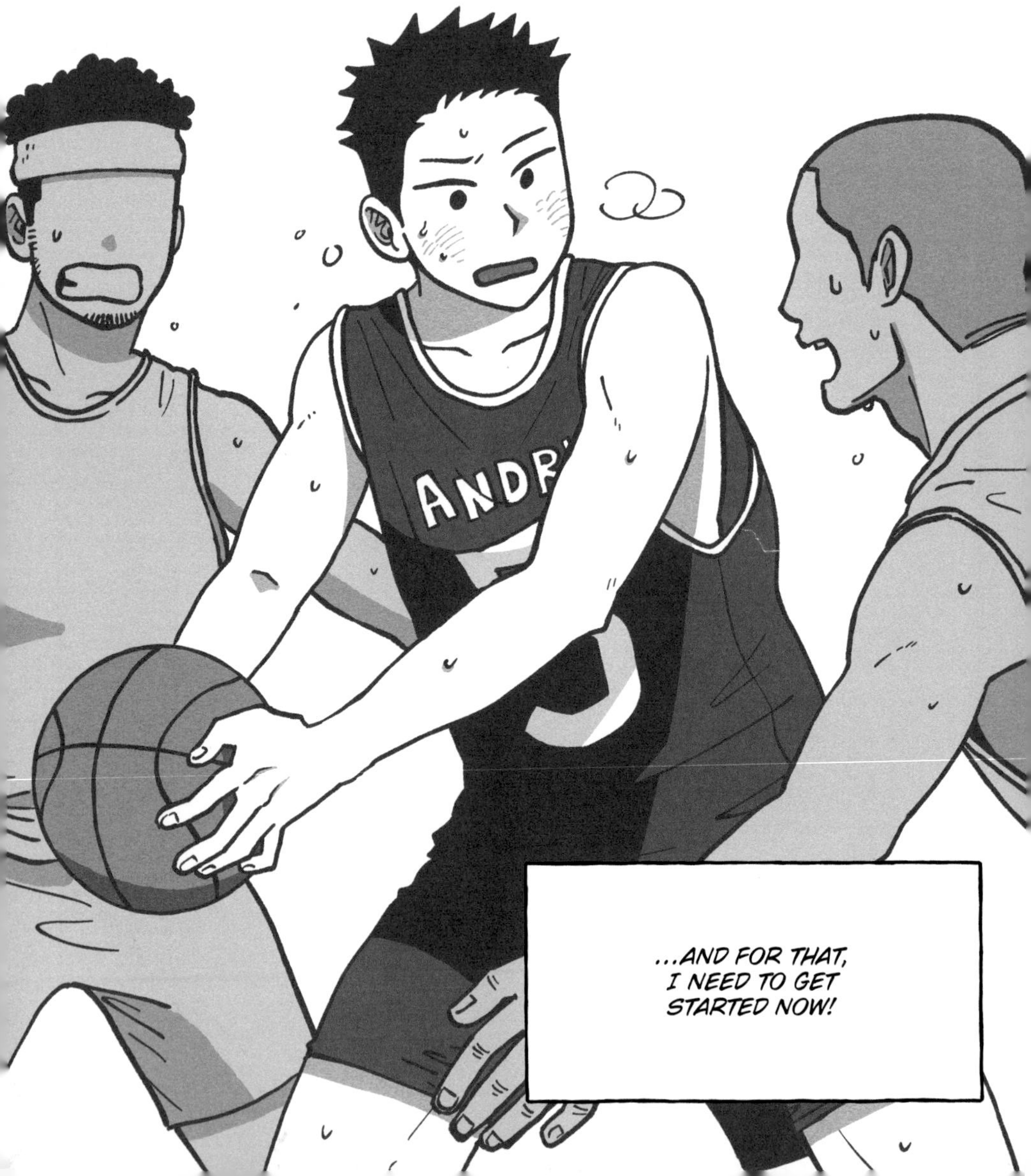
ANDR
...AND FOR THAT, I NEED TO GET STARTED NOW!

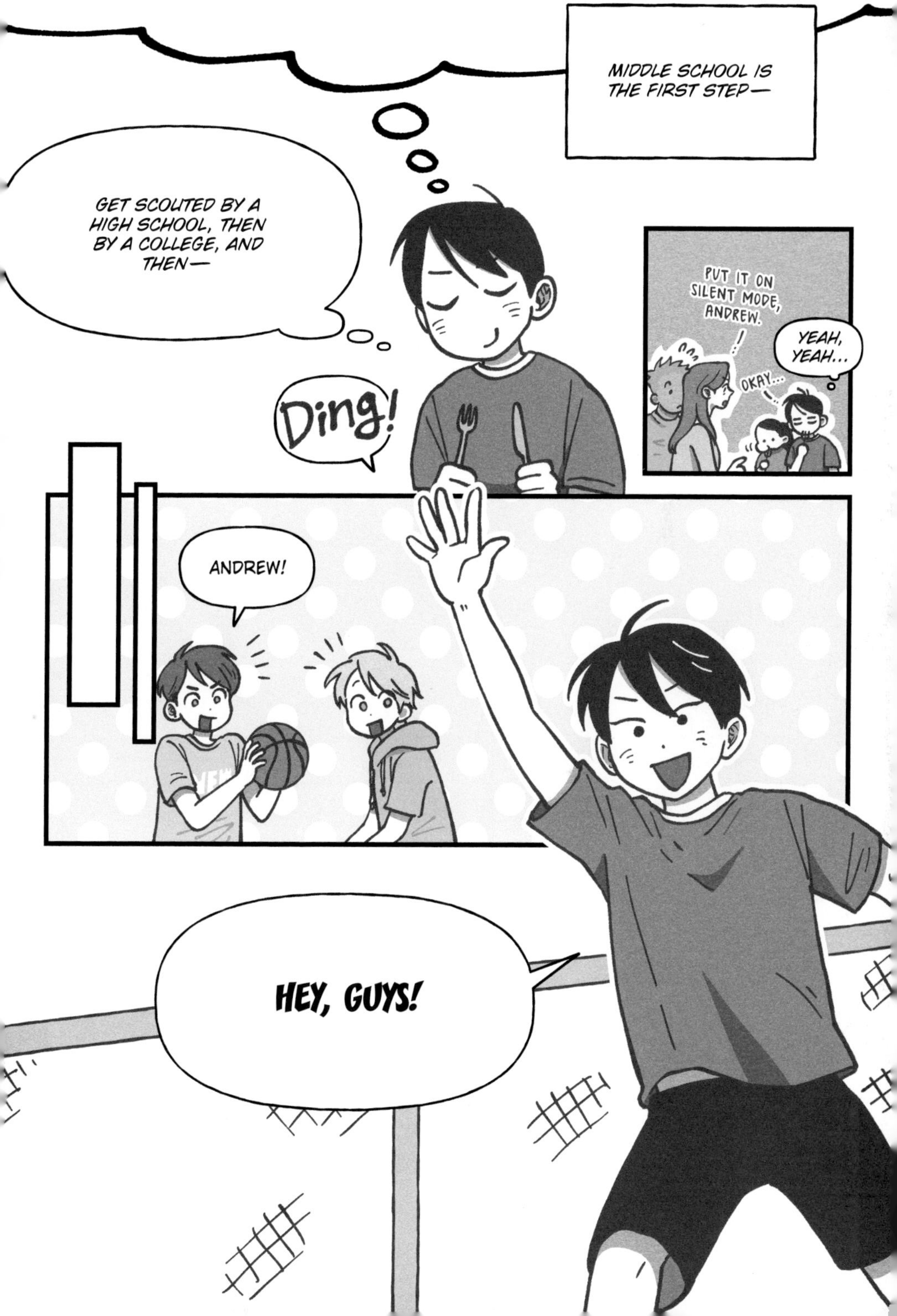
MIDDLE SCHOOL IS THE FIRST STEP—
GET SCOUTED BY A HIGH SCHOOL, THEN BY A COLLEGE, AND THEN—
Ding!
PUT IT ON SILENT MODE, ANDREW.
YEAH, YEAH...
OKAY...
ANDREW!
HEY, GUYS!

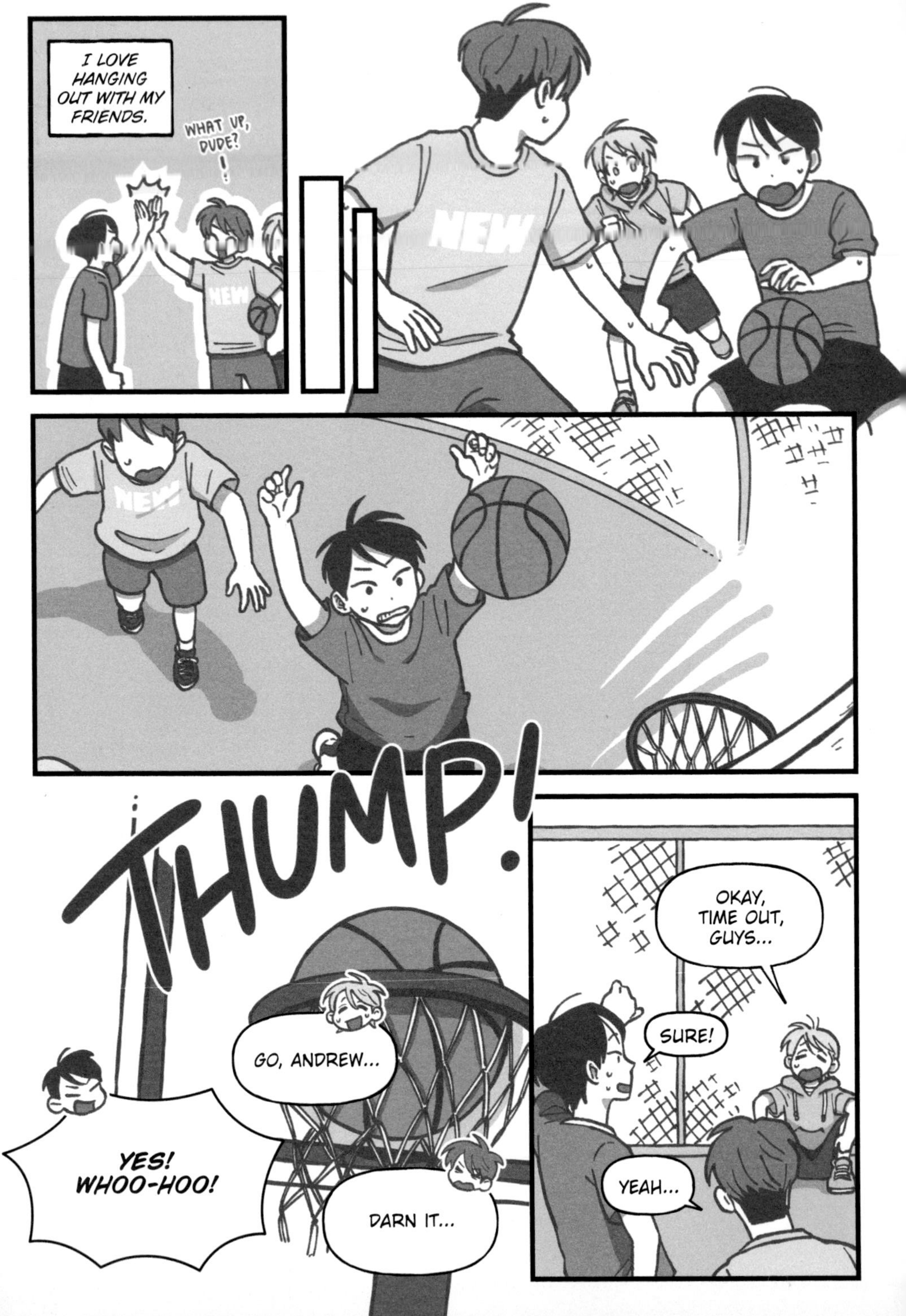
I LOVE HANGING OUT WITH MY FRIENDS.
WHAT UP, DUDE?
THUMP!
GO, ANDREW...
YES! WHOO-HOO!
DARN IT...
OKAY, TIME OUT, GUYS...
SURE!
YEAH...

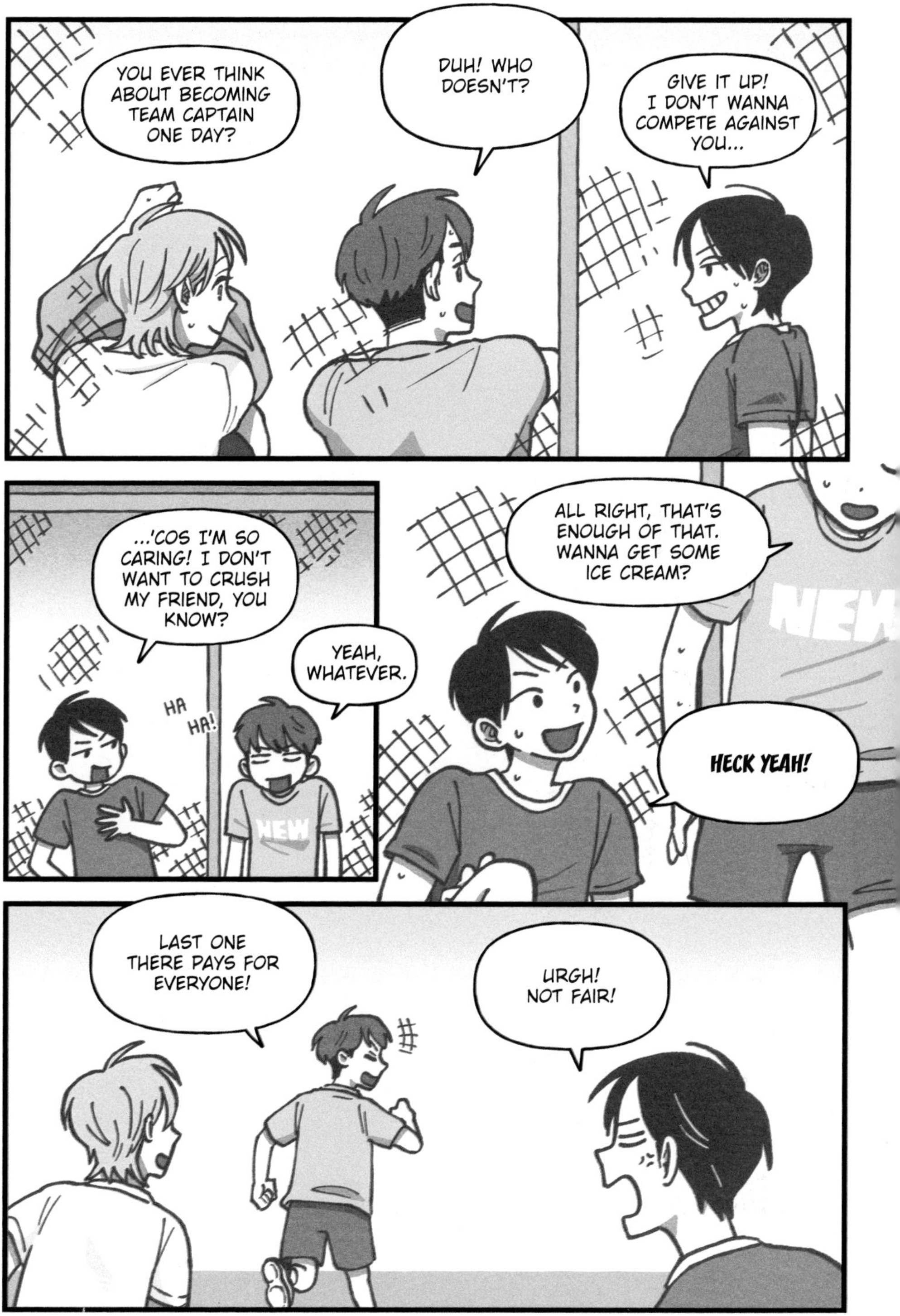
YOU EVER THINK ABOUT BECOMING TEAM CAPTAIN ONE DAY?
DUH! WHO DOESN'T?
GIVE IT UP! I DON'T WANNA COMPETE AGAINST YOU...
...'COS I'M SO CARING! I DON'T WANT TO CRUSH MY FRIEND, YOU KNOW?
HA HA!
YEAH, WHATEVER.
NEW
ALL RIGHT, THAT'S ENOUGH OF THAT. WANNA GET SOME ICE CREAM?
NEW
HECK YEAH!
LAST ONE THERE PAYS FOR EVERYONE!
URGH! NOT FAIR!

AHHHHH,

HA

HA

HA

WAIT
FOR
ME
~!

HA

Chapter 2

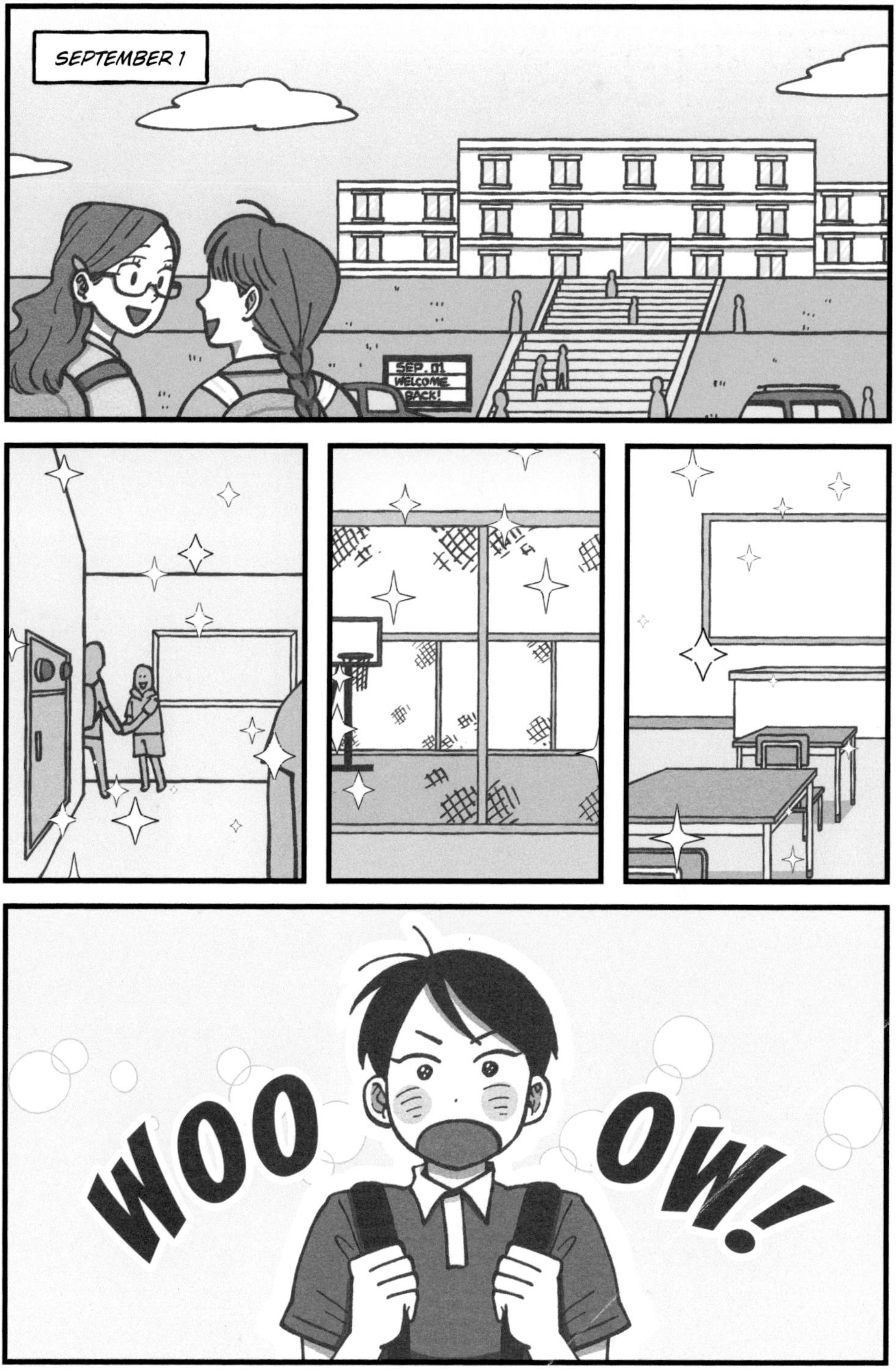
SEPTEMBER 1
SEP. 01
WELCOME
BACK!
WOO
OW!

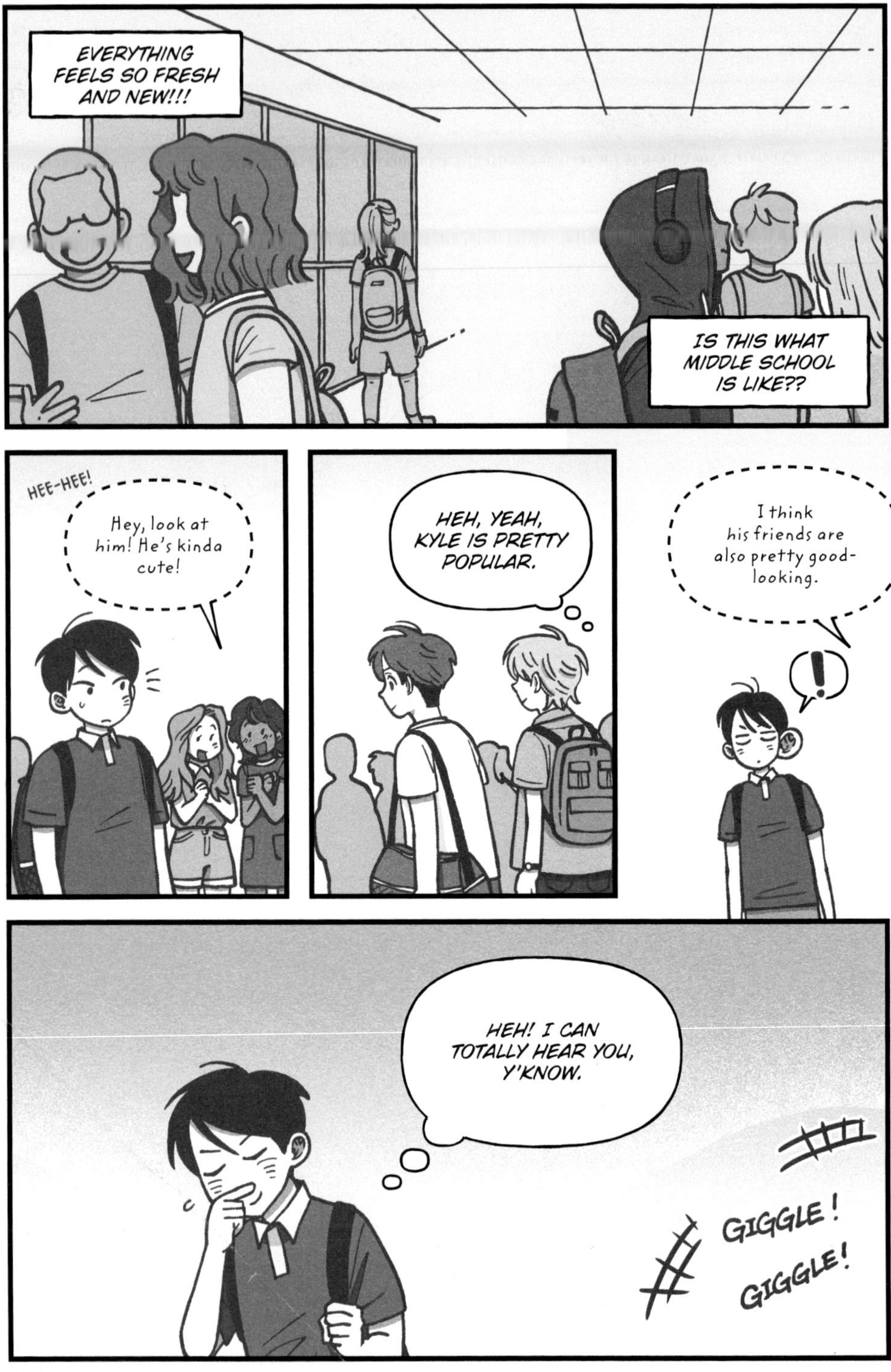
EVERYTHING FEELS SO FRESH AND NEW!!!
IS THIS WHAT MIDDLE SCHOOL IS LIKE??
HEE-HEE!
Hey, look at him! He's kinda cute!
HEH, YEAH, KYLE IS PRETTY POPULAR.
I think his friends are also pretty good-looking.
!
HEH! I CAN TOTALLY HEAR YOU, Y'KNOW.
GIGGLE!
GIGGLE!

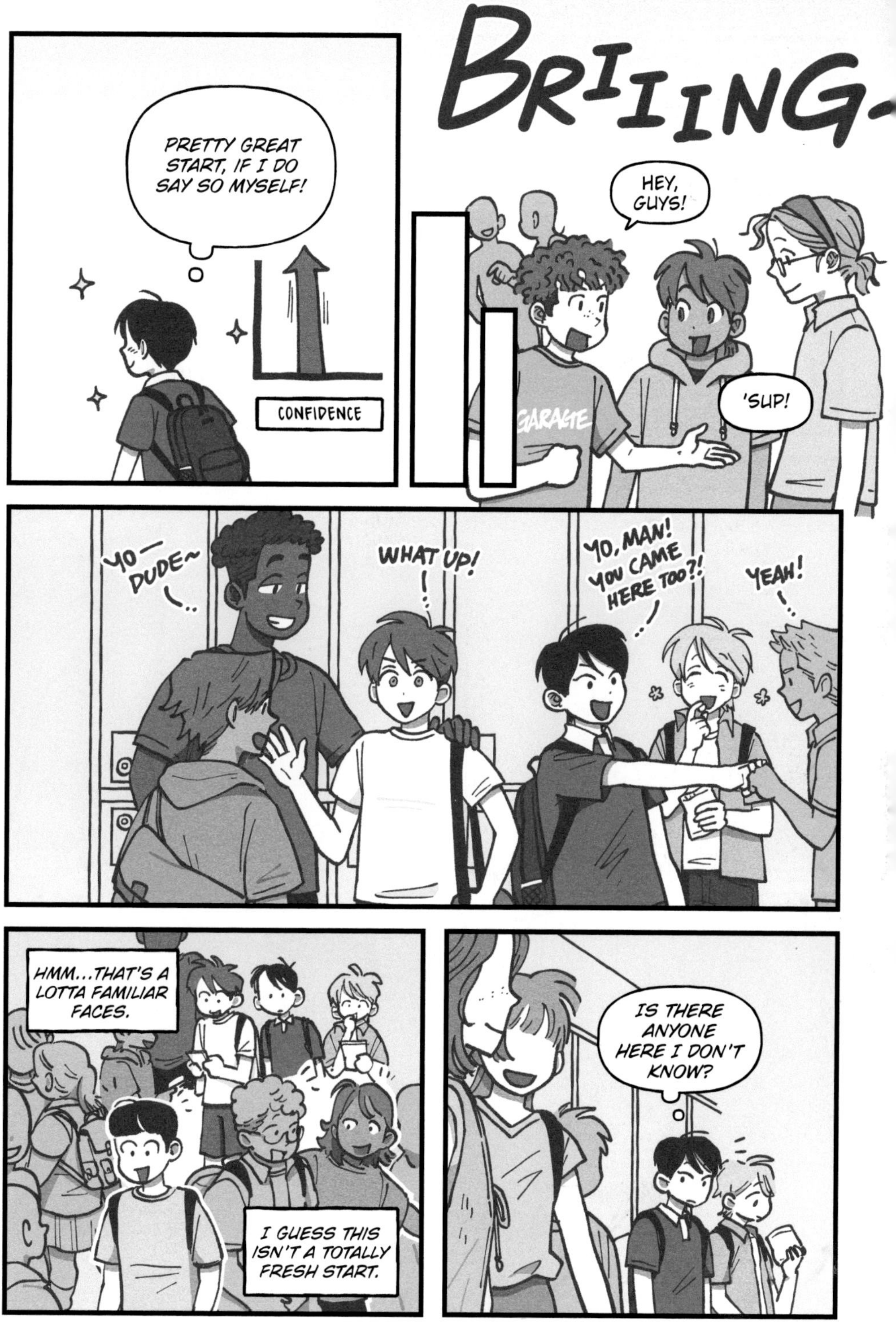
PRETTY GREAT START, IF I DO SAY SO MYSELF!
CONFIDENCE
BRIIING-
HEY, GUYS!
GARAGE
'SUP!
YO— DUDE~
WHAT UP!
YO, MAN! YOU CAME HERE TOO?!
YEAH!
HMM...THAT'S A LOTTA FAMILIAR FACES.
I GUESS THIS ISN'T A TOTALLY FRESH START.
IS THERE ANYONE HERE I DON'T KNOW?

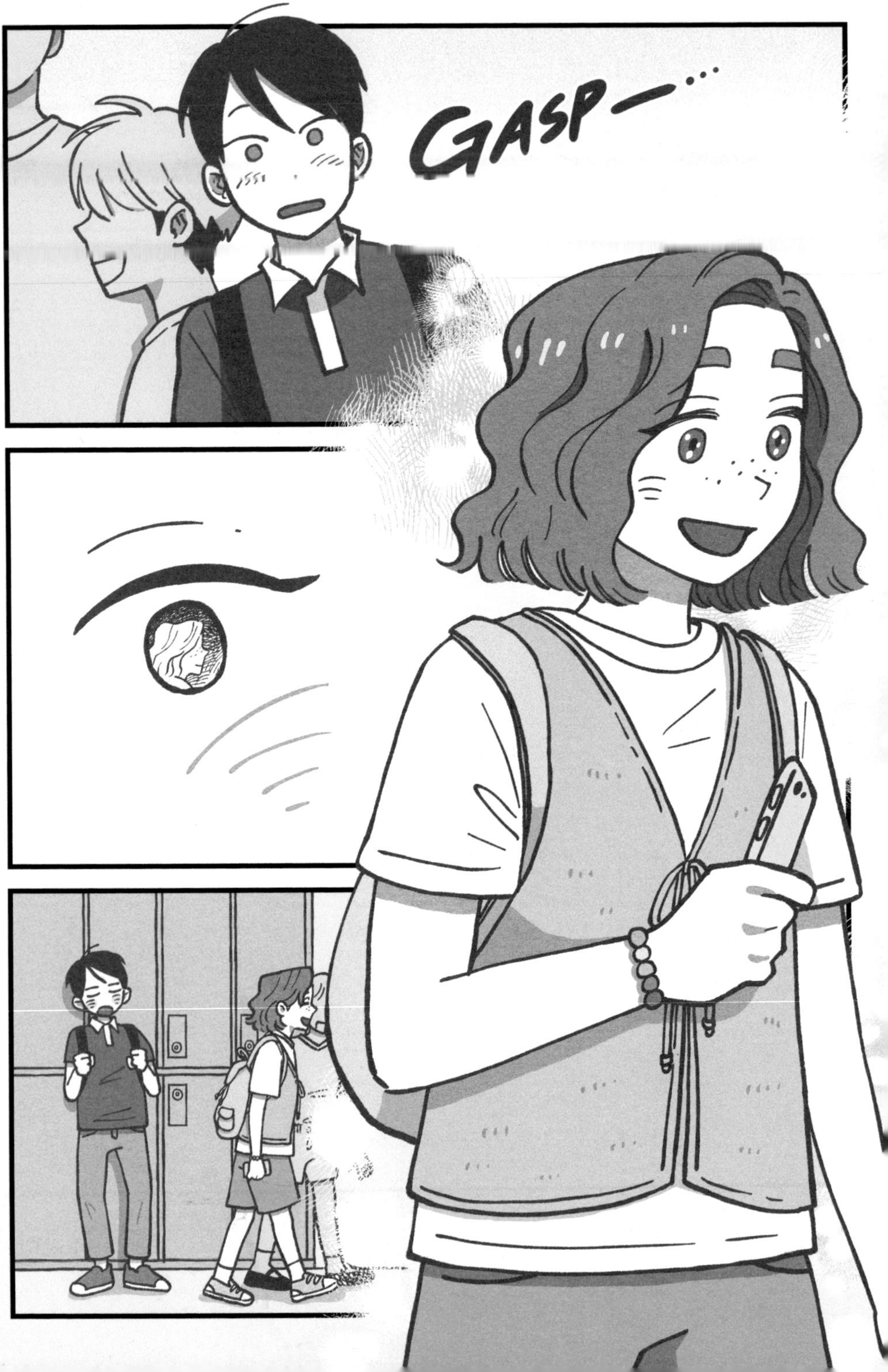
GASP—...

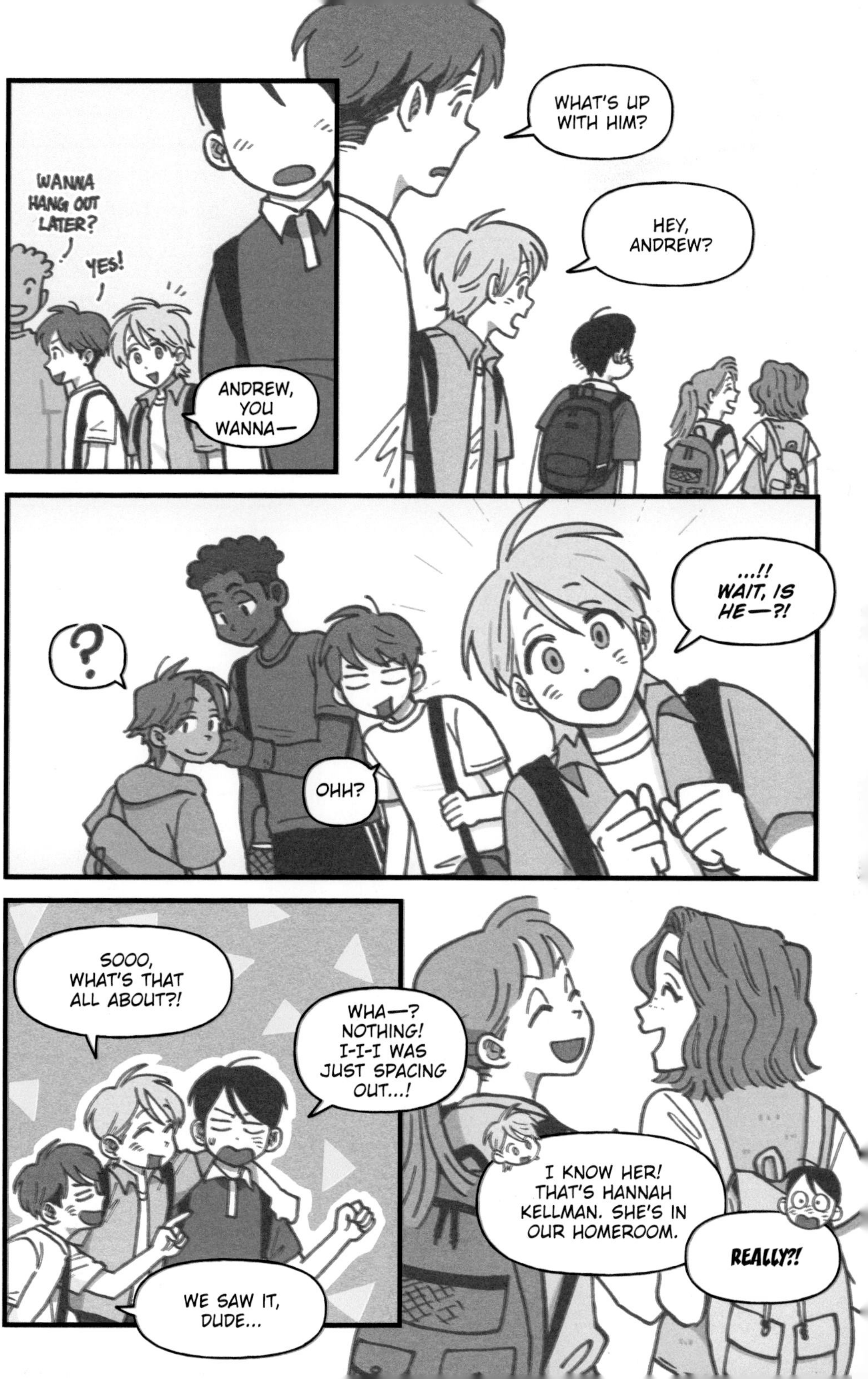
WHAT'S UP WITH HIM?
HEY, ANDREW?
WANNA HANG OUT LATER?
YES!
ANDREW, YOU WANNA—
?
...!! WAIT, IS HE—?!
OHH?
SOOO, WHAT'S THAT ALL ABOUT?!
WHA—? NOTHING! I-I-I WAS JUST SPACING OUT...!
WE SAW IT, DUDE...
I KNOW HER! THAT'S HANNAH KELLMAN. SHE'S IN OUR HOMEROOM.
REALLY?!

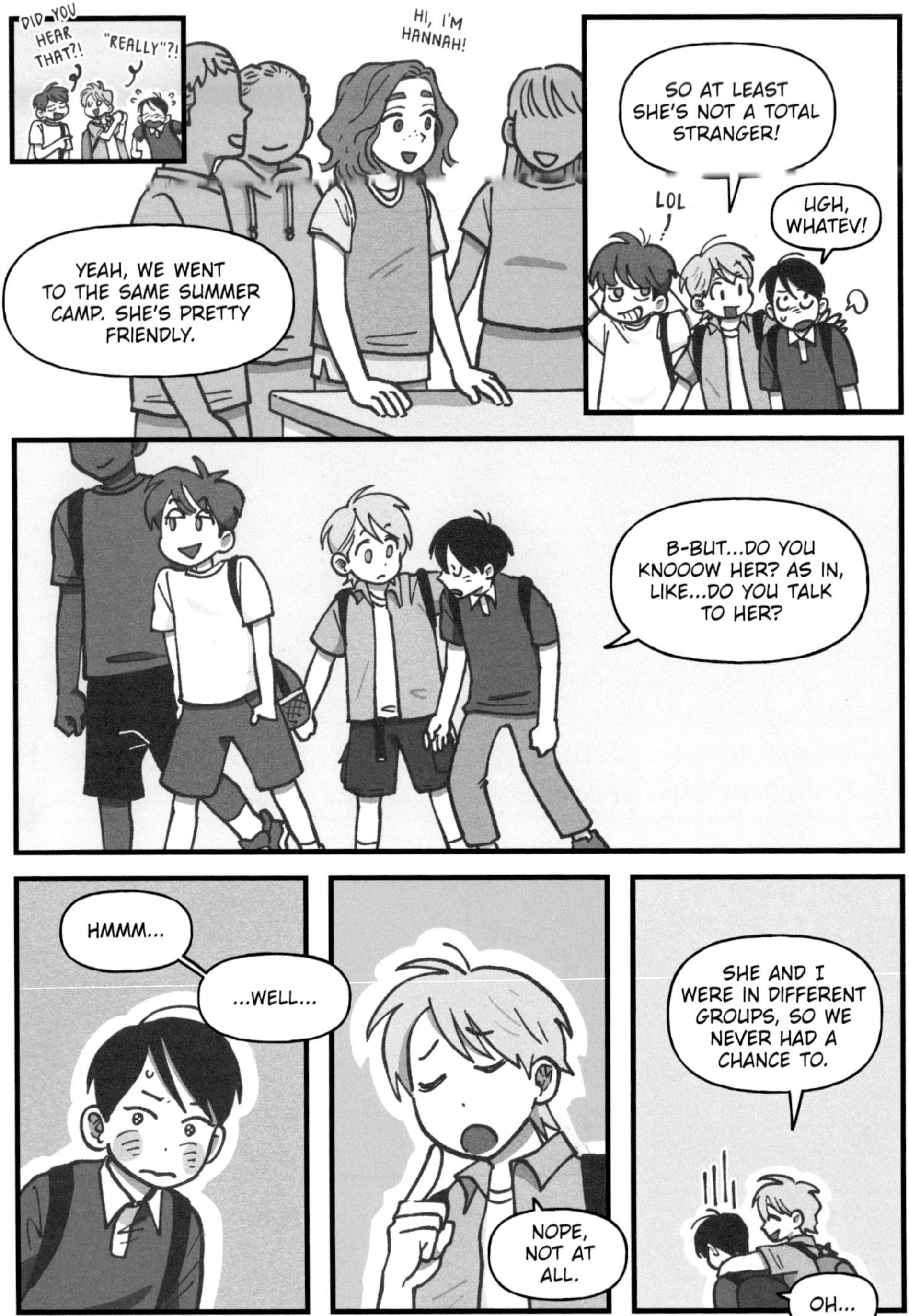
DID YOU HEAR THAT?!
"REALLY"?!
HI, I'M HANNAH!
YEAH, WE WENT TO THE SAME SUMMER CAMP. SHE'S PRETTY FRIENDLY.
SO AT LEAST SHE'S NOT A TOTAL STRANGER!
LOL
UGH, WHATEV!
B-BUT...DO YOU KNOOOW HER? AS IN, LIKE...DO YOU TALK TO HER?
HMMM...
...WELL...
NOPE, NOT AT ALL.
SHE AND I WERE IN DIFFERENT GROUPS, SO WE NEVER HAD A CHANCE TO.
OH...

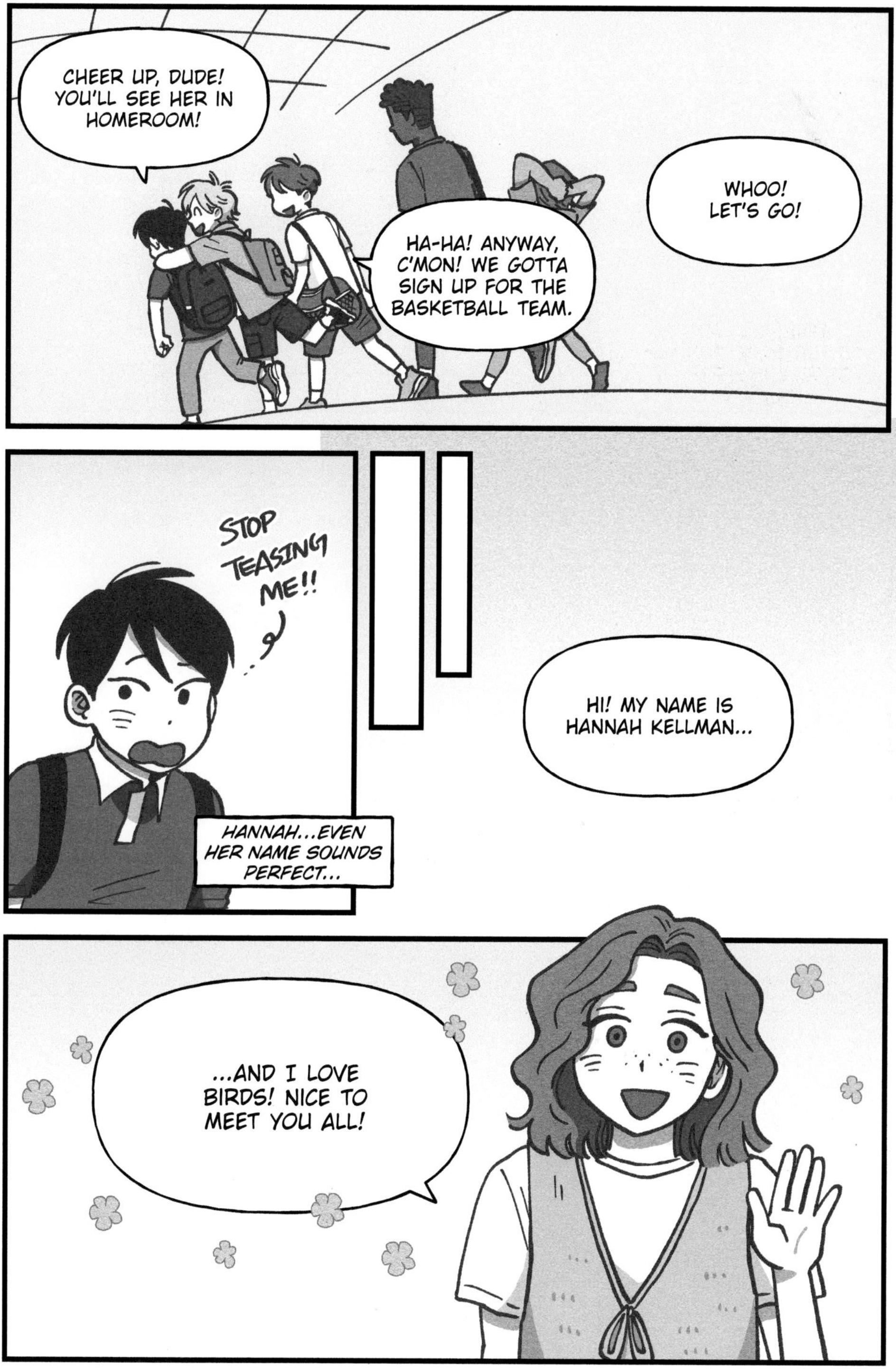
CHEER UP, DUDE! YOU'LL SEE HER IN HOMEROOM!
HA-HA! ANYWAY, C'MON! WE GOTTA SIGN UP FOR THE BASKETBALL TEAM.
WHOO! LET'S GO!
STOP TEASING ME!!
HANNAH...EVEN HER NAME SOUNDS PERFECT...
HI! MY NAME IS HANNAH KELLMAN...
...AND I LOVE BIRDS! NICE TO MEET YOU ALL!

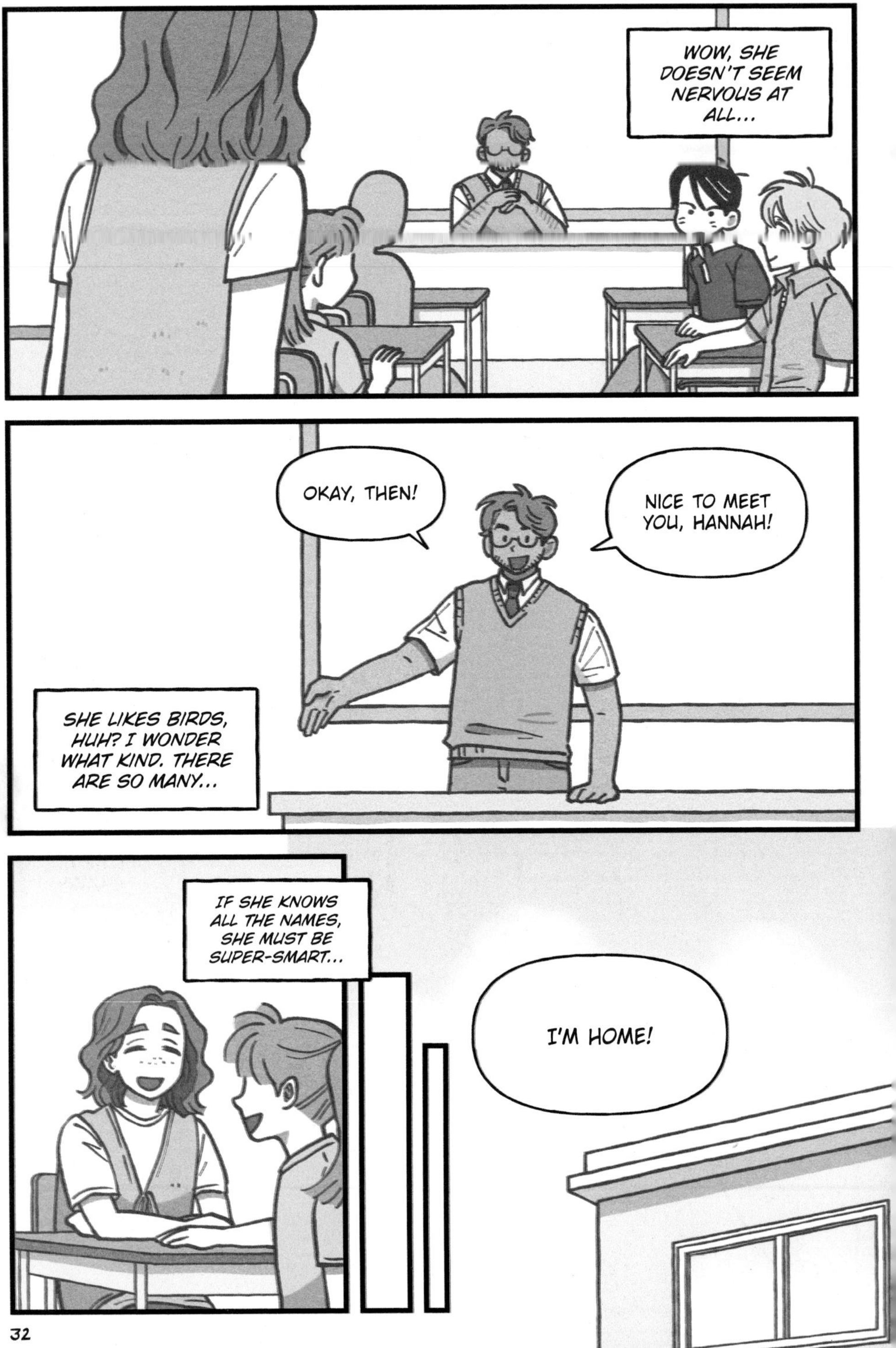
WOW, SHE DOESN'T SEEM NERVOUS AT ALL...
OKAY, THEN!
NICE TO MEET YOU, HANNAH!
SHE LIKES BIRDS, HUH? I WONDER WHAT KIND. THERE ARE SO MANY...
IF SHE KNOWS ALL THE NAMES, SHE MUST BE SUPER-SMART...
I'M HOME!

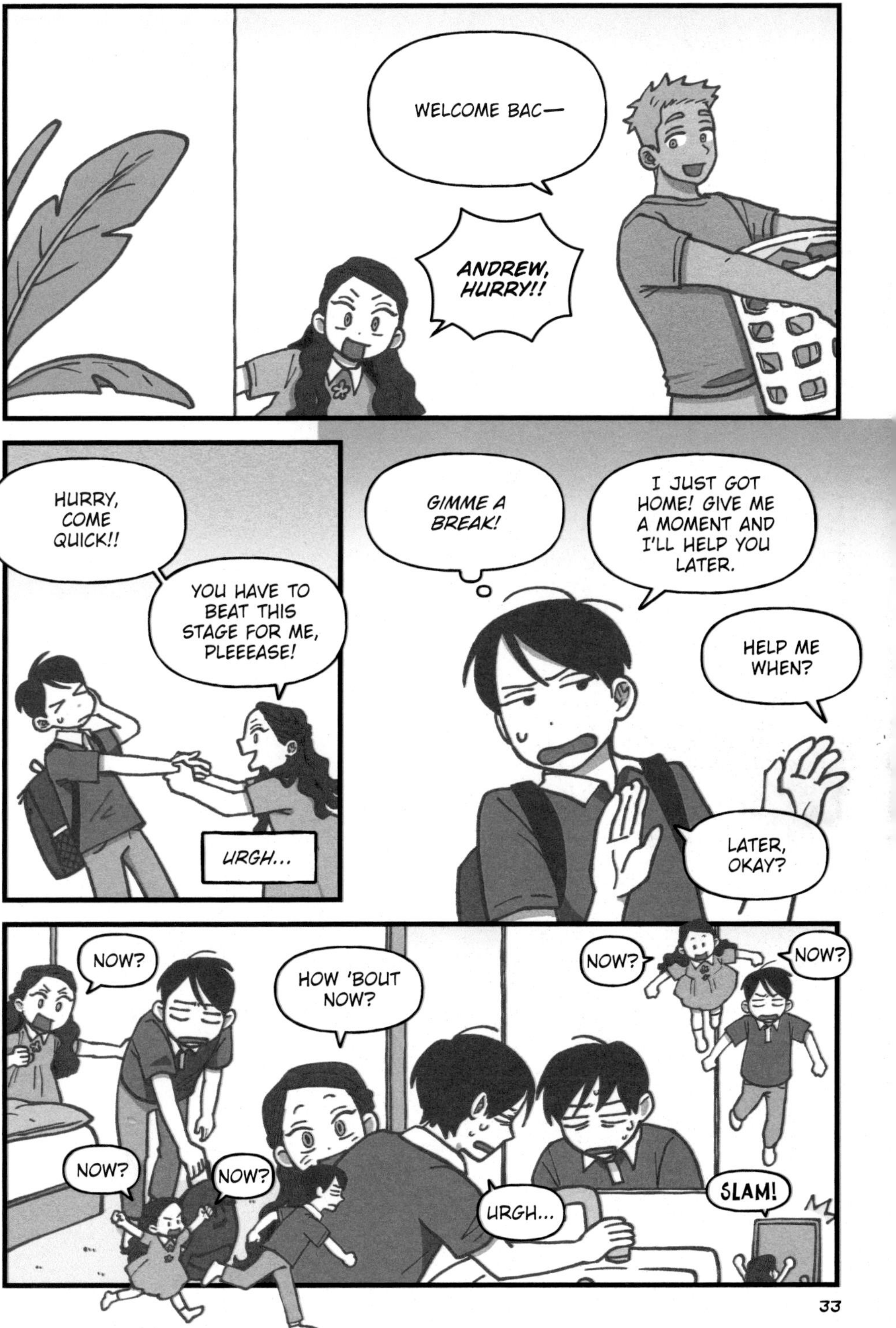
WELCOME BAC—
ANDREW, HURRY!!
HURRY, COME QUICK!!
YOU HAVE TO BEAT THIS STAGE FOR ME, PLEEEASE!
URGH...
GIMME A BREAK!
I JUST GOT HOME! GIVE ME A MOMENT AND I'LL HELP YOU LATER.
HELP ME WHEN?
LATER, OKAY?
NOW?
HOW 'BOUT NOW?
NOW?
NOW?
NOW?
NOW?
URGH...
SLAM!

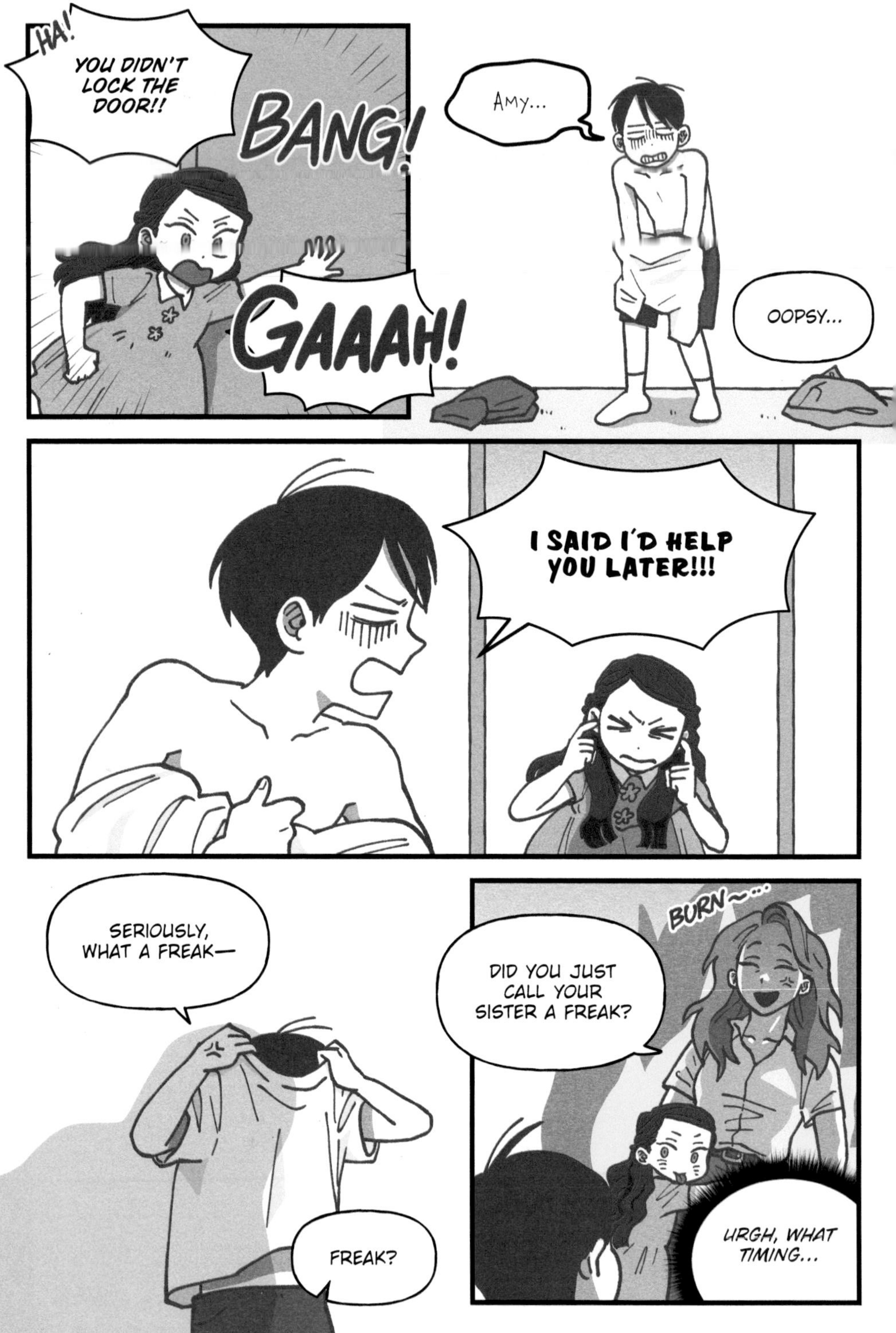
HA!
YOU DIDN'T LOCK THE DOOR!!
BANG!
GAAAH!
AMY...
OOPSY...
I SAID I'D HELP YOU LATER!!!
SERIOUSLY, WHAT A FREAK—
FREAK?
BURN~...
DID YOU JUST CALL YOUR SISTER A FREAK?
URGH, WHAT TIMING...

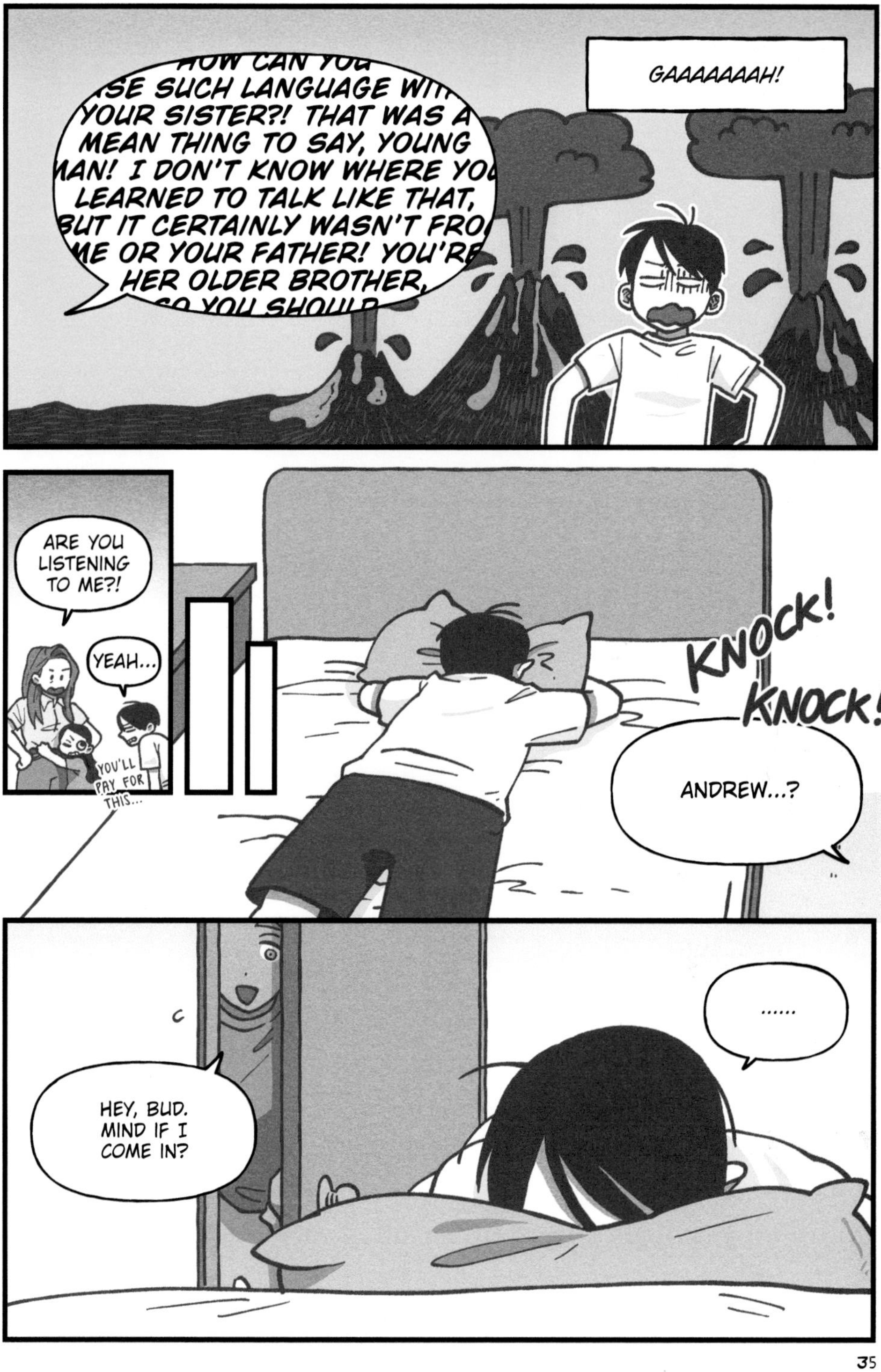
HOW CAN YOU USE SUCH LANGUAGE WITH YOUR SISTER?! THAT WAS A MEAN THING TO SAY, YOUNG MAN! I DON'T KNOW WHERE YOU LEARNED TO TALK LIKE THAT, BUT IT CERTAINLY WASN'T FROM ME OR YOUR FATHER! YOU'RE HER OLDER BROTHER, SO YOU SHOULD
GAAAAAAAH!
ARE YOU LISTENING TO ME?!
YEAH...
YOU'LL PAY FOR THIS...
KNOCK! KNOCK!
ANDREW...?
HEY, BUD. MIND IF I COME IN?
......

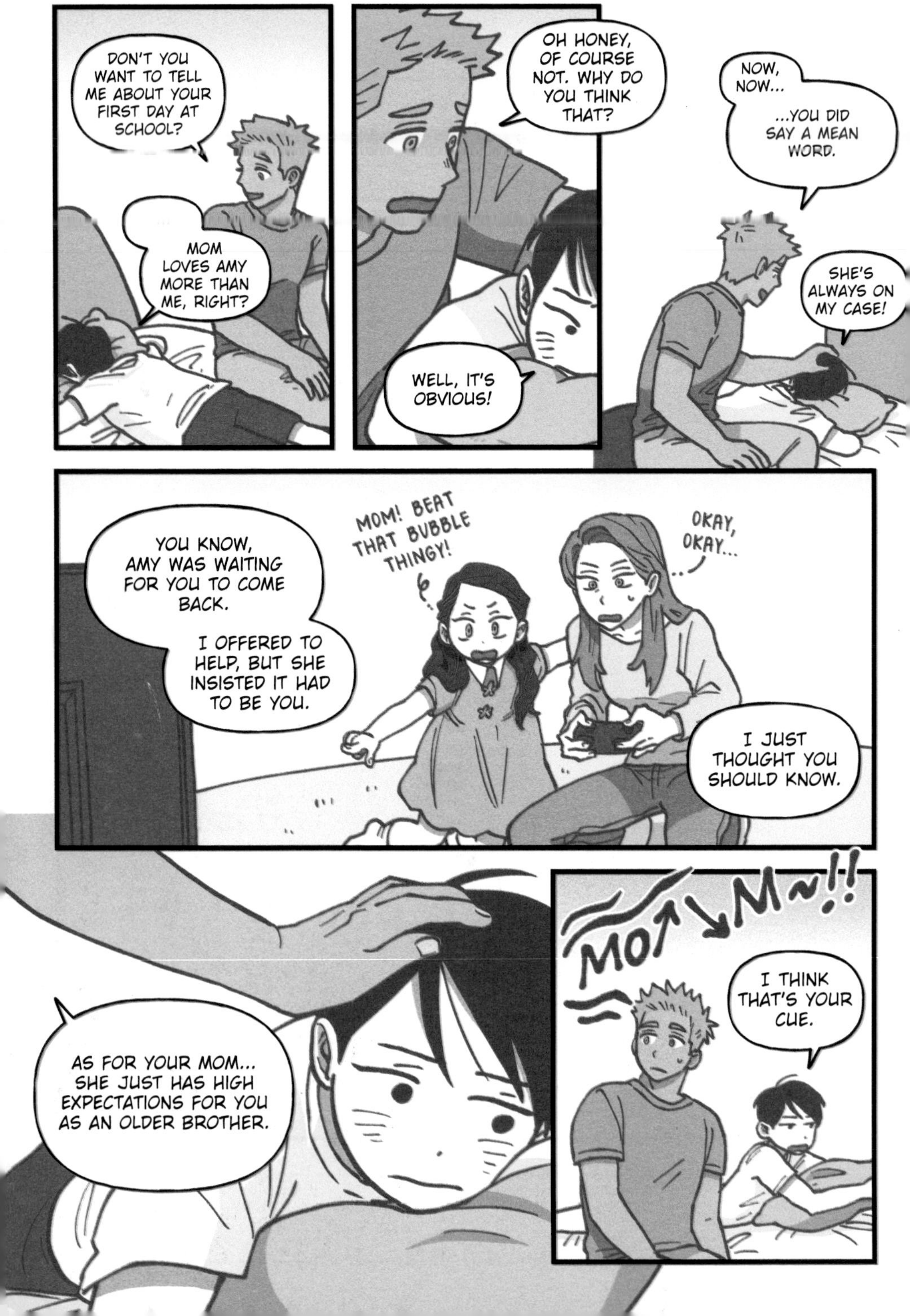
DON'T YOU WANT TO TELL ME ABOUT YOUR FIRST DAY AT SCHOOL?
MOM LOVES AMY MORE THAN ME, RIGHT?
OH HONEY, OF COURSE NOT. WHY DO YOU THINK THAT?
WELL, IT'S OBVIOUS!
NOW, NOW...
...YOU DID SAY A MEAN WORD.
SHE'S ALWAYS ON MY CASE!
YOU KNOW, AMY WAS WAITING FOR YOU TO COME BACK.
I OFFERED TO HELP, BUT SHE INSISTED IT HAD TO BE YOU.
MOM! BEAT THAT BUBBLE THINGY!
OKAY, OKAY...
I JUST THOUGHT YOU SHOULD KNOW.
AS FOR YOUR MOM... SHE JUST HAS HIGH EXPECTATIONS FOR YOU AS AN OLDER BROTHER.
MOM~M~!!
I THINK THAT'S YOUR CUE.

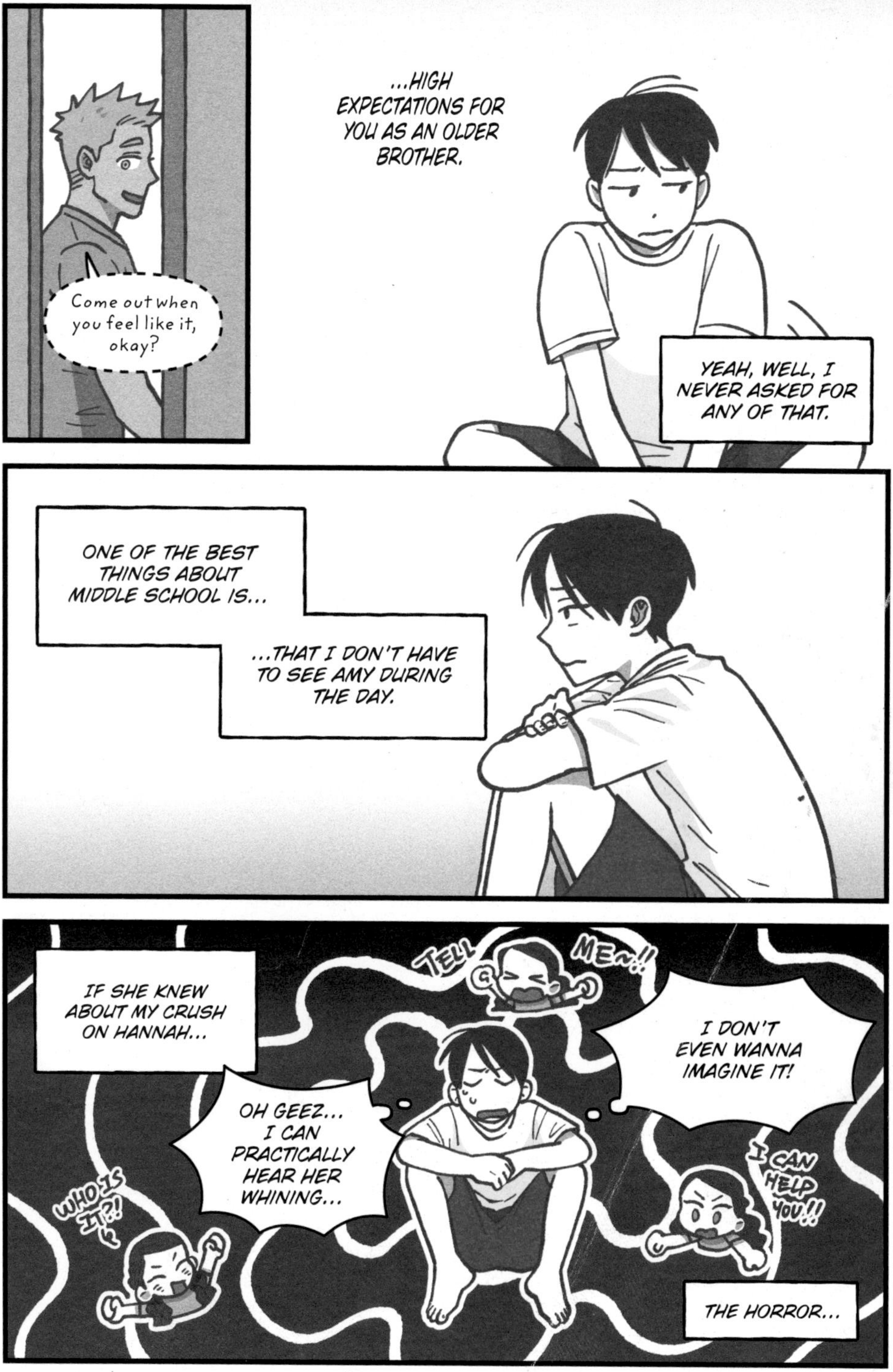
Come out when you feel like it, okay?
...HIGH EXPECTATIONS FOR YOU AS AN OLDER BROTHER.
YEAH, WELL, I NEVER ASKED FOR ANY OF THAT.
ONE OF THE BEST THINGS ABOUT MIDDLE SCHOOL IS...
...THAT I DON'T HAVE TO SEE AMY DURING THE DAY.
IF SHE KNEW ABOUT MY CRUSH ON HANNAH...
TELL ME~!!
I DON'T EVEN WANNA IMAGINE IT!
OH GEEZ... I CAN PRACTICALLY HEAR HER WHINING...
WHO IS IT?!
I CAN HELP YOU!!
THE HORROR...

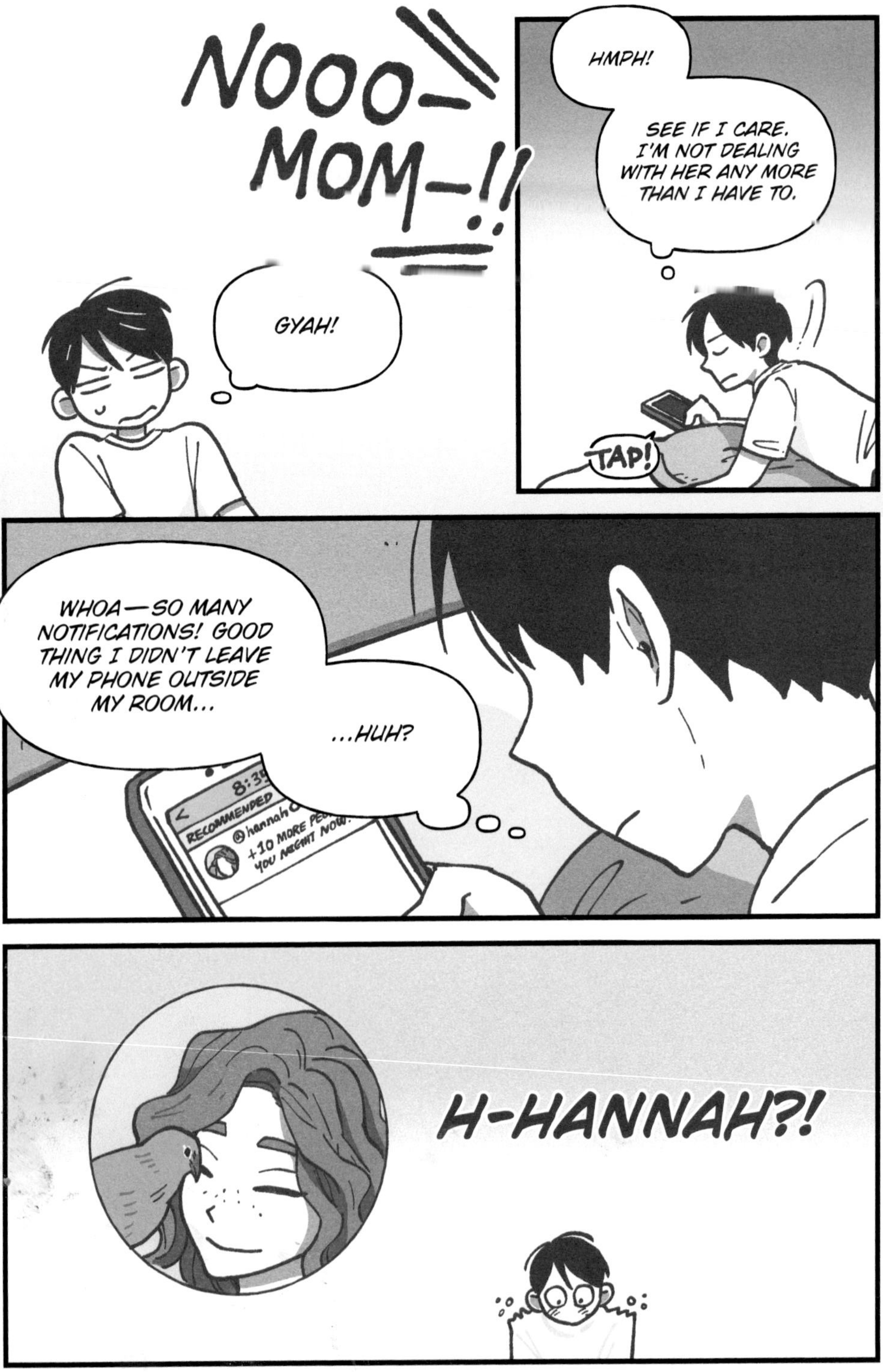
NOOO—
MOM—!!
GYAH!
HMPH!
SEE IF I CARE. I'M NOT DEALING WITH HER ANY MORE THAN I HAVE TO.
TAP!
WHOA—SO MANY NOTIFICATIONS! GOOD THING I DIDN'T LEAVE MY PHONE OUTSIDE MY ROOM...
...HUH?
H-HANNAH?!

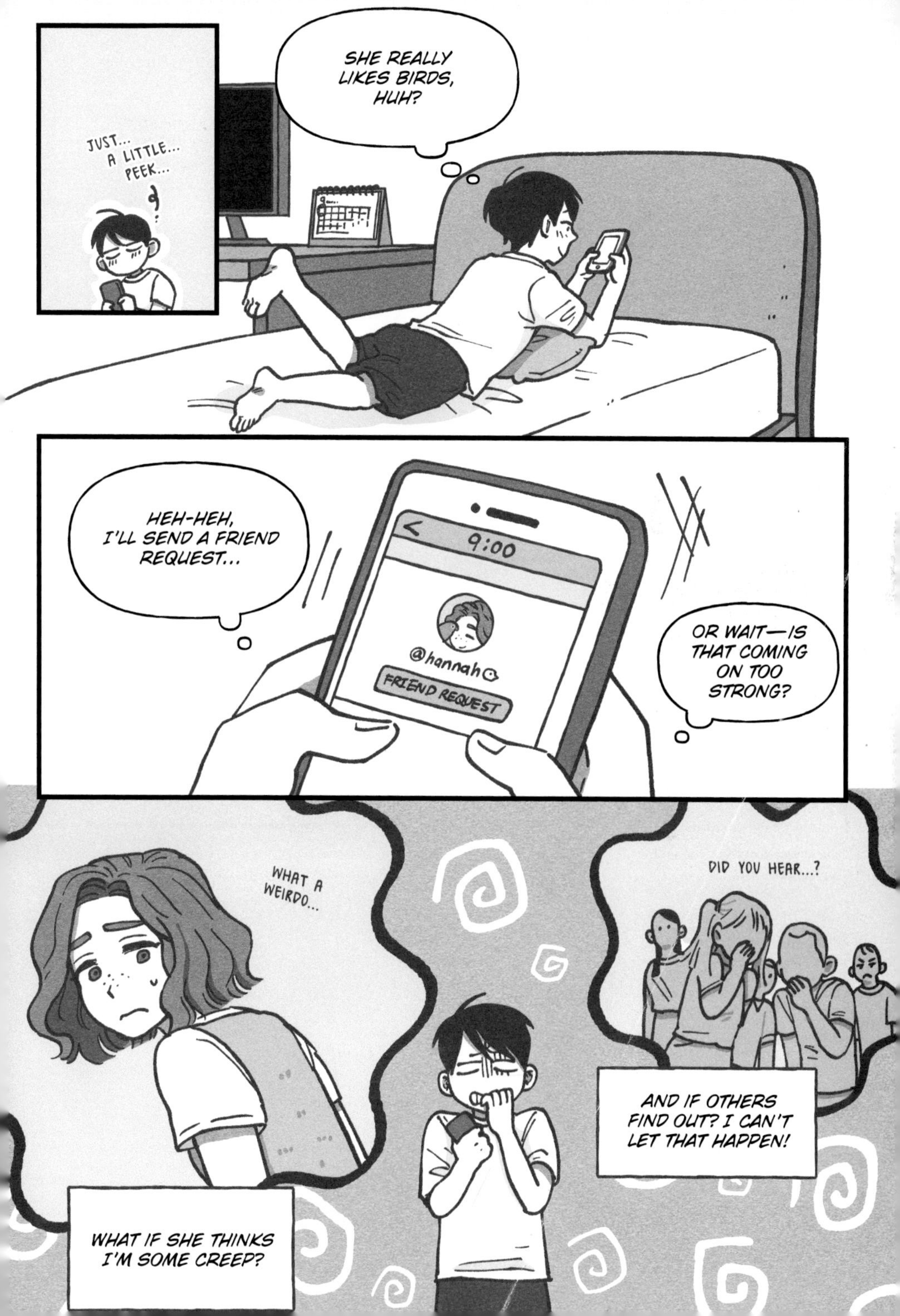
JUST... A LITTLE... PEEK...
SHE REALLY LIKES BIRDS, HUH?
HEH-HEH, I'LL SEND A FRIEND REQUEST...
9:00
@hannah
FRIEND REQUEST
OR WAIT—IS THAT COMING ON TOO STRONG?
WHAT A WEIRDO...
DID YOU HEAR...?
AND IF OTHERS FIND OUT? I CAN'T LET THAT HAPPEN!
WHAT IF SHE THINKS I'M SOME CREEP?

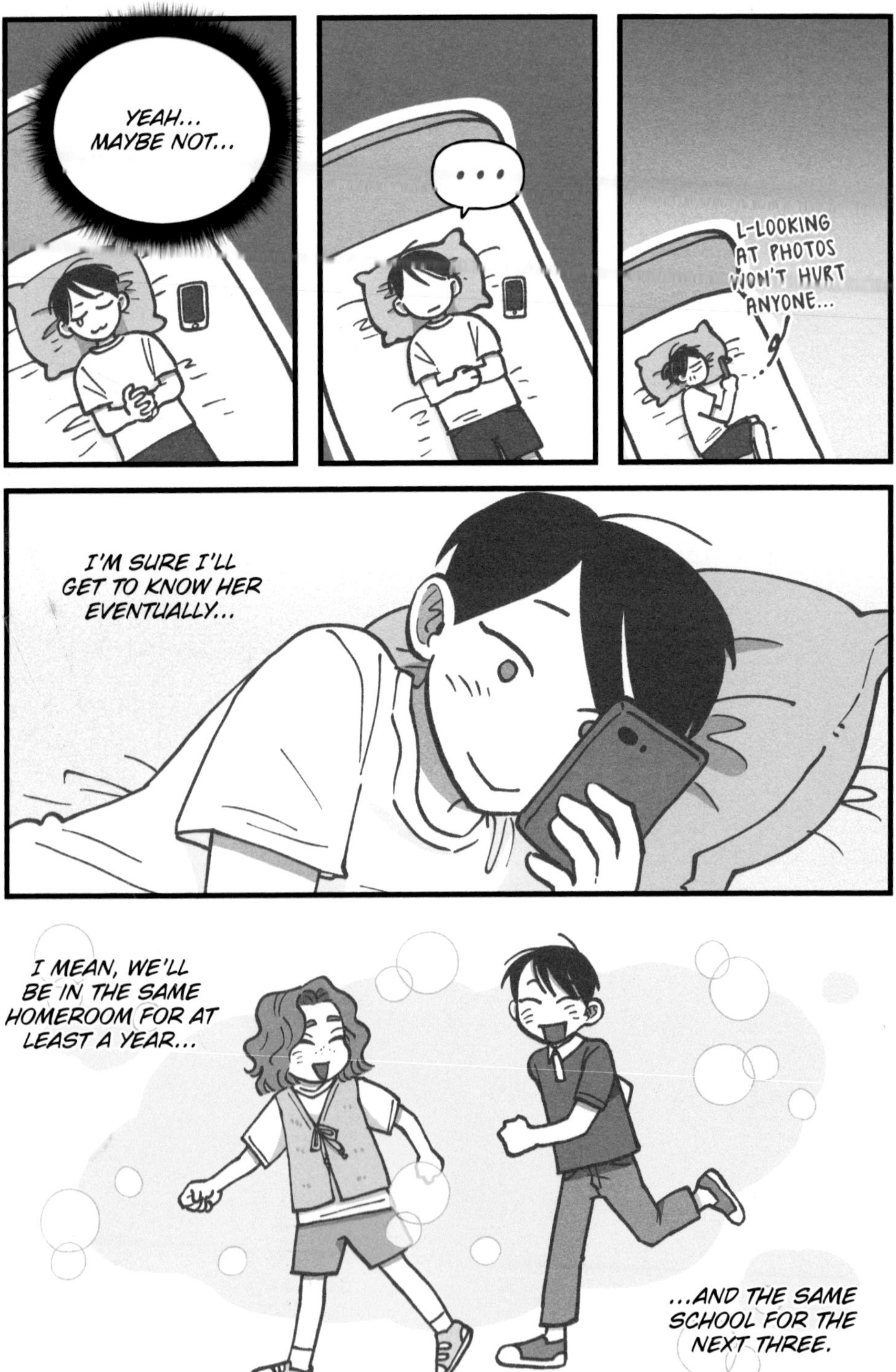
YEAH... MAYBE NOT...
...
L-LOOKING AT PHOTOS WON'T HURT ANYONE...
I'M SURE I'LL GET TO KNOW HER EVENTUALLY...
I MEAN, WE'LL BE IN THE SAME HOMEROOM FOR AT LEAST A YEAR...
...AND THE SAME SCHOOL FOR THE NEXT THREE.

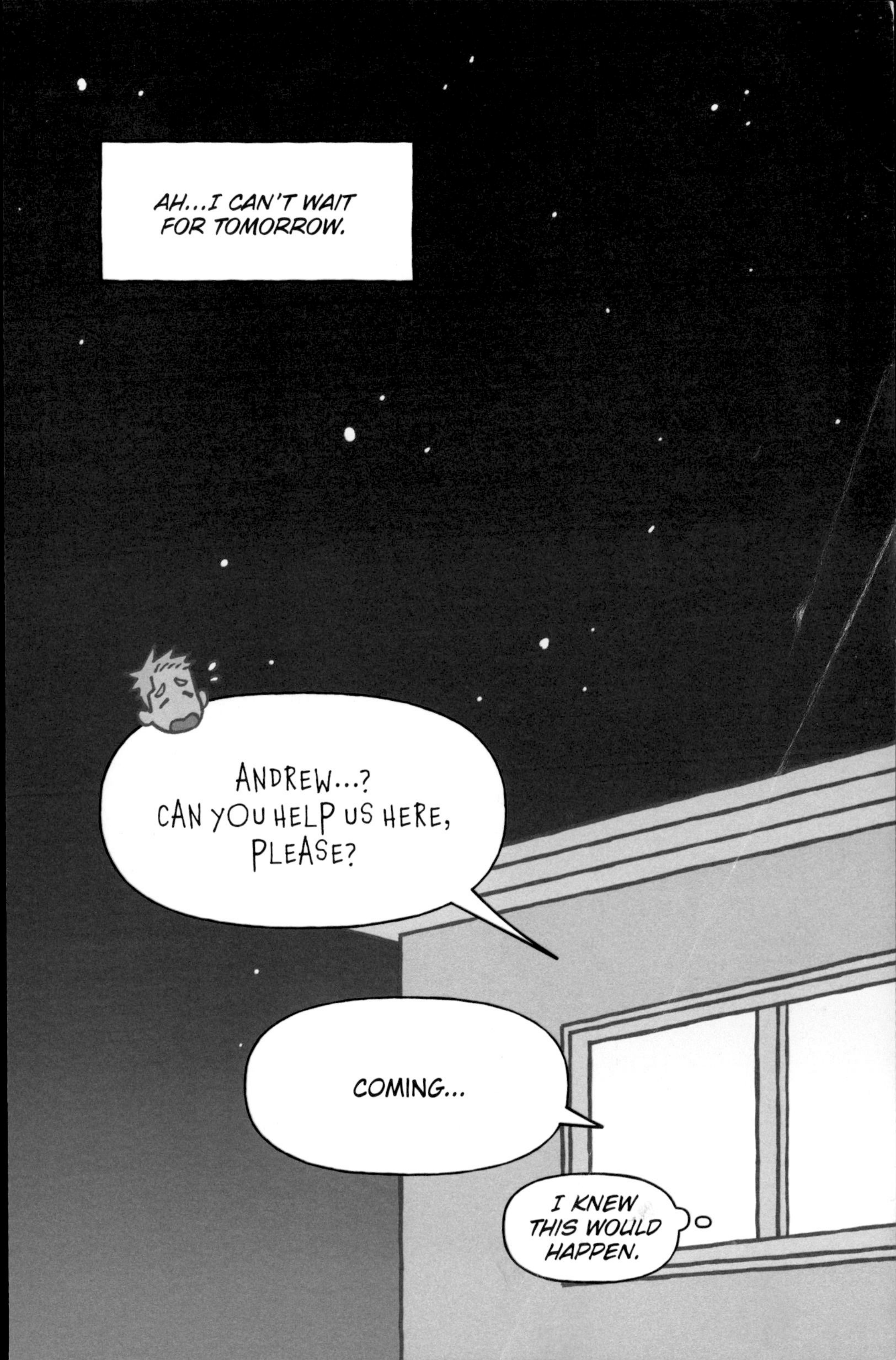
AH...I CAN'T WAIT FOR TOMORROW.
ANDREW...? CAN YOU HELP US HERE, PLEASE?
COMING...
I KNEW THIS WOULD HAPPEN.

Chapter 3

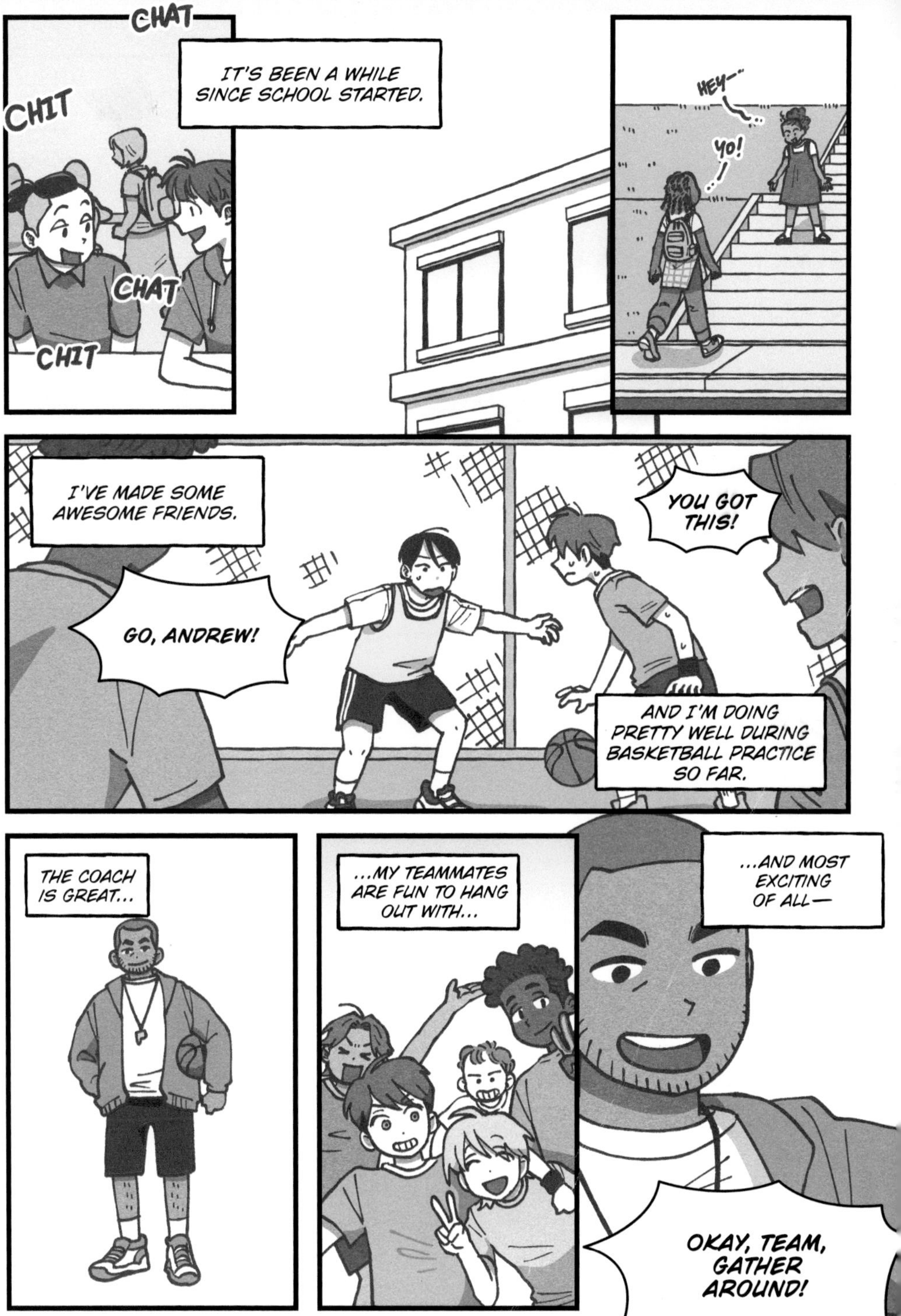
CHAT
IT'S BEEN A WHILE SINCE SCHOOL STARTED.
CHIT
CHAT
CHIT
HEY--
YO!
I'VE MADE SOME AWESOME FRIENDS.
GO, ANDREW!
YOU GOT THIS!
AND I'M DOING PRETTY WELL DURING BASKETBALL PRACTICE SO FAR.
THE COACH IS GREAT...
...MY TEAMMATES ARE FUN TO HANG OUT WITH...
...AND MOST EXCITING OF ALL—
OKAY, TEAM, GATHER AROUND!

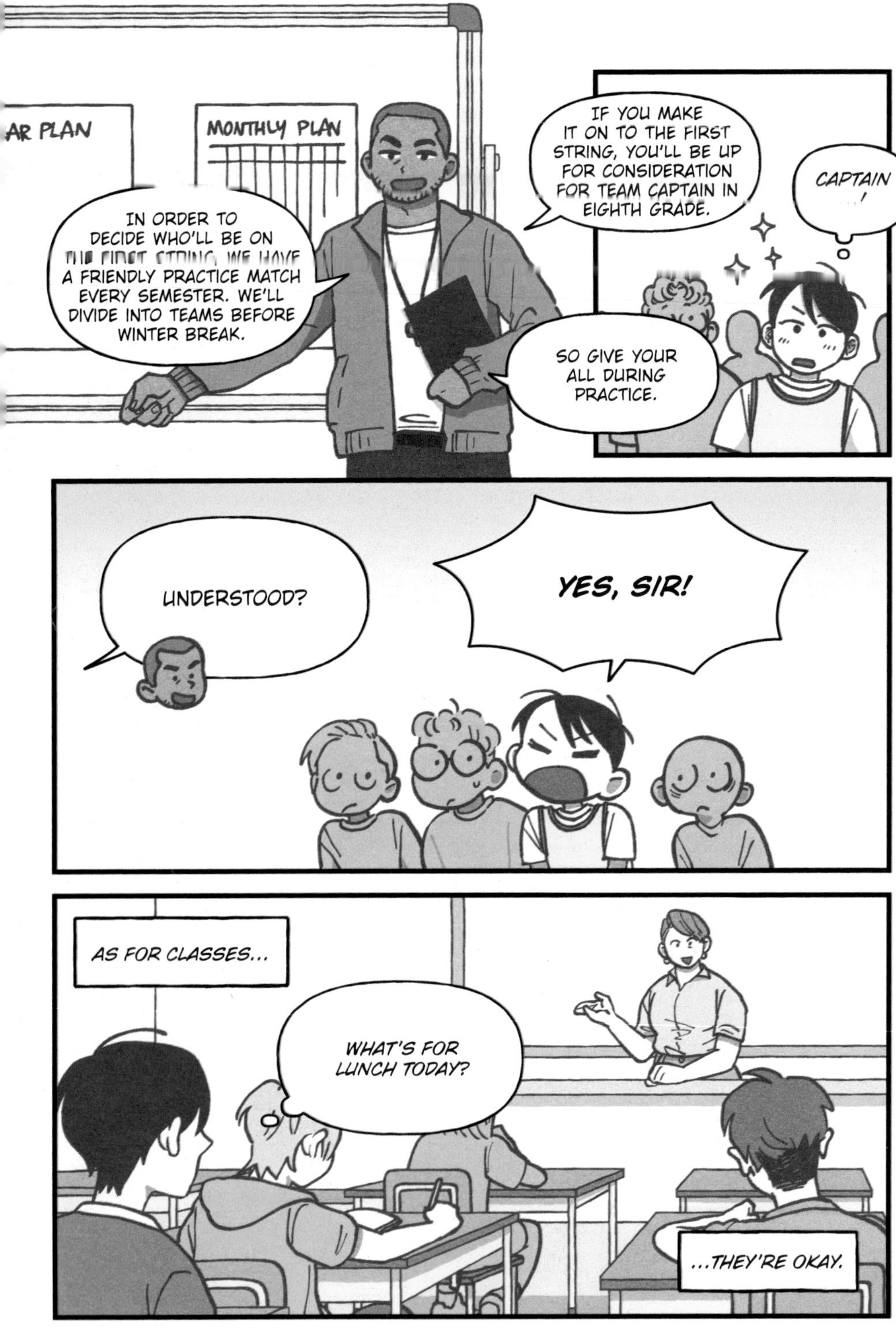
AR PLAN
MONTHLY PLAN
IN ORDER TO DECIDE WHO'LL BE ON THE FIRST STRING, WE HAVE A FRIENDLY PRACTICE MATCH EVERY SEMESTER. WE'LL DIVIDE INTO TEAMS BEFORE WINTER BREAK.
IF YOU MAKE IT ON TO THE FIRST STRING, YOU'LL BE UP FOR CONSIDERATION FOR TEAM CAPTAIN IN EIGHTH GRADE.
CAPTAIN...!
SO GIVE YOUR ALL DURING PRACTICE.
UNDERSTOOD?
YES, SIR!
AS FOR CLASSES...
WHAT'S FOR LUNCH TODAY?
...THEY'RE OKAY.

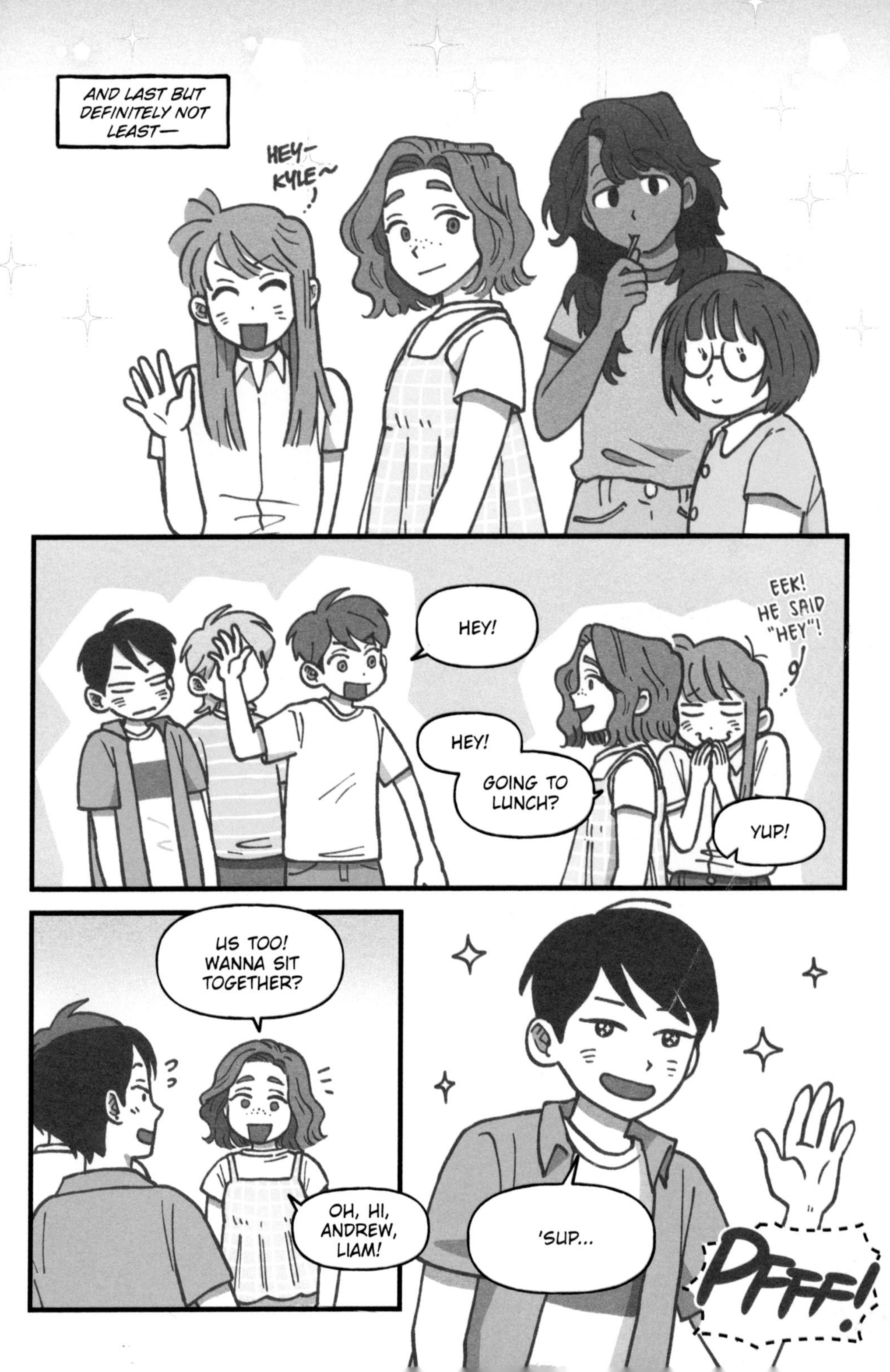
AND LAST BUT DEFINITELY NOT LEAST—
HEY- KYLE~
HEY!
EEK! HE SAID "HEY"!
HEY!
GOING TO LUNCH?
YUP!
US TOO! WANNA SIT TOGETHER?
OH, HI, ANDREW, LIAM!
'SUP...
PFFF!

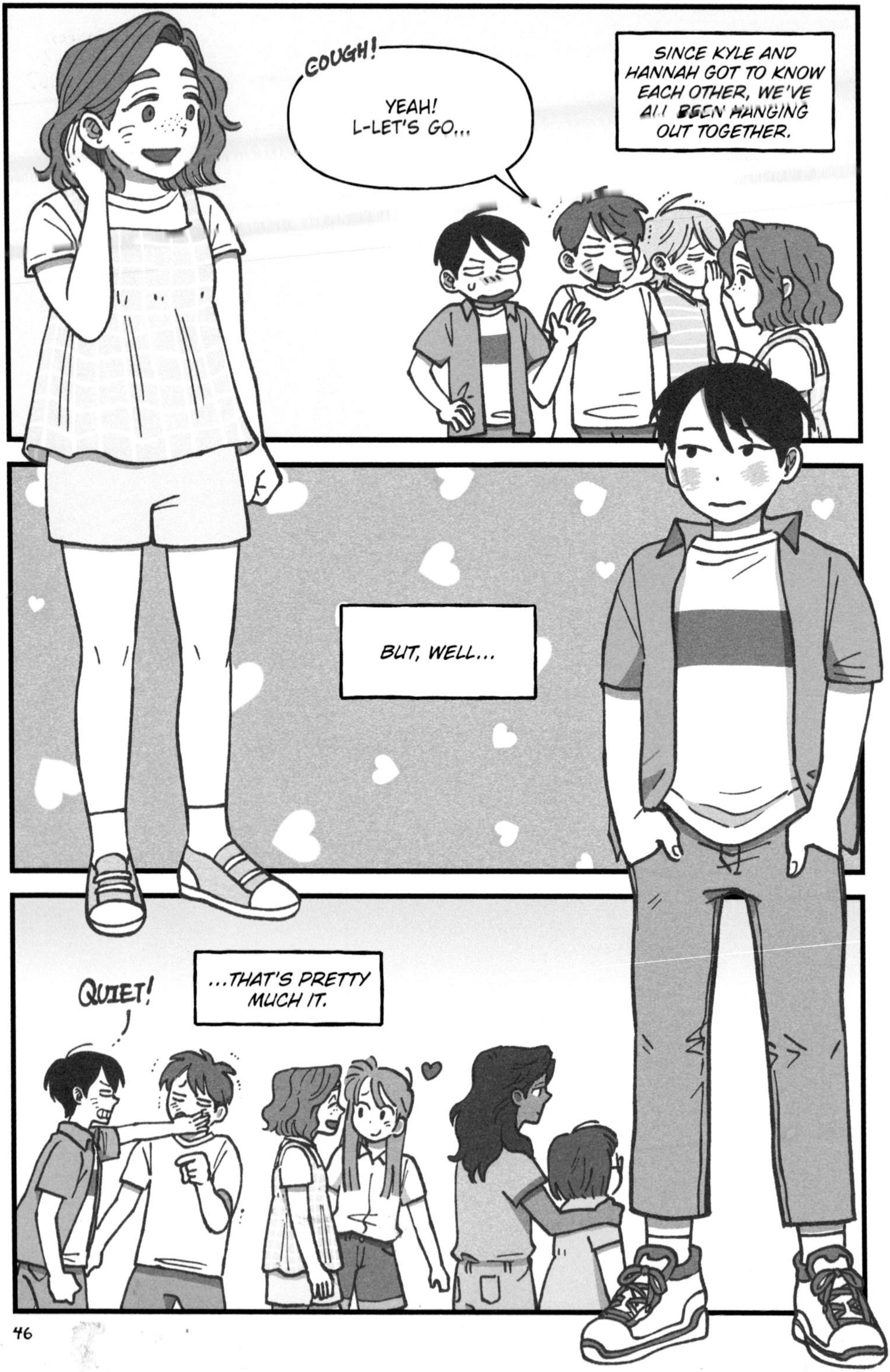
COUGH!
YEAH! L-LET'S GO...
SINCE KYLE AND HANNAH GOT TO KNOW EACH OTHER, WE'VE ALL BEEN HANGING OUT TOGETHER.
BUT, WELL...
...THAT'S PRETTY MUCH IT.
QUIET!

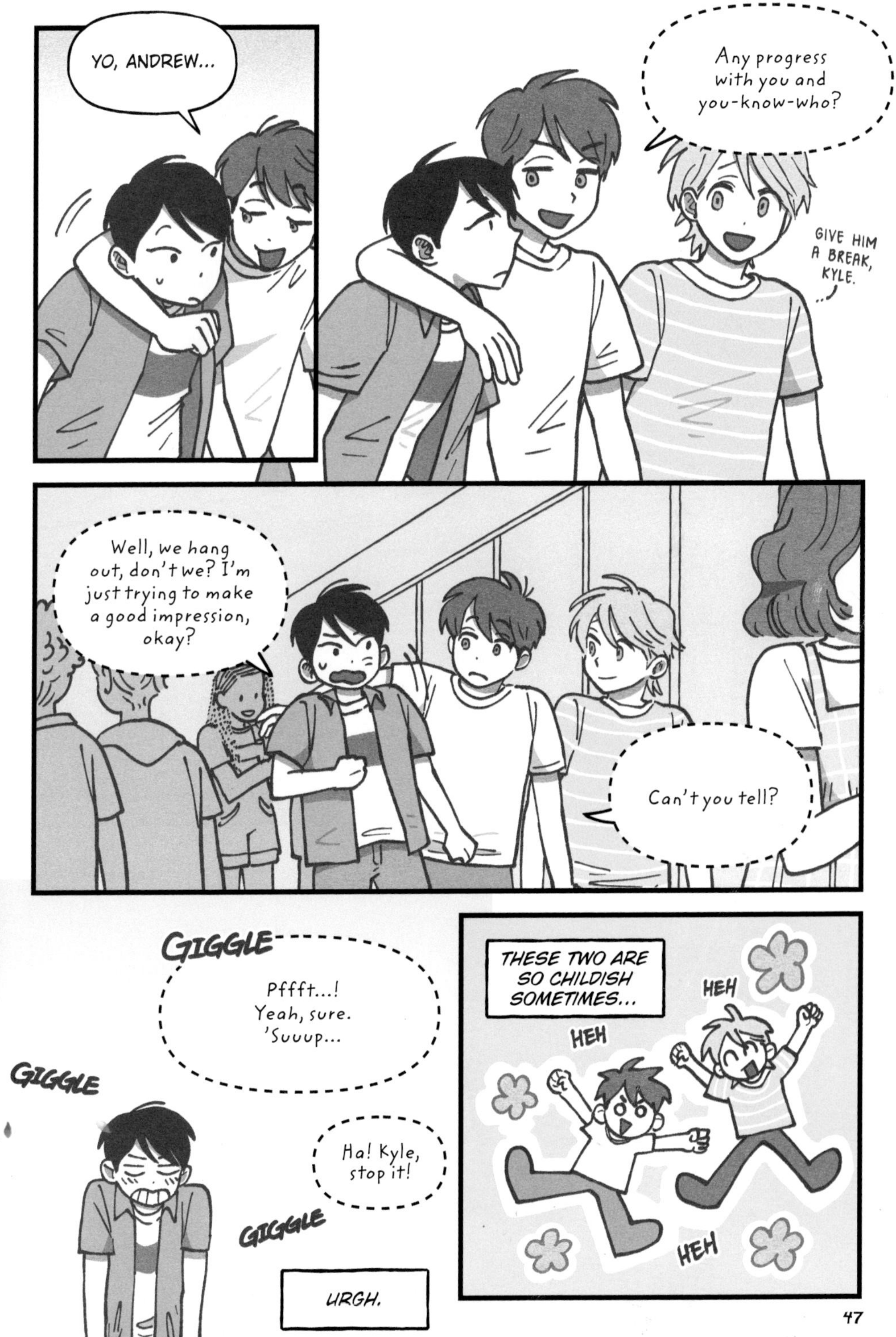
YO, ANDREW...
Any progress with you and you-know-who?
GIVE HIM A BREAK, KYLE.
Well, we hang out, don't we? I'm just trying to make a good impression, okay?
Can't you tell?
GIGGLE
Pffft...! Yeah, sure. 'Suuup...
GIGGLE
Ha! Kyle, stop it!
GIGGLE
URGH.
THESE TWO ARE SO CHILDISH SOMETIMES...
HEH
HEH
HEH

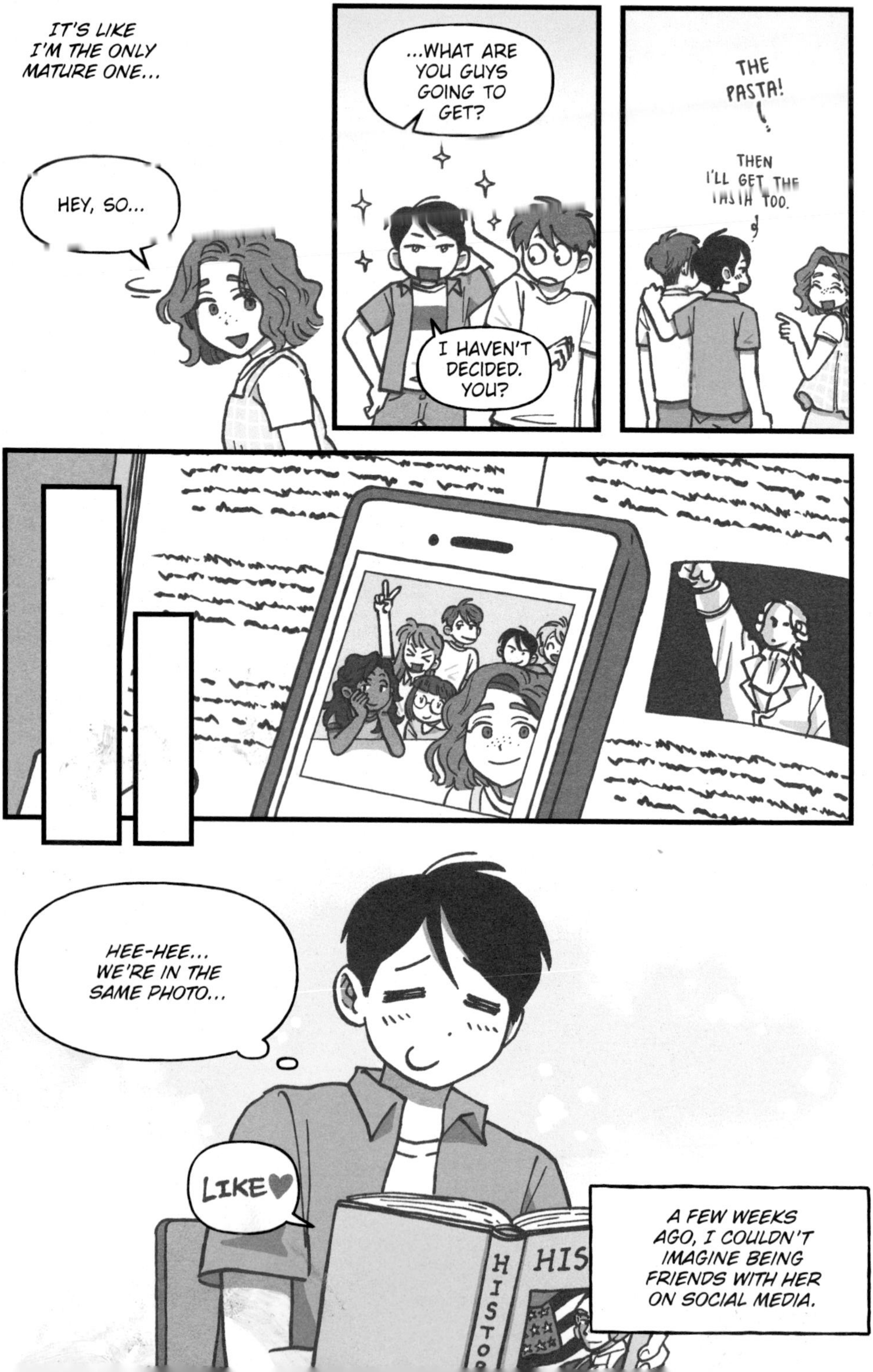
IT'S LIKE I'M THE ONLY MATURE ONE...
HEY, SO...
...WHAT ARE YOU GUYS GOING TO GET?
I HAVEN'T DECIDED. YOU?
THE PASTA!
THEN I'LL GET THE PASTA TOO.
HEE-HEE... WE'RE IN THE SAME PHOTO...
LIKE♥
A FEW WEEKS AGO, I COULDN'T IMAGINE BEING FRIENDS WITH HER ON SOCIAL MEDIA.
HIS
HISTO

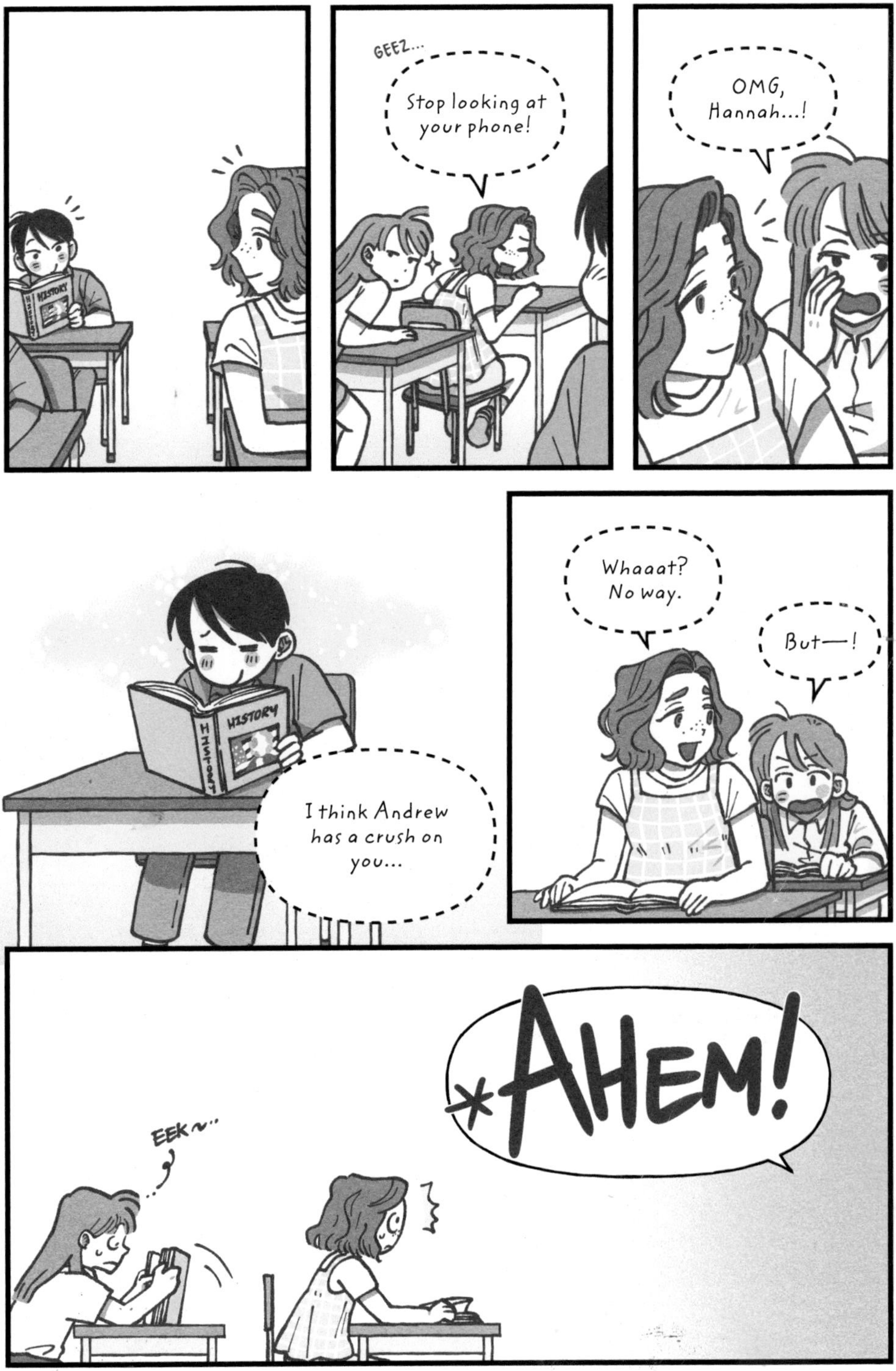
GEEZ...
Stop looking at your phone!
OMG, Hannah...!
I think Andrew has a crush on you...
Whaaat? No way.
But—!
*AHEM!
EEK~..

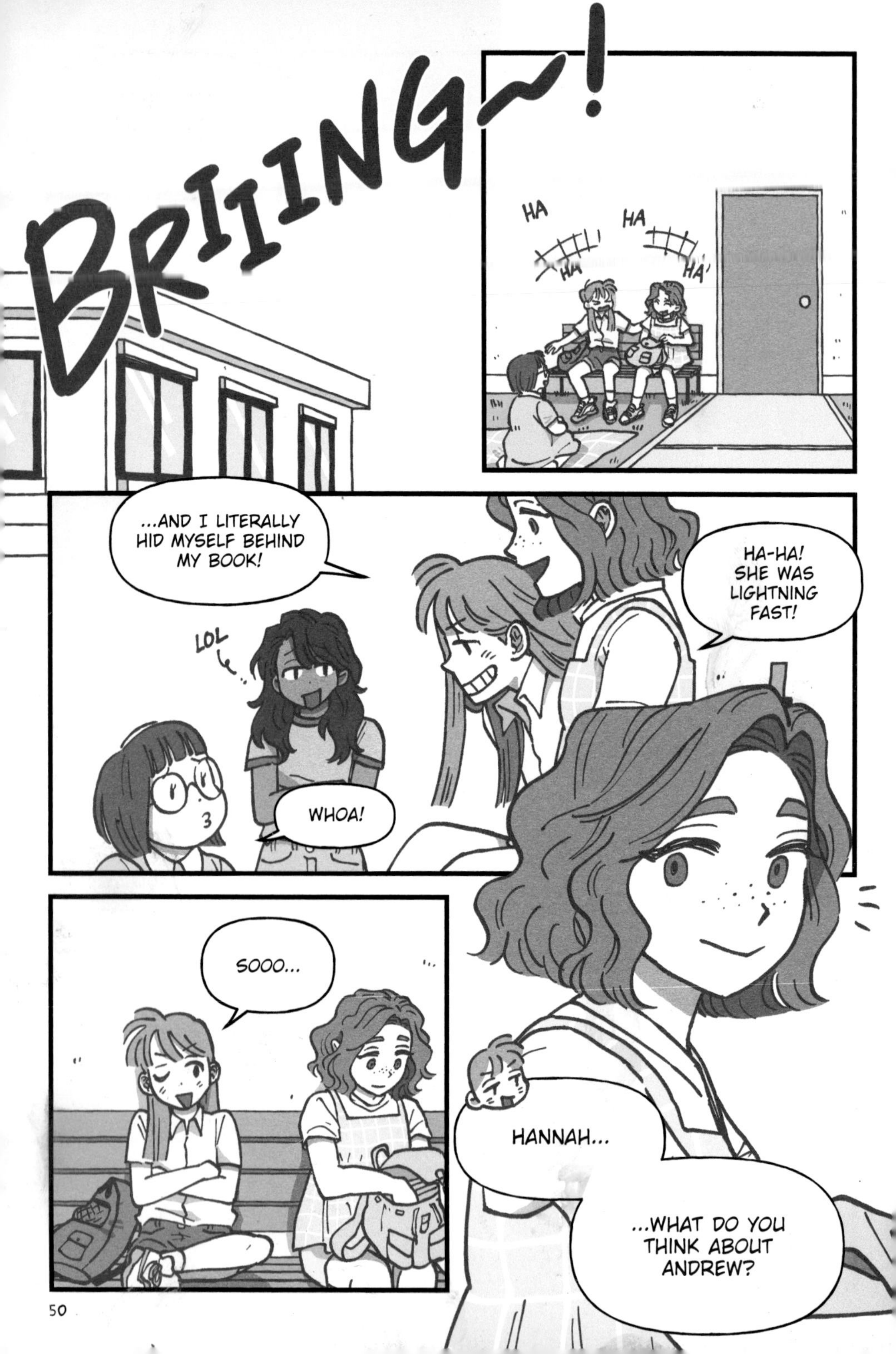
BRIIING~!
HA
HA
HA
HA
...AND I LITERALLY HID MYSELF BEHIND MY BOOK!
HA-HA! SHE WAS LIGHTNING FAST!
LOL
WHOA!
SOOO...
HANNAH...
...WHAT DO YOU THINK ABOUT ANDREW?

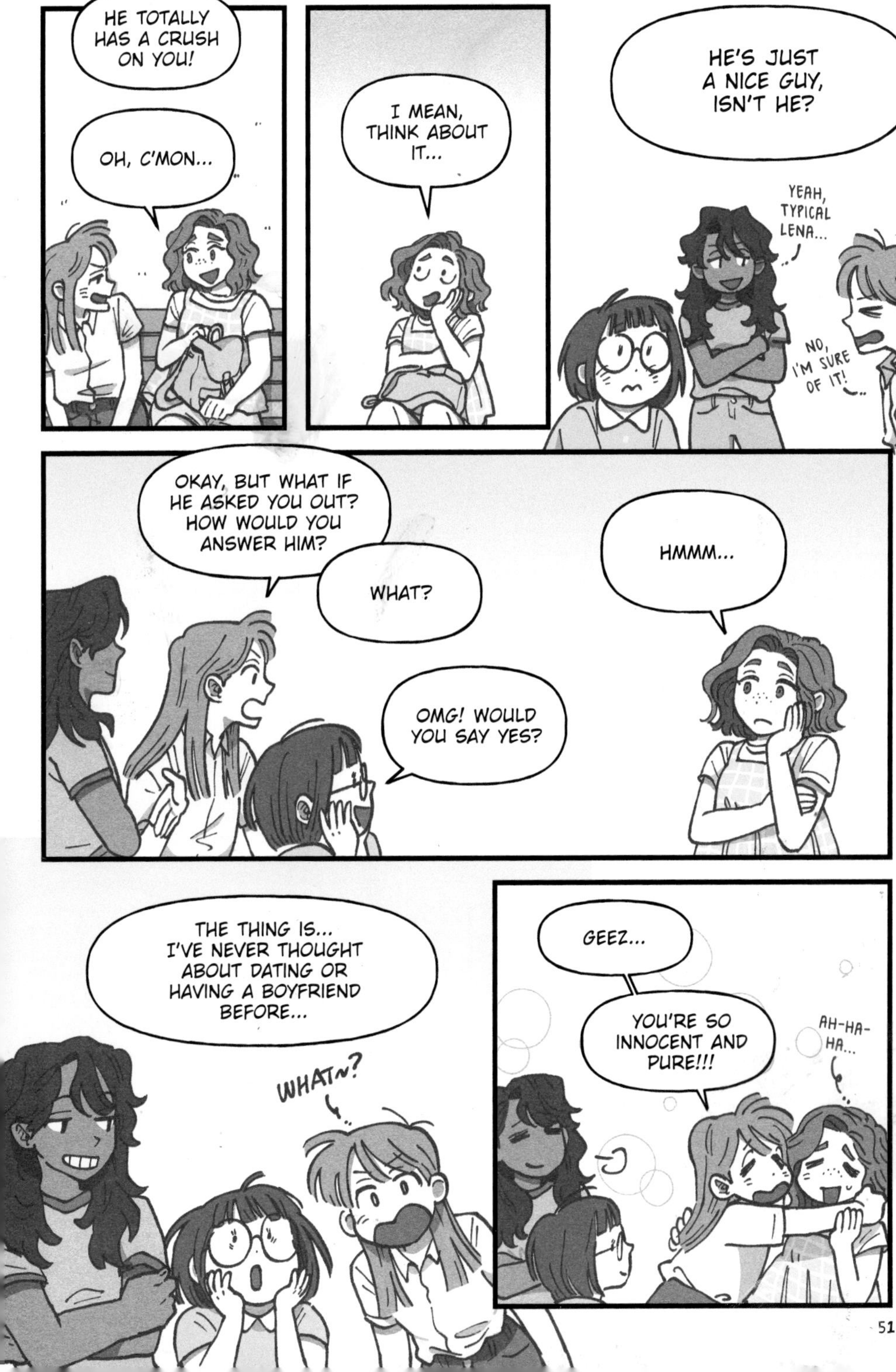
HE TOTALLY HAS A CRUSH ON YOU!
OH, C'MON...
I MEAN, THINK ABOUT IT...
HE'S JUST A NICE GUY, ISN'T HE?
YEAH, TYPICAL LENA...
NO, I'M SURE OF IT!
OKAY, BUT WHAT IF HE ASKED YOU OUT? HOW WOULD YOU ANSWER HIM?
WHAT?
OMG! WOULD YOU SAY YES?
HMMM...
THE THING IS... I'VE NEVER THOUGHT ABOUT DATING OR HAVING A BOYFRIEND BEFORE...
WHAT~?
GEEZ...
YOU'RE SO INNOCENT AND PURE!!!
AH-HA-HA...

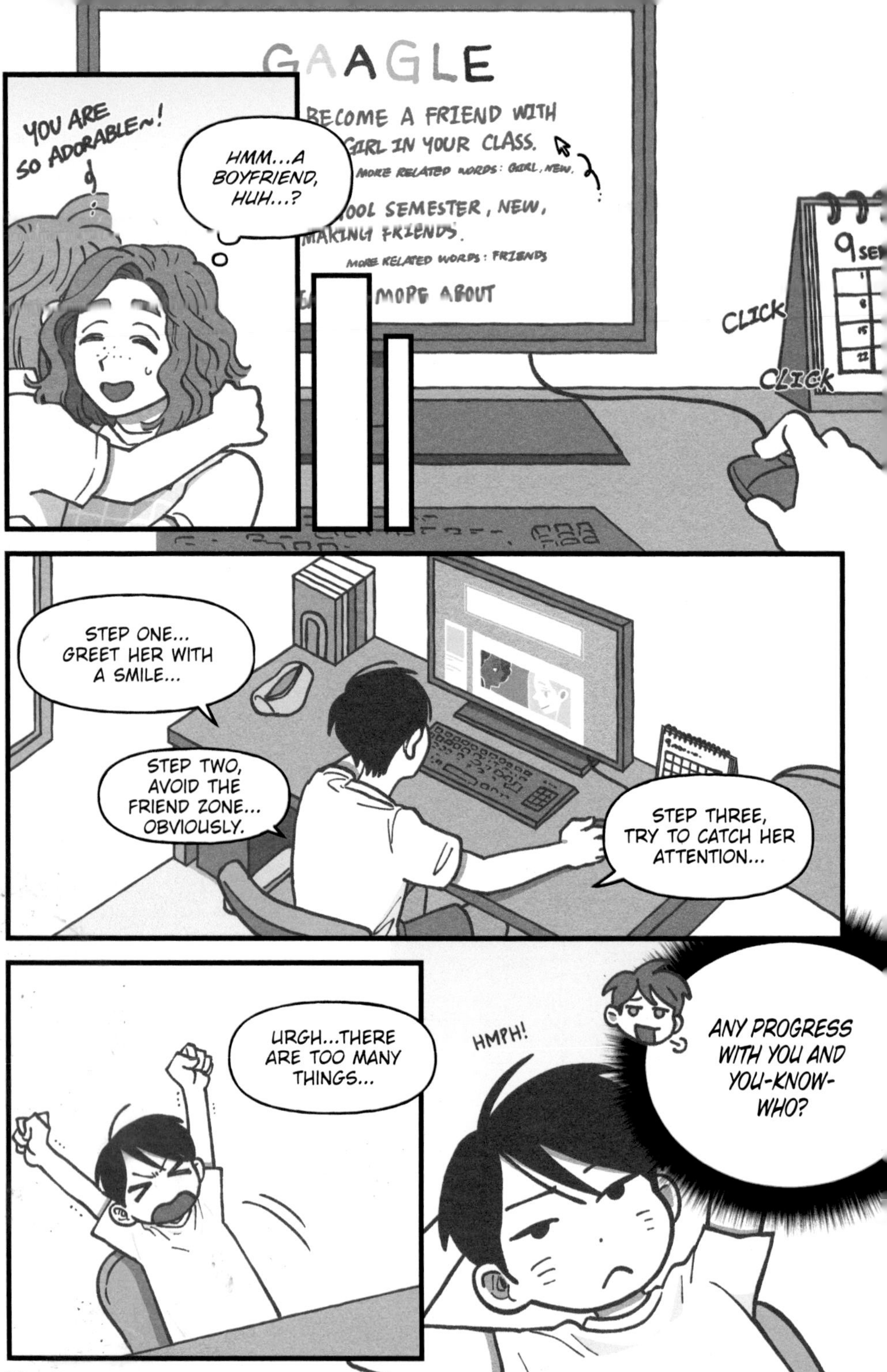
GAAGLE
BECOME A FRIEND WITH
GIRL IN YOUR CLASS.
MORE RELATED WORDS: GIRL, NEW.
HOOL SEMESTER, NEW,
MAKING FRIENDS.
MORE RELATED WORDS: FRIENDS
MORE ABOUT
YOU ARE SO ADORABLE~!
HMM...A BOYFRIEND, HUH...?
CLICK
CLICK
STEP ONE... GREET HER WITH A SMILE...
STEP TWO, AVOID THE FRIEND ZONE... OBVIOUSLY.
STEP THREE, TRY TO CATCH HER ATTENTION...
URGH...THERE ARE TOO MANY THINGS...
HMPH!
ANY PROGRESS WITH YOU AND YOU-KNOW-WHO?

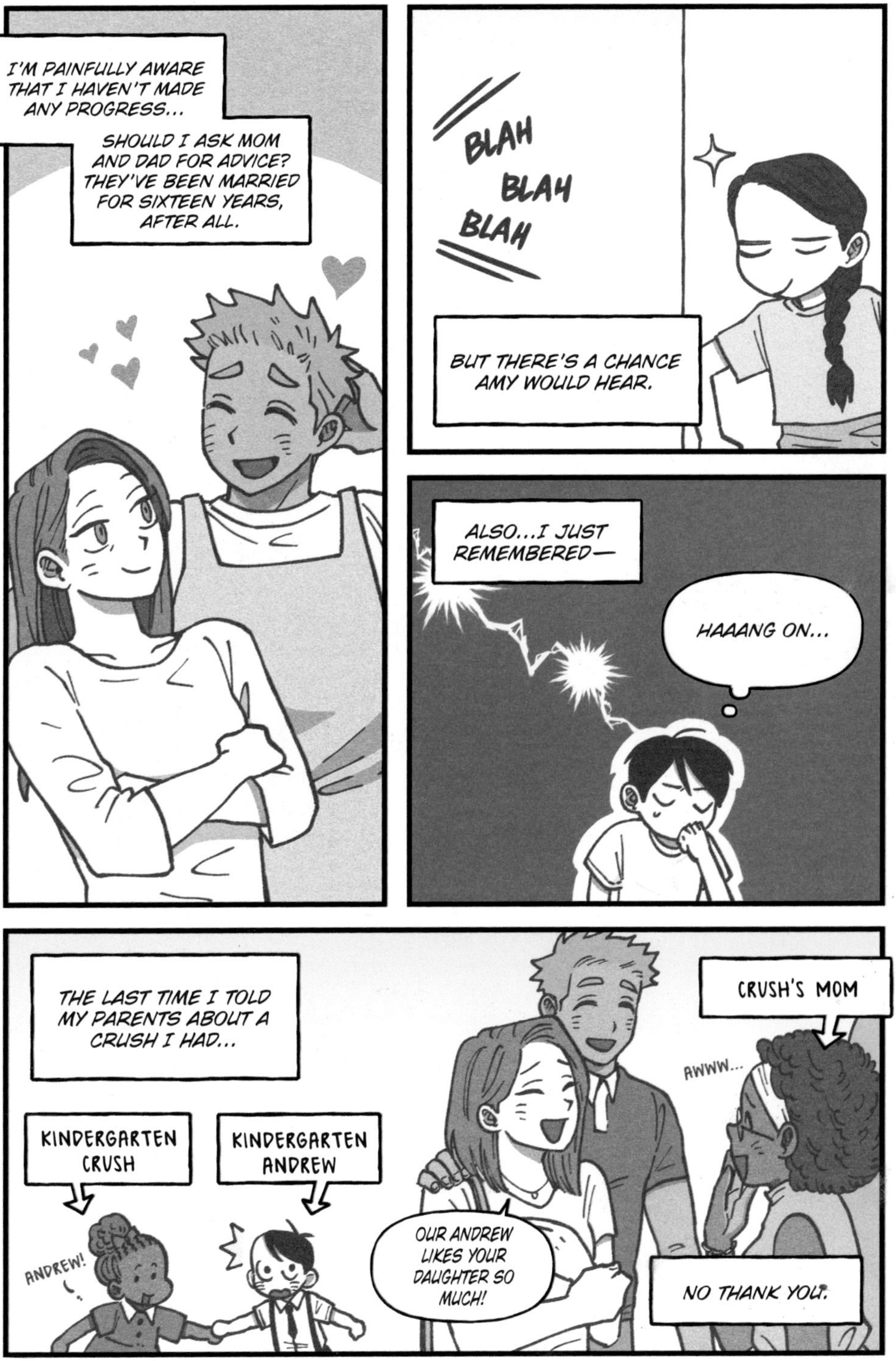
I'M PAINFULLY AWARE THAT I HAVEN'T MADE ANY PROGRESS...
SHOULD I ASK MOM AND DAD FOR ADVICE? THEY'VE BEEN MARRIED FOR SIXTEEN YEARS, AFTER ALL.
BLAH
BLAH
BLAH
BUT THERE'S A CHANCE AMY WOULD HEAR.
ALSO...I JUST REMEMBERED—
HAAANG ON...
THE LAST TIME I TOLD MY PARENTS ABOUT A CRUSH I HAD...
KINDERGARTEN CRUSH
KINDERGARTEN ANDREW
ANDREW!
OUR ANDREW LIKES YOUR DAUGHTER SO MUCH!
CRUSH'S MOM
AWWW...
NO THANK YOU.

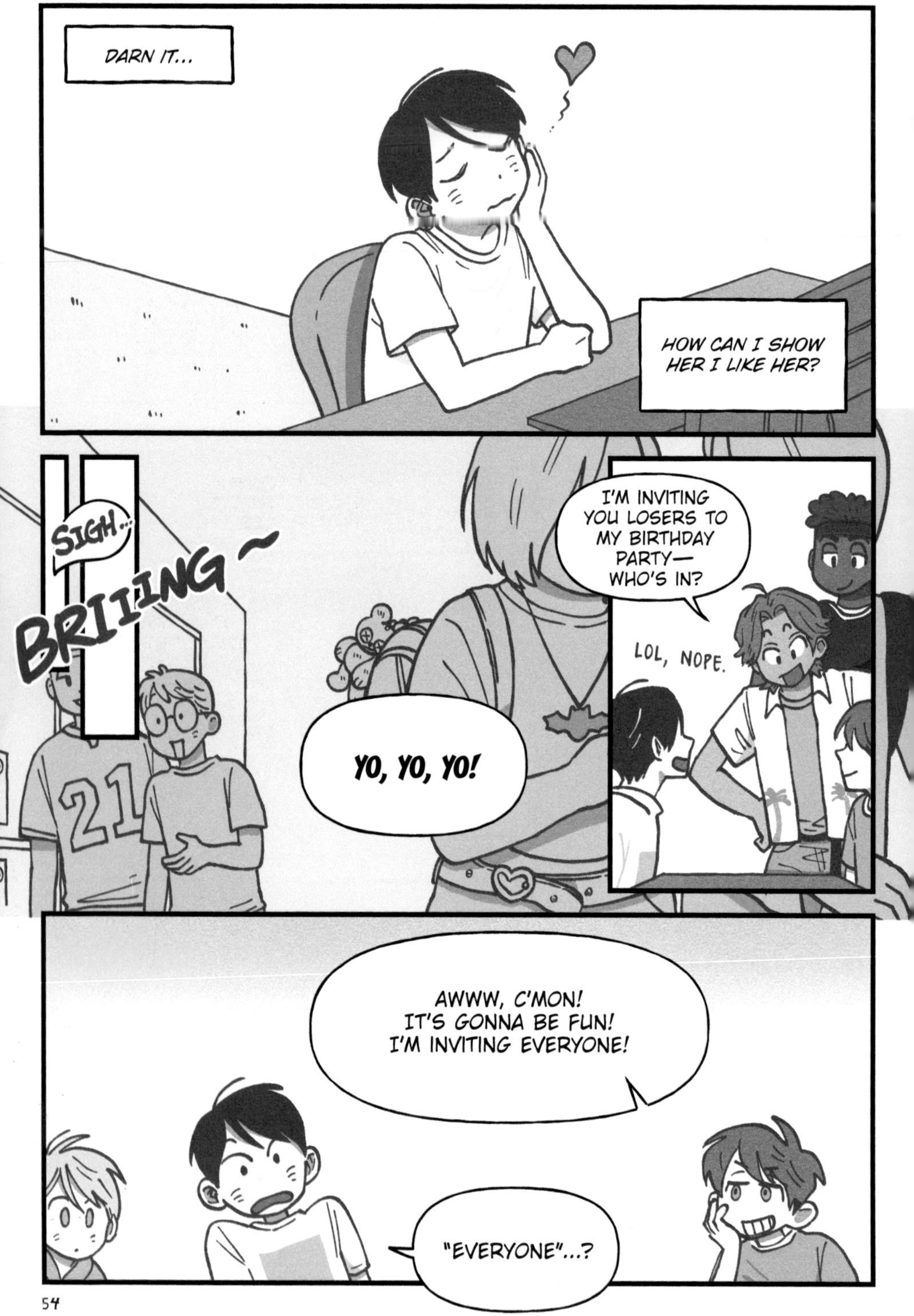
DARN IT...
HOW CAN I SHOW HER I LIKE HER?
SIGH...
BRIIING~
YO, YO, YO!
I'M INVITING YOU LOSERS TO MY BIRTHDAY PARTY— WHO'S IN?
LOL, NOPE.
AWWW, C'MON! IT'S GONNA BE FUN! I'M INVITING EVERYONE!
"EVERYONE"...?

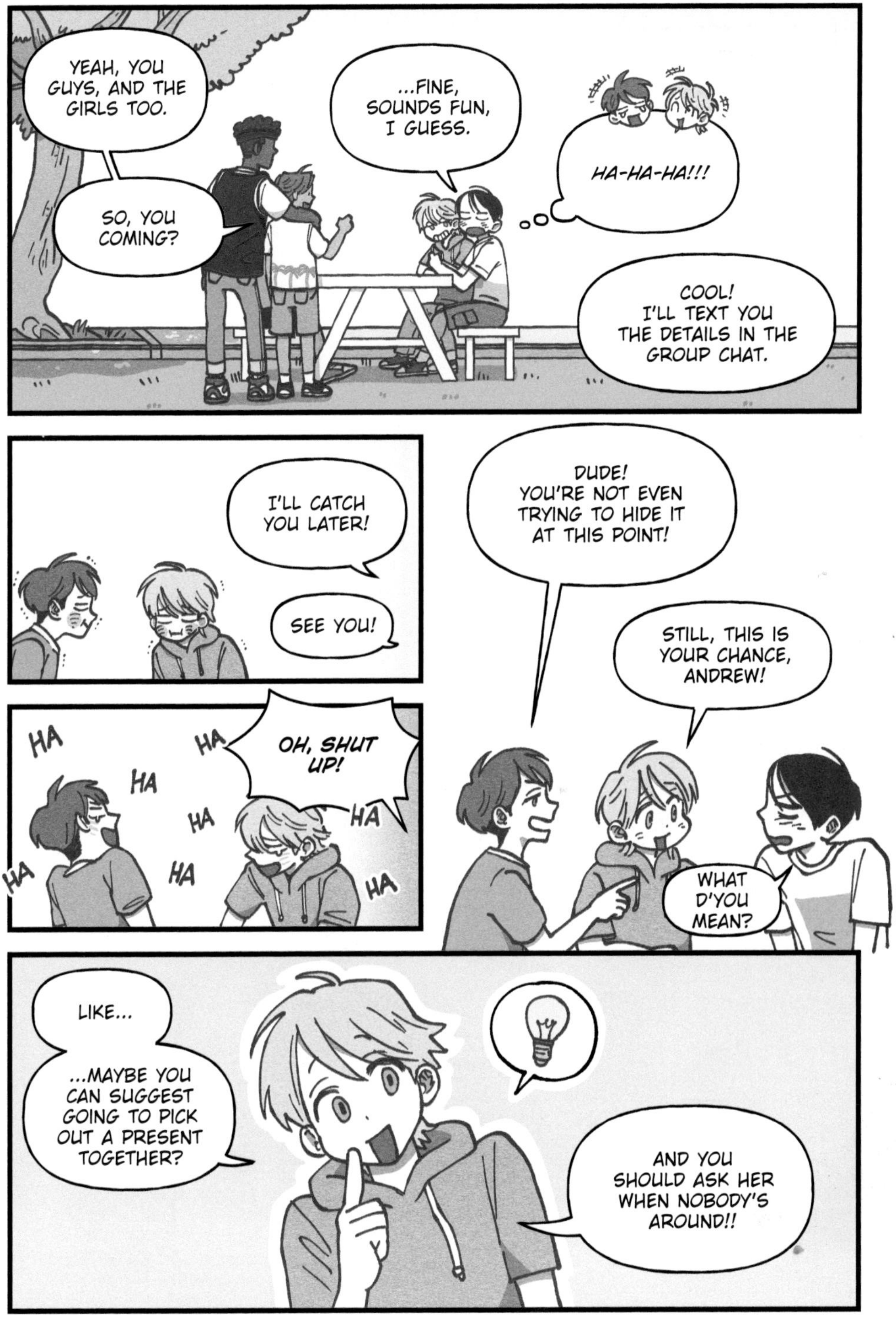
YEAH, YOU GUYS, AND THE GIRLS TOO.
SO, YOU COMING?
...FINE, SOUNDS FUN, I GUESS.
HA-HA-HA!!!
COOL! I'LL TEXT YOU THE DETAILS IN THE GROUP CHAT.
I'LL CATCH YOU LATER!
SEE YOU!
HA
HA
HA
HA
HA
OH, SHUT UP!
HA
HA
HA
DUDE! YOU'RE NOT EVEN TRYING TO HIDE IT AT THIS POINT!
STILL, THIS IS YOUR CHANCE, ANDREW!
WHAT D'YOU MEAN?
LIKE...
...MAYBE YOU CAN SUGGEST GOING TO PICK OUT A PRESENT TOGETHER?
AND YOU SHOULD ASK HER WHEN NOBODY'S AROUND!!

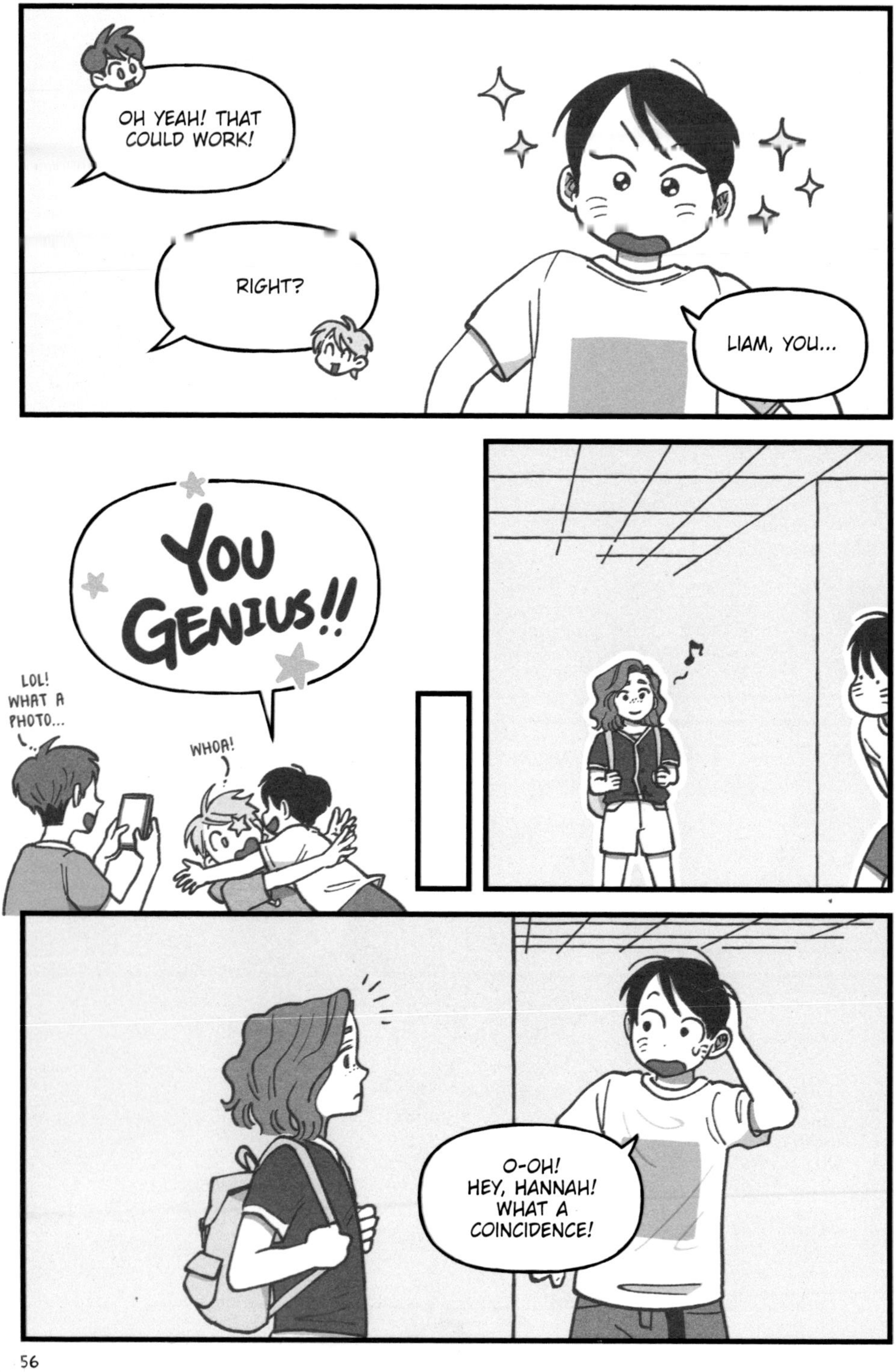
OH YEAH! THAT COULD WORK!
RIGHT?
LIAM, YOU...
YOU GENIUS!!
LOL! WHAT A PHOTO...
WHOA!
O-OH! HEY, HANNAH! WHAT A COINCIDENCE!

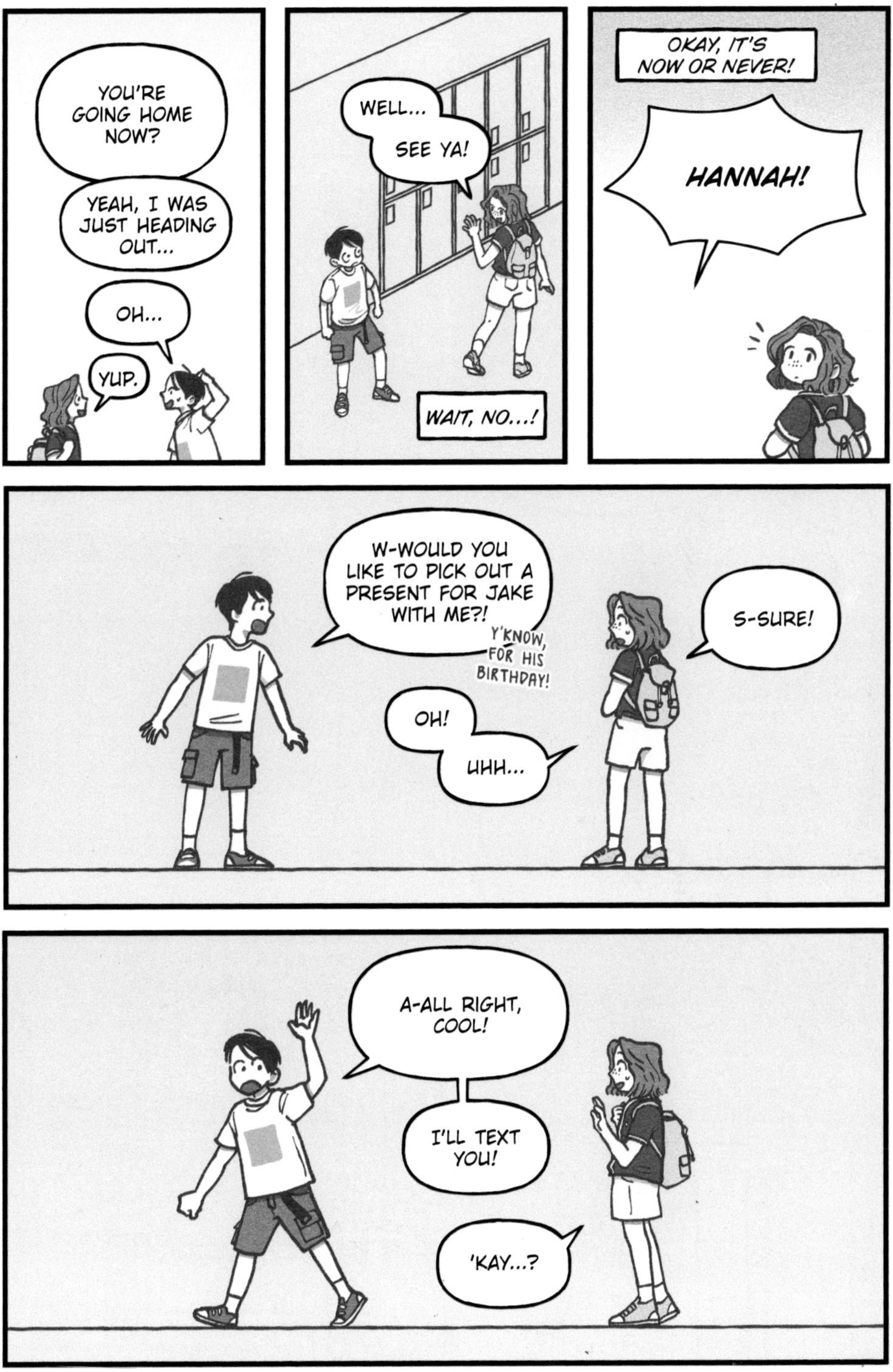

YOU'RE GOING HOME NOW?
YEAH, I WAS JUST HEADING OUT...
OH...
YUP.
WELL...
SEE YA!
WAIT, NO...!
OKAY, IT'S NOW OR NEVER!
HANNAH!
W-WOULD YOU LIKE TO PICK OUT A PRESENT FOR JAKE WITH ME?!
Y'KNOW, FOR HIS BIRTHDAY!
OH!
UHH...
S-SURE!
A-ALL RIGHT, COOL!
I'LL TEXT YOU!
'KAY...?

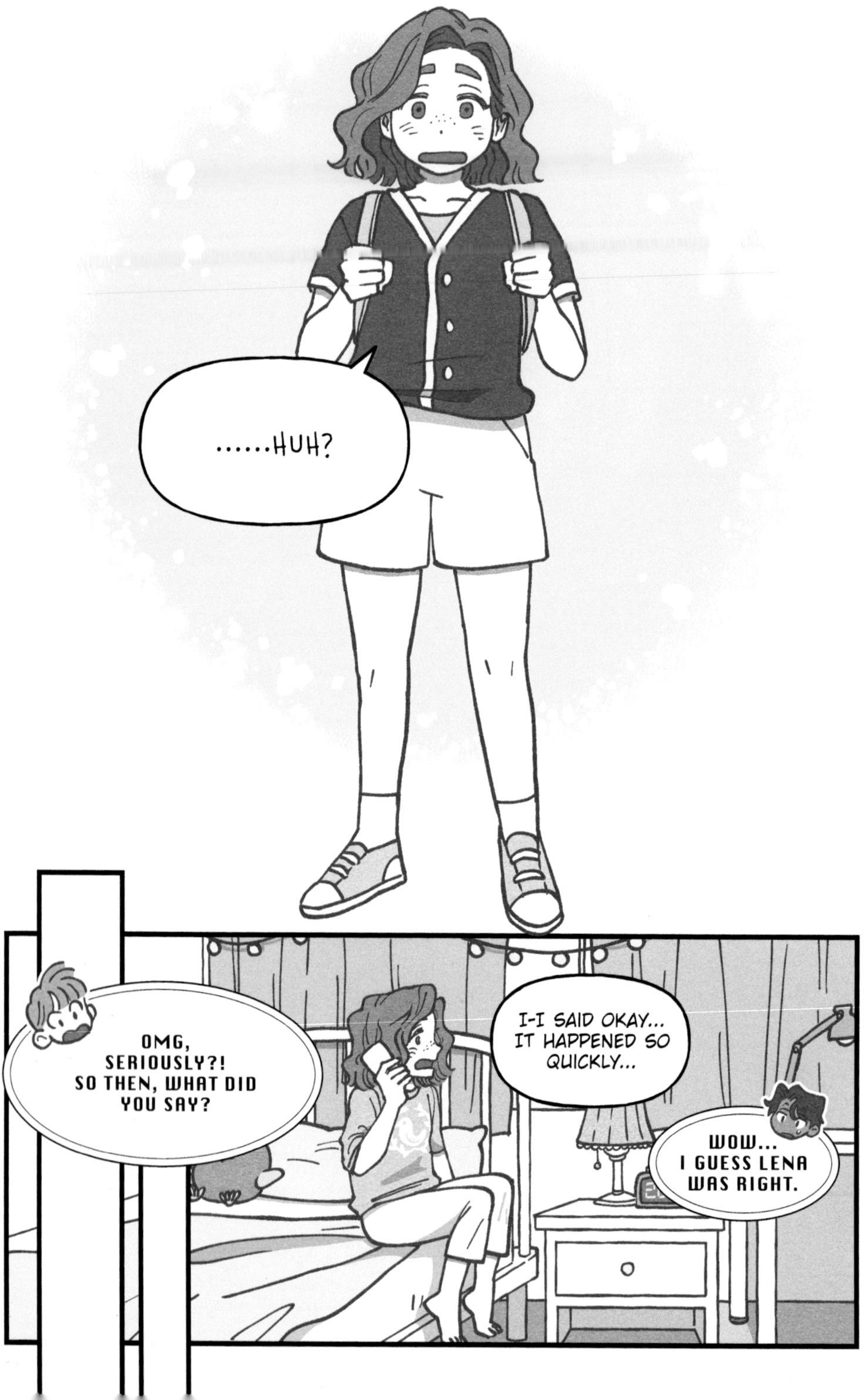
......HUH?
OMG, SERIOUSLY?! SO THEN, WHAT DID YOU SAY?
I-I SAID OKAY... IT HAPPENED SO QUICKLY...
WOW... I GUESS LENA WAS RIGHT.

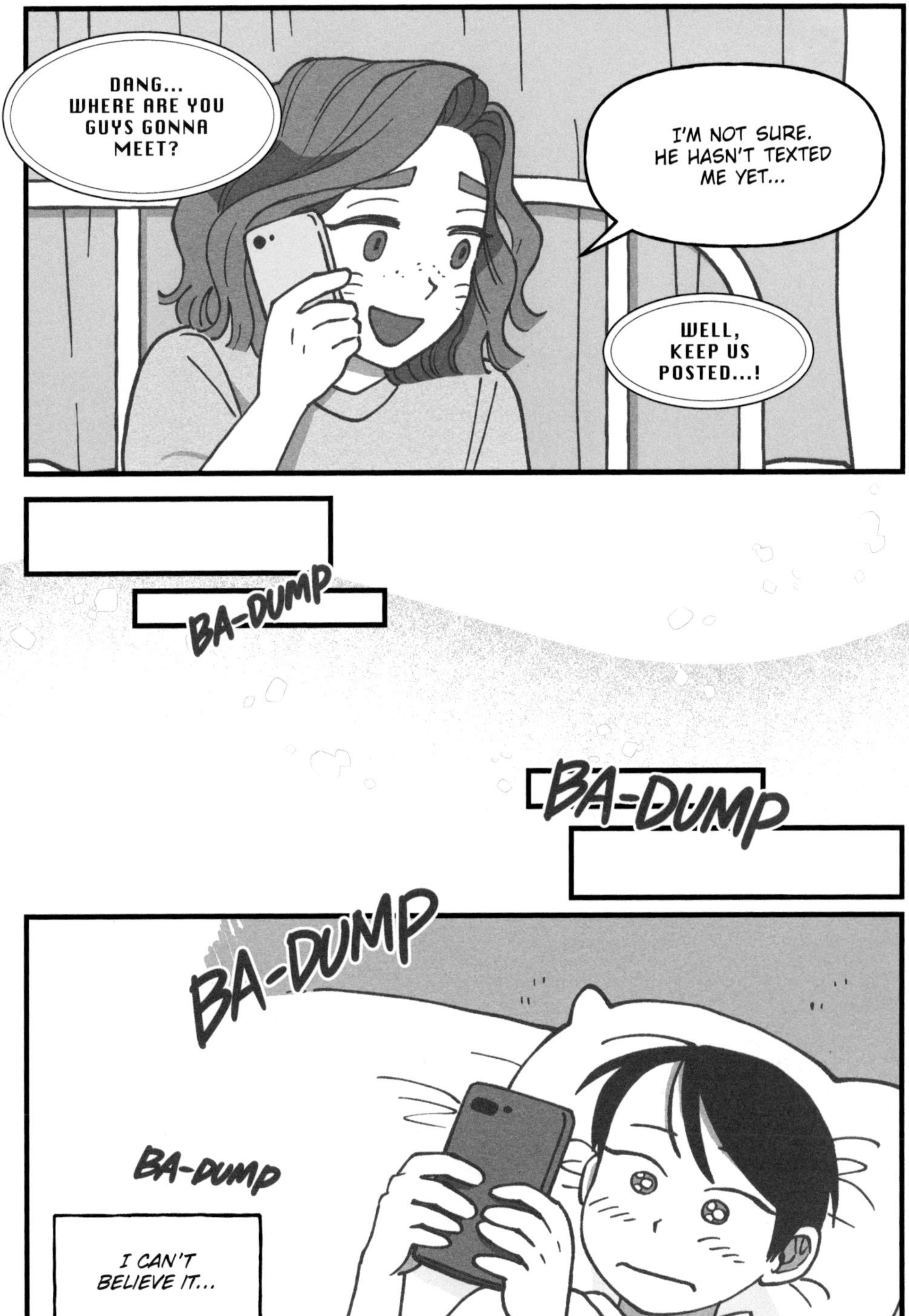
DANG... WHERE ARE YOU GUYS GONNA MEET?
I'M NOT SURE. HE HASN'T TEXTED ME YET...
WELL, KEEP US POSTED...!
BA-DUMP
BA-DUMP
BA-DUMP
BA-DUMP
I CAN'T BELIEVE IT...

I MADE PROGRESS!

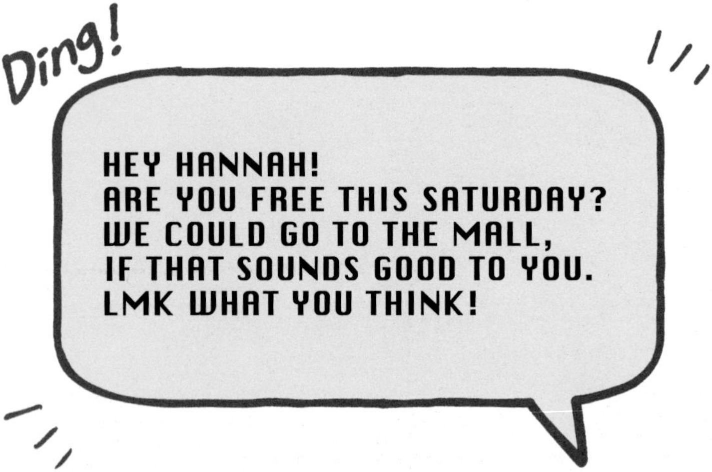

Chapter 4

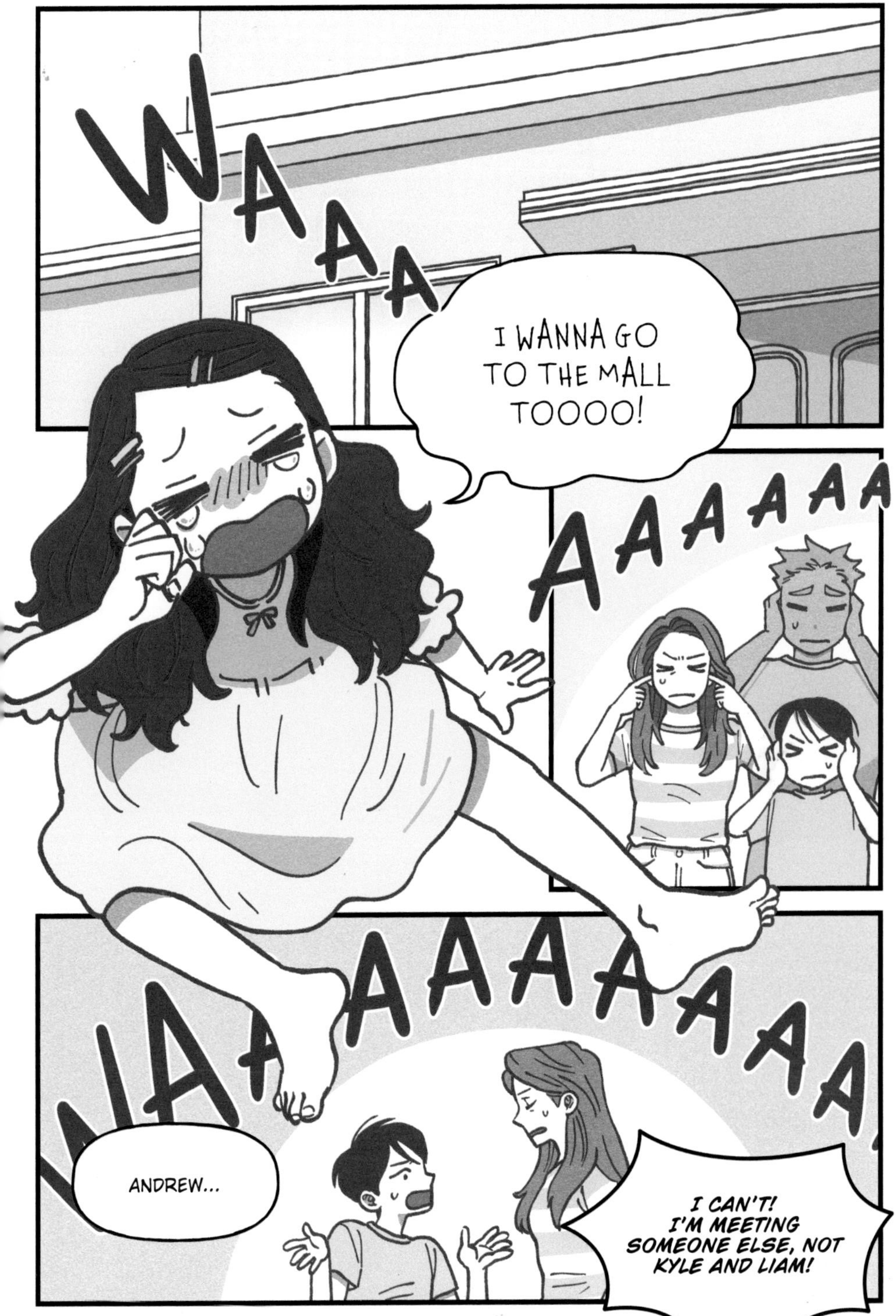
WAAA
I WANNA GO TO THE MALL TOOOO!
AAAAAAA
WAAAAAAAAAAA
ANDREW...
I CAN'T! I'M MEETING SOMEONE ELSE, NOT KYLE AND LIAM!

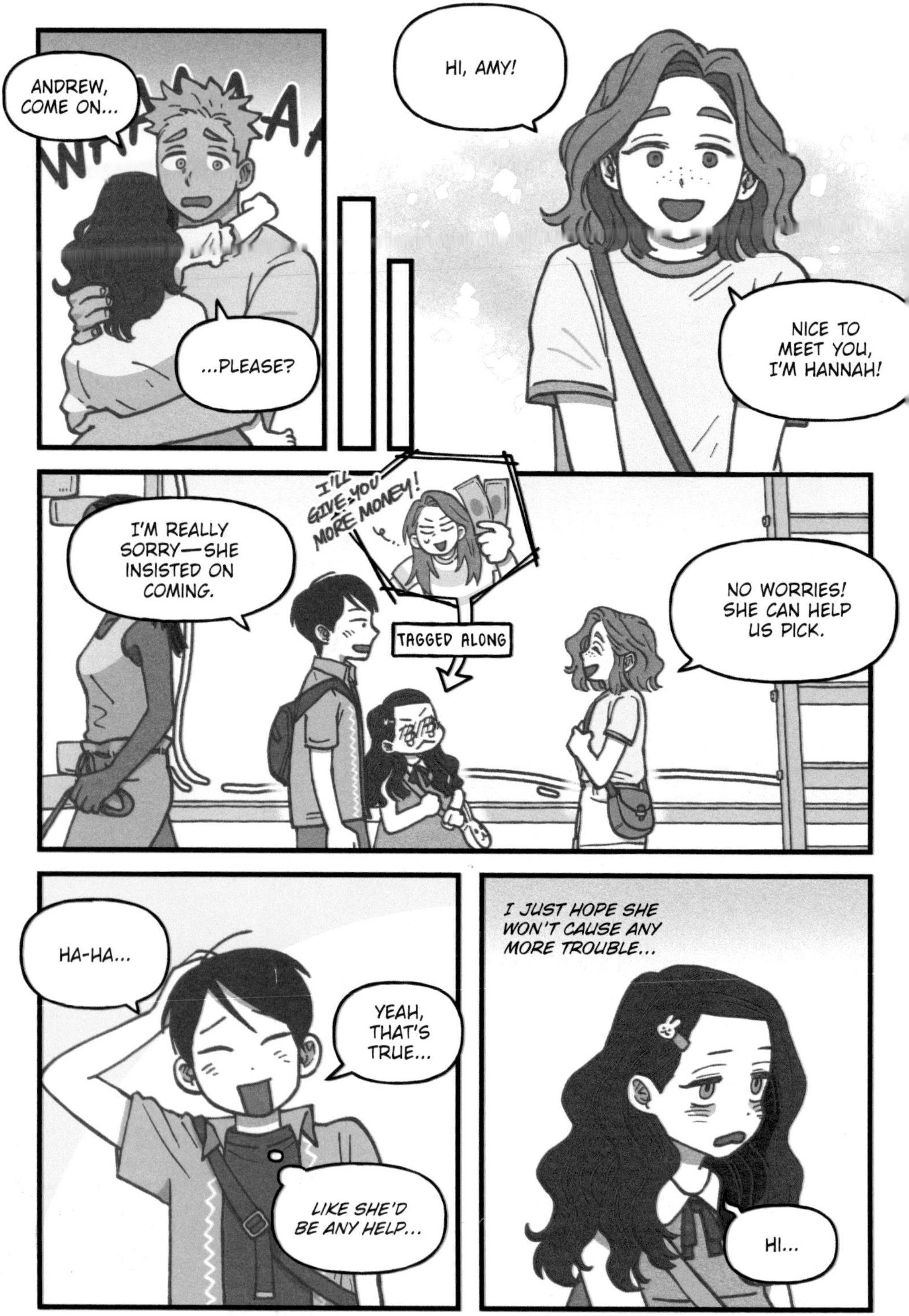
ANDREW, COME ON...
...PLEASE?
HI, AMY!
NICE TO MEET YOU, I'M HANNAH!
I'M REALLY SORRY—SHE INSISTED ON COMING.
I'LL GIVE YOU MORE MONEY!
TAGGED ALONG
NO WORRIES! SHE CAN HELP US PICK.
HA-HA...
YEAH, THAT'S TRUE...
LIKE SHE'D BE ANY HELP...
I JUST HOPE SHE WON'T CAUSE ANY MORE TROUBLE...
HI...

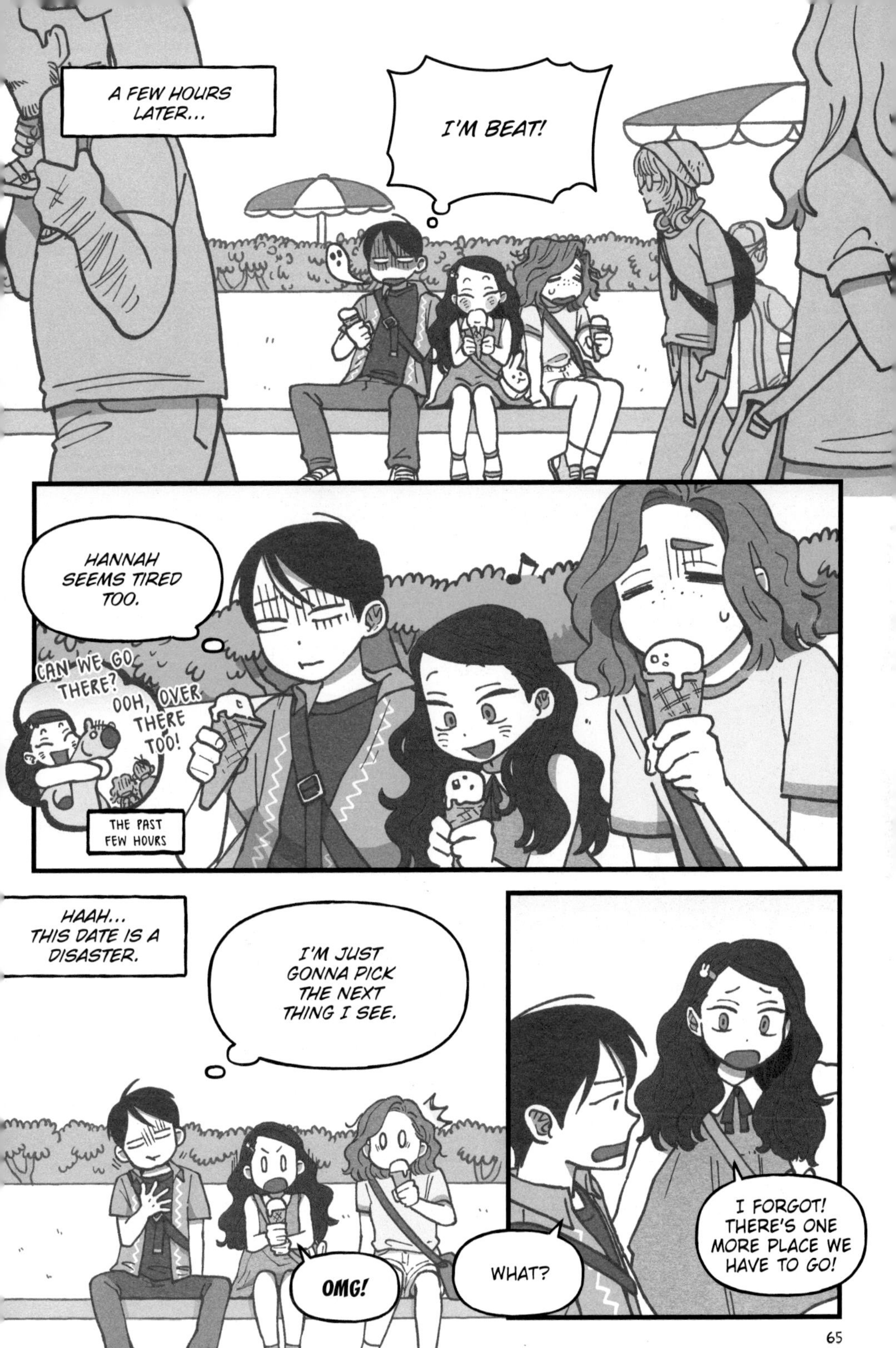
A FEW HOURS LATER...
I'M BEAT!
HANNAH SEEMS TIRED TOO.
CAN WE GO THERE?
OOH, OVER THERE TOO!
THE PAST FEW HOURS
HAAH... THIS DATE IS A DISASTER.
I'M JUST GONNA PICK THE NEXT THING I SEE.
OMG!
WHAT?
I FORGOT! THERE'S ONE MORE PLACE WE HAVE TO GO!

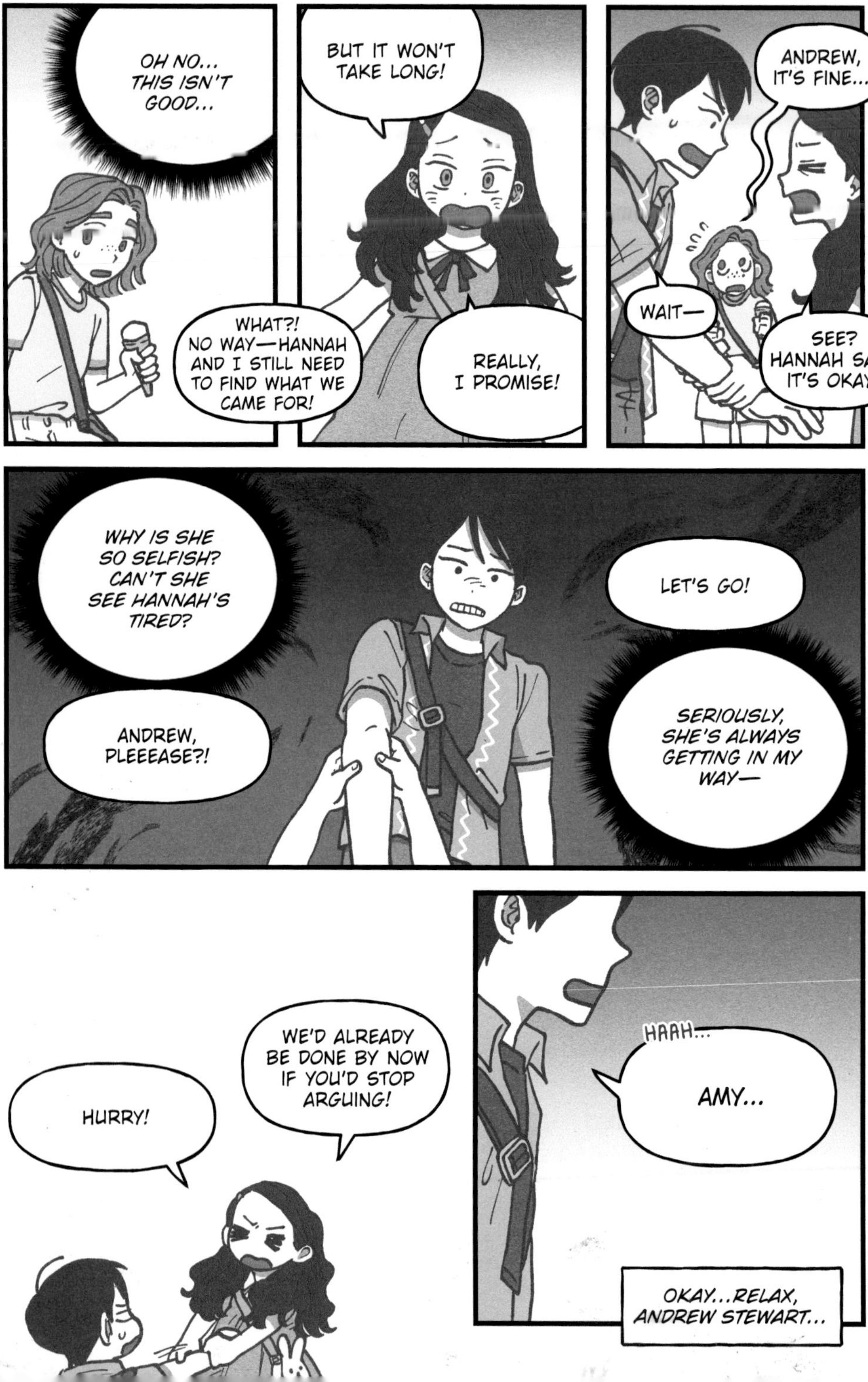
OH NO... THIS ISN'T GOOD...
WHAT?! NO WAY—HANNAH AND I STILL NEED TO FIND WHAT WE CAME FOR!
BUT IT WON'T TAKE LONG!
REALLY, I PROMISE!
ANDREW, IT'S FINE...
WAIT—
SEE? HANNAH SAYS IT'S OKAY!
WHY IS SHE SO SELFISH? CAN'T SHE SEE HANNAH'S TIRED?
ANDREW, PLEEEASE?!
LET'S GO!
SERIOUSLY, SHE'S ALWAYS GETTING IN MY WAY—
HURRY!
WE'D ALREADY BE DONE BY NOW IF YOU'D STOP ARGUING!
HAAH...
AMY...
OKAY...RELAX, ANDREW STEWART...

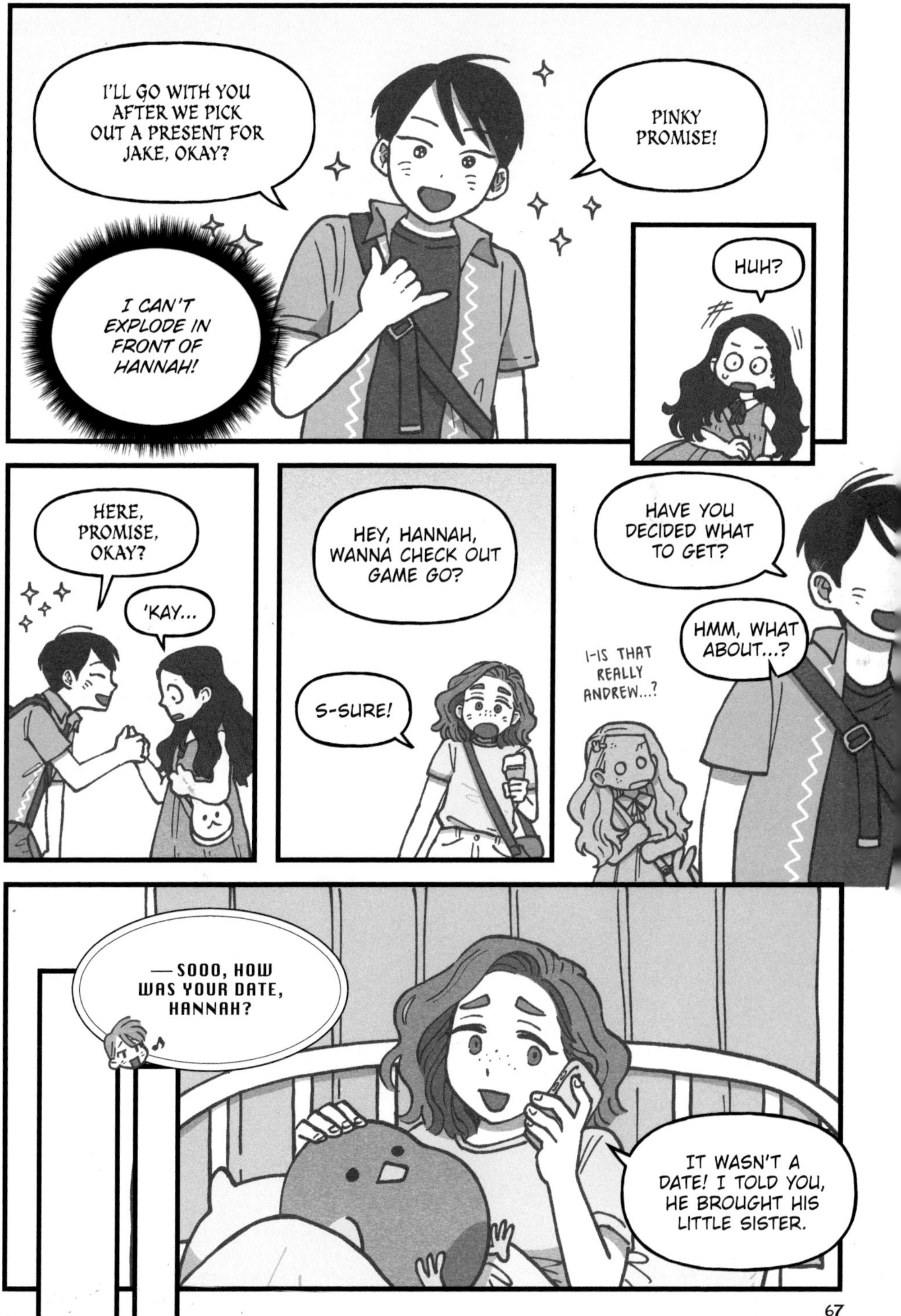
I'LL GO WITH YOU AFTER WE PICK OUT A PRESENT FOR JAKE, OKAY?
PINKY PROMISE!
I CAN'T EXPLODE IN FRONT OF HANNAH!
HUH?
HERE, PROMISE, OKAY?
'KAY...
HEY, HANNAH, WANNA CHECK OUT GAME GO?
S-SURE!
HAVE YOU DECIDED WHAT TO GET?
HMM, WHAT ABOUT...?
I-IS THAT REALLY ANDREW...?
—SOOO, HOW WAS YOUR DATE, HANNAH?
IT WASN'T A DATE! I TOLD YOU, HE BROUGHT HIS LITTLE SISTER.

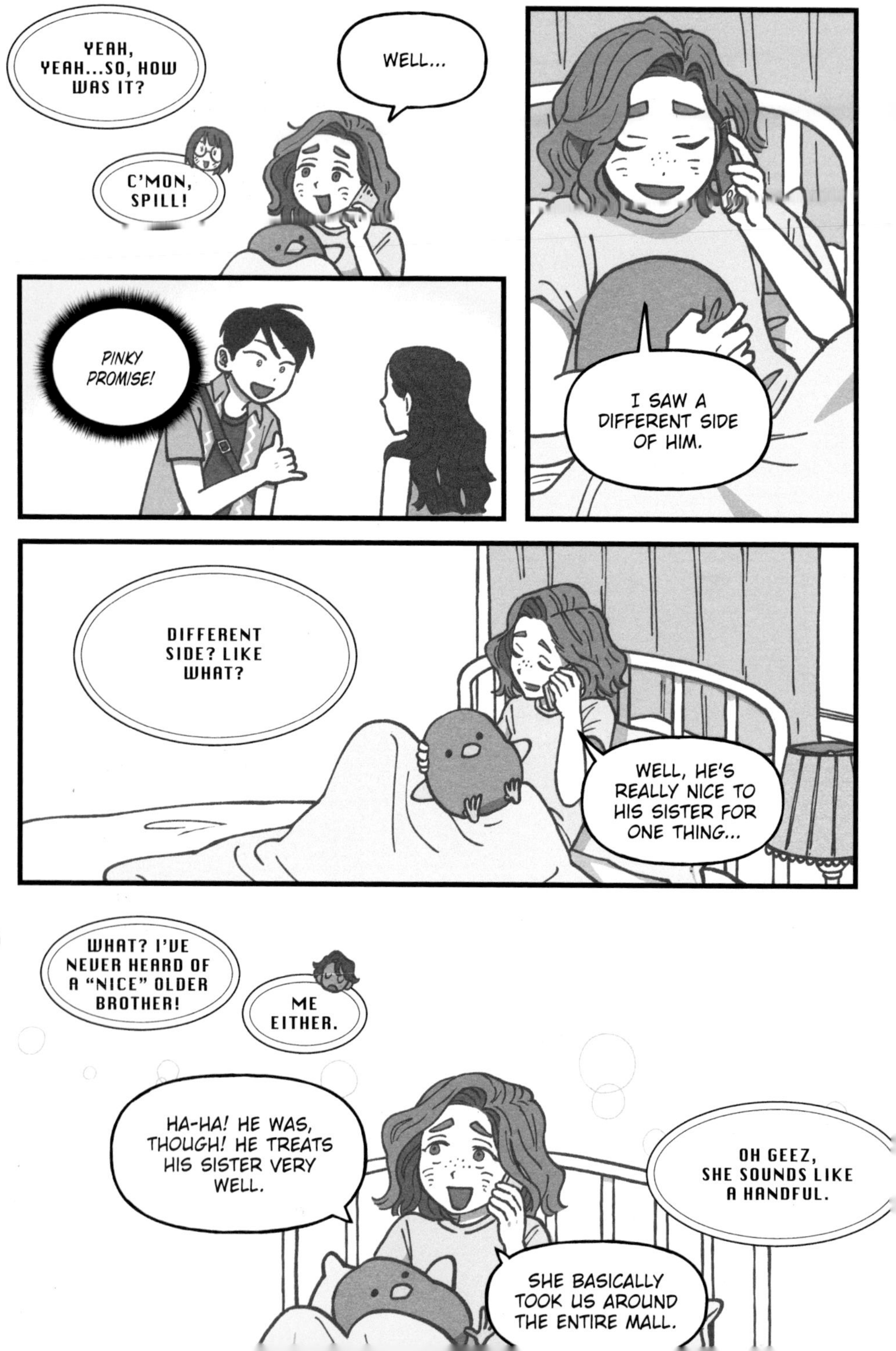
YEAH, YEAH...SO, HOW WAS IT?
WELL...
C'MON, SPILL!
I SAW A DIFFERENT SIDE OF HIM.
PINKY PROMISE!
DIFFERENT SIDE? LIKE WHAT?
WELL, HE'S REALLY NICE TO HIS SISTER FOR ONE THING...
WHAT? I'VE NEVER HEARD OF A "NICE" OLDER BROTHER!
ME EITHER.
HA-HA! HE WAS, THOUGH! HE TREATS HIS SISTER VERY WELL.
OH GEEZ, SHE SOUNDS LIKE A HANDFUL.
SHE BASICALLY TOOK US AROUND THE ENTIRE MALL.

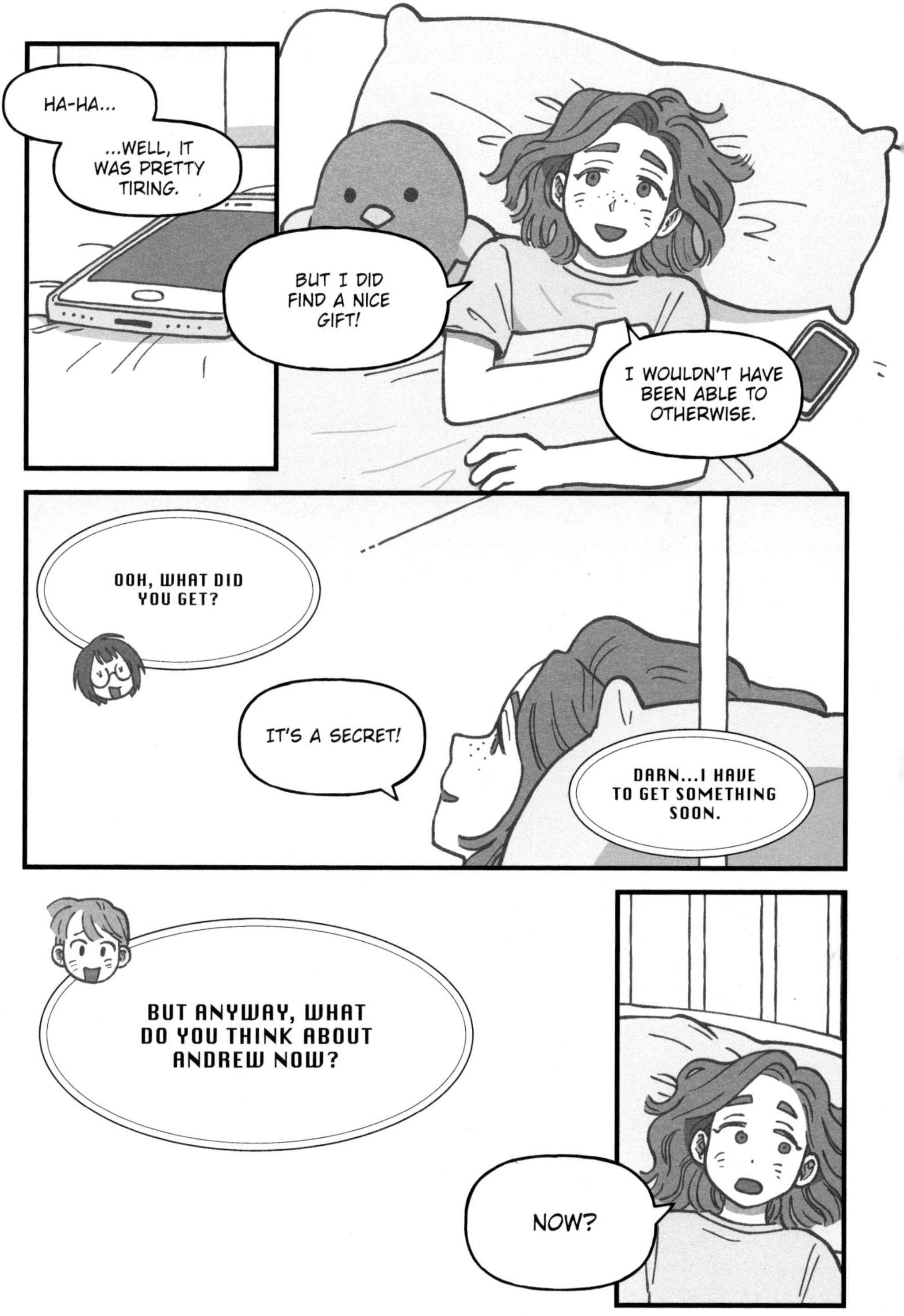
HA-HA...
...WELL, IT WAS PRETTY TIRING.
BUT I DID FIND A NICE GIFT!
I WOULDN'T HAVE BEEN ABLE TO OTHERWISE.
OOH, WHAT DID YOU GET?
IT'S A SECRET!
DARN...I HAVE TO GET SOMETHING SOON.
BUT ANYWAY, WHAT DO YOU THINK ABOUT ANDREW NOW?
NOW?

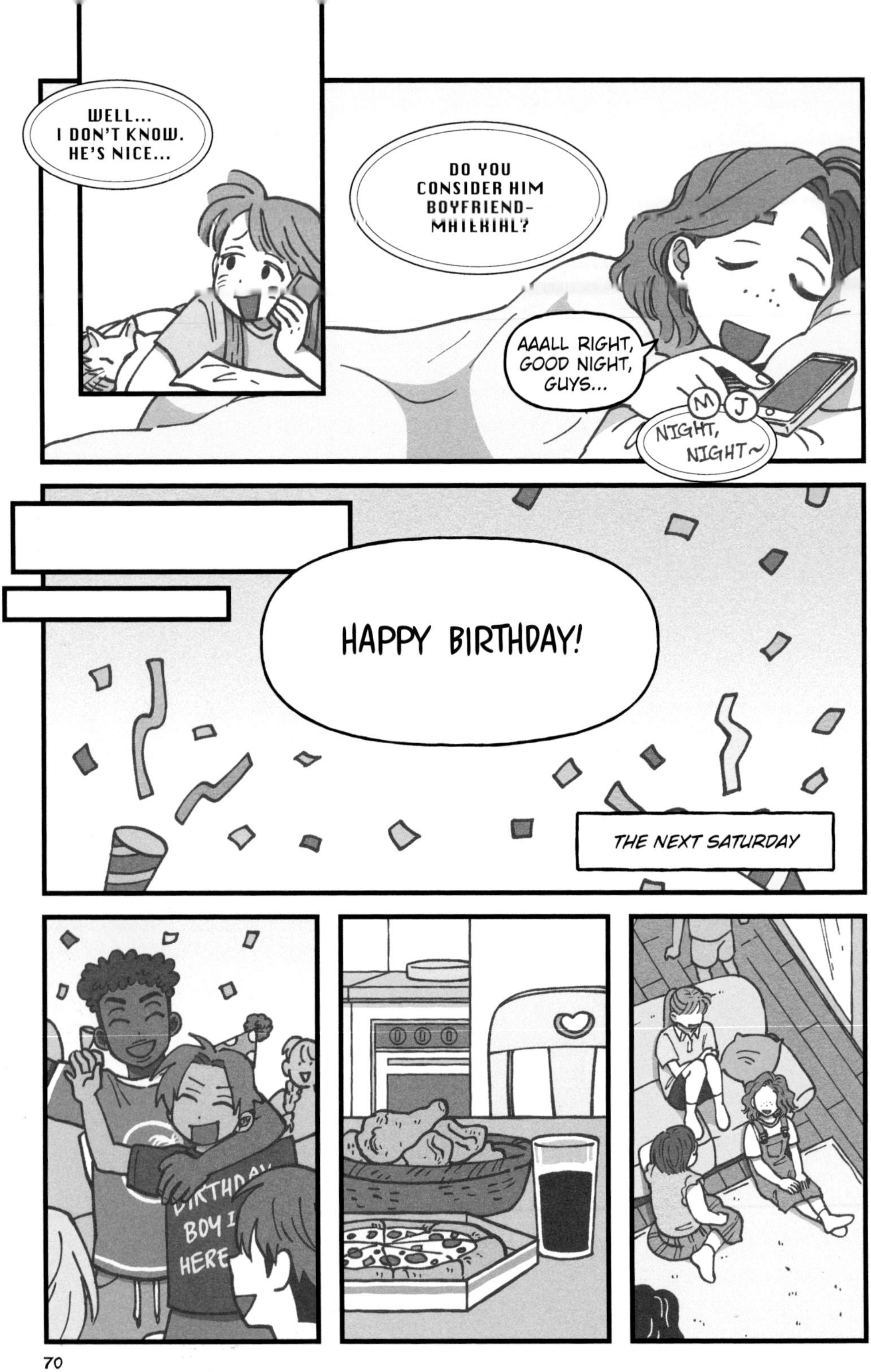
WELL...
I DON'T KNOW.
HE'S NICE...
DO YOU
CONSIDER HIM
BOYFRIEND-
MATERIAL?
AAALL RIGHT,
GOOD NIGHT,
GUYS...
M
J
NIGHT,
NIGHT~
HAPPY BIRTHDAY!
THE NEXT SATURDAY

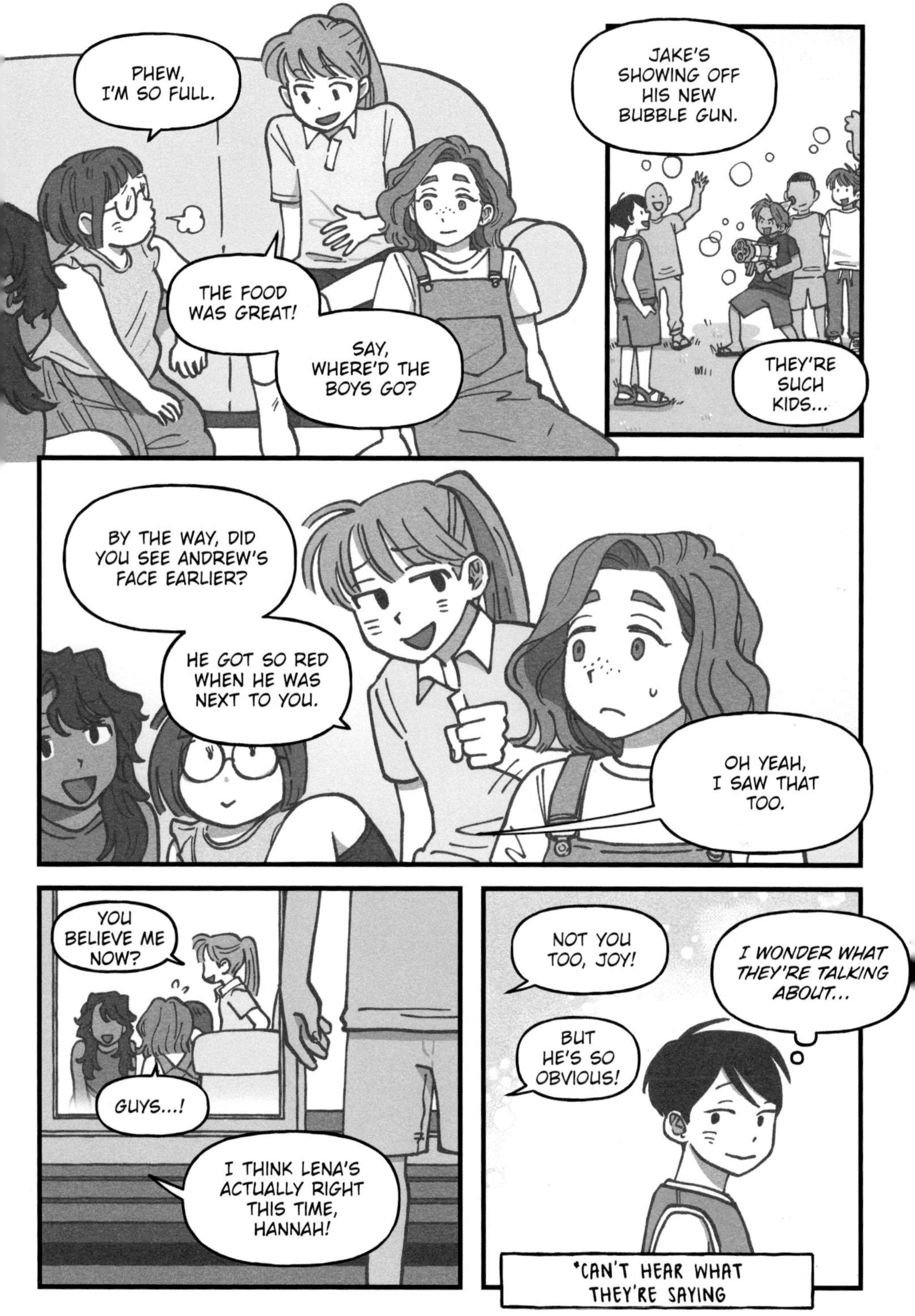
PHEW, I'M SO FULL.
THE FOOD WAS GREAT!
SAY, WHERE'D THE BOYS GO?
JAKE'S SHOWING OFF HIS NEW BUBBLE GUN.
THEY'RE SUCH KIDS...
BY THE WAY, DID YOU SEE ANDREW'S FACE EARLIER?
HE GOT SO RED WHEN HE WAS NEXT TO YOU.
OH YEAH, I SAW THAT TOO.
YOU BELIEVE ME NOW?
GUYS...!
I THINK LENA'S ACTUALLY RIGHT THIS TIME, HANNAH!
NOT YOU TOO, JOY!
BUT HE'S SO OBVIOUS!
I WONDER WHAT THEY'RE TALKING ABOUT...
*CAN'T HEAR WHAT THEY'RE SAYING

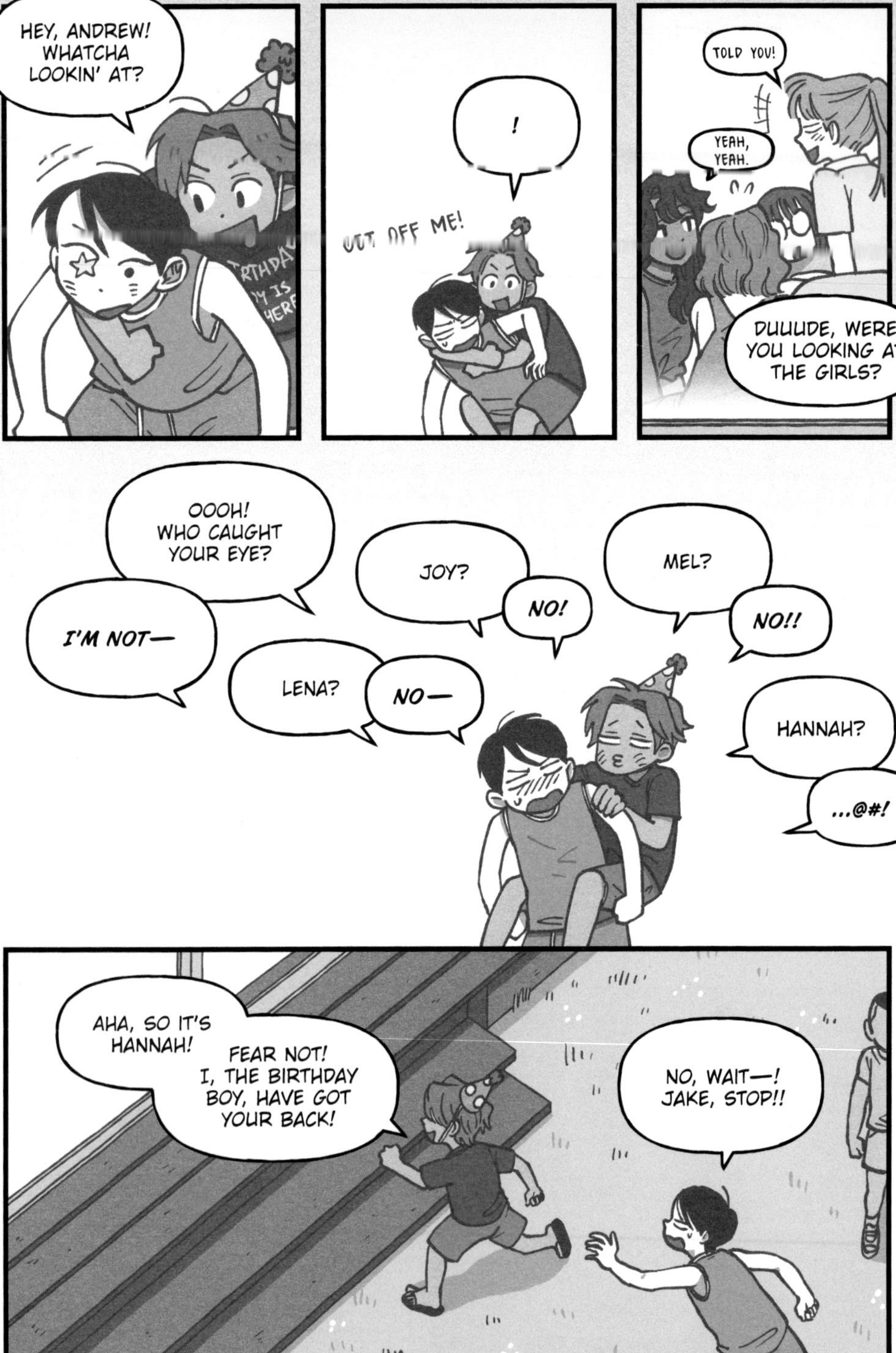
HEY, ANDREW! WHATCHA LOOKIN' AT?
BIRTHDAY BOY IS HERE
!
OFF ME!
TOLD YOU!
YEAH, YEAH.
DUUUDE, WERE YOU LOOKING AT THE GIRLS?
OOOH! WHO CAUGHT YOUR EYE?
I'M NOT—
JOY?
NO!
MEL?
NO!!
LENA?
NO—
HANNAH?
...@#!
AHA, SO IT'S HANNAH!
FEAR NOT! I, THE BIRTHDAY BOY, HAVE GOT YOUR BACK!
NO, WAIT—! JAKE, STOP!!

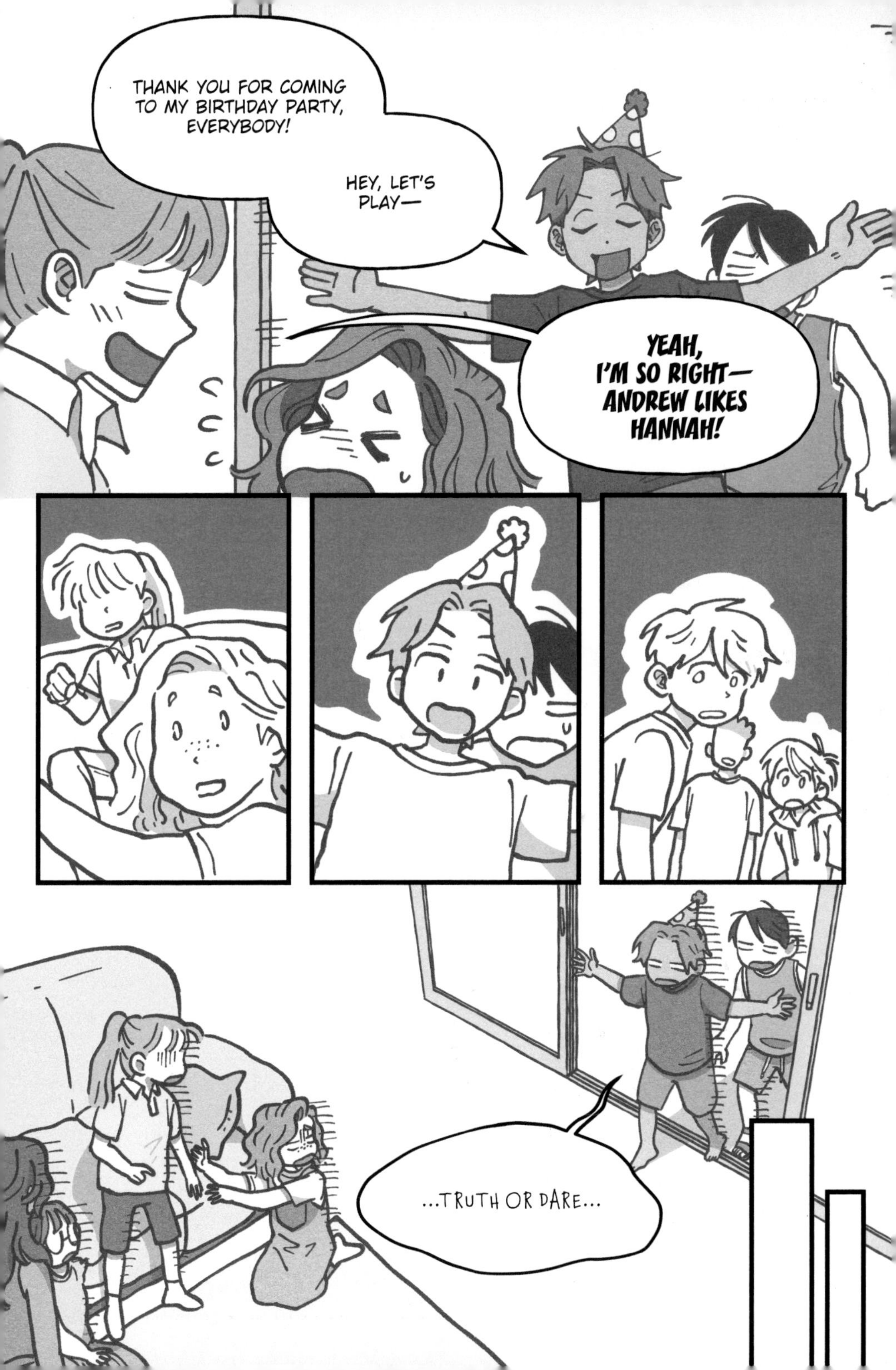
THANK YOU FOR COMING TO MY BIRTHDAY PARTY, EVERYBODY!
HEY, LET'S PLAY—
YEAH, I'M SO RIGHT—ANDREW LIKES HANNAH!
...TRUTH OR DARE...

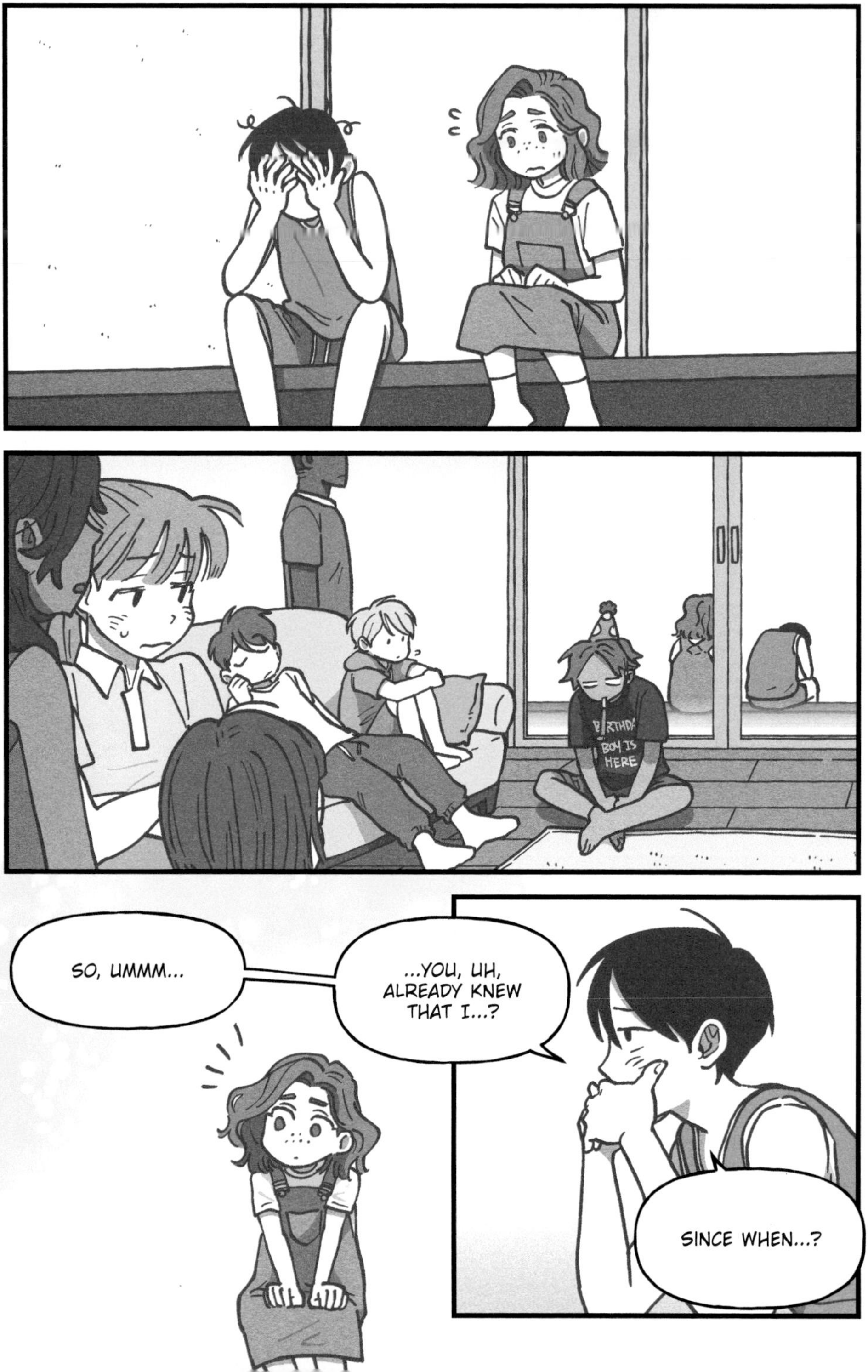
BIRTHDAY BOY IS HERE
SO, UMMM...
...YOU, UH, ALREADY KNEW THAT I...?
SINCE WHEN...?

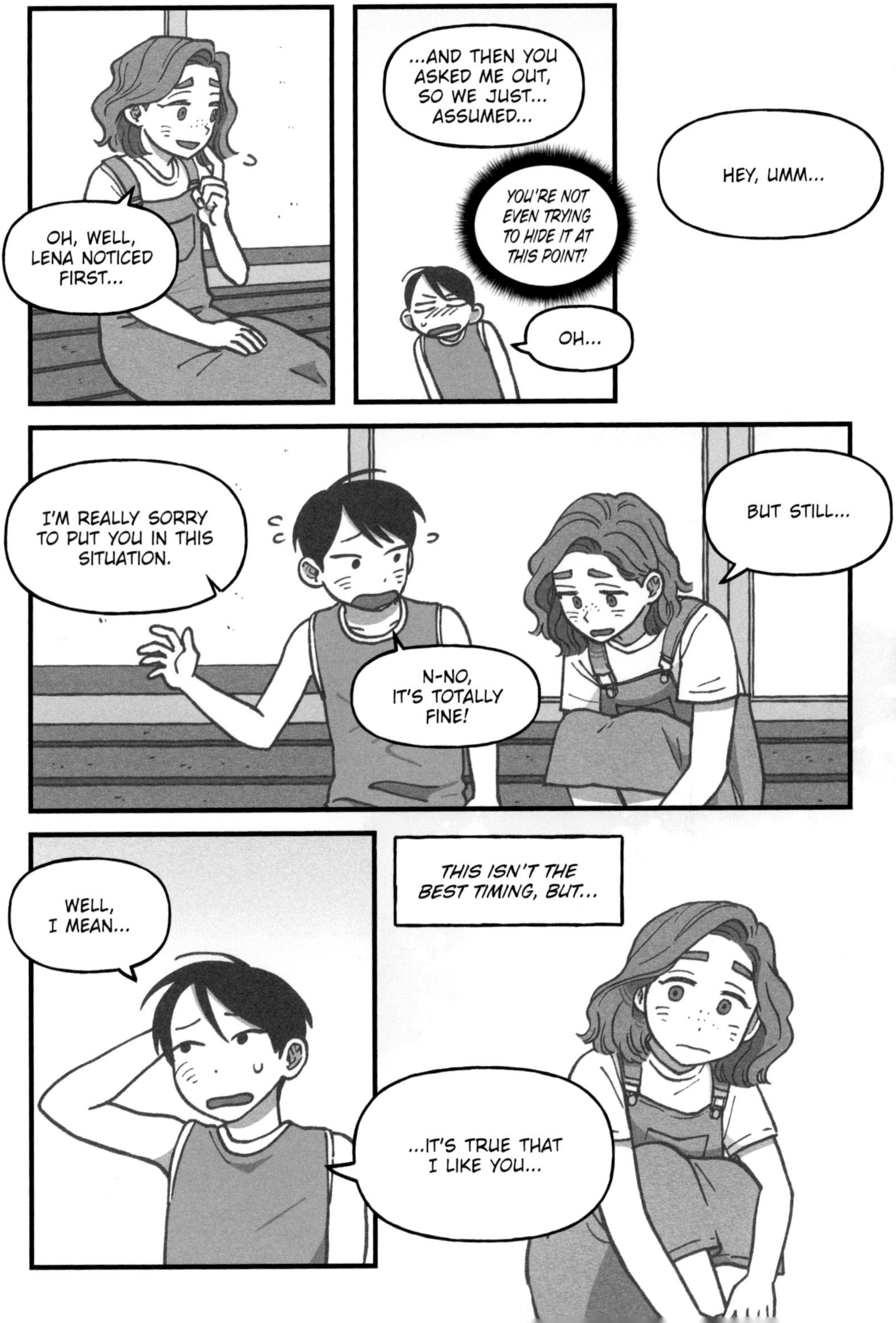
OH, WELL, LENA NOTICED FIRST...
...AND THEN YOU ASKED ME OUT, SO WE JUST... ASSUMED...
YOU'RE NOT EVEN TRYING TO HIDE IT AT THIS POINT!
OH...
HEY, UMM...
I'M REALLY SORRY TO PUT YOU IN THIS SITUATION.
N-NO, IT'S TOTALLY FINE!
BUT STILL...
WELL, I MEAN...
THIS ISN'T THE BEST TIMING, BUT...
...IT'S TRUE THAT I LIKE YOU...

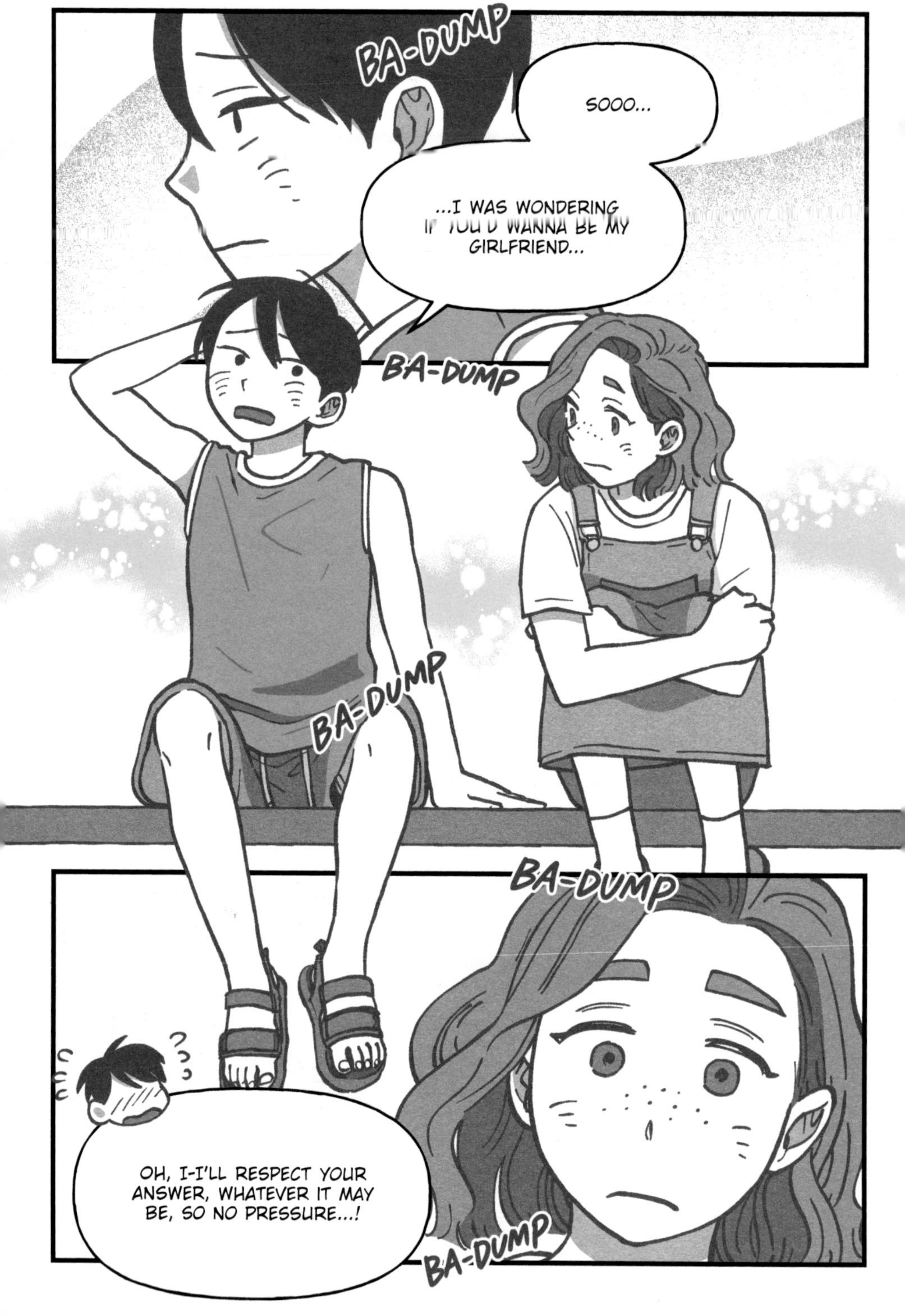
BA-DUMP
SOOO...
...I WAS WONDERING IF YOU'D WANNA BE MY GIRLFRIEND...
BA-DUMP
BA-DUMP
BA-DUMP
OH, I-I'LL RESPECT YOUR ANSWER, WHATEVER IT MAY BE, SO NO PRESSURE...!
BA-DUMP

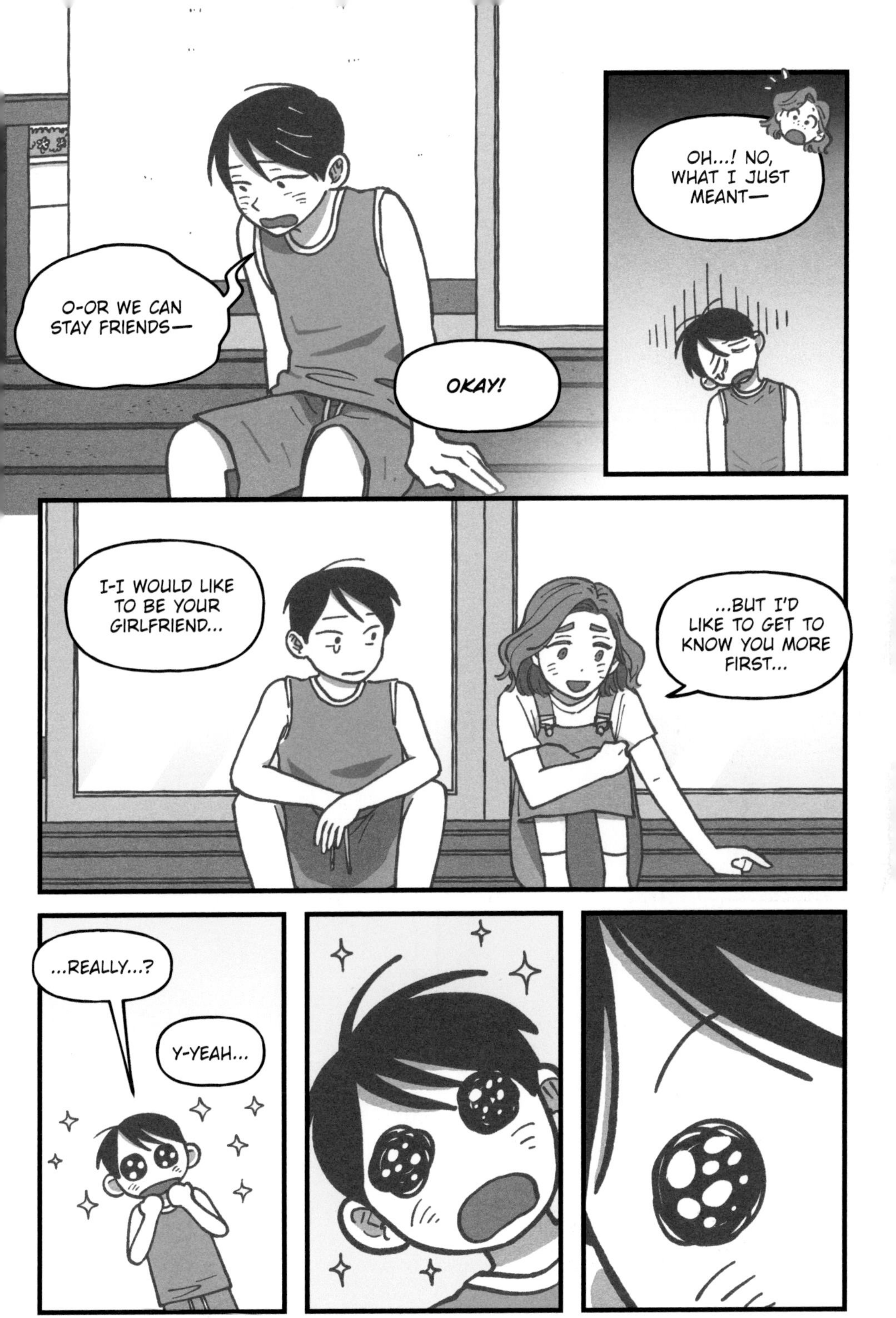
O-OR WE CAN
STAY FRIENDS—
OKAY!
OH...! NO,
WHAT I JUST
MEANT—
I-I WOULD LIKE
TO BE YOUR
GIRLFRIEND...
...BUT I'D
LIKE TO GET TO
KNOW YOU MORE
FIRST...
...REALLY...?
Y-YEAH...

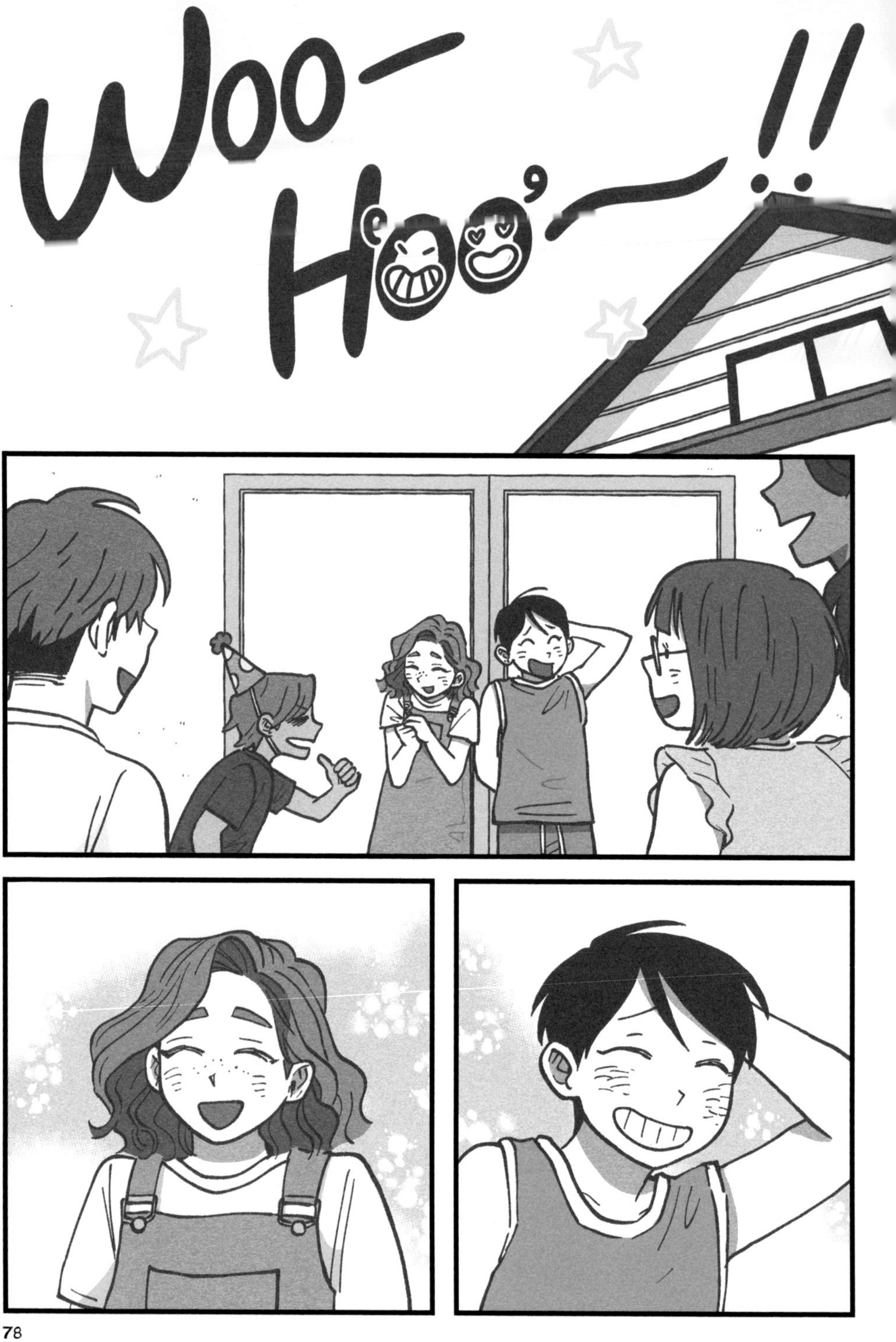
WOO-HOO—!!

AT THAT TIME, WE HAD
NO IDEA WHAT FUTURE
AWAITED US...

Chapter 5

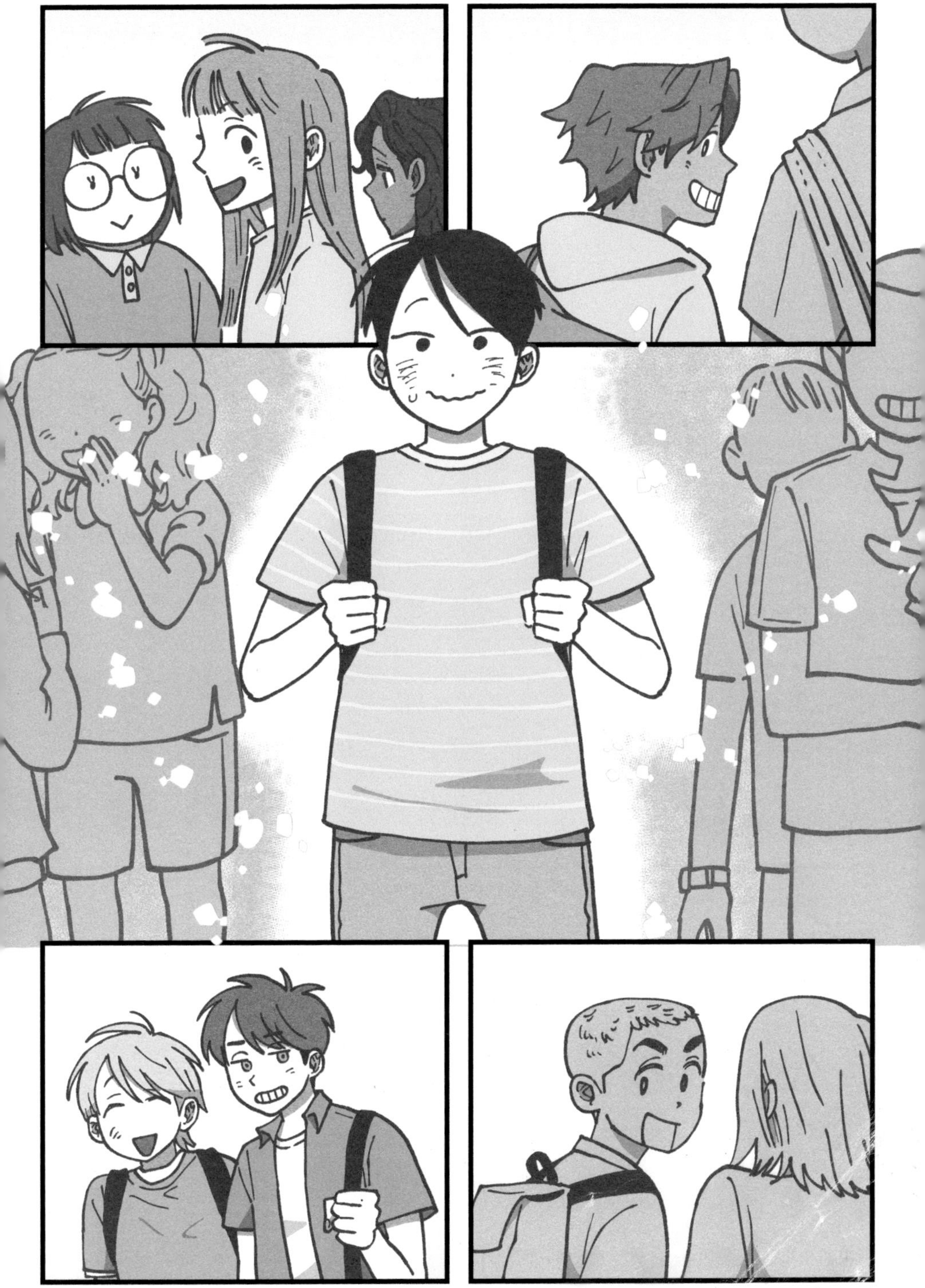

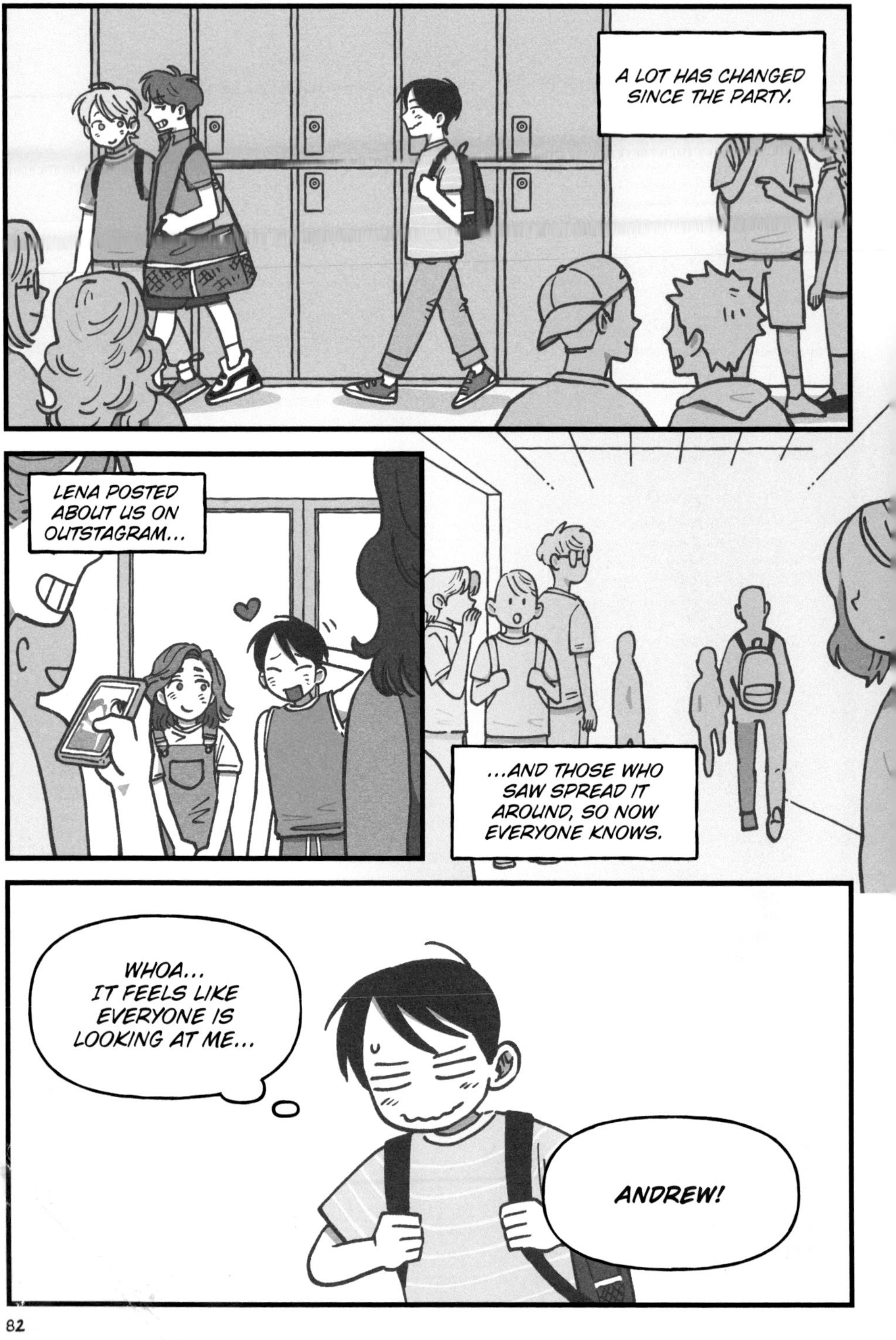
A LOT HAS CHANGED SINCE THE PARTY.
LENA POSTED ABOUT US ON OUTSTAGRAM...
...AND THOSE WHO SAW SPREAD IT AROUND, SO NOW EVERYONE KNOWS.
WHOA... IT FEELS LIKE EVERYONE IS LOOKING AT ME...
ANDREW!

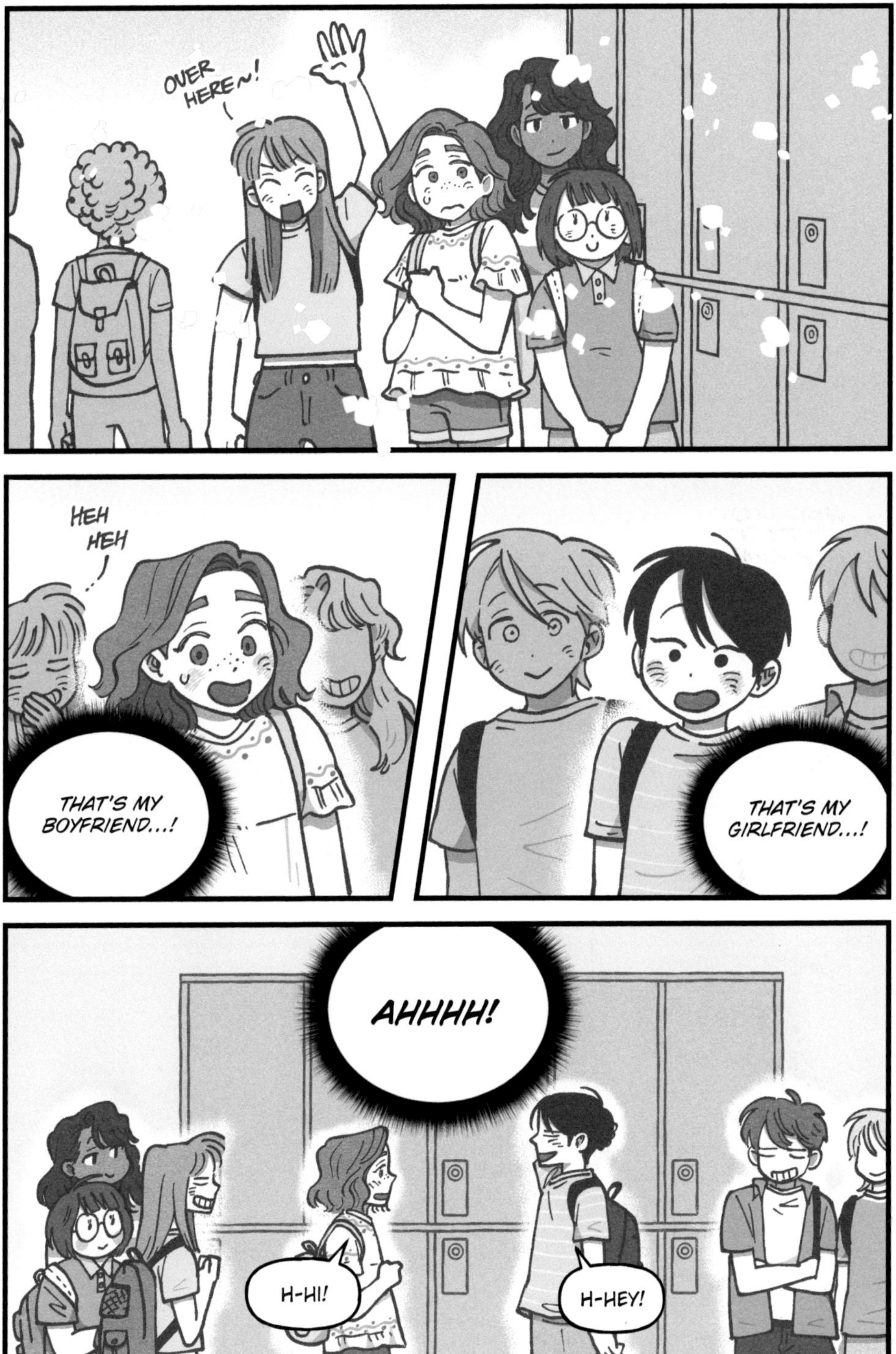
OVER HERE~!
HEH HEH
THAT'S MY BOYFRIEND...!
THAT'S MY GIRLFRIEND...!
AHHHH!
H-HI!
H-HEY!

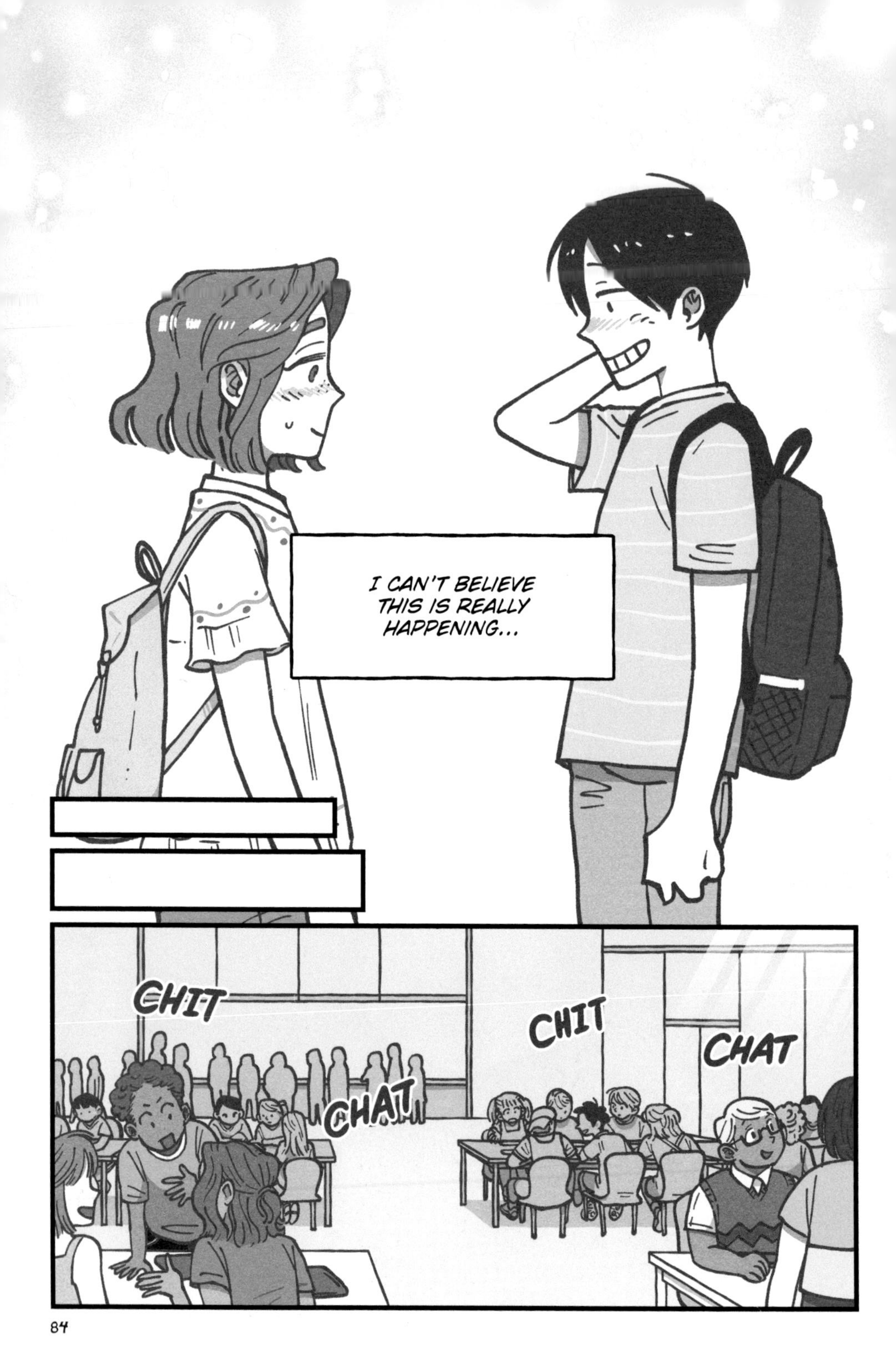
I CAN'T BELIEVE THIS IS REALLY HAPPENING...
CHIT
CHAT
CHIT
CHAT

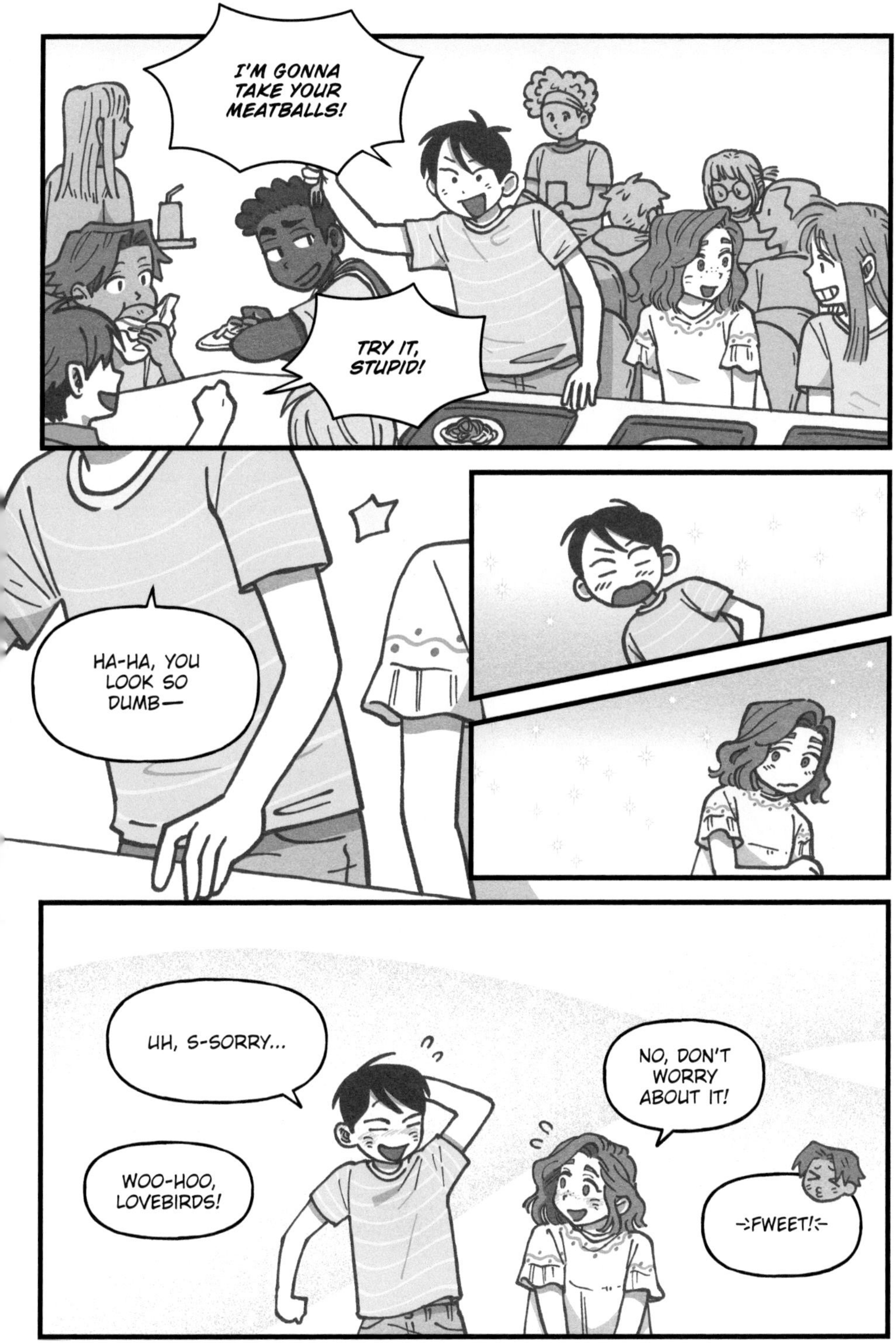
I'M GONNA TAKE YOUR MEATBALLS!
TRY IT, STUPID!
HA-HA, YOU LOOK SO DUMB—
UH, S-SORRY...
NO, DON'T WORRY ABOUT IT!
WOO-HOO, LOVEBIRDS!
FWEET!

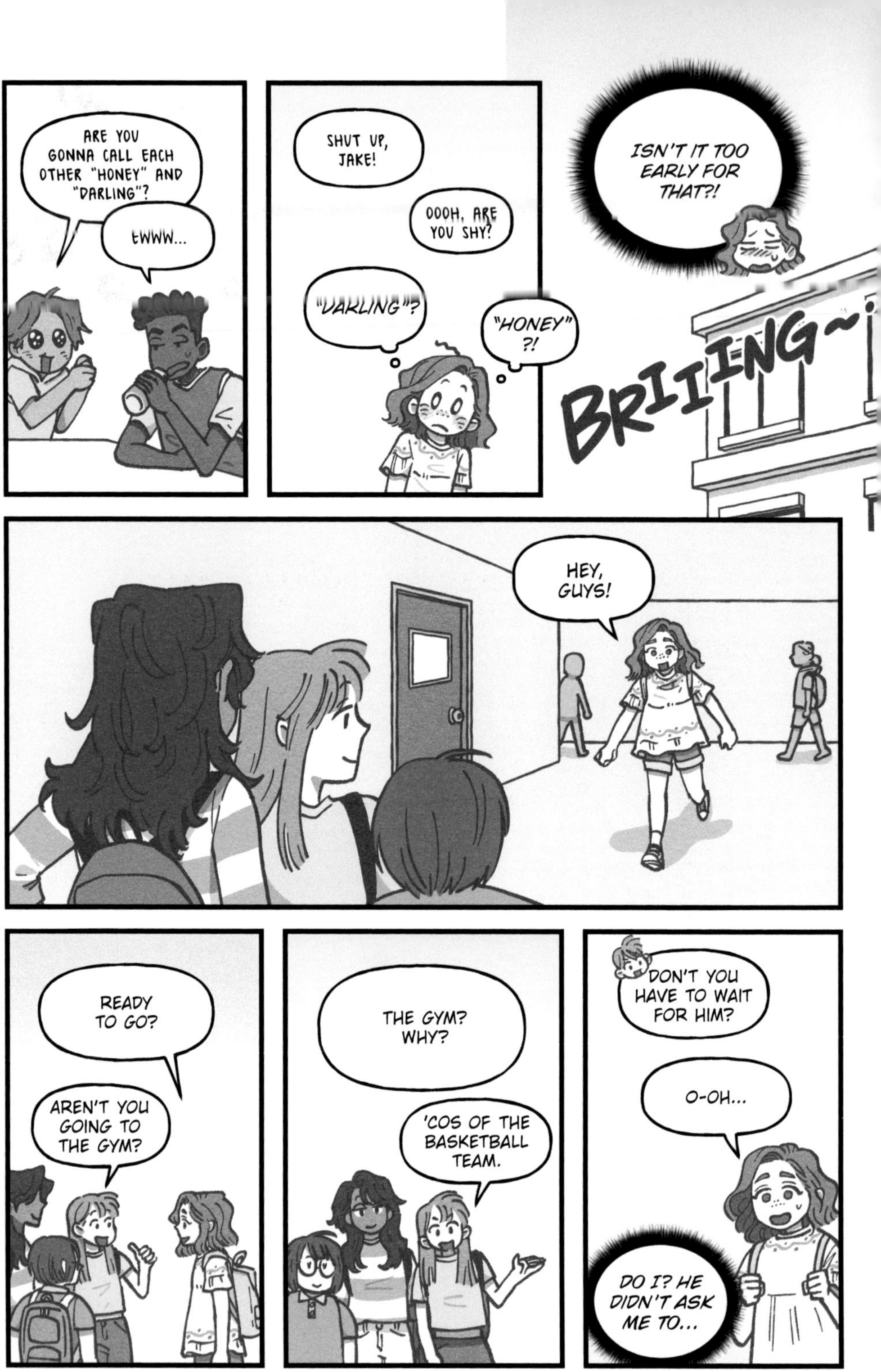
ARE YOU GONNA CALL EACH OTHER "HONEY" AND "DARLING"?
EWWW...
SHUT UP, JAKE!
OOOH, ARE YOU SHY?
"DARLING"?
"HONEY"?!
ISN'T IT TOO EARLY FOR THAT?!
BRIIING~
HEY, GUYS!
READY TO GO?
AREN'T YOU GOING TO THE GYM?
THE GYM? WHY?
'COS OF THE BASKETBALL TEAM.
DON'T YOU HAVE TO WAIT FOR HIM?
O-OH...
DO I? HE DIDN'T ASK ME TO...

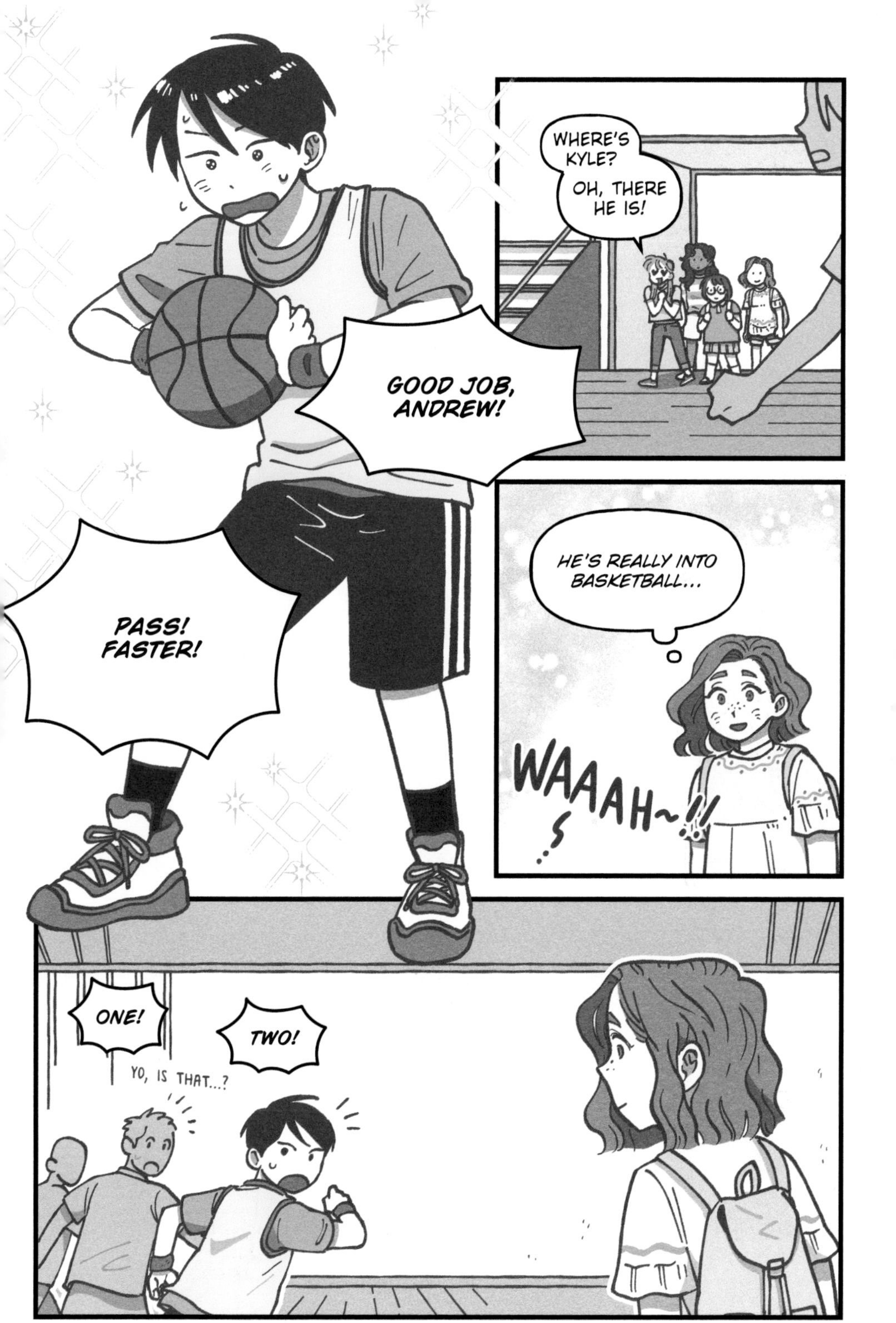
WHERE'S KYLE?
OH, THERE HE IS!
GOOD JOB, ANDREW!
HE'S REALLY INTO BASKETBALL...
PASS! FASTER!
WAAAH~!!
ONE!
TWO!
YO, IS THAT...?

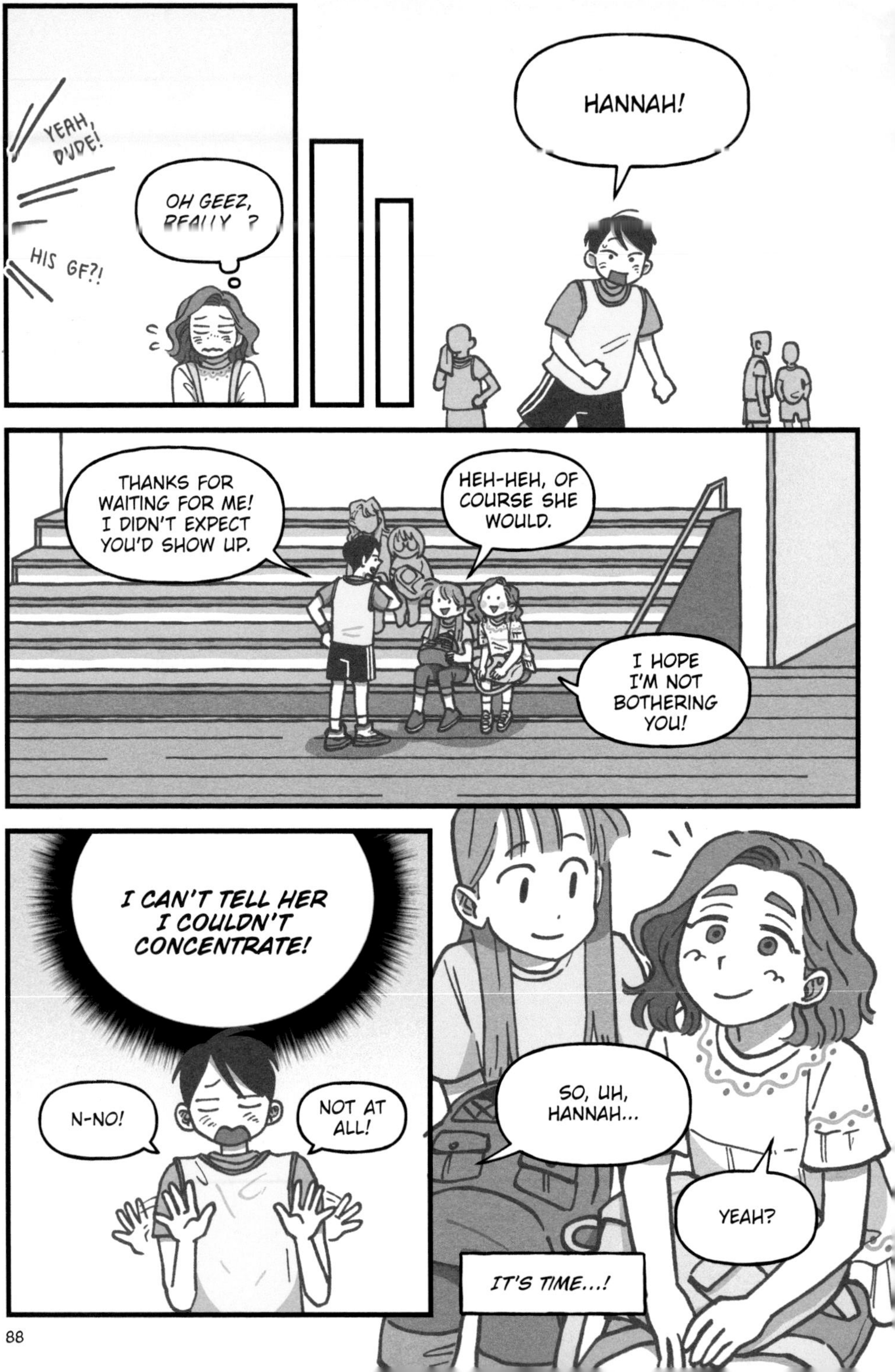
YEAH, DUDE!
HIS GF?!
OH GEEZ, REALLY...?
HANNAH!
THANKS FOR WAITING FOR ME! I DIDN'T EXPECT YOU'D SHOW UP.
HEH-HEH, OF COURSE SHE WOULD.
I HOPE I'M NOT BOTHERING YOU!
I CAN'T TELL HER I COULDN'T CONCENTRATE!
N-NO!
NOT AT ALL!
SO, UH, HANNAH...
YEAH?
IT'S TIME...!

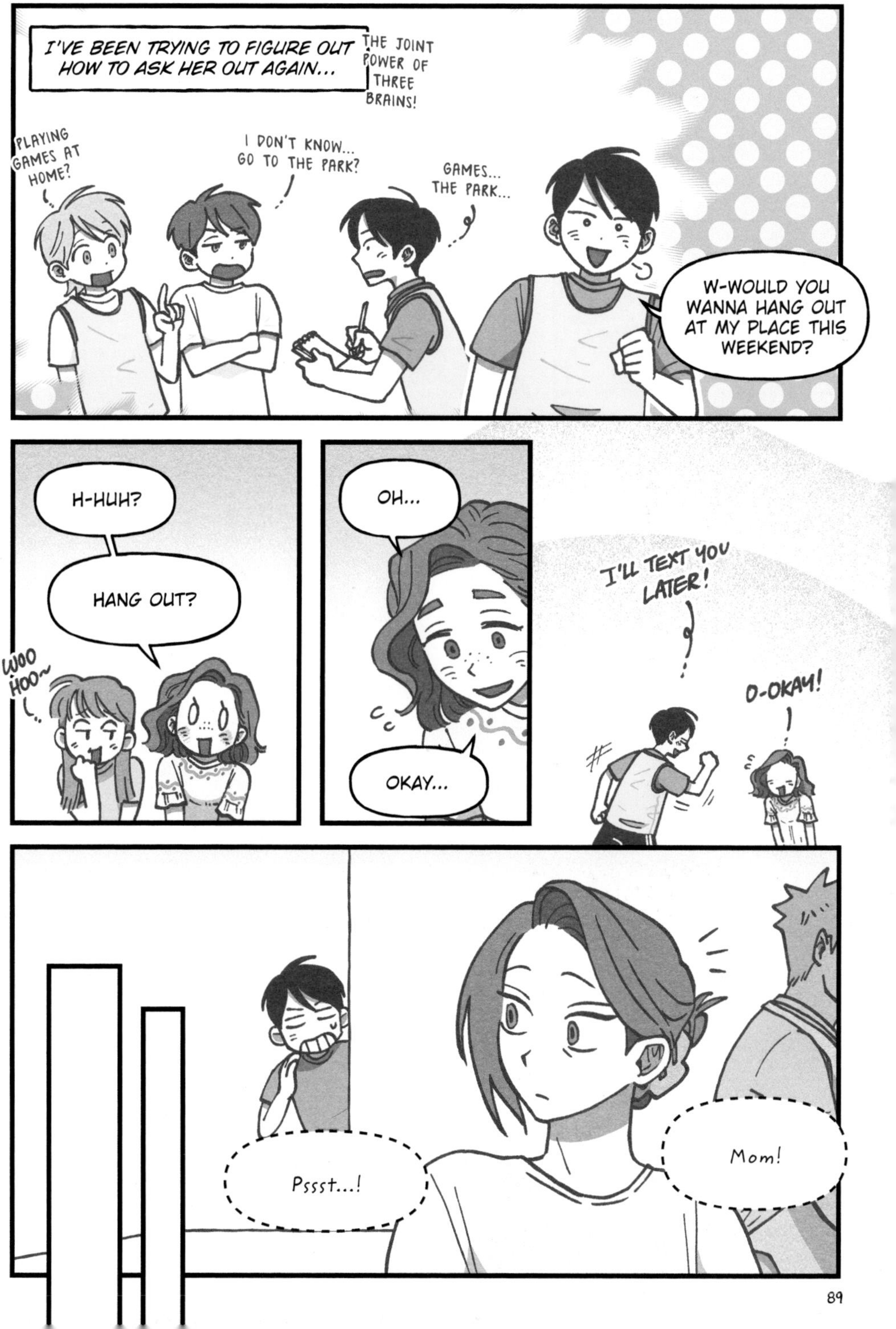

I'VE BEEN TRYING TO FIGURE OUT HOW TO ASK HER OUT AGAIN...
THE JOINT POWER OF THREE BRAINS!
PLAYING GAMES AT HOME?
I DON'T KNOW... GO TO THE PARK?
GAMES... THE PARK...
W-WOULD YOU WANNA HANG OUT AT MY PLACE THIS WEEKEND?
H-HUH?
HANG OUT?
WOO HOO~
OH...
OKAY...
I'LL TEXT YOU LATER!
O-OKAY!
Pssst...!
Mom!

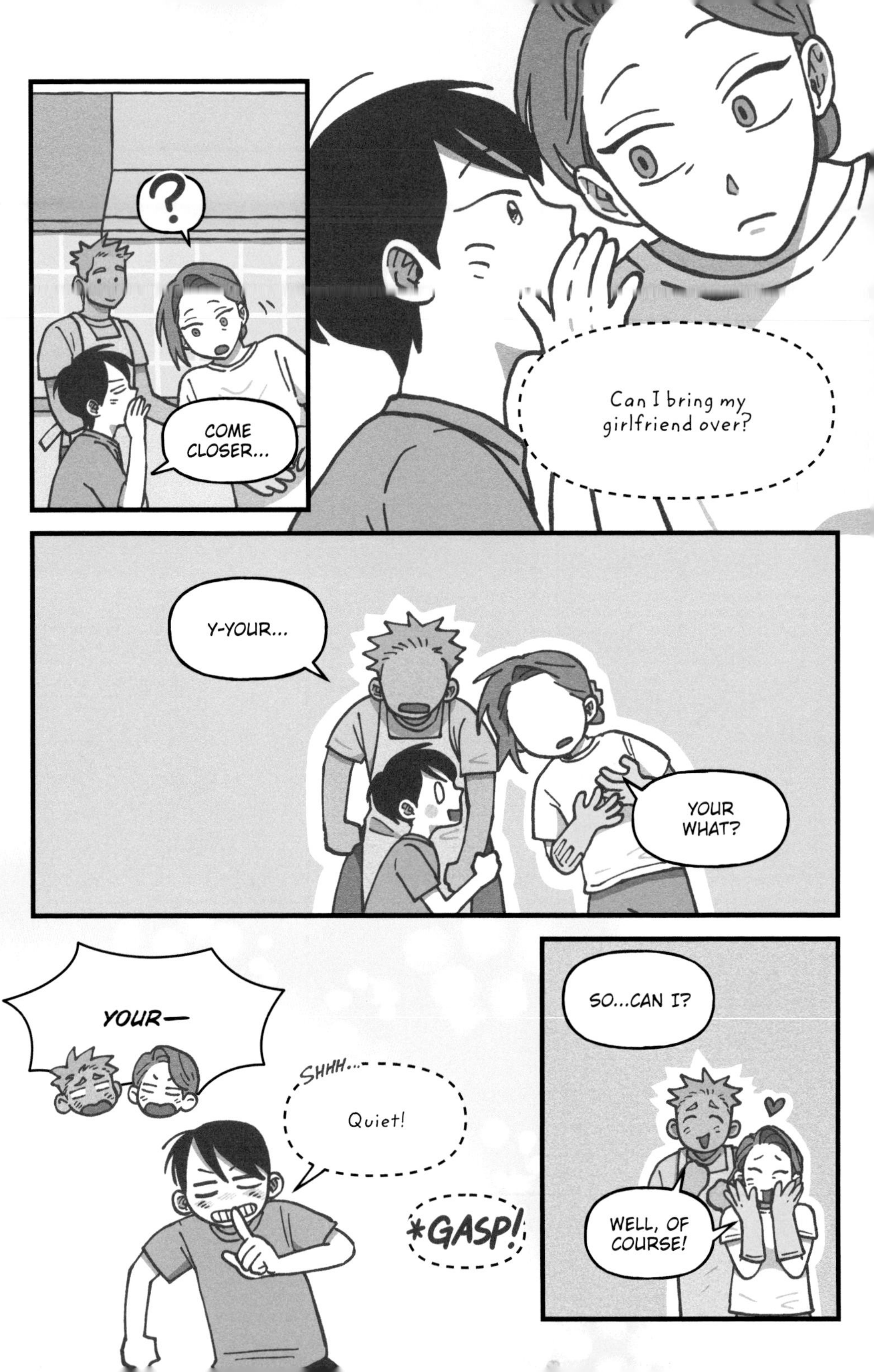
?
COME CLOSER...
Can I bring my girlfriend over?
Y-YOUR...
YOUR WHAT?
YOUR—
SHHH...
Quiet!
*GASP!
SO...CAN I?
WELL, OF COURSE!

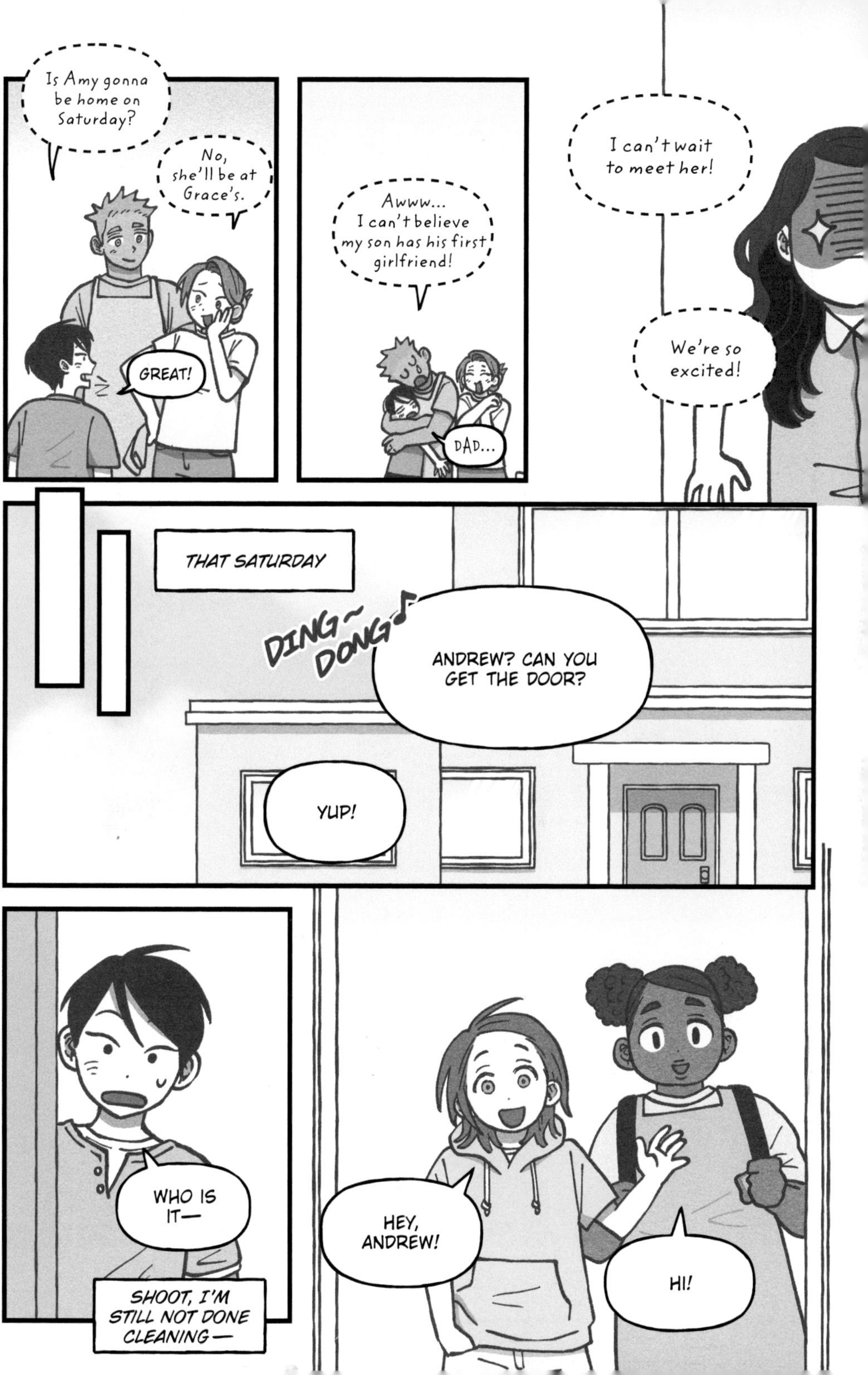
Is Amy gonna be home on Saturday?
No, she'll be at Grace's.
GREAT!
Awww... I can't believe my son has his first girlfriend!
DAD...
I can't wait to meet her!
We're so excited!
THAT SATURDAY
DING~ DONG♪
ANDREW? CAN YOU GET THE DOOR?
YUP!
WHO IS IT—
SHOOT, I'M STILL NOT DONE CLEANING—
HEY, ANDREW!
HI!

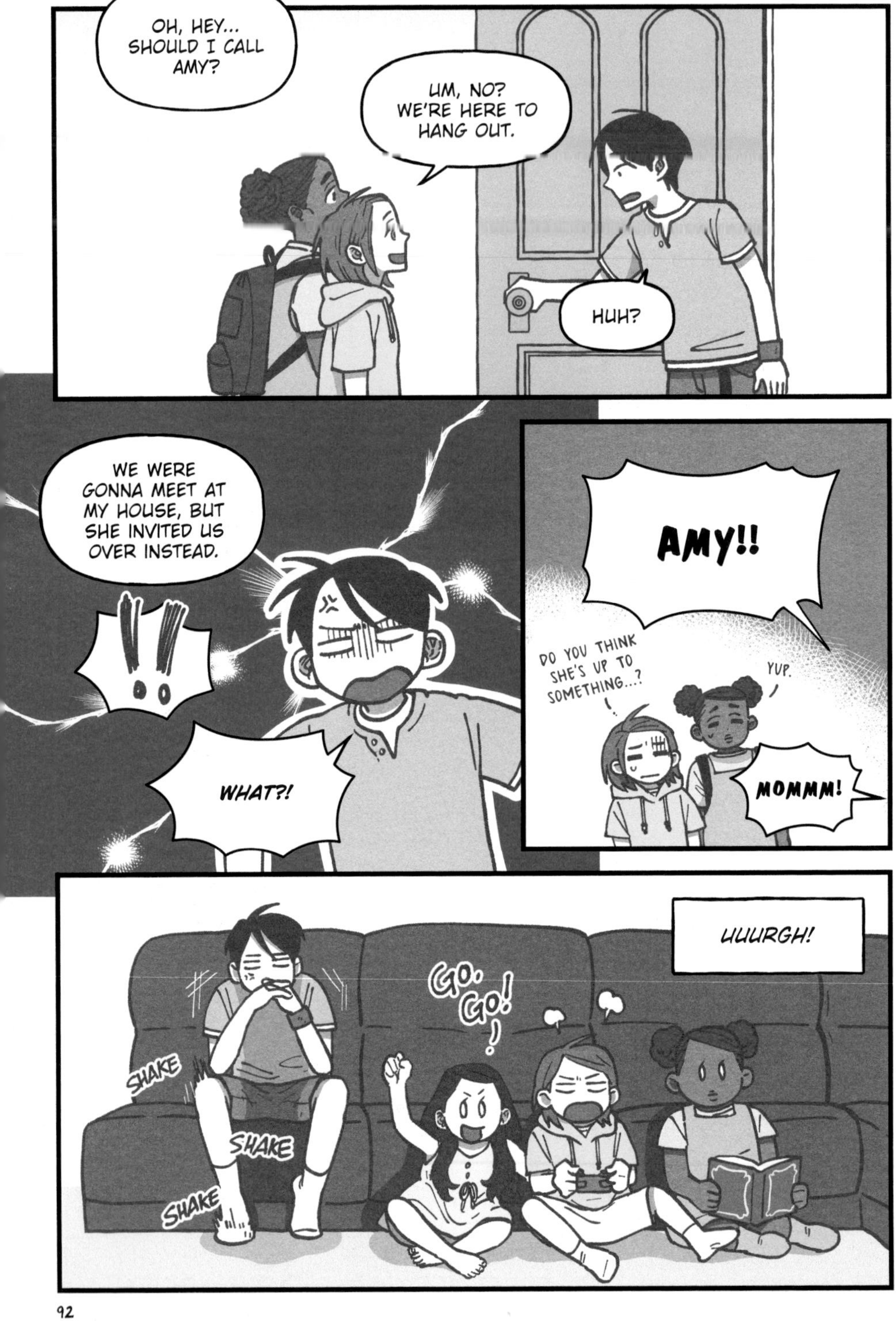
OH, HEY... SHOULD I CALL AMY?
UM, NO? WE'RE HERE TO HANG OUT.
HUH?
WE WERE GONNA MEET AT MY HOUSE, BUT SHE INVITED US OVER INSTEAD.
!!
WHAT?!
AMY!!
DO YOU THINK SHE'S UP TO SOMETHING...?
YUP.
MOMMM!
UUURGH!
SHAKE
SHAKE
SHAKE
GO. GO!

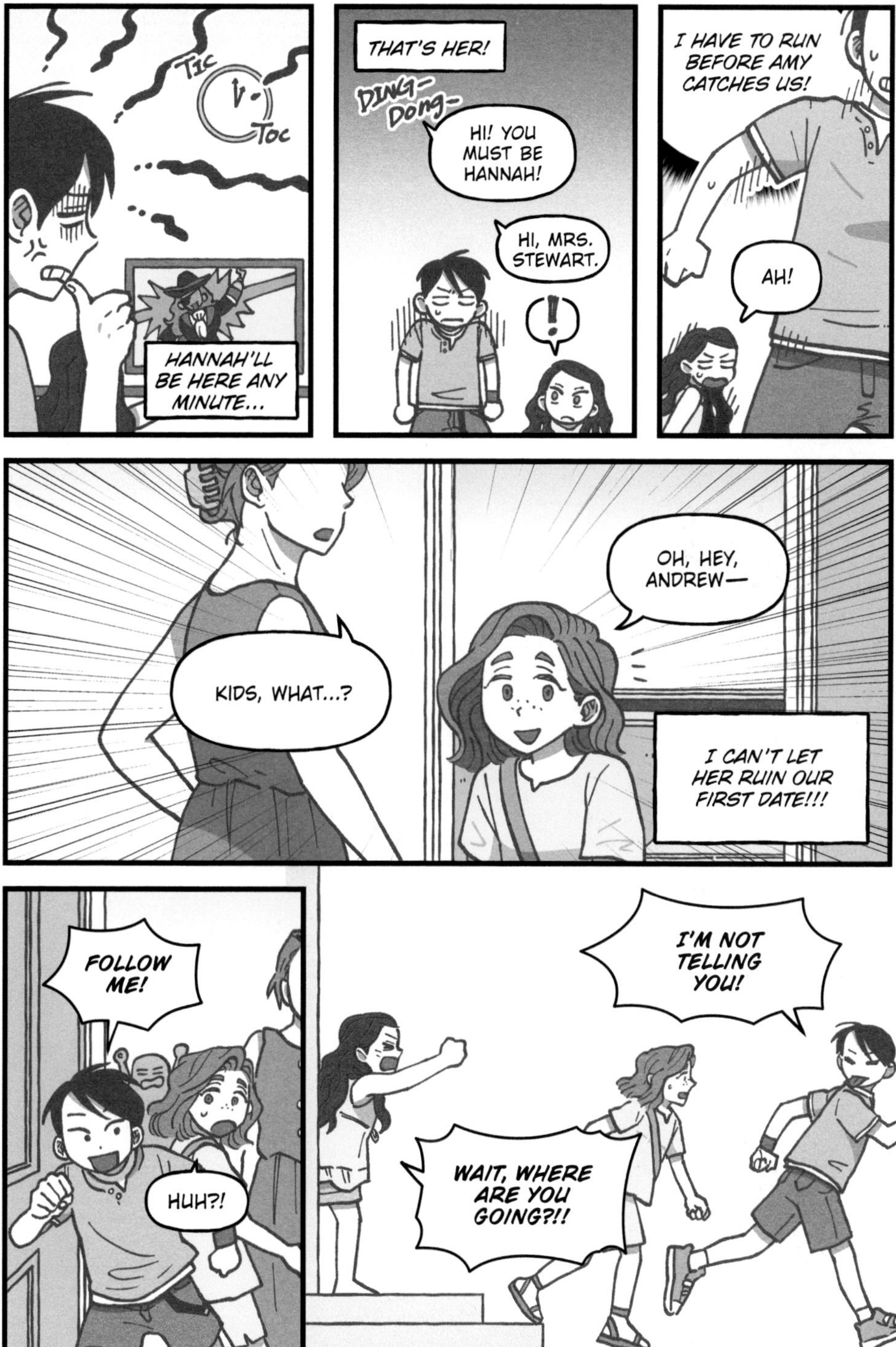
TIC
TOC
HANNAH'LL BE HERE ANY MINUTE...
THAT'S HER!
DING-Dong-
HI! YOU MUST BE HANNAH!
HI, MRS. STEWART.
!
I HAVE TO RUN BEFORE AMY CATCHES US!
AH!
KIDS, WHAT...?
OH, HEY, ANDREW—
I CAN'T LET HER RUIN OUR FIRST DATE!!!
FOLLOW ME!
HUH?!
I'M NOT TELLING YOU!
WAIT, WHERE ARE YOU GOING?!!

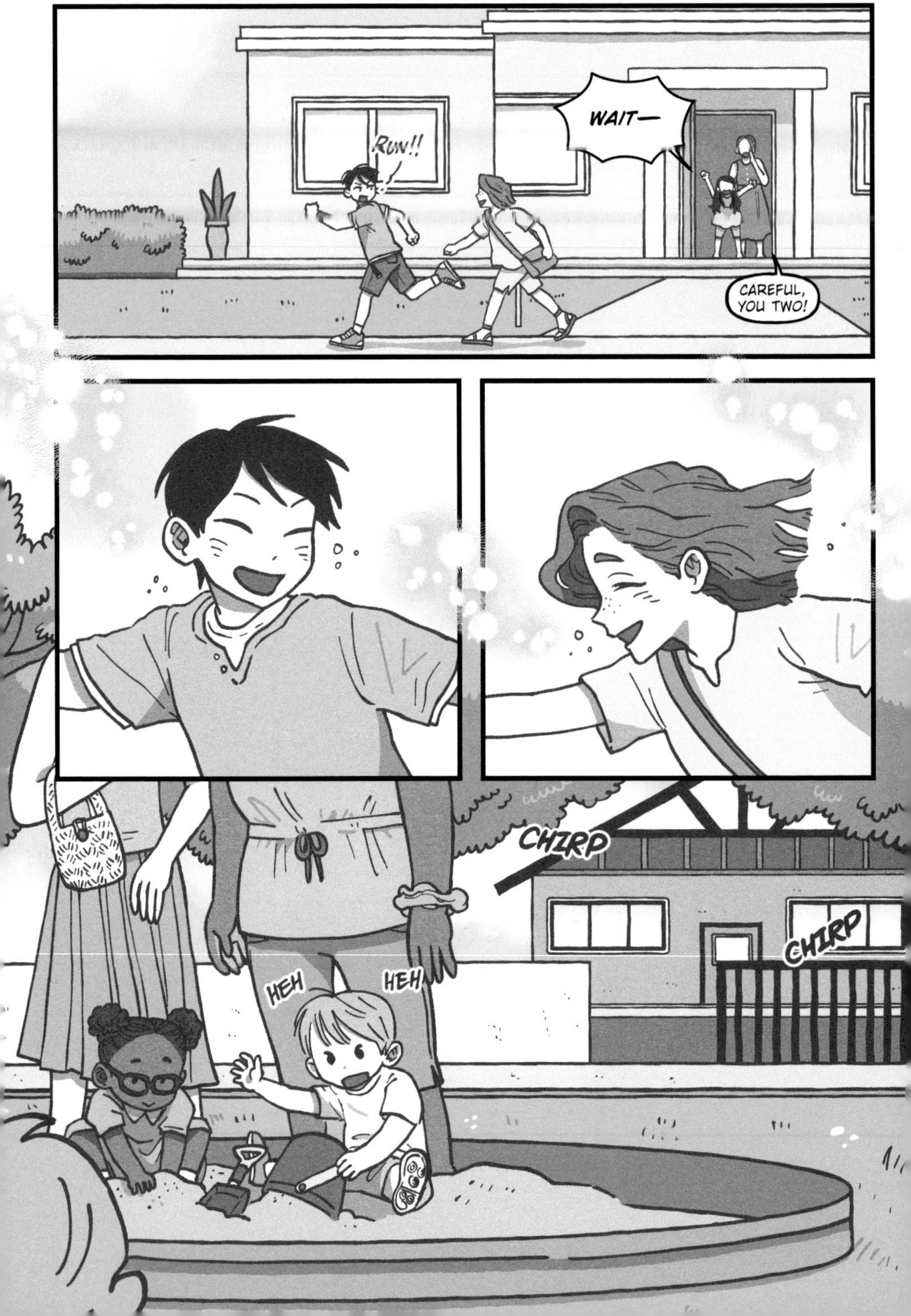
RUN!!
WAIT—
CAREFUL, YOU TWO!
CHIRP
CHIRP
HEH
HEH

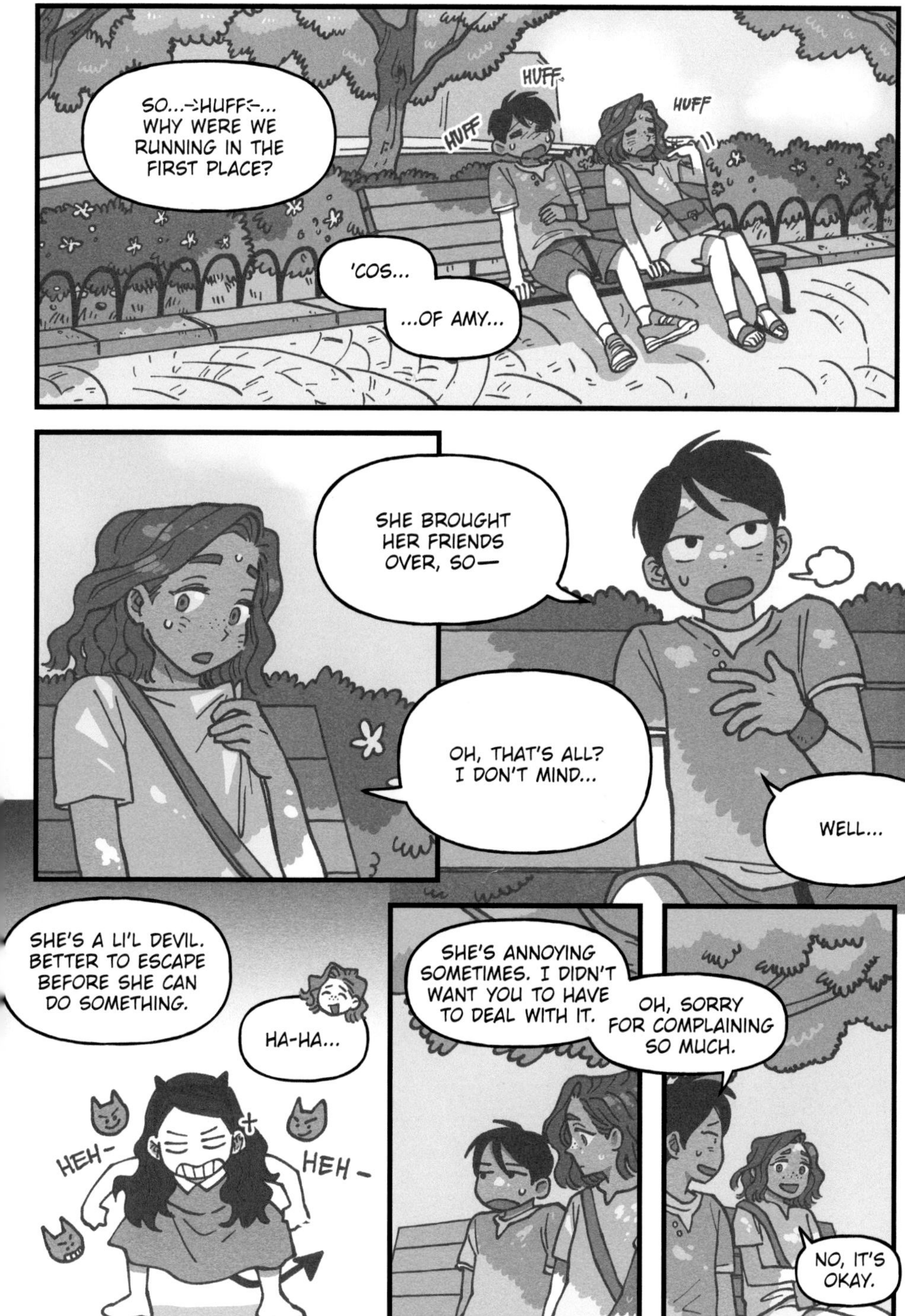
HUFF
HUFF
HUFF
SO...⇒HUFF⇐... WHY WERE WE RUNNING IN THE FIRST PLACE?
'COS...
...OF AMY...
SHE BROUGHT HER FRIENDS OVER, SO—
OH, THAT'S ALL? I DON'T MIND...
WELL...
SHE'S A LI'L DEVIL. BETTER TO ESCAPE BEFORE SHE CAN DO SOMETHING.
HA-HA...
HEH-
HEH-
SHE'S ANNOYING SOMETIMES. I DIDN'T WANT YOU TO HAVE TO DEAL WITH IT.
OH, SORRY FOR COMPLAINING SO MUCH.
NO, IT'S OKAY.

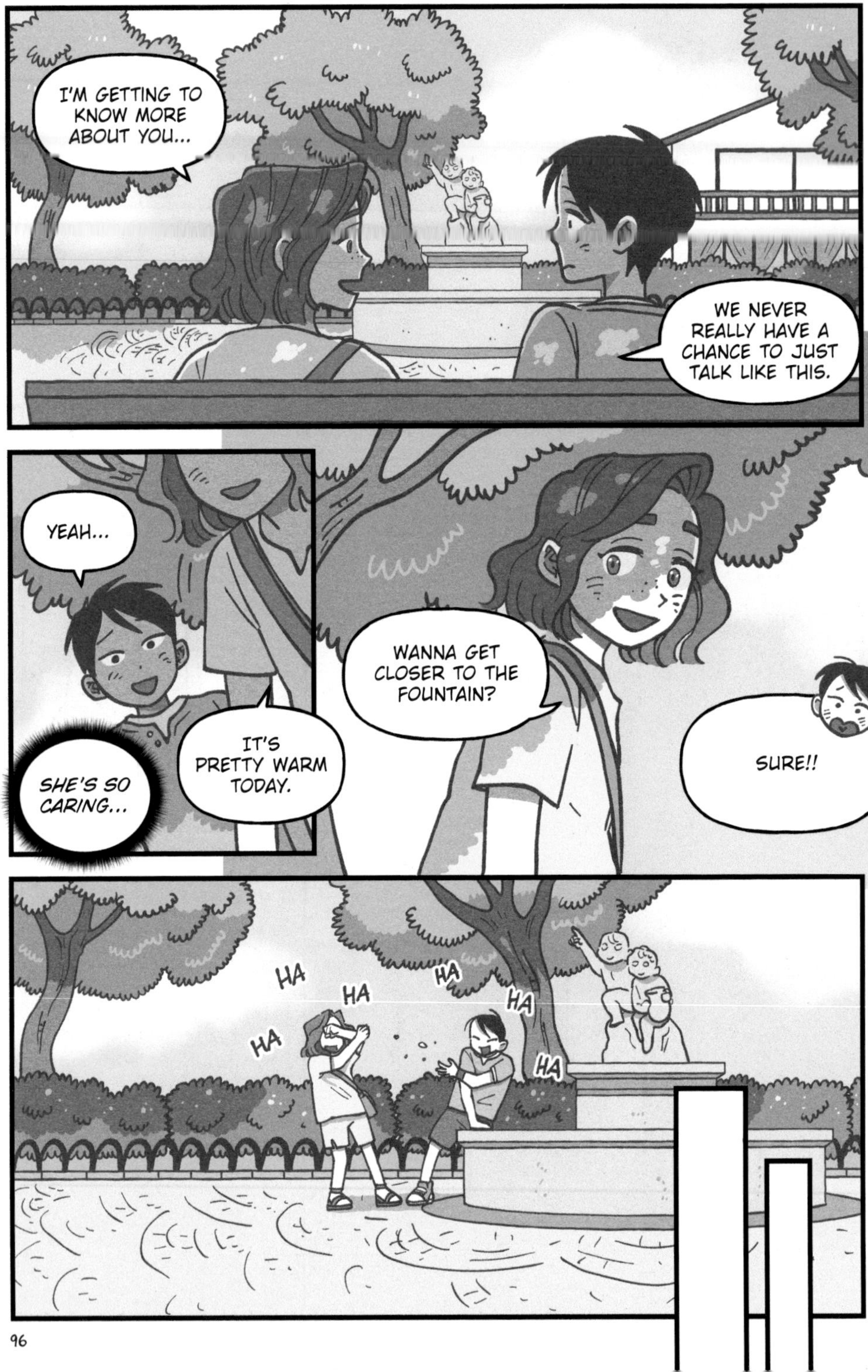
I'M GETTING TO KNOW MORE ABOUT YOU...
WE NEVER REALLY HAVE A CHANCE TO JUST TALK LIKE THIS.
YEAH...
IT'S PRETTY WARM TODAY.
SHE'S SO CARING...
WANNA GET CLOSER TO THE FOUNTAIN?
SURE!!
HA
HA
HA
HA
HA
HA

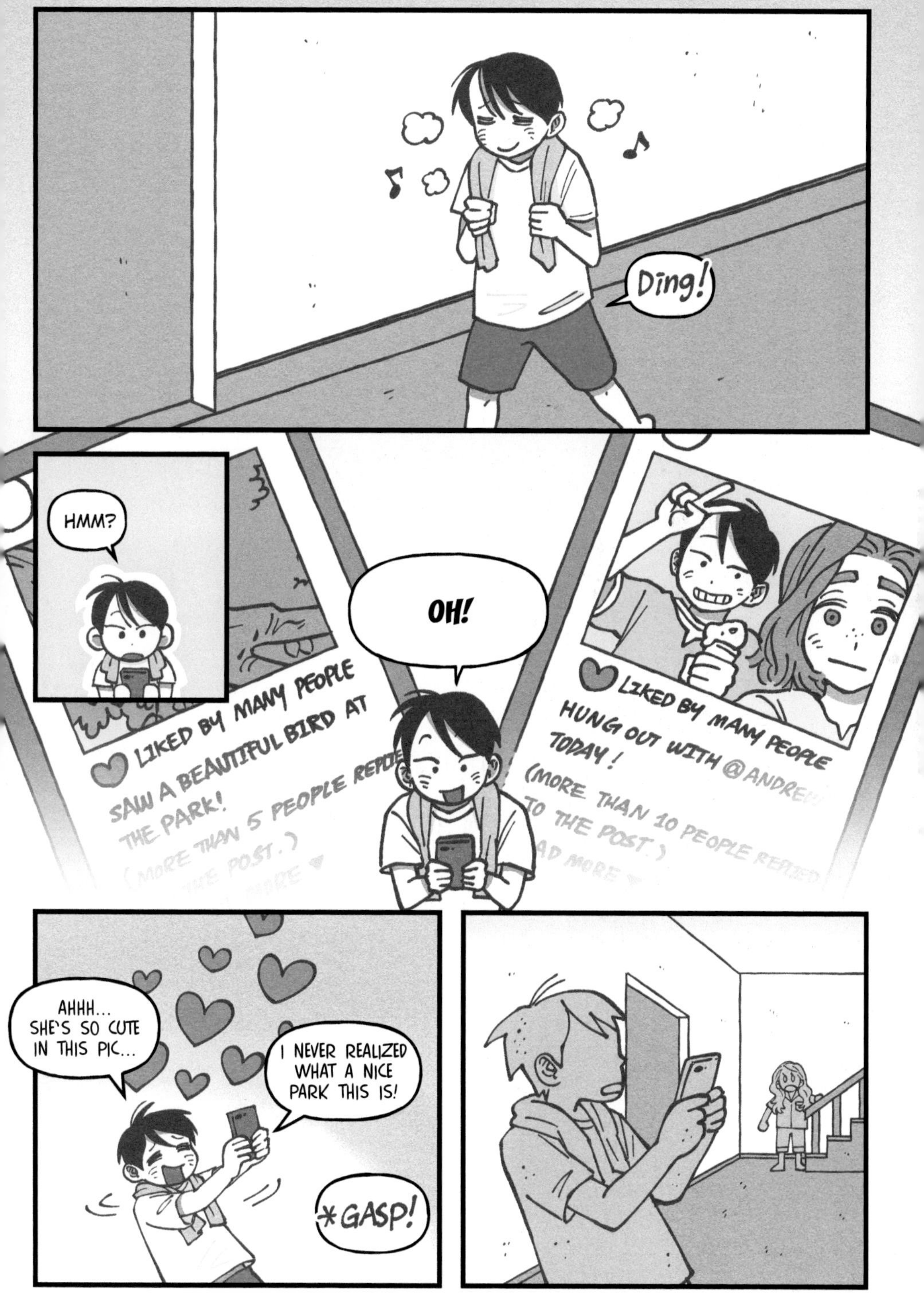

Ding!
HMM?
OH!
LIKED BY MANY PEOPLE
SAW A BEAUTIFUL BIRD AT THE PARK!
LIKED BY MANY PEOPLE
HUNG OUT WITH
TODAY!
AHHH... SHE'S SO CUTE IN THIS PIC...
I NEVER REALIZED WHAT A NICE PARK THIS IS!
*GASP!

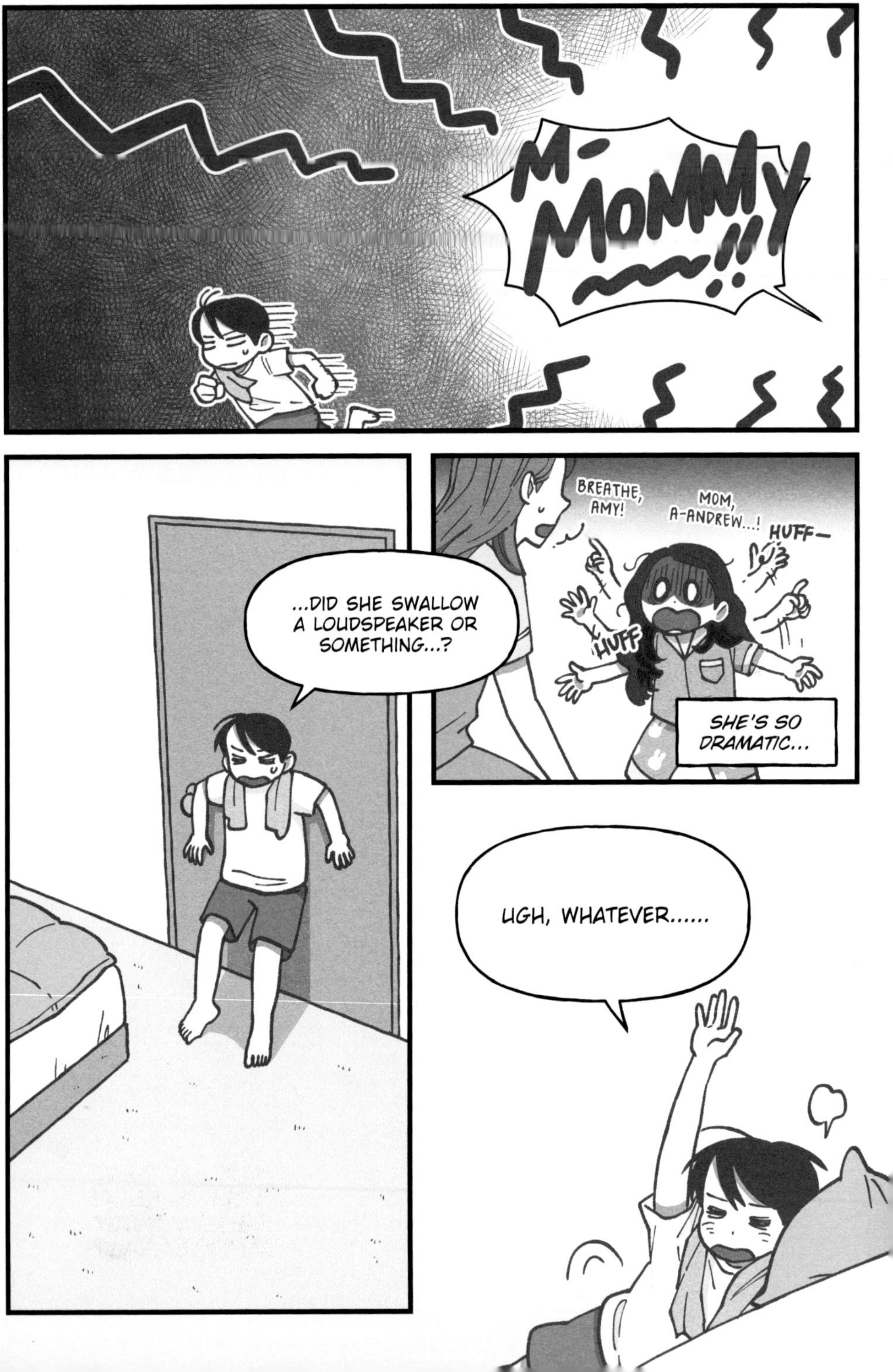
M-MOMMY~~~!!
...DID SHE SWALLOW A LOUDSPEAKER OR SOMETHING...?
BREATHE, AMY!
MOM, A-ANDREW...!
HUFF—
HUFF
SHE'S SO DRAMATIC...
UGH, WHATEVER......

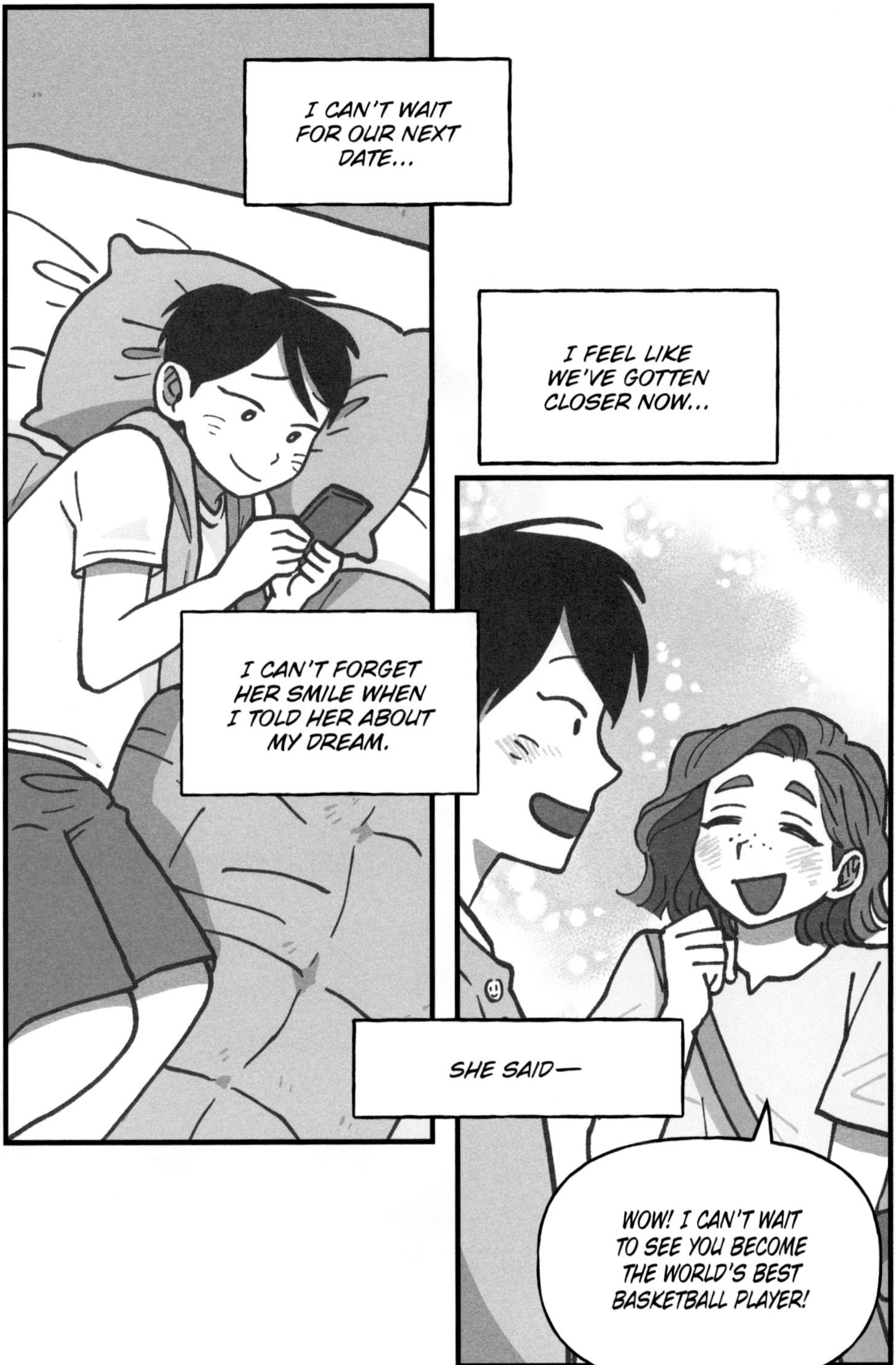
I CAN'T WAIT FOR OUR NEXT DATE...
I FEEL LIKE WE'VE GOTTEN CLOSER NOW...
I CAN'T FORGET HER SMILE WHEN I TOLD HER ABOUT MY DREAM.
SHE SAID—
WOW! I CAN'T WAIT TO SEE YOU BECOME THE WORLD'S BEST BASKETBALL PLAYER!

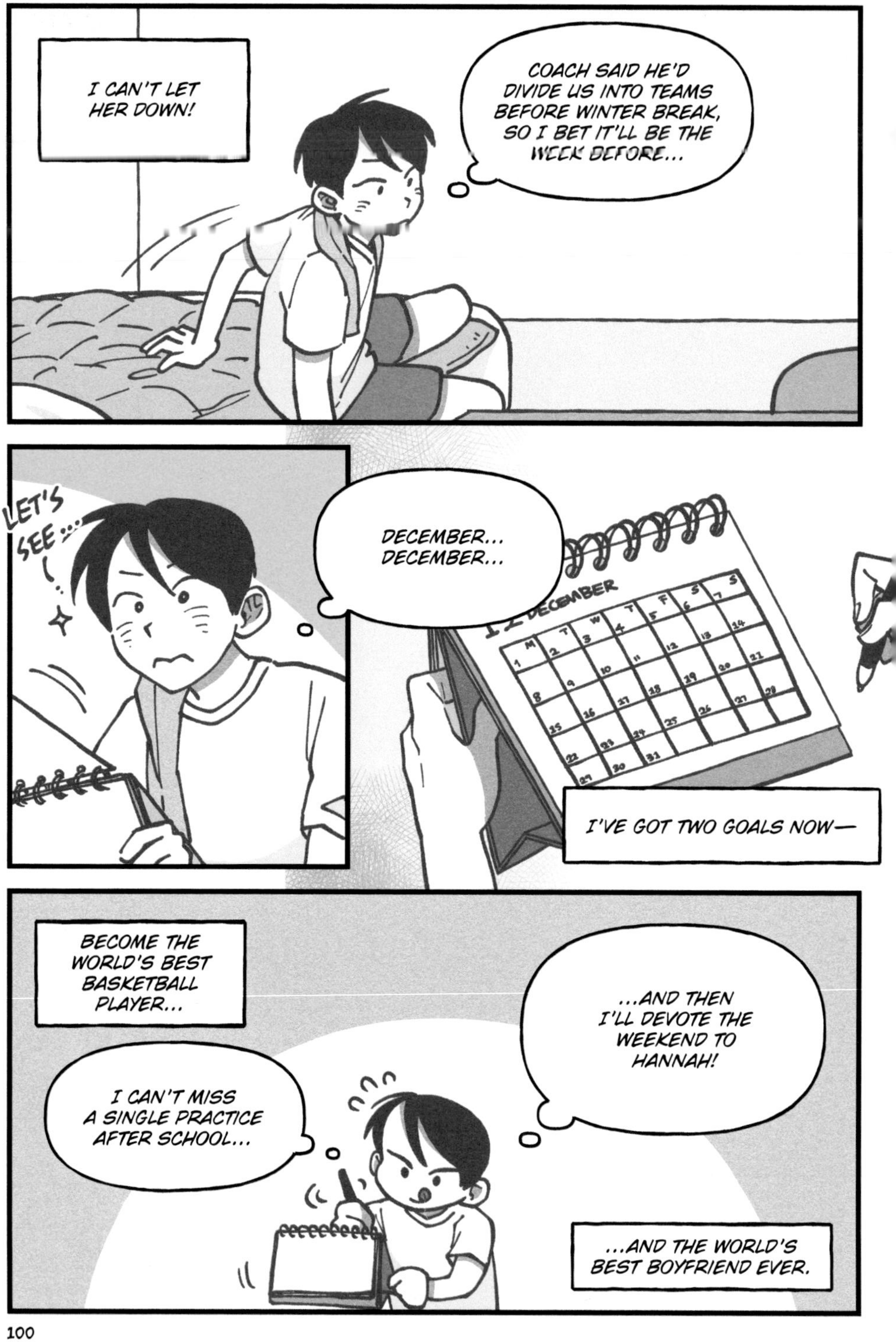
I CAN'T LET HER DOWN!
COACH SAID HE'D DIVIDE US INTO TEAMS BEFORE WINTER BREAK, SO I BET IT'LL BE THE WEEK BEFORE...
LET'S SEE...
DECEMBER... DECEMBER...
12 DECEMBER
I'VE GOT TWO GOALS NOW—
BECOME THE WORLD'S BEST BASKETBALL PLAYER...
...AND THEN I'LL DEVOTE THE WEEKEND TO HANNAH!
I CAN'T MISS A SINGLE PRACTICE AFTER SCHOOL...
...AND THE WORLD'S BEST BOYFRIEND EVER.

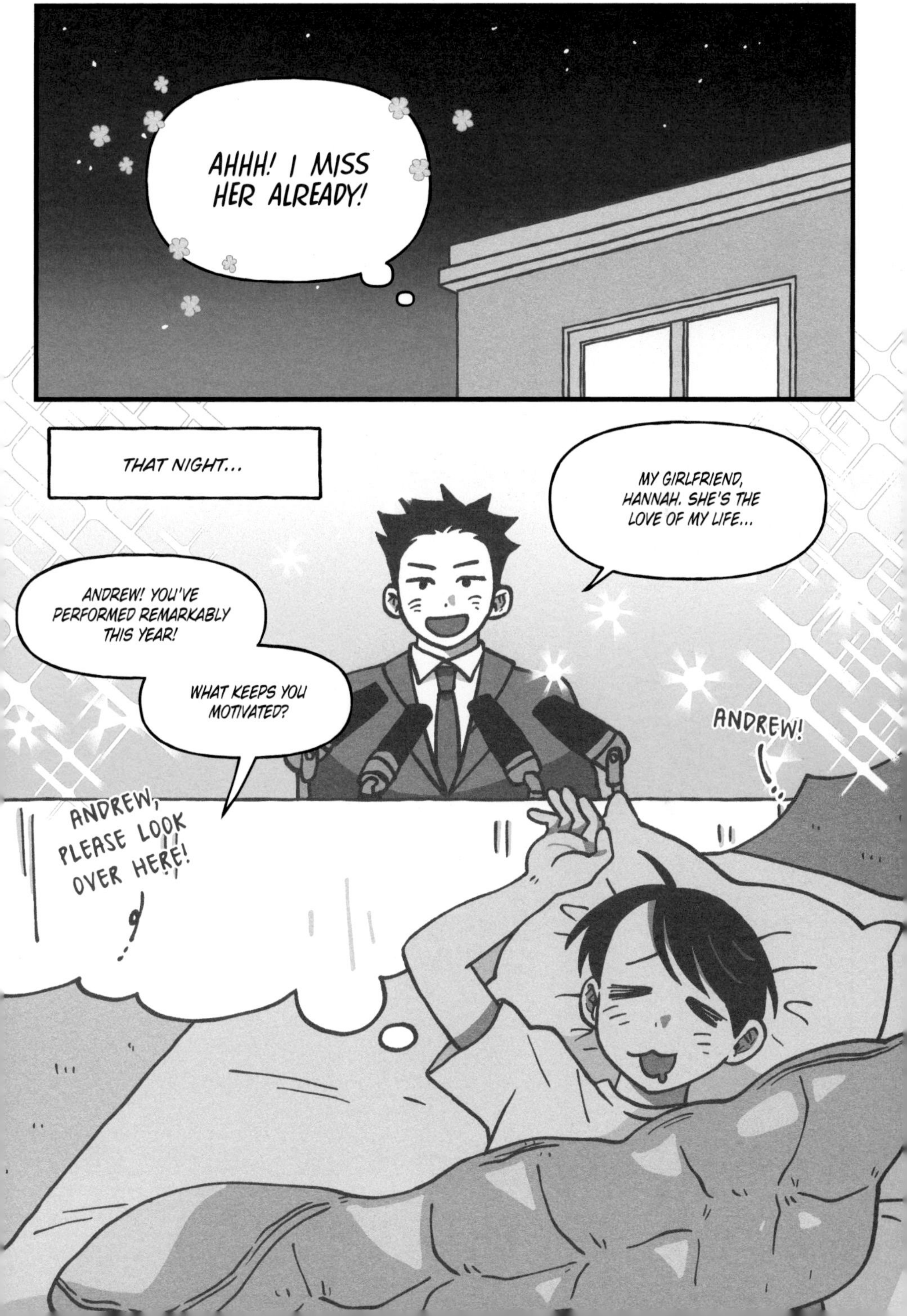
AHHH! I MISS HER ALREADY!
THAT NIGHT...
MY GIRLFRIEND, HANNAH. SHE'S THE LOVE OF MY LIFE...
ANDREW! YOU'VE PERFORMED REMARKABLY THIS YEAR!
WHAT KEEPS YOU MOTIVATED?
ANDREW!
ANDREW, PLEASE LOOK OVER HERE!

Chapter 6

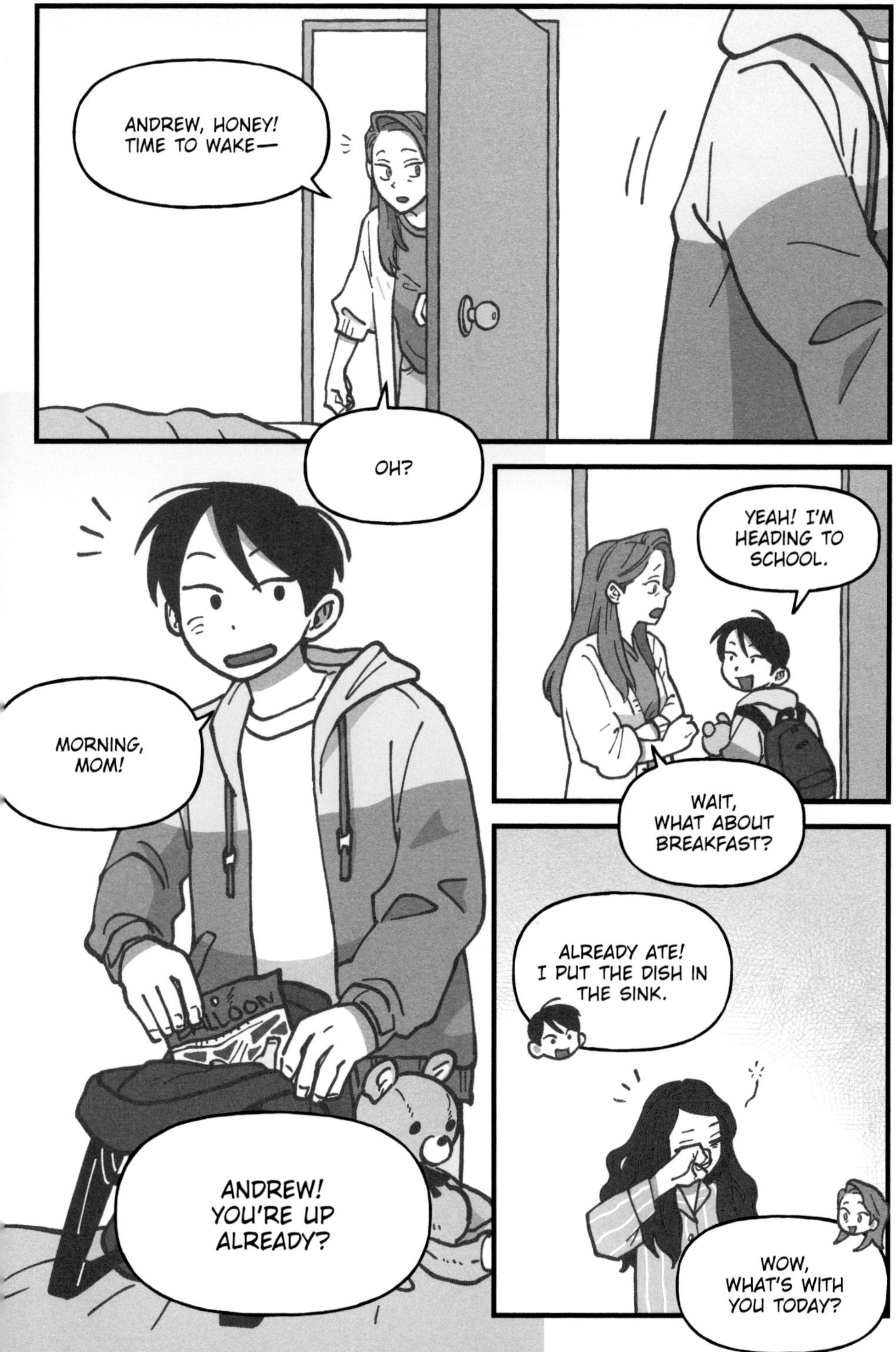
ANDREW, HONEY! TIME TO WAKE—
OH?
MORNING, MOM!
ANDREW! YOU'RE UP ALREADY?
YEAH! I'M HEADING TO SCHOOL.
WAIT, WHAT ABOUT BREAKFAST?
ALREADY ATE! I PUT THE DISH IN THE SINK.
WOW, WHAT'S WITH YOU TODAY?
BALLOON

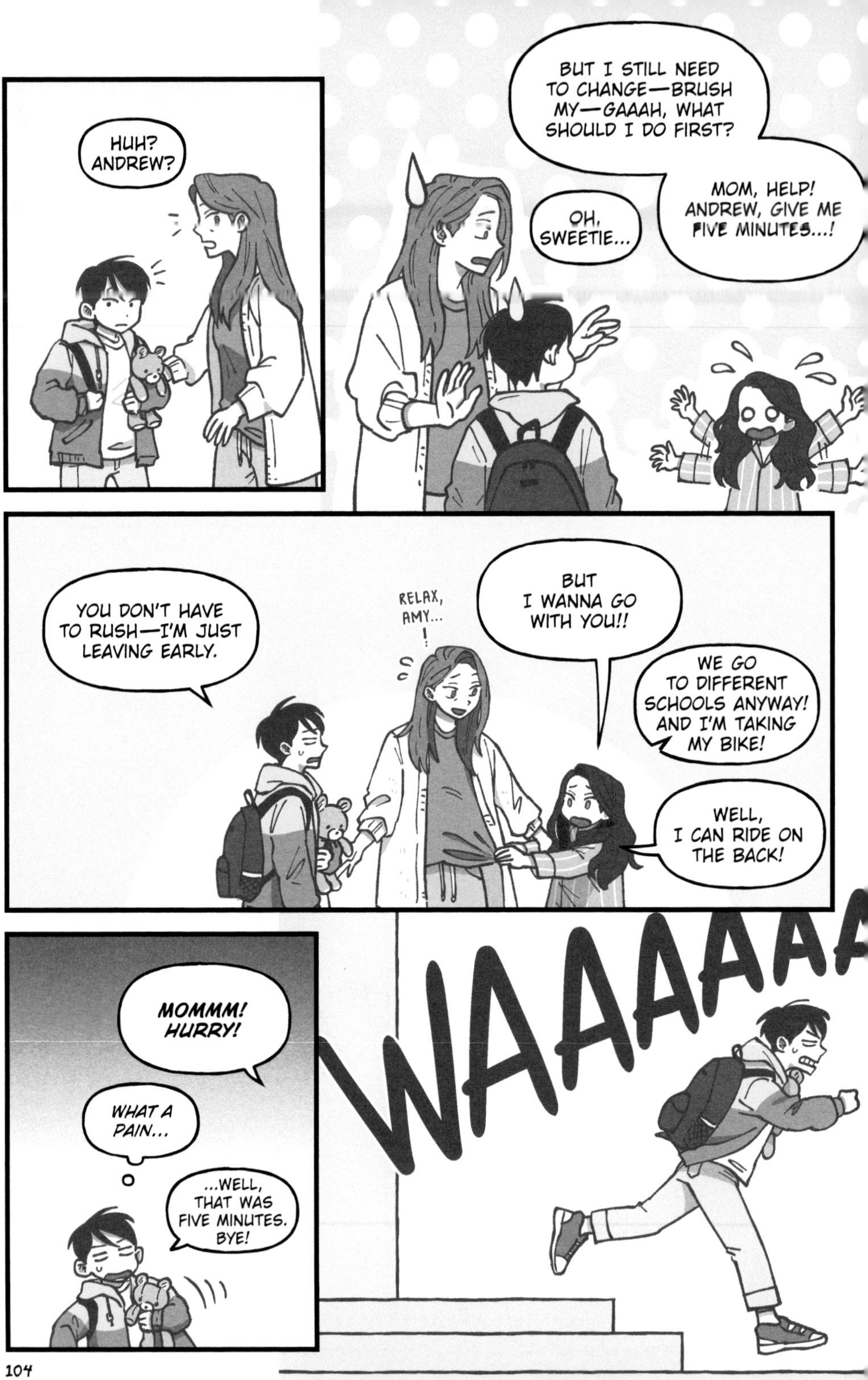
HUH? ANDREW?
BUT I STILL NEED TO CHANGE—BRUSH MY—GAAAH, WHAT SHOULD I DO FIRST?
MOM, HELP! ANDREW, GIVE ME FIVE MINUTES...!
OH, SWEETIE...
YOU DON'T HAVE TO RUSH—I'M JUST LEAVING EARLY.
RELAX, AMY...
BUT I WANNA GO WITH YOU!!
WE GO TO DIFFERENT SCHOOLS ANYWAY! AND I'M TAKING MY BIKE!
WELL, I CAN RIDE ON THE BACK!
MOMMM! HURRY!
WHAT A PAIN...
...WELL, THAT WAS FIVE MINUTES. BYE!
WAAAAAA

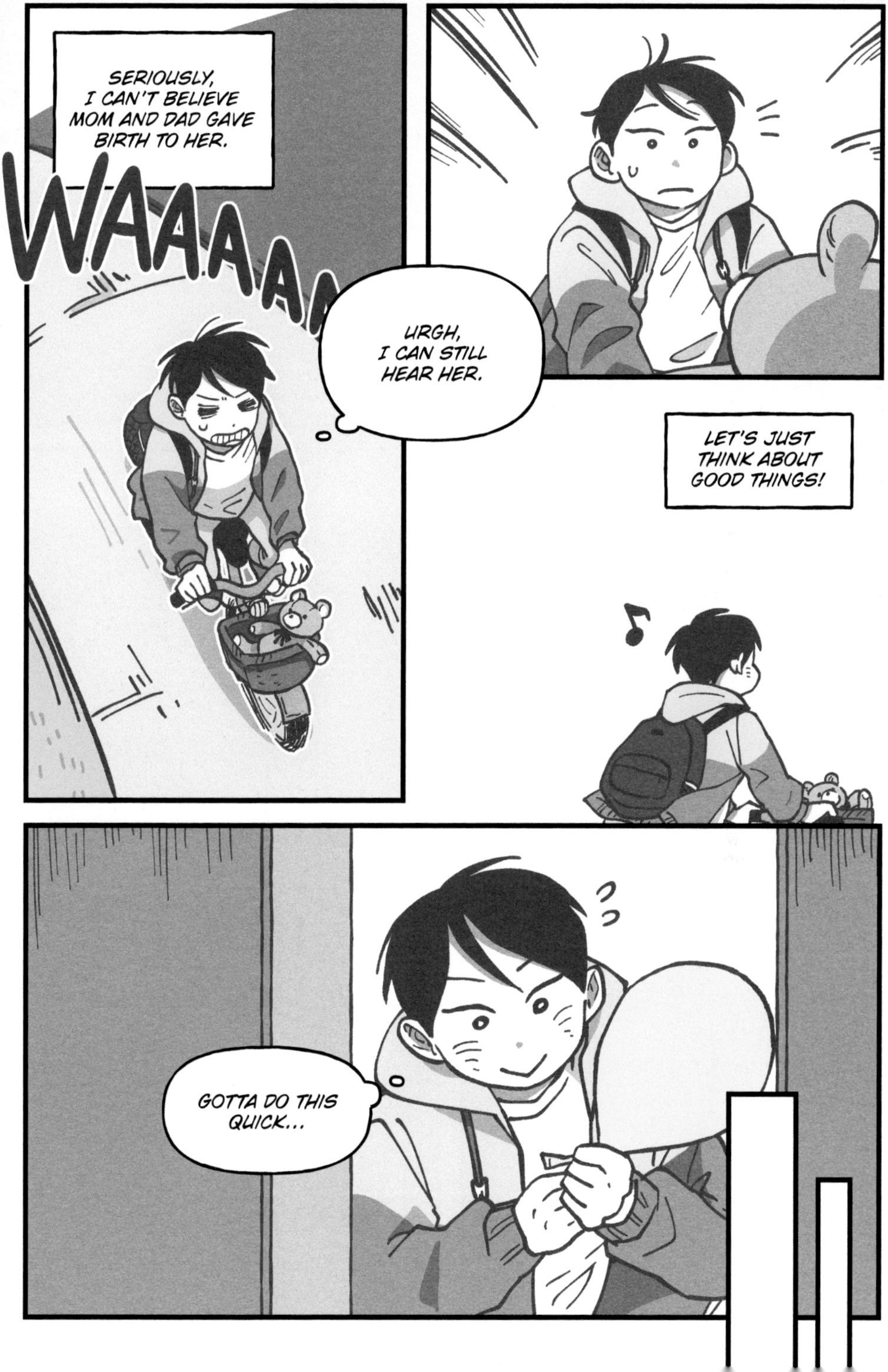
SERIOUSLY, I CAN'T BELIEVE MOM AND DAD GAVE BIRTH TO HER.
WAAAAA
URGH, I CAN STILL HEAR HER.
LET'S JUST THINK ABOUT GOOD THINGS!
GOTTA DO THIS QUICK...

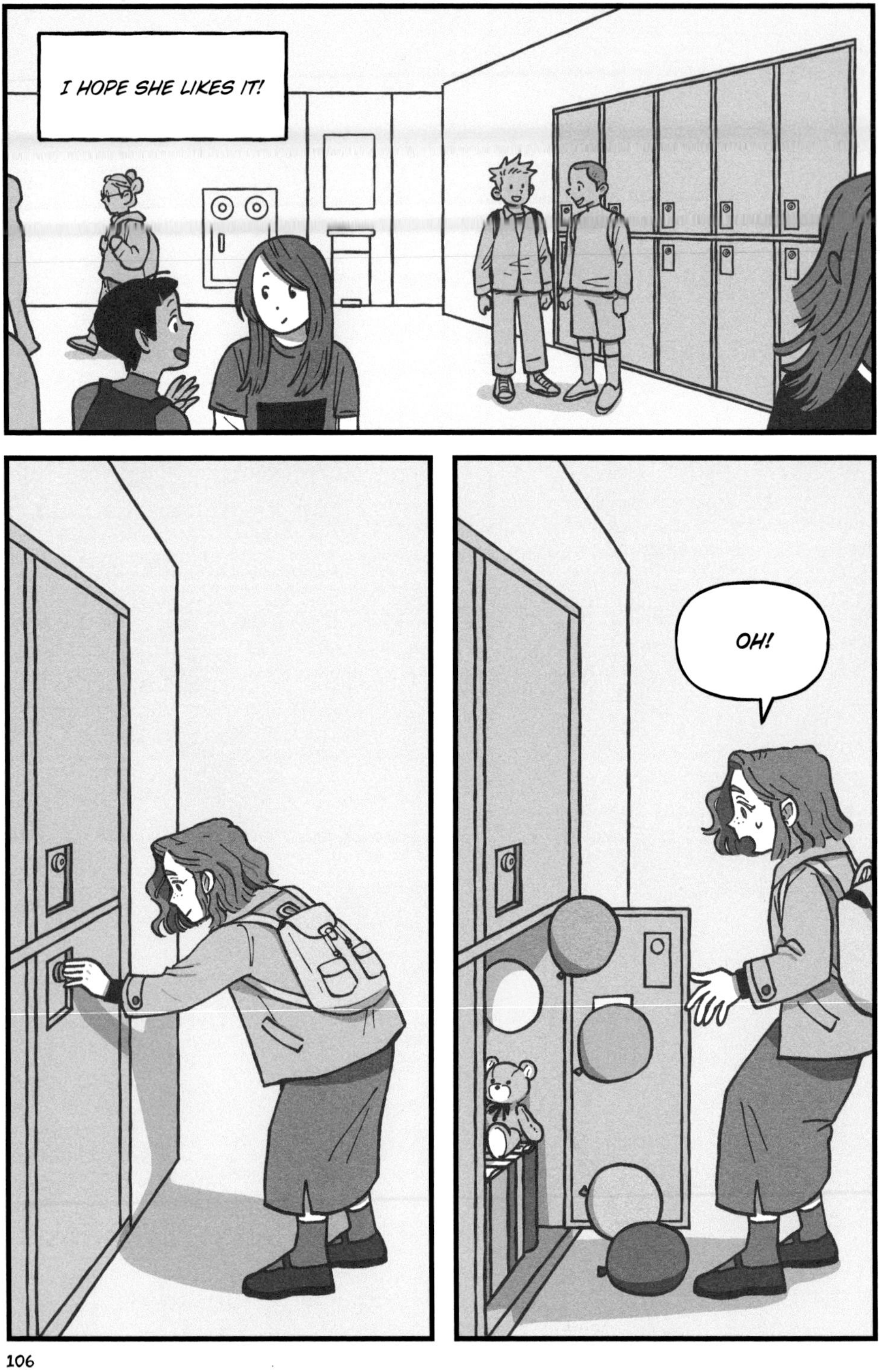
I HOPE SHE LIKES IT!
OH!

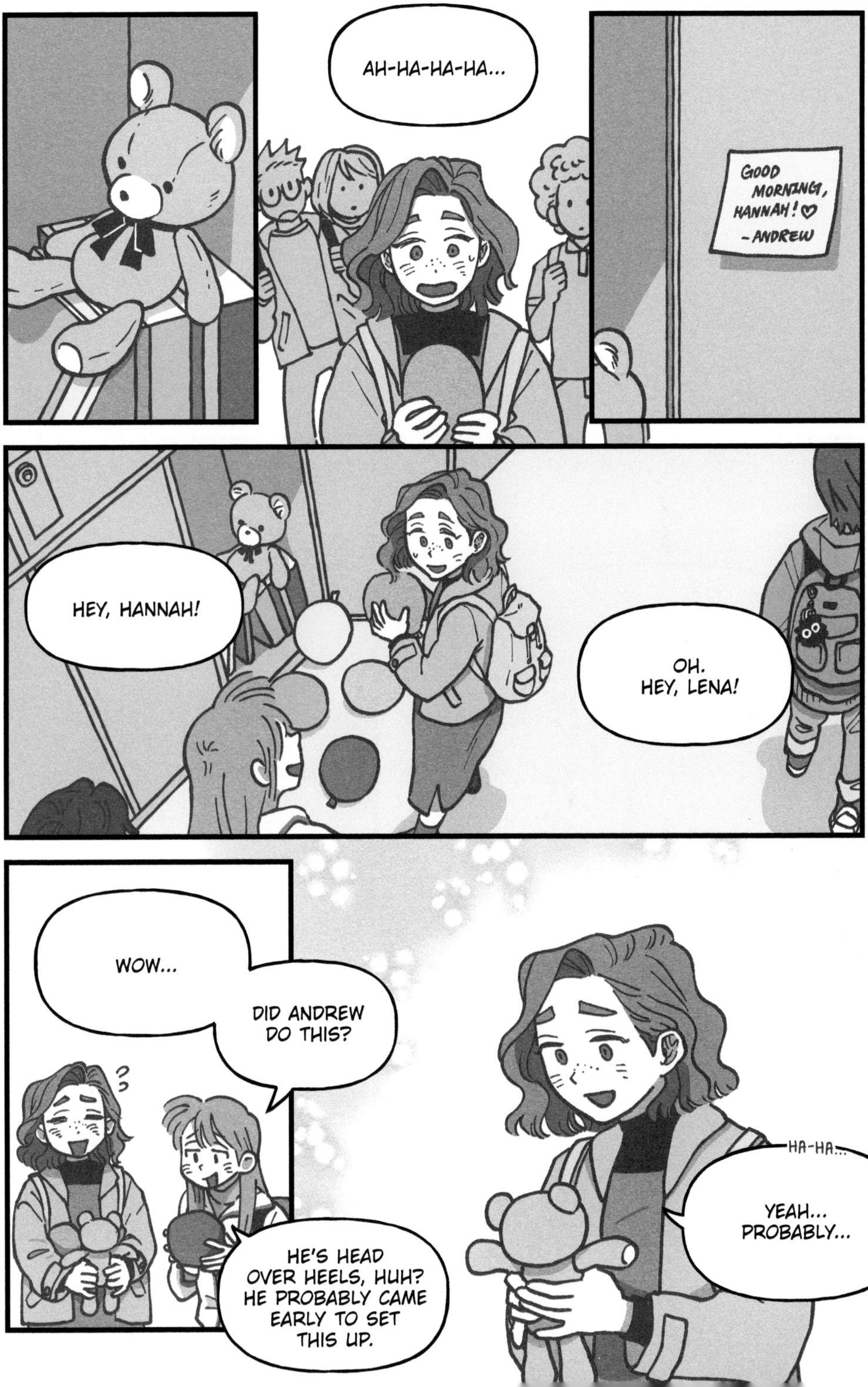
AH-HA-HA-HA...
GOOD MORNING, HANNAH! ♡ -ANDREW
HEY, HANNAH!
OH. HEY, LENA!
WOW...
DID ANDREW DO THIS?
HE'S HEAD OVER HEELS, HUH? HE PROBABLY CAME EARLY TO SET THIS UP.
HA-HA...
YEAH... PROBABLY...

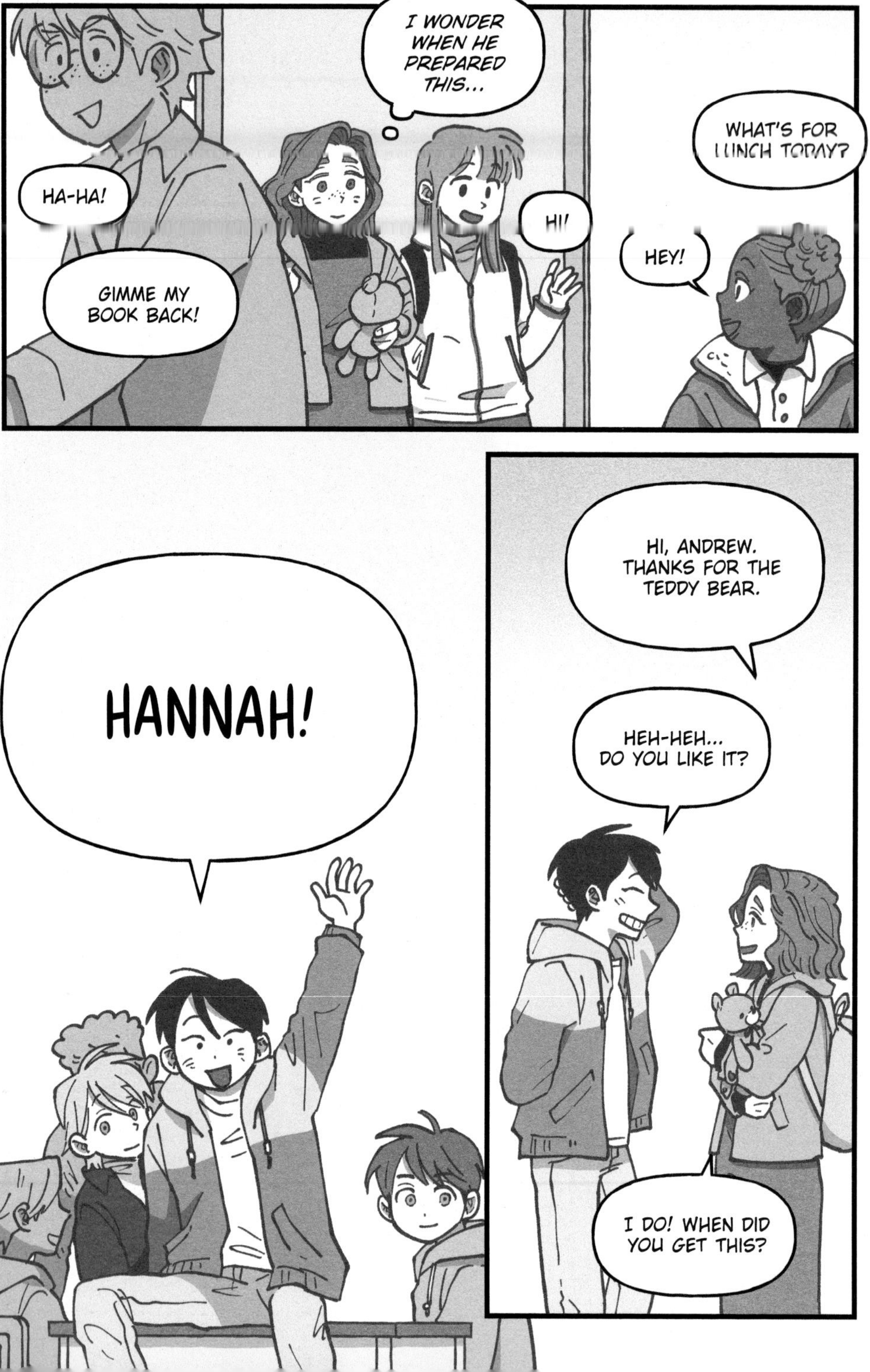
I WONDER WHEN HE PREPARED THIS...
WHAT'S FOR LUNCH TODAY?
HA-HA!
HI!
HEY!
GIMME MY BOOK BACK!
HANNAH!
HI, ANDREW. THANKS FOR THE TEDDY BEAR.
HEH-HEH... DO YOU LIKE IT?
I DO! WHEN DID YOU GET THIS?

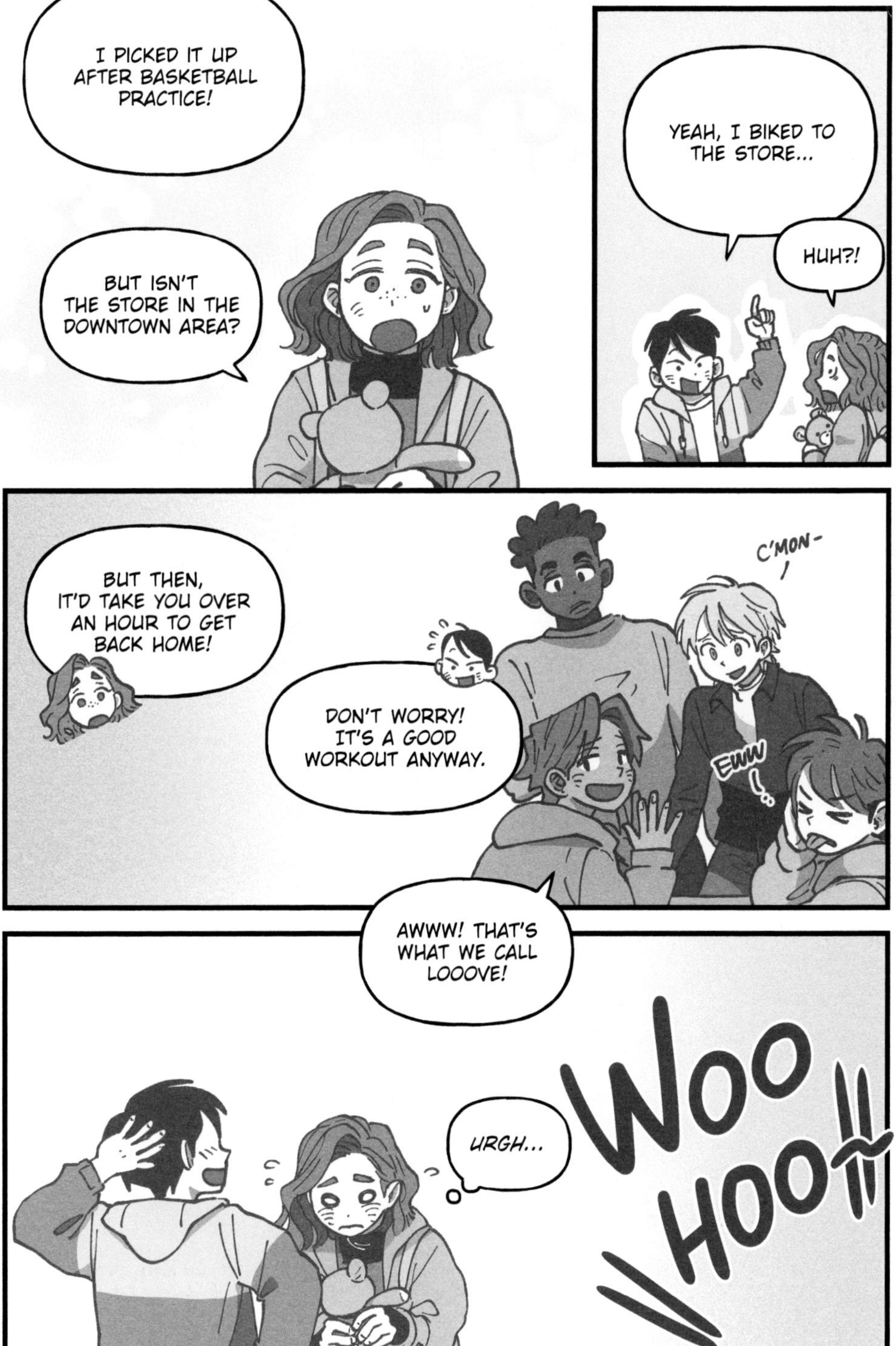
I PICKED IT UP AFTER BASKETBALL PRACTICE!
BUT ISN'T THE STORE IN THE DOWNTOWN AREA?
YEAH, I BIKED TO THE STORE...
HUH?!
BUT THEN, IT'D TAKE YOU OVER AN HOUR TO GET BACK HOME!
C'MON-
DON'T WORRY! IT'S A GOOD WORKOUT ANYWAY.
EWW
AWWW! THAT'S WHAT WE CALL LOOOVE!
URGH...
WOO HOO!!

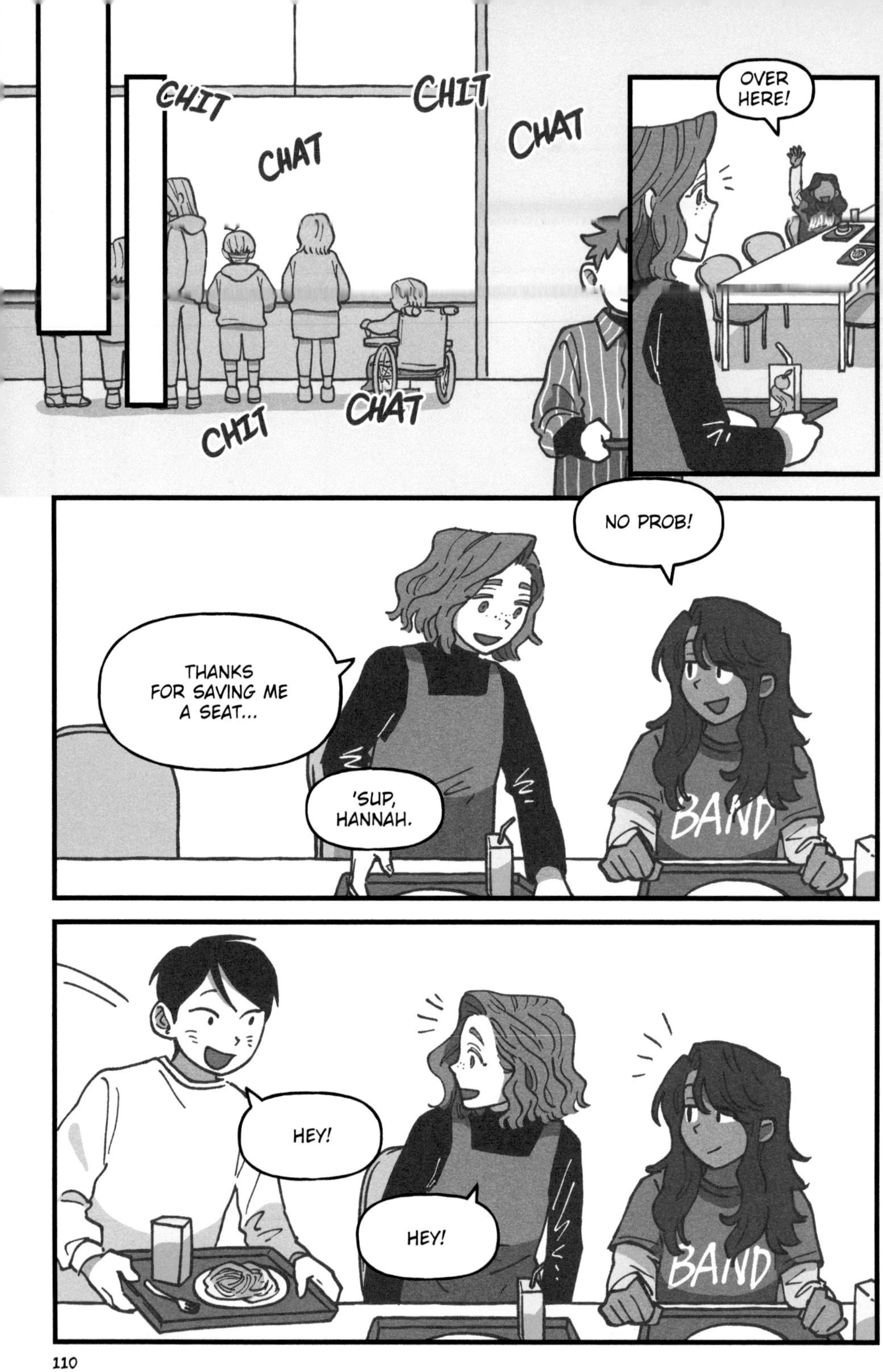
CHIT
CHAT
CHIT
CHAT
CHIT
CHAT
OVER HERE!
THANKS FOR SAVING ME A SEAT...
NO PROB!
'SUP, HANNAH.
BAND
HEY!
HEY!
BAND

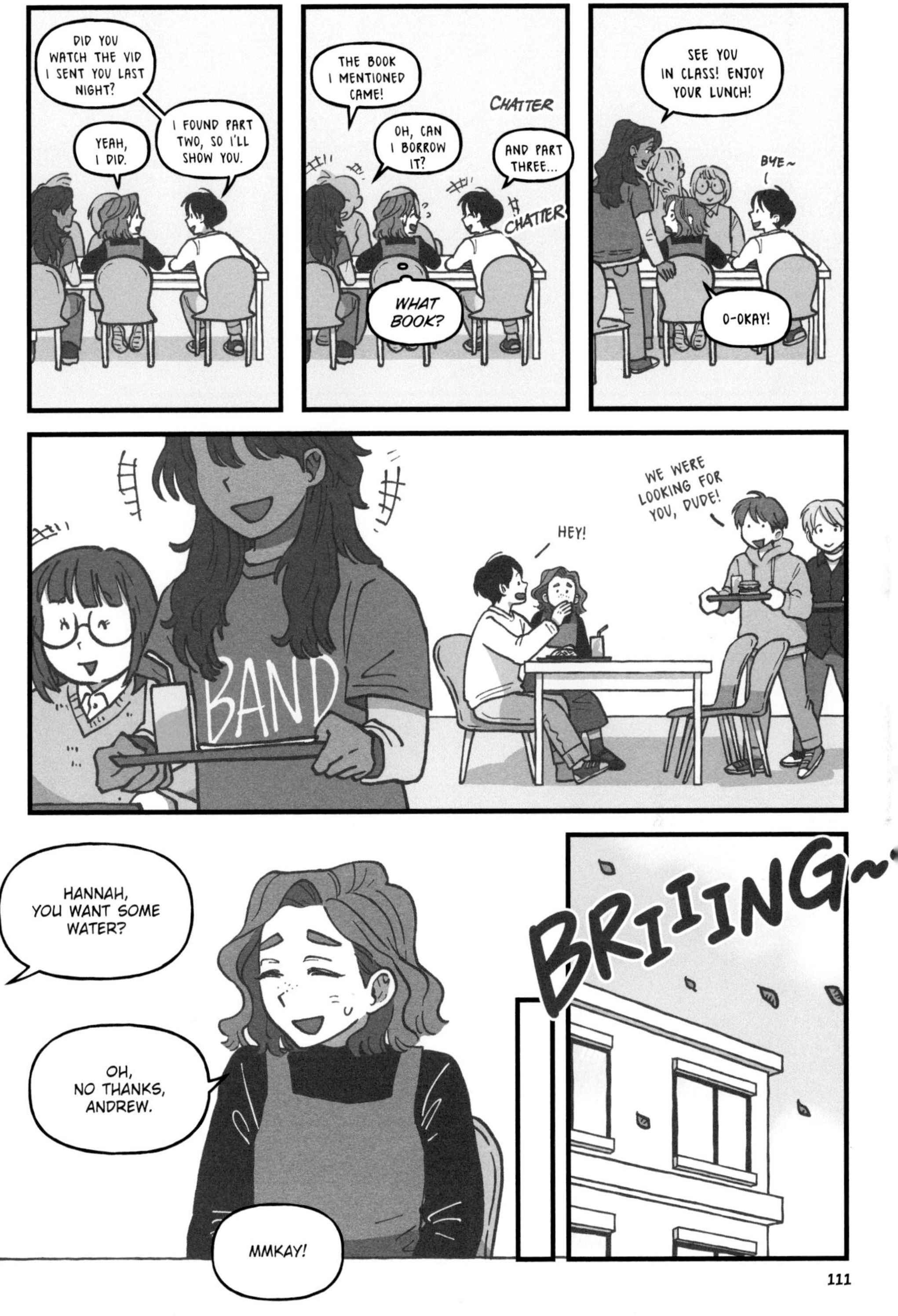
DID YOU WATCH THE VID I SENT YOU LAST NIGHT?
YEAH, I DID.
I FOUND PART TWO, SO I'LL SHOW YOU.
THE BOOK I MENTIONED CAME!
OH, CAN I BORROW IT?
CHATTER
AND PART THREE...
CHATTER
WHAT BOOK?
SEE YOU IN CLASS! ENJOY YOUR LUNCH!
BYE~
O-OKAY!
BAND
WE WERE LOOKING FOR YOU, DUDE!
HEY!
HANNAH, YOU WANT SOME WATER?
OH, NO THANKS, ANDREW.
MMKAY!
BRIIING~

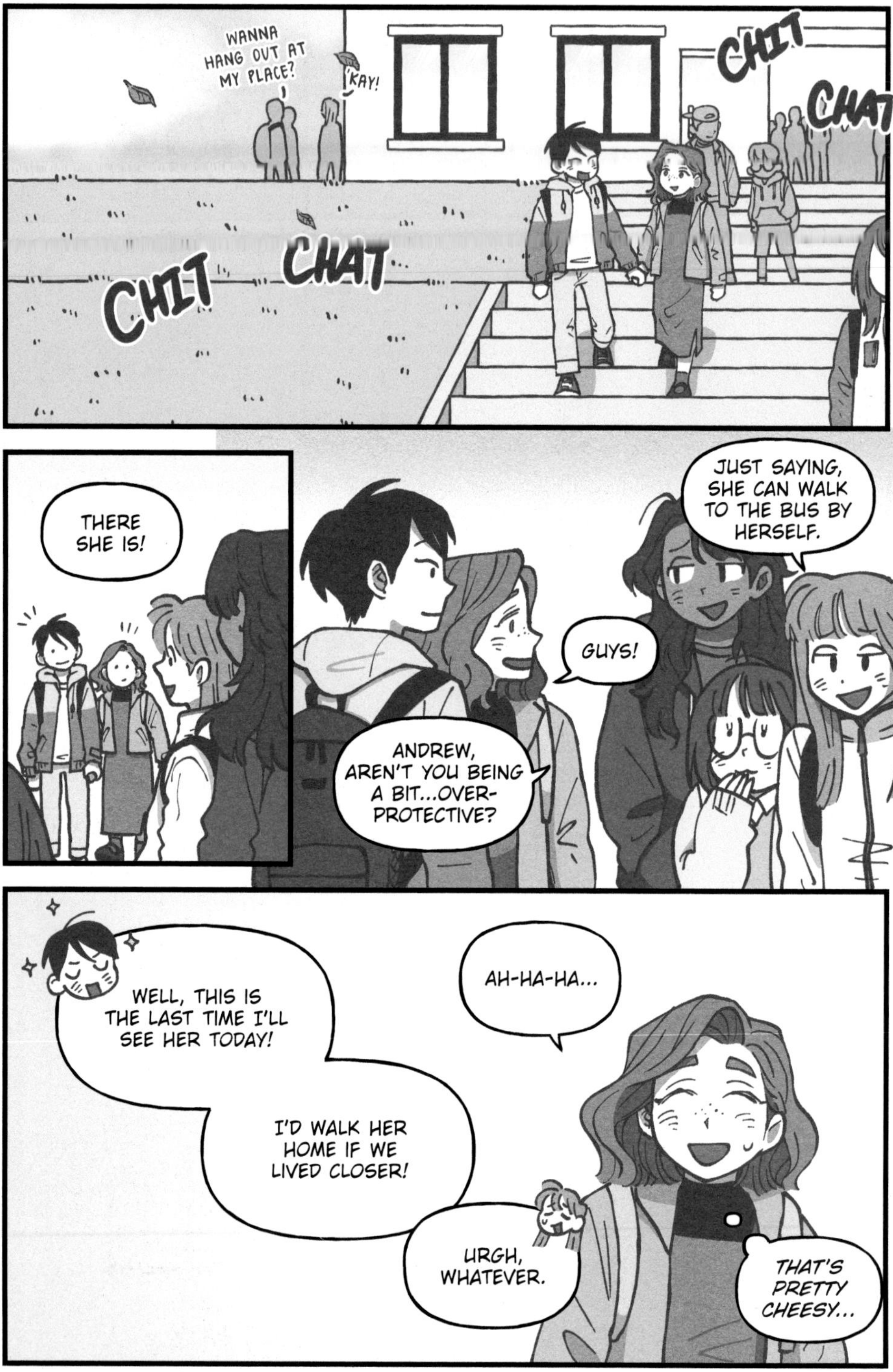
WANNA HANG OUT AT MY PLACE?
'KAY!
CHIT
CHAT
CHIT
CHAT
THERE SHE IS!
JUST SAYING, SHE CAN WALK TO THE BUS BY HERSELF.
GUYS!
ANDREW, AREN'T YOU BEING A BIT...OVER-PROTECTIVE?
WELL, THIS IS THE LAST TIME I'LL SEE HER TODAY!
I'D WALK HER HOME IF WE LIVED CLOSER!
AH-HA-HA...
URGH, WHATEVER.
THAT'S PRETTY CHEESY...

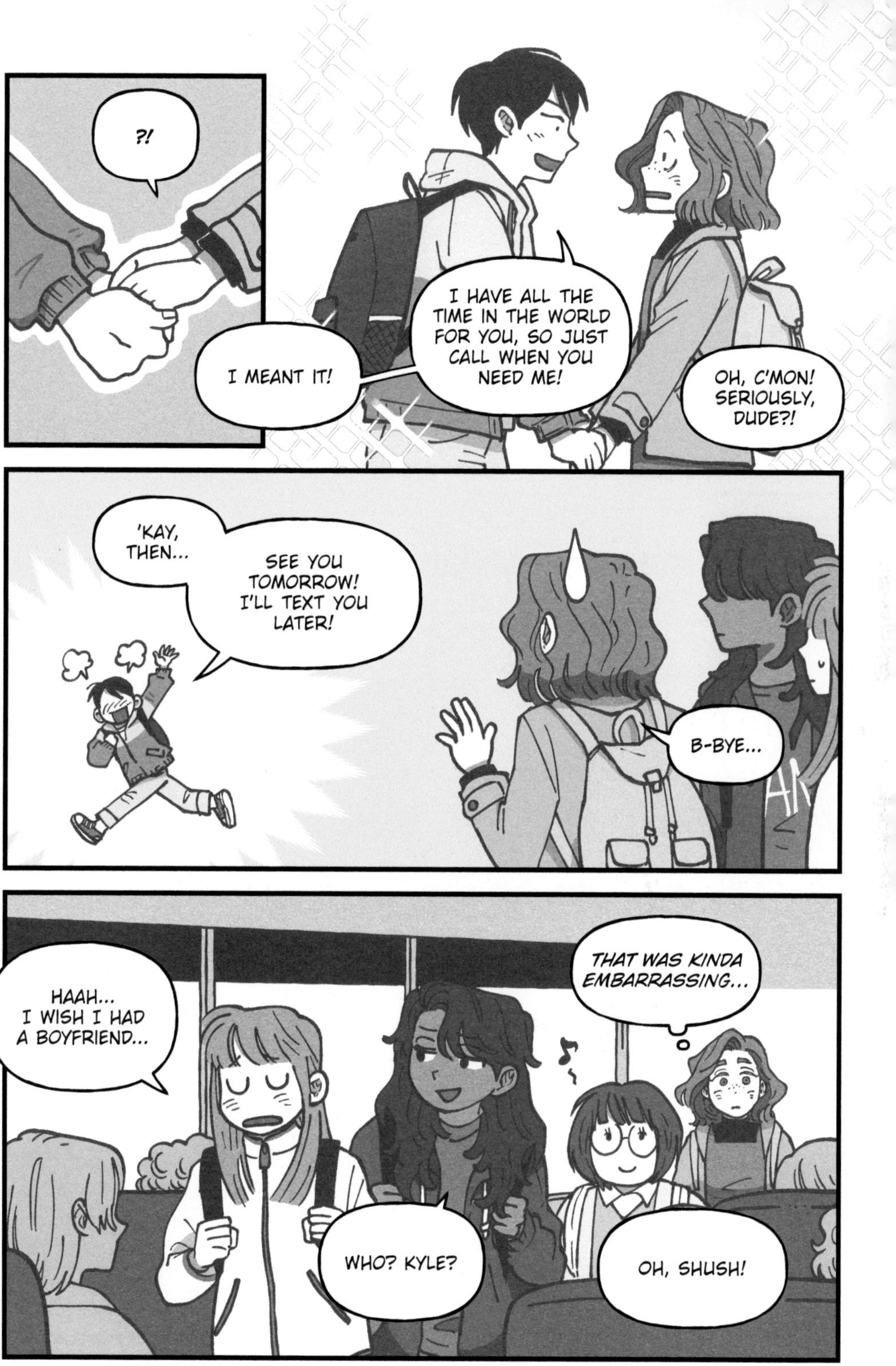
?!
I HAVE ALL THE TIME IN THE WORLD FOR YOU, SO JUST CALL WHEN YOU NEED ME!
I MEANT IT!
OH, C'MON! SERIOUSLY, DUDE?!
'KAY, THEN...
SEE YOU TOMORROW! I'LL TEXT YOU LATER!
B-BYE...
HAAH... I WISH I HAD A BOYFRIEND...
THAT WAS KINDA EMBARRASSING...
WHO? KYLE?
OH, SHUSH!

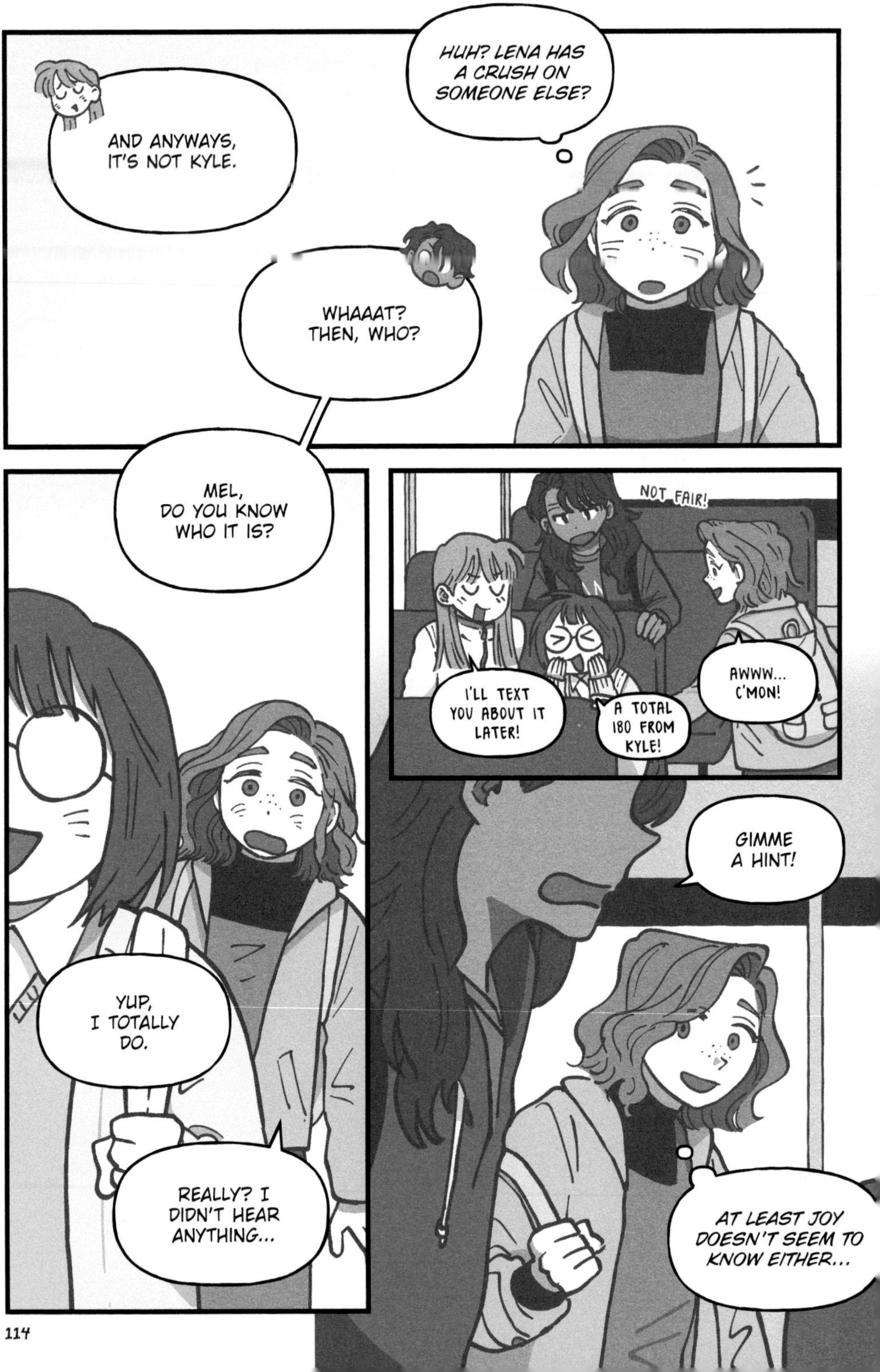
HUH? LENA HAS A CRUSH ON SOMEONE ELSE?
AND ANYWAYS, IT'S NOT KYLE.
WHAAAT? THEN, WHO?
MEL, DO YOU KNOW WHO IT IS?
NOT FAIR!
I'LL TEXT YOU ABOUT IT LATER!
A TOTAL 180 FROM KYLE!
AWWW... C'MON!
YUP, I TOTALLY DO.
REALLY? I DIDN'T HEAR ANYTHING...
GIMME A HINT!
AT LEAST JOY DOESN'T SEEM TO KNOW EITHER...

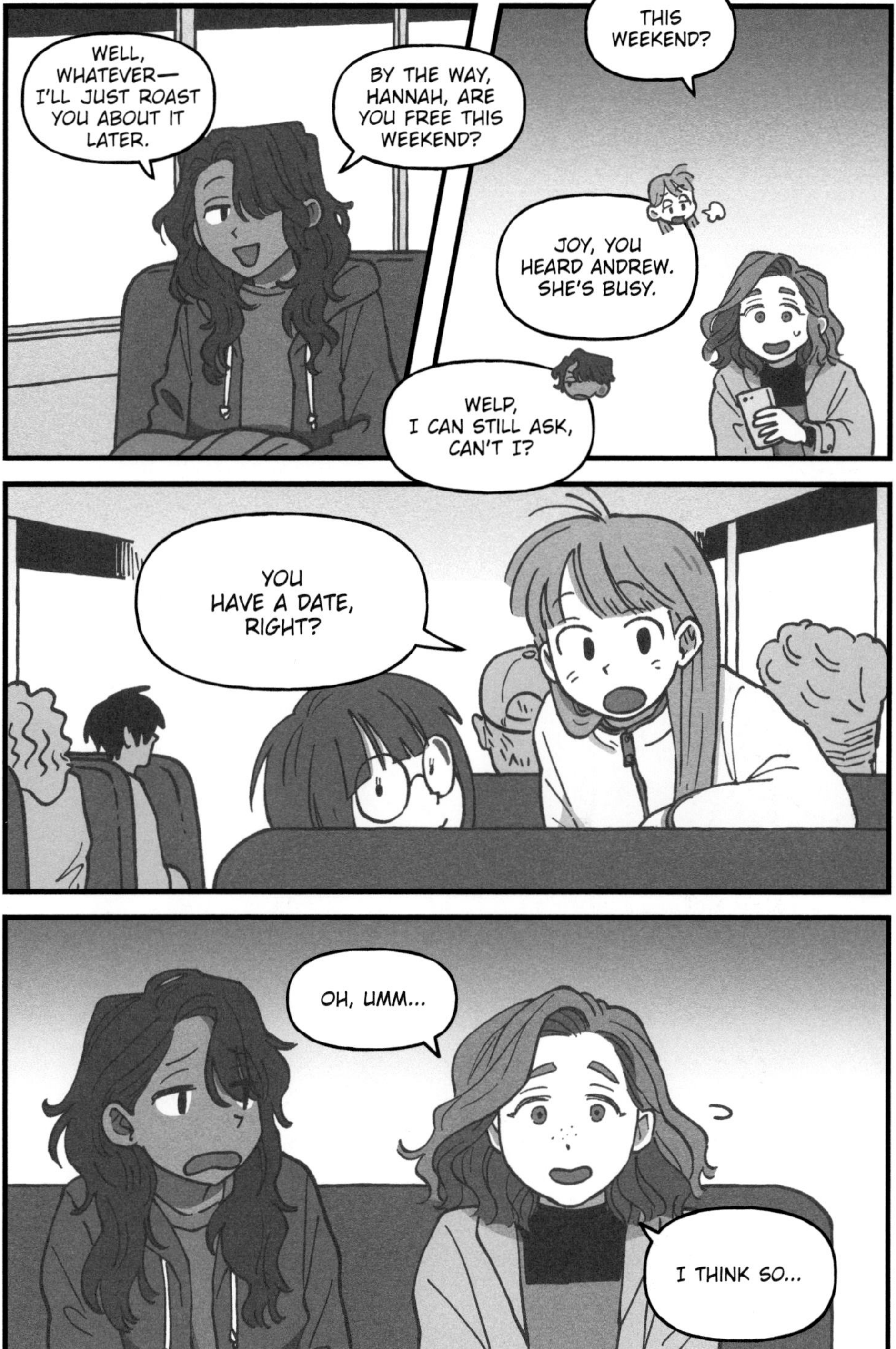
WELL, WHATEVER— I'LL JUST ROAST YOU ABOUT IT LATER.
BY THE WAY, HANNAH, ARE YOU FREE THIS WEEKEND?
THIS WEEKEND?
JOY, YOU HEARD ANDREW. SHE'S BUSY.
WELP, I CAN STILL ASK, CAN'T I?
YOU HAVE A DATE, RIGHT?
OH, UMM...
I THINK SO...

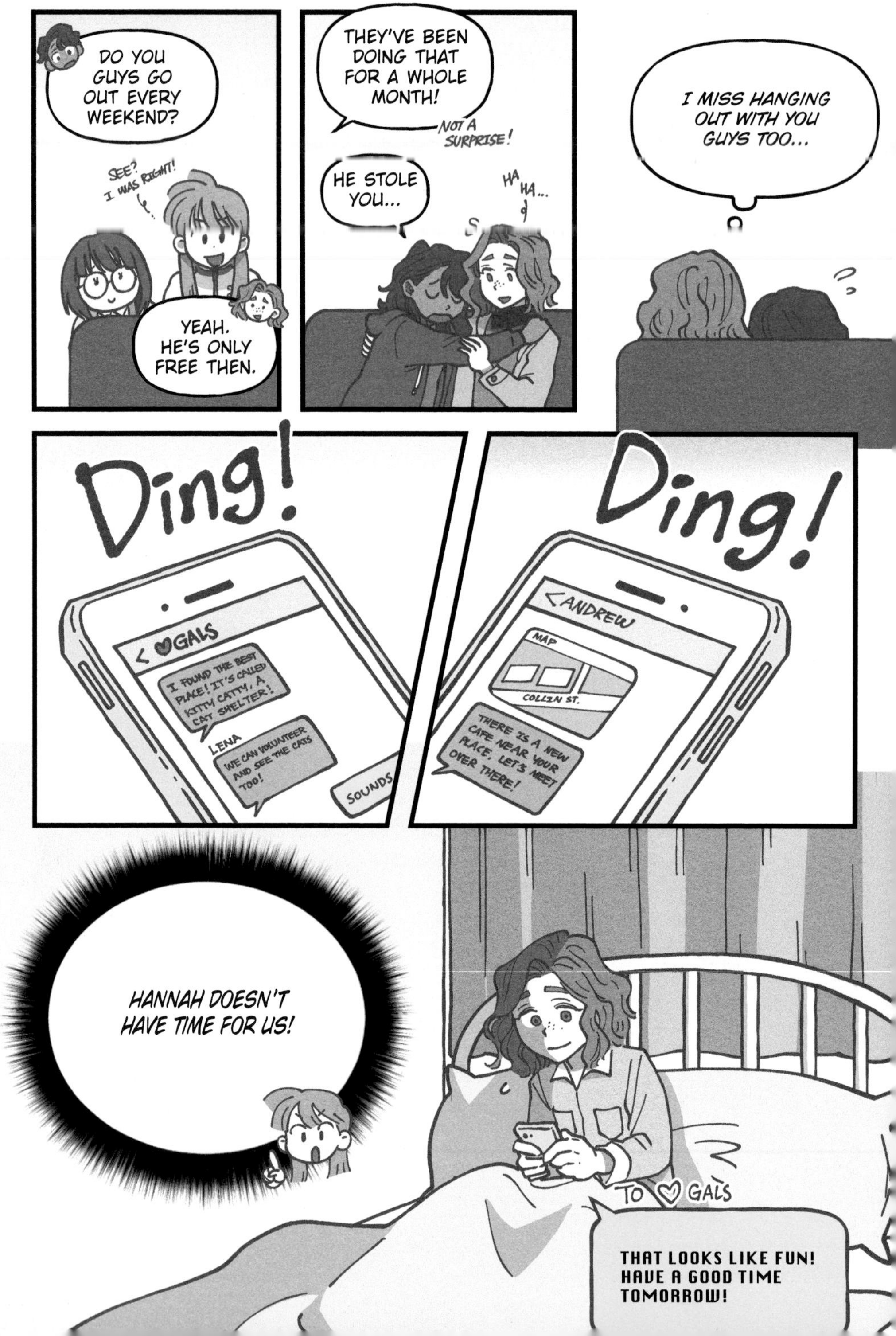

DO YOU GUYS GO OUT EVERY WEEKEND?
SEE? I WAS RIGHT!
YEAH. HE'S ONLY FREE THEN.
THEY'VE BEEN DOING THAT FOR A WHOLE MONTH!
NOT A SURPRISE!
HE STOLE YOU...
HA HA...
I MISS HANGING OUT WITH YOU GUYS TOO...
Ding!
< ♡GALS
I FOUND THE BEST PLACE! IT'S CALLED KITTY CATTY, A CAT SHELTER!
LENA
WE CAN VOLUNTEER AND SEE THE CATS TOO!
SOUNDS
Ding!
< ANDREW
MAP
COLLIN ST.
THERE IS A NEW CAFE NEAR YOUR PLACE, LET'S MEET OVER THERE!
HANNAH DOESN'T HAVE TIME FOR US!
TO ♡ GALS
THAT LOOKS LIKE FUN! HAVE A GOOD TIME TOMORROW!

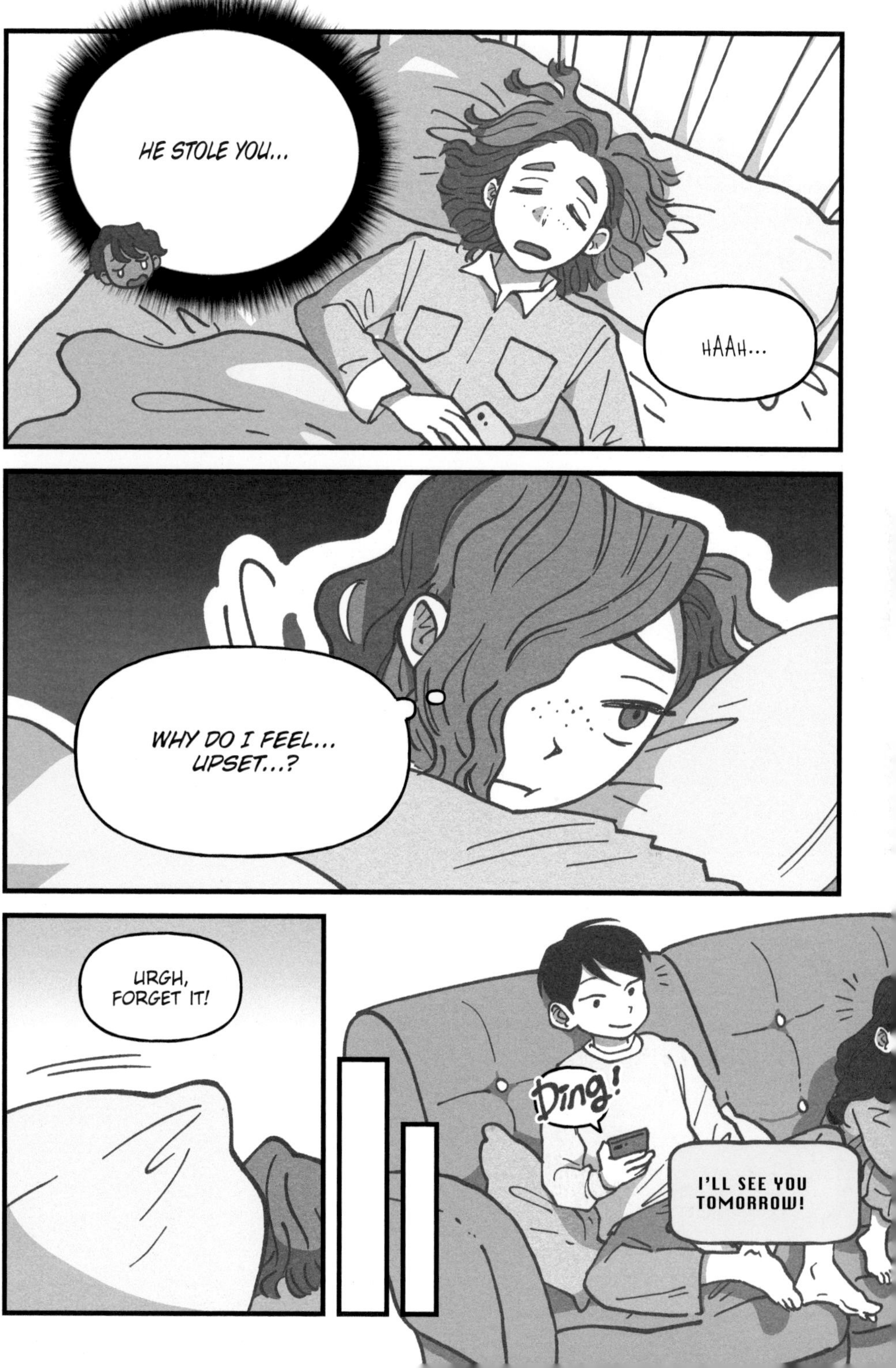
HE STOLE YOU...
HAAH...
WHY DO I FEEL... UPSET...?
URGH, FORGET IT!
Ding!
I'LL SEE YOU TOMORROW!

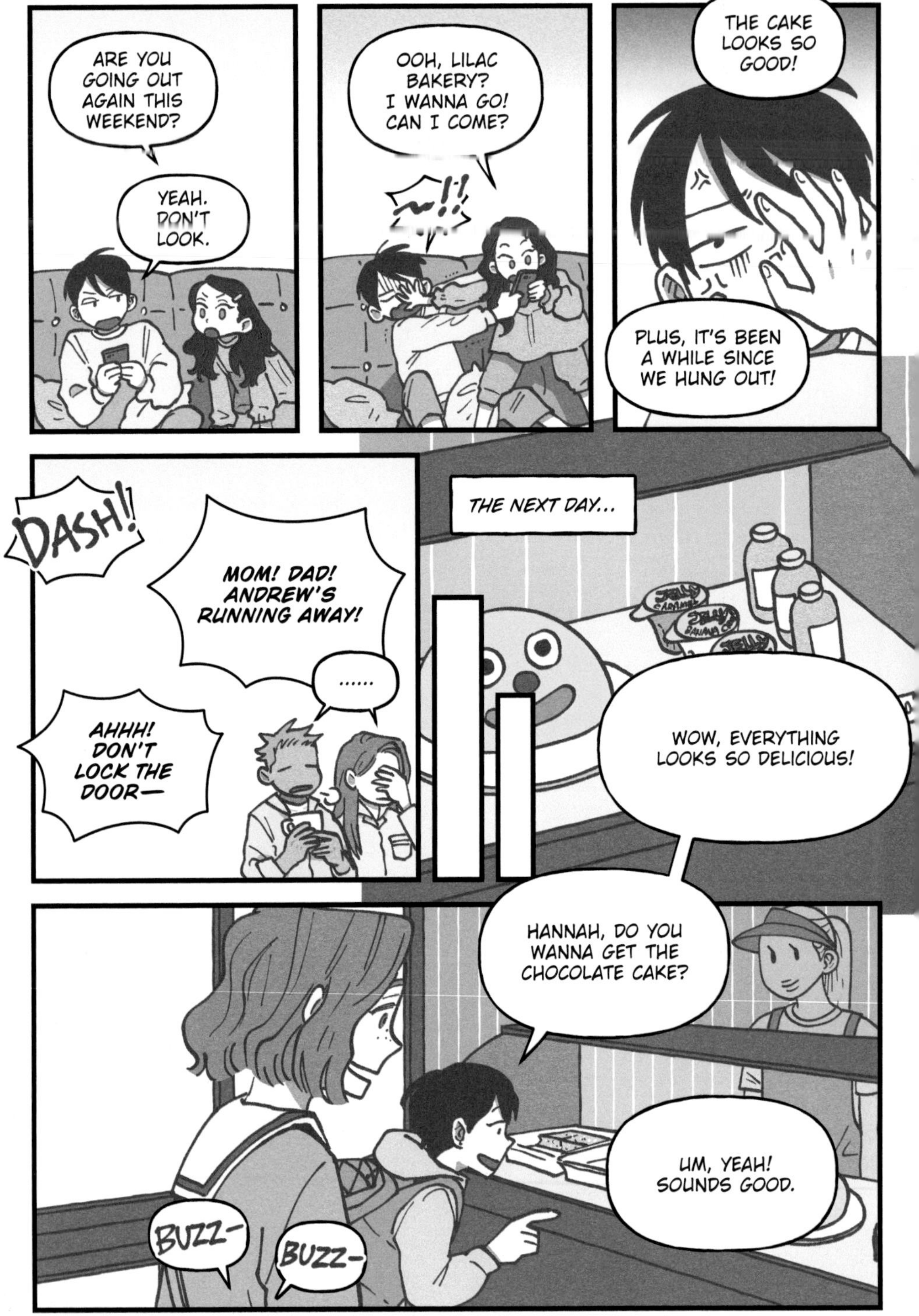
ARE YOU GOING OUT AGAIN THIS WEEKEND?
YEAH. DON'T LOOK.
OOH, LILAC BAKERY? I WANNA GO! CAN I COME?
~!!
THE CAKE LOOKS SO GOOD!
PLUS, IT'S BEEN A WHILE SINCE WE HUNG OUT!
DASH!
MOM! DAD! ANDREW'S RUNNING AWAY!
AHHH! DON'T LOCK THE DOOR—
......
THE NEXT DAY...
WOW, EVERYTHING LOOKS SO DELICIOUS!
HANNAH, DO YOU WANNA GET THE CHOCOLATE CAKE?
UM, YEAH! SOUNDS GOOD.
BUZZ-
BUZZ-

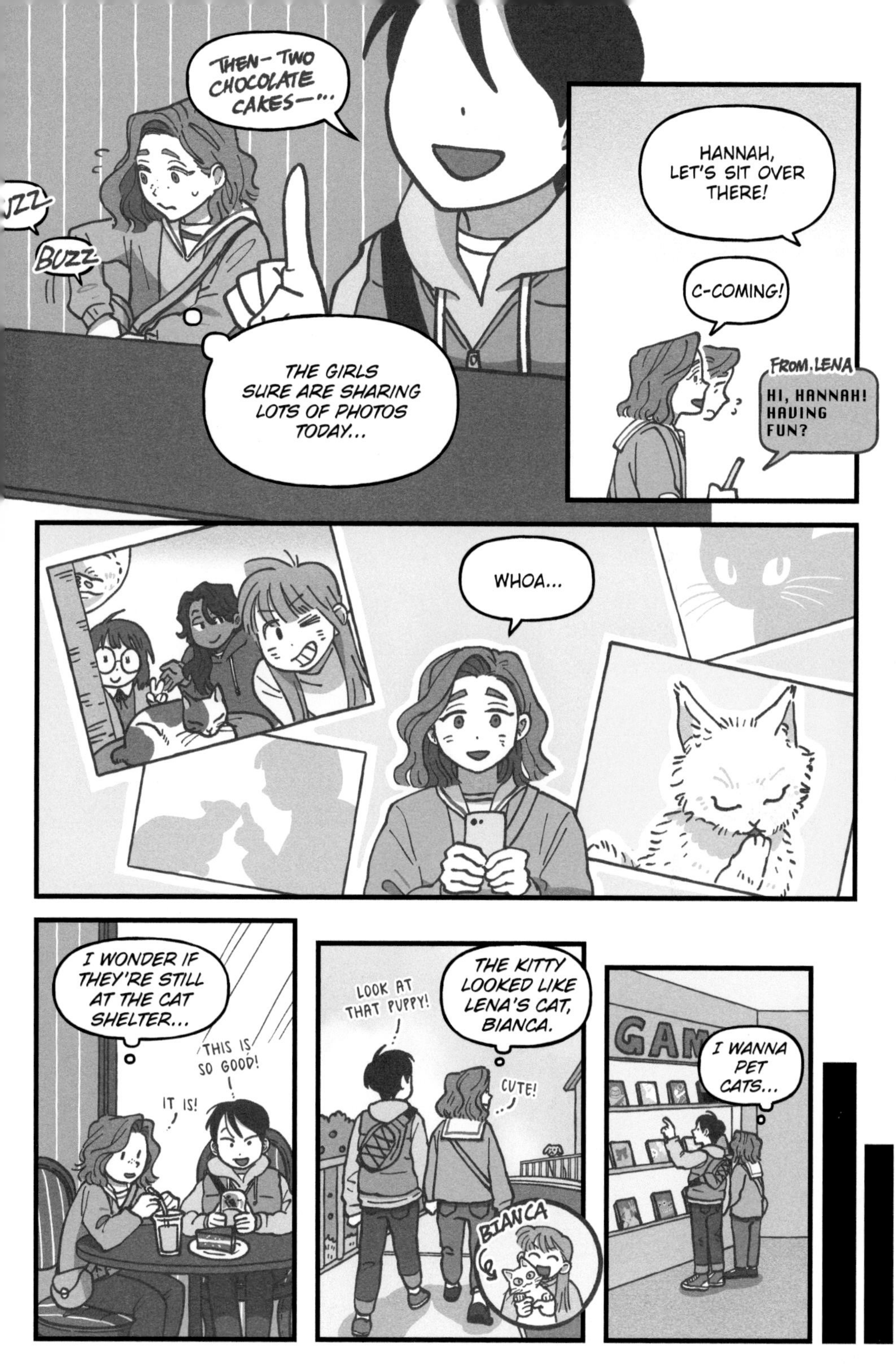
THEN- TWO CHOCOLATE CAKES—...
JZZ
BUZZ
THE GIRLS SURE ARE SHARING LOTS OF PHOTOS TODAY...
HANNAH, LET'S SIT OVER THERE!
C-COMING!
FROM.LENA
HI, HANNAH! HAVING FUN?
WHOA...
I WONDER IF THEY'RE STILL AT THE CAT SHELTER...
THIS IS SO GOOD!
IT IS!
LOOK AT THAT PUPPY!
THE KITTY LOOKED LIKE LENA'S CAT, BIANCA.
CUTE!
BIANCA
GAM
I WANNA PET CATS...

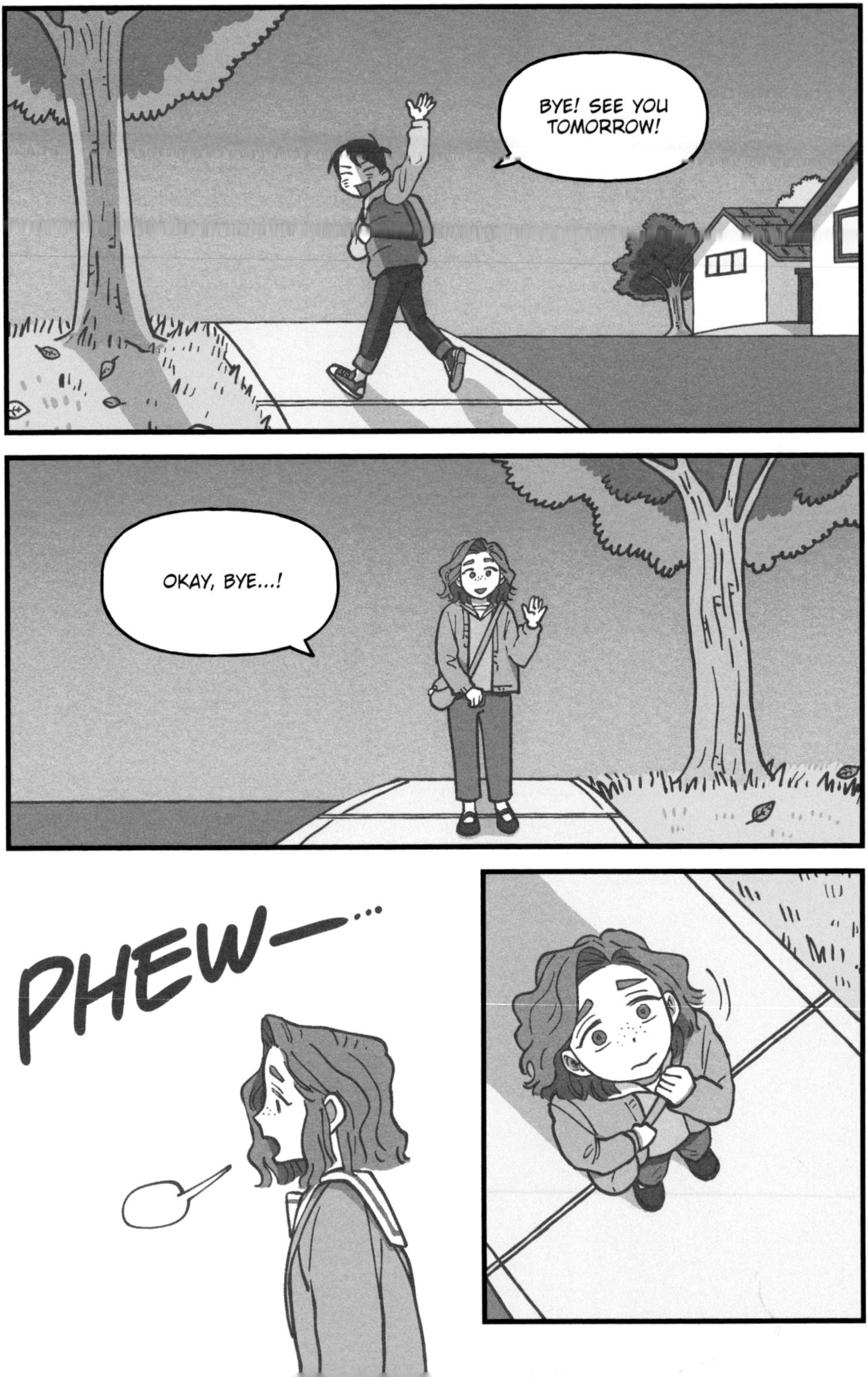
BYE! SEE YOU TOMORROW!
OKAY, BYE...!
PHEW—...

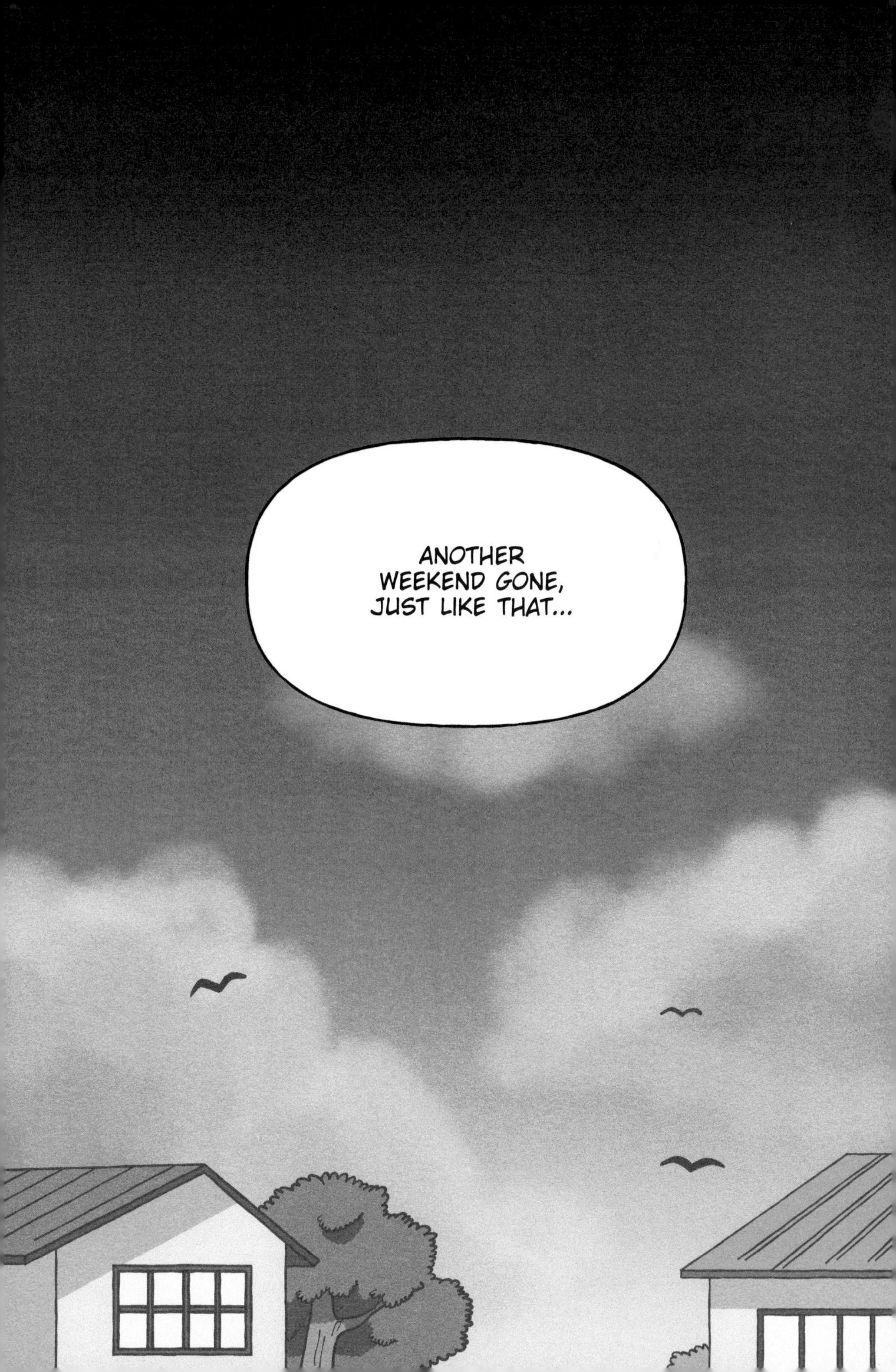
ANOTHER WEEKEND GONE, JUST LIKE THAT...

Chapter 7

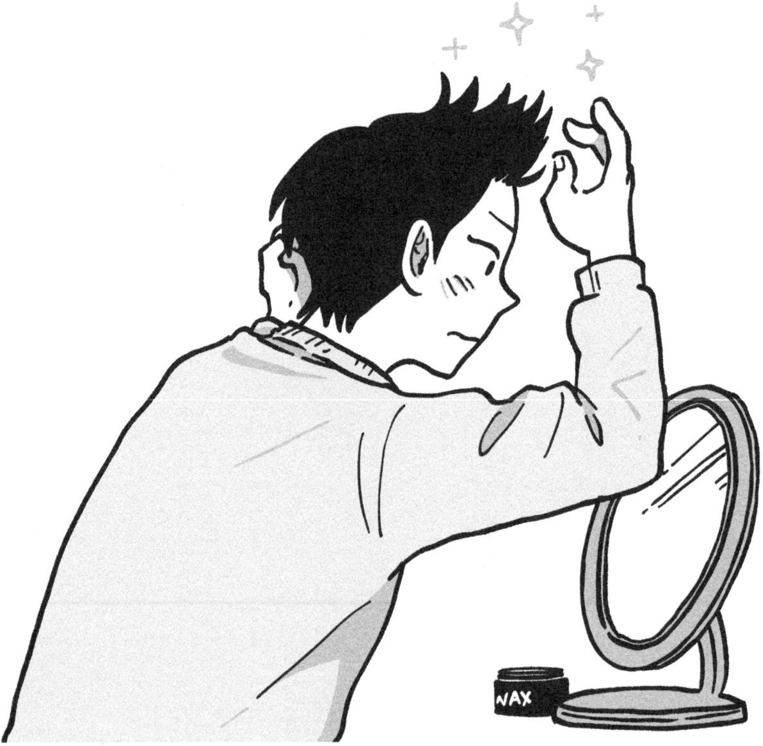
WAX

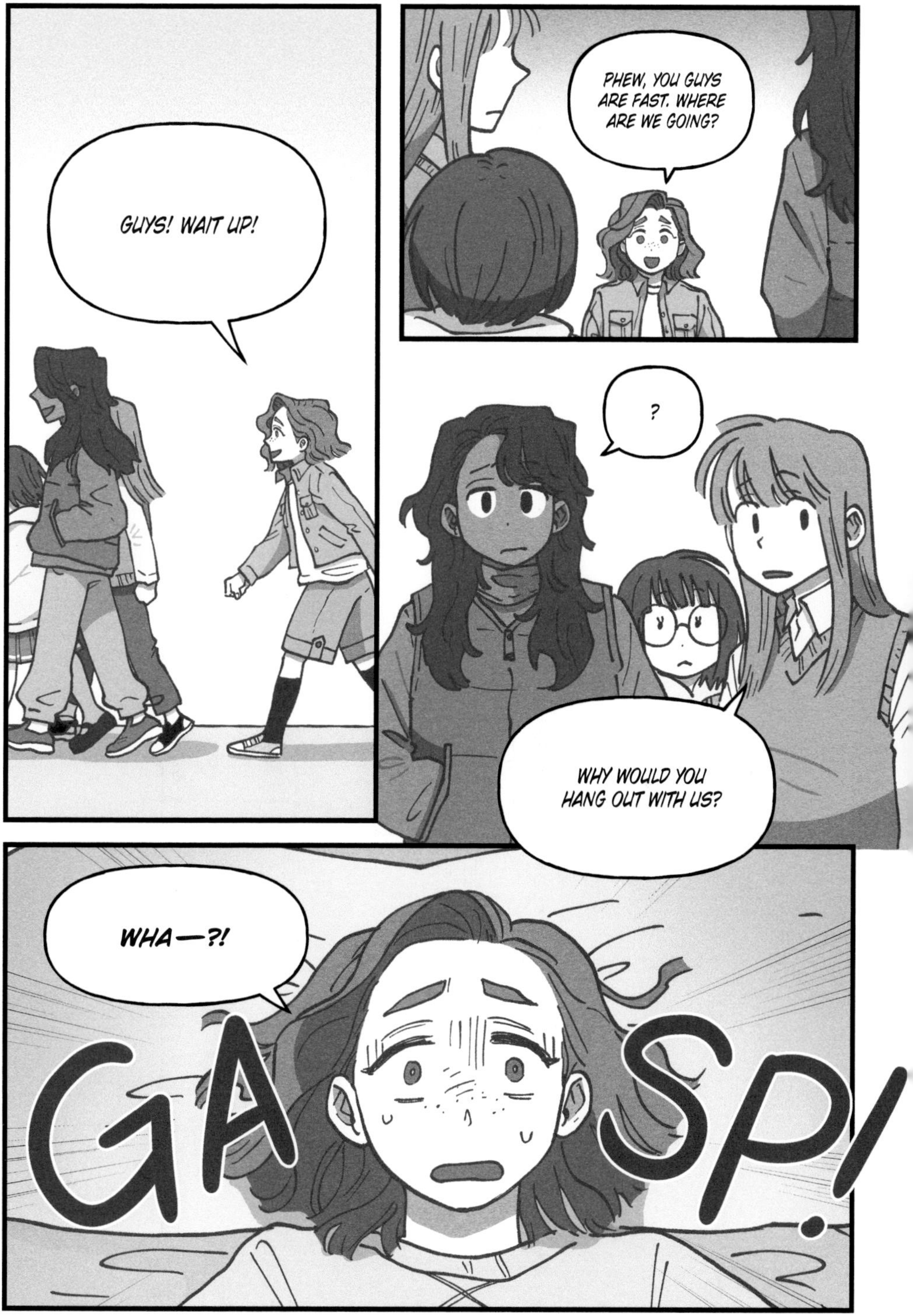
GUYS! WAIT UP!
PHEW, YOU GUYS ARE FAST. WHERE ARE WE GOING?
?
WHY WOULD YOU HANG OUT WITH US?
WHA—?!
GASP!

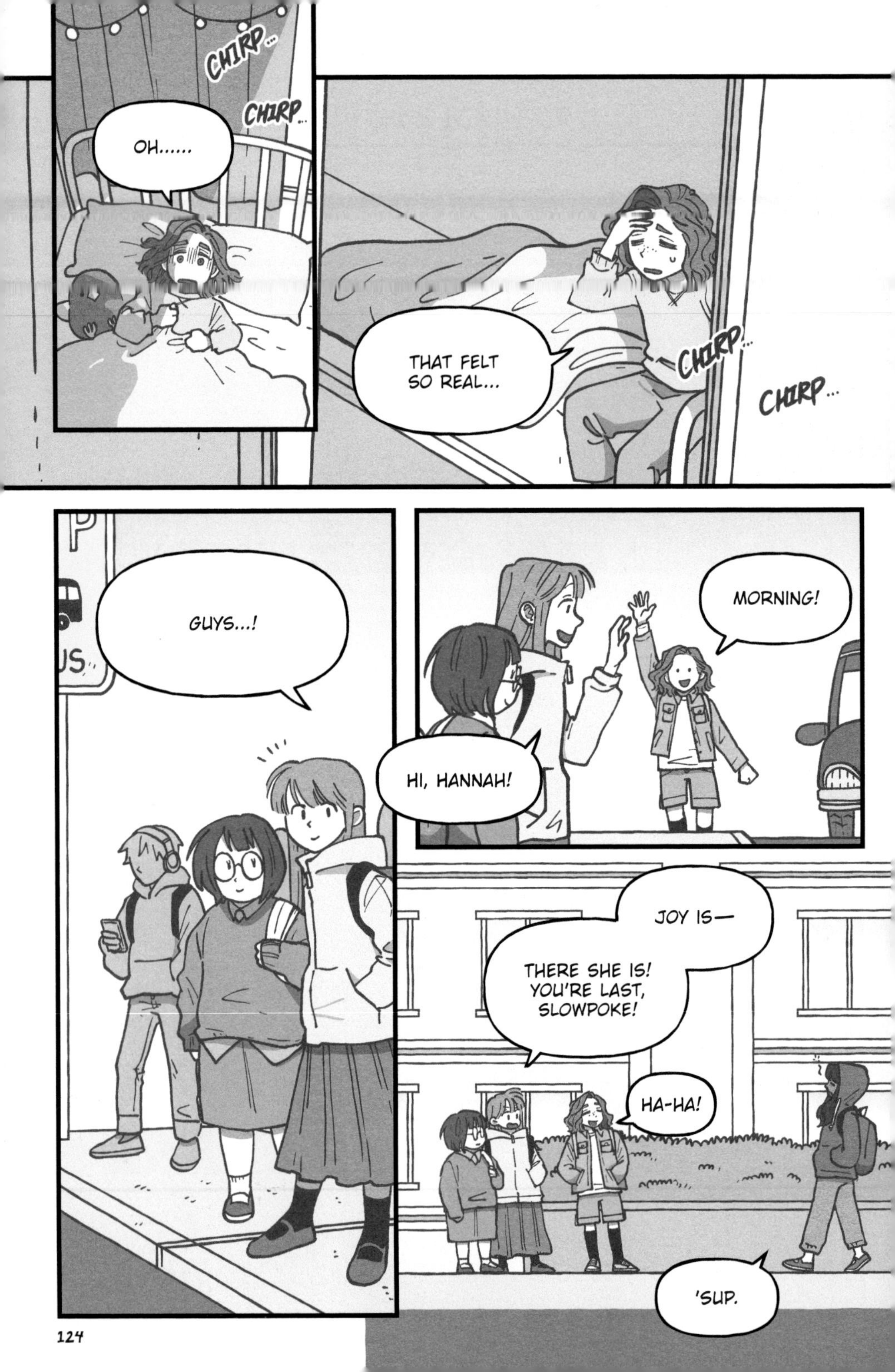
CHIRP...
CHIRP...
OH......
THAT FELT SO REAL...
CHIRP...
CHIRP...
GUYS...!
P
US
HI, HANNAH!
MORNING!
JOY IS—
THERE SHE IS! YOU'RE LAST, SLOWPOKE!
HA-HA!
'SUP.

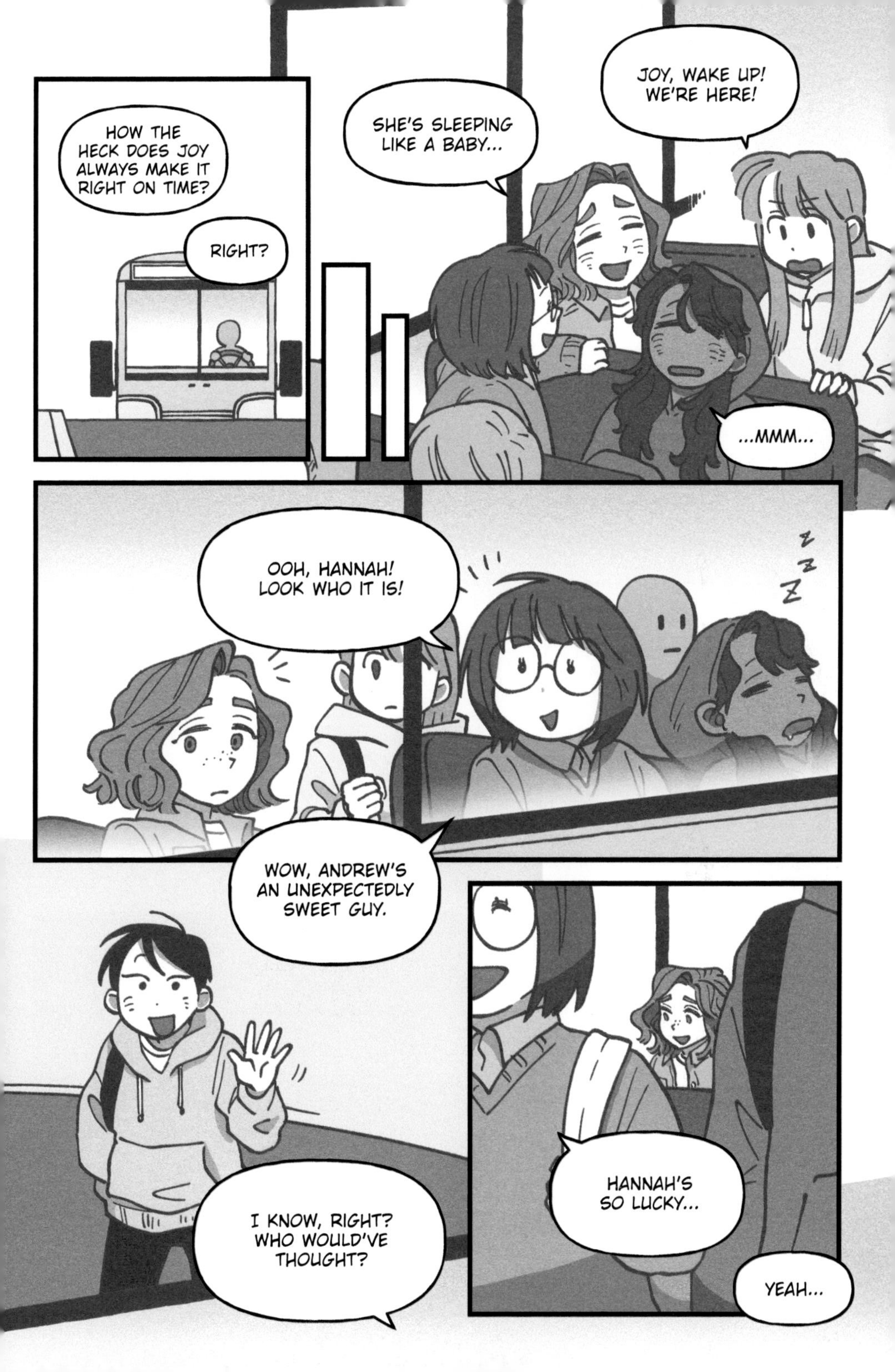
HOW THE HECK DOES JOY ALWAYS MAKE IT RIGHT ON TIME?
RIGHT?
JOY, WAKE UP! WE'RE HERE!
SHE'S SLEEPING LIKE A BABY...
...MMM...
OOH, HANNAH! LOOK WHO IT IS!
Z Z Z
WOW, ANDREW'S AN UNEXPECTEDLY SWEET GUY.
I KNOW, RIGHT? WHO WOULD'VE THOUGHT?
HANNAH'S SO LUCKY...
YEAH...

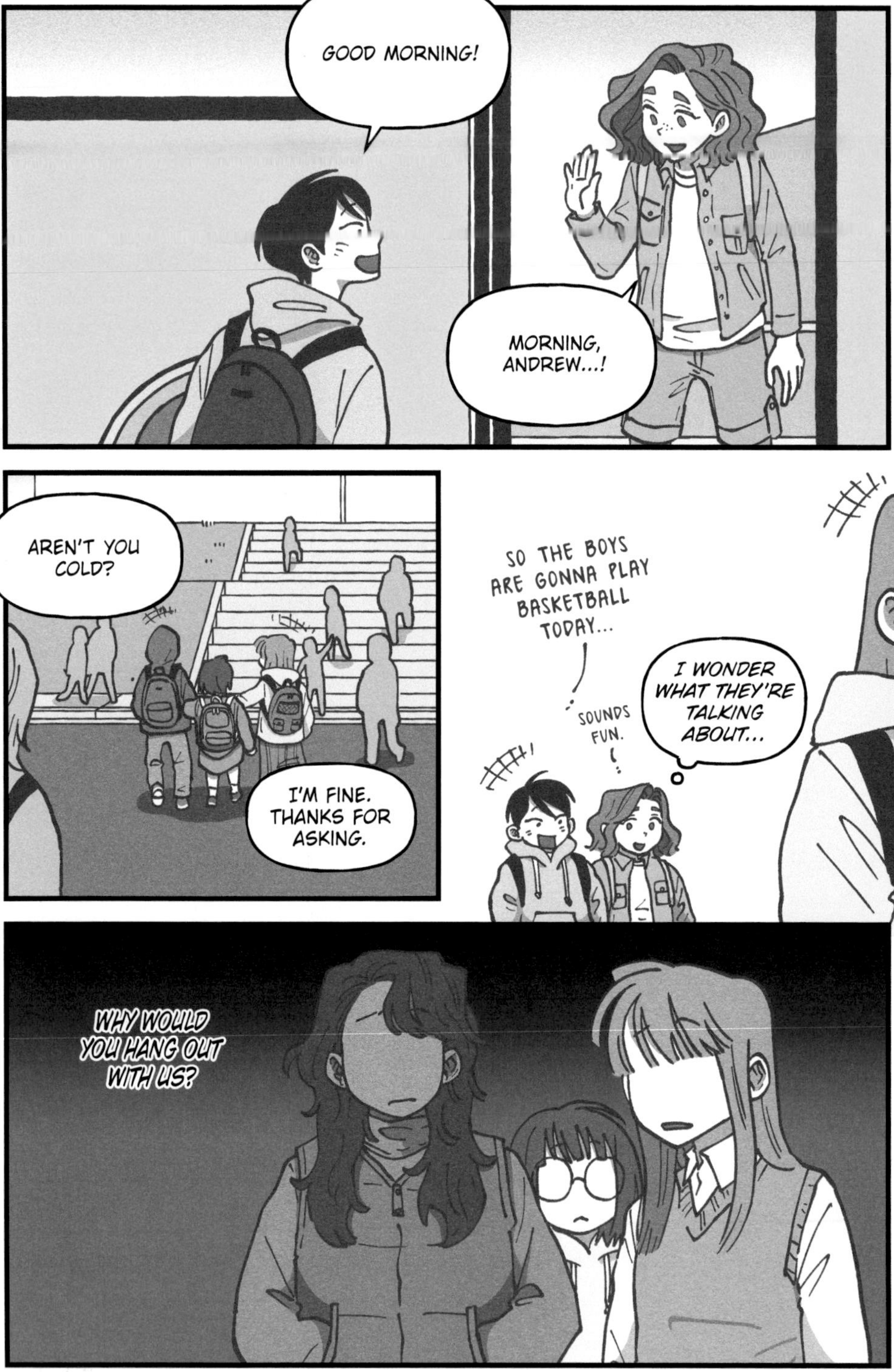
GOOD MORNING!
MORNING, ANDREW...!
AREN'T YOU COLD?
I'M FINE. THANKS FOR ASKING.
SO THE BOYS ARE GONNA PLAY BASKETBALL TODAY...
SOUNDS FUN.
I WONDER WHAT THEY'RE TALKING ABOUT...
WHY WOULD YOU HANG OUT WITH US?

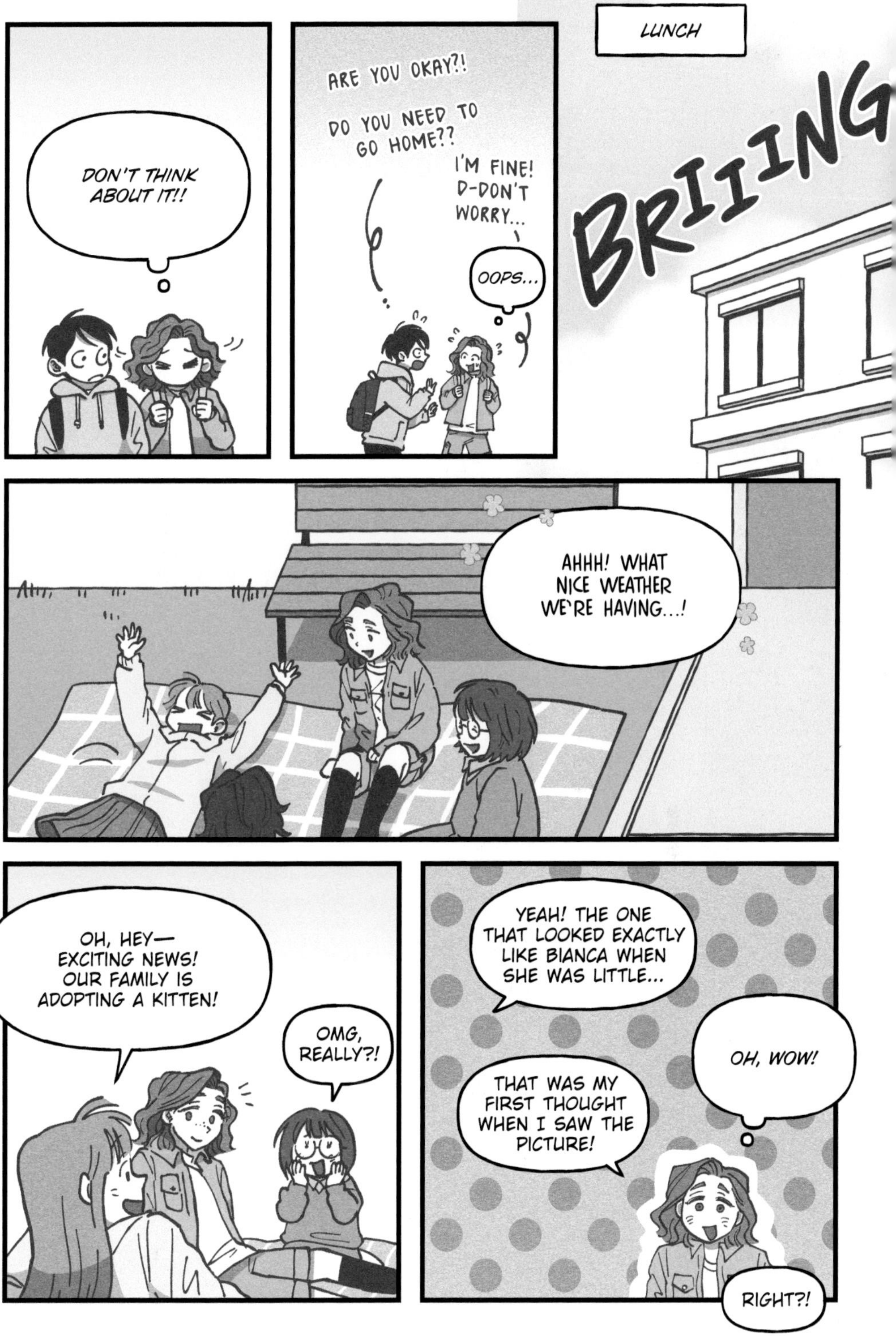
DON'T THINK ABOUT IT!!
ARE YOU OKAY?!
DO YOU NEED TO GO HOME??
I'M FINE! D-DON'T WORRY...
OOPS...
LUNCH
BRIIING
AHHH! WHAT NICE WEATHER WE'RE HAVING...!
OH, HEY— EXCITING NEWS! OUR FAMILY IS ADOPTING A KITTEN!
OMG, REALLY?!
YEAH! THE ONE THAT LOOKED EXACTLY LIKE BIANCA WHEN SHE WAS LITTLE...
OH, WOW!
THAT WAS MY FIRST THOUGHT WHEN I SAW THE PICTURE!
RIGHT?!

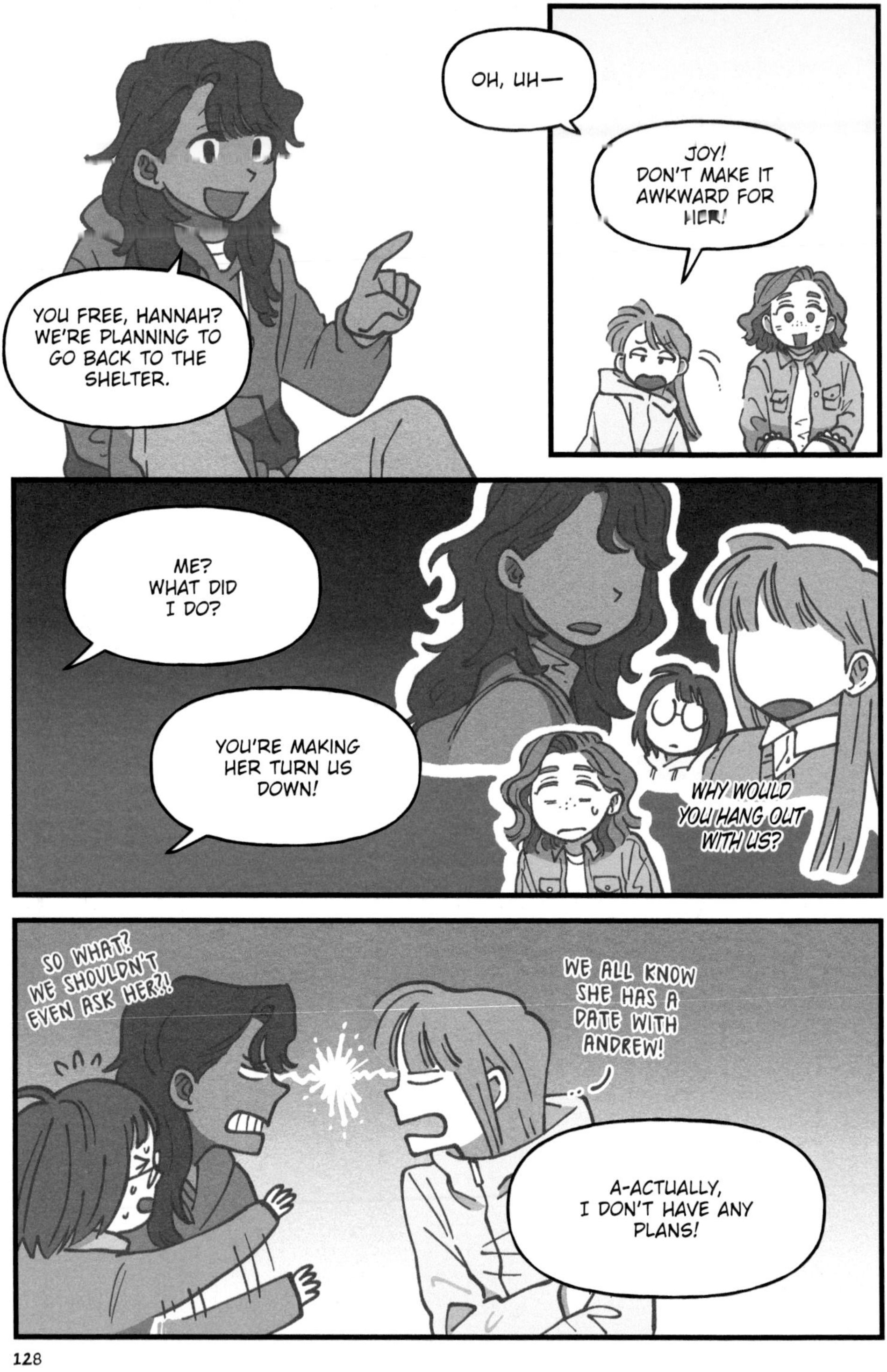
YOU FREE, HANNAH? WE'RE PLANNING TO GO BACK TO THE SHELTER.
OH, UH—
JOY! DON'T MAKE IT AWKWARD FOR HER!
ME? WHAT DID I DO?
YOU'RE MAKING HER TURN US DOWN!
WHY WOULD YOU HANG OUT WITH US?
SO WHAT? WE SHOULDN'T EVEN ASK HER?!
WE ALL KNOW SHE HAS A DATE WITH ANDREW!
A-ACTUALLY, I DON'T HAVE ANY PLANS!

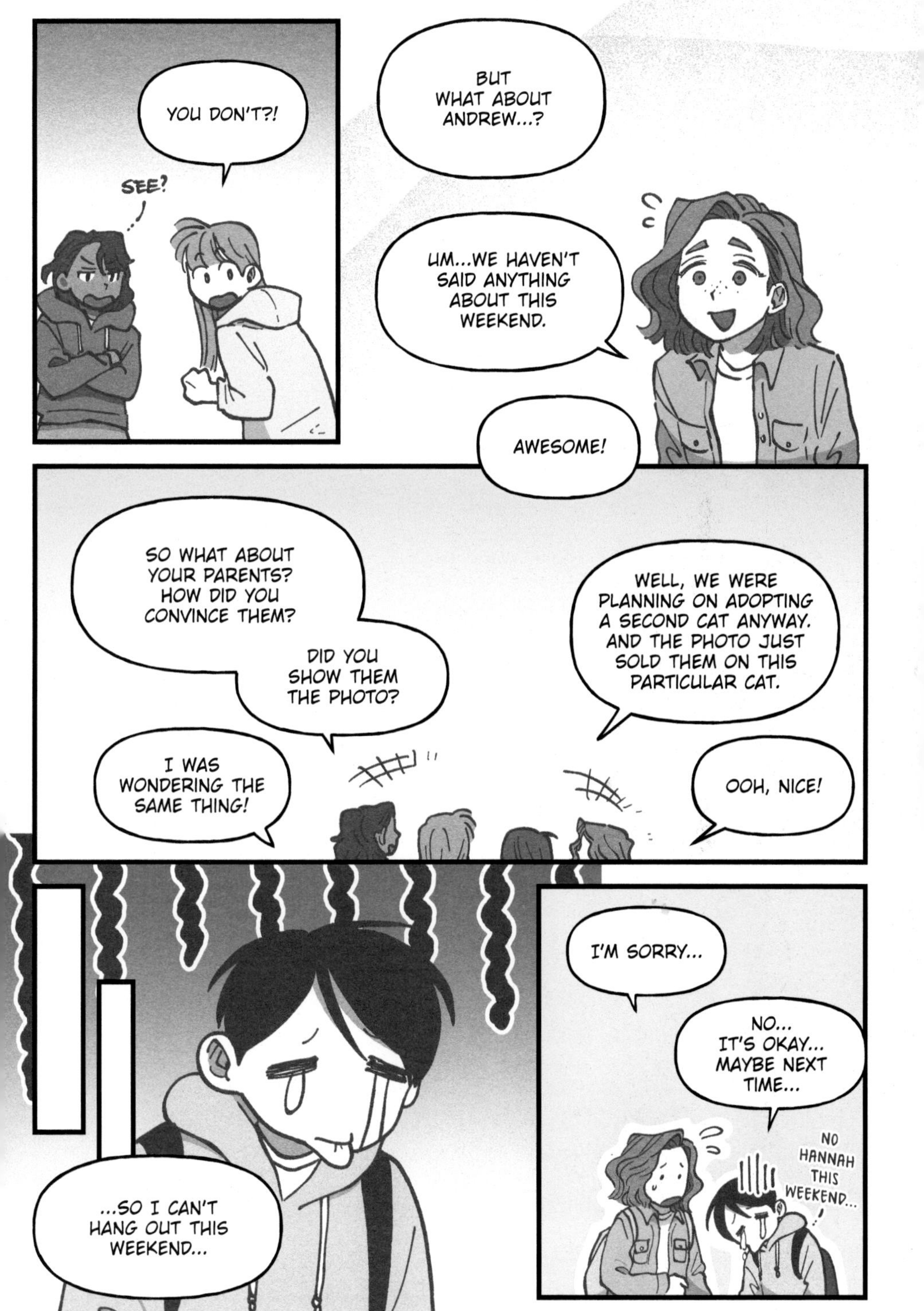
YOU DON'T?!
SEE?
BUT WHAT ABOUT ANDREW...?
UM...WE HAVEN'T SAID ANYTHING ABOUT THIS WEEKEND.
AWESOME!
SO WHAT ABOUT YOUR PARENTS? HOW DID YOU CONVINCE THEM?
DID YOU SHOW THEM THE PHOTO?
I WAS WONDERING THE SAME THING!
WELL, WE WERE PLANNING ON ADOPTING A SECOND CAT ANYWAY. AND THE PHOTO JUST SOLD THEM ON THIS PARTICULAR CAT.
OOH, NICE!
...SO I CAN'T HANG OUT THIS WEEKEND...
I'M SORRY...
NO... IT'S OKAY... MAYBE NEXT TIME...
NO HANNAH THIS WEEKEND...

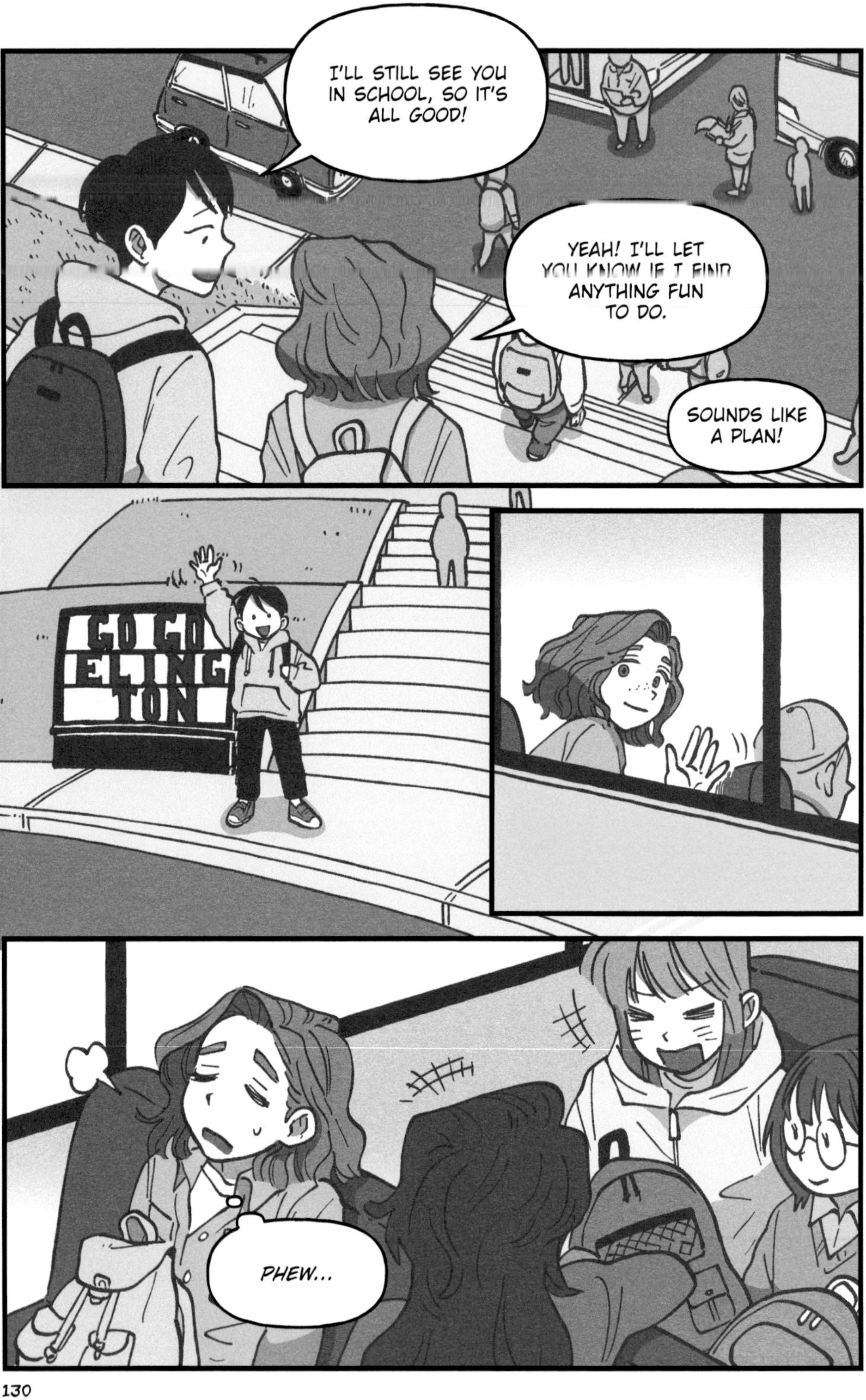
I'LL STILL SEE YOU IN SCHOOL, SO IT'S ALL GOOD!
YEAH! I'LL LET YOU KNOW IF I FIND ANYTHING FUN TO DO.
SOUNDS LIKE A PLAN!
GO GO ELLINGTON
PHEW...

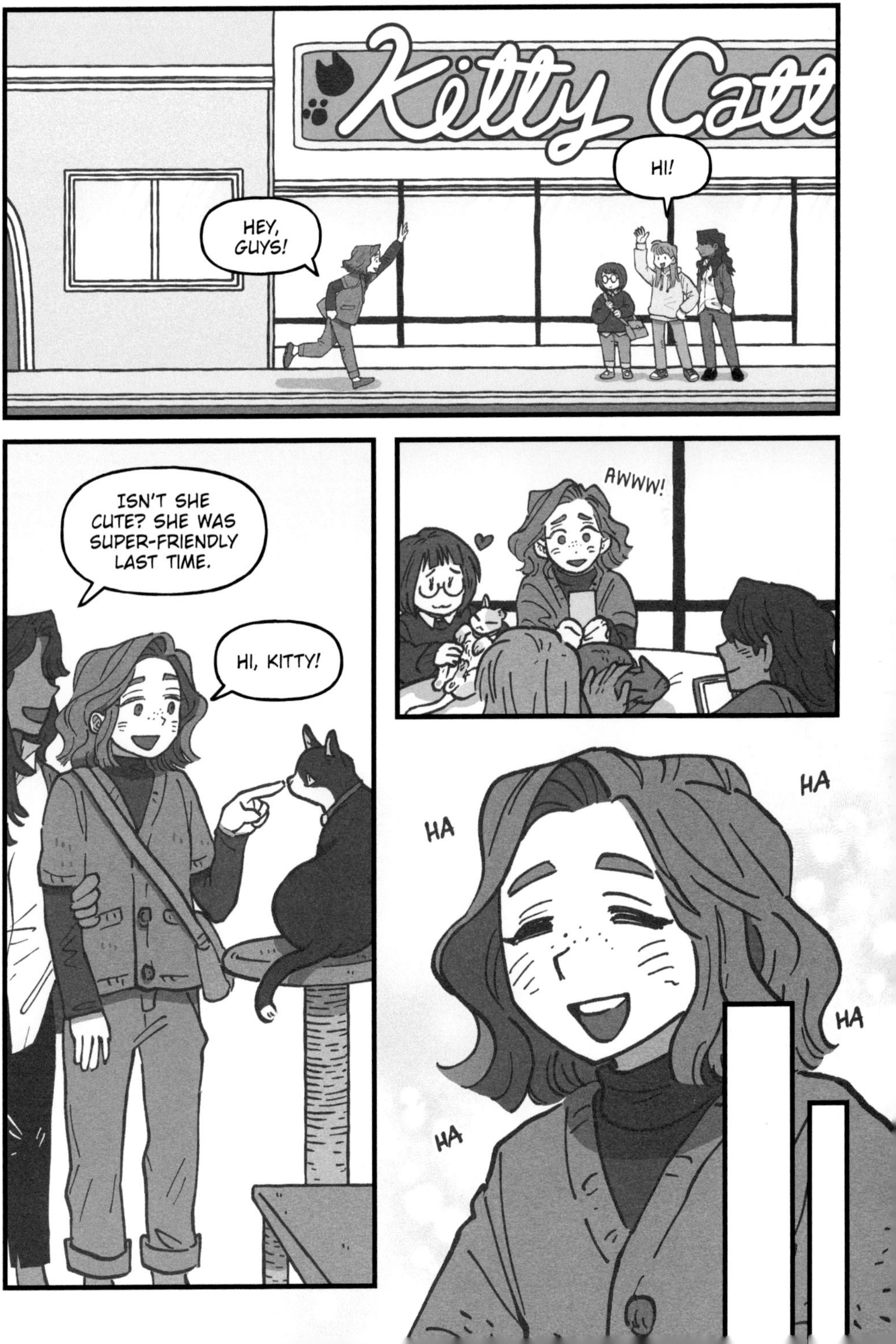
Kitty Catt
HEY, GUYS!
HI!
ISN'T SHE CUTE? SHE WAS SUPER-FRIENDLY LAST TIME.
HI, KITTY!
AWWW!
HA
HA
HA
HA

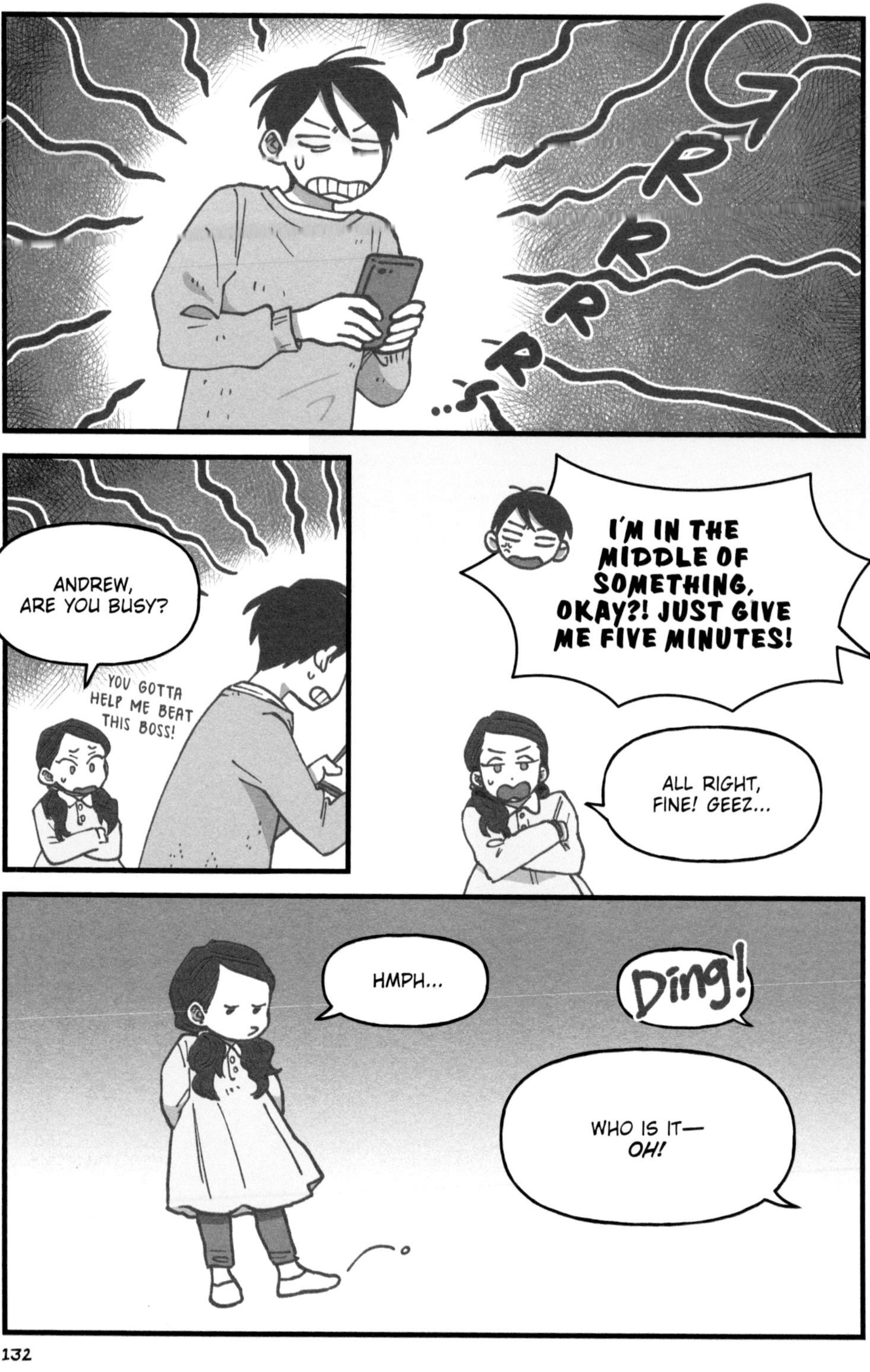
GRRRRRS...
ANDREW, ARE YOU BUSY?
YOU GOTTA HELP ME BEAT THIS BOSS!
I'M IN THE MIDDLE OF SOMETHING, OKAY?! JUST GIVE ME FIVE MINUTES!
ALL RIGHT, FINE! GEEZ...
HMPH...
Ding!
WHO IS IT— OH!

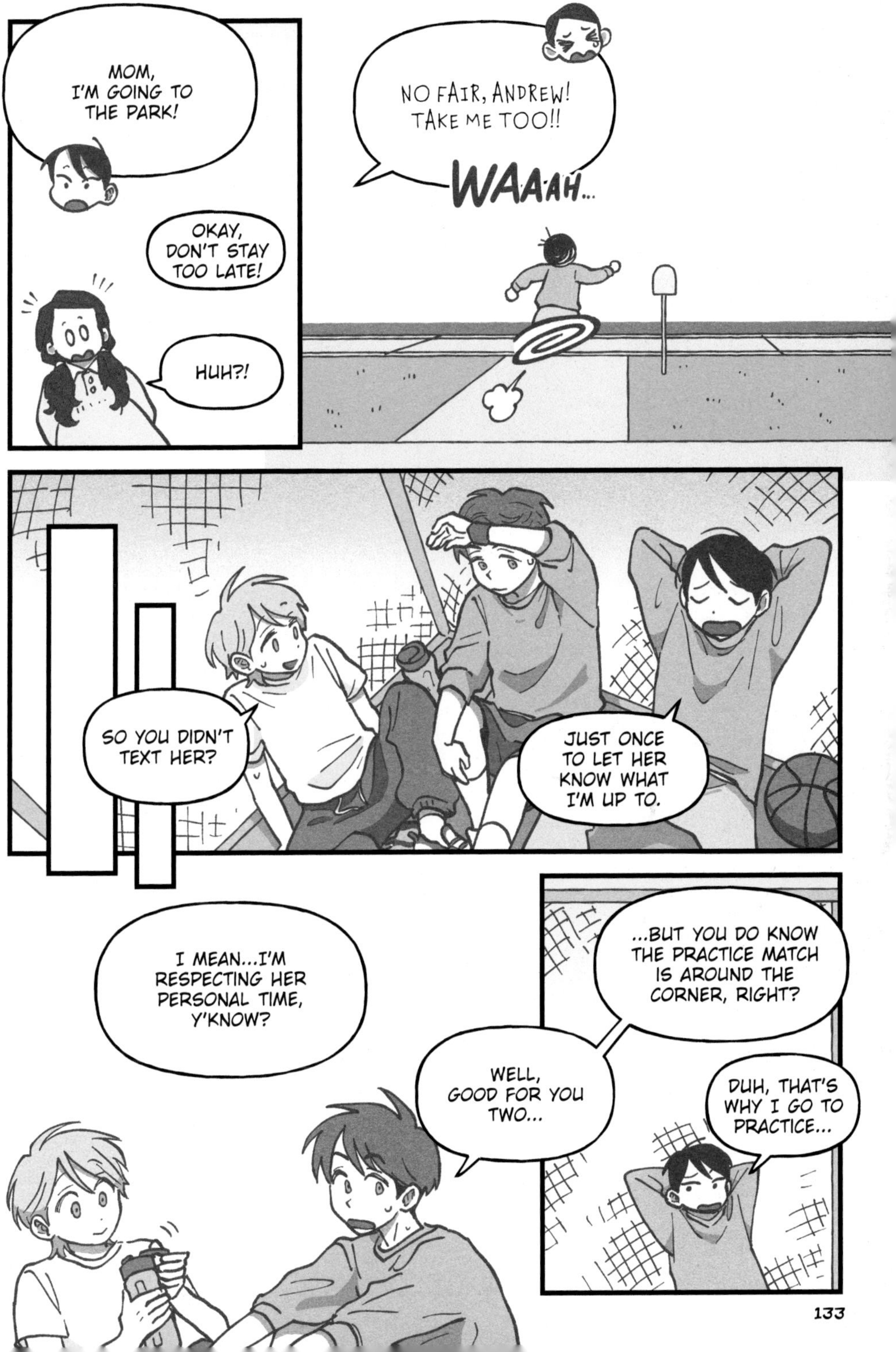
MOM, I'M GOING TO THE PARK!
NO FAIR, ANDREW! TAKE ME TOO!!
WAAAH...
OKAY, DON'T STAY TOO LATE!
HUH?!
SO YOU DIDN'T TEXT HER?
JUST ONCE TO LET HER KNOW WHAT I'M UP TO.
I MEAN...I'M RESPECTING HER PERSONAL TIME, Y'KNOW?
WELL, GOOD FOR YOU TWO...
...BUT YOU DO KNOW THE PRACTICE MATCH IS AROUND THE CORNER, RIGHT?
DUH, THAT'S WHY I GO TO PRACTICE...

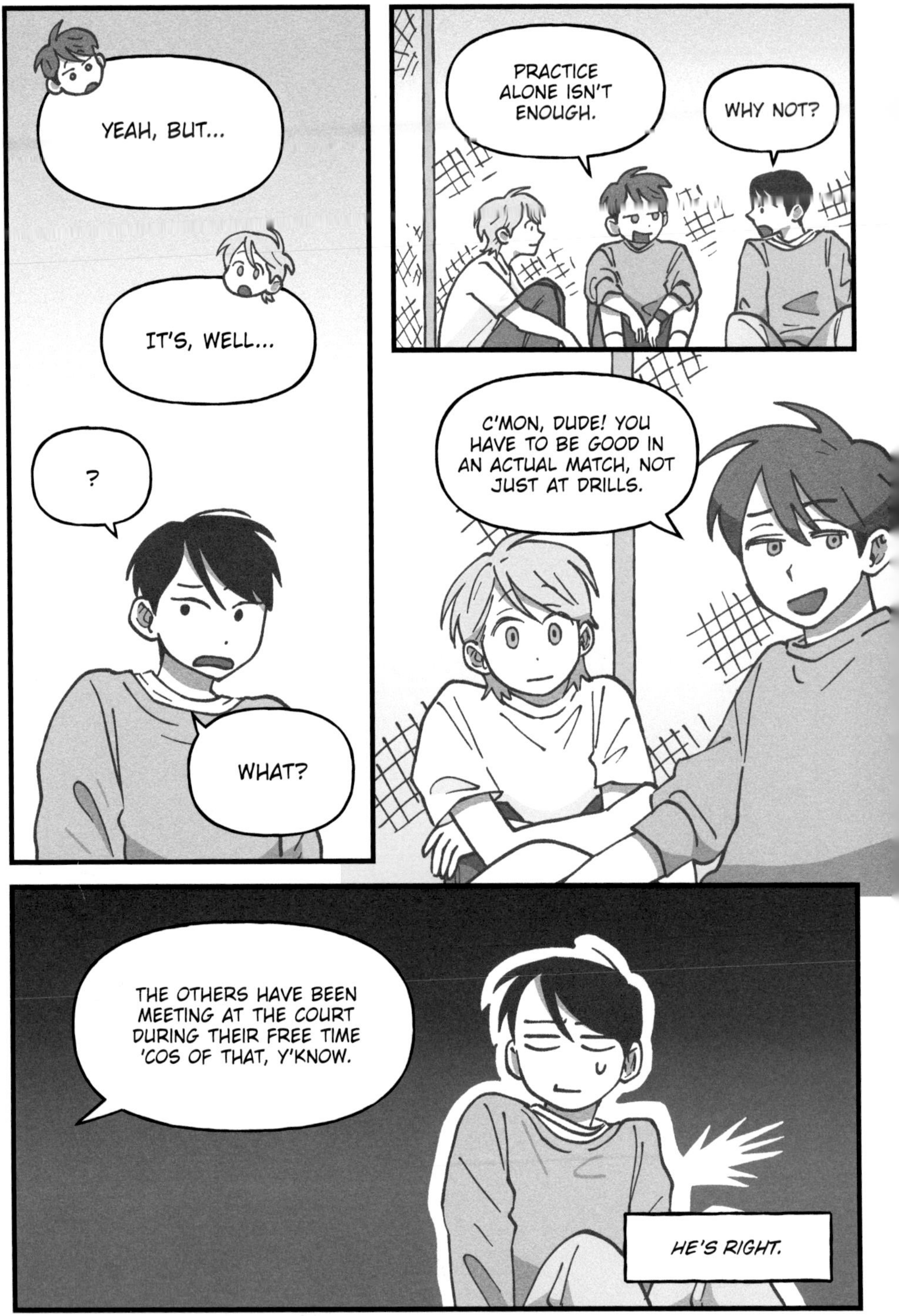
YEAH, BUT...
IT'S, WELL...
?
WHAT?
PRACTICE ALONE ISN'T ENOUGH.
WHY NOT?
C'MON, DUDE! YOU HAVE TO BE GOOD IN AN ACTUAL MATCH, NOT JUST AT DRILLS.
THE OTHERS HAVE BEEN MEETING AT THE COURT DURING THEIR FREE TIME 'COS OF THAT, Y'KNOW.
HE'S RIGHT.

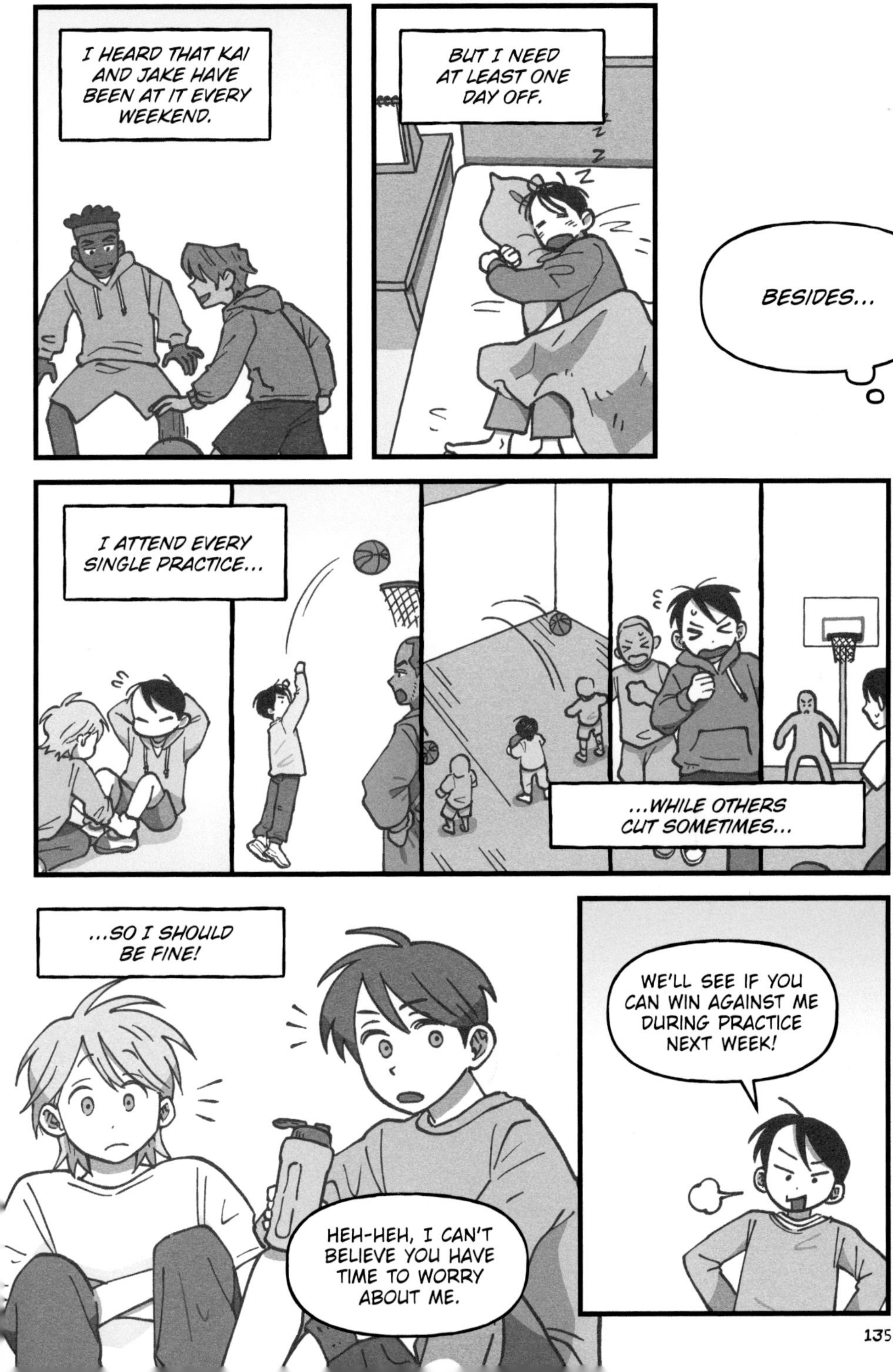
I HEARD THAT KAI AND JAKE HAVE BEEN AT IT EVERY WEEKEND.
BUT I NEED AT LEAST ONE DAY OFF.
BESIDES...
I ATTEND EVERY SINGLE PRACTICE...
...WHILE OTHERS CUT SOMETIMES...
...SO I SHOULD BE FINE!
HEH-HEH, I CAN'T BELIEVE YOU HAVE TIME TO WORRY ABOUT ME.
WE'LL SEE IF YOU CAN WIN AGAINST ME DURING PRACTICE NEXT WEEK!

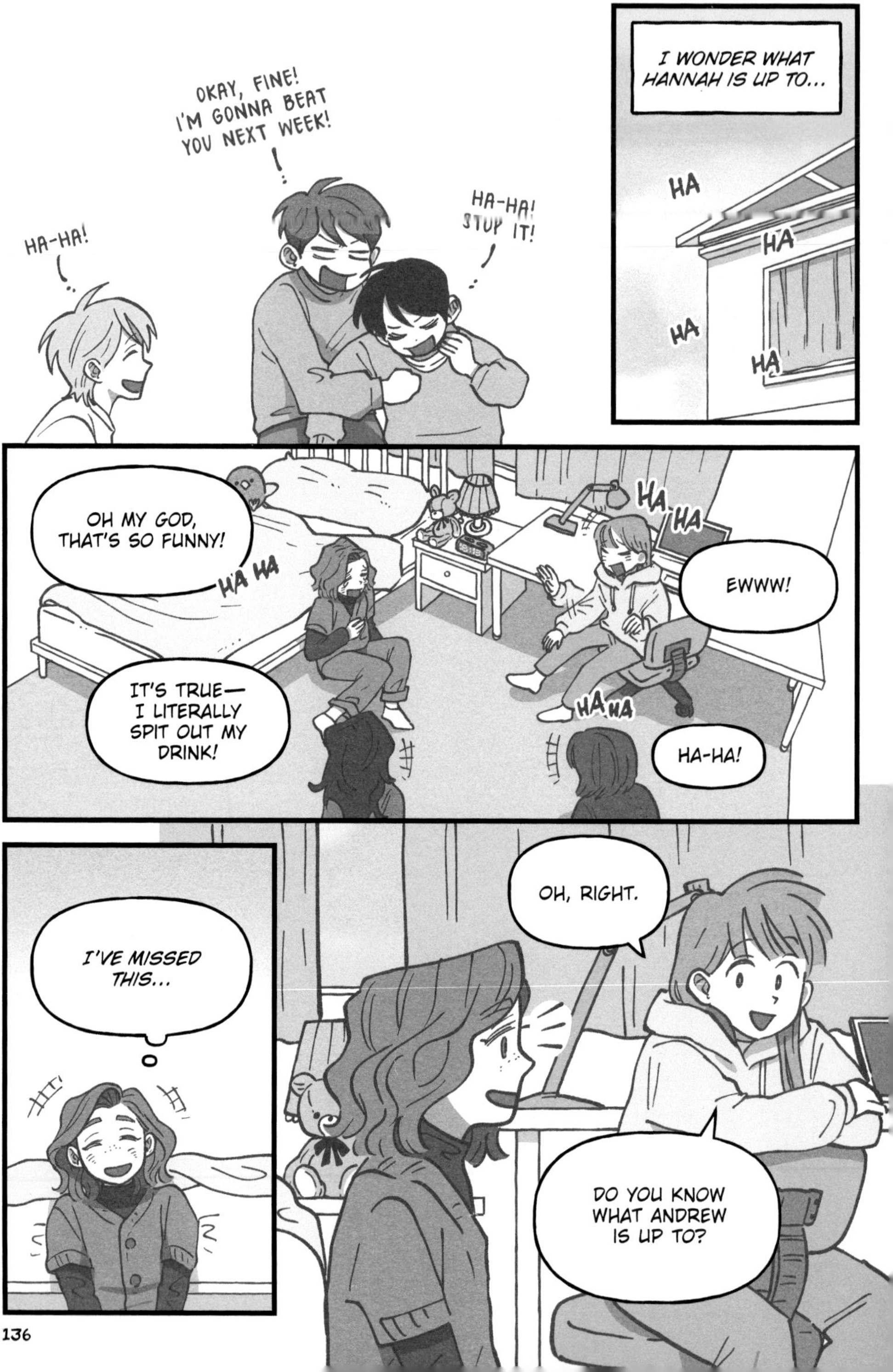
OKAY, FINE! I'M GONNA BEAT YOU NEXT WEEK!
HA-HA!
HA-HA! STOP IT!
I WONDER WHAT HANNAH IS UP TO...
HA
HA
HA
HA
OH MY GOD, THAT'S SO FUNNY!
HA HA
HA HA
EWWW!
IT'S TRUE— I LITERALLY SPIT OUT MY DRINK!
HA HA
HA-HA!
OH, RIGHT.
I'VE MISSED THIS...
DO YOU KNOW WHAT ANDREW IS UP TO?

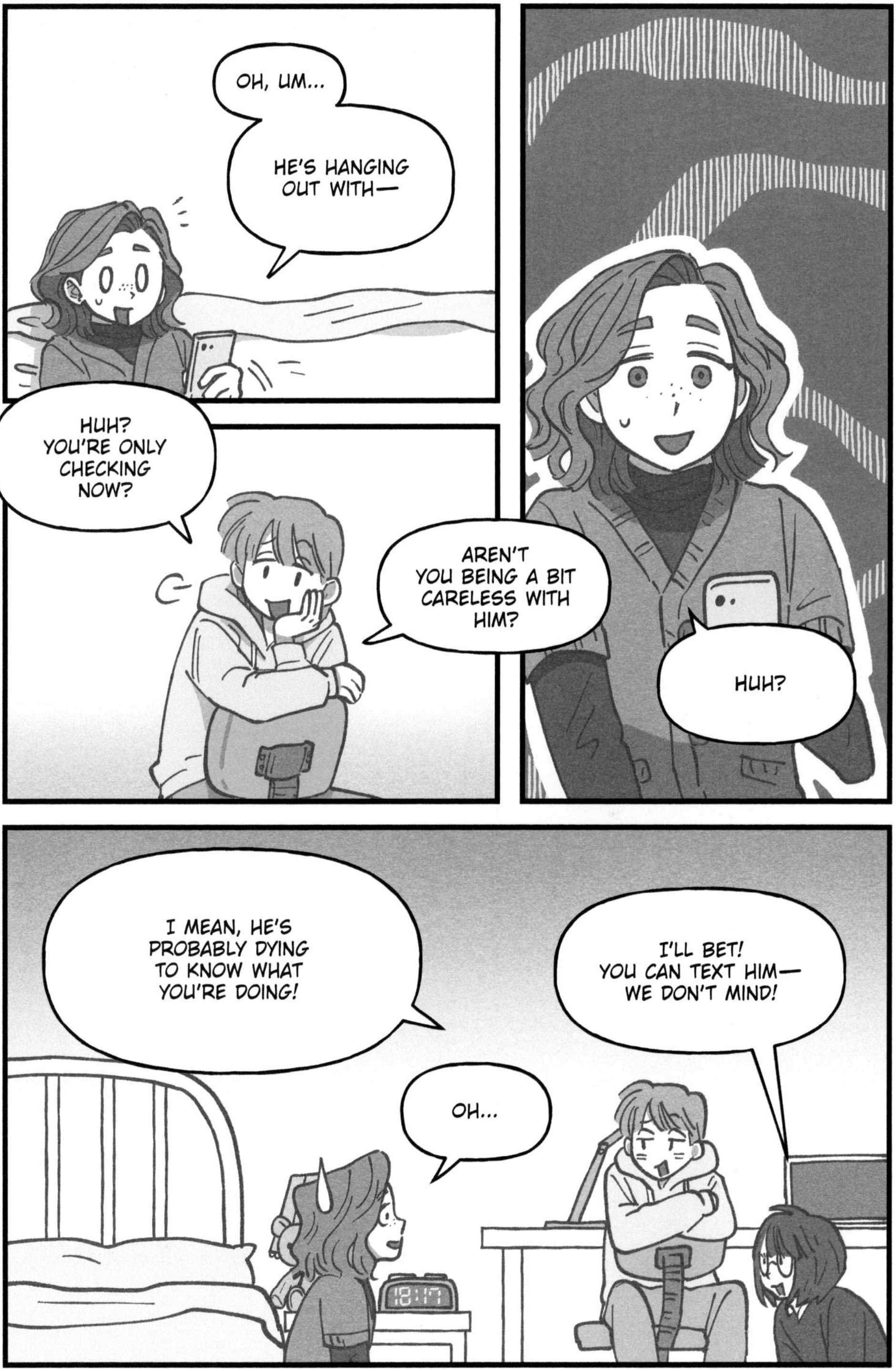
OH, UM...
HE'S HANGING OUT WITH—
HUH? YOU'RE ONLY CHECKING NOW?
AREN'T YOU BEING A BIT CARELESS WITH HIM?
HUH?
I MEAN, HE'S PROBABLY DYING TO KNOW WHAT YOU'RE DOING!
I'LL BET! YOU CAN TEXT HIM— WE DON'T MIND!
OH...

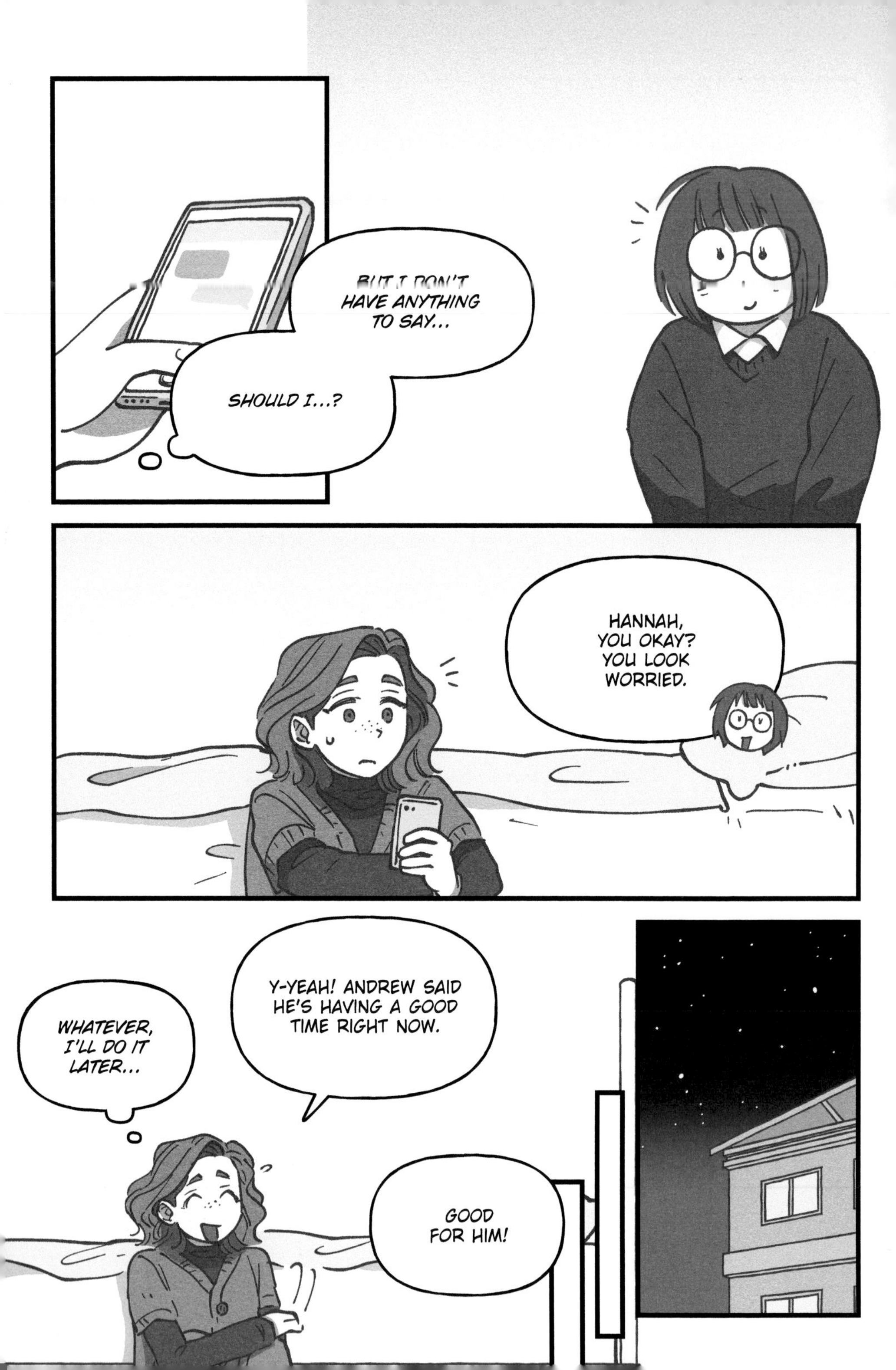
BUT I DON'T HAVE ANYTHING TO SAY...
SHOULD I...?
HANNAH, YOU OKAY? YOU LOOK WORRIED.
Y-YEAH! ANDREW SAID HE'S HAVING A GOOD TIME RIGHT NOW.
WHATEVER, I'LL DO IT LATER...
GOOD FOR HIM!

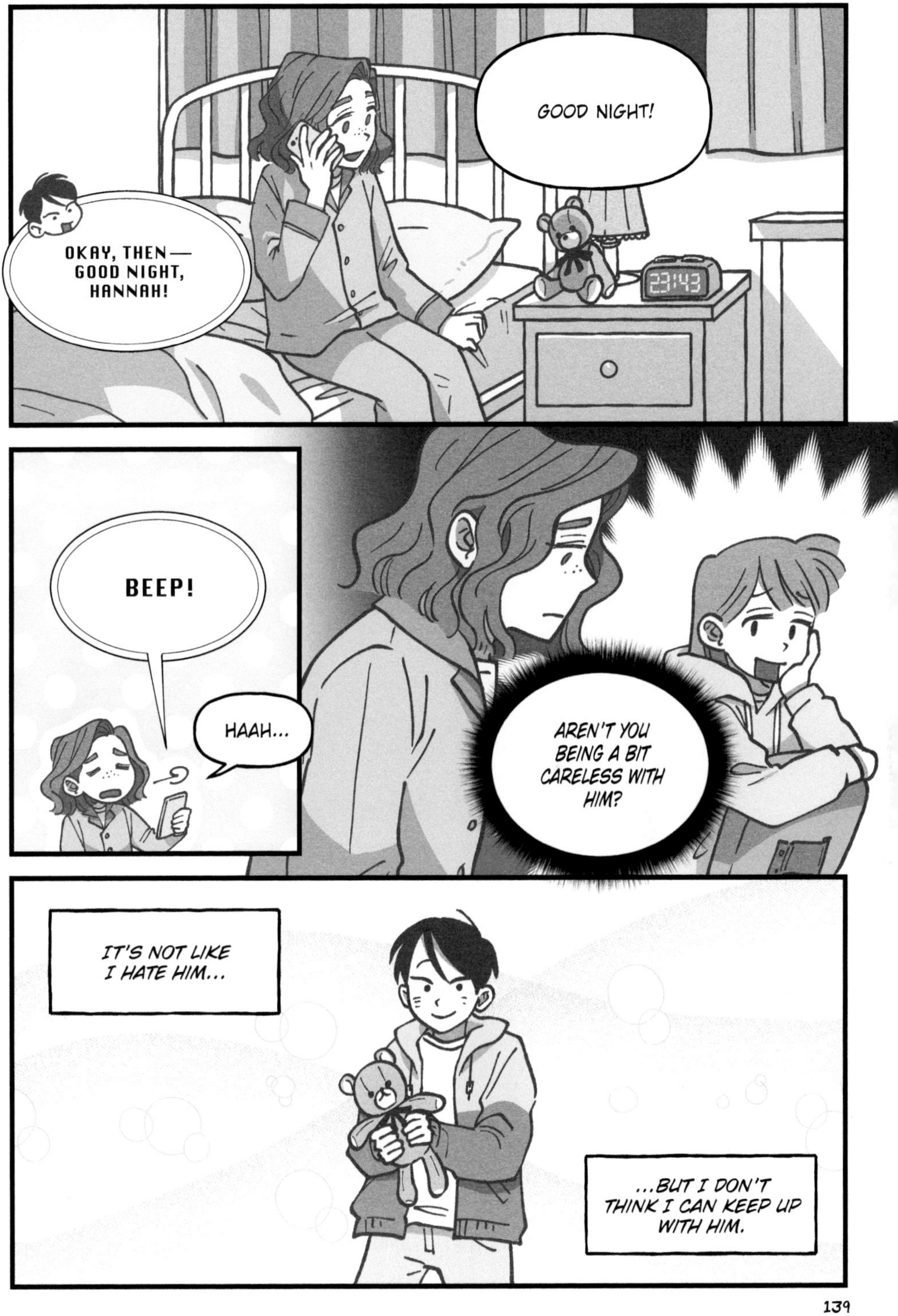
GOOD NIGHT!
OKAY, THEN— GOOD NIGHT, HANNAH!
BEEP!
HAAH...
AREN'T YOU BEING A BIT CARELESS WITH HIM?
IT'S NOT LIKE I HATE HIM...
...BUT I DON'T THINK I CAN KEEP UP WITH HIM.

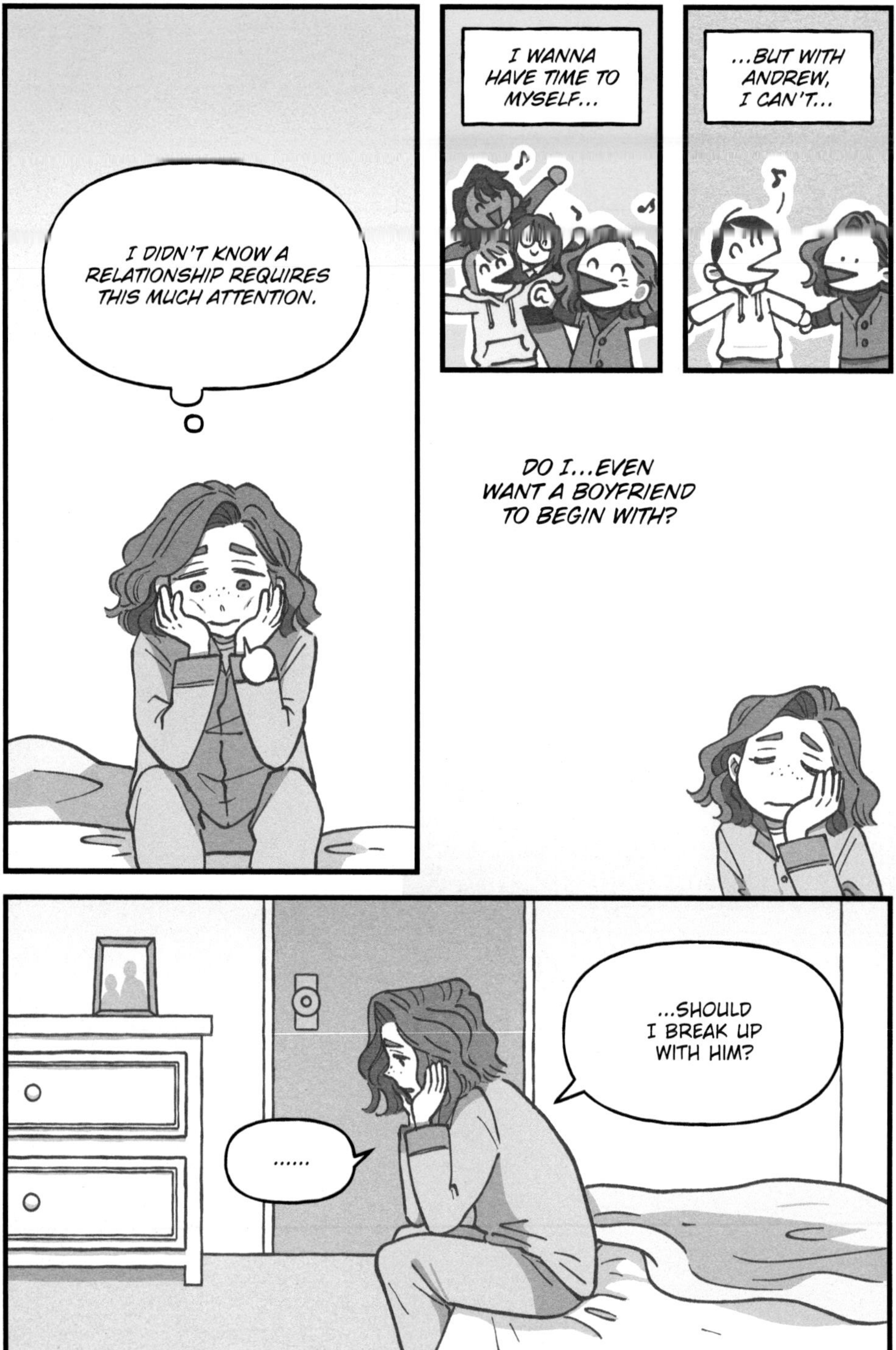

I DIDN'T KNOW A RELATIONSHIP REQUIRES THIS MUCH ATTENTION.
I WANNA HAVE TIME TO MYSELF...
...BUT WITH ANDREW, I CAN'T...
DO I...EVEN WANT A BOYFRIEND TO BEGIN WITH?
...SHOULD I BREAK UP WITH HIM?
......

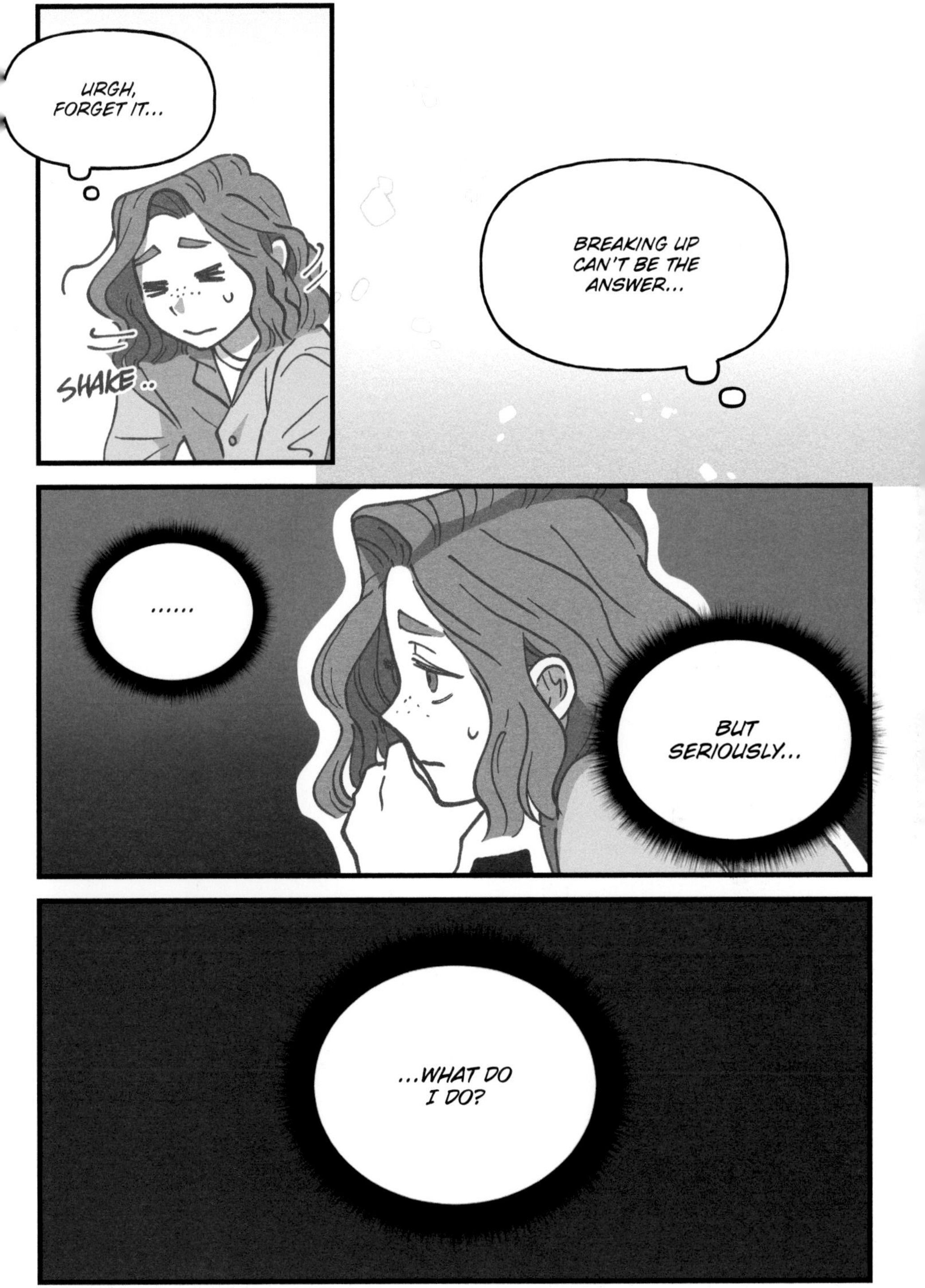
URGH, FORGET IT...
SHAKE
BREAKING UP CAN'T BE THE ANSWER...
......
BUT SERIOUSLY...
...WHAT DO I DO?

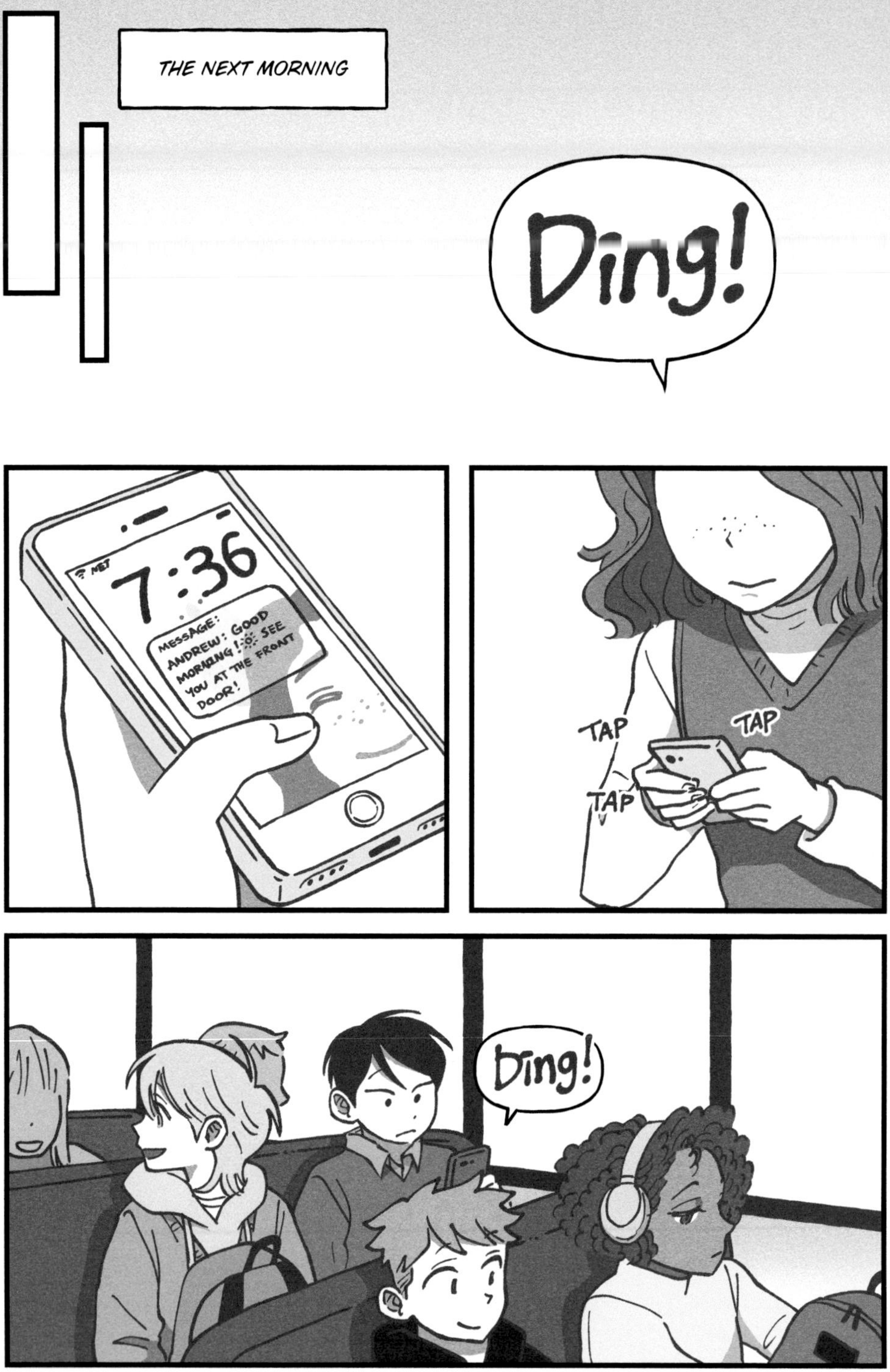
THE NEXT MORNING
Ding!
NET
7:36
MESSAGE: ANDREW: GOOD MORNING! SEE YOU AT THE FRONT DOOR!
TAP
TAP
TAP
Ding!

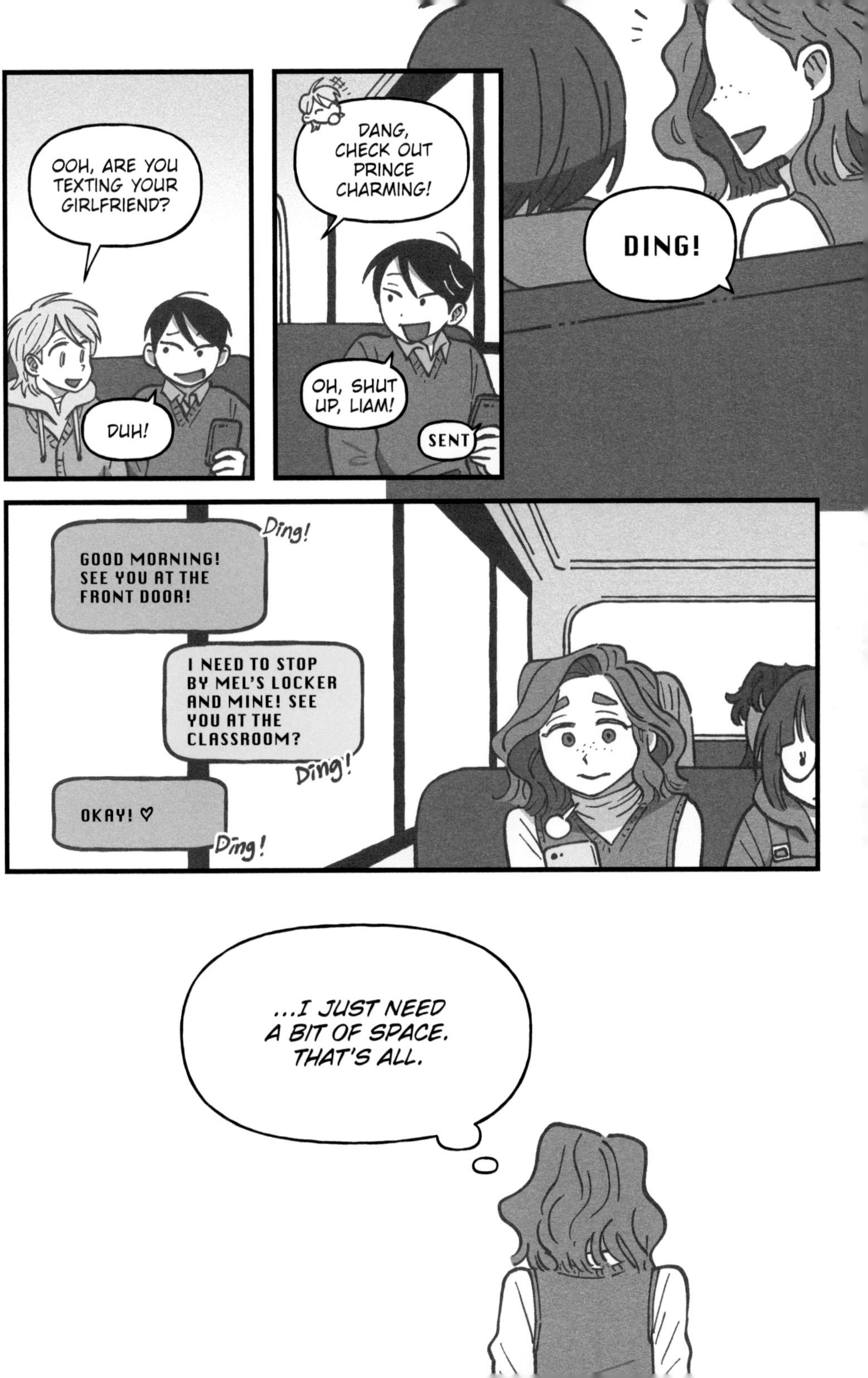

OOH, ARE YOU TEXTING YOUR GIRLFRIEND?
DUH!
DANG, CHECK OUT PRINCE CHARMING!
OH, SHUT UP, LIAM!
SENT
DING!
Ding!
GOOD MORNING! SEE YOU AT THE FRONT DOOR!
I NEED TO STOP BY MEL'S LOCKER AND MINE! SEE YOU AT THE CLASSROOM?
Ding!
OKAY! ♡
Ding!
...I JUST NEED A BIT OF SPACE. THAT'S ALL.

Chapter 8

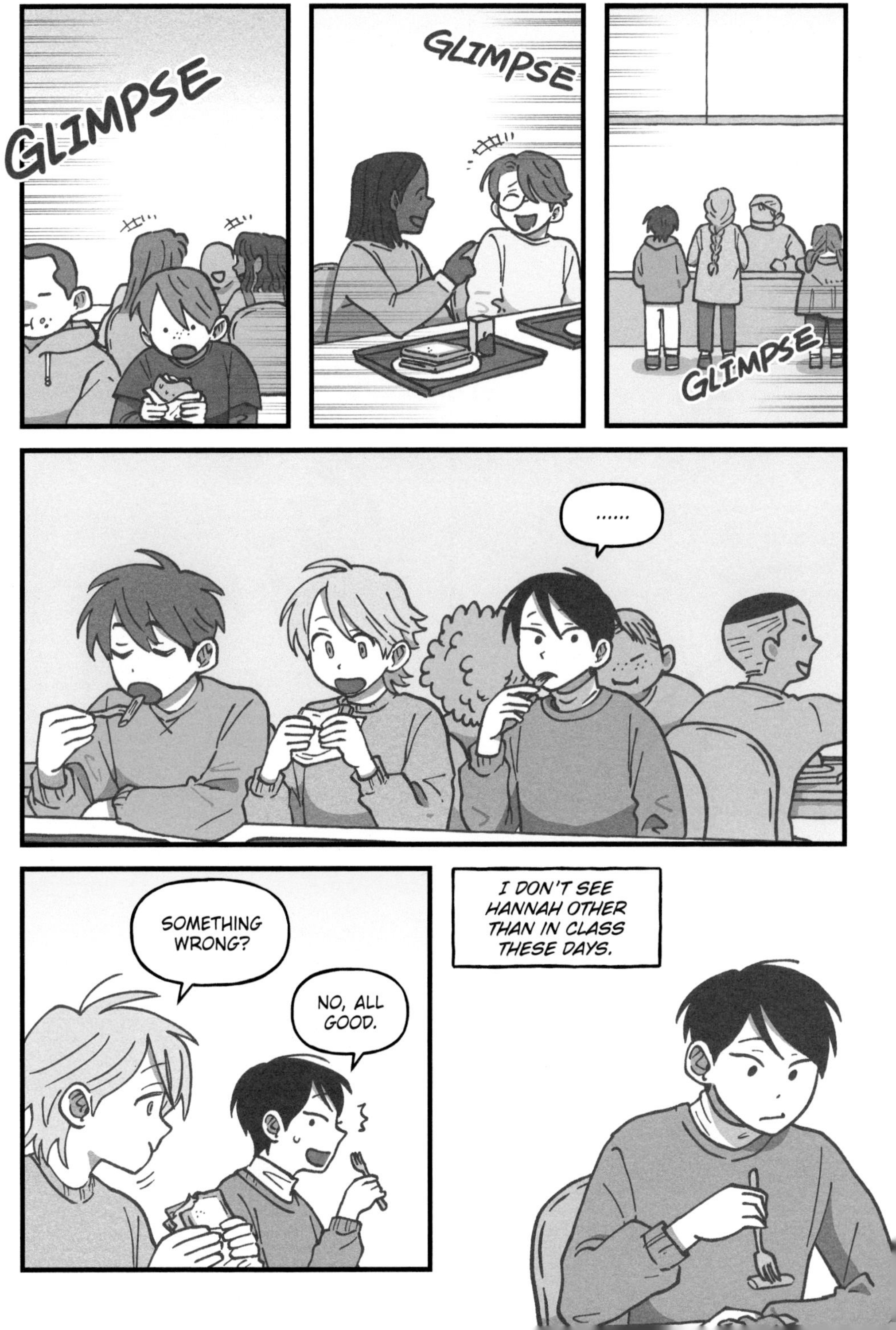
GLIMPSE
GLIMPSE
GLIMPSE
......
SOMETHING WRONG?
NO, ALL GOOD.
I DON'T SEE HANNAH OTHER THAN IN CLASS THESE DAYS.

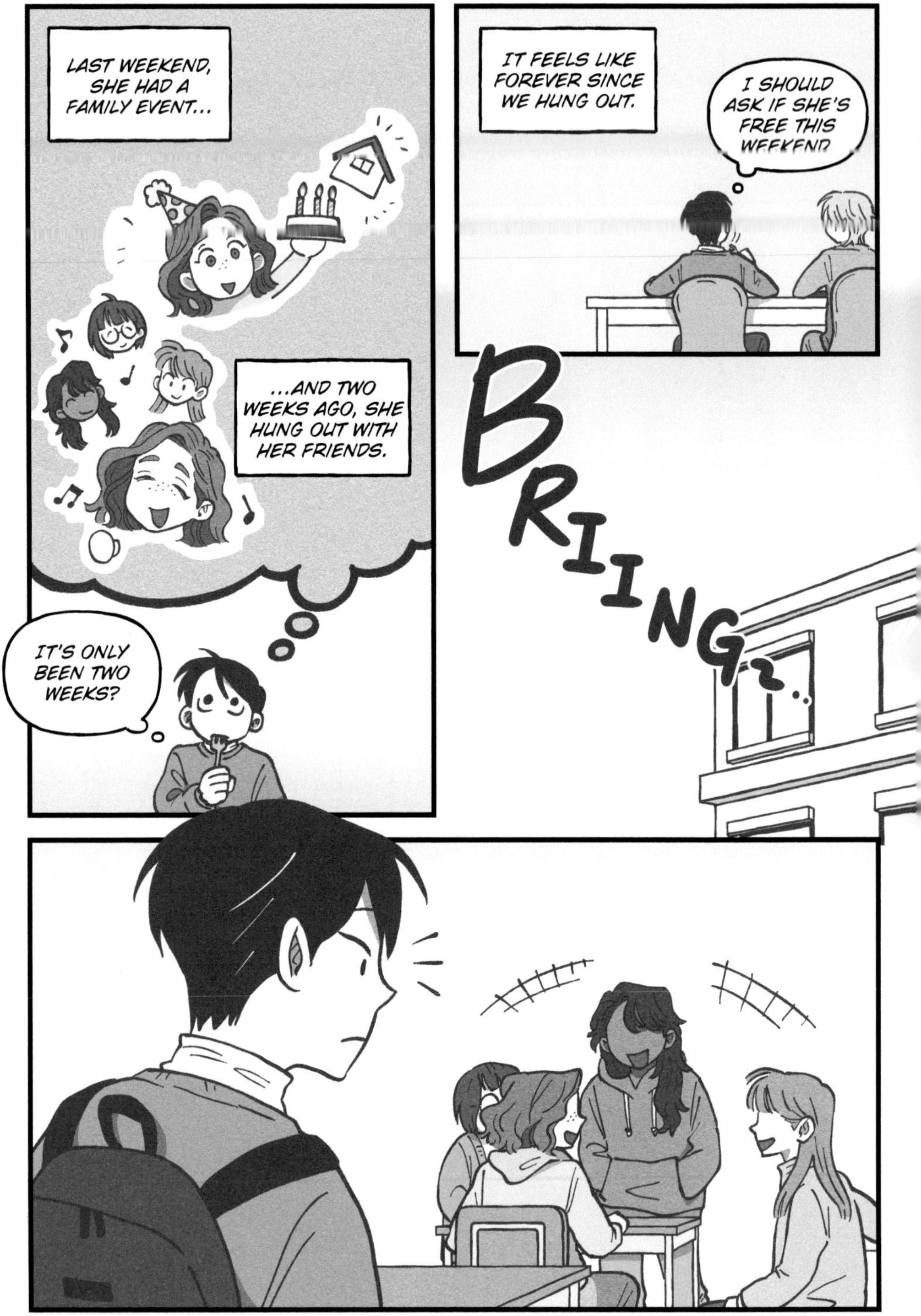
LAST WEEKEND, SHE HAD A FAMILY EVENT...
...AND TWO WEEKS AGO, SHE HUNG OUT WITH HER FRIENDS.
IT'S ONLY BEEN TWO WEEKS?
IT FEELS LIKE FOREVER SINCE WE HUNG OUT.
I SHOULD ASK IF SHE'S FREE THIS WEEKEND
BRIING...

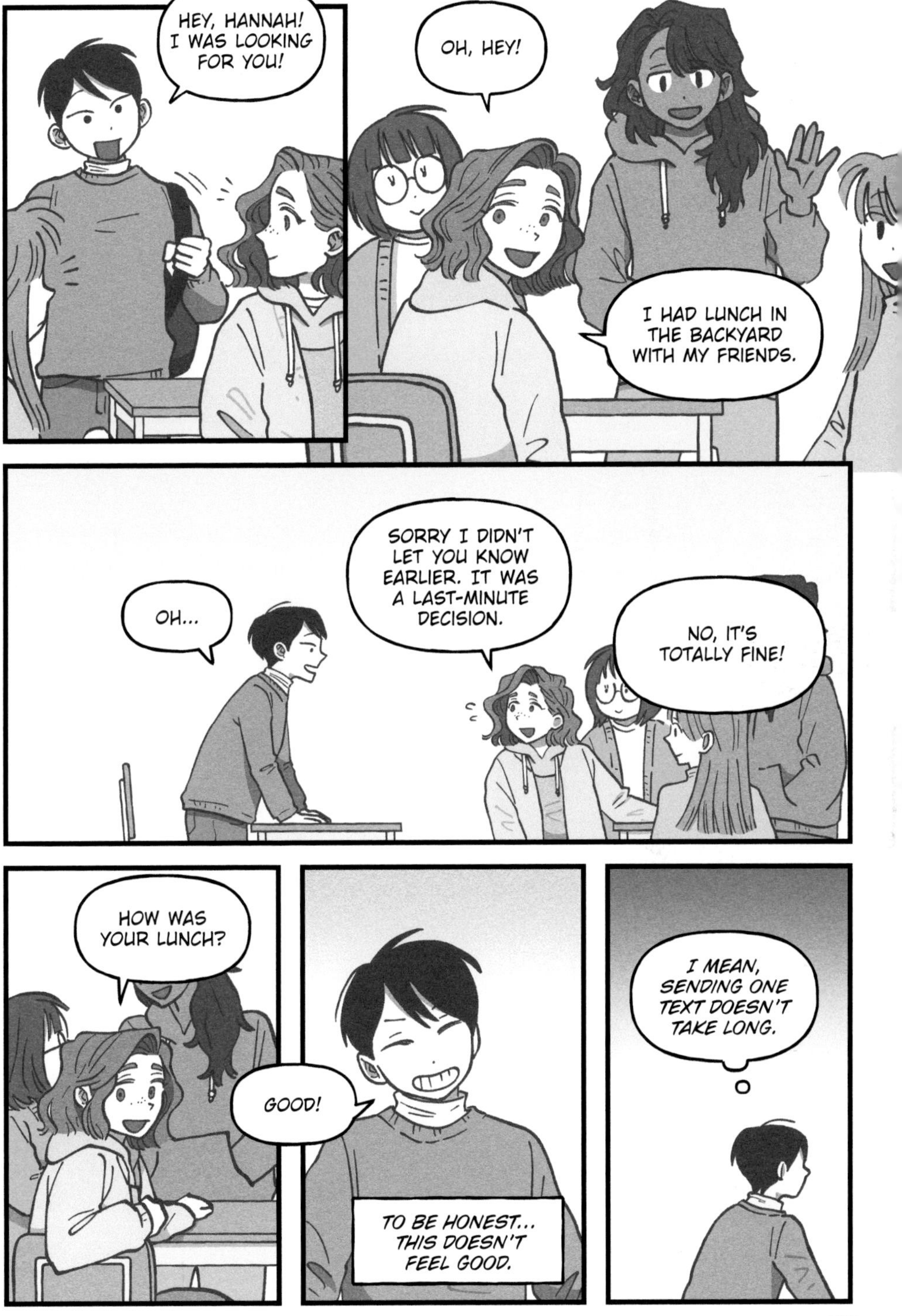
HEY, HANNAH! I WAS LOOKING FOR YOU!
OH, HEY!
I HAD LUNCH IN THE BACKYARD WITH MY FRIENDS.
OH...
SORRY I DIDN'T LET YOU KNOW EARLIER. IT WAS A LAST-MINUTE DECISION.
NO, IT'S TOTALLY FINE!
HOW WAS YOUR LUNCH?
GOOD!
TO BE HONEST... THIS DOESN'T FEEL GOOD.
I MEAN, SENDING ONE TEXT DOESN'T TAKE LONG.

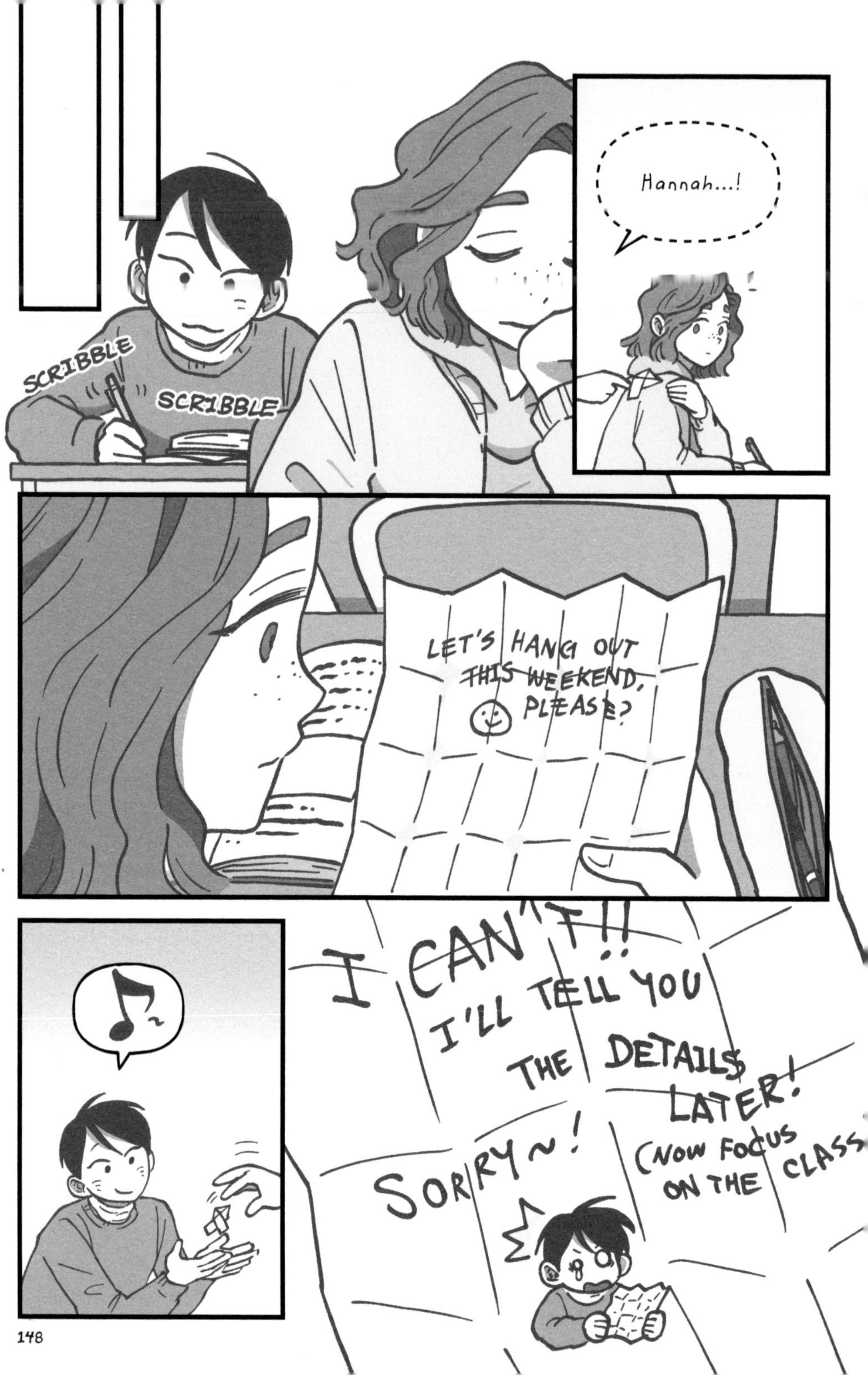
SCRIBBLE
SCRIBBLE
Hannah...!
LET'S HANG OUT THIS WEEKEND, PLEASE?
I CAN'T!!
I'LL TELL YOU THE DETAILS LATER!
SORRY~!
(NOW FOCUS ON THE CLASS

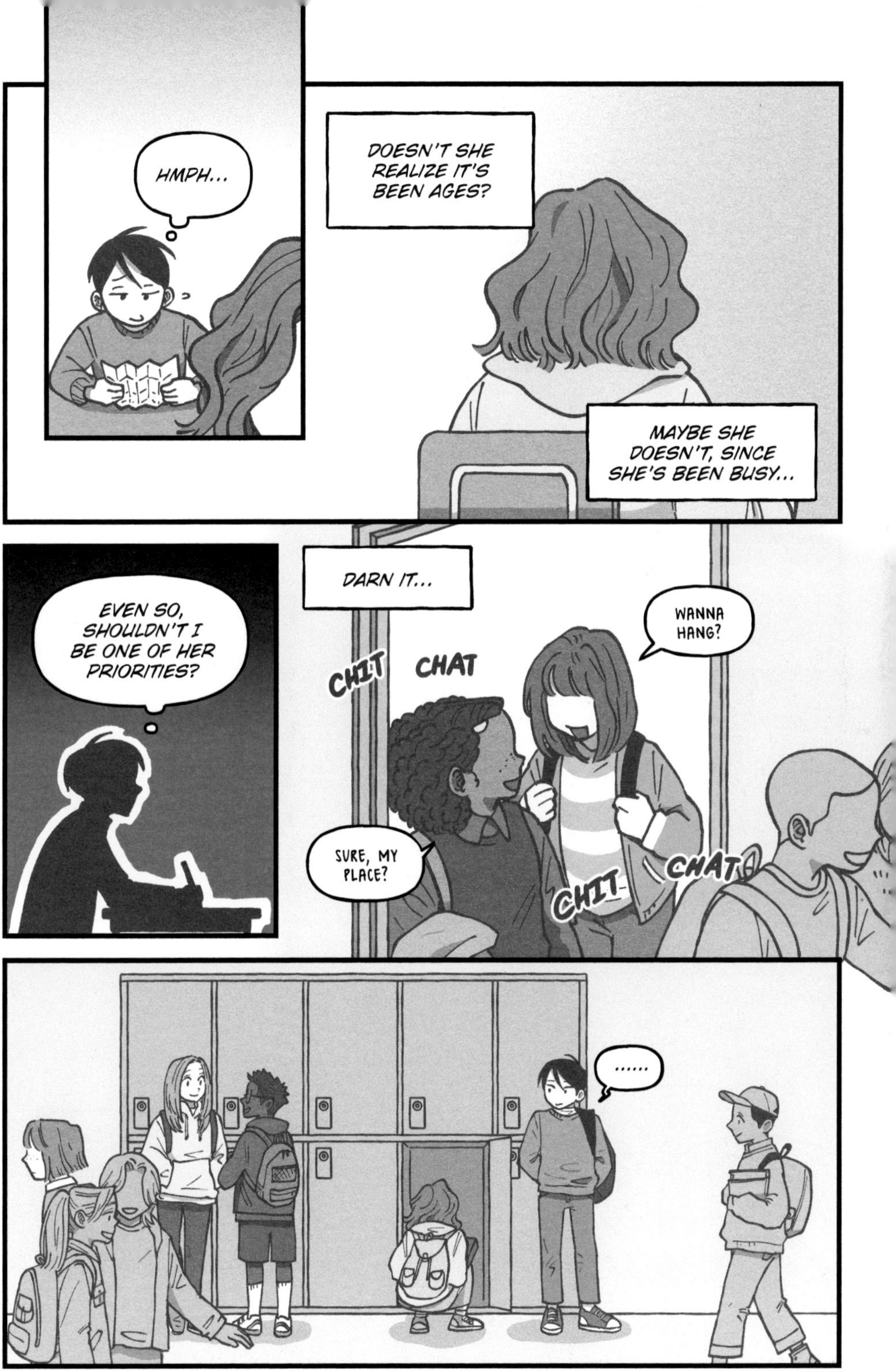
HMPH...
DOESN'T SHE REALIZE IT'S BEEN AGES?
MAYBE SHE DOESN'T, SINCE SHE'S BEEN BUSY...
EVEN SO, SHOULDN'T I BE ONE OF HER PRIORITIES?
DARN IT...
WANNA HANG?
CHIT CHAT
SURE, MY PLACE?
CHIT CHAT
......

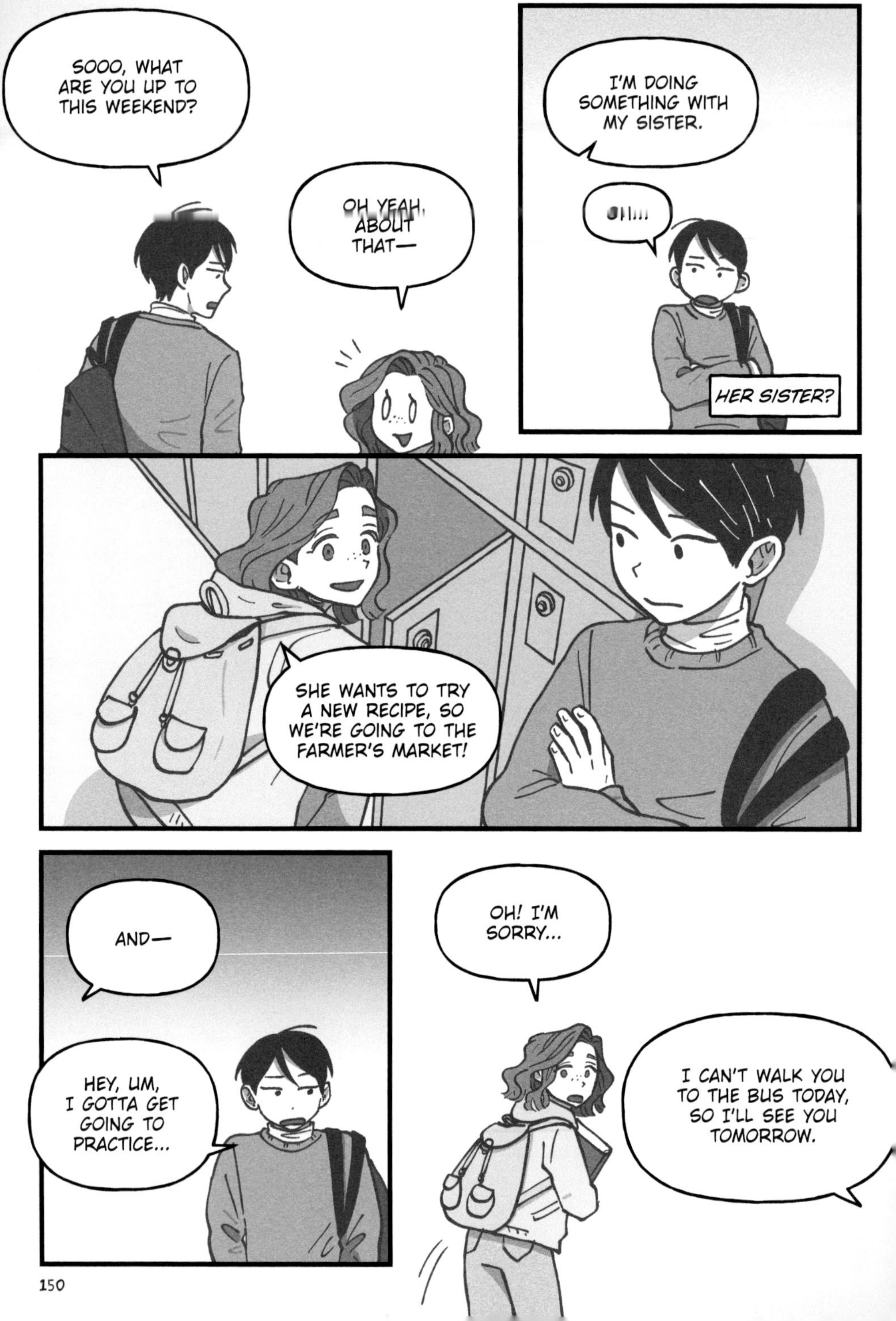
SOOO, WHAT ARE YOU UP TO THIS WEEKEND?
OH YEAH, ABOUT THAT—
I'M DOING SOMETHING WITH MY SISTER.
HER SISTER?
SHE WANTS TO TRY A NEW RECIPE, SO WE'RE GOING TO THE FARMER'S MARKET!
AND—
HEY, UM, I GOTTA GET GOING TO PRACTICE...
OH! I'M SORRY...
I CAN'T WALK YOU TO THE BUS TODAY, SO I'LL SEE YOU TOMORROW.

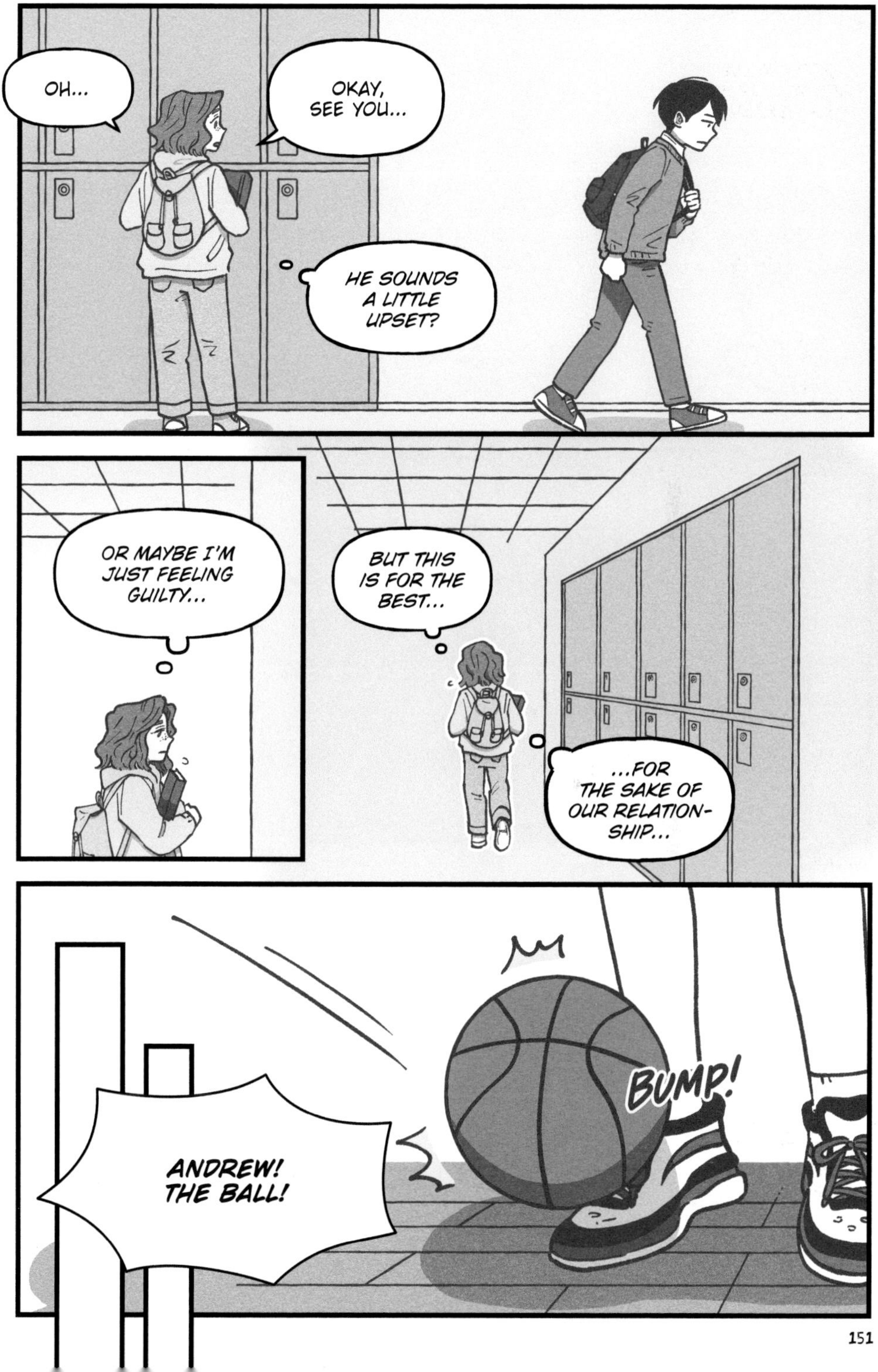
OH...
OKAY, SEE YOU...
HE SOUNDS A LITTLE UPSET?
OR MAYBE I'M JUST FEELING GUILTY...
BUT THIS IS FOR THE BEST...
...FOR THE SAKE OF OUR RELATION-SHIP...
BUMP!
ANDREW! THE BALL!

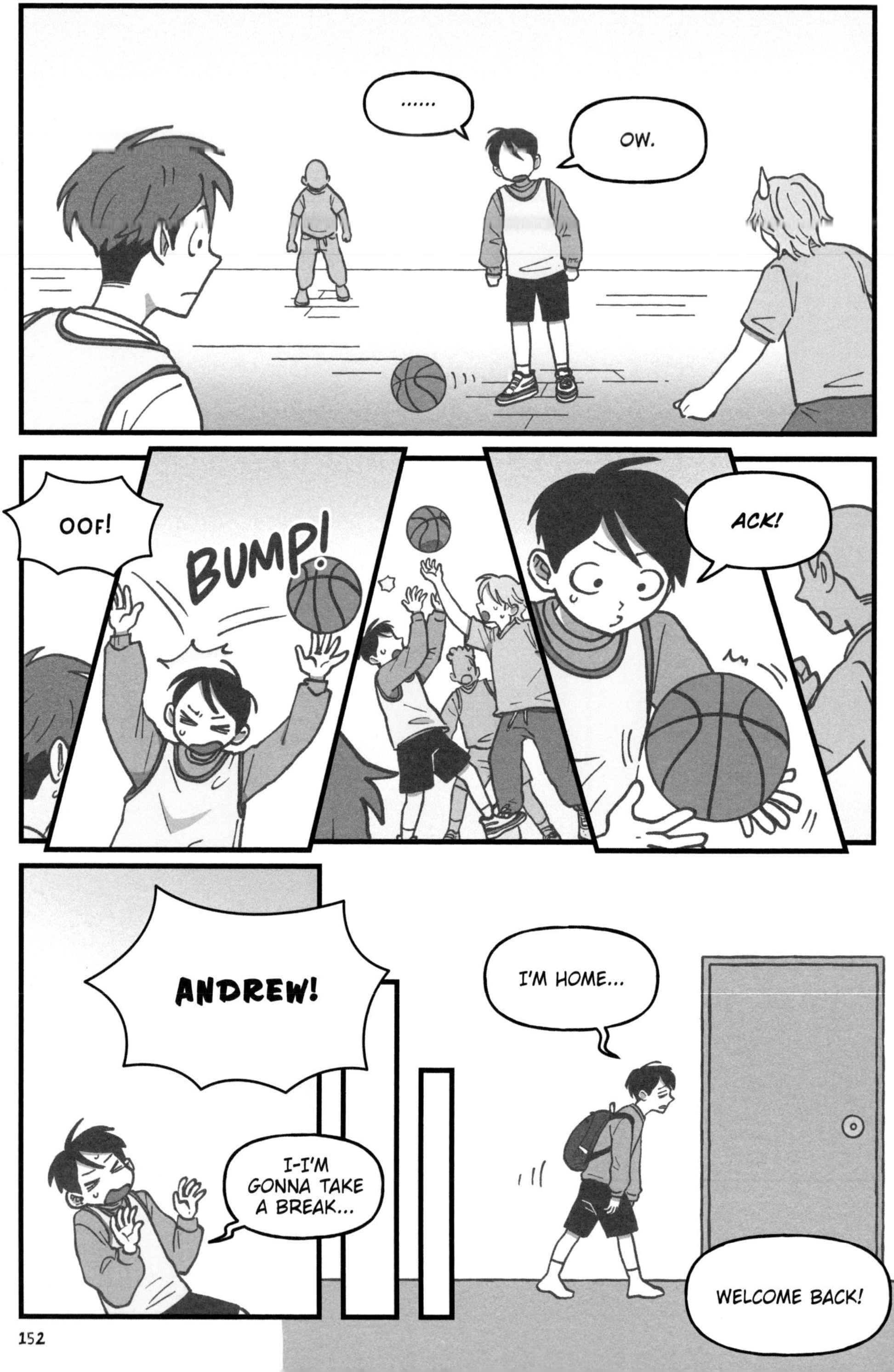
......
OW.
OOF!
BUMP!
ACK!
ANDREW!
I-I'M GONNA TAKE A BREAK...
I'M HOME...
WELCOME BACK!

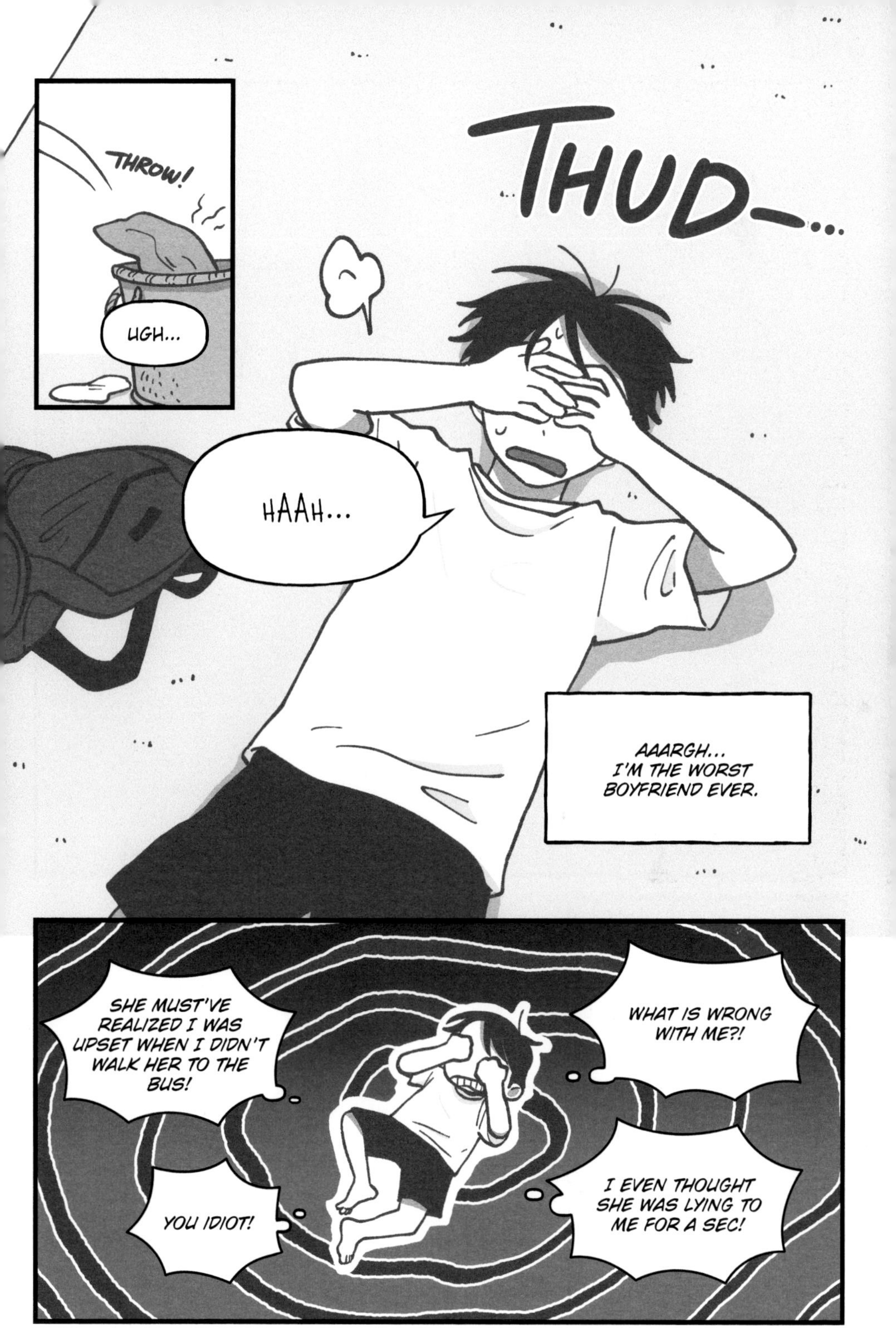
THROW!
UGH...
THUD—...
HAAH...
AAARGH... I'M THE WORST BOYFRIEND EVER.
SHE MUST'VE REALIZED I WAS UPSET WHEN I DIDN'T WALK HER TO THE BUS!
WHAT IS WRONG WITH ME?!
YOU IDIOT!
I EVEN THOUGHT SHE WAS LYING TO ME FOR A SEC!

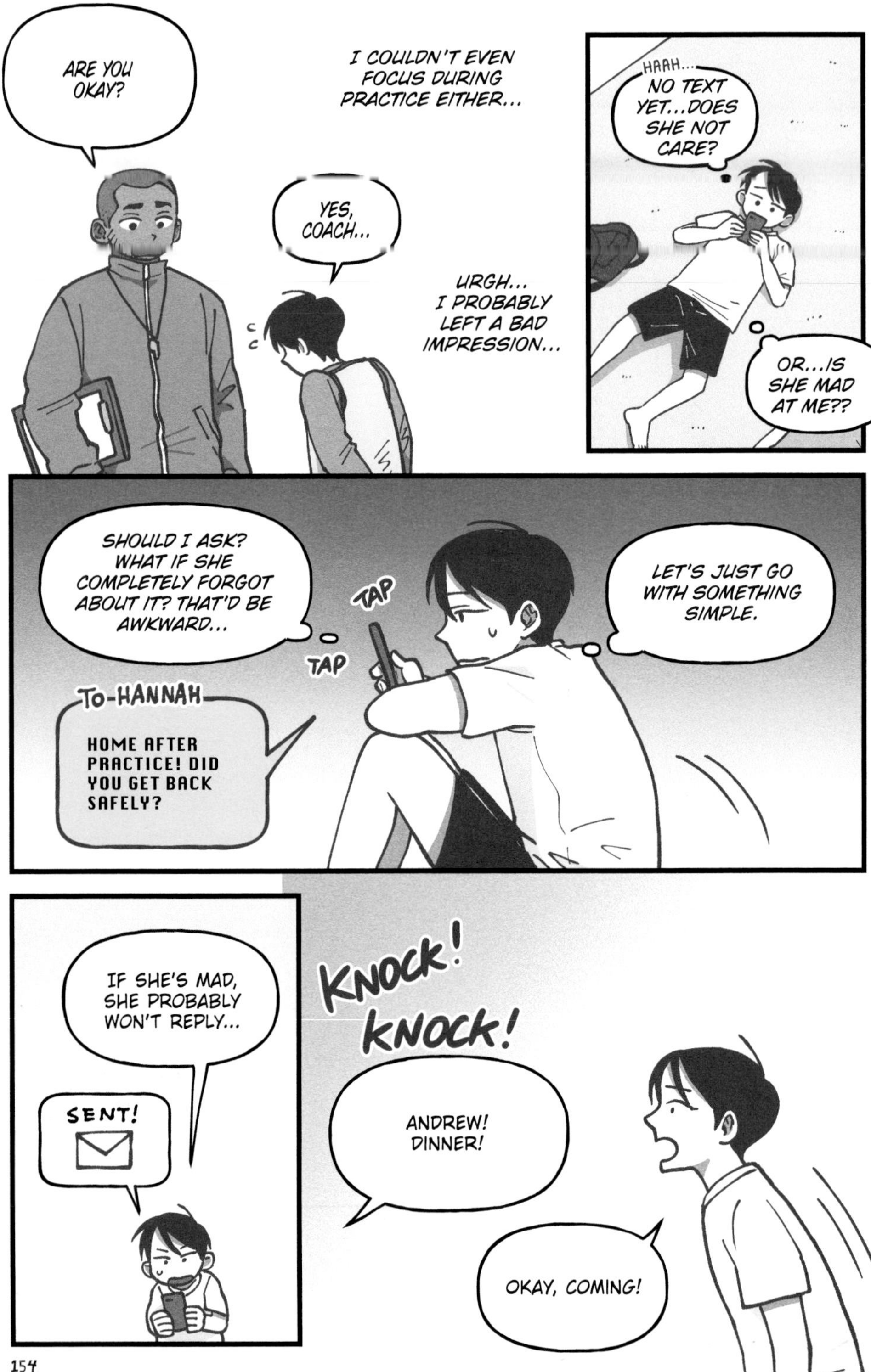
ARE YOU OKAY?
I COULDN'T EVEN FOCUS DURING PRACTICE EITHER...
YES, COACH...
URGH... I PROBABLY LEFT A BAD IMPRESSION...
HAAH...
NO TEXT YET...DOES SHE NOT CARE?
OR...IS SHE MAD AT ME??
SHOULD I ASK? WHAT IF SHE COMPLETELY FORGOT ABOUT IT? THAT'D BE AWKWARD...
TAP
TAP
LET'S JUST GO WITH SOMETHING SIMPLE.
TO-HANNAH
HOME AFTER PRACTICE! DID YOU GET BACK SAFELY?
IF SHE'S MAD, SHE PROBABLY WON'T REPLY...
SENT!
KNOCK! KNOCK!
ANDREW! DINNER!
OKAY, COMING!

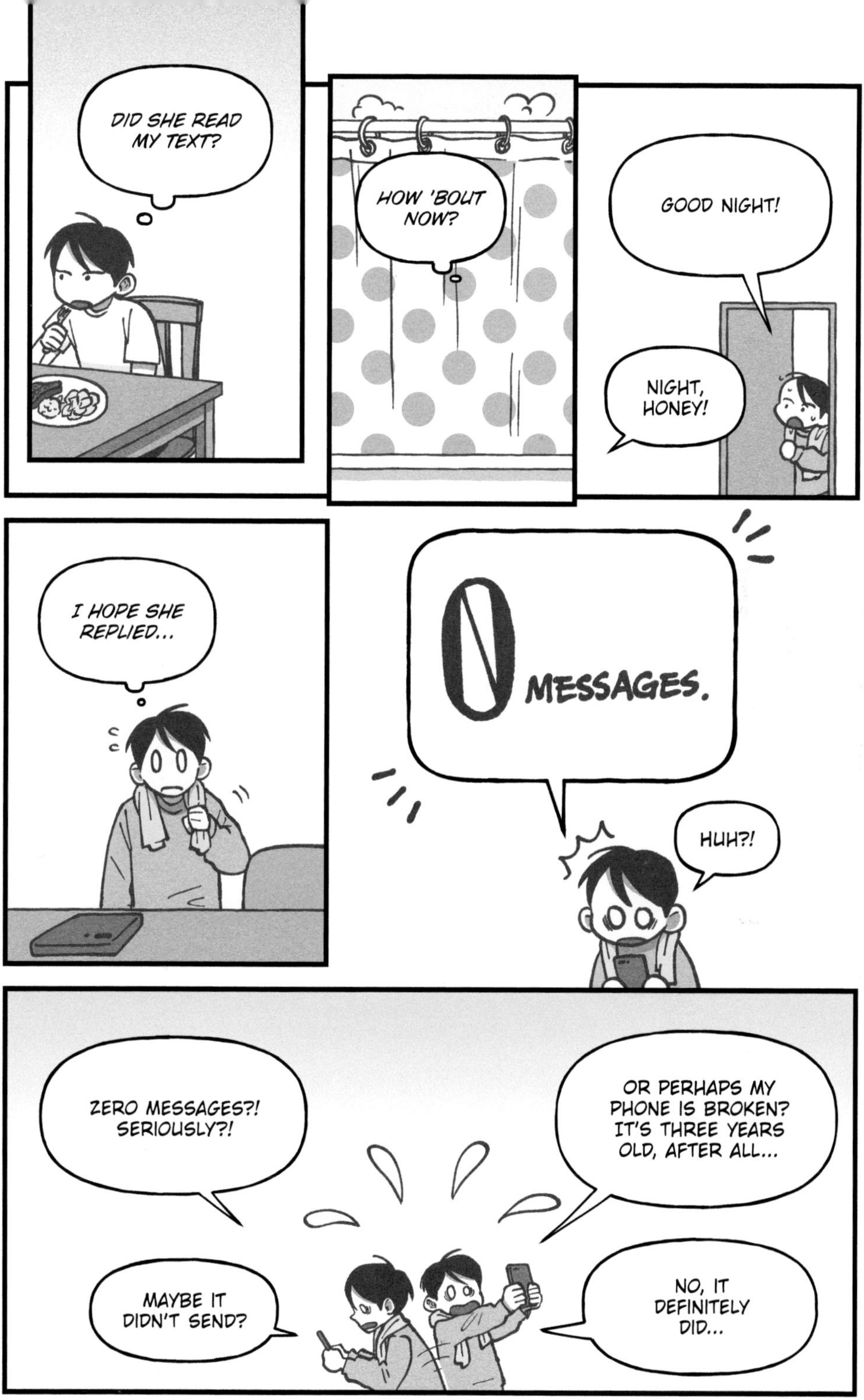
DID SHE READ MY TEXT?
HOW 'BOUT NOW?
GOOD NIGHT!
NIGHT, HONEY!
I HOPE SHE REPLIED...
0 MESSAGES.
HUH?!
ZERO MESSAGES?! SERIOUSLY?!
OR PERHAPS MY PHONE IS BROKEN? IT'S THREE YEARS OLD, AFTER ALL...
MAYBE IT DIDN'T SEND?
NO, IT DEFINITELY DID...

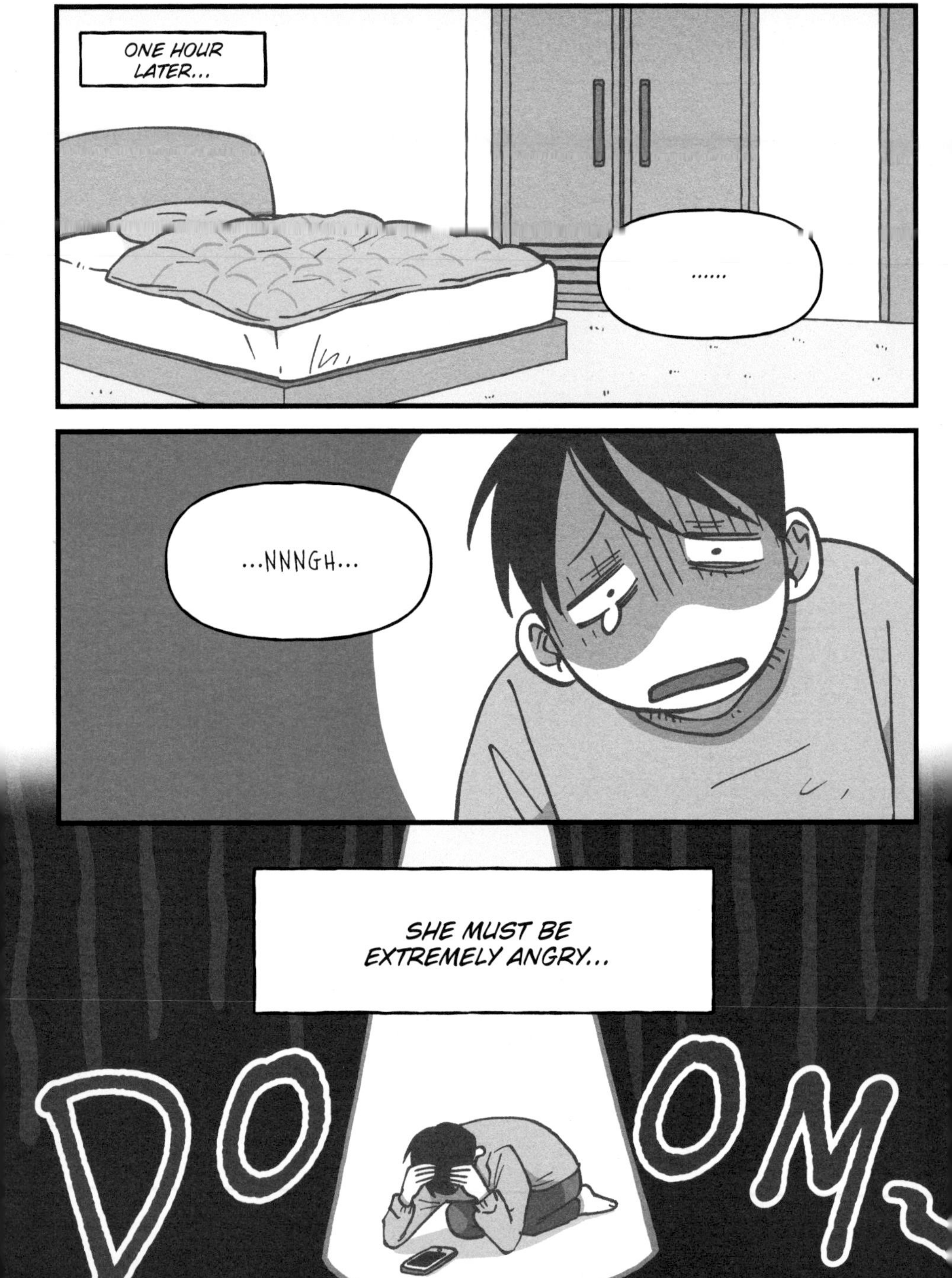
ONE HOUR LATER...
......
...NNNGH...
SHE MUST BE EXTREMELY ANGRY...
DOOM~

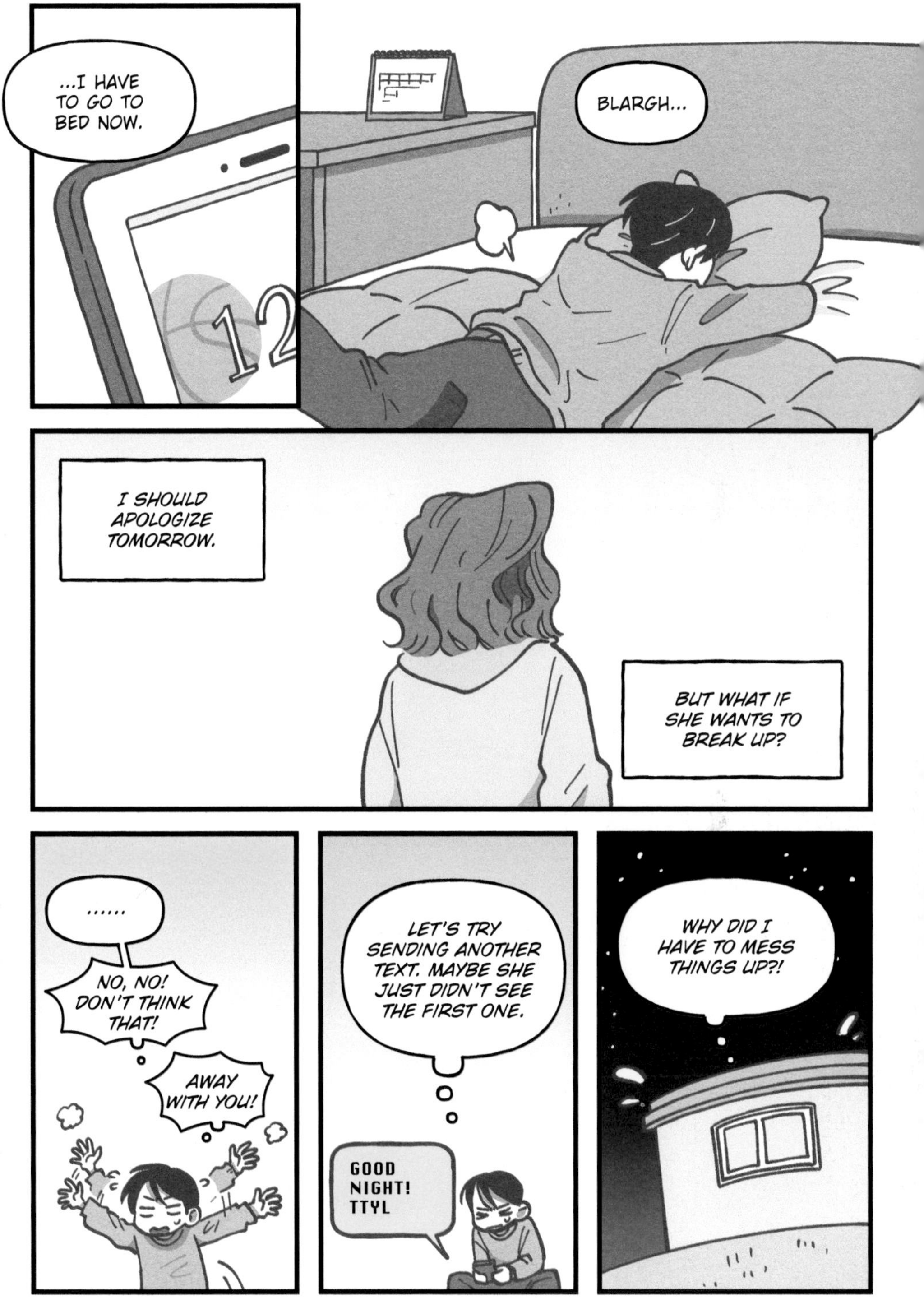
...I HAVE TO GO TO BED NOW.
12
BLARGH...
I SHOULD APOLOGIZE TOMORROW.
BUT WHAT IF SHE WANTS TO BREAK UP?
......
NO, NO! DON'T THINK THAT!
AWAY WITH YOU!
LET'S TRY SENDING ANOTHER TEXT. MAYBE SHE JUST DIDN'T SEE THE FIRST ONE.
GOOD NIGHT! TTYL
WHY DID I HAVE TO MESS THINGS UP?!

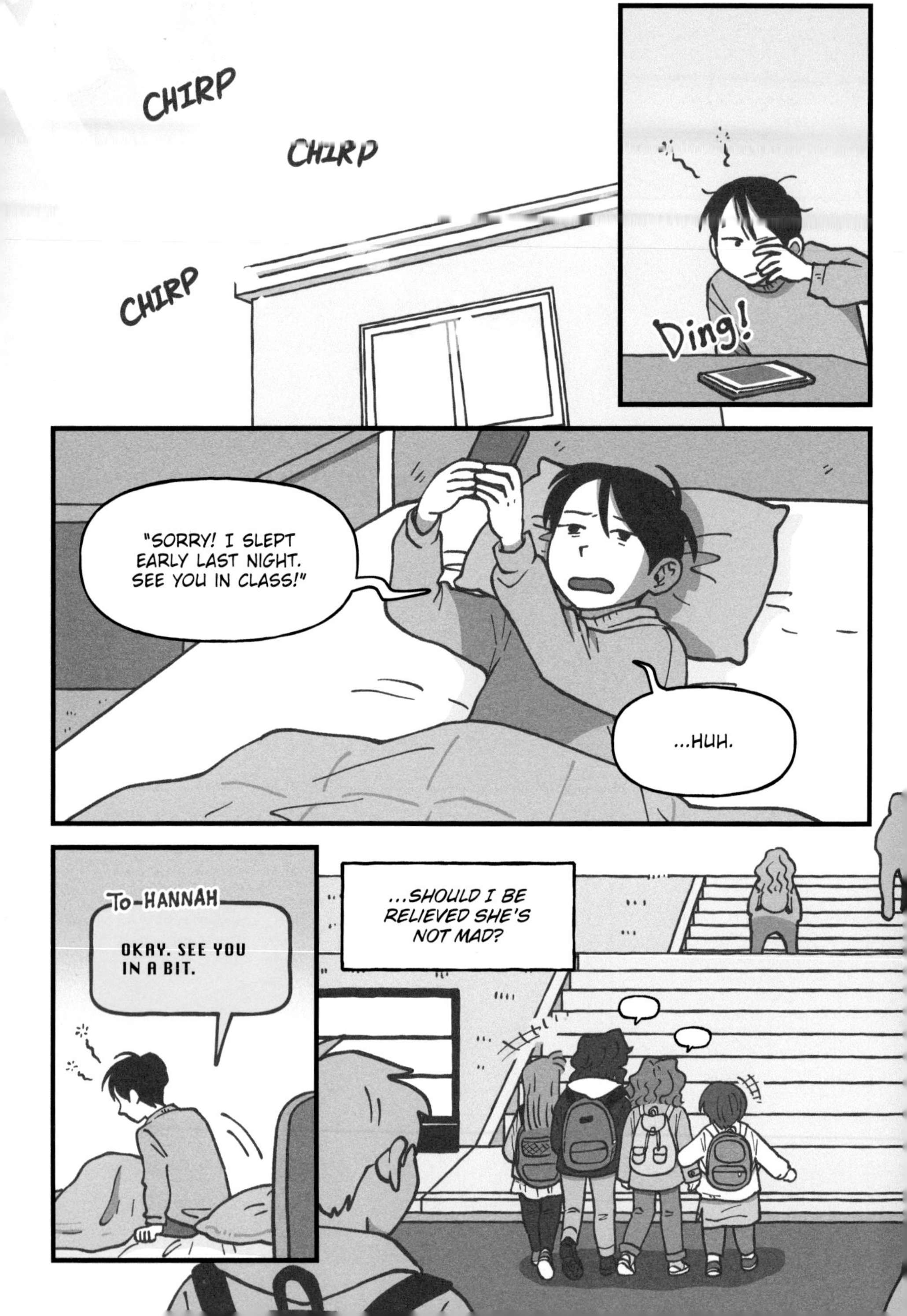
CHIRP
CHIRP
CHIRP
Ding!
"SORRY! I SLEPT EARLY LAST NIGHT. SEE YOU IN CLASS!"
...HUH.
To-HANNAH
OKAY. SEE YOU IN A BIT.
...SHOULD I BE RELIEVED SHE'S NOT MAD?

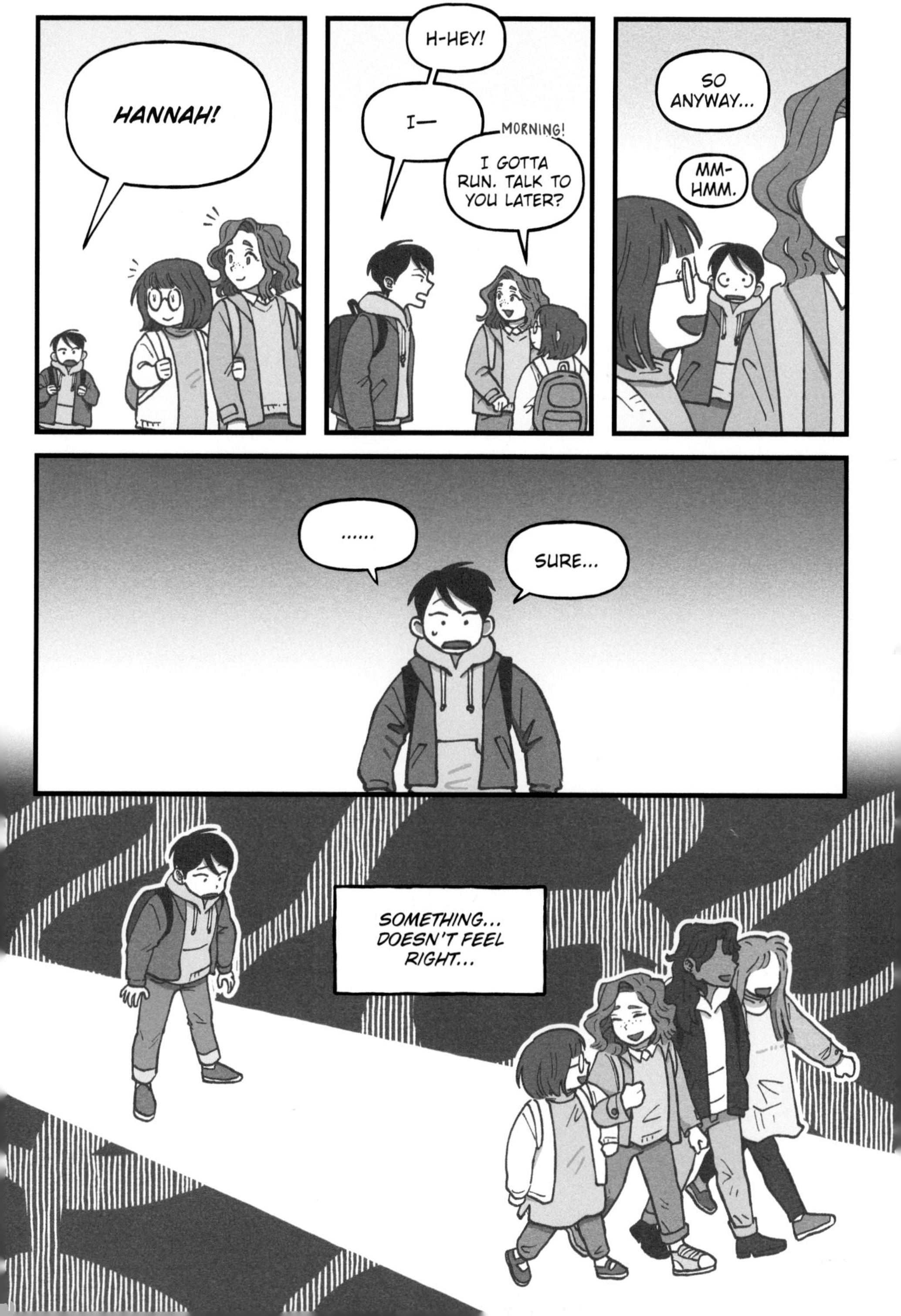
HANNAH!
H-HEY!
I—
MORNING!
I GOTTA RUN. TALK TO YOU LATER?
SO ANYWAY...
MM-HMM.
......
SURE...
SOMETHING... DOESN'T FEEL RIGHT...

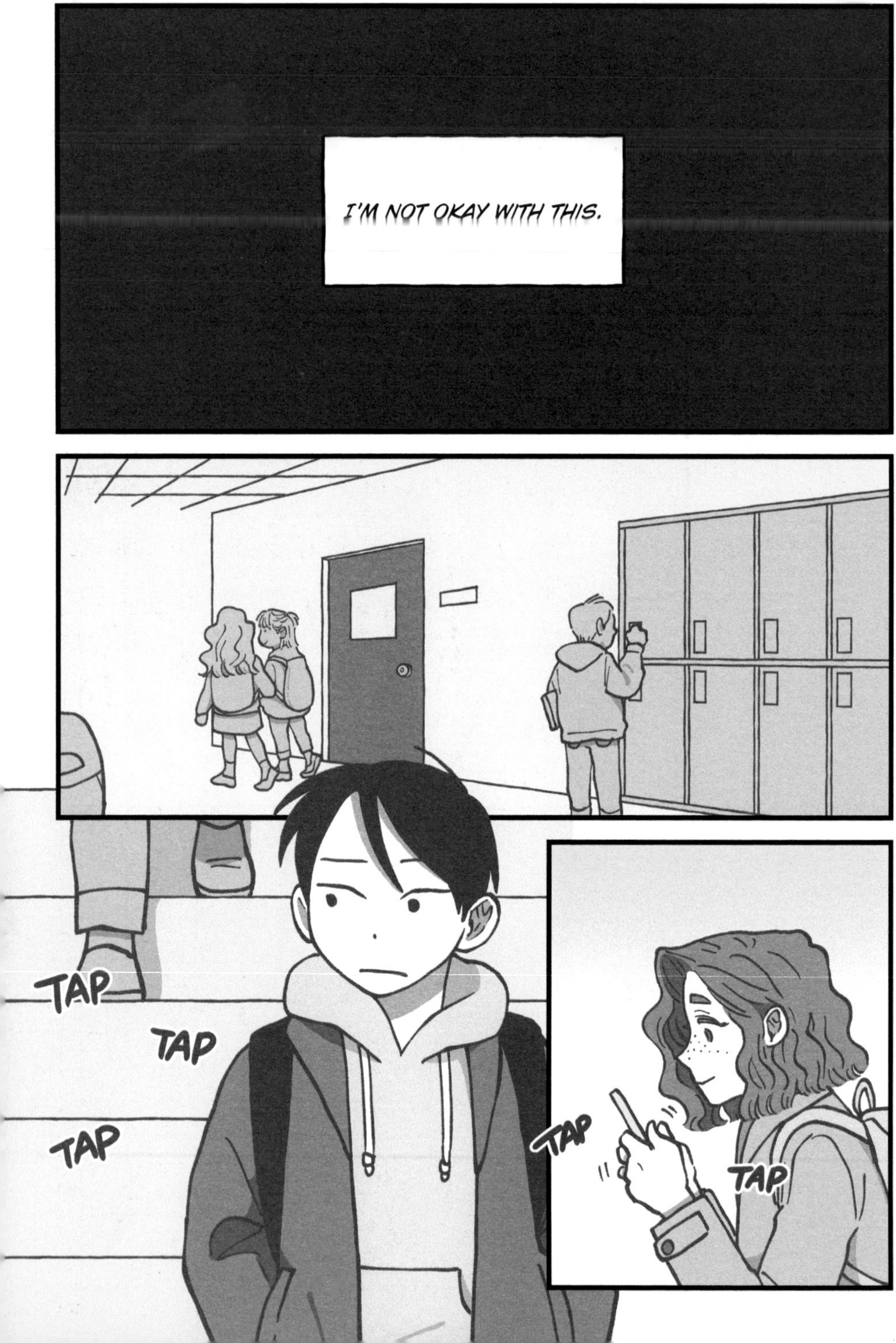
I'M NOT OKAY WITH THIS.
TAP
TAP
TAP
TAP
TAP

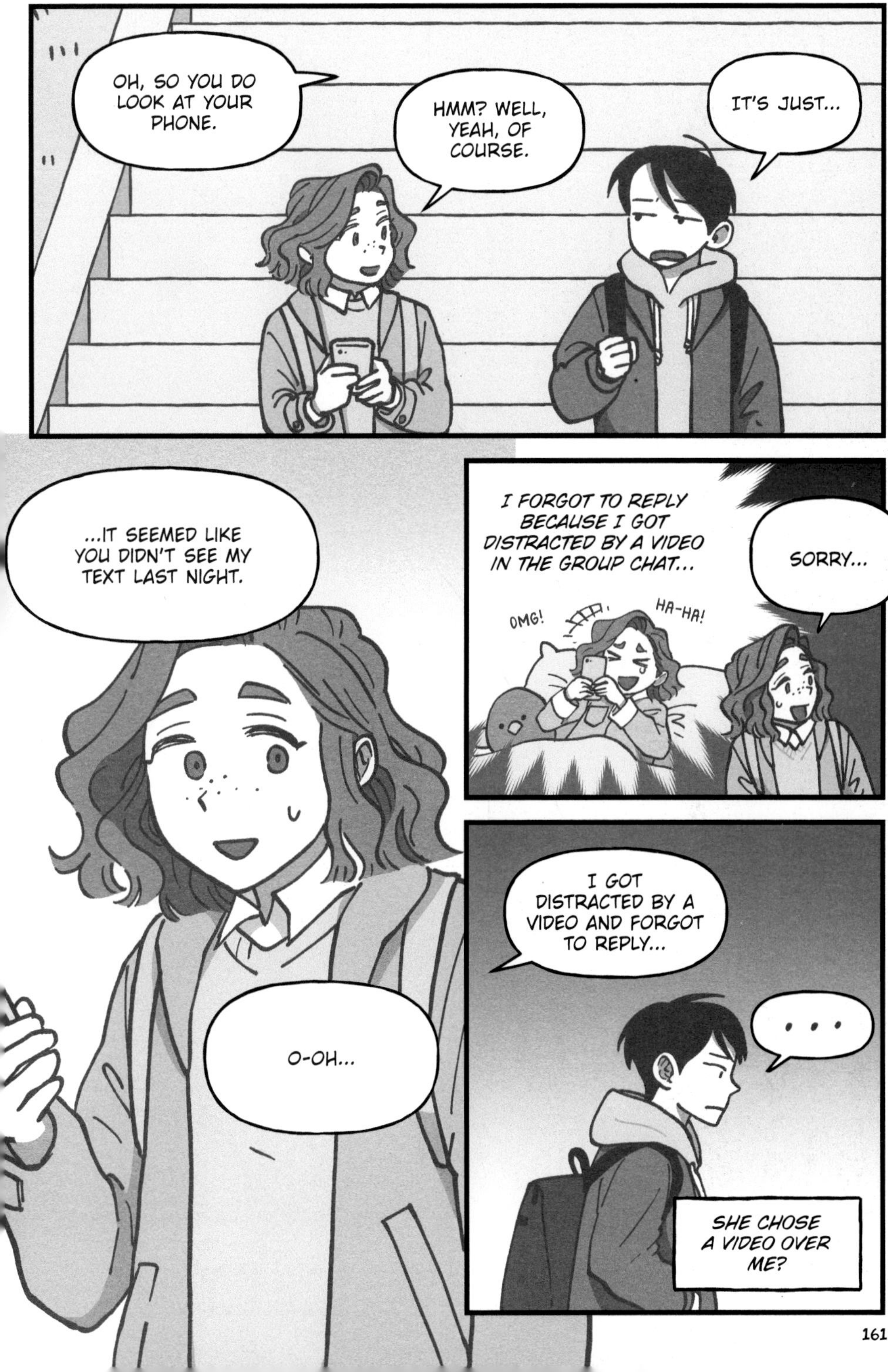
OH, SO YOU DO LOOK AT YOUR PHONE.
HMM? WELL, YEAH, OF COURSE.
IT'S JUST...
...IT SEEMED LIKE YOU DIDN'T SEE MY TEXT LAST NIGHT.
I FORGOT TO REPLY BECAUSE I GOT DISTRACTED BY A VIDEO IN THE GROUP CHAT...
SORRY...
OMG!
HA-HA!
O-OH...
I GOT DISTRACTED BY A VIDEO AND FORGOT TO REPLY...
...
SHE CHOSE A VIDEO OVER ME?

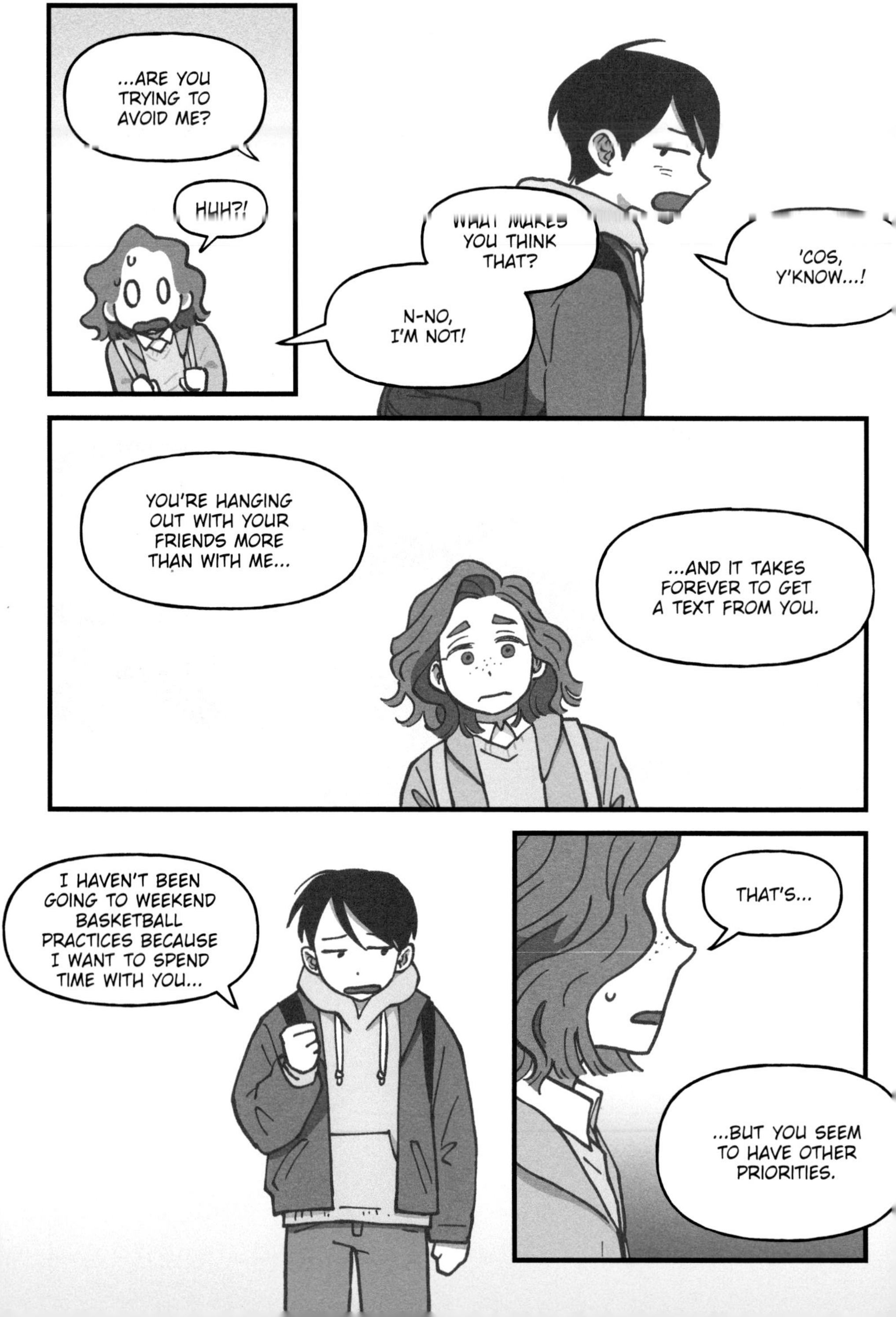
...ARE YOU TRYING TO AVOID ME?
HUH?!
YOU THINK THAT?
N-NO, I'M NOT!
'COS, Y'KNOW...!
YOU'RE HANGING OUT WITH YOUR FRIENDS MORE THAN WITH ME...
...AND IT TAKES FOREVER TO GET A TEXT FROM YOU.
I HAVEN'T BEEN GOING TO WEEKEND BASKETBALL PRACTICES BECAUSE I WANT TO SPEND TIME WITH YOU...
THAT'S...
...BUT YOU SEEM TO HAVE OTHER PRIORITIES.

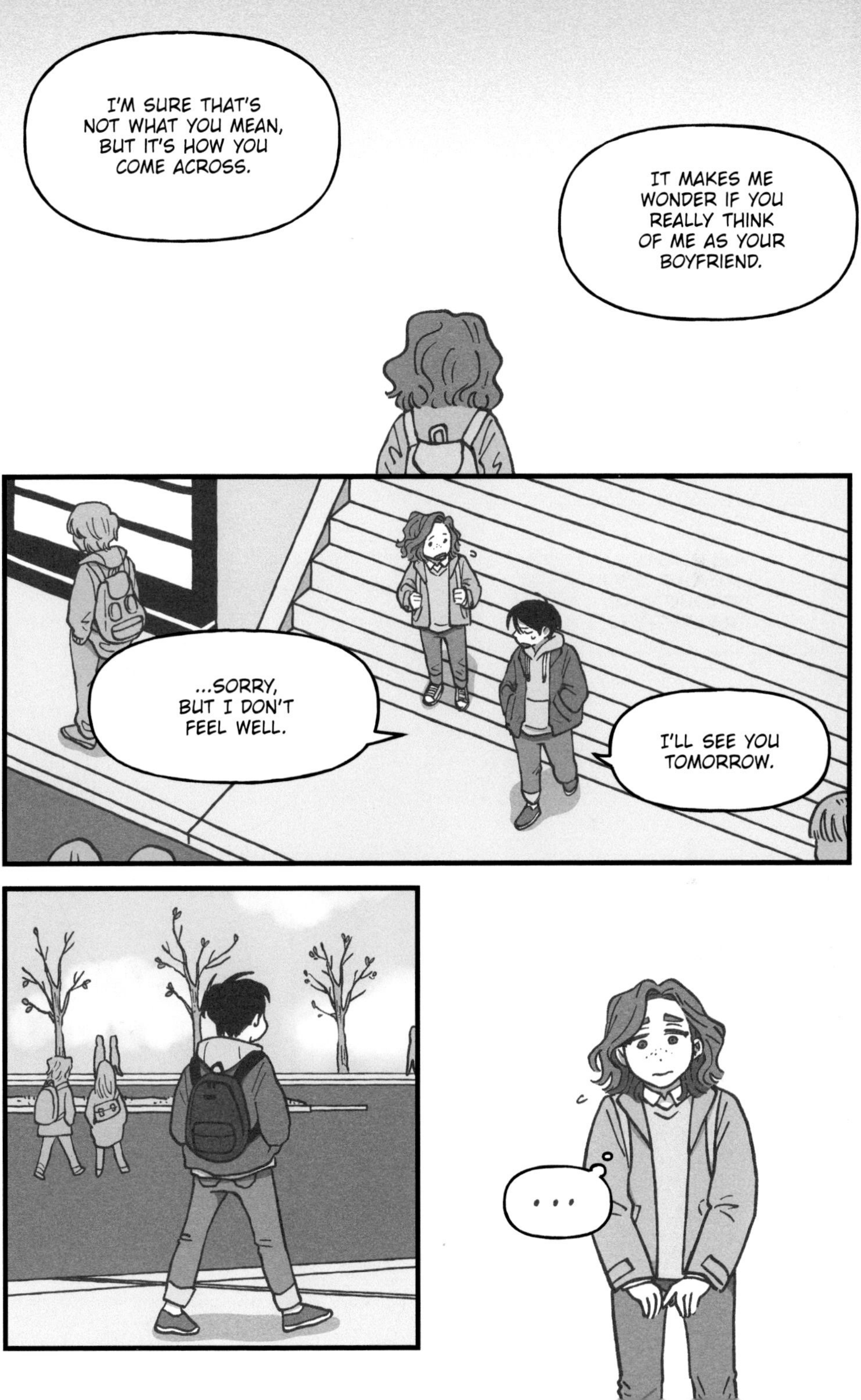
I'M SURE THAT'S NOT WHAT YOU MEAN, BUT IT'S HOW YOU COME ACROSS.
IT MAKES ME WONDER IF YOU REALLY THINK OF ME AS YOUR BOYFRIEND.
...SORRY, BUT I DON'T FEEL WELL.
I'LL SEE YOU TOMORROW.
...

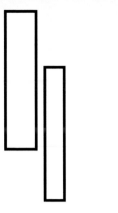

HAAH...

I MIGHT HAVE OVERREACTED YESTERDAY, BUT I HAD A RIGHT TO BE UPSET TODAY!

LAST NIGHT WAS THE WORST NIGHT OF MY LIFE!

SHE SHOULD APOLOGIZE!

HANNAH?!

BNNN

OH.

<KYLE, LIAM

KYLE

DON'T FORGET WE'RE HITTING THE COURT TOMORROW!

LIAM

ok!

TO KYLE & LIAM

GOTCHA.

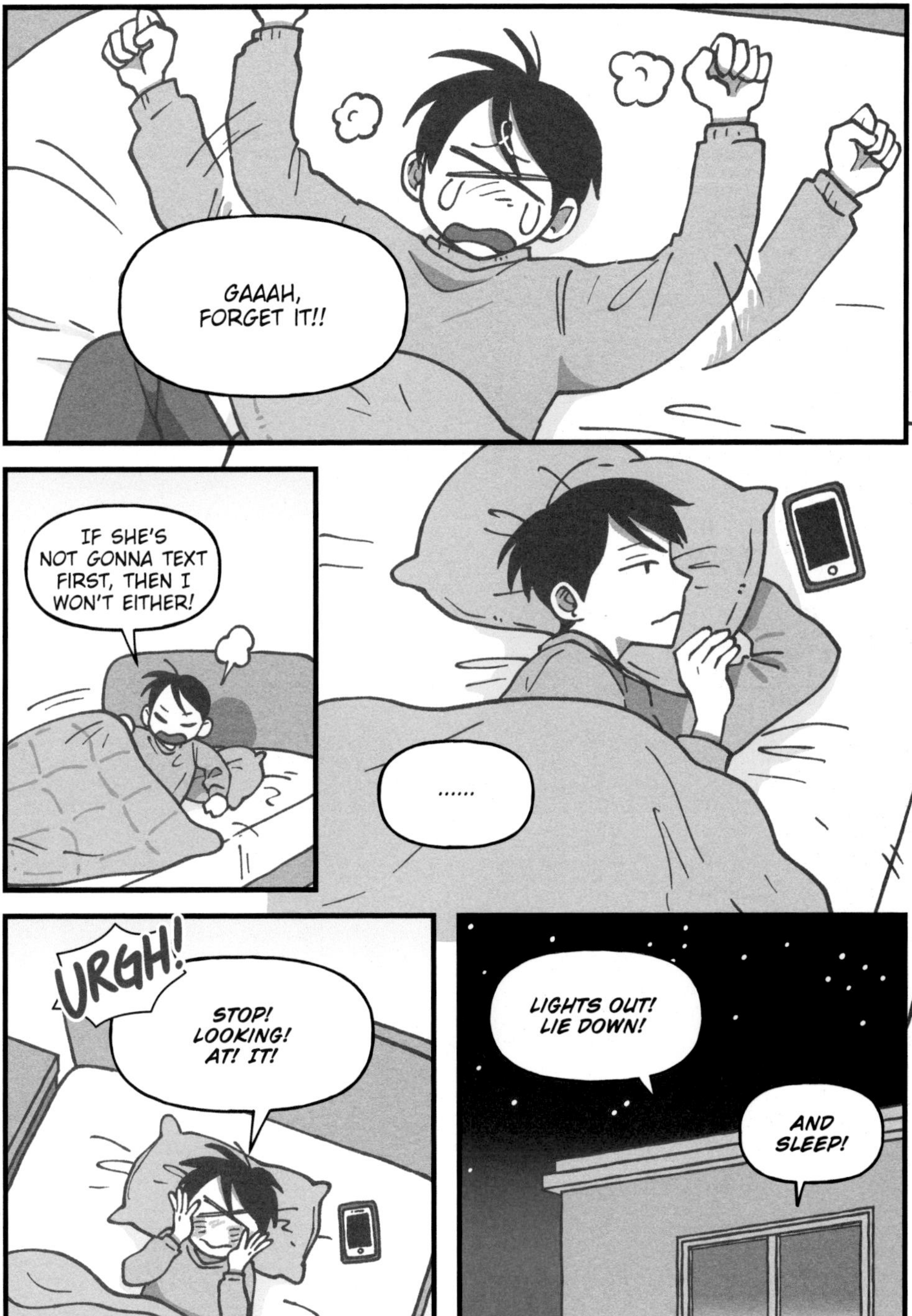
GAAAH, FORGET IT!!
IF SHE'S NOT GONNA TEXT FIRST, THEN I WON'T EITHER!
......
URGH!
STOP! LOOKING! AT! IT!
LIGHTS OUT! LIE DOWN!
AND SLEEP!

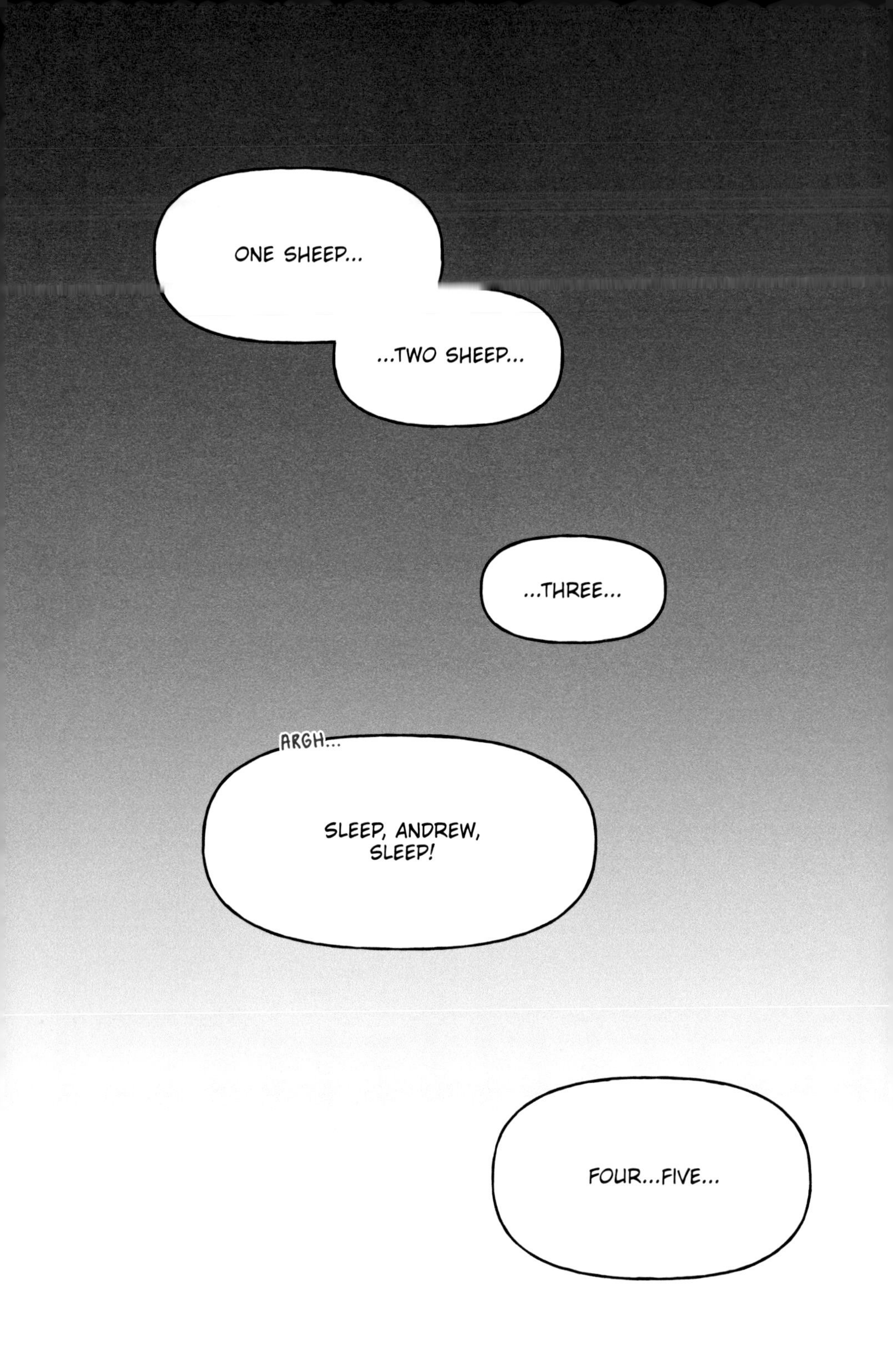
ONE SHEEP...
...TWO SHEEP...
...THREE...
ARGH...
SLEEP, ANDREW, SLEEP!
FOUR...FIVE...

Chapter 9

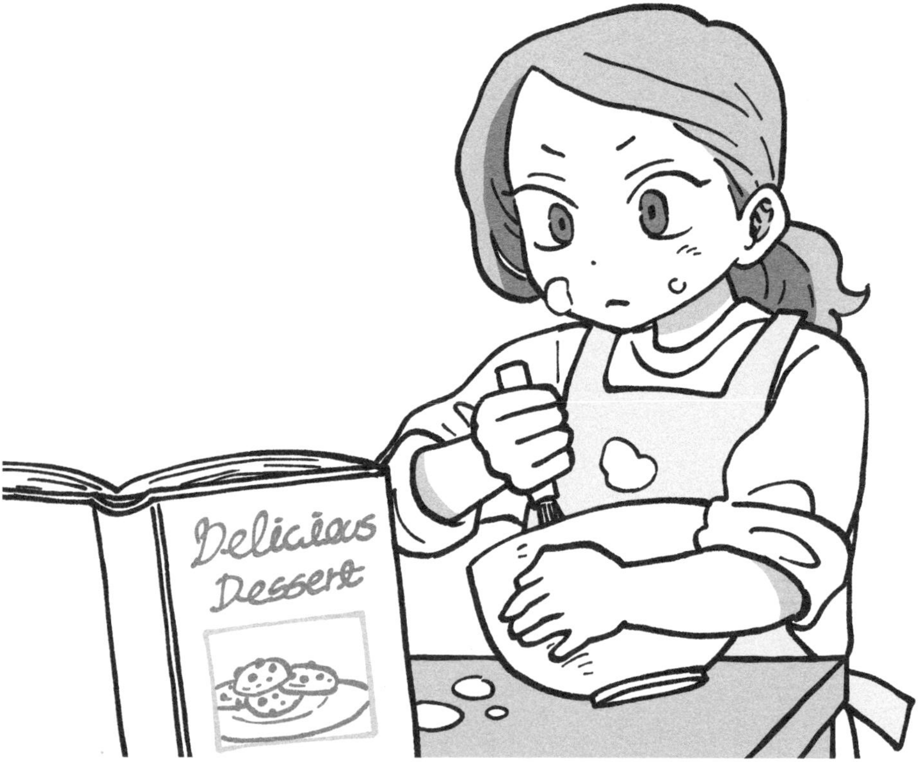
Delicious Dessert

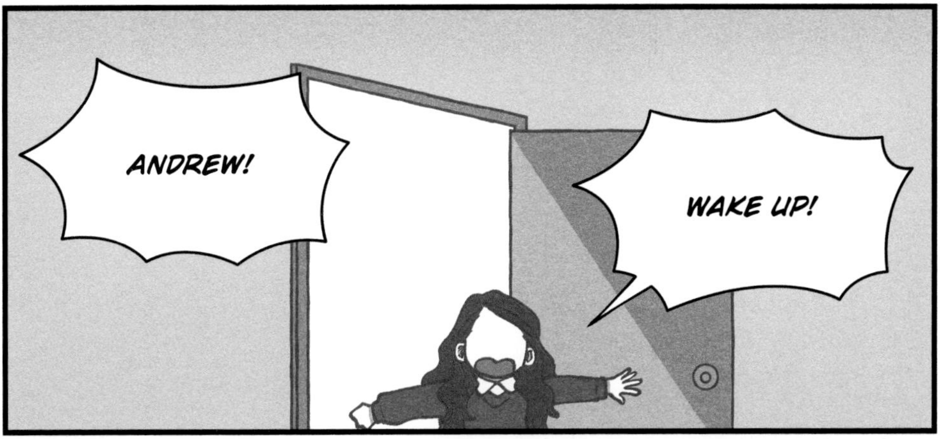
ANDREW!
WAKE UP!

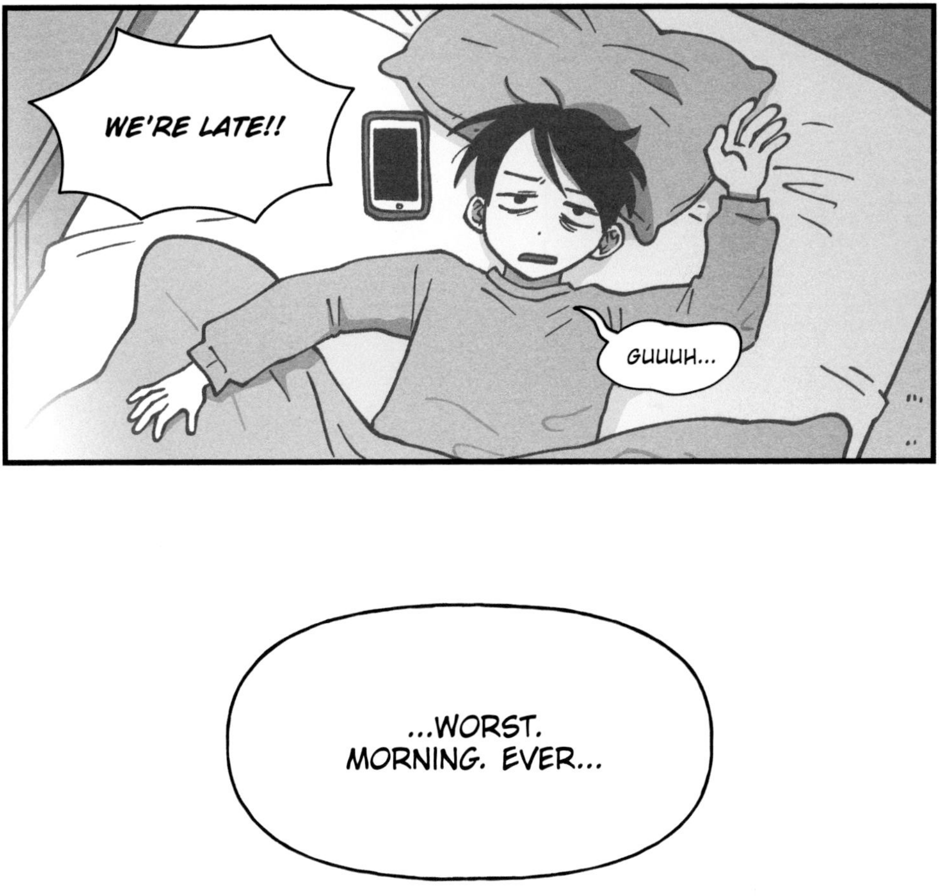
WE'RE LATE!!
GUUUH...

...WORST.
MORNING. EVER...

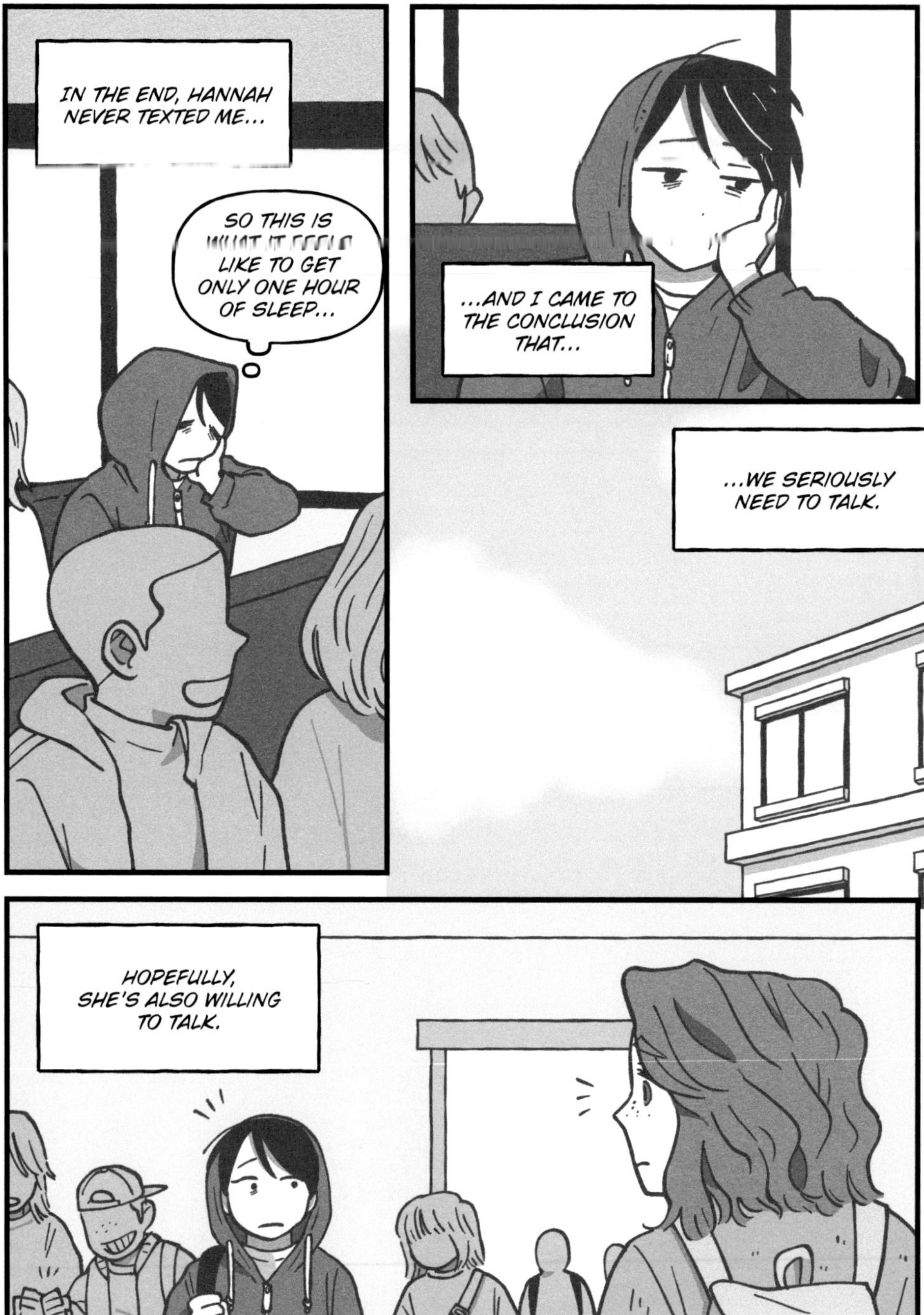
IN THE END, HANNAH NEVER TEXTED ME...
SO THIS IS LIKE TO GET ONLY ONE HOUR OF SLEEP...
...AND I CAME TO THE CONCLUSION THAT...
...WE SERIOUSLY NEED TO TALK.
HOPEFULLY, SHE'S ALSO WILLING TO TALK.

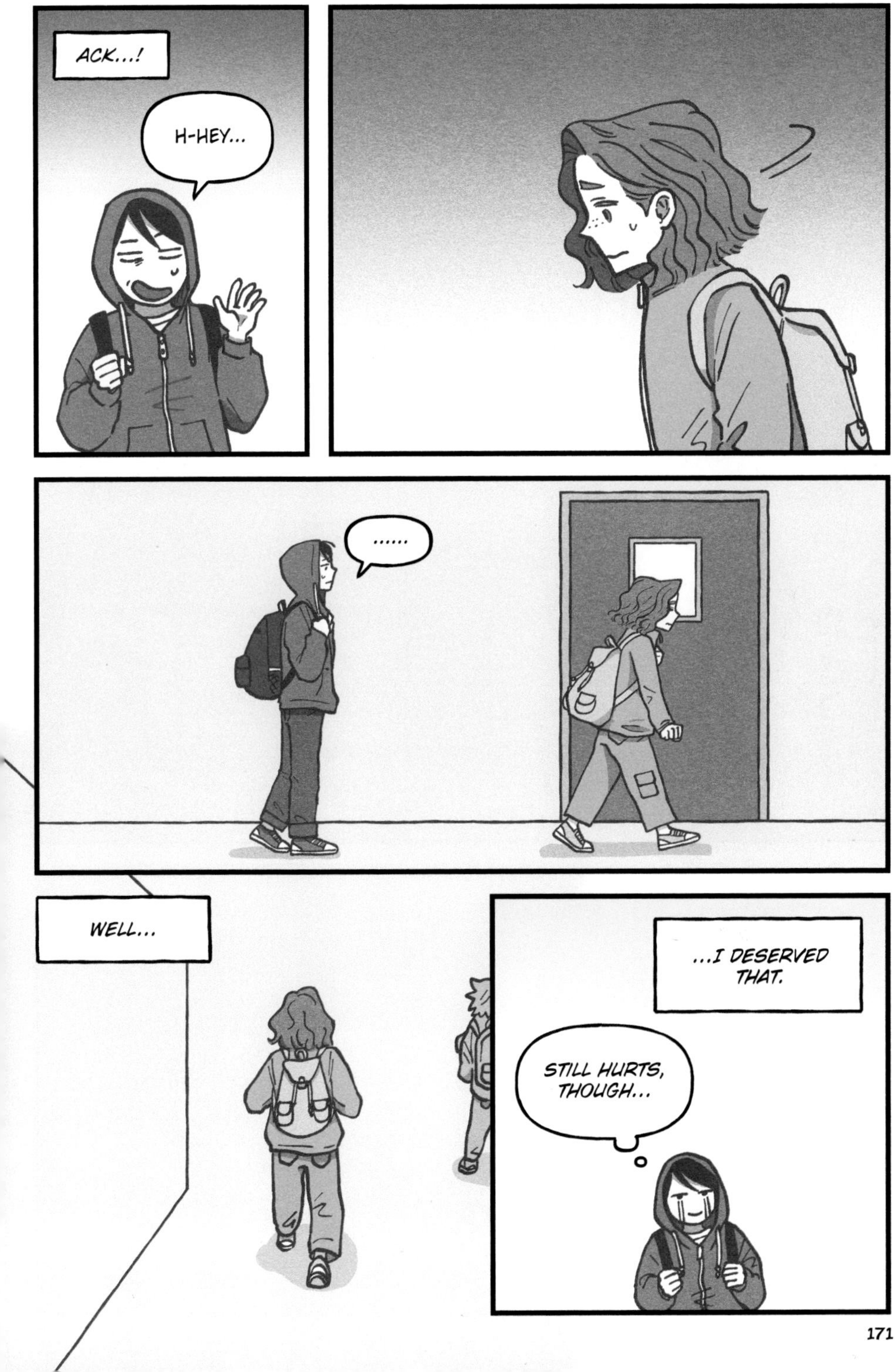
ACK...!
H-HEY...
......
WELL...
...I DESERVED THAT.
STILL HURTS, THOUGH...

I...

HAN...

...SHOULD...

...NAH—!

...BE...

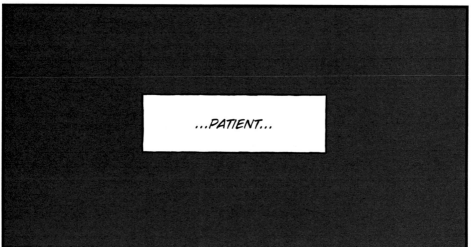

...PATIENT...

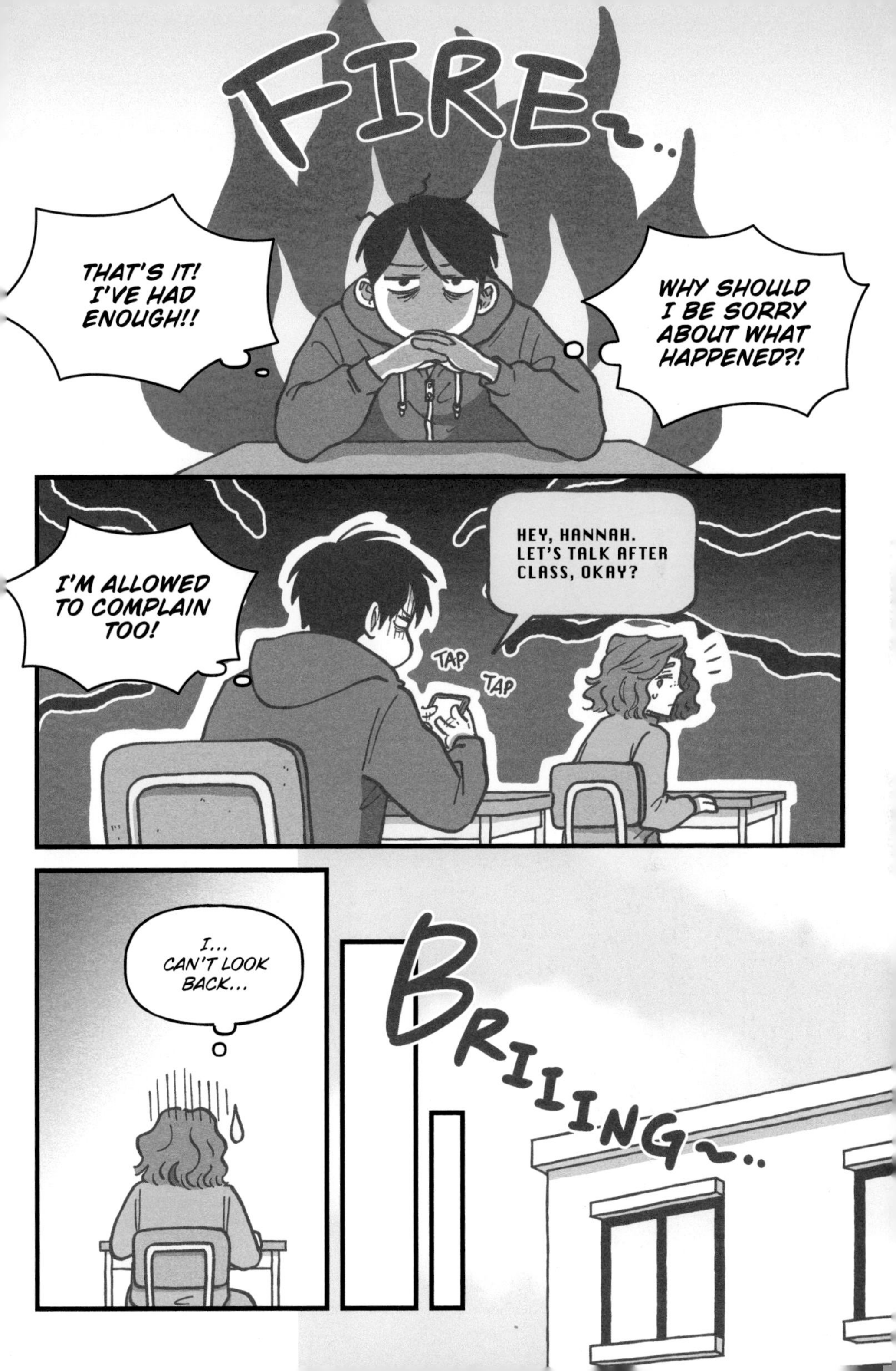
FIRE~..
THAT'S IT! I'VE HAD ENOUGH!!
WHY SHOULD I BE SORRY ABOUT WHAT HAPPENED?!
I'M ALLOWED TO COMPLAIN TOO!
HEY, HANNAH. LET'S TALK AFTER CLASS, OKAY?
TAP
TAP
I... CAN'T LOOK BACK...
BRIIING~..

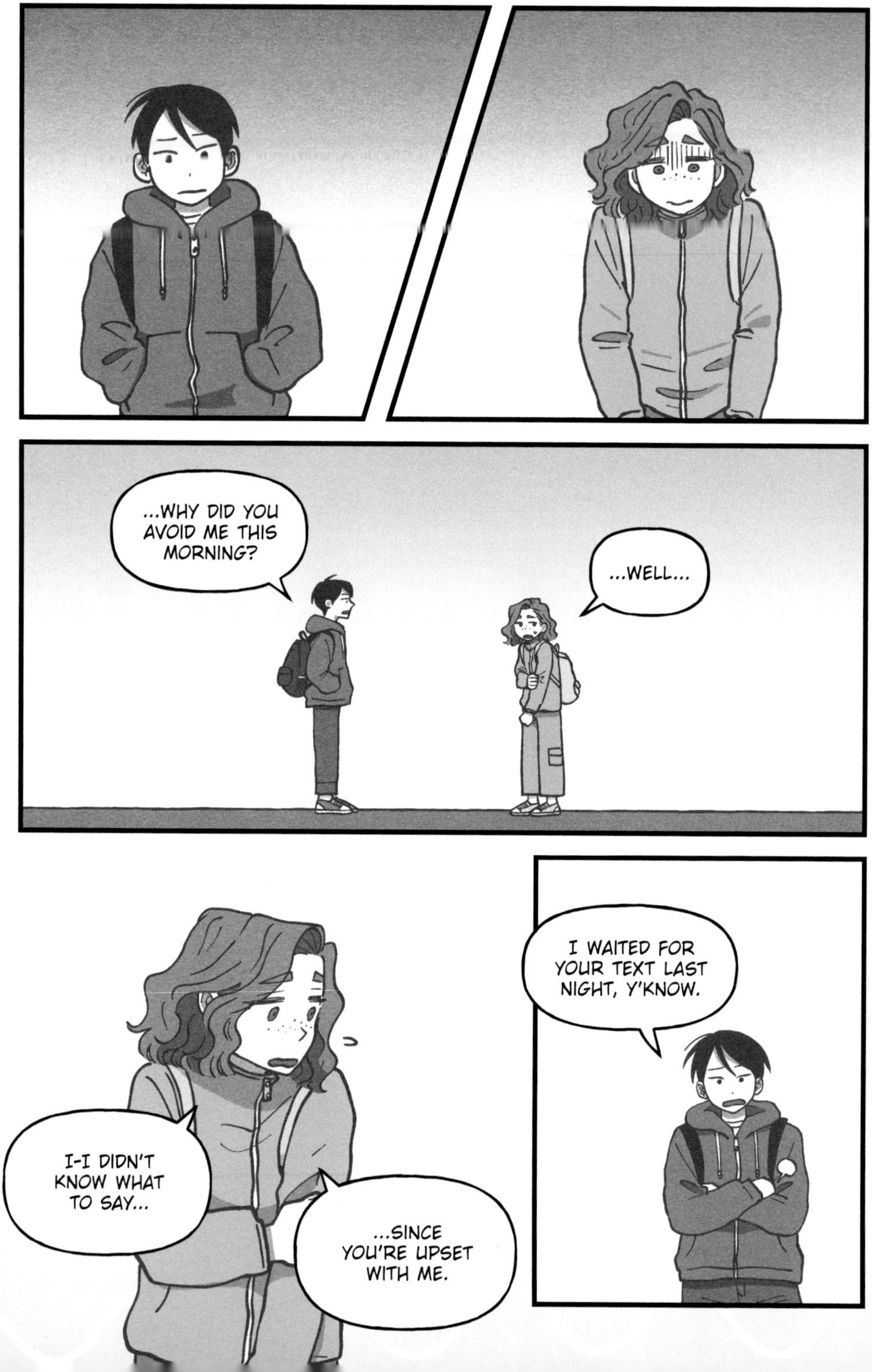
...WHY DID YOU AVOID ME THIS MORNING?
...WELL...
I WAITED FOR YOUR TEXT LAST NIGHT, Y'KNOW.
I-I DIDN'T KNOW WHAT TO SAY...
...SINCE YOU'RE UPSET WITH ME.

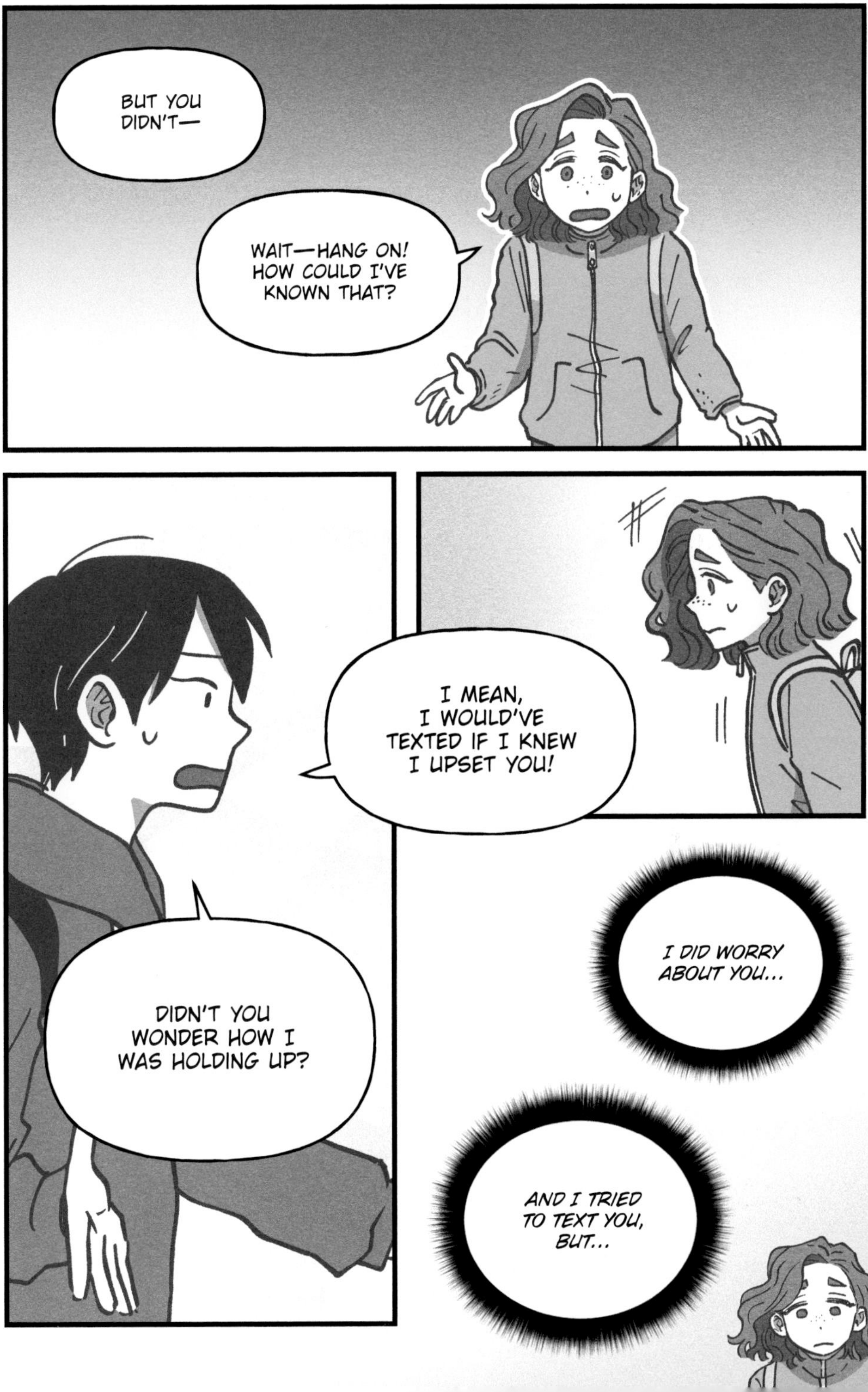
BUT YOU DIDN'T—
WAIT—HANG ON! HOW COULD I'VE KNOWN THAT?
I MEAN, I WOULD'VE TEXTED IF I KNEW I UPSET YOU!
DIDN'T YOU WONDER HOW I WAS HOLDING UP?
I DID WORRY ABOUT YOU...
AND I TRIED TO TEXT YOU, BUT...

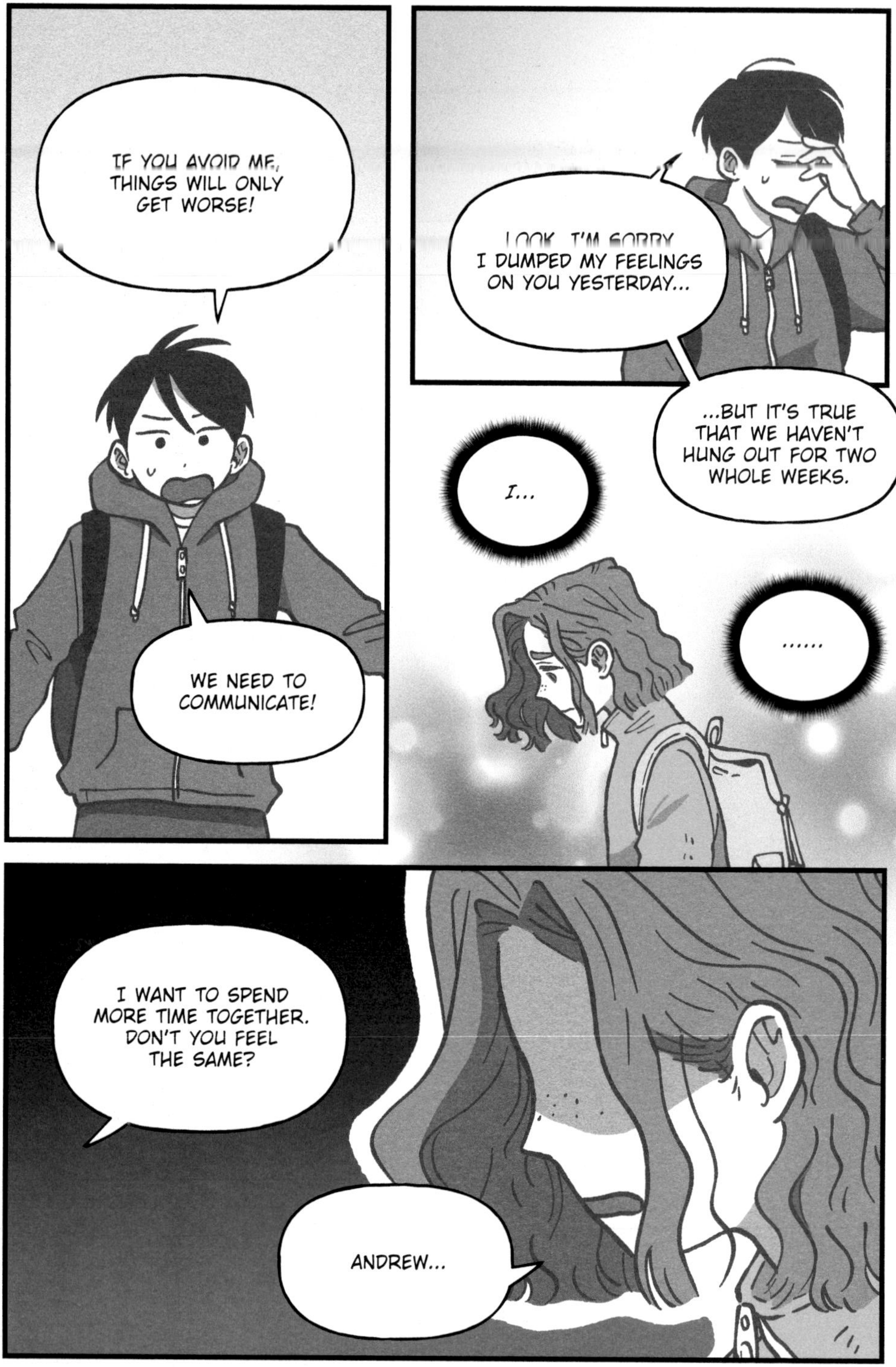
IF YOU AVOID ME, THINGS WILL ONLY GET WORSE!
WE NEED TO COMMUNICATE!
LOOK, I'M SORRY I DUMPED MY FEELINGS ON YOU YESTERDAY...
...BUT IT'S TRUE THAT WE HAVEN'T HUNG OUT FOR TWO WHOLE WEEKS.
I...
......
I WANT TO SPEND MORE TIME TOGETHER. DON'T YOU FEEL THE SAME?
ANDREW...

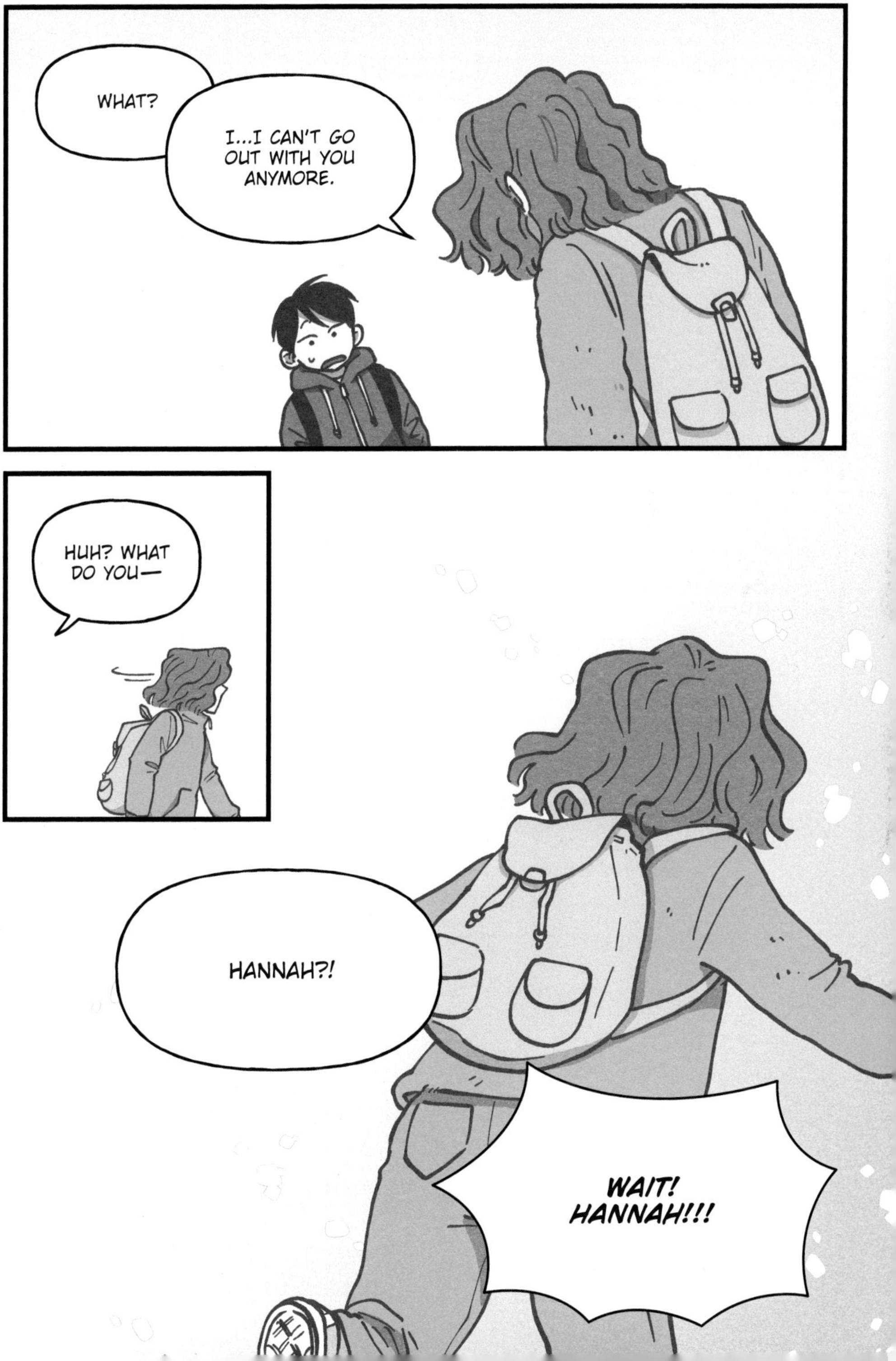
WHAT?
I...I CAN'T GO OUT WITH YOU ANYMORE.
HUH? WHAT DO YOU—
HANNAH?!
WAIT! HANNAH!!!

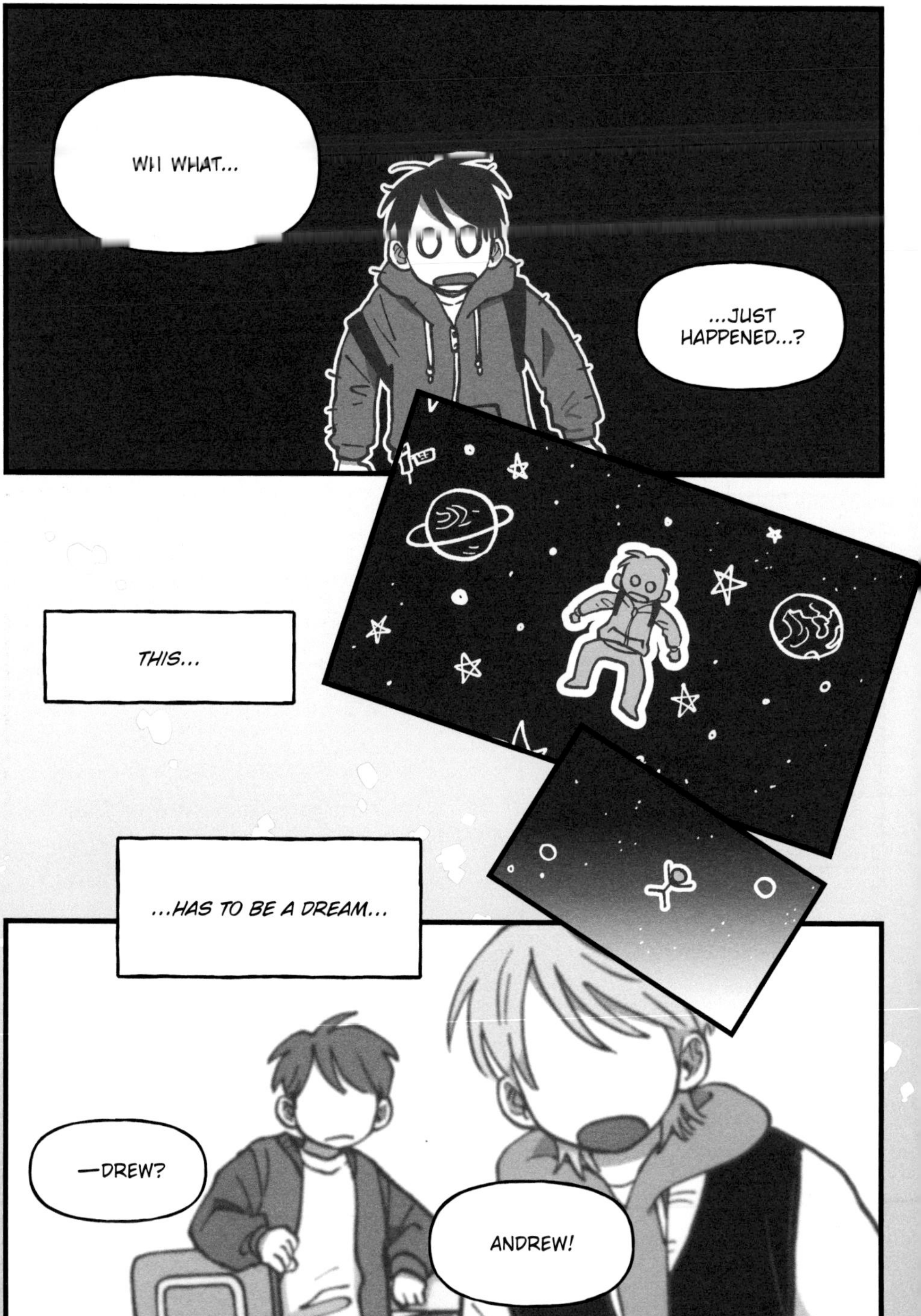

WH WHAT...
...JUST HAPPENED...?
THIS...
...HAS TO BE A DREAM...
—DREW?
ANDREW!

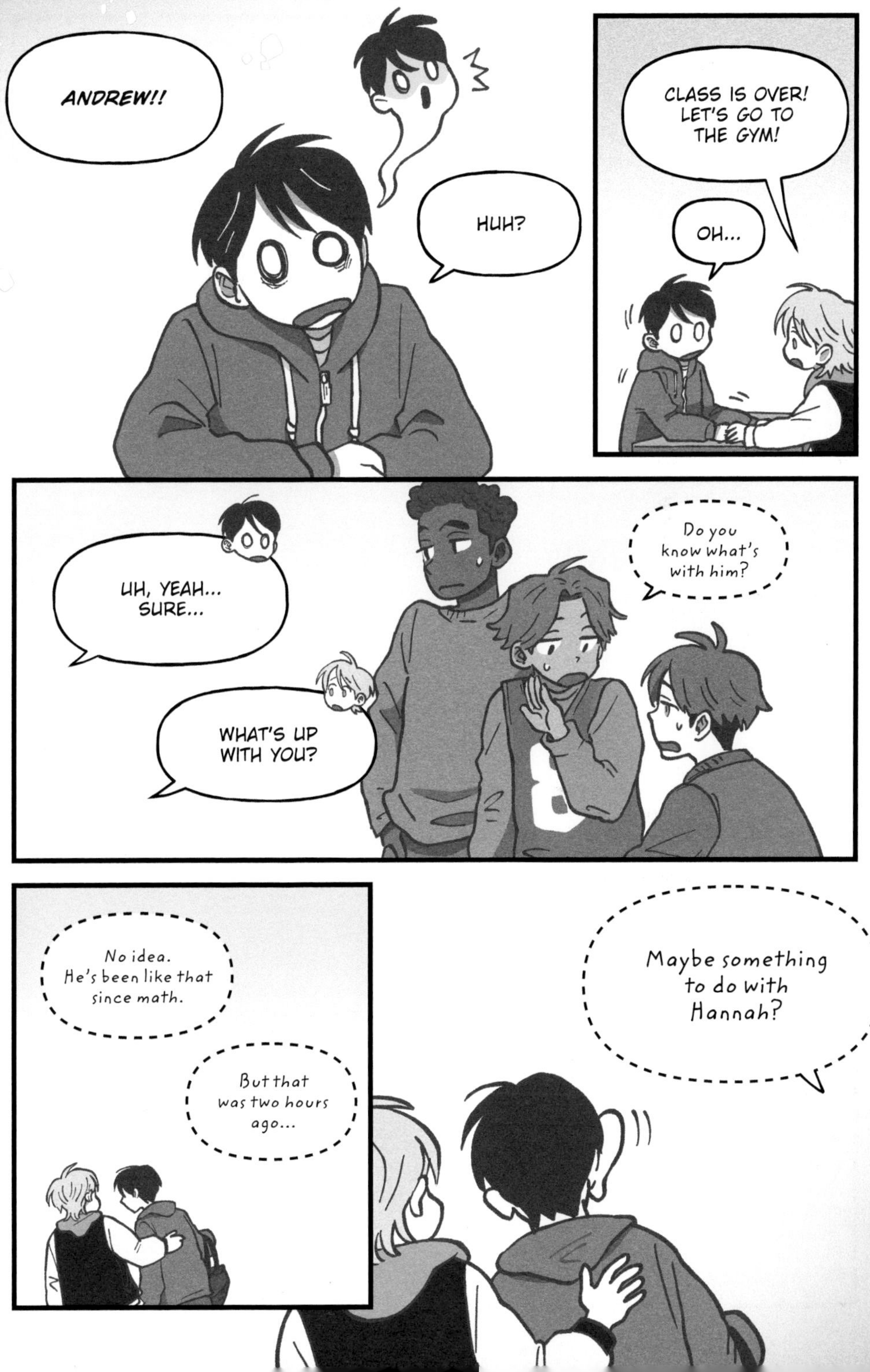
ANDREW!!
HUH?
CLASS IS OVER! LET'S GO TO THE GYM!
OH...
UH, YEAH... SURE...
WHAT'S UP WITH YOU?
Do you know what's with him?
No idea. He's been like that since math.
But that was two hours ago...
Maybe something to do with Hannah?

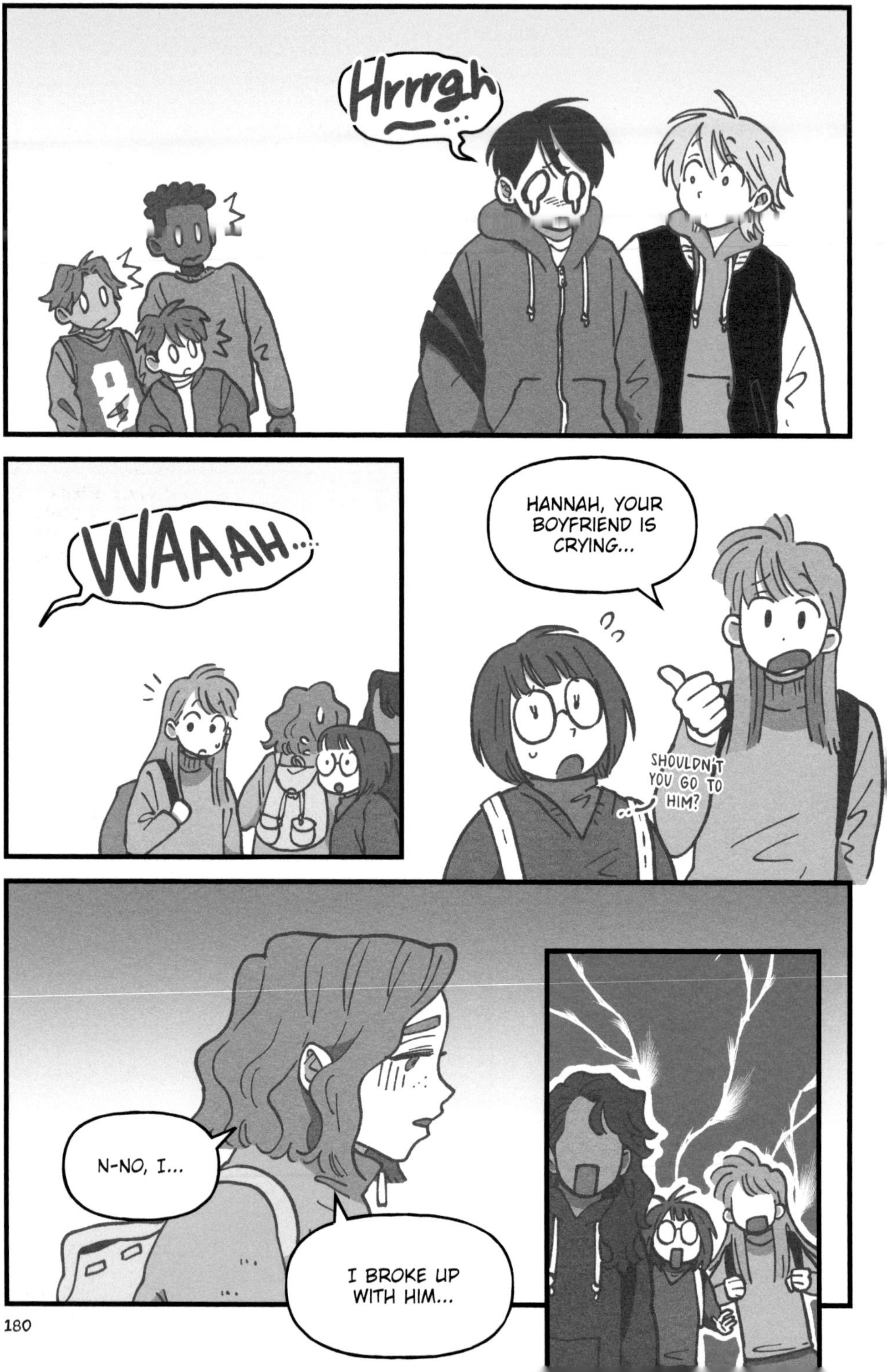
Hrrrgh...
WAAAH...
HANNAH, YOUR BOYFRIEND IS CRYING...
SHOULDN'T YOU GO TO HIM?
N-NO, I...
I BROKE UP WITH HIM...

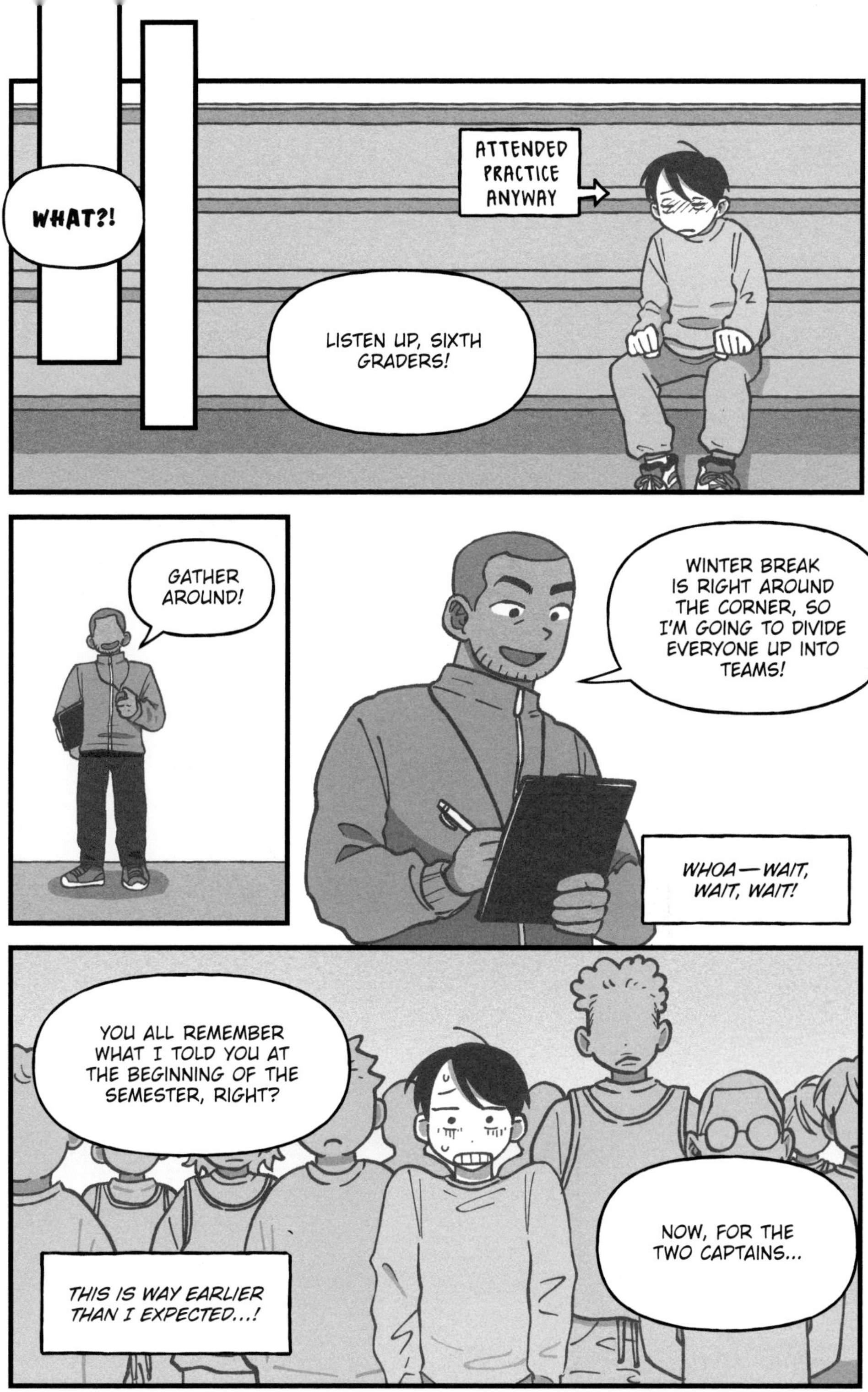

WHAT?!
ATTENDED PRACTICE ANYWAY
LISTEN UP, SIXTH GRADERS!
GATHER AROUND!
WINTER BREAK IS RIGHT AROUND THE CORNER, SO I'M GOING TO DIVIDE EVERYONE UP INTO TEAMS!
WHOA—WAIT, WAIT, WAIT!
YOU ALL REMEMBER WHAT I TOLD YOU AT THE BEGINNING OF THE SEMESTER, RIGHT?
THIS IS WAY EARLIER THAN I EXPECTED...!
NOW, FOR THE TWO CAPTAINS...

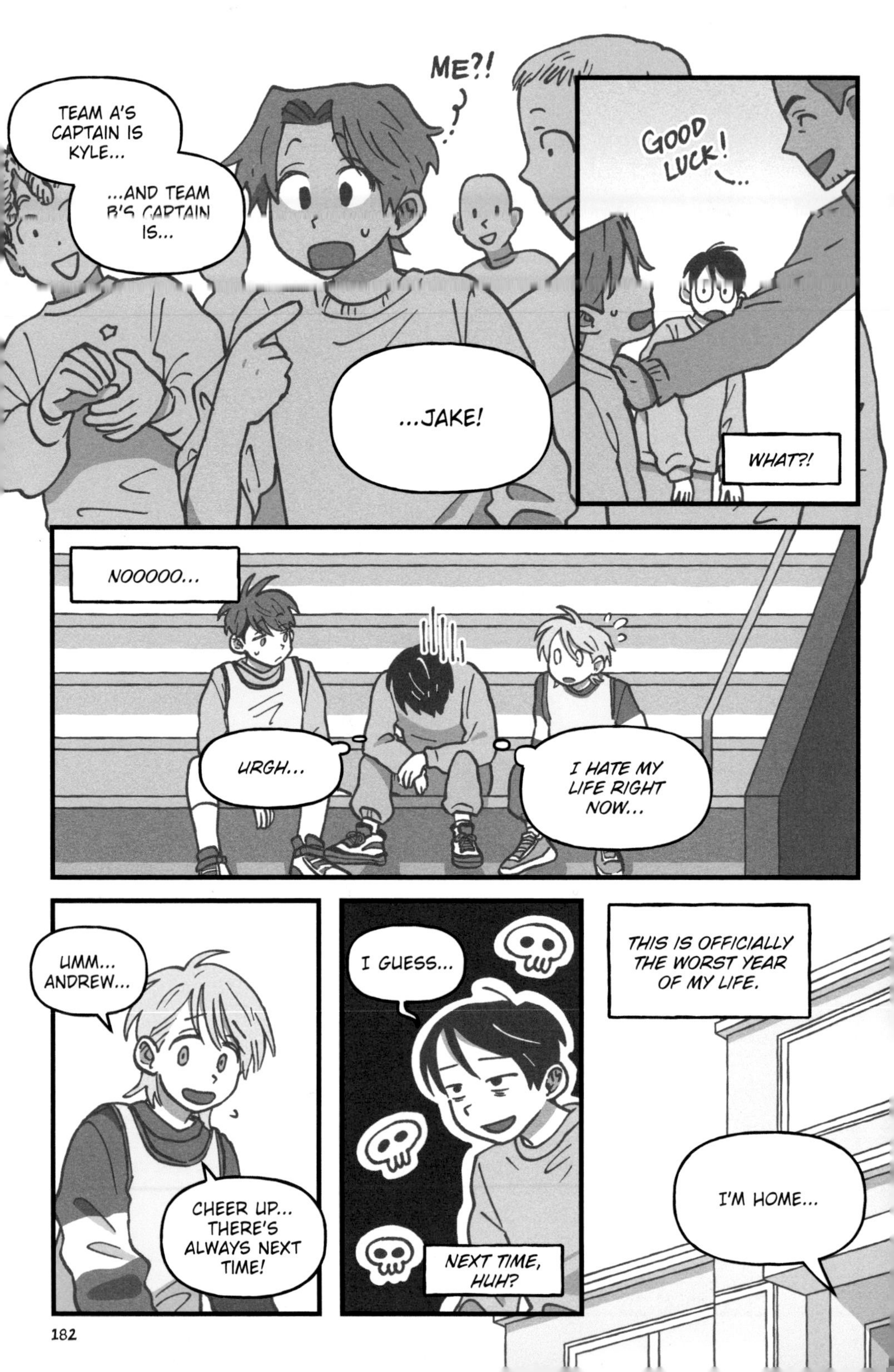
TEAM A'S CAPTAIN IS KYLE...
...AND TEAM B'S CAPTAIN IS...
ME?!
GOOD LUCK!
...JAKE!
WHAT?!
NOOOOO...
URGH...
I HATE MY LIFE RIGHT NOW...
UMM... ANDREW...
CHEER UP... THERE'S ALWAYS NEXT TIME!
I GUESS...
NEXT TIME, HUH?
THIS IS OFFICIALLY THE WORST YEAR OF MY LIFE.
I'M HOME...

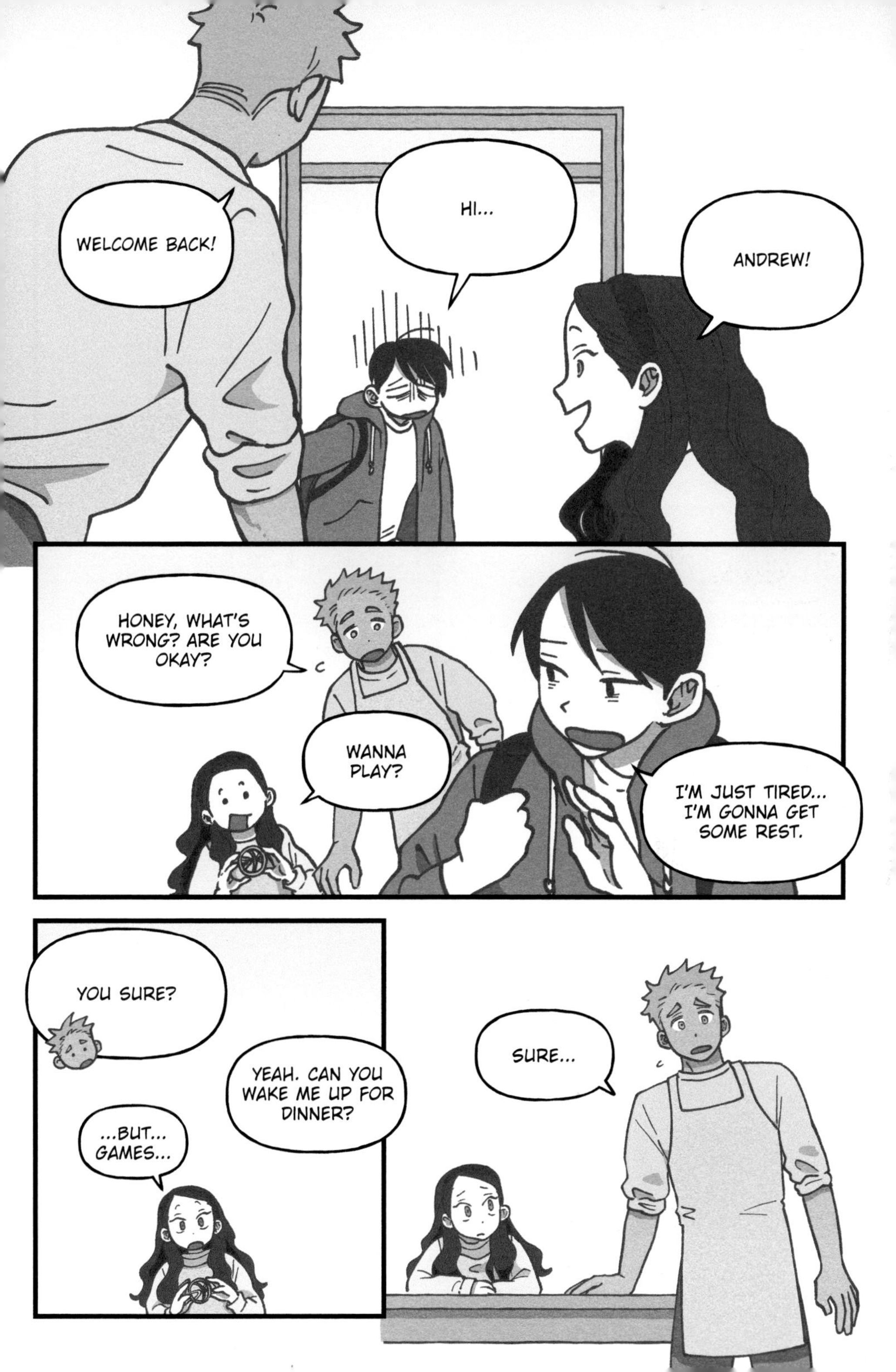
WELCOME BACK!
HI...
ANDREW!
HONEY, WHAT'S WRONG? ARE YOU OKAY?
WANNA PLAY?
I'M JUST TIRED... I'M GONNA GET SOME REST.
YOU SURE?
YEAH. CAN YOU WAKE ME UP FOR DINNER?
...BUT... GAMES...
SURE...

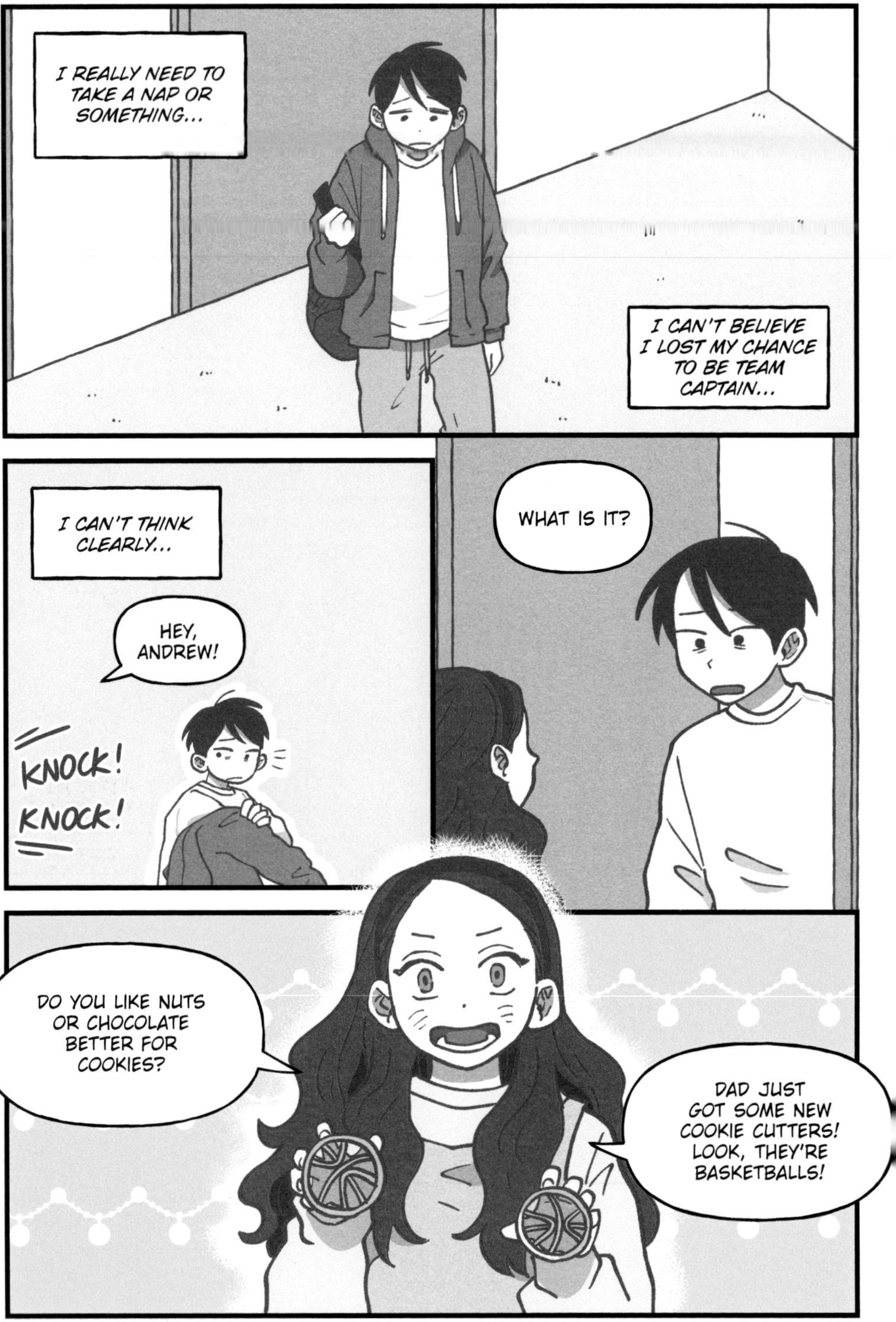
I REALLY NEED TO TAKE A NAP OR SOMETHING...
I CAN'T BELIEVE I LOST MY CHANCE TO BE TEAM CAPTAIN...
I CAN'T THINK CLEARLY...
HEY, ANDREW!
KNOCK! KNOCK!
WHAT IS IT?
DO YOU LIKE NUTS OR CHOCOLATE BETTER FOR COOKIES?
DAD JUST GOT SOME NEW COOKIE CUTTERS! LOOK, THEY'RE BASKETBALLS!

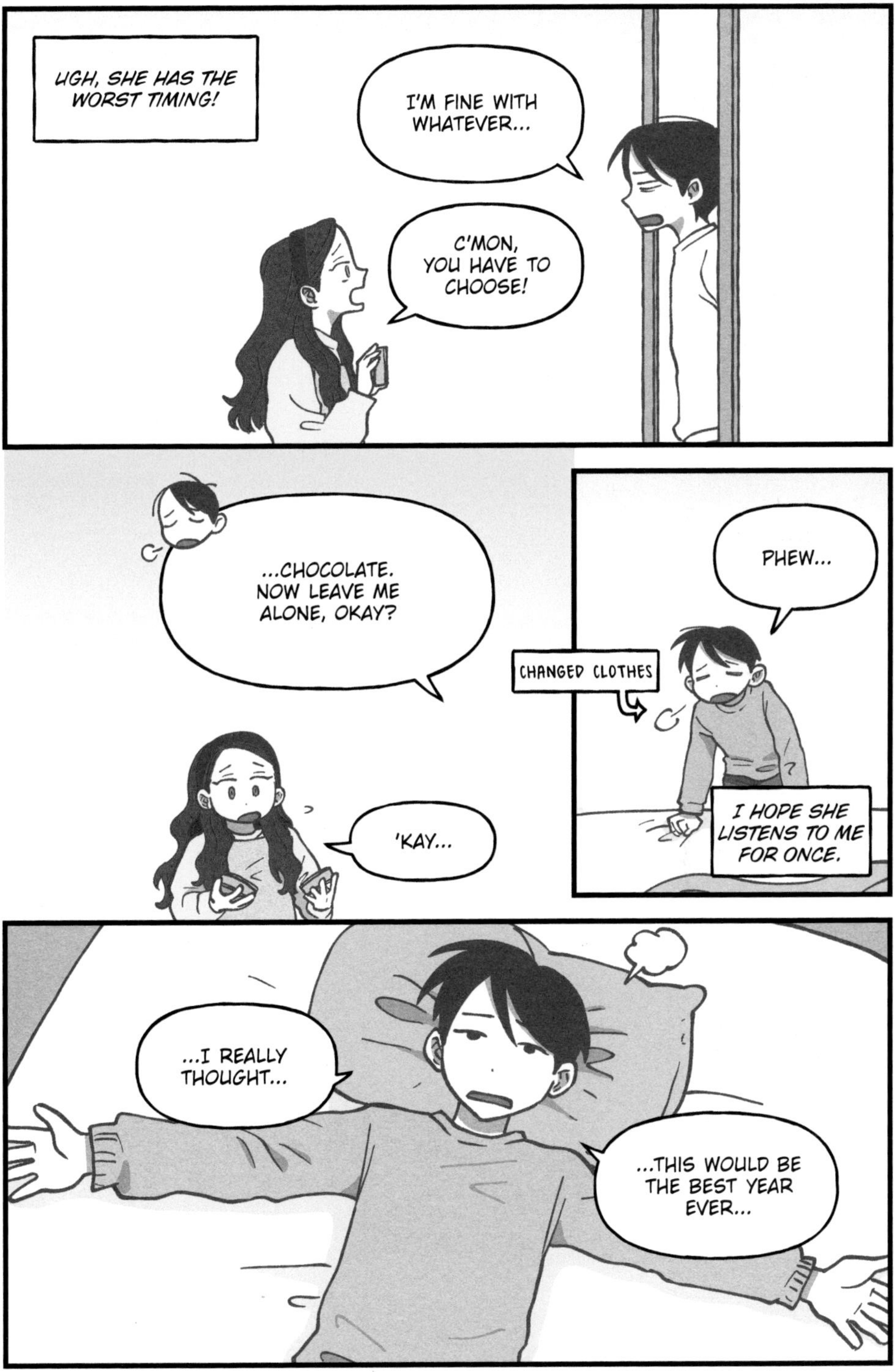
UGH, SHE HAS THE WORST TIMING!
I'M FINE WITH WHATEVER...
C'MON, YOU HAVE TO CHOOSE!
...CHOCOLATE. NOW LEAVE ME ALONE, OKAY?
'KAY...
PHEW...
CHANGED CLOTHES
I HOPE SHE LISTENS TO ME FOR ONCE.
...I REALLY THOUGHT...
...THIS WOULD BE THE BEST YEAR EVER...

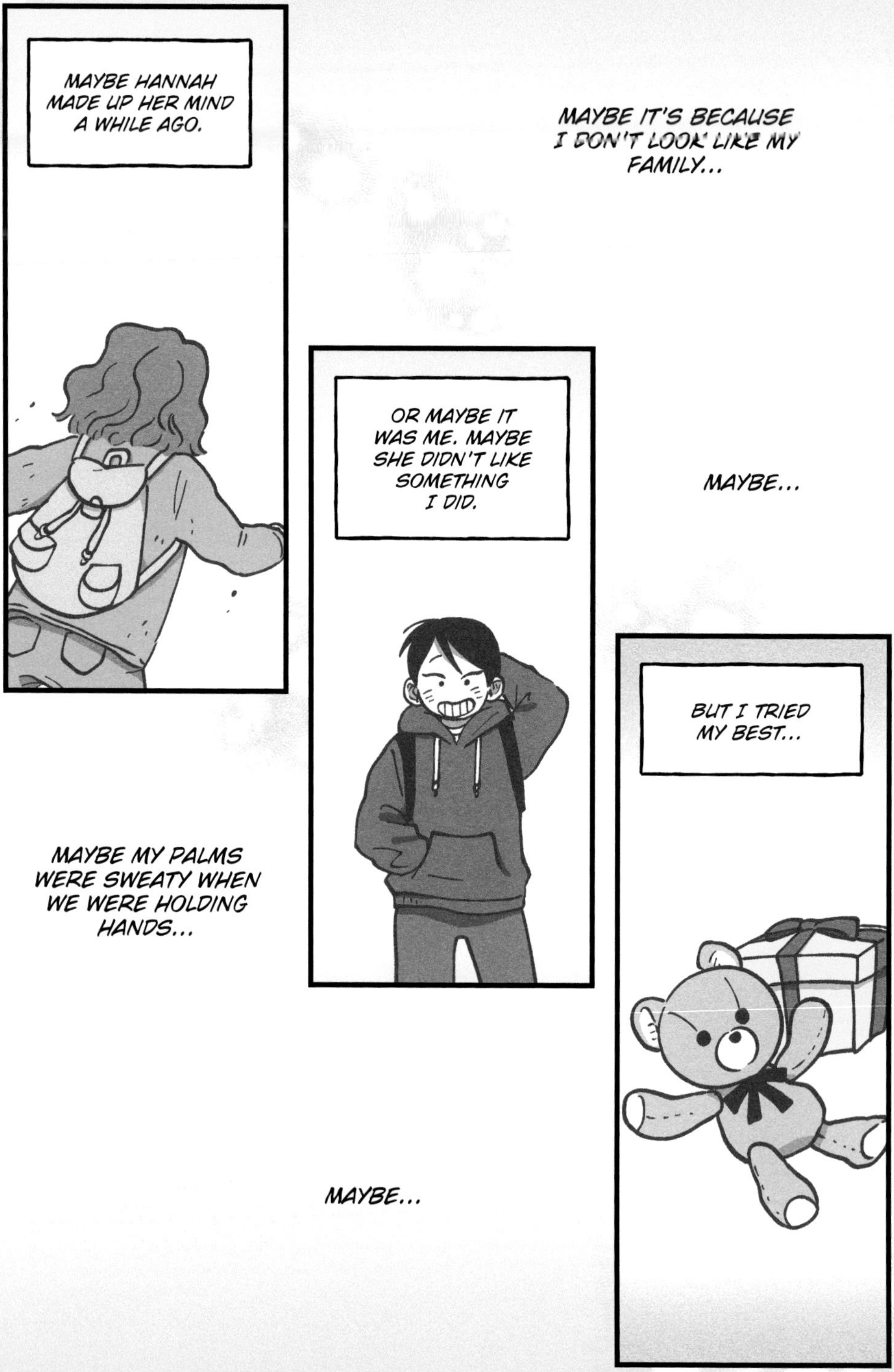
MAYBE HANNAH MADE UP HER MIND A WHILE AGO.
MAYBE IT'S BECAUSE I DON'T LOOK LIKE MY FAMILY...
OR MAYBE IT WAS ME. MAYBE SHE DIDN'T LIKE SOMETHING I DID.
MAYBE...
MAYBE MY PALMS WERE SWEATY WHEN WE WERE HOLDING HANDS...
BUT I TRIED MY BEST...
MAYBE...

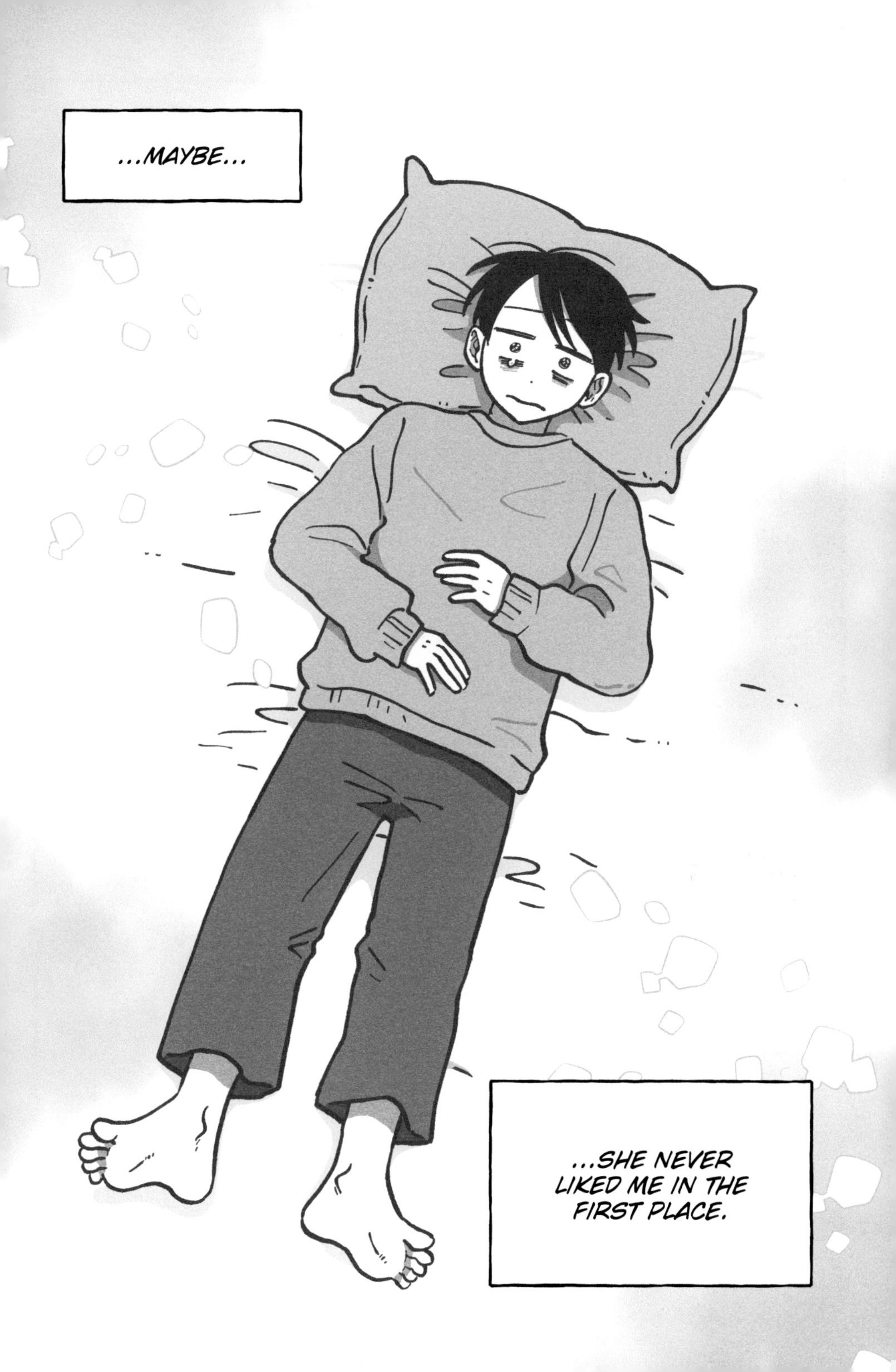
...MAYBE...
...SHE NEVER LIKED ME IN THE FIRST PLACE.

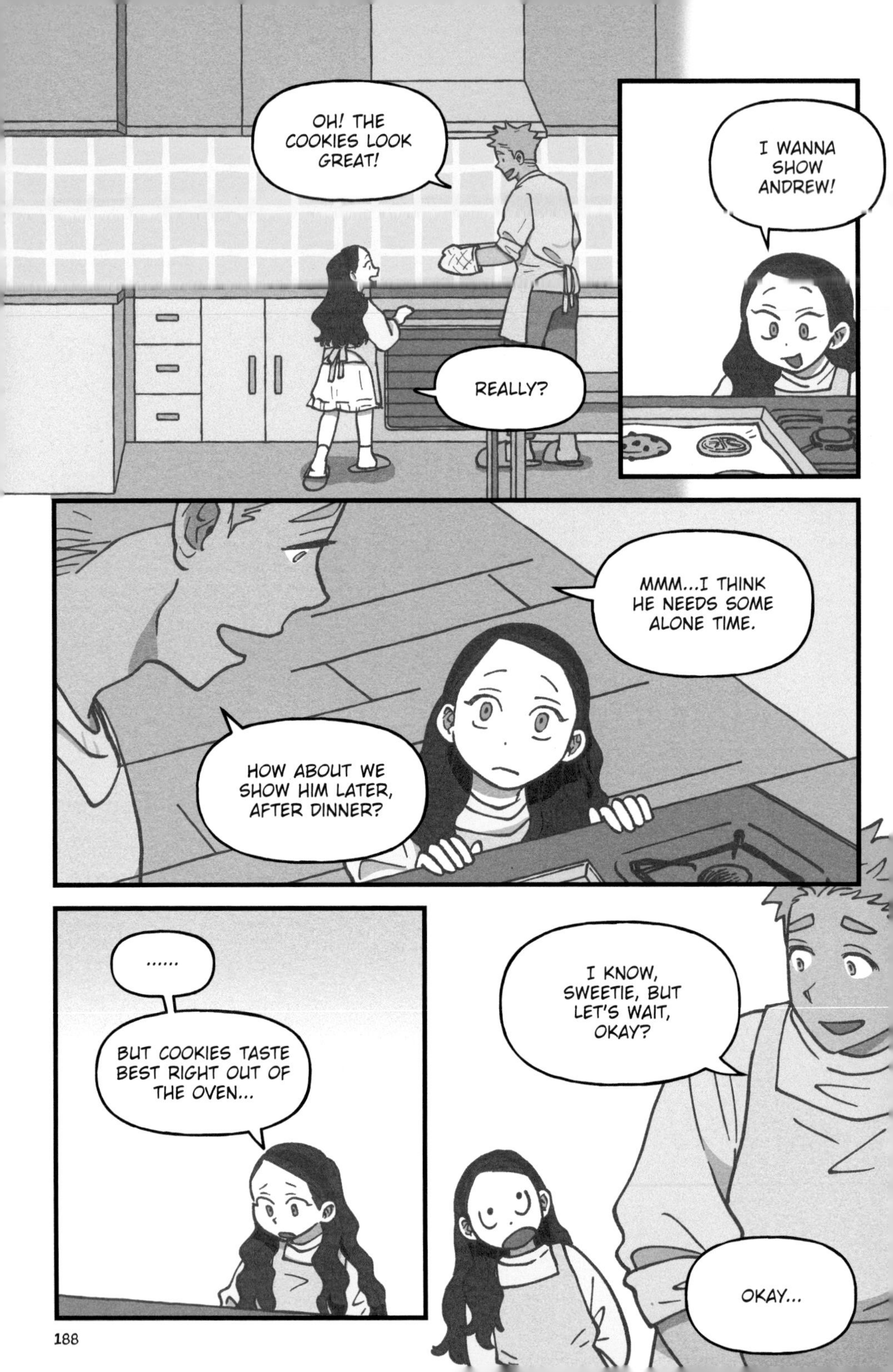
OH! THE COOKIES LOOK GREAT!
REALLY?
I WANNA SHOW ANDREW!
MMM...I THINK HE NEEDS SOME ALONE TIME.
HOW ABOUT WE SHOW HIM LATER, AFTER DINNER?
......
BUT COOKIES TASTE BEST RIGHT OUT OF THE OVEN...
I KNOW, SWEETIE, BUT LET'S WAIT, OKAY?
OKAY...

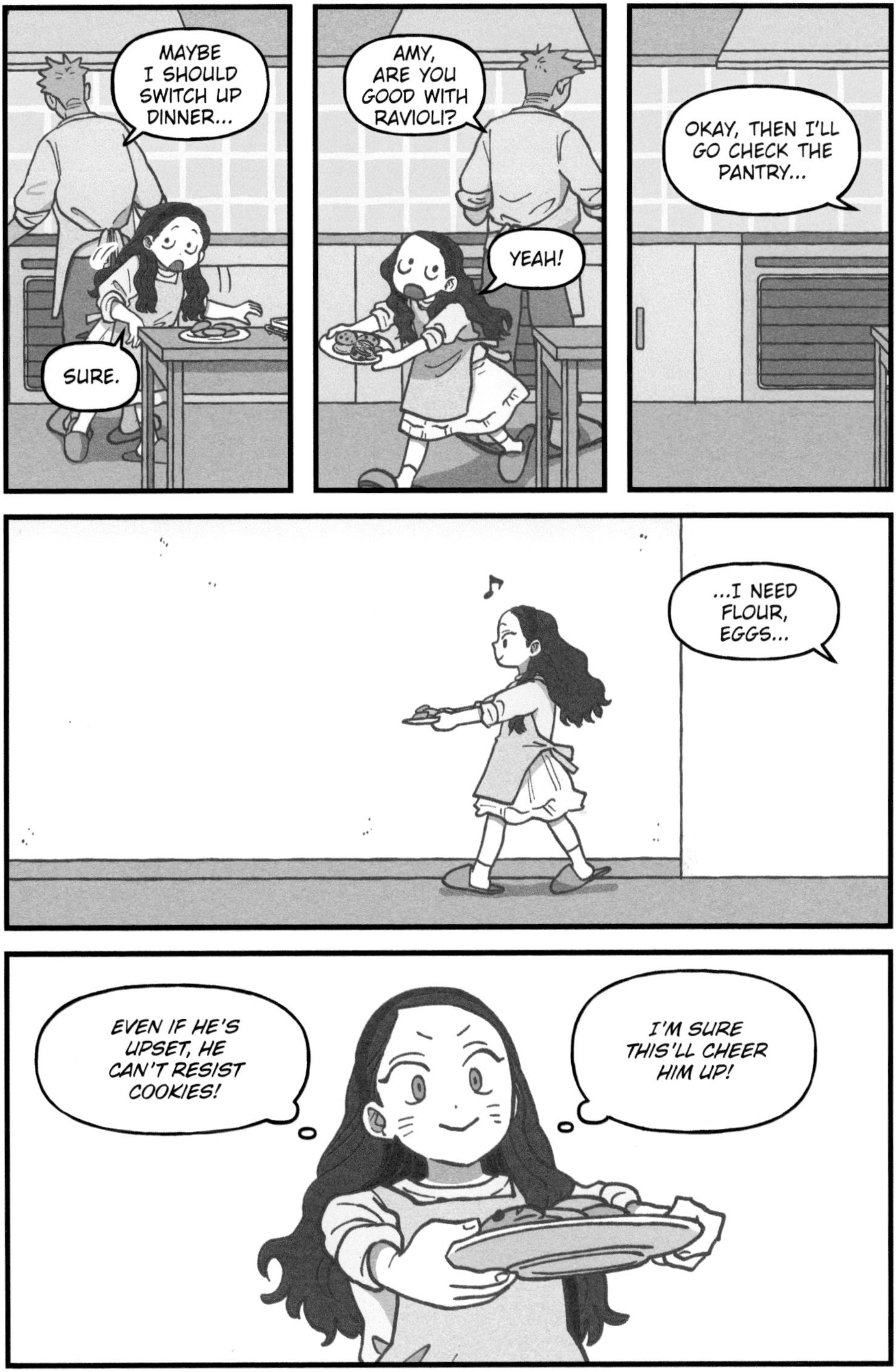
MAYBE I SHOULD SWITCH UP DINNER...
SURE.
AMY, ARE YOU GOOD WITH RAVIOLI?
YEAH!
OKAY, THEN I'LL GO CHECK THE PANTRY...
...I NEED FLOUR, EGGS...
EVEN IF HE'S UPSET, HE CAN'T RESIST COOKIES!
I'M SURE THIS'LL CHEER HIM UP!

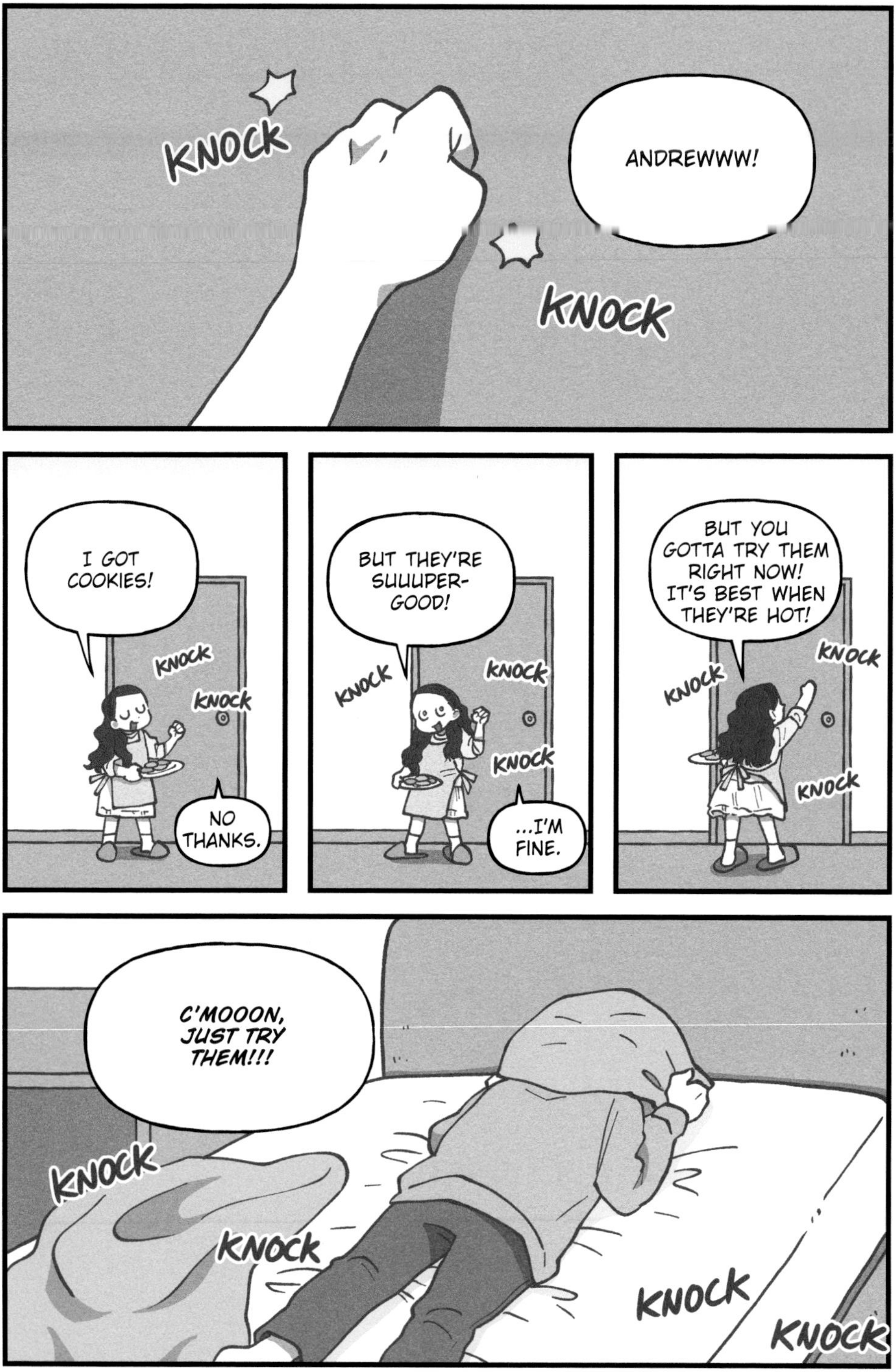
KNOCK
ANDREWWW!
KNOCK
I GOT COOKIES!
KNOCK
KNOCK
NO THANKS.
BUT THEY'RE SUUUPER-GOOD!
KNOCK
KNOCK
KNOCK
...I'M FINE.
BUT YOU GOTTA TRY THEM RIGHT NOW! IT'S BEST WHEN THEY'RE HOT!
KNOCK
KNOCK
KNOCK
C'MOOON, JUST TRY THEM!!!
KNOCK
KNOCK
KNOCK
KNOCK

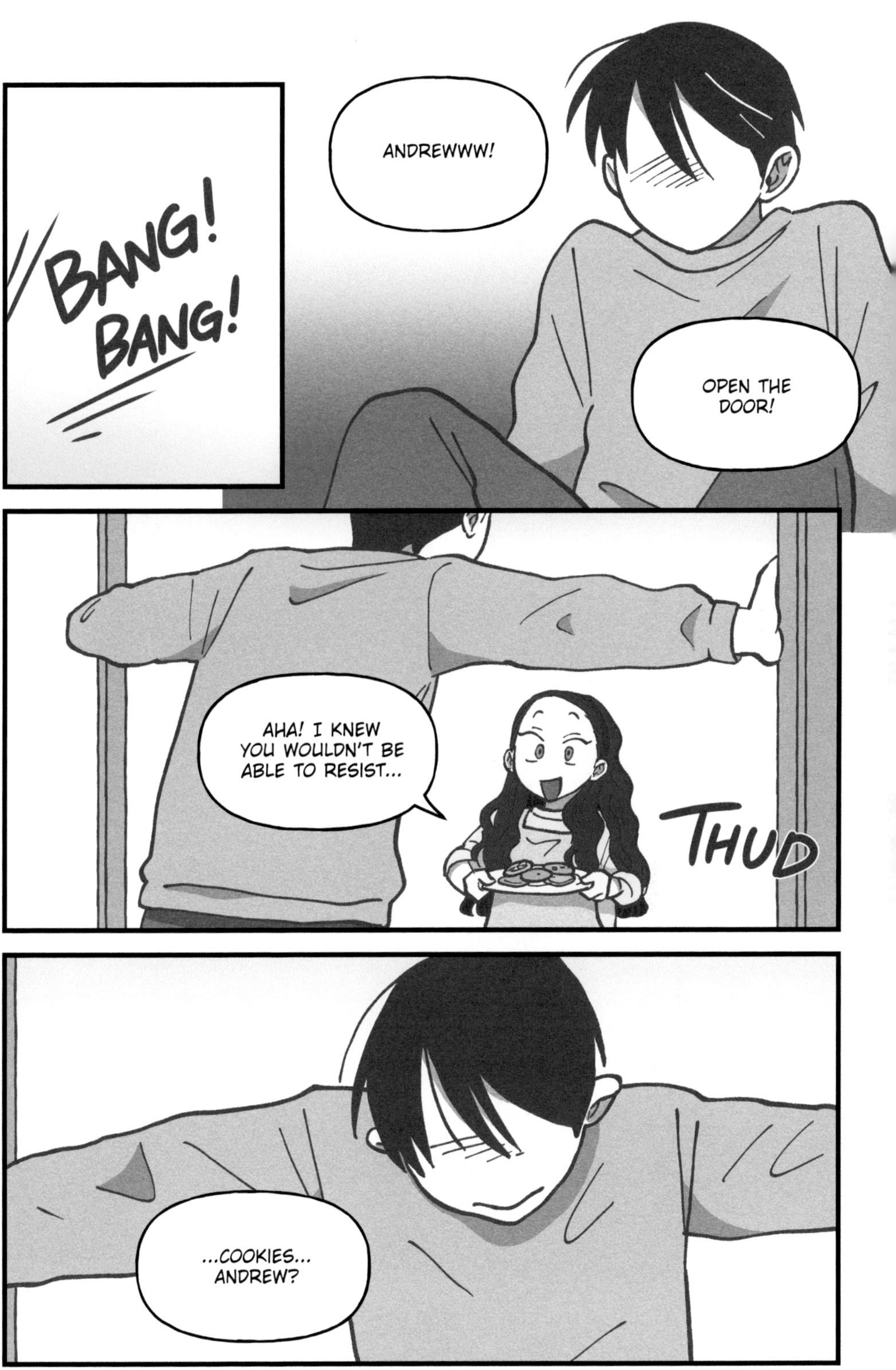
BANG! BANG!
ANDREWWW!
OPEN THE DOOR!
AHA! I KNEW YOU WOULDN'T BE ABLE TO RESIST...
THUD
...COOKIES... ANDREW?

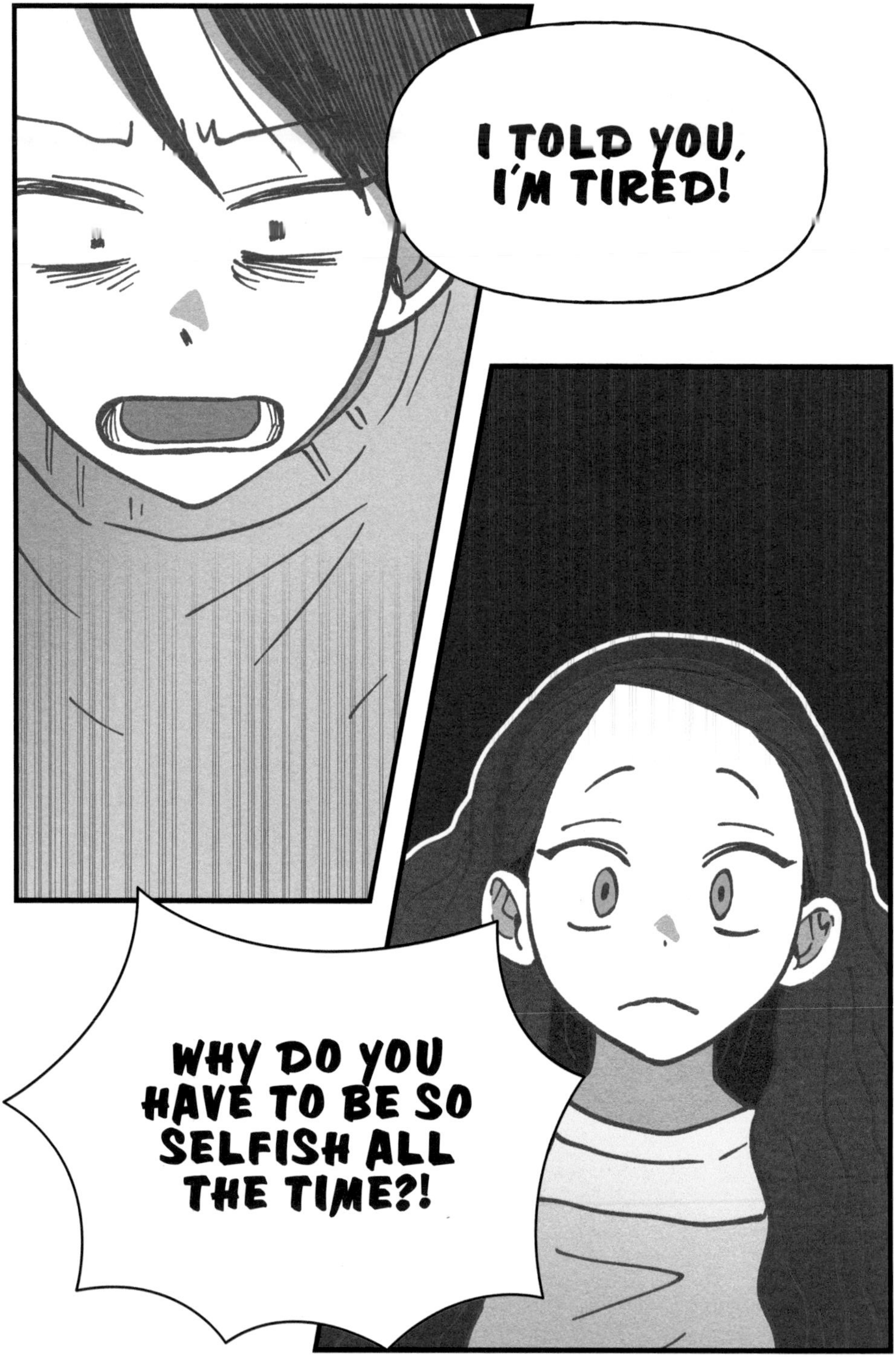
I TOLD YOU, I'M TIRED!
WHY DO YOU HAVE TO BE SO SELFISH ALL THE TIME?!

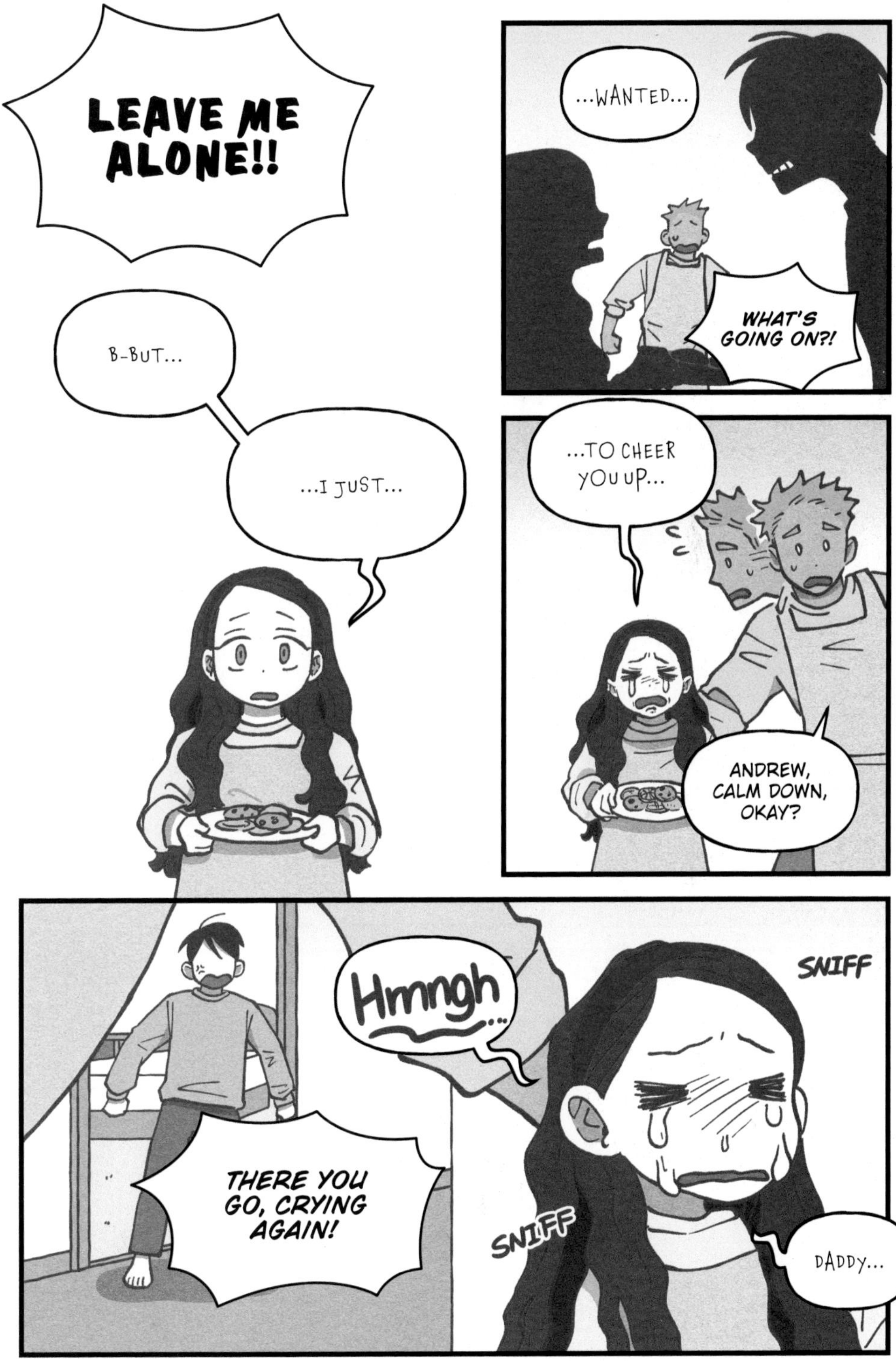
LEAVE ME ALONE!!
...WANTED...
WHAT'S GOING ON?!
B-BUT...
...I JUST...
...TO CHEER YOU UP...
ANDREW, CALM DOWN, OKAY?
Hmngh...
SNIFF
THERE YOU GO, CRYING AGAIN!
SNIFF
DADDY...

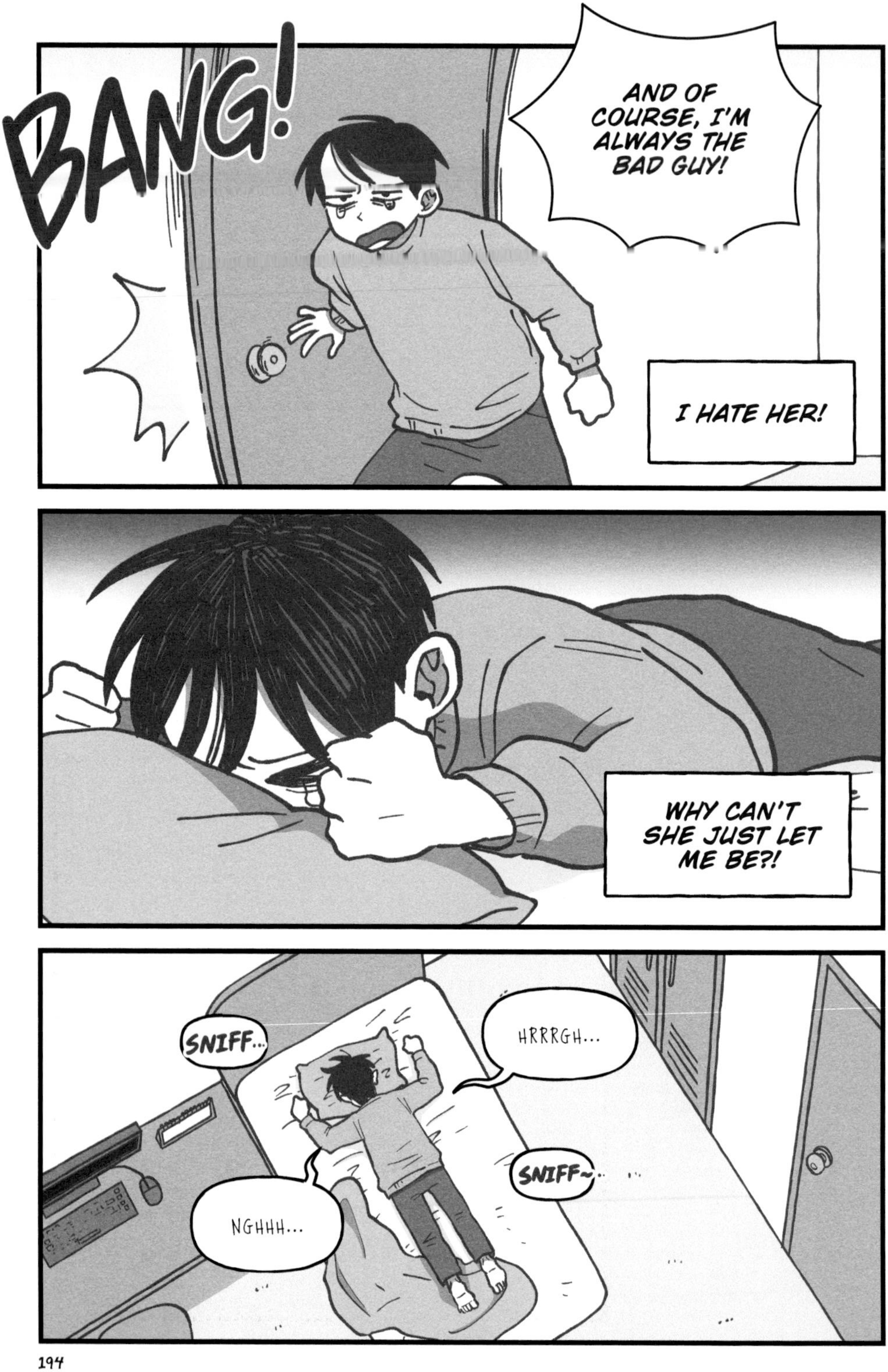
BANG!
AND OF COURSE, I'M ALWAYS THE BAD GUY!
I HATE HER!
WHY CAN'T SHE JUST LET ME BE?!
SNIFF...
HRRRGH...
SNIFF~...
NGHHH...

Chapter 10

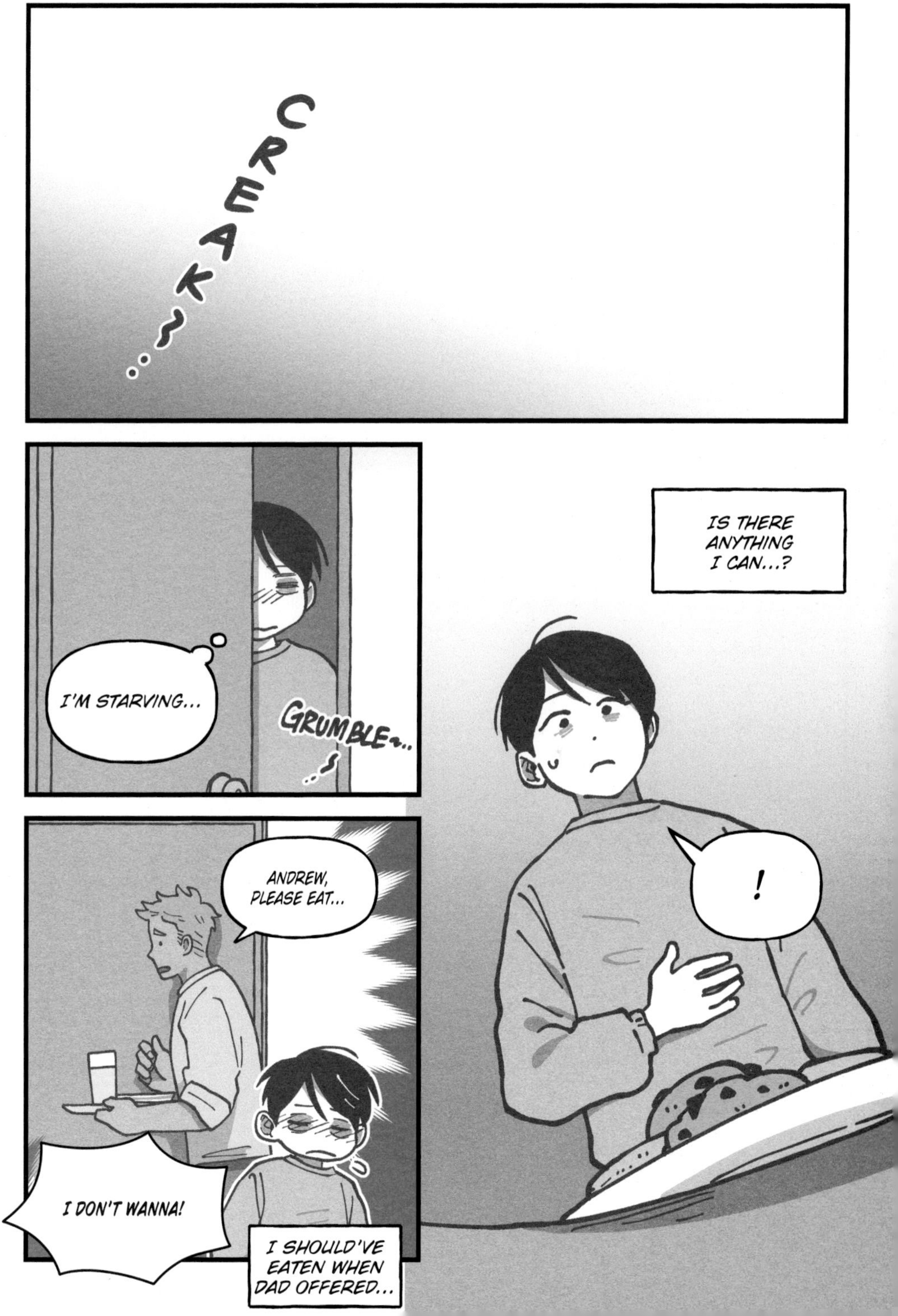
CREAK...
IS THERE ANYTHING I CAN...?
I'M STARVING...
GRUMBLE...
!
ANDREW, PLEASE EAT...
I DON'T WANNA!
I SHOULD'VE EATEN WHEN DAD OFFERED...

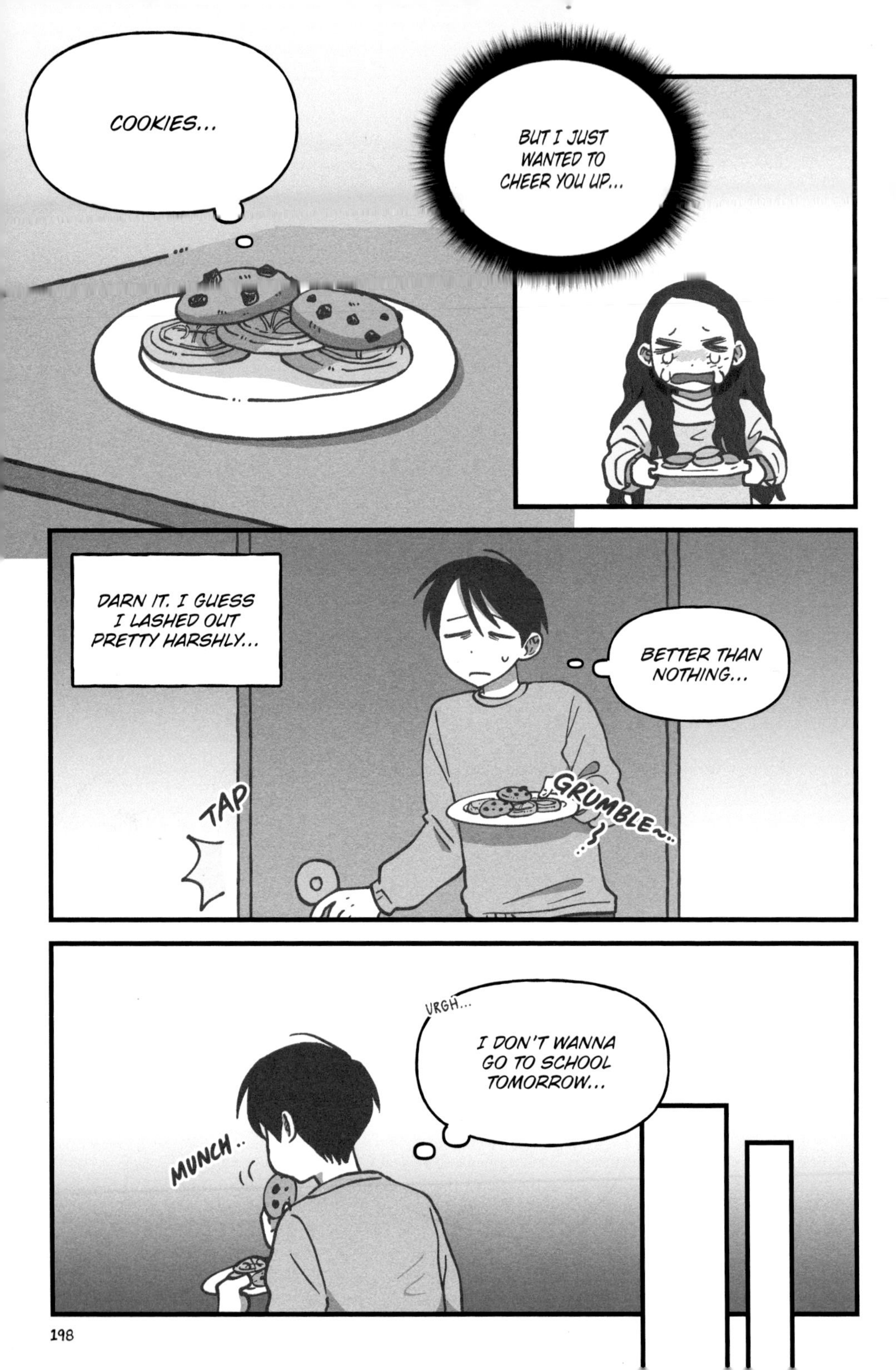
COOKIES...
BUT I JUST WANTED TO CHEER YOU UP...
DARN IT. I GUESS I LASHED OUT PRETTY HARSHLY...
BETTER THAN NOTHING...
TAP
GRUMBLE~...
URGH...
I DON'T WANNA GO TO SCHOOL TOMORROW...
MUNCH..

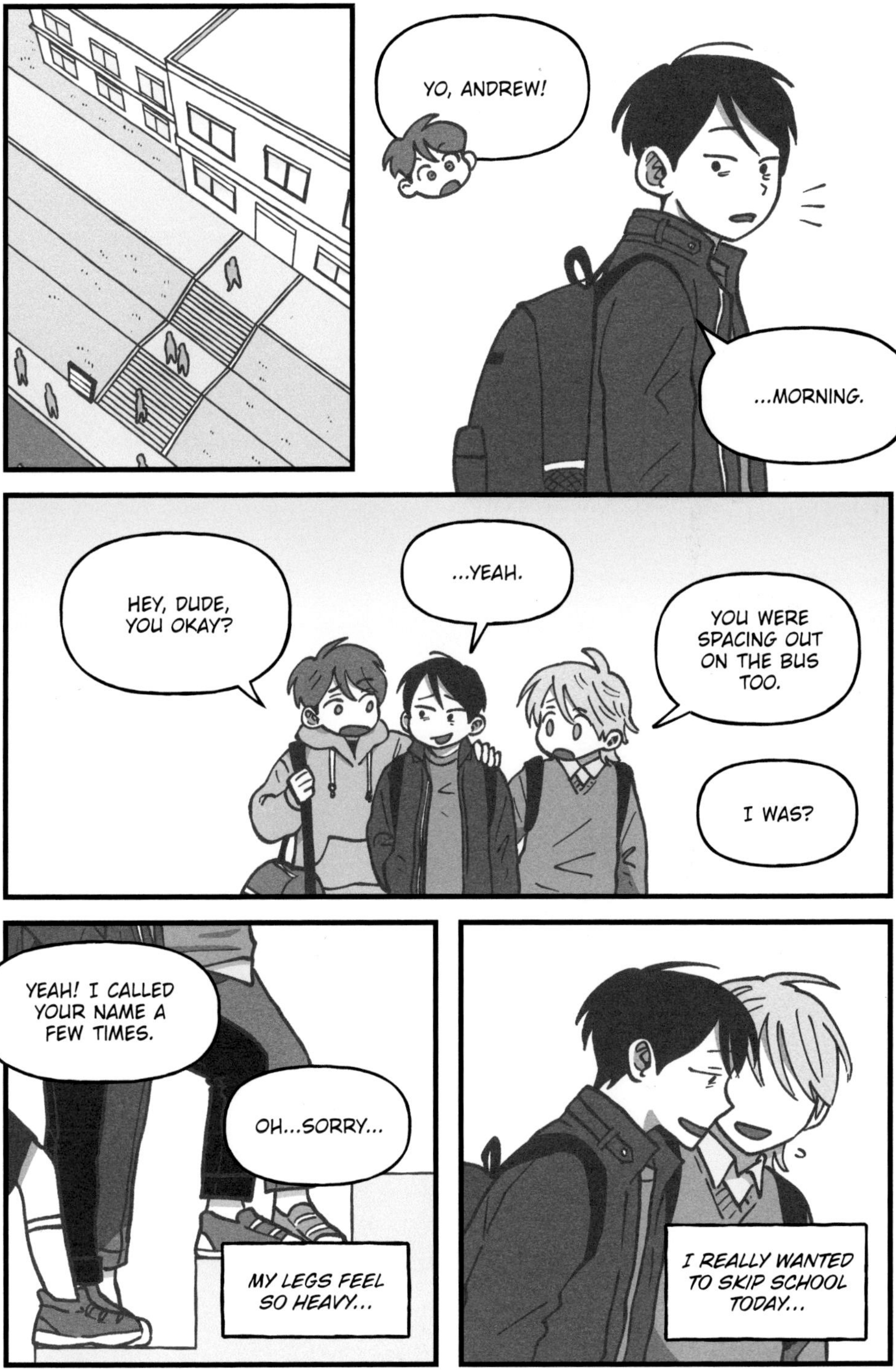
YO, ANDREW!
...MORNING.
HEY, DUDE, YOU OKAY?
...YEAH.
YOU WERE SPACING OUT ON THE BUS TOO.
I WAS?
YEAH! I CALLED YOUR NAME A FEW TIMES.
OH...SORRY...
MY LEGS FEEL SO HEAVY...
I REALLY WANTED TO SKIP SCHOOL TODAY...

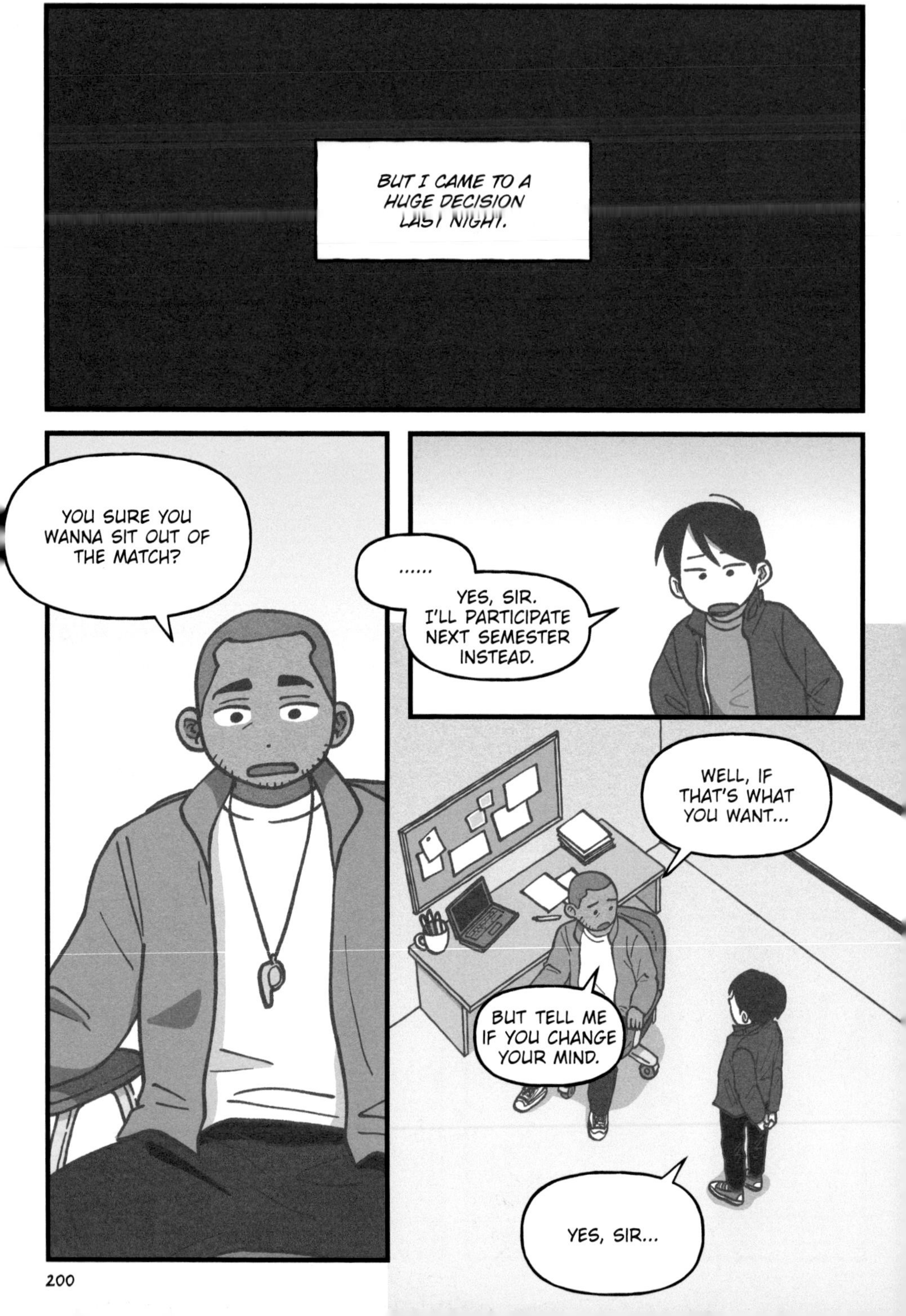
BUT I CAME TO A HUGE DECISION LAST NIGHT.
YOU SURE YOU WANNA SIT OUT OF THE MATCH?
......
YES, SIR. I'LL PARTICIPATE NEXT SEMESTER INSTEAD.
WELL, IF THAT'S WHAT YOU WANT...
BUT TELL ME IF YOU CHANGE YOUR MIND.
YES, SIR...

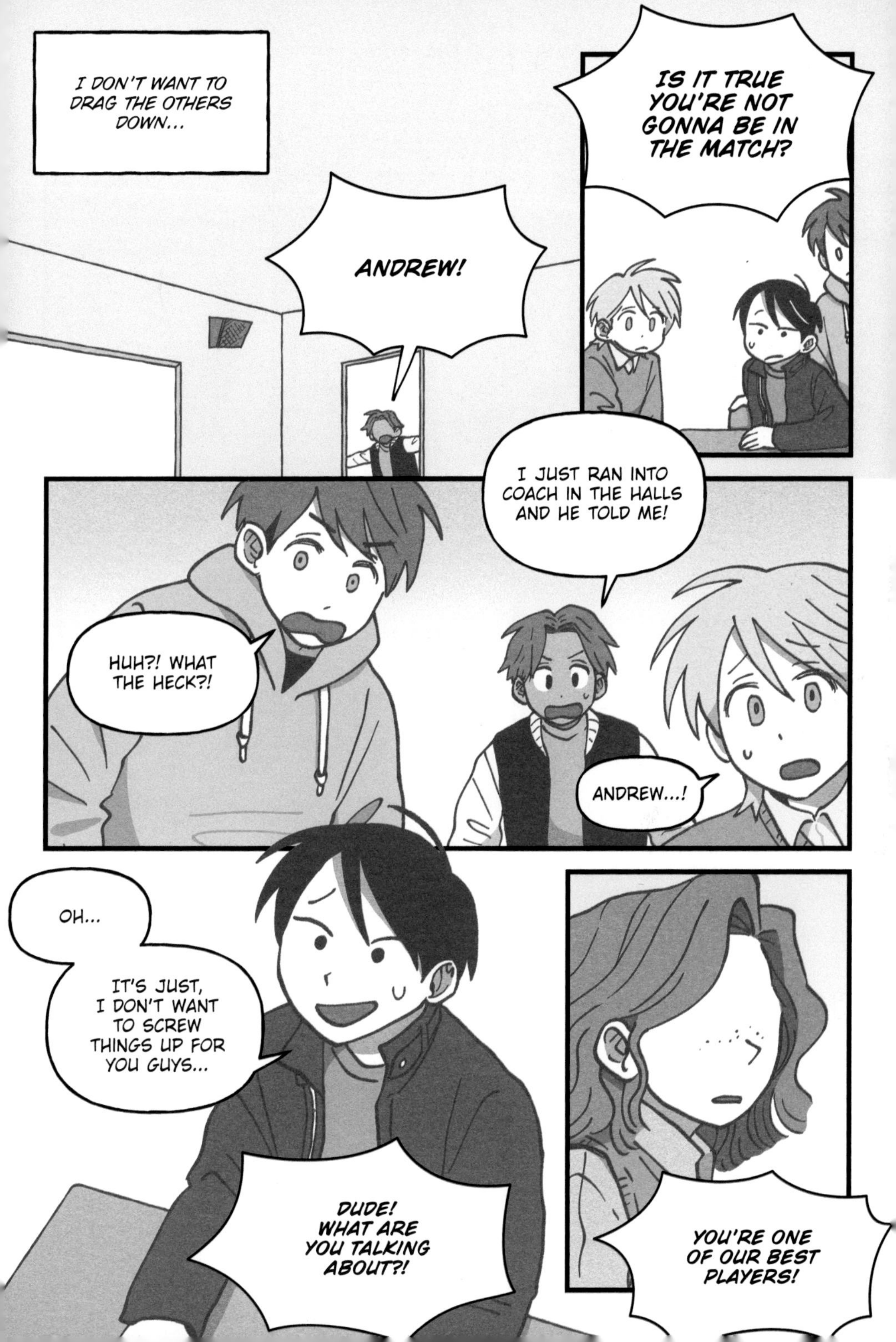
I DON'T WANT TO DRAG THE OTHERS DOWN...
IS IT TRUE YOU'RE NOT GONNA BE IN THE MATCH?
ANDREW!
I JUST RAN INTO COACH IN THE HALLS AND HE TOLD ME!
HUH?! WHAT THE HECK?!
ANDREW...!
OH...
IT'S JUST, I DON'T WANT TO SCREW THINGS UP FOR YOU GUYS...
DUDE! WHAT ARE YOU TALKING ABOUT?!
YOU'RE ONE OF OUR BEST PLAYERS!

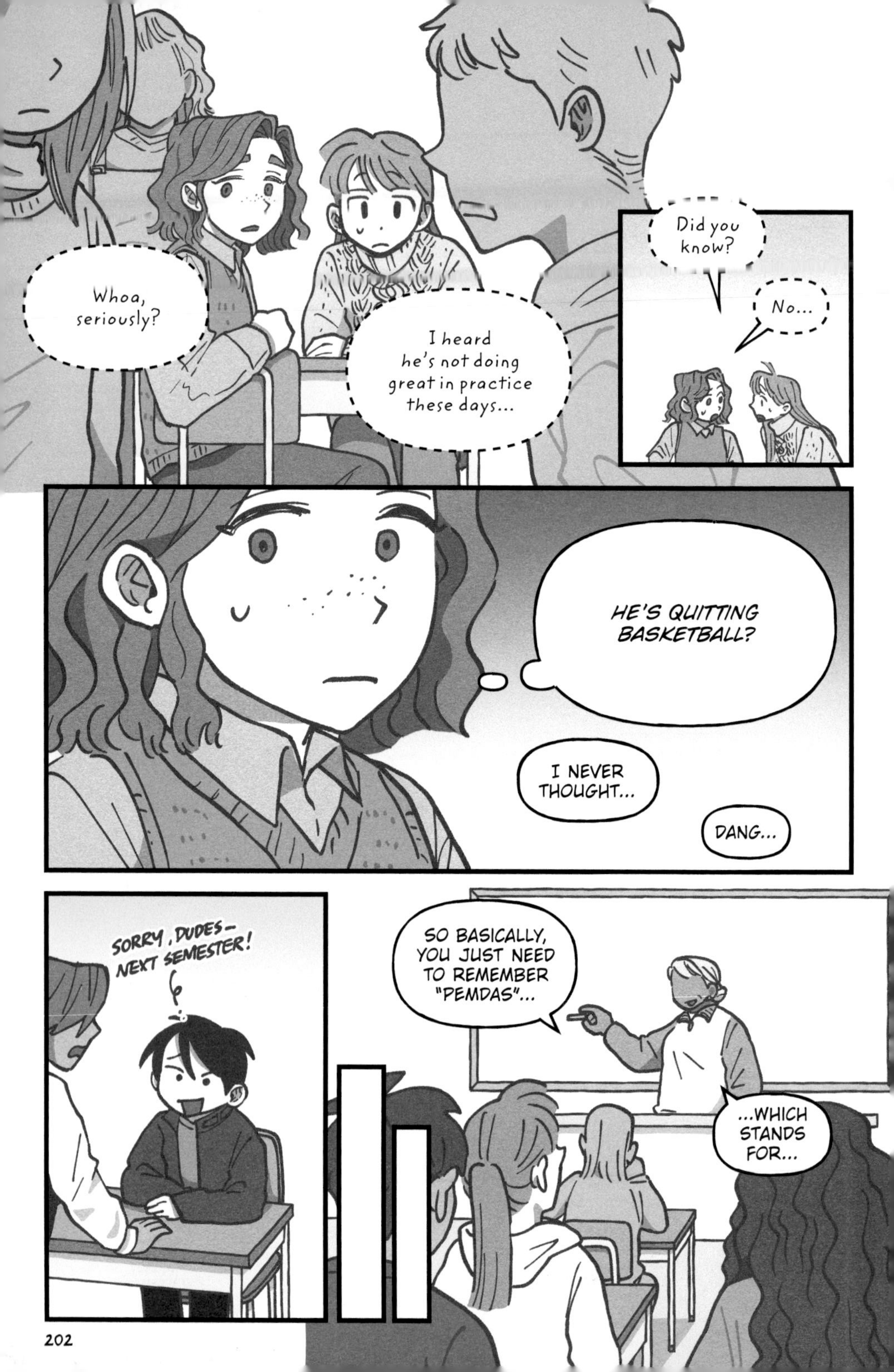
Whoa, seriously?
I heard he's not doing great in practice these days...
Did you know?
No...
HE'S QUITTING BASKETBALL?
I NEVER THOUGHT...
DANG...
SORRY, DUDES— NEXT SEMESTER!
SO BASICALLY, YOU JUST NEED TO REMEMBER "PEMDAS"...
...WHICH STANDS FOR...

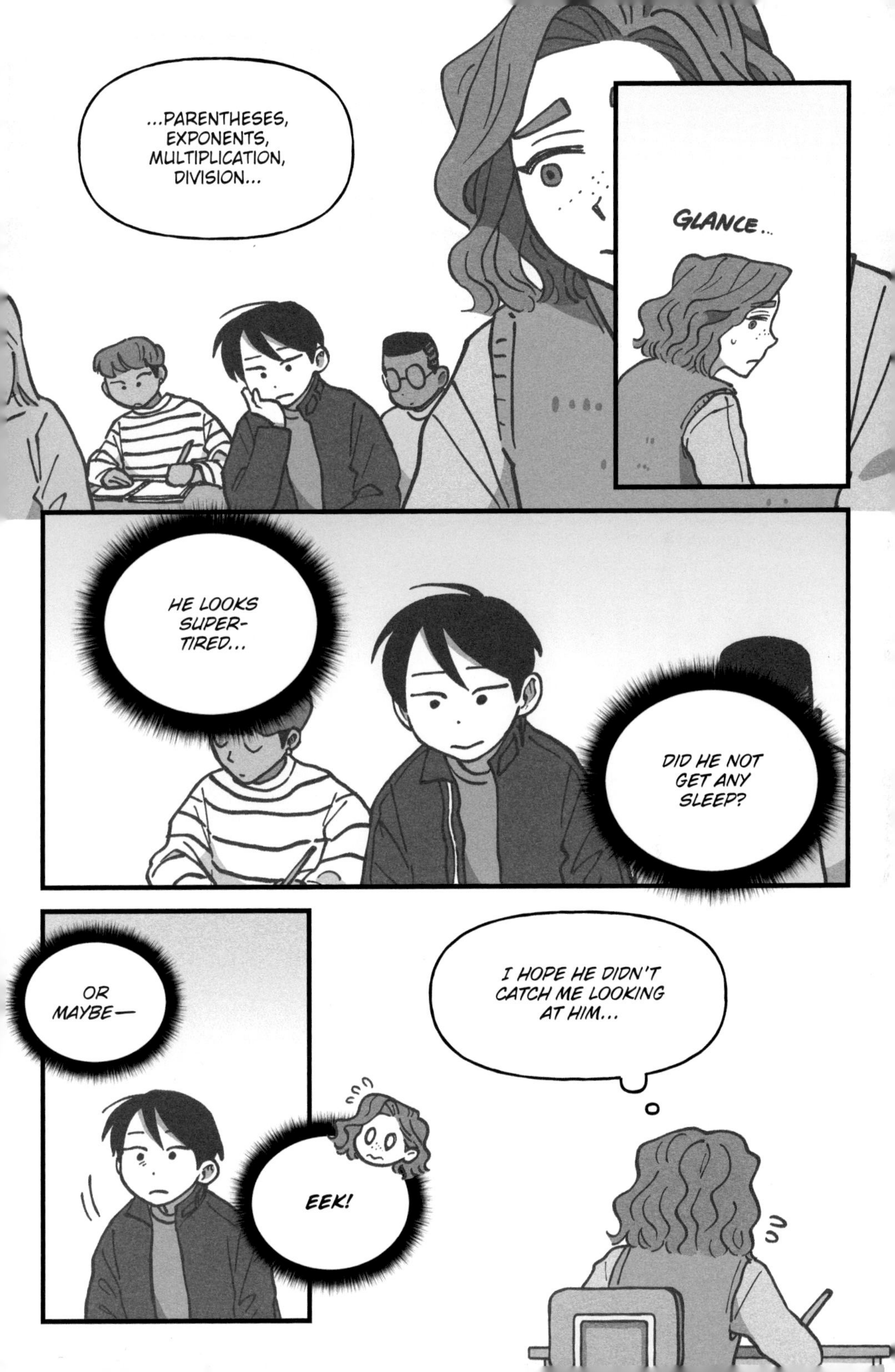
...PARENTHESES, EXPONENTS, MULTIPLICATION, DIVISION...
GLANCE...
HE LOOKS SUPER-TIRED...
DID HE NOT GET ANY SLEEP?
OR MAYBE—
EEK!
I HOPE HE DIDN'T CATCH ME LOOKING AT HIM...

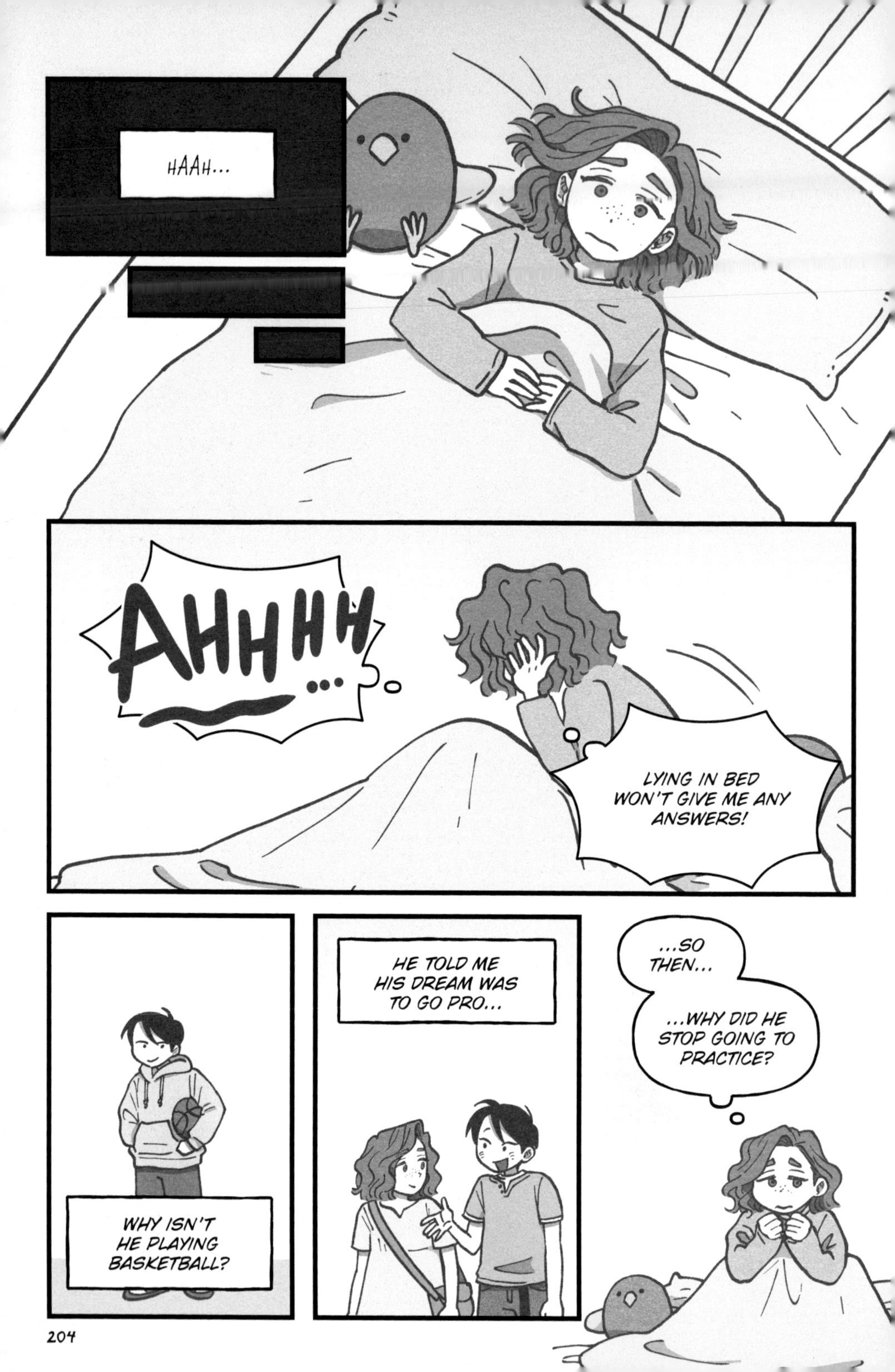
[redacted]
HAAH...
[redacted]
AHHHH...
LYING IN BED WON'T GIVE ME ANY ANSWERS!
WHY ISN'T HE PLAYING BASKETBALL?
HE TOLD ME HIS DREAM WAS TO GO PRO...
...SO THEN...
...WHY DID HE STOP GOING TO PRACTICE?

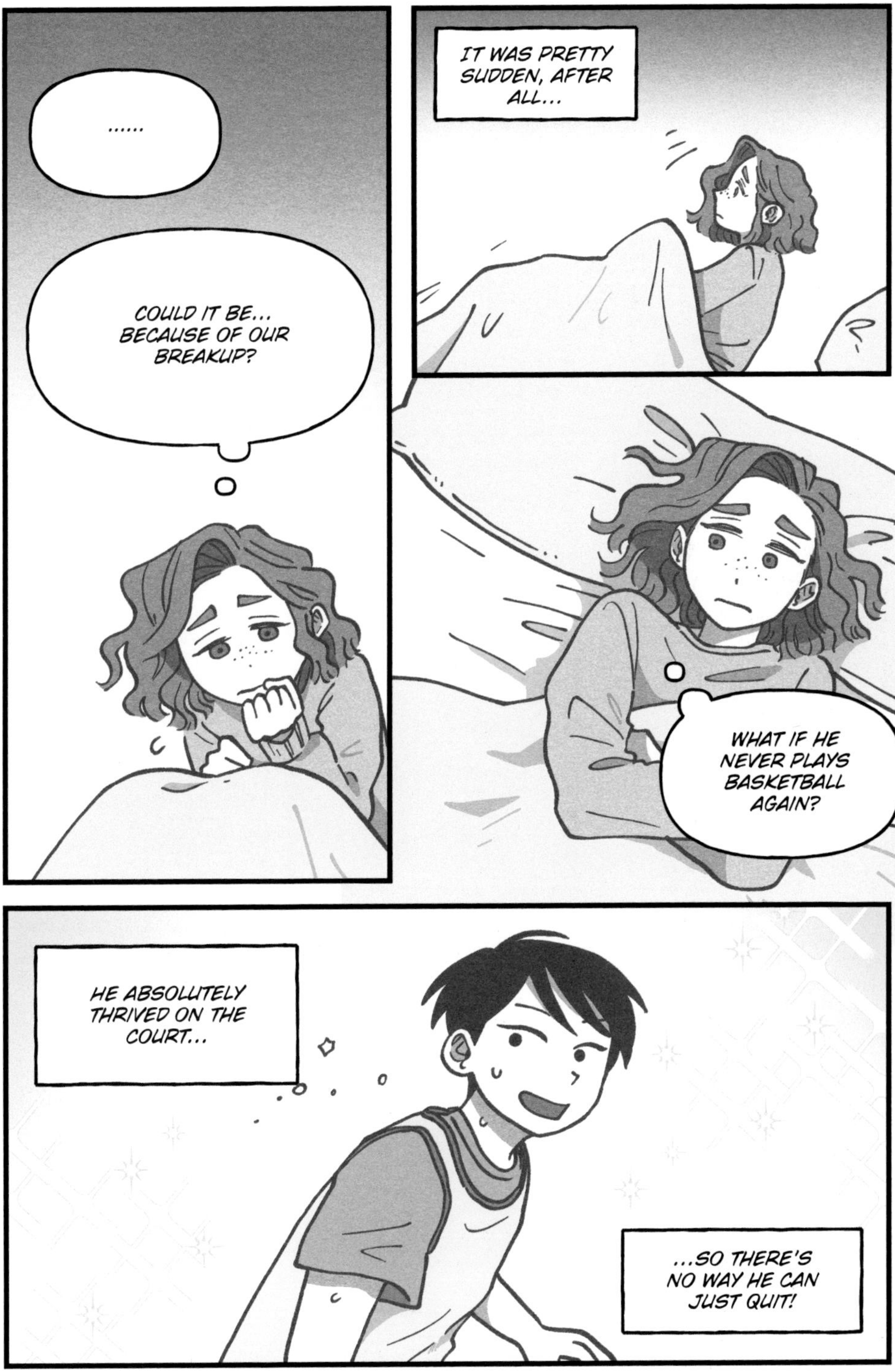
......
COULD IT BE... BECAUSE OF OUR BREAKUP?
IT WAS PRETTY SUDDEN, AFTER ALL...
WHAT IF HE NEVER PLAYS BASKETBALL AGAIN?
HE ABSOLUTELY THRIVED ON THE COURT...
...SO THERE'S NO WAY HE CAN JUST QUIT!

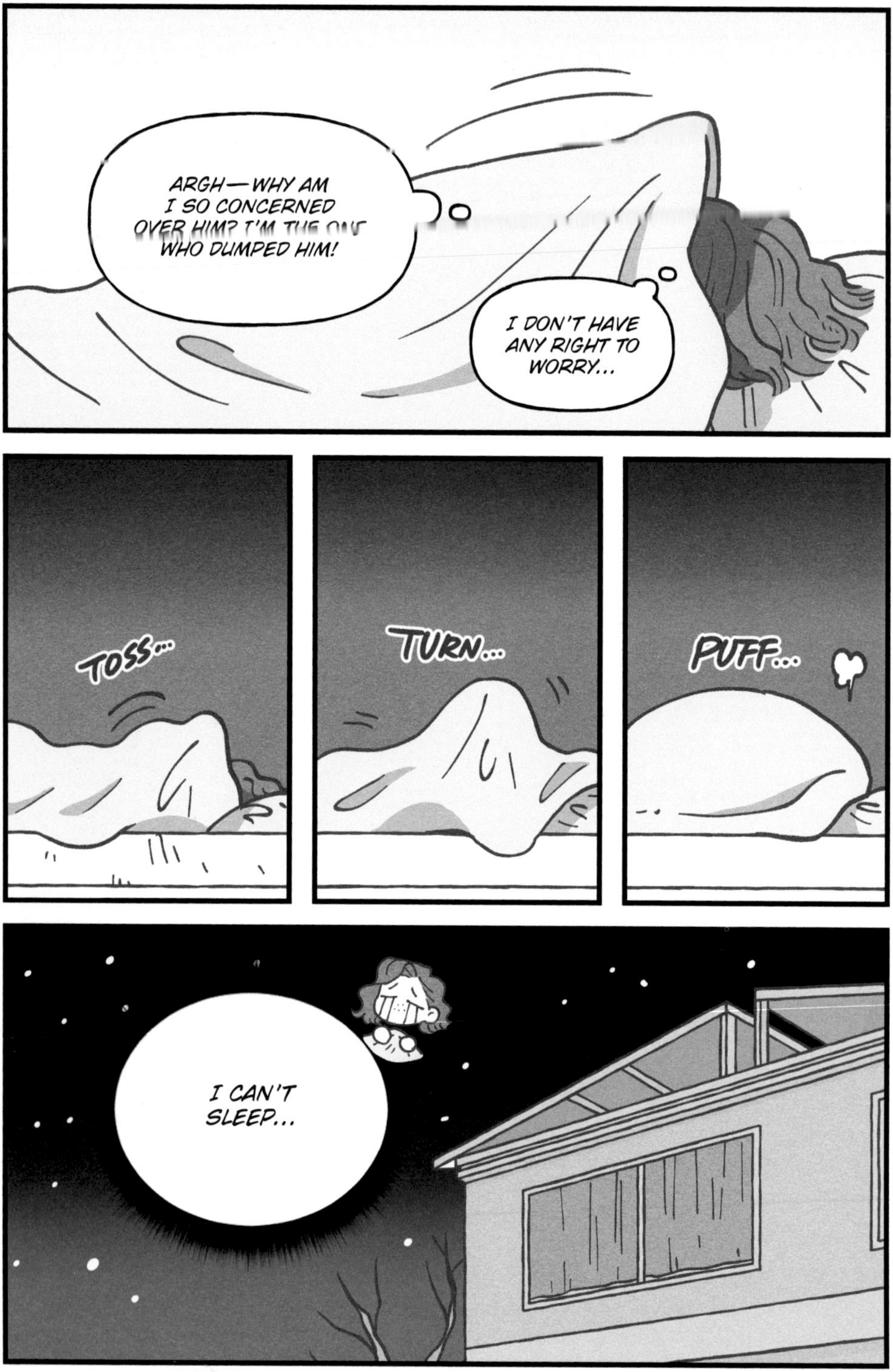
ARGH—WHY AM I SO CONCERNED OVER HIM? I'M THE ONE WHO DUMPED HIM!
I DON'T HAVE ANY RIGHT TO WORRY...
TOSS...
TURN...
PUFF...
I CAN'T SLEEP...

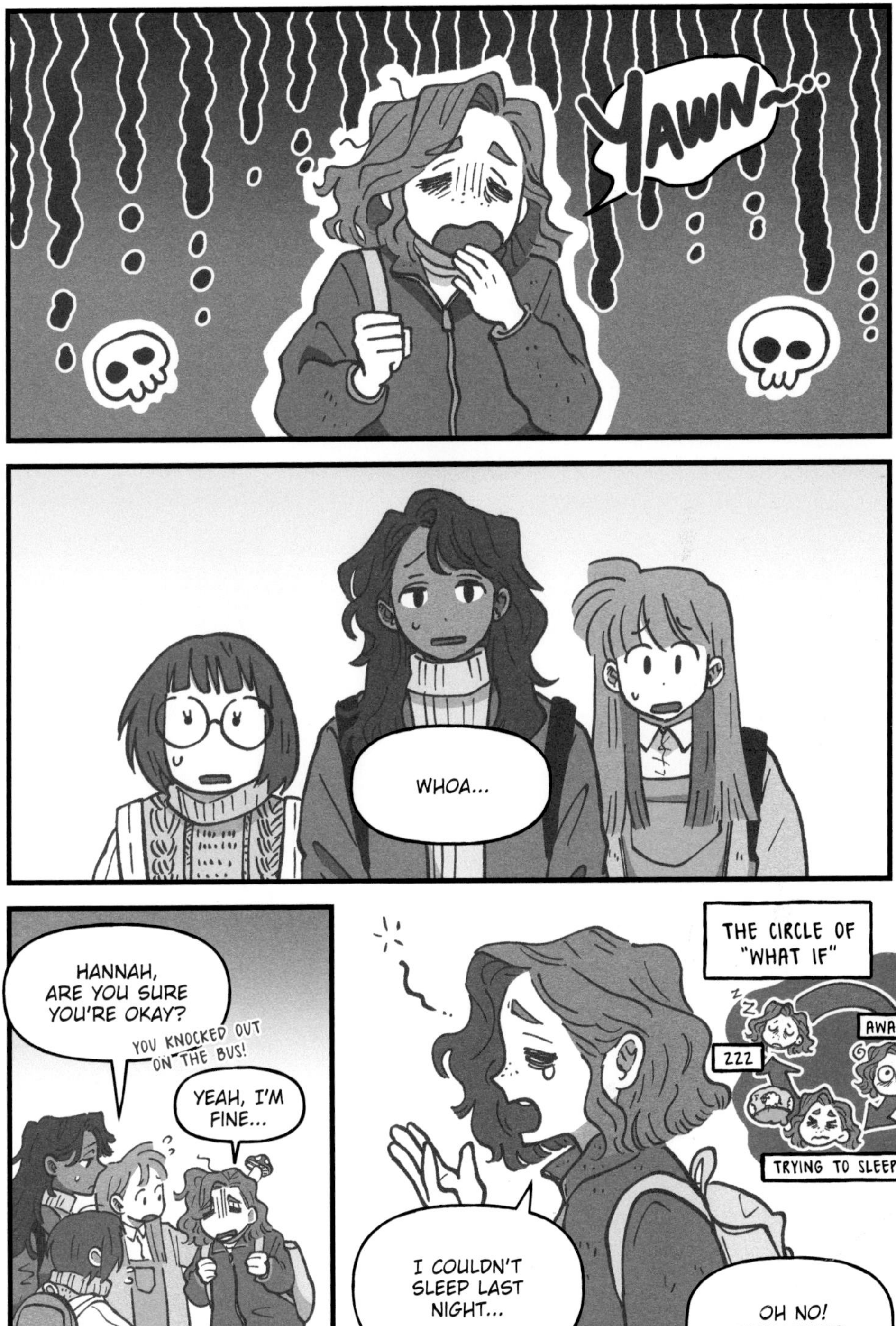
YAWN~
WHOA...
HANNAH, ARE YOU SURE YOU'RE OKAY?
YOU KNOCKED OUT ON THE BUS!
YEAH, I'M FINE...
THE CIRCLE OF "WHAT IF"
AWAKE
ZZZ
TRYING TO SLEEP
I COULDN'T SLEEP LAST NIGHT...
OH NO! WHY NOT?

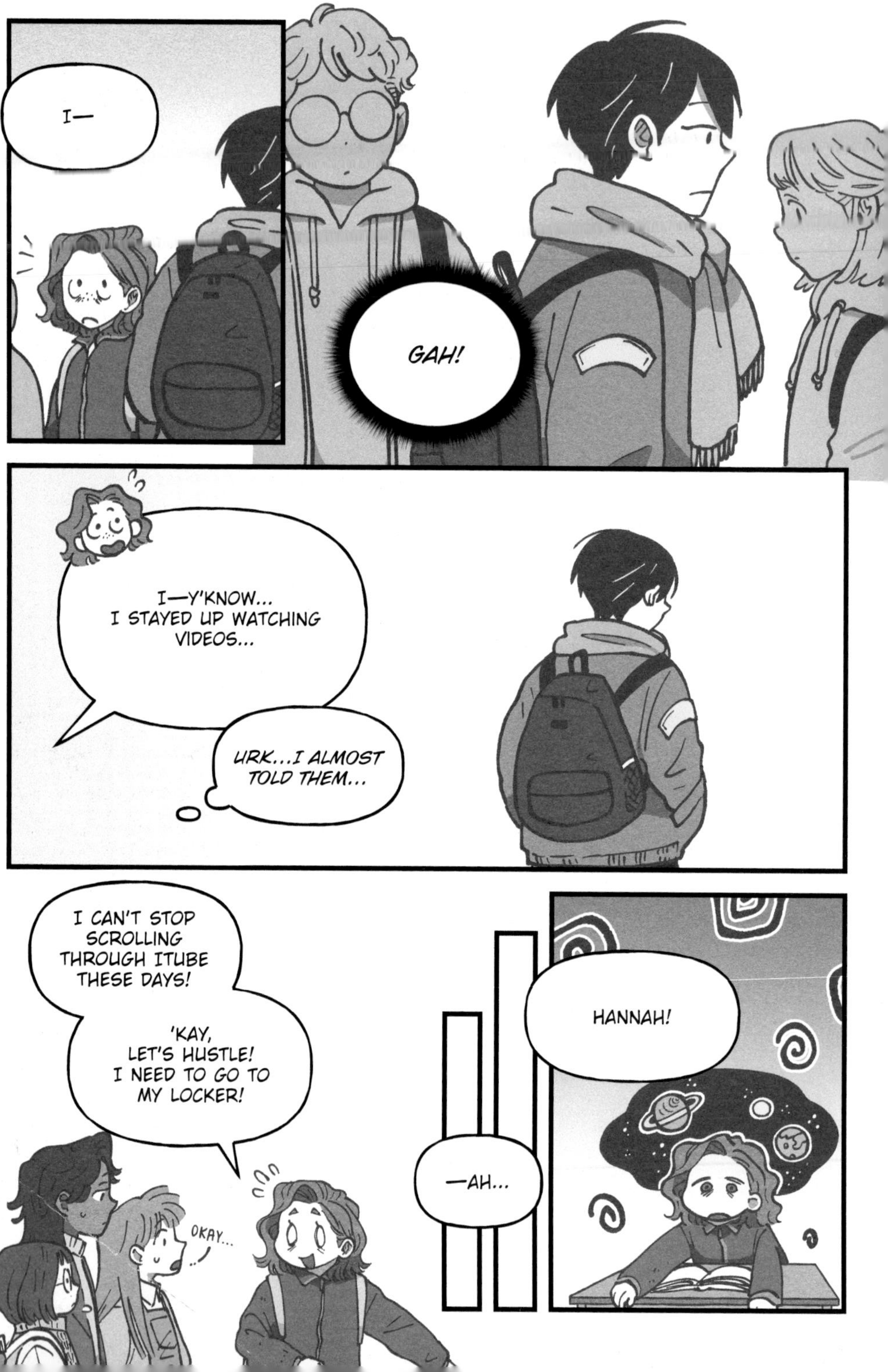
I—
GAH!
I—Y'KNOW... I STAYED UP WATCHING VIDEOS...
URK...I ALMOST TOLD THEM...
I CAN'T STOP SCROLLING THROUGH ITUBE THESE DAYS!
'KAY, LET'S HUSTLE! I NEED TO GO TO MY LOCKER!
OKAY...
HANNAH!
—AH...

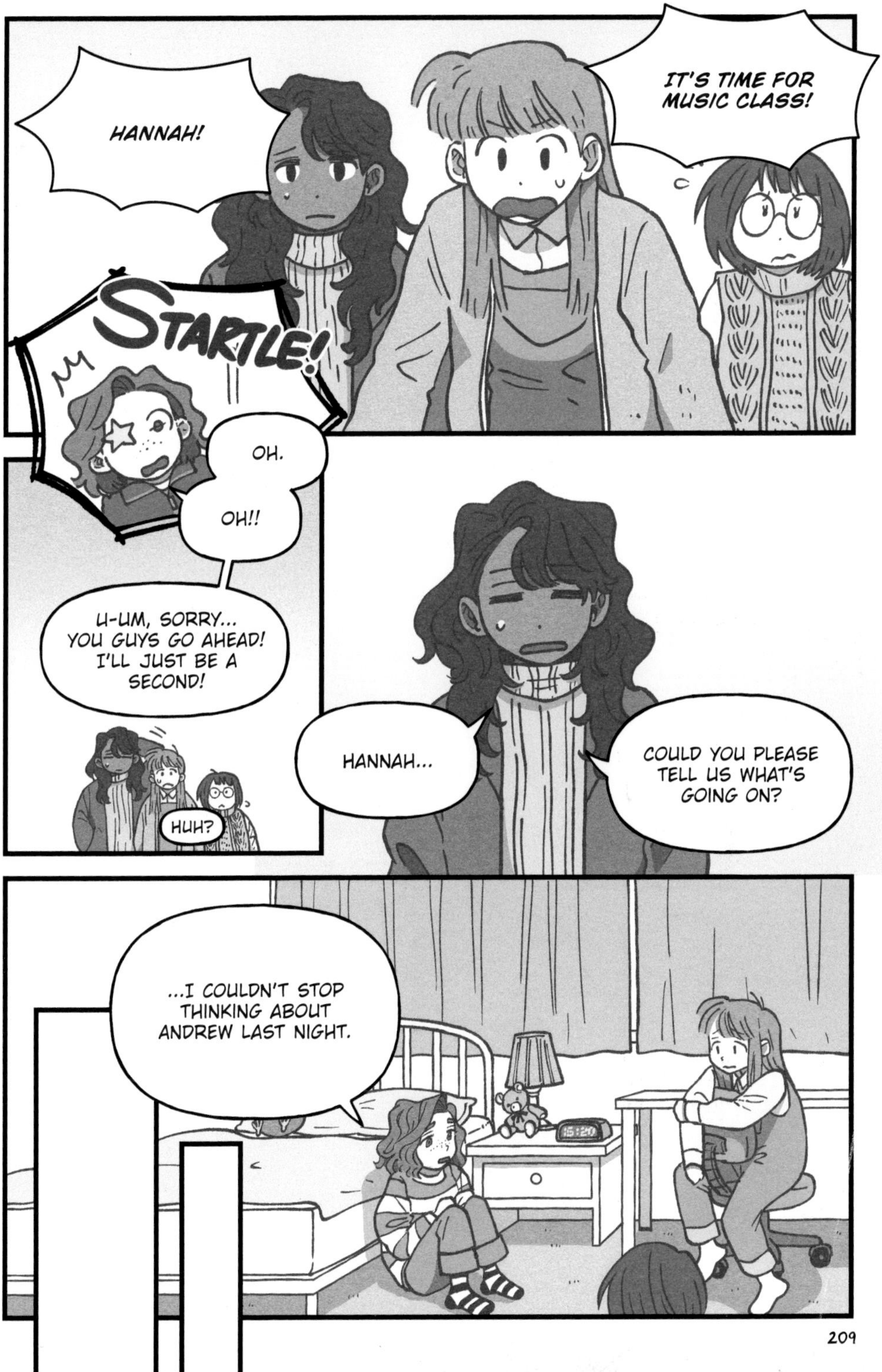
HANNAH!
IT'S TIME FOR MUSIC CLASS!
STARTLE!
OH.
OH!!
U-UM, SORRY... YOU GUYS GO AHEAD! I'LL JUST BE A SECOND!
HUH?
HANNAH...
COULD YOU PLEASE TELL US WHAT'S GOING ON?
...I COULDN'T STOP THINKING ABOUT ANDREW LAST NIGHT.
15:20

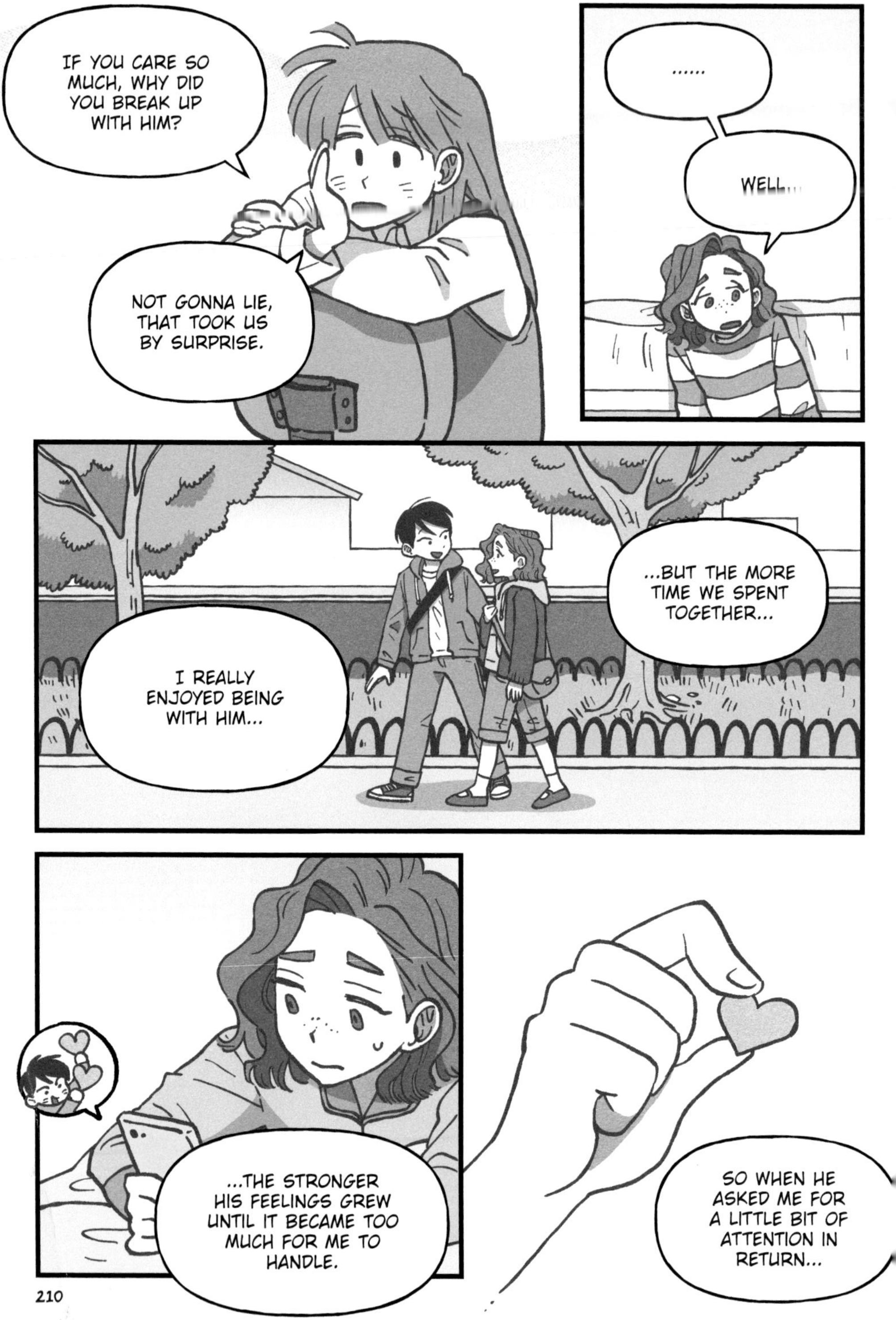
IF YOU CARE SO MUCH, WHY DID YOU BREAK UP WITH HIM?
NOT GONNA LIE, THAT TOOK US BY SURPRISE.
......
WELL...
I REALLY ENJOYED BEING WITH HIM...
...BUT THE MORE TIME WE SPENT TOGETHER...
...THE STRONGER HIS FEELINGS GREW UNTIL IT BECAME TOO MUCH FOR ME TO HANDLE.
SO WHEN HE ASKED ME FOR A LITTLE BIT OF ATTENTION IN RETURN...

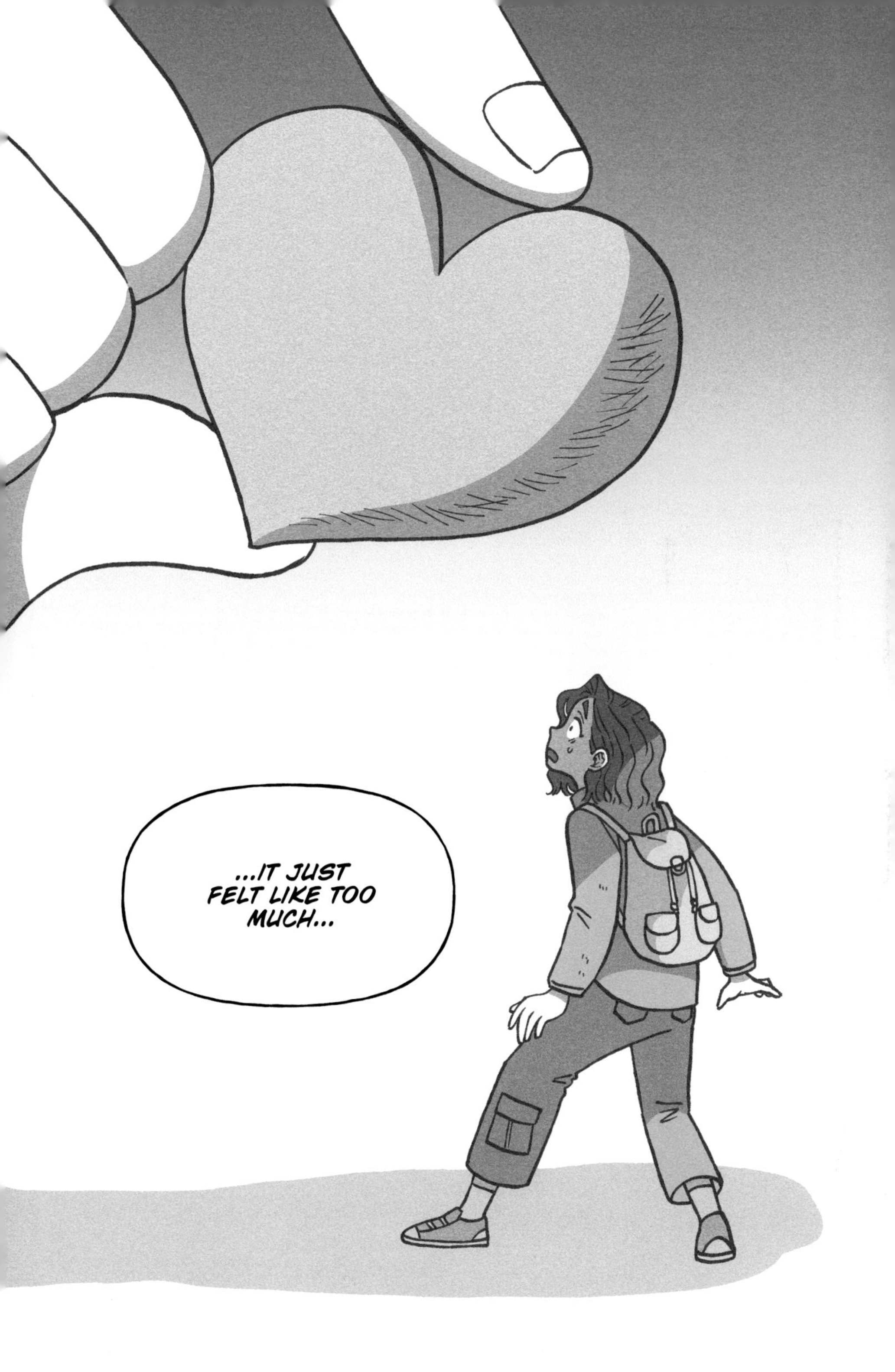
...IT JUST FELT LIKE TOO MUCH...

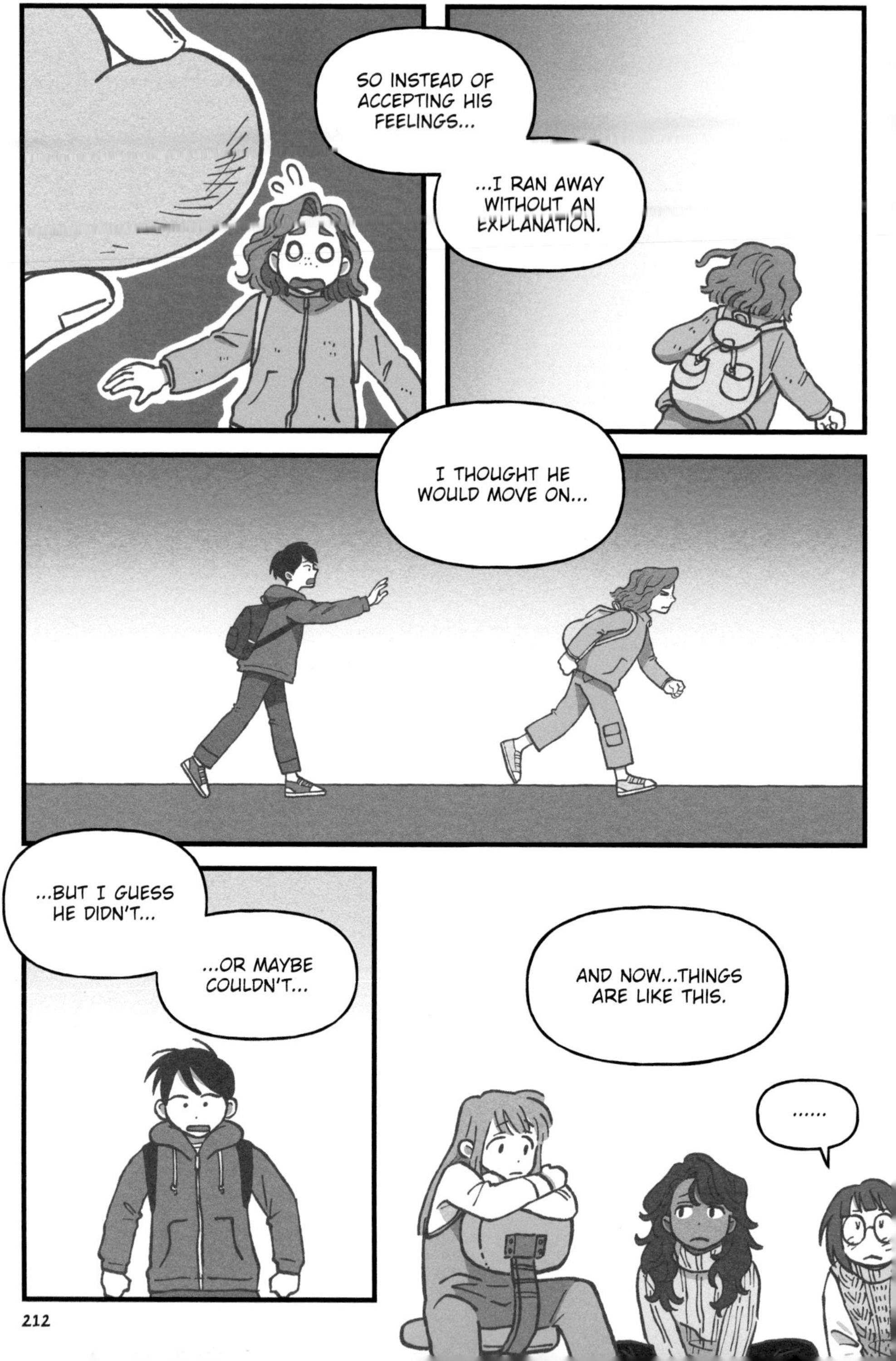
SO INSTEAD OF ACCEPTING HIS FEELINGS...
...I RAN AWAY WITHOUT AN EXPLANATION.
I THOUGHT HE WOULD MOVE ON...
...BUT I GUESS HE DIDN'T...
...OR MAYBE COULDN'T...
AND NOW...THINGS ARE LIKE THIS.
......

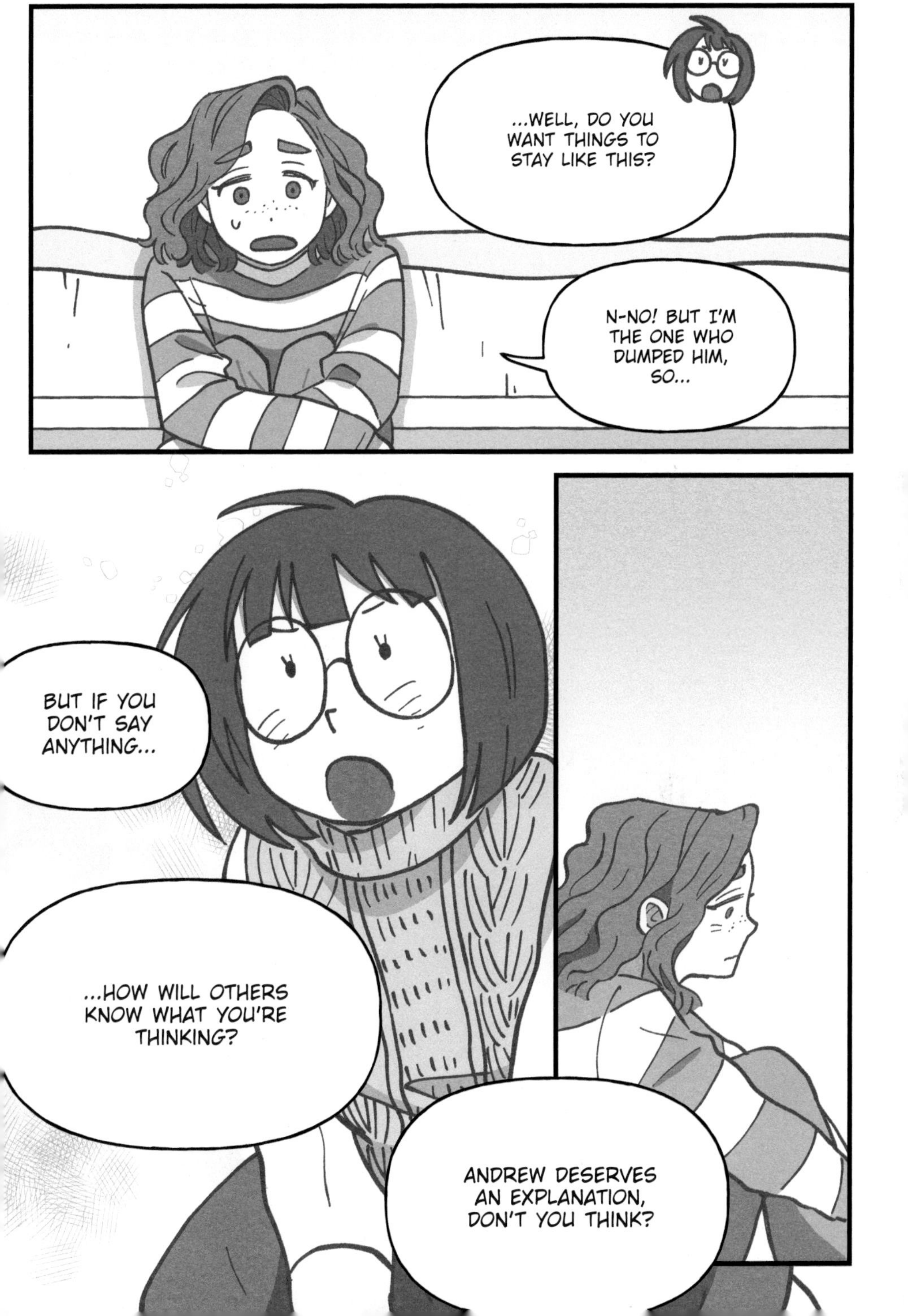
...WELL, DO YOU WANT THINGS TO STAY LIKE THIS?
N-NO! BUT I'M THE ONE WHO DUMPED HIM, SO...
BUT IF YOU DON'T SAY ANYTHING...
...HOW WILL OTHERS KNOW WHAT YOU'RE THINKING?
ANDREW DESERVES AN EXPLANATION, DON'T YOU THINK?

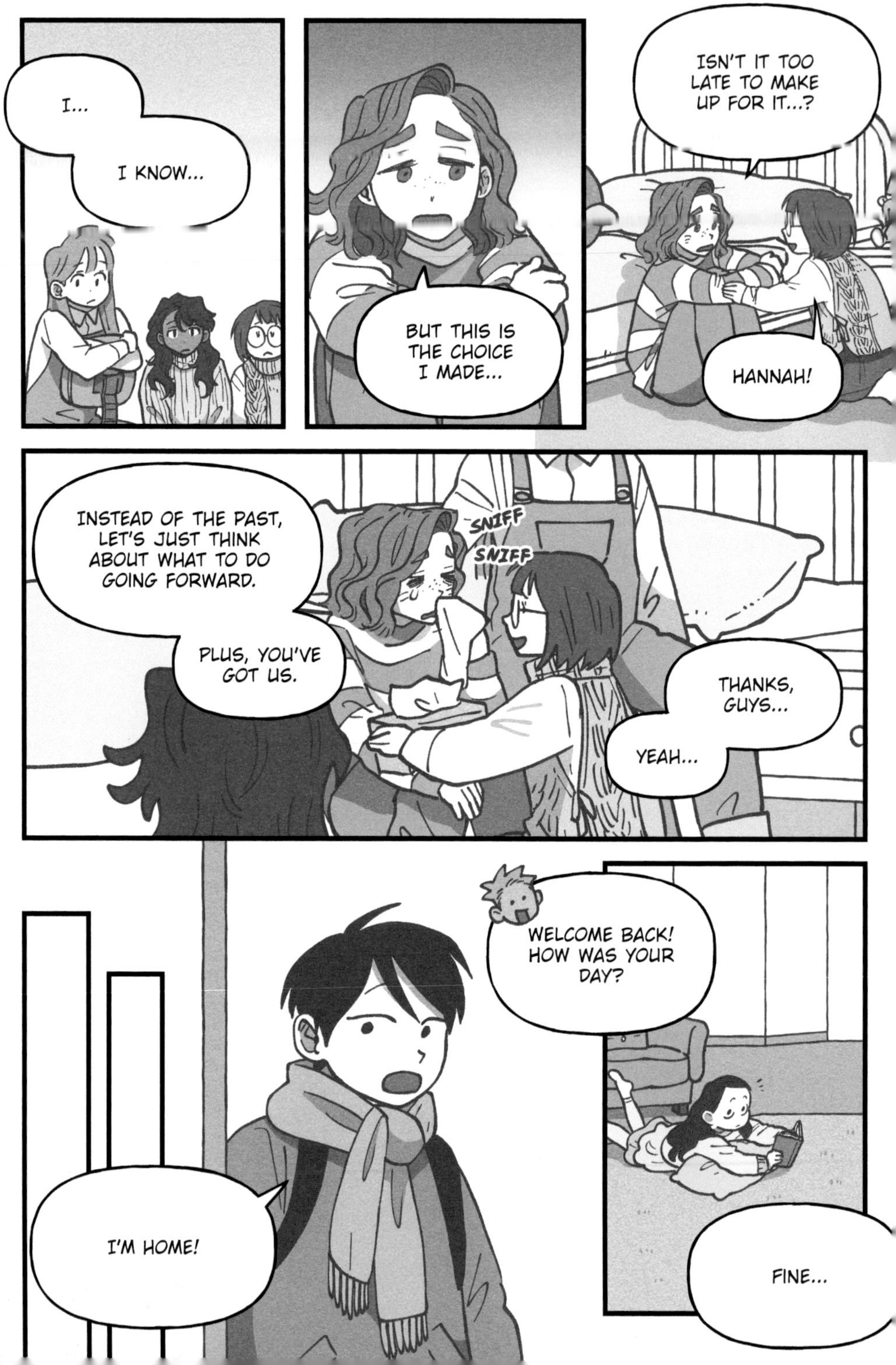
I...
I KNOW...
BUT THIS IS THE CHOICE I MADE...
ISN'T IT TOO LATE TO MAKE UP FOR IT...?
HANNAH!
INSTEAD OF THE PAST, LET'S JUST THINK ABOUT WHAT TO DO GOING FORWARD.
PLUS, YOU'VE GOT US.
SNIFF
SNIFF
THANKS, GUYS...
YEAH...
I'M HOME!
WELCOME BACK! HOW WAS YOUR DAY?
FINE...

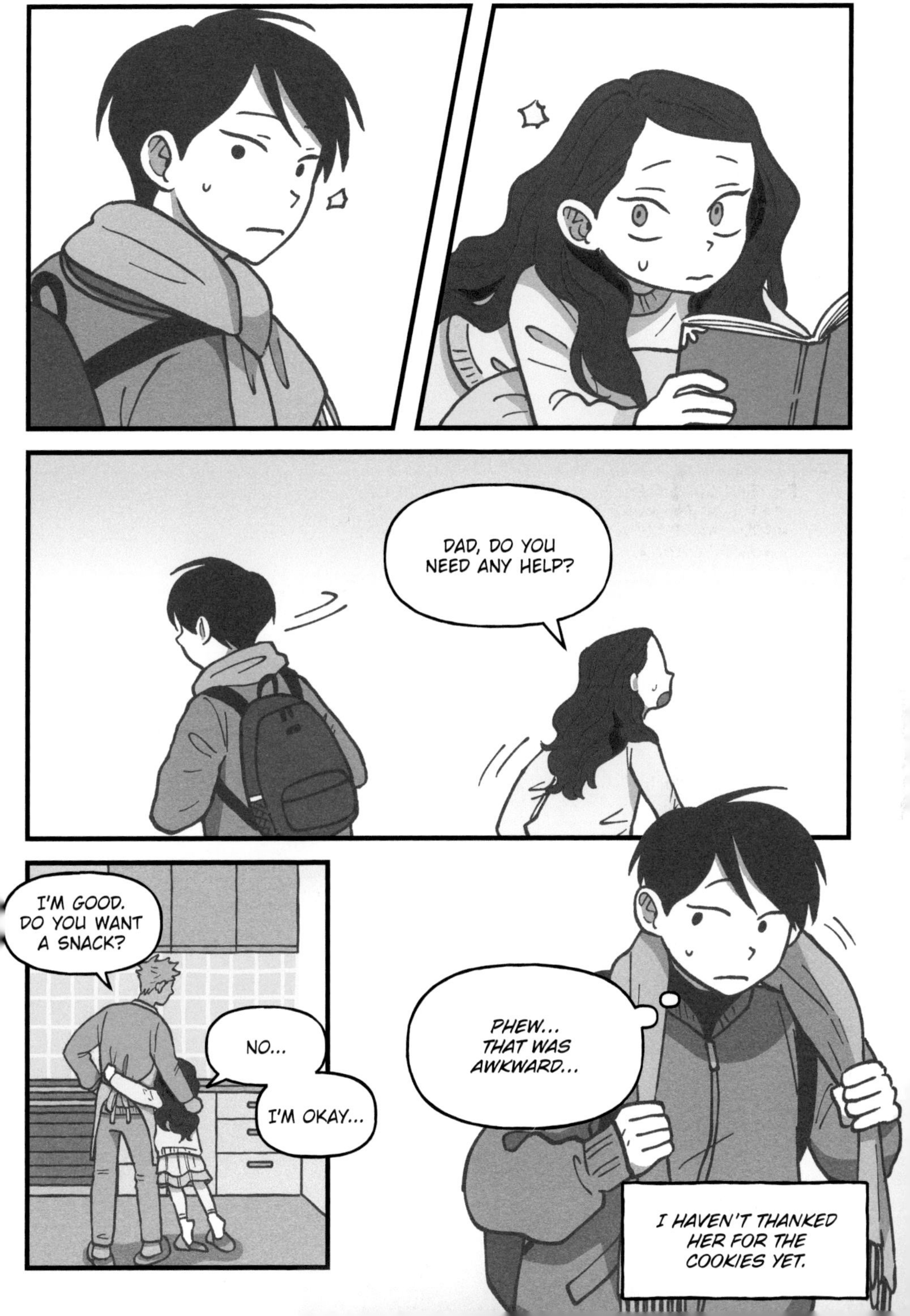
DAD, DO YOU NEED ANY HELP?
I'M GOOD. DO YOU WANT A SNACK?
NO...
I'M OKAY...
PHEW... THAT WAS AWKWARD...
I HAVEN'T THANKED HER FOR THE COOKIES YET.

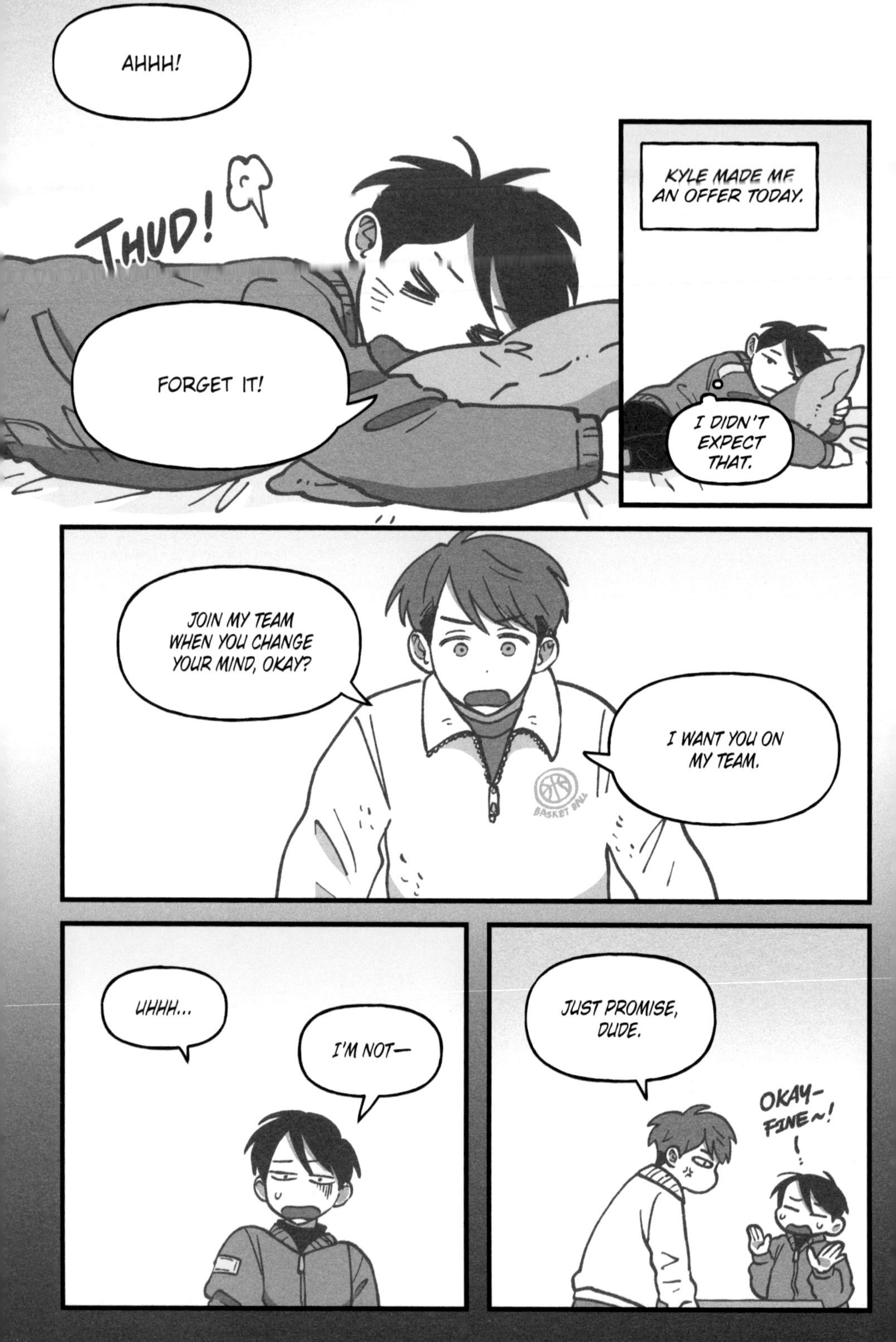
AHHH!
THUD!
FORGET IT!
KYLE MADE ME AN OFFER TODAY.
I DIDN'T EXPECT THAT.
JOIN MY TEAM WHEN YOU CHANGE YOUR MIND, OKAY?
I WANT YOU ON MY TEAM.
BASKET BALL
UHHH...
I'M NOT—
JUST PROMISE, DUDE.
OKAY-FINE~!

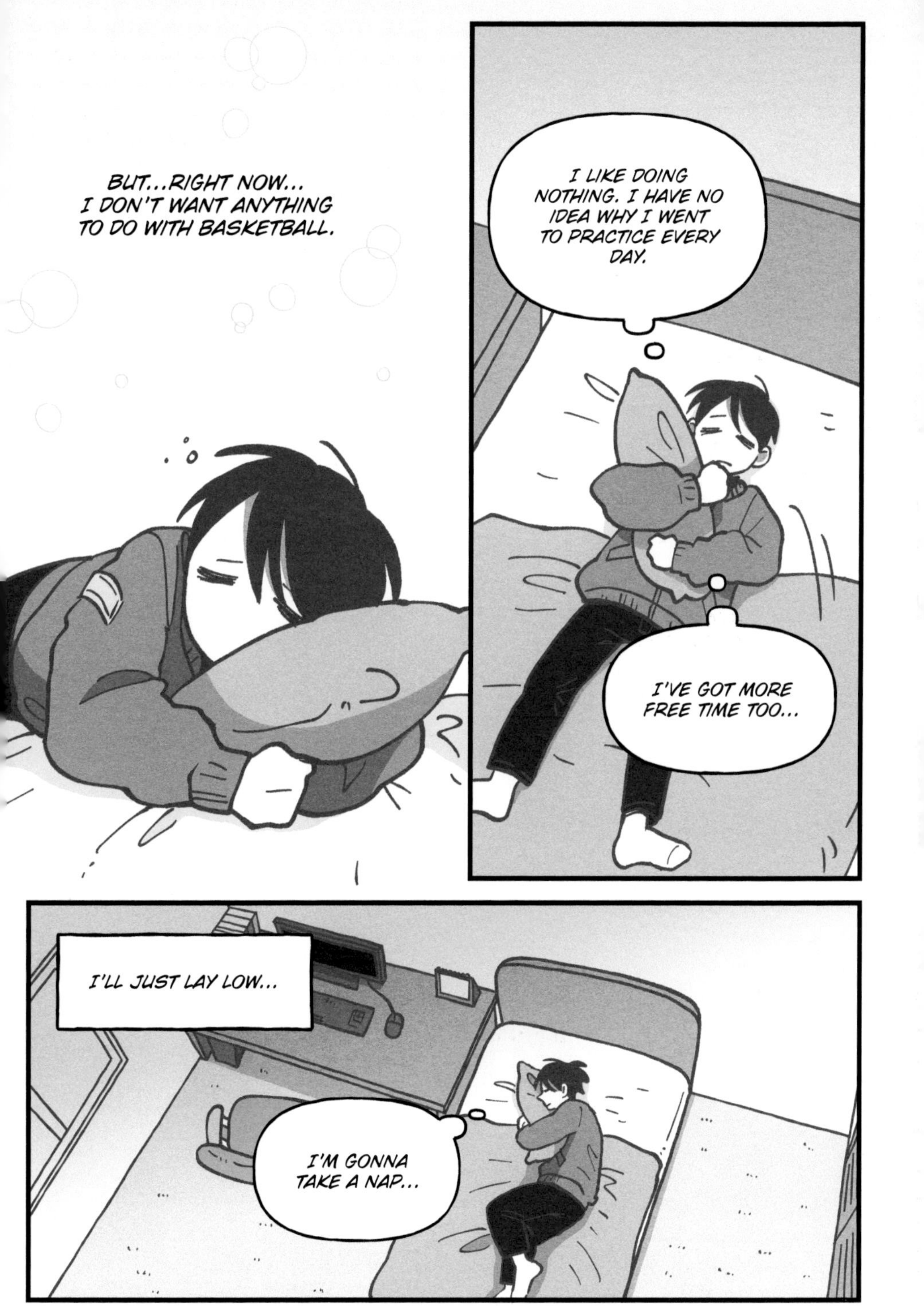
BUT...RIGHT NOW... I DON'T WANT ANYTHING TO DO WITH BASKETBALL.
I LIKE DOING NOTHING. I HAVE NO IDEA WHY I WENT TO PRACTICE EVERY DAY.
I'VE GOT MORE FREE TIME TOO...
I'LL JUST LAY LOW...
I'M GONNA TAKE A NAP...

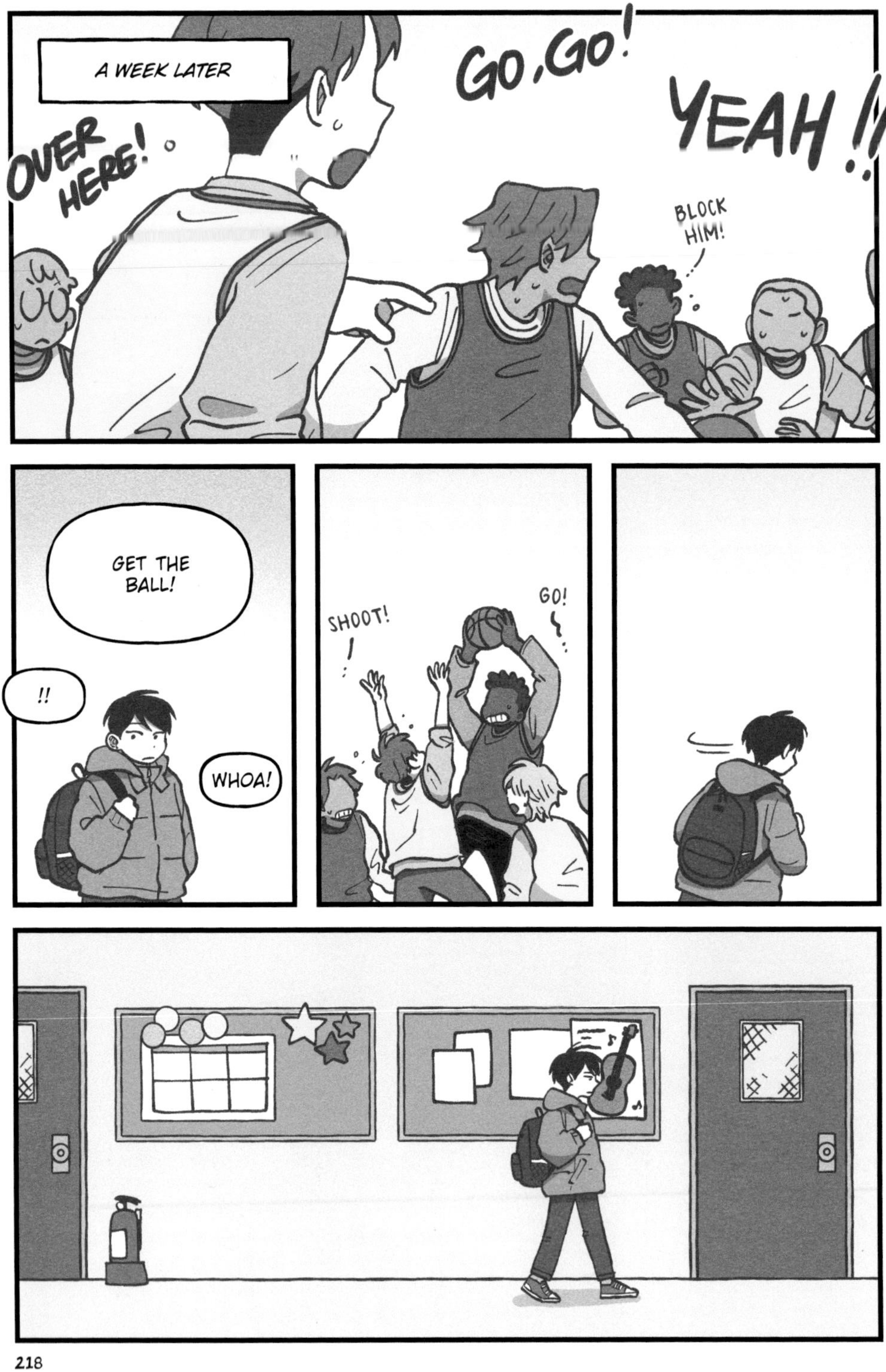
A WEEK LATER
OVER HERE!
GO, GO!
YEAH!!
BLOCK HIM!
GET THE BALL!
!!
WHOA!
SHOOT!
GO!

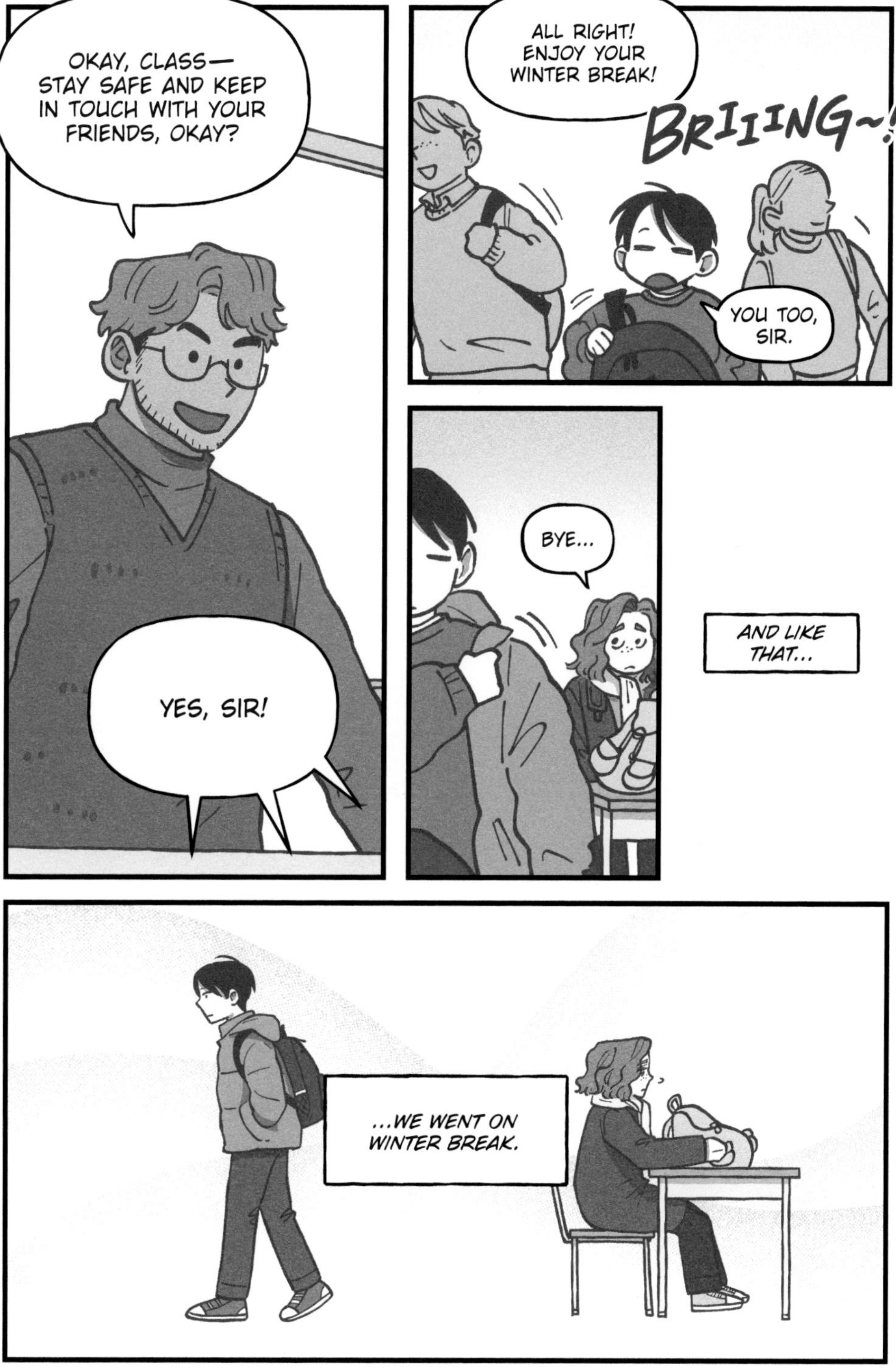
OKAY, CLASS—STAY SAFE AND KEEP IN TOUCH WITH YOUR FRIENDS, OKAY?
YES, SIR!
ALL RIGHT! ENJOY YOUR WINTER BREAK!
BRIIING~!
YOU TOO, SIR.
BYE...
AND LIKE THAT...
...WE WENT ON WINTER BREAK.

Chapter 11

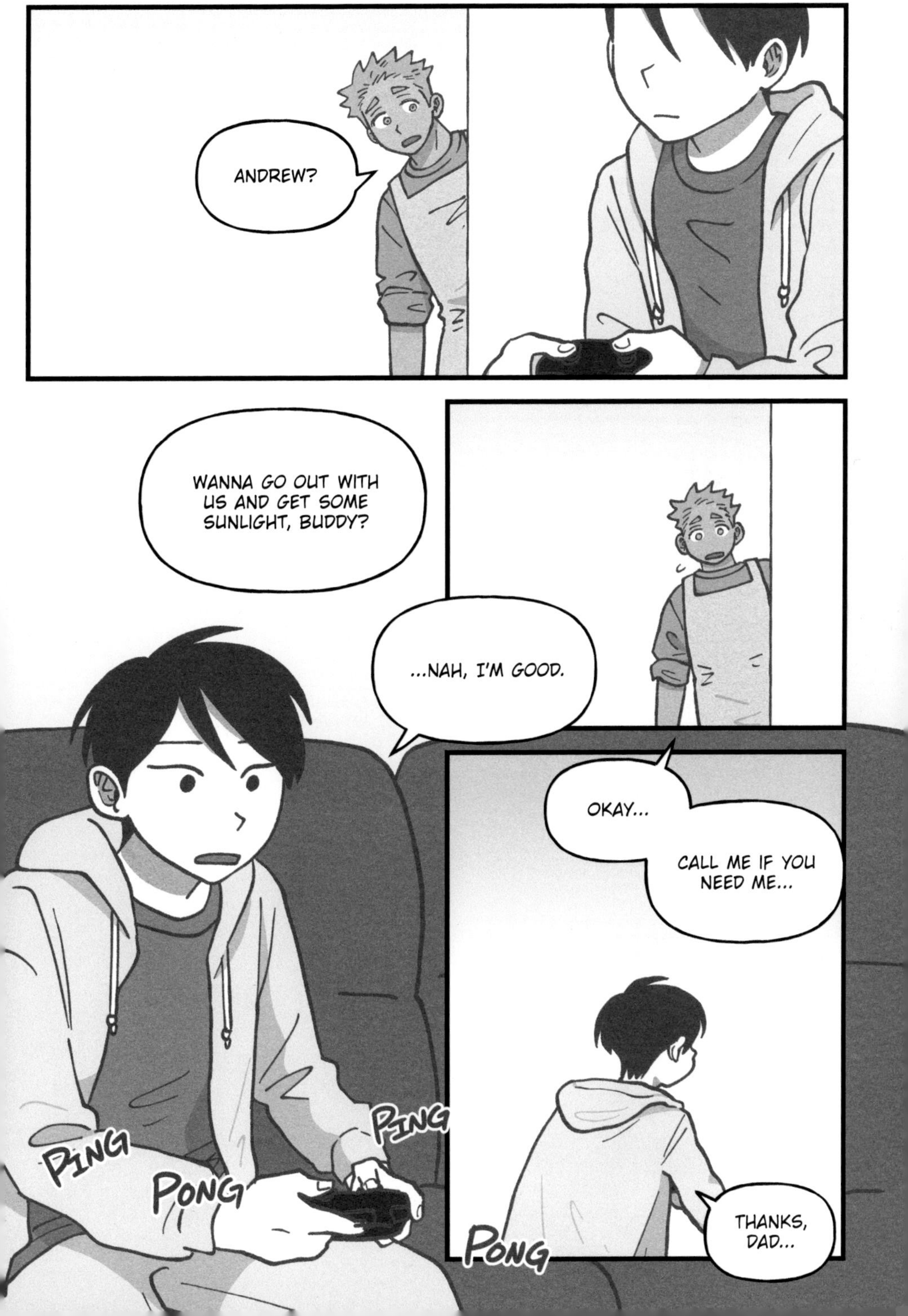
ANDREW?
WANNA GO OUT WITH US AND GET SOME SUNLIGHT, BUDDY?
...NAH, I'M GOOD.
OKAY...
CALL ME IF YOU NEED ME...
PING
PING
PONG
PONG
THANKS, DAD...

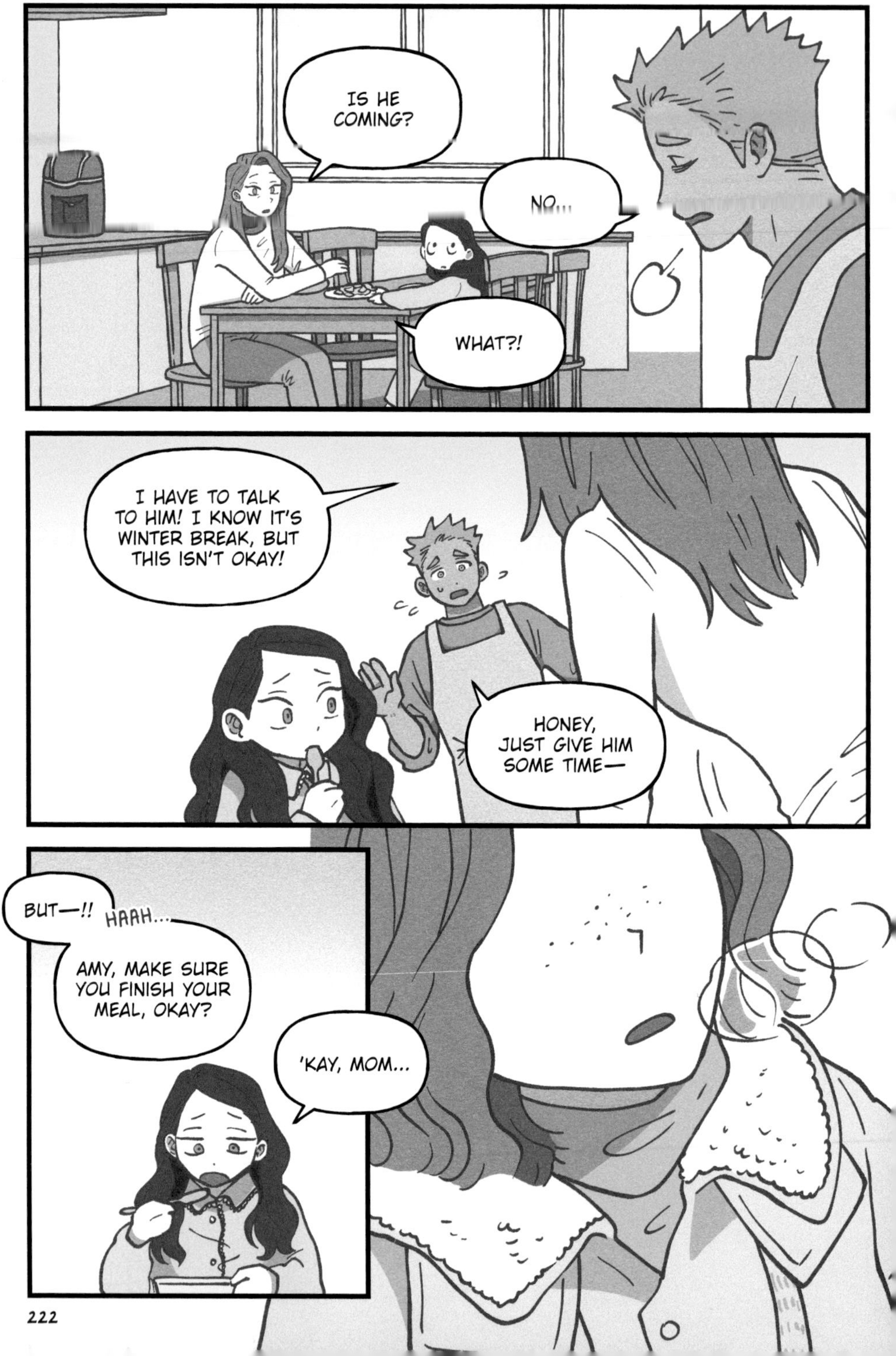
IS HE COMING?
NO...
WHAT?!
I HAVE TO TALK TO HIM! I KNOW IT'S WINTER BREAK, BUT THIS ISN'T OKAY!
HONEY, JUST GIVE HIM SOME TIME—
BUT—!!
HAAH...
AMY, MAKE SURE YOU FINISH YOUR MEAL, OKAY?
'KAY, MOM...

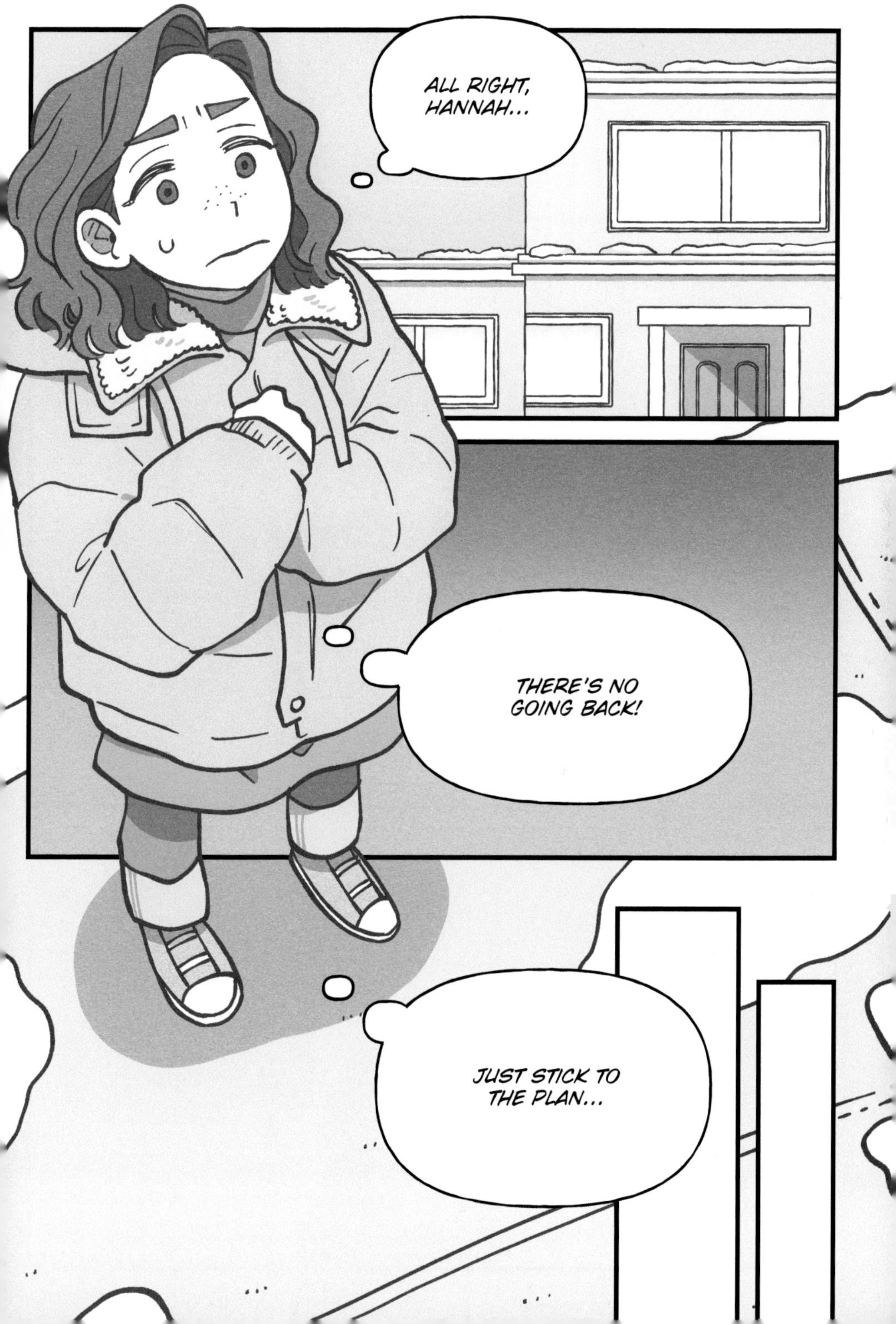
ALL RIGHT, HANNAH...
THERE'S NO GOING BACK!
JUST STICK TO THE PLAN...

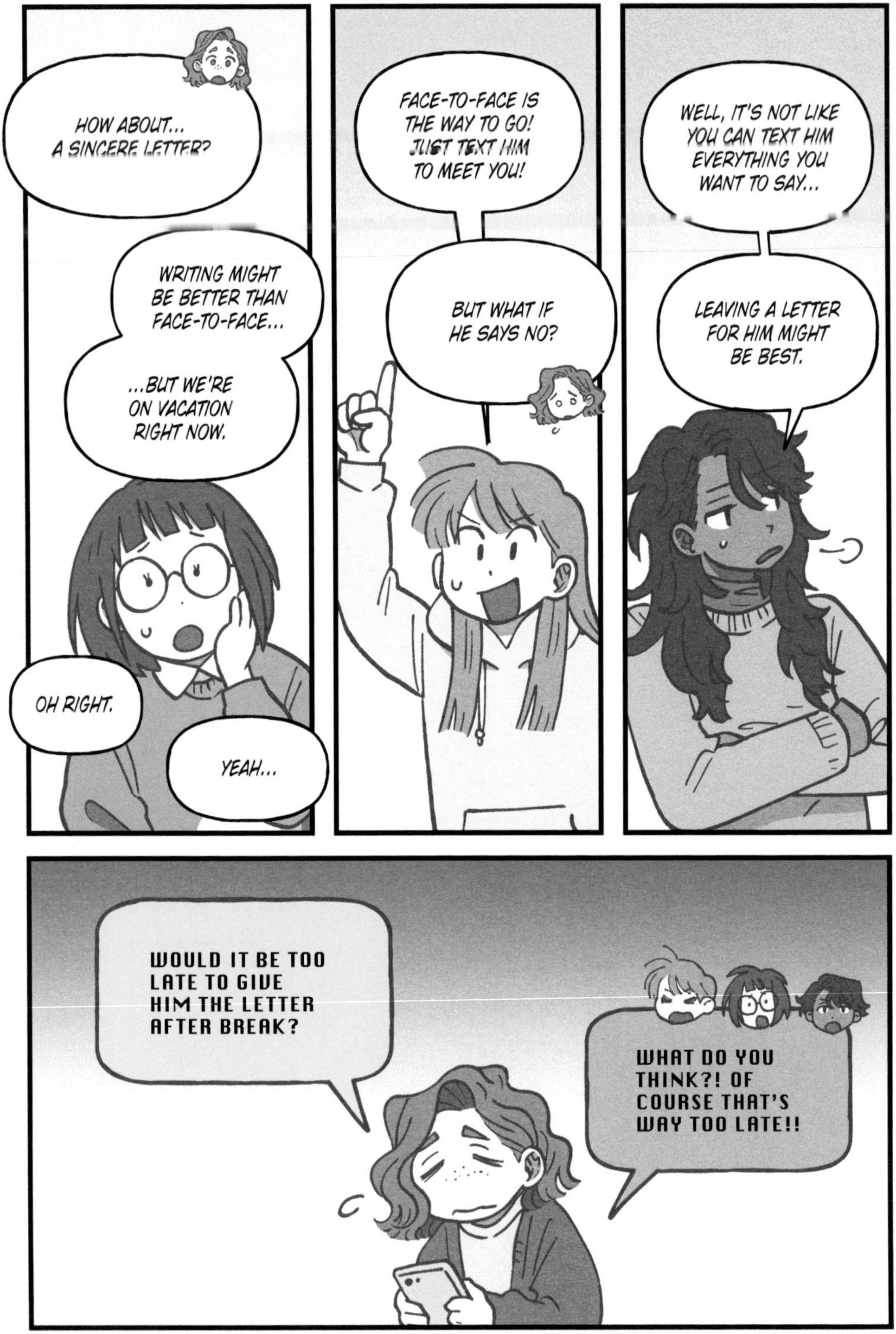
HOW ABOUT... A SINCERE LETTER?
WRITING MIGHT BE BETTER THAN FACE-TO-FACE...
...BUT WE'RE ON VACATION RIGHT NOW.
OH RIGHT.
YEAH...
FACE-TO-FACE IS THE WAY TO GO! JUST TEXT HIM TO MEET YOU!
BUT WHAT IF HE SAYS NO?
WELL, IT'S NOT LIKE YOU CAN TEXT HIM EVERYTHING YOU WANT TO SAY...
LEAVING A LETTER FOR HIM MIGHT BE BEST.
WOULD IT BE TOO LATE TO GIVE HIM THE LETTER AFTER BREAK?
WHAT DO YOU THINK?! OF COURSE THAT'S WAY TOO LATE!!

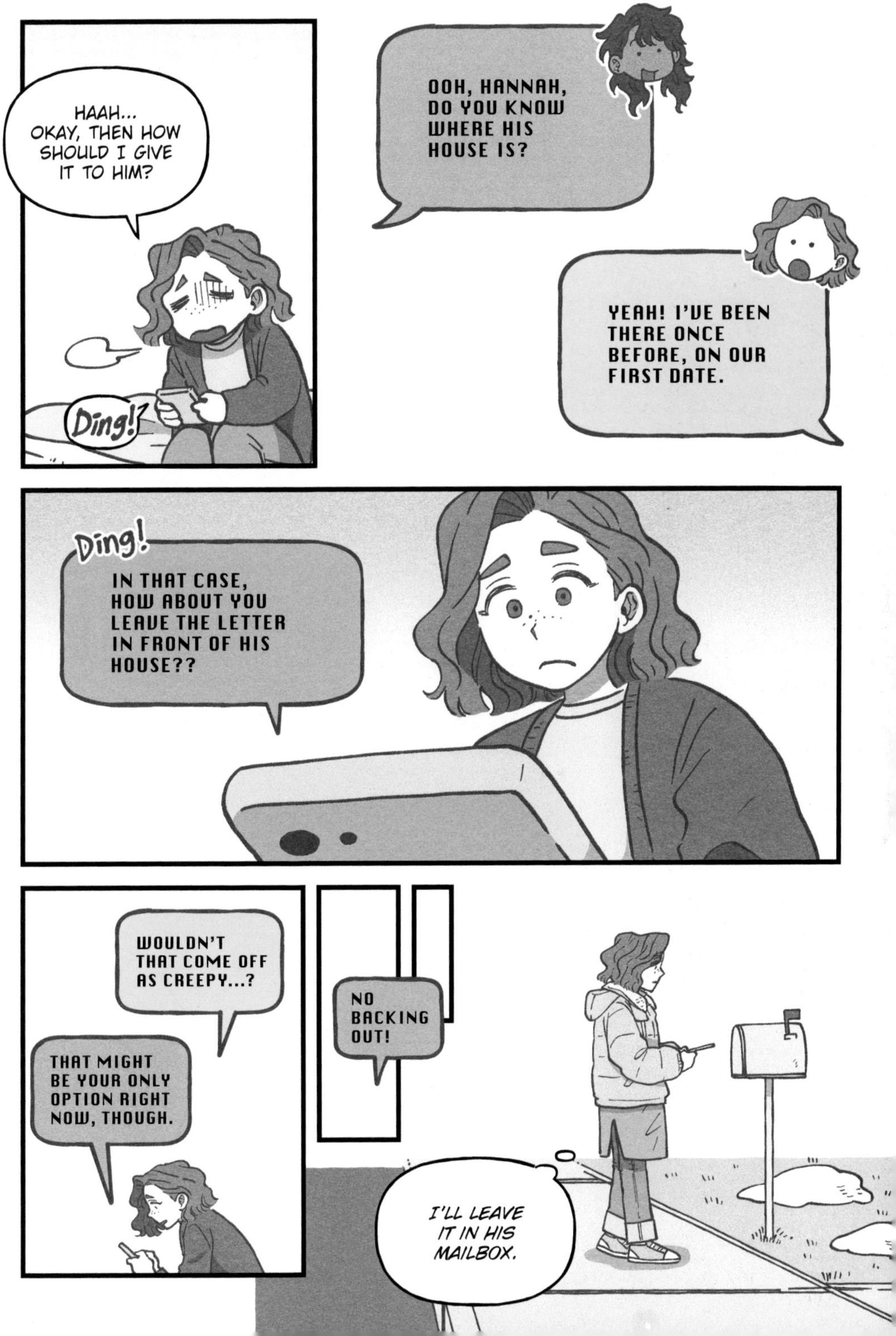
HAAH... OKAY, THEN HOW SHOULD I GIVE IT TO HIM?
Ding!
OOH, HANNAH, DO YOU KNOW WHERE HIS HOUSE IS?
YEAH! I'VE BEEN THERE ONCE BEFORE, ON OUR FIRST DATE.
Ding!
IN THAT CASE, HOW ABOUT YOU LEAVE THE LETTER IN FRONT OF HIS HOUSE??
WOULDN'T THAT COME OFF AS CREEPY...?
THAT MIGHT BE YOUR ONLY OPTION RIGHT NOW, THOUGH.
NO BACKING OUT!
I'LL LEAVE IT IN HIS MAILBOX.

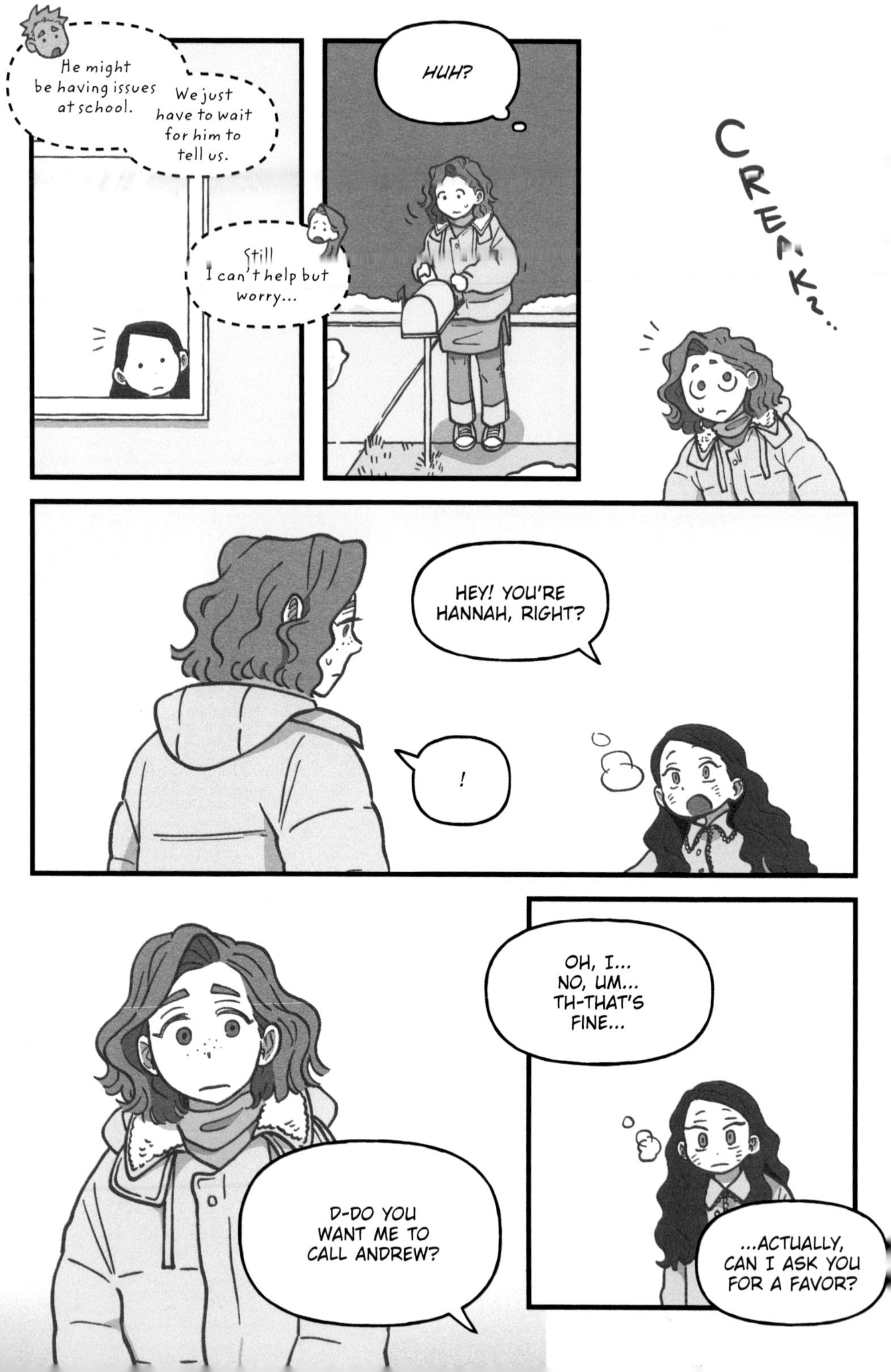
He might be having issues at school.
We just have to wait for him to tell us.
Still I can't help but worry...
HUH?
CREAK..
HEY! YOU'RE HANNAH, RIGHT?
!
OH, I... NO, UM... TH-THAT'S FINE...
D-DO YOU WANT ME TO CALL ANDREW?
...ACTUALLY, CAN I ASK YOU FOR A FAVOR?

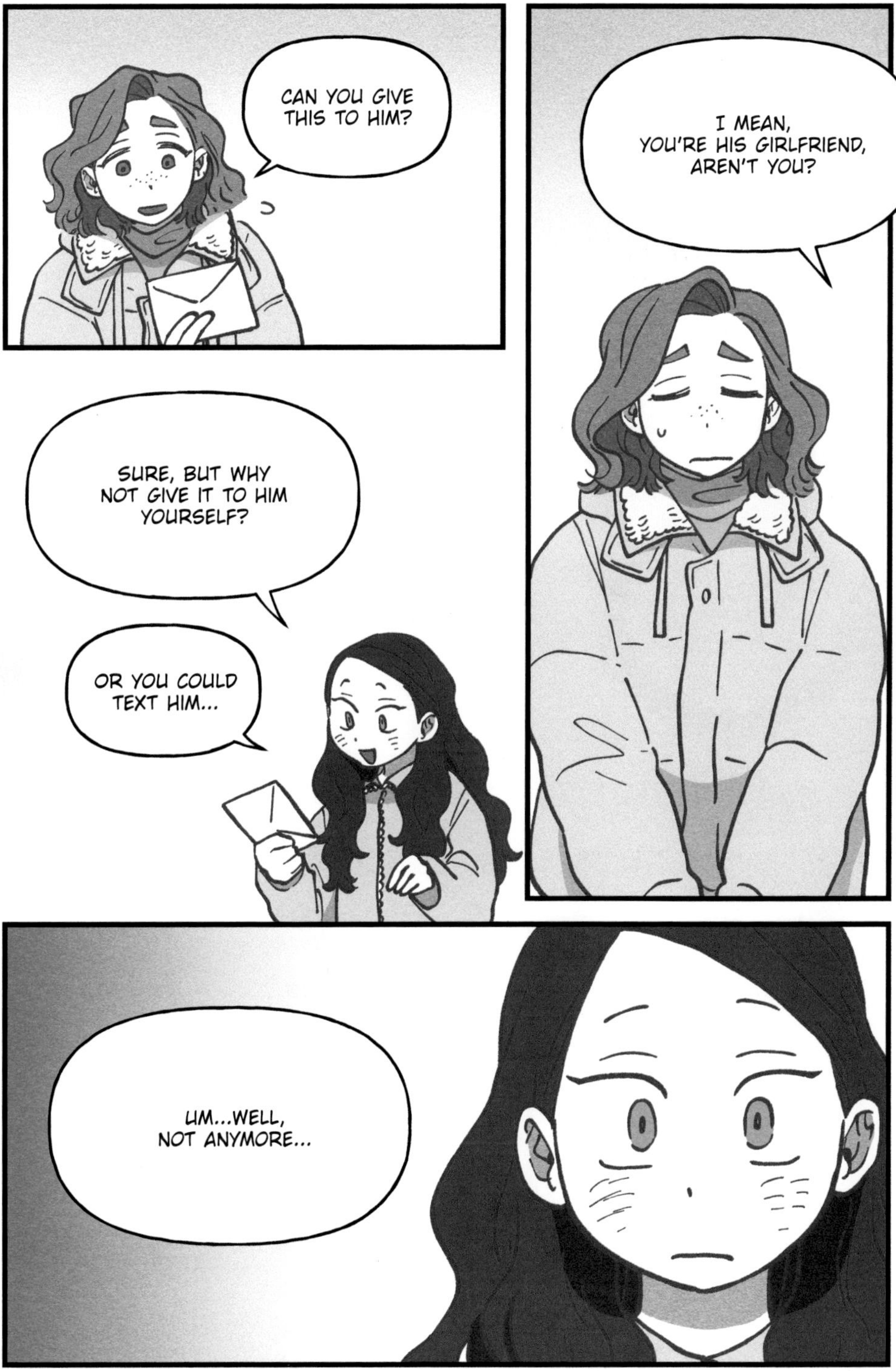
CAN YOU GIVE THIS TO HIM?
I MEAN, YOU'RE HIS GIRLFRIEND, AREN'T YOU?
SURE, BUT WHY NOT GIVE IT TO HIM YOURSELF?
OR YOU COULD TEXT HIM...
UM...WELL, NOT ANYMORE...

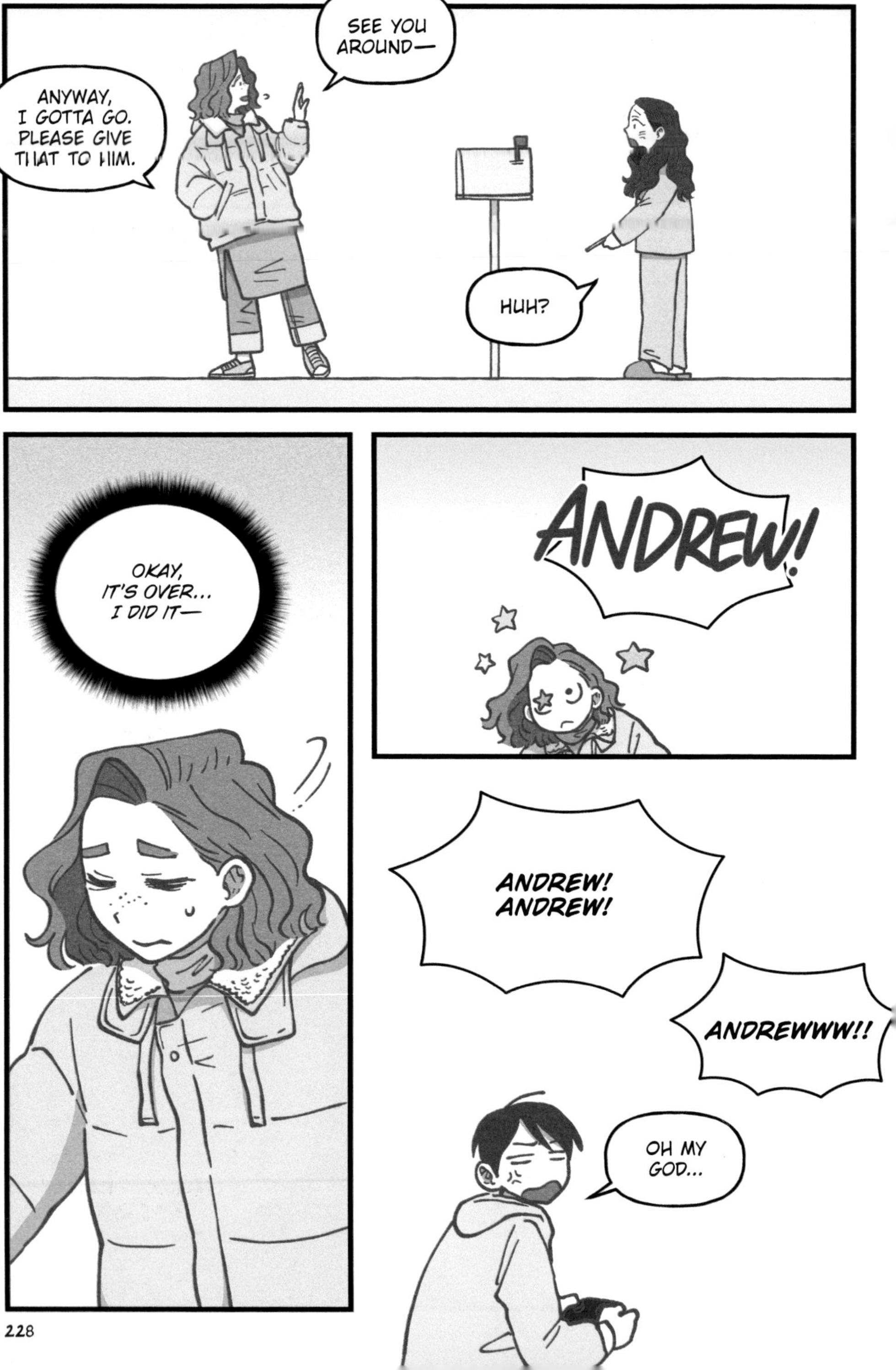
ANYWAY, I GOTTA GO. PLEASE GIVE THAT TO HIM.
SEE YOU AROUND—
HUH?
OKAY, IT'S OVER... I DID IT—
ANDREW!
ANDREW! ANDREW!
ANDREWWW!!
OH MY GOD...

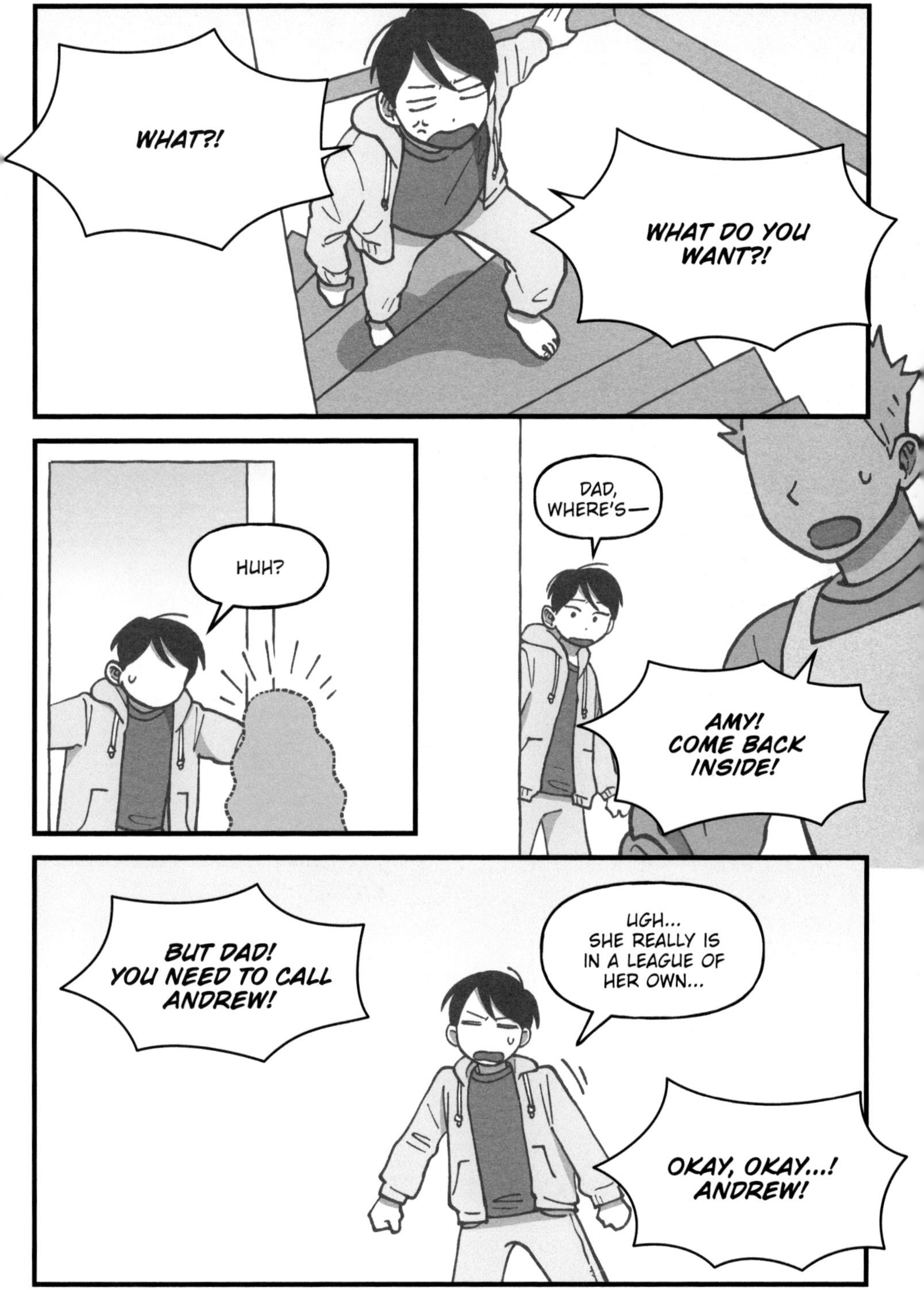
WHAT?!
WHAT DO YOU WANT?!
HUH?
DAD, WHERE'S—
AMY! COME BACK INSIDE!
BUT DAD! YOU NEED TO CALL ANDREW!
UGH... SHE REALLY IS IN A LEAGUE OF HER OWN...
OKAY, OKAY...! ANDREW!

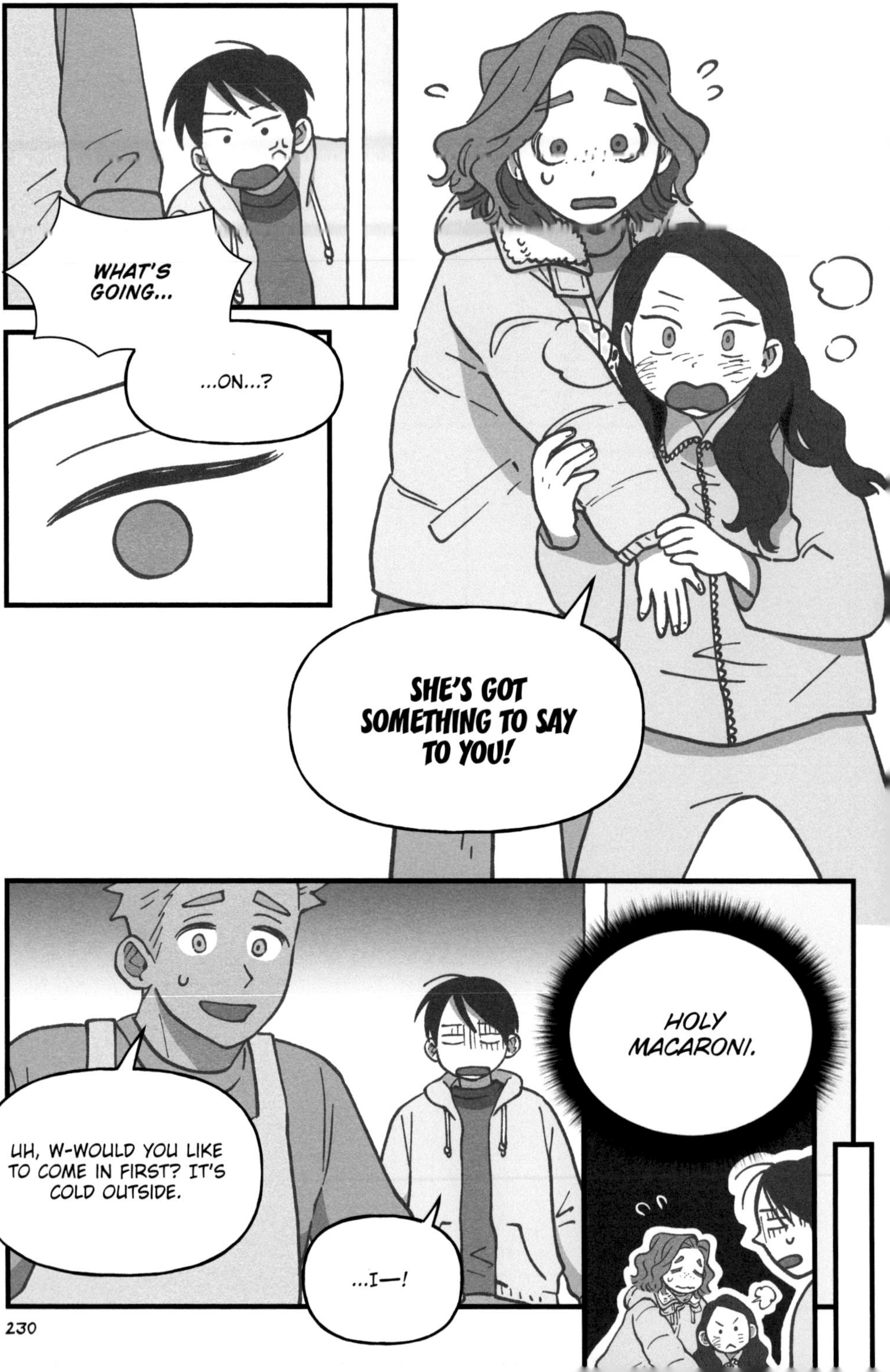
WHAT'S GOING...
...ON...?
SHE'S GOT SOMETHING TO SAY TO YOU!
HOLY MACARONI.
UH, W-WOULD YOU LIKE TO COME IN FIRST? IT'S COLD OUTSIDE.
...I—!

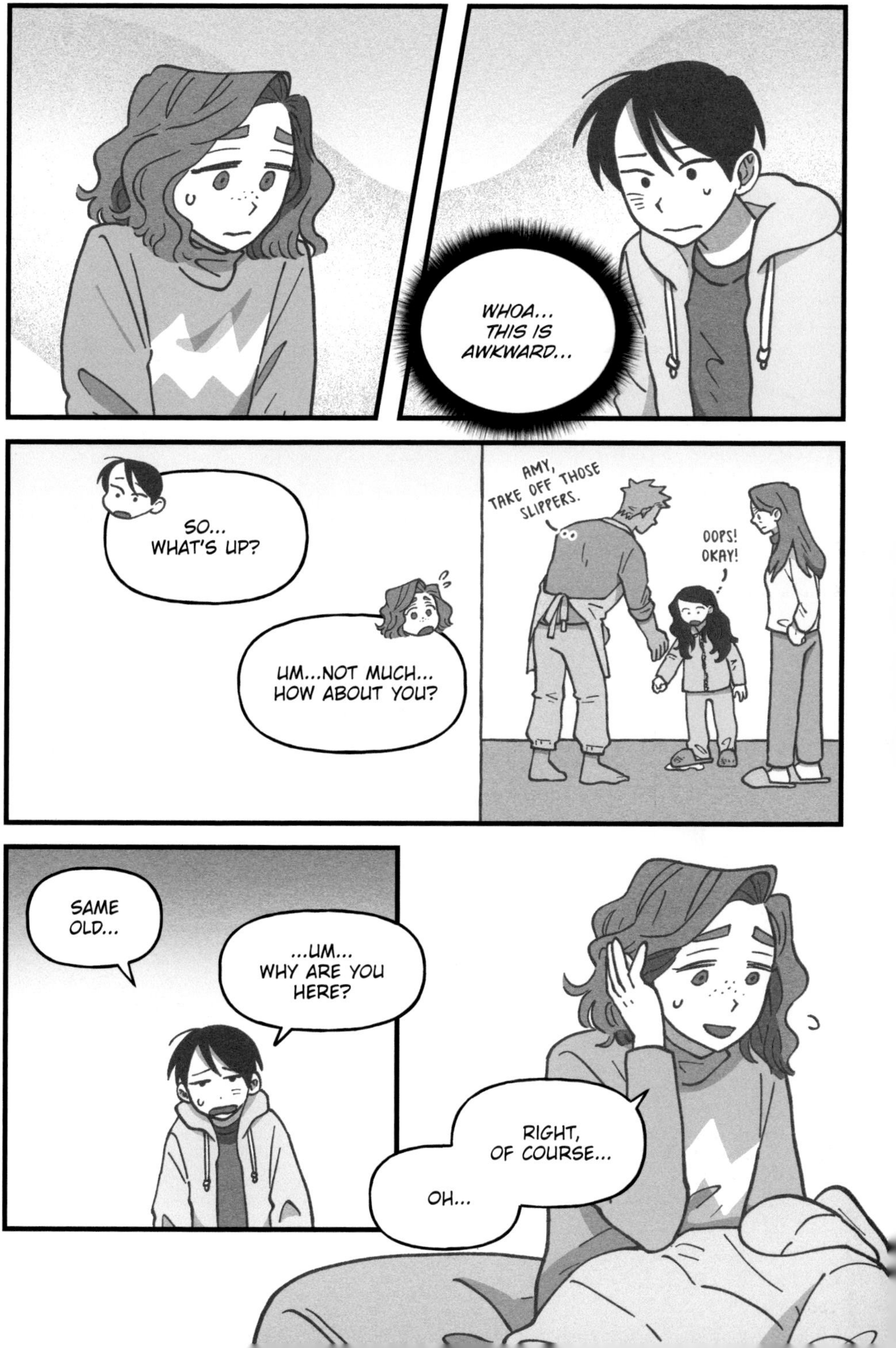
WHOA... THIS IS AWKWARD...
SO... WHAT'S UP?
UM...NOT MUCH... HOW ABOUT YOU?
AMY, TAKE OFF THOSE SLIPPERS.
OOPS! OKAY!
SAME OLD...
...UM... WHY ARE YOU HERE?
RIGHT, OF COURSE...
OH...

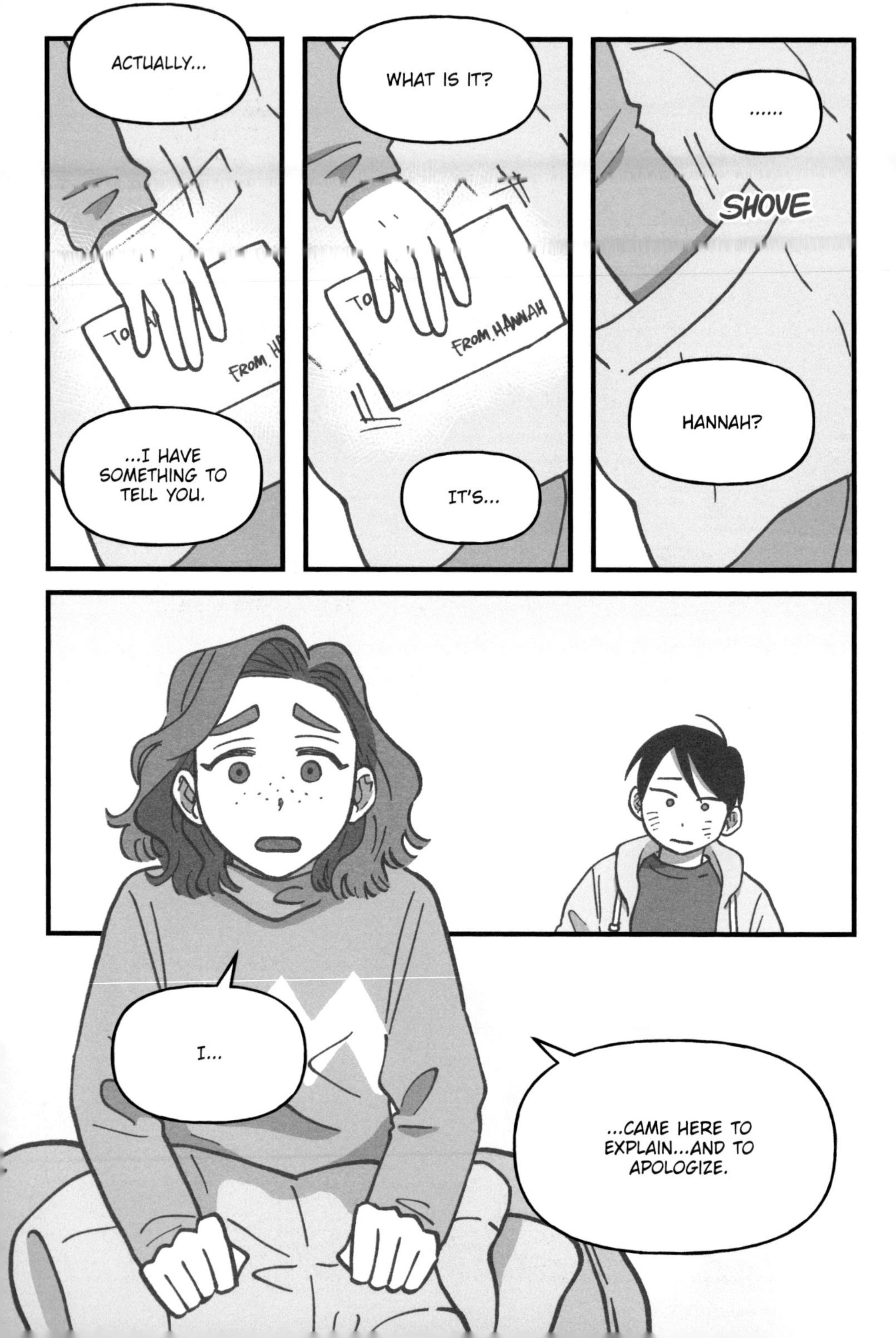
ACTUALLY...
...I HAVE SOMETHING TO TELL YOU.
TO
FROM, H
WHAT IS IT?
TO
FROM, HANNAH
IT'S...
......
SHOVE
HANNAH?
I...
...CAME HERE TO EXPLAIN...AND TO APOLOGIZE.

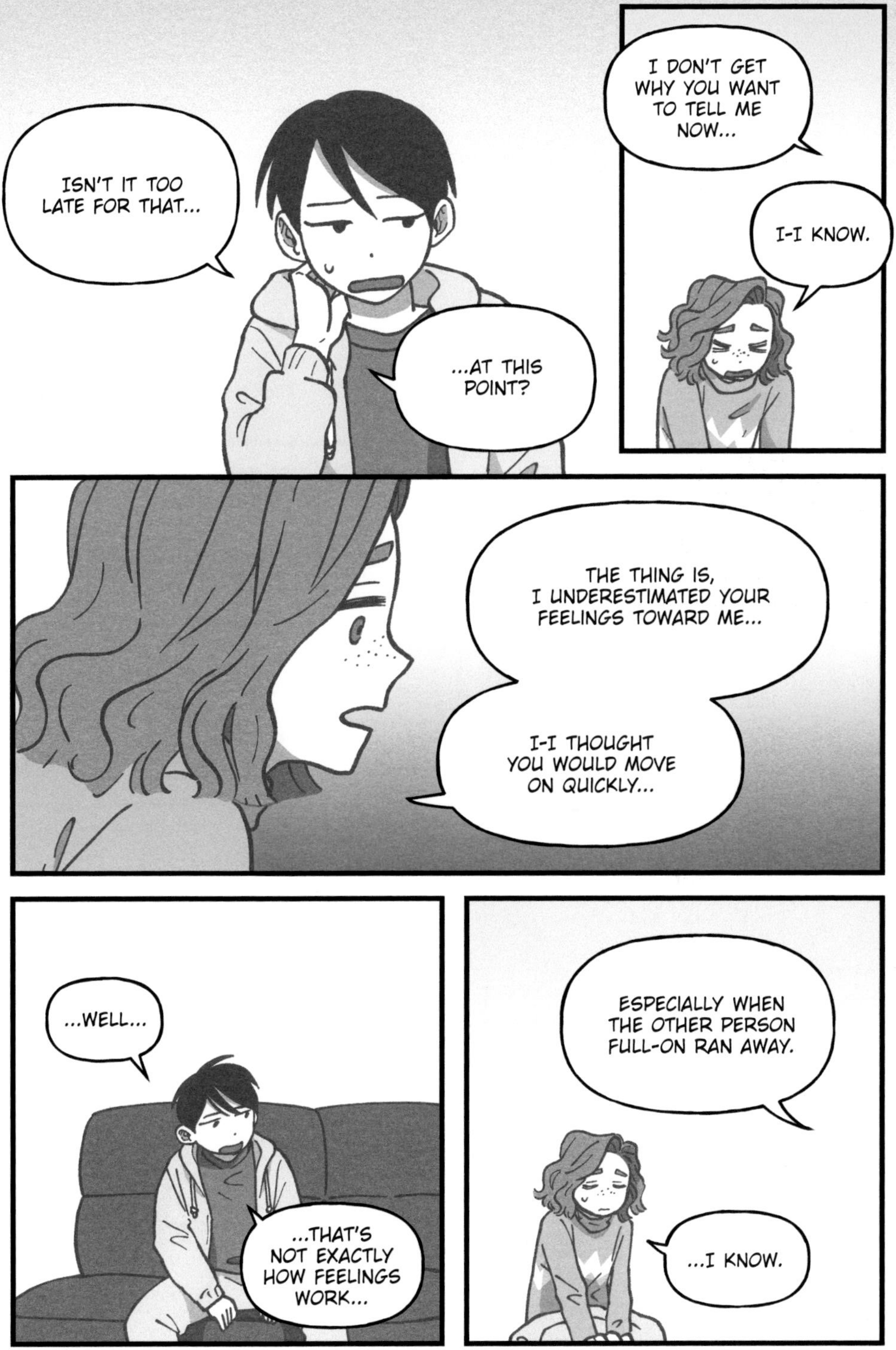
I DON'T GET WHY YOU WANT TO TELL ME NOW...
I-I KNOW.
ISN'T IT TOO LATE FOR THAT...
...AT THIS POINT?
THE THING IS, I UNDERESTIMATED YOUR FEELINGS TOWARD ME...
I-I THOUGHT YOU WOULD MOVE ON QUICKLY...
...WELL...
...THAT'S NOT EXACTLY HOW FEELINGS WORK...
ESPECIALLY WHEN THE OTHER PERSON FULL-ON RAN AWAY.
...I KNOW.

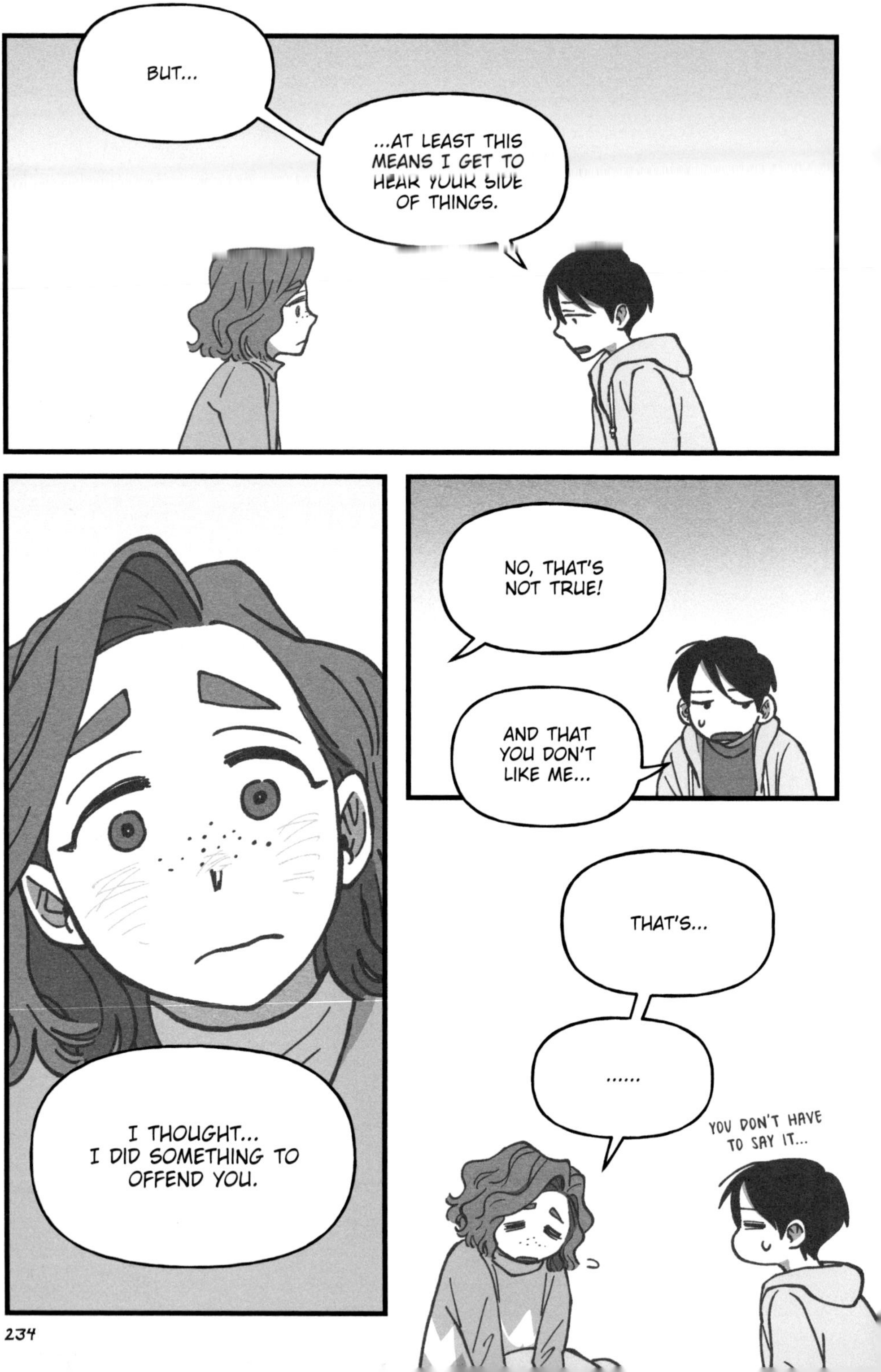
BUT...
...AT LEAST THIS MEANS I GET TO HEAR YOUR SIDE OF THINGS.
I THOUGHT... I DID SOMETHING TO OFFEND YOU.
NO, THAT'S NOT TRUE!
AND THAT YOU DON'T LIKE ME...
THAT'S...
......
YOU DON'T HAVE TO SAY IT...

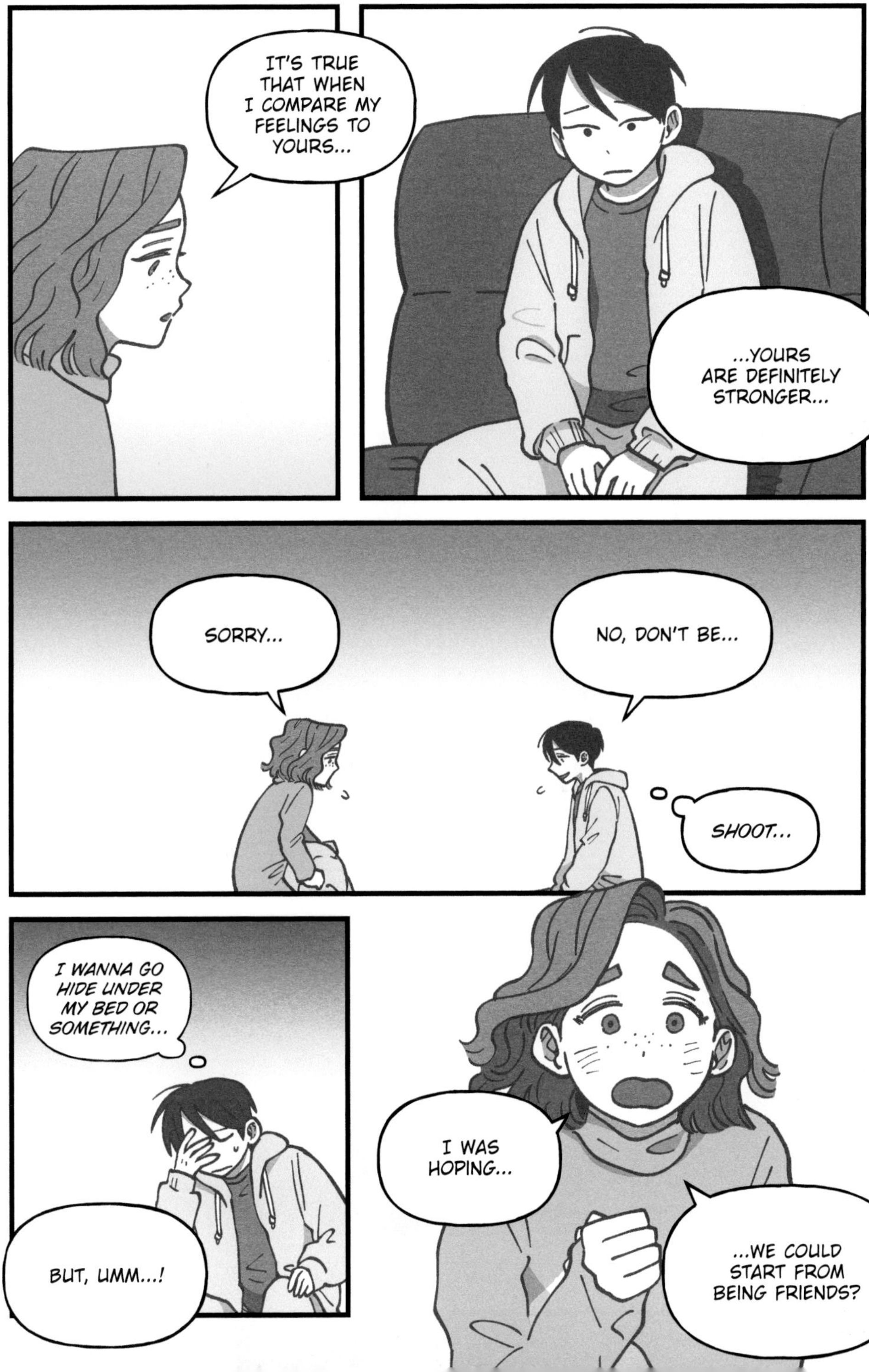
IT'S TRUE THAT WHEN I COMPARE MY FEELINGS TO YOURS...
...YOURS ARE DEFINITELY STRONGER...
SORRY...
NO, DON'T BE...
SHOOT...
I WANNA GO HIDE UNDER MY BED OR SOMETHING...
BUT, UMM...!
I WAS HOPING...
...WE COULD START FROM BEING FRIENDS?

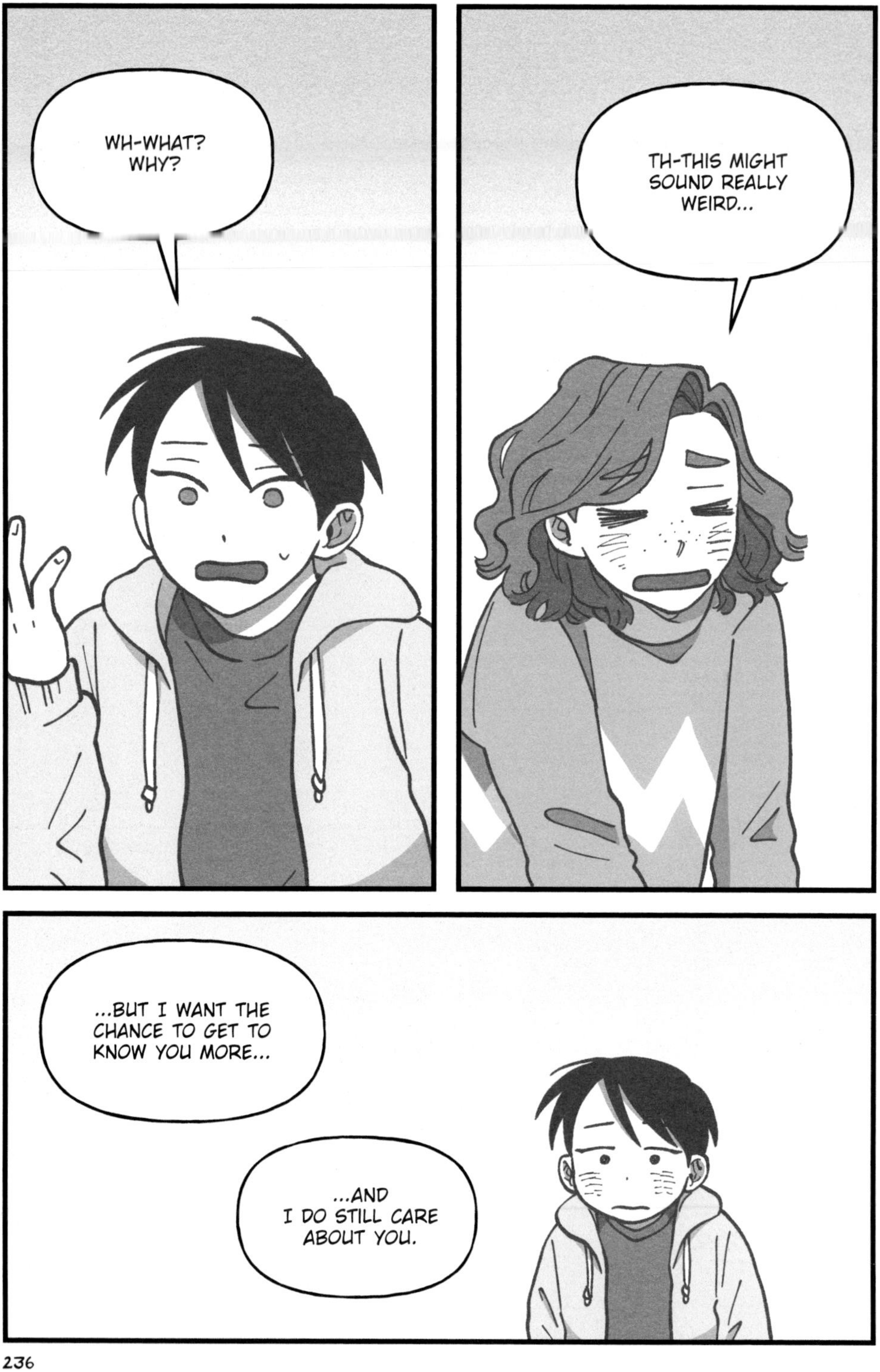
WH-WHAT? WHY?
TH-THIS MIGHT SOUND REALLY WEIRD...
...BUT I WANT THE CHANCE TO GET TO KNOW YOU MORE...
...AND I DO STILL CARE ABOUT YOU.

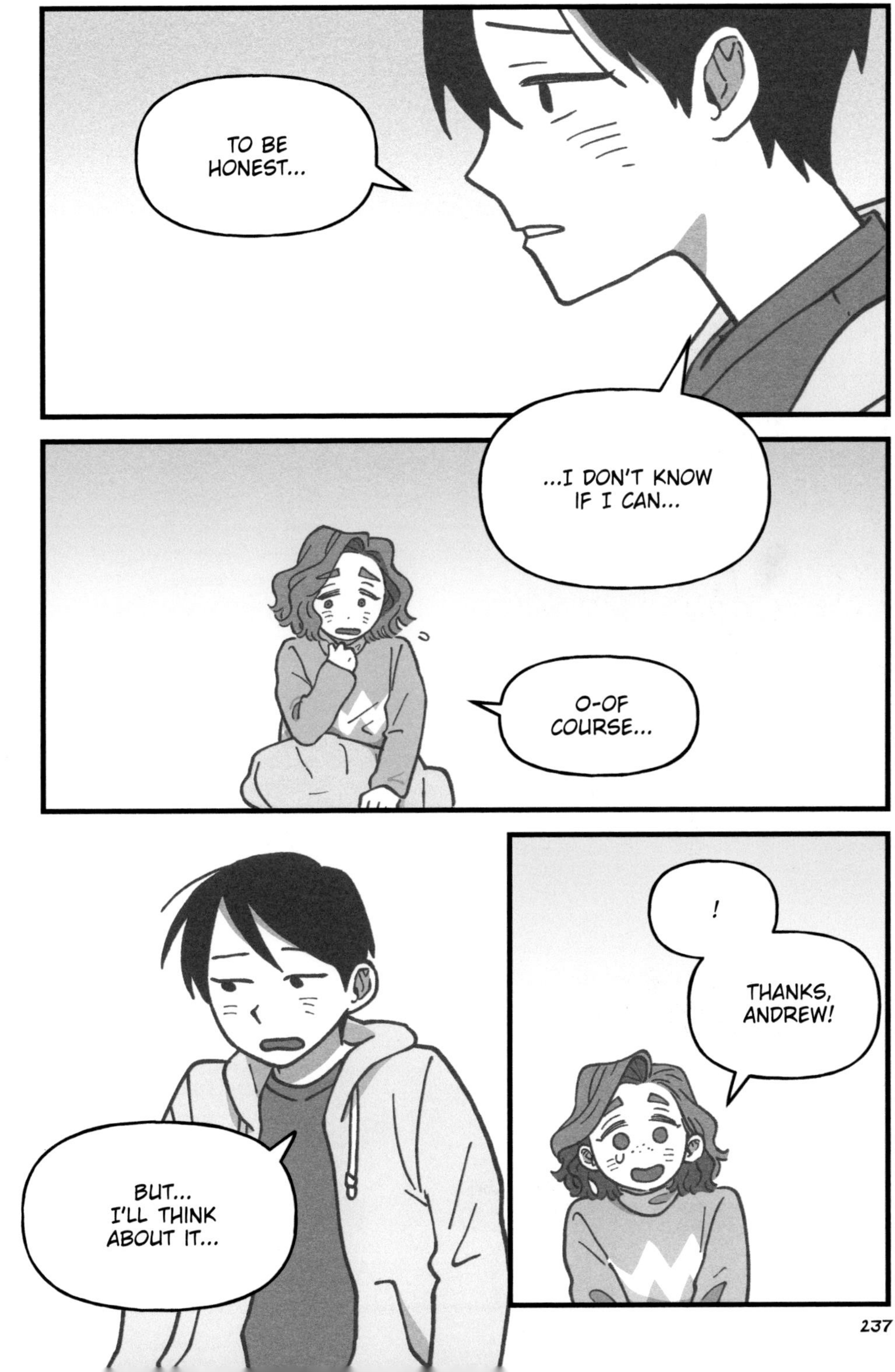
TO BE HONEST...
...I DON'T KNOW IF I CAN...
O-OF COURSE...
BUT... I'LL THINK ABOUT IT...
!
THANKS, ANDREW!

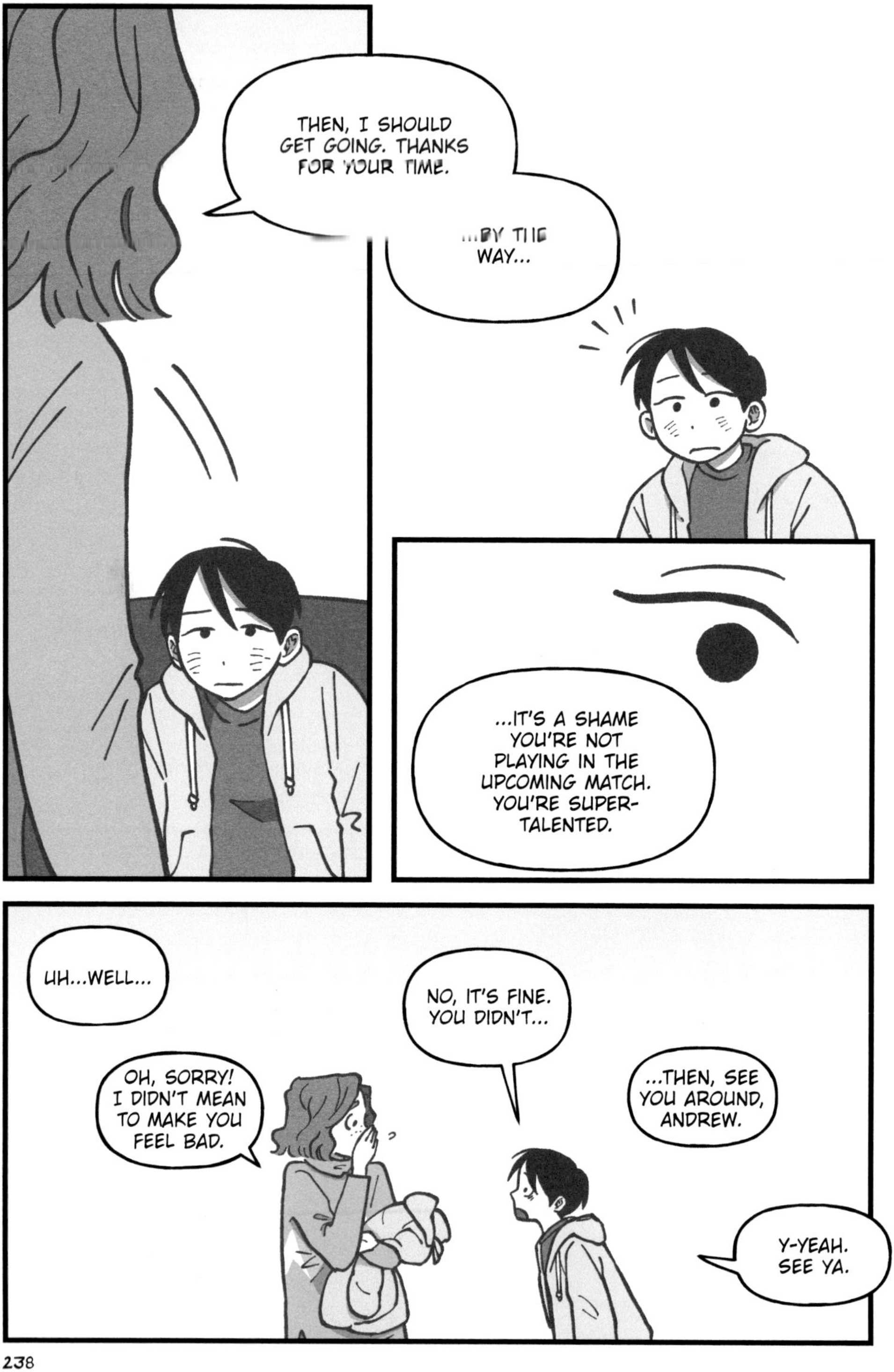
THEN, I SHOULD GET GOING. THANKS FOR YOUR TIME.
...BY THE WAY...
...IT'S A SHAME YOU'RE NOT PLAYING IN THE UPCOMING MATCH. YOU'RE SUPER-TALENTED.
UH...WELL...
OH, SORRY! I DIDN'T MEAN TO MAKE YOU FEEL BAD.
NO, IT'S FINE. YOU DIDN'T...
...THEN, SEE YOU AROUND, ANDREW.
Y-YEAH. SEE YA.

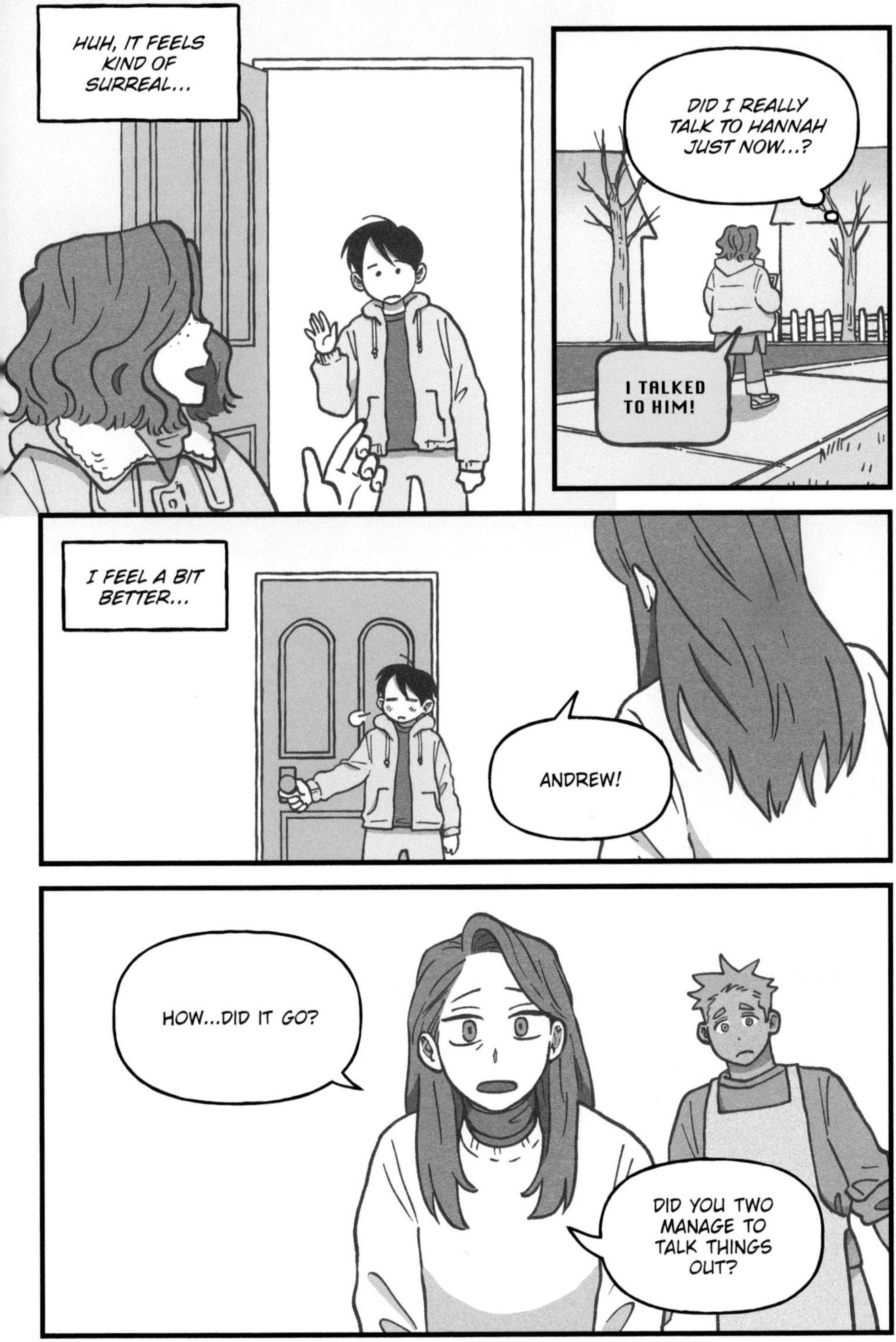
HUH, IT FEELS KIND OF SURREAL...
DID I REALLY TALK TO HANNAH JUST NOW...?
I TALKED TO HIM!
I FEEL A BIT BETTER...
ANDREW!
HOW...DID IT GO?
DID YOU TWO MANAGE TO TALK THINGS OUT?

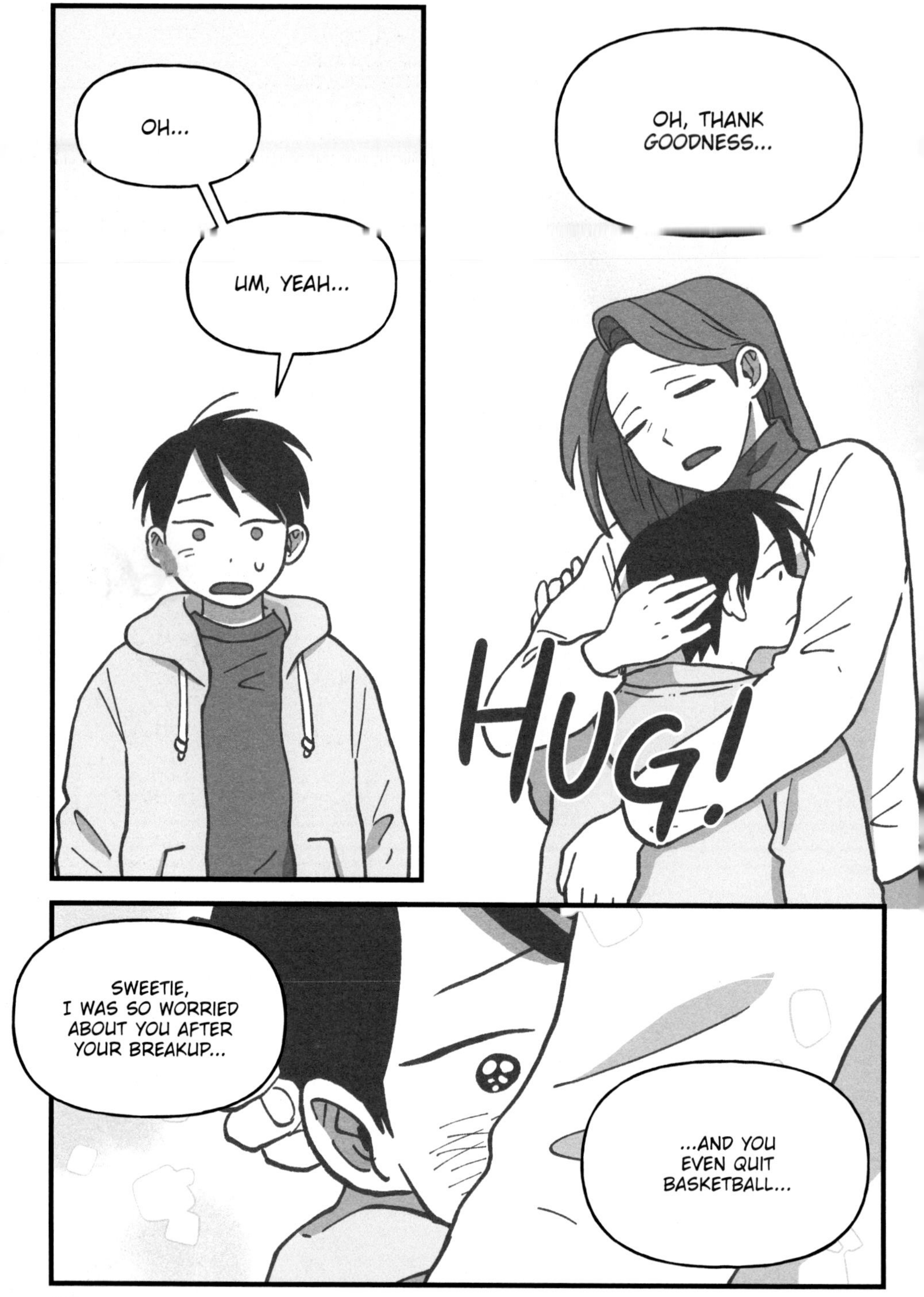
OH...
UM, YEAH...
OH, THANK GOODNESS...
HUG!
SWEETIE, I WAS SO WORRIED ABOUT YOU AFTER YOUR BREAKUP...
...AND YOU EVEN QUIT BASKETBALL...

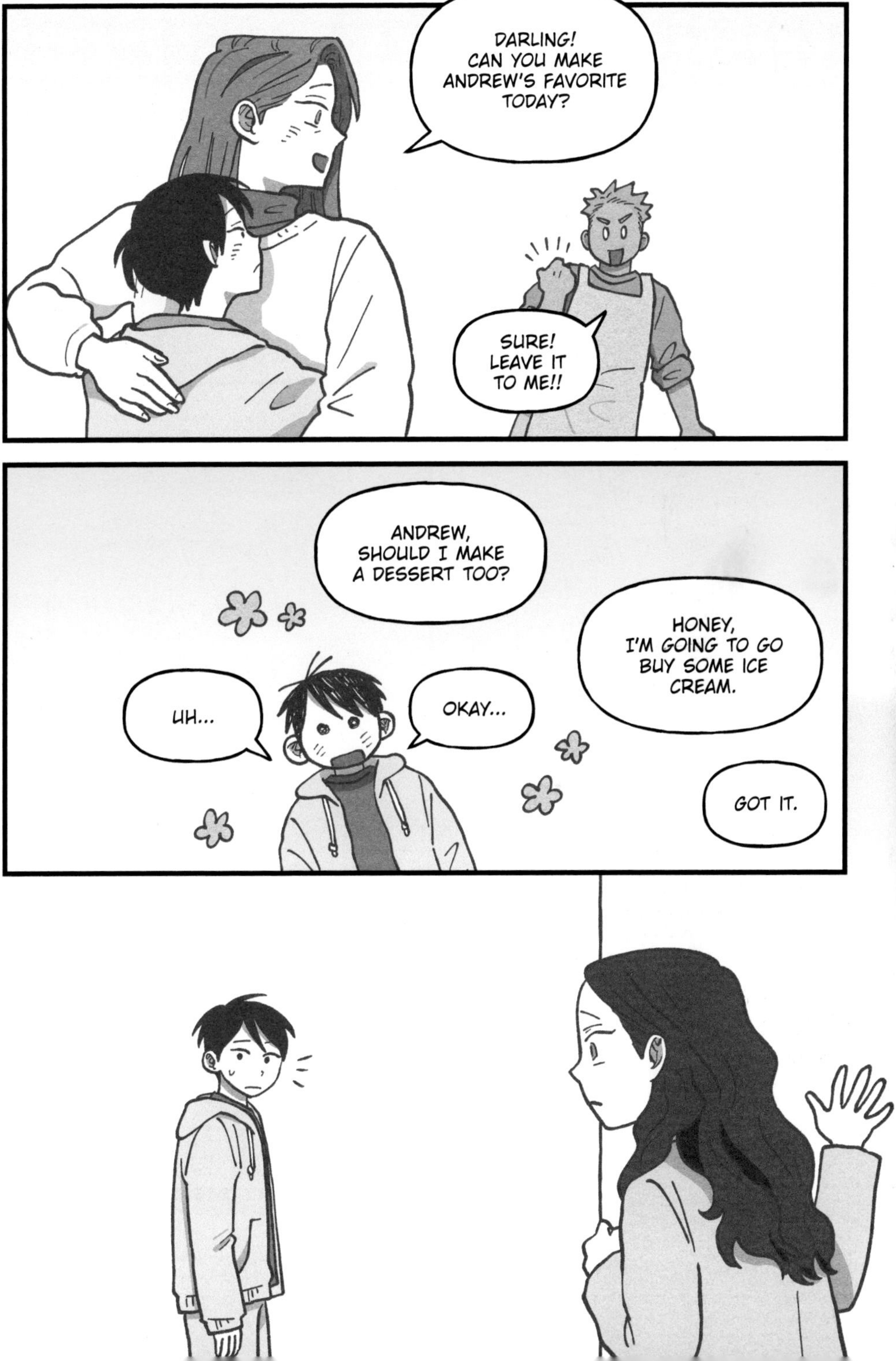
DARLING! CAN YOU MAKE ANDREW'S FAVORITE TODAY?
SURE! LEAVE IT TO ME!!
ANDREW, SHOULD I MAKE A DESSERT TOO?
HONEY, I'M GOING TO GO BUY SOME ICE CREAM.
OKAY...
UH...
GOT IT.

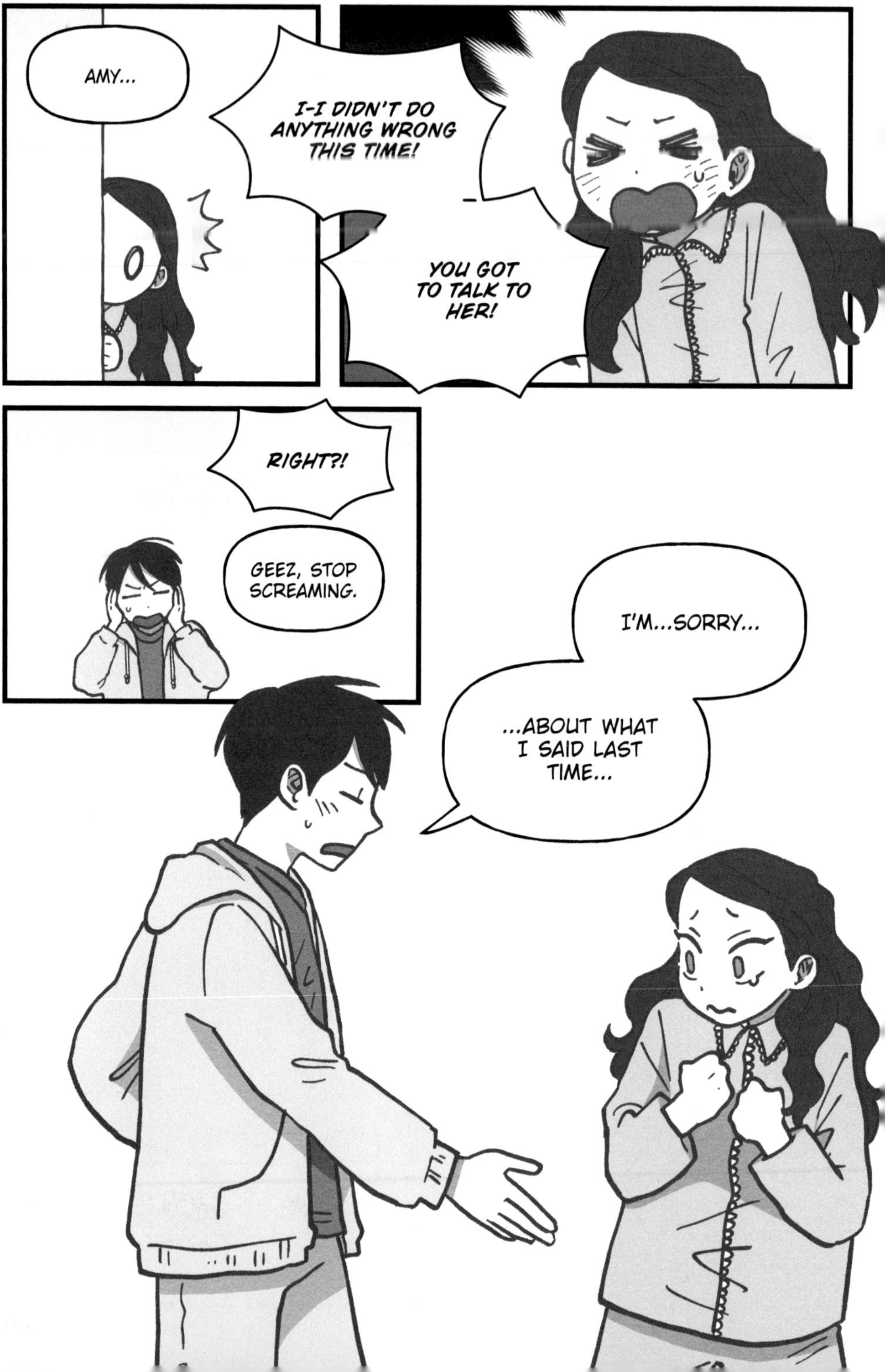
AMY...
I-I DIDN'T DO ANYTHING WRONG THIS TIME!
YOU GOT TO TALK TO HER!
RIGHT?!
GEEZ, STOP SCREAMING.
I'M...SORRY...
...ABOUT WHAT I SAID LAST TIME...

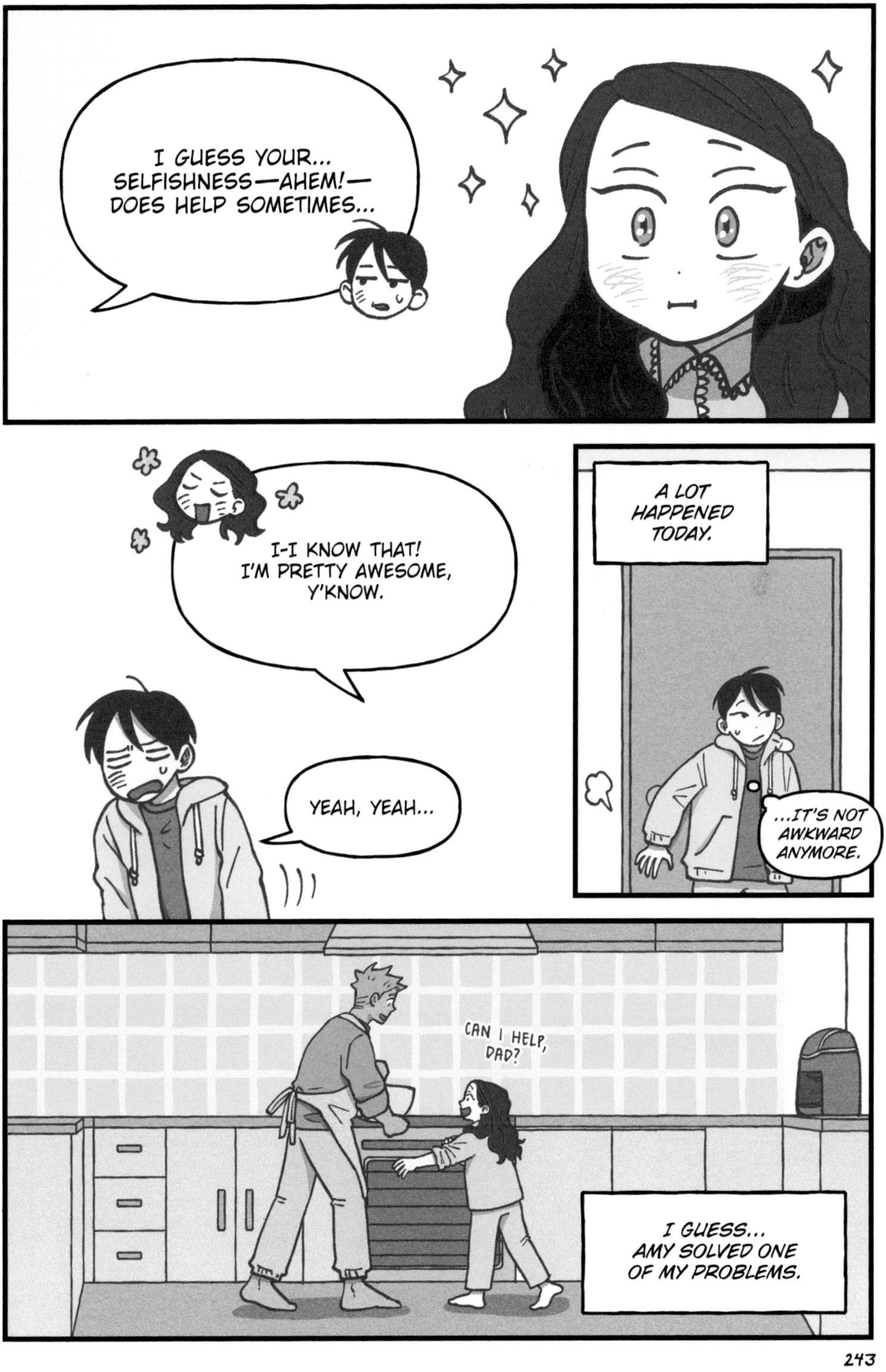
I GUESS YOUR... SELFISHNESS—AHEM!—DOES HELP SOMETIMES...
I-I KNOW THAT! I'M PRETTY AWESOME, Y'KNOW.
YEAH, YEAH...
A LOT HAPPENED TODAY.
...IT'S NOT AWKWARD ANYMORE.
CAN I HELP, DAD?
I GUESS... AMY SOLVED ONE OF MY PROBLEMS.

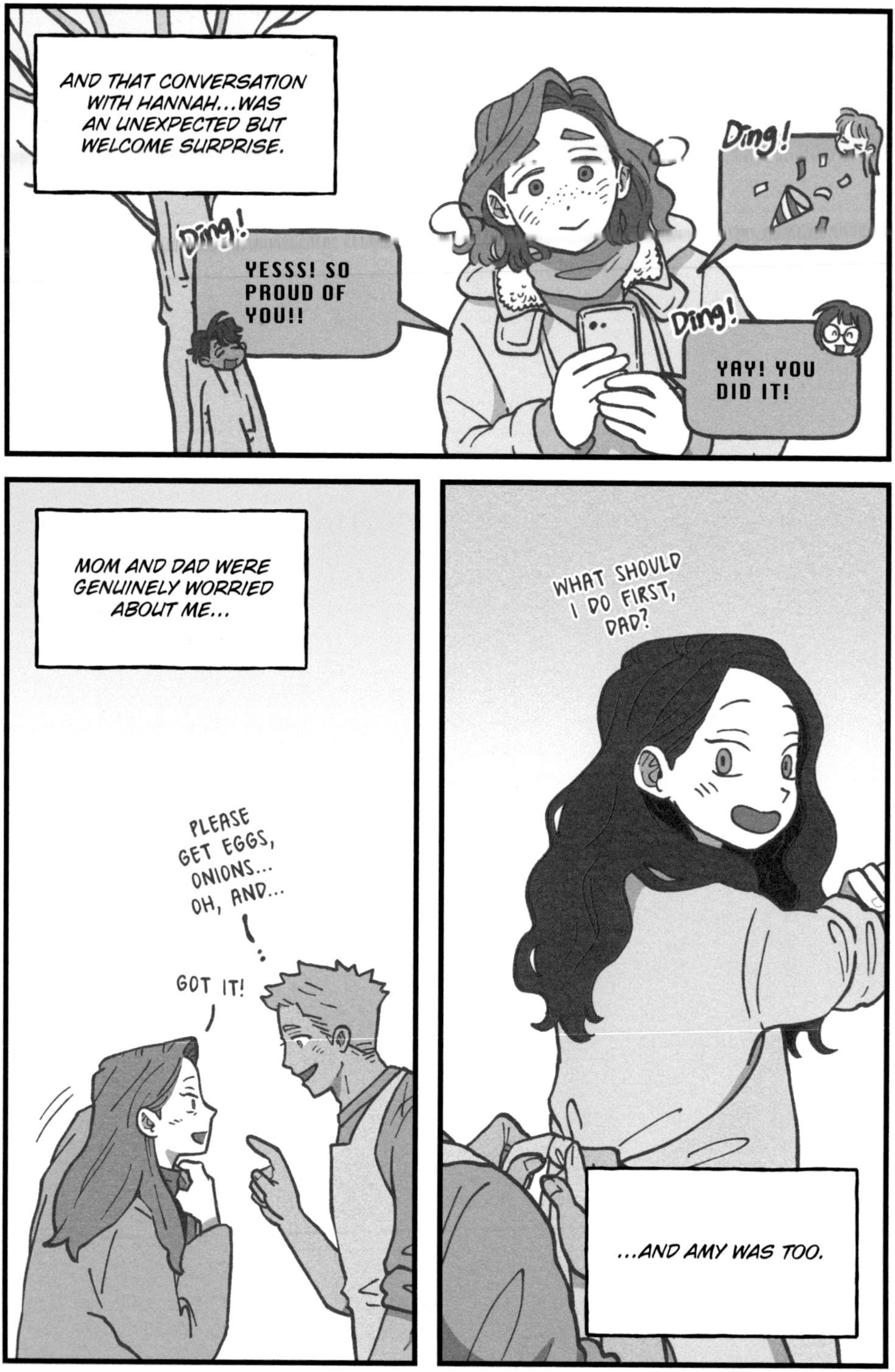
AND THAT CONVERSATION WITH HANNAH...WAS AN UNEXPECTED BUT WELCOME SURPRISE.
Ding!
YESSS! SO PROUD OF YOU!!
Ding!
Ding!
YAY! YOU DID IT!
MOM AND DAD WERE GENUINELY WORRIED ABOUT ME...
PLEASE GET EGGS, ONIONS... OH, AND...
GOT IT!
WHAT SHOULD I DO FIRST, DAD?
...AND AMY WAS TOO.

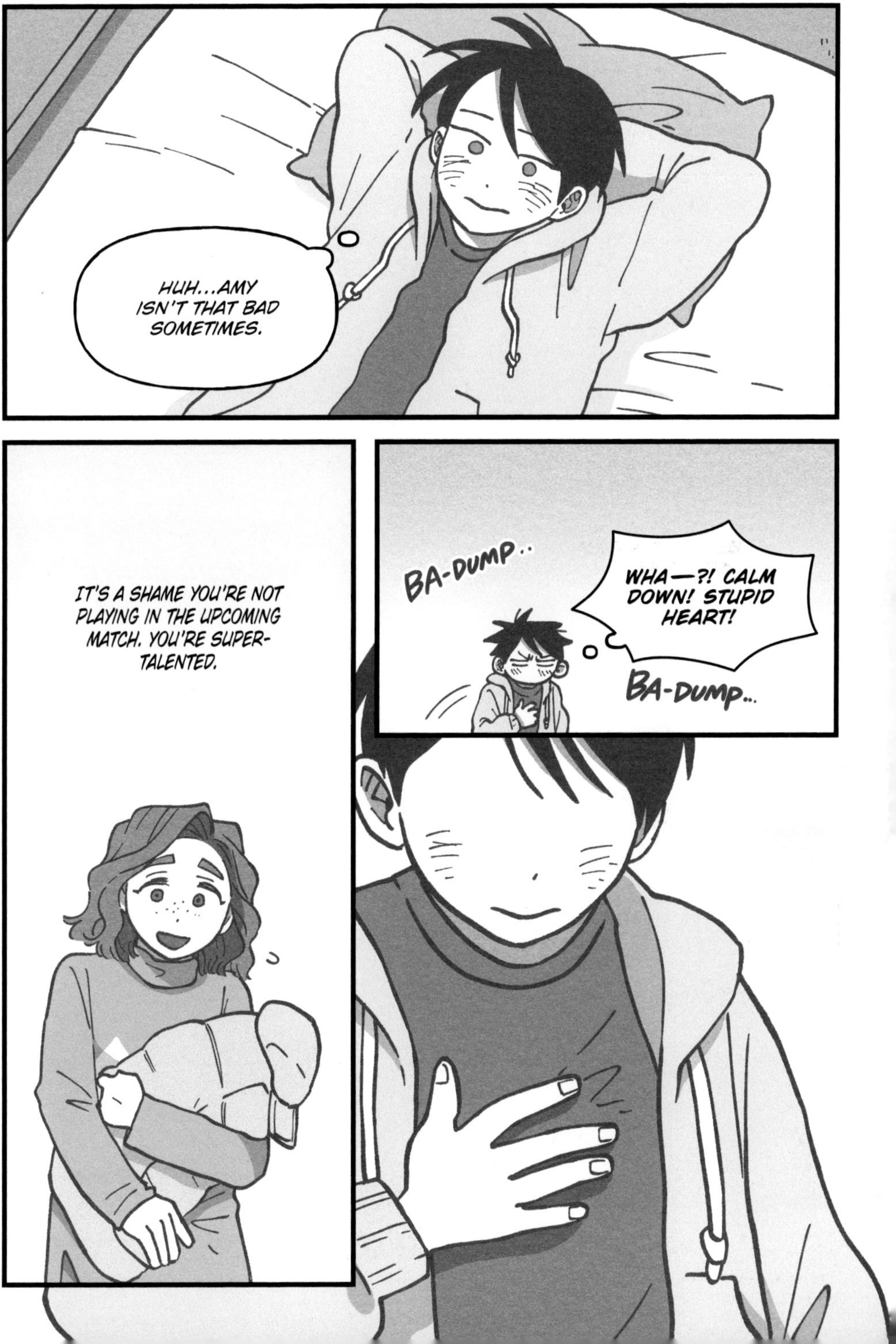
HUH...AMY ISN'T THAT BAD SOMETIMES.
IT'S A SHAME YOU'RE NOT PLAYING IN THE UPCOMING MATCH. YOU'RE SUPER-TALENTED.
BA-DUMP..
WHA—?! CALM DOWN! STUPID HEART!
BA-DUMP...

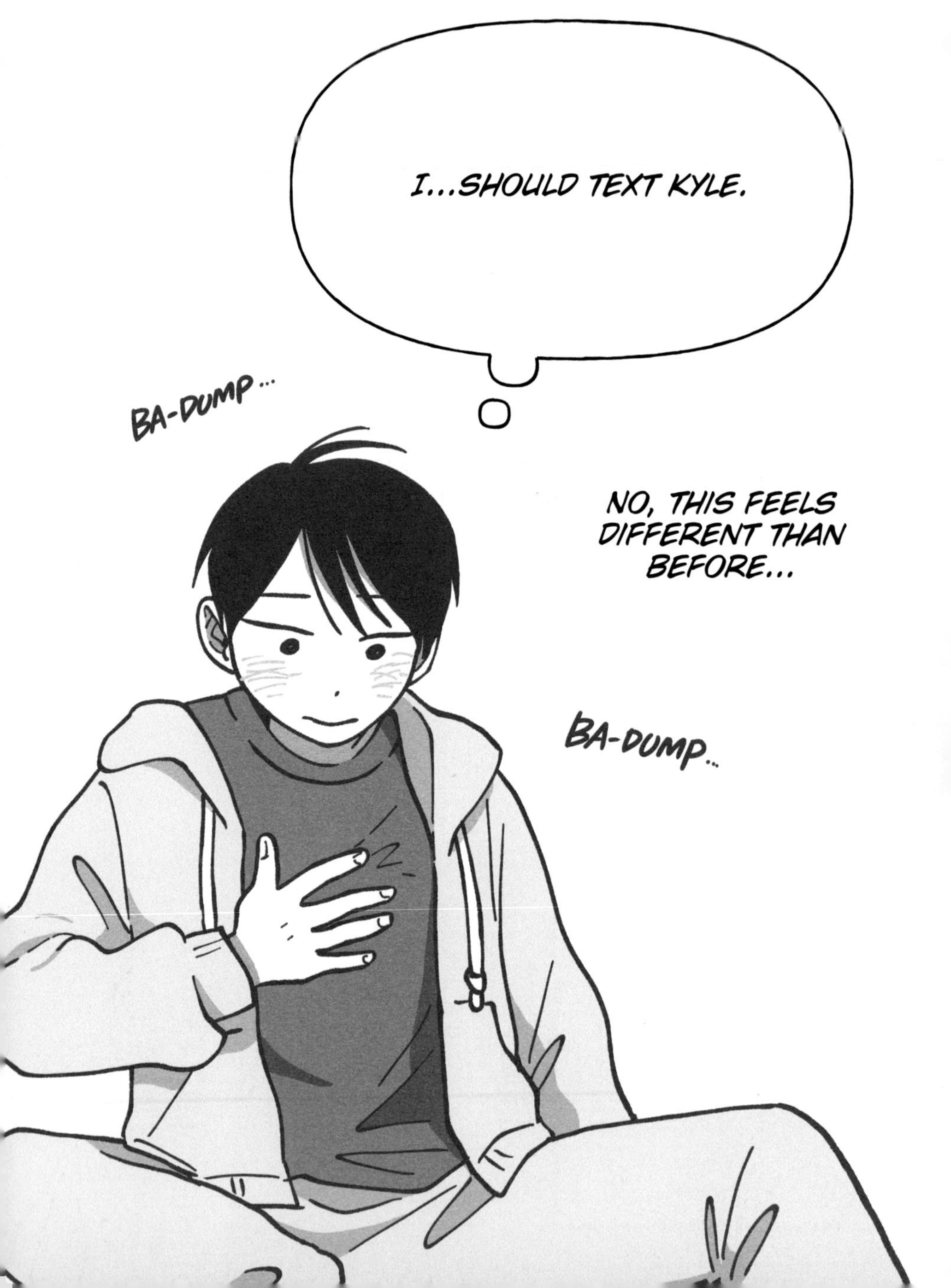
I...SHOULD TEXT KYLE.
BA-DUMP...
NO, THIS FEELS DIFFERENT THAN BEFORE...
BA-DUMP...

I...WANT TO PLAY BASKETBALL AGAIN.

DUDE!!

AMY'S BiG BROTHER
THE END

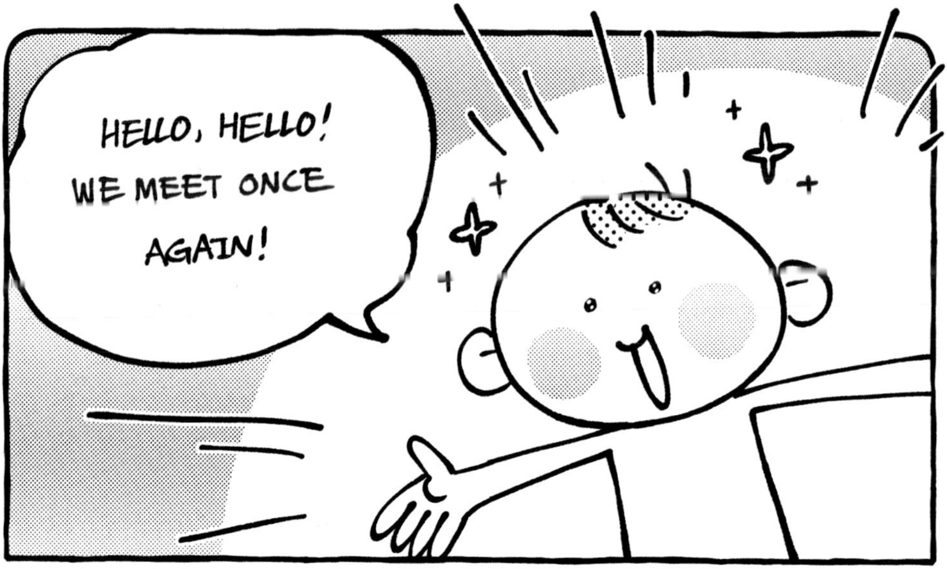
HELLO, HELLO! WE MEET ONCE AGAIN!

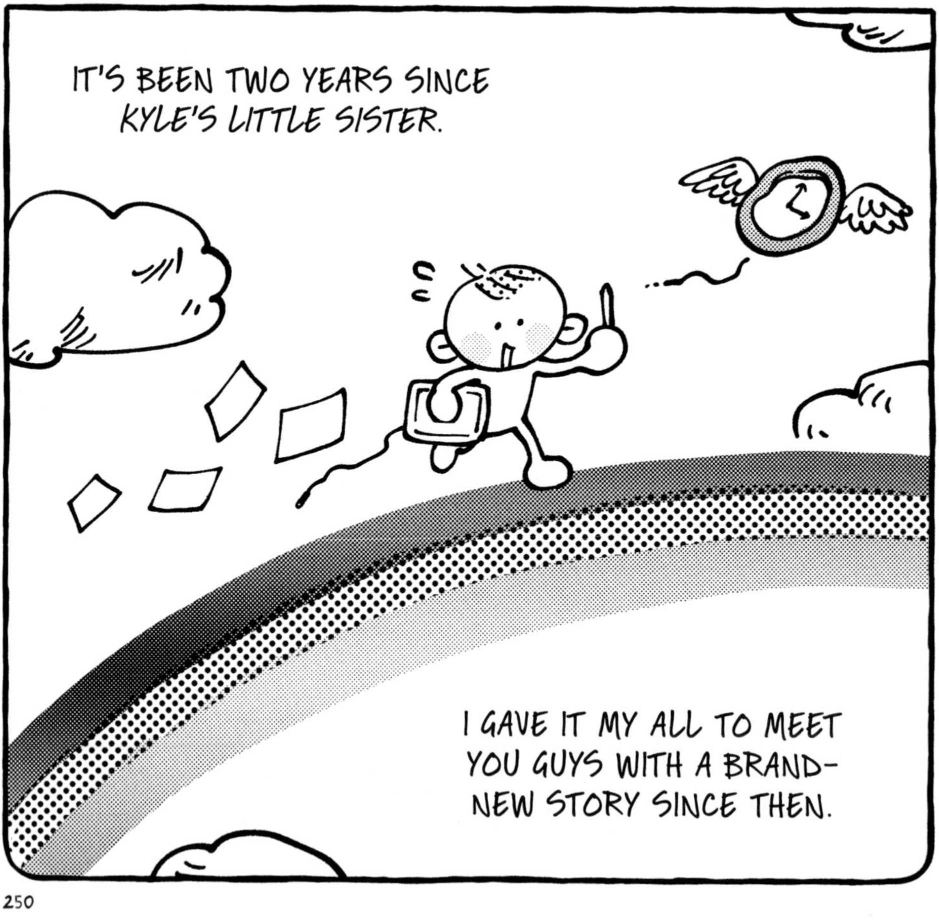
IT'S BEEN TWO YEARS SINCE KYLE'S LITTLE SISTER.
I GAVE IT MY ALL TO MEET YOU GUYS WITH A BRAND-NEW STORY SINCE THEN.

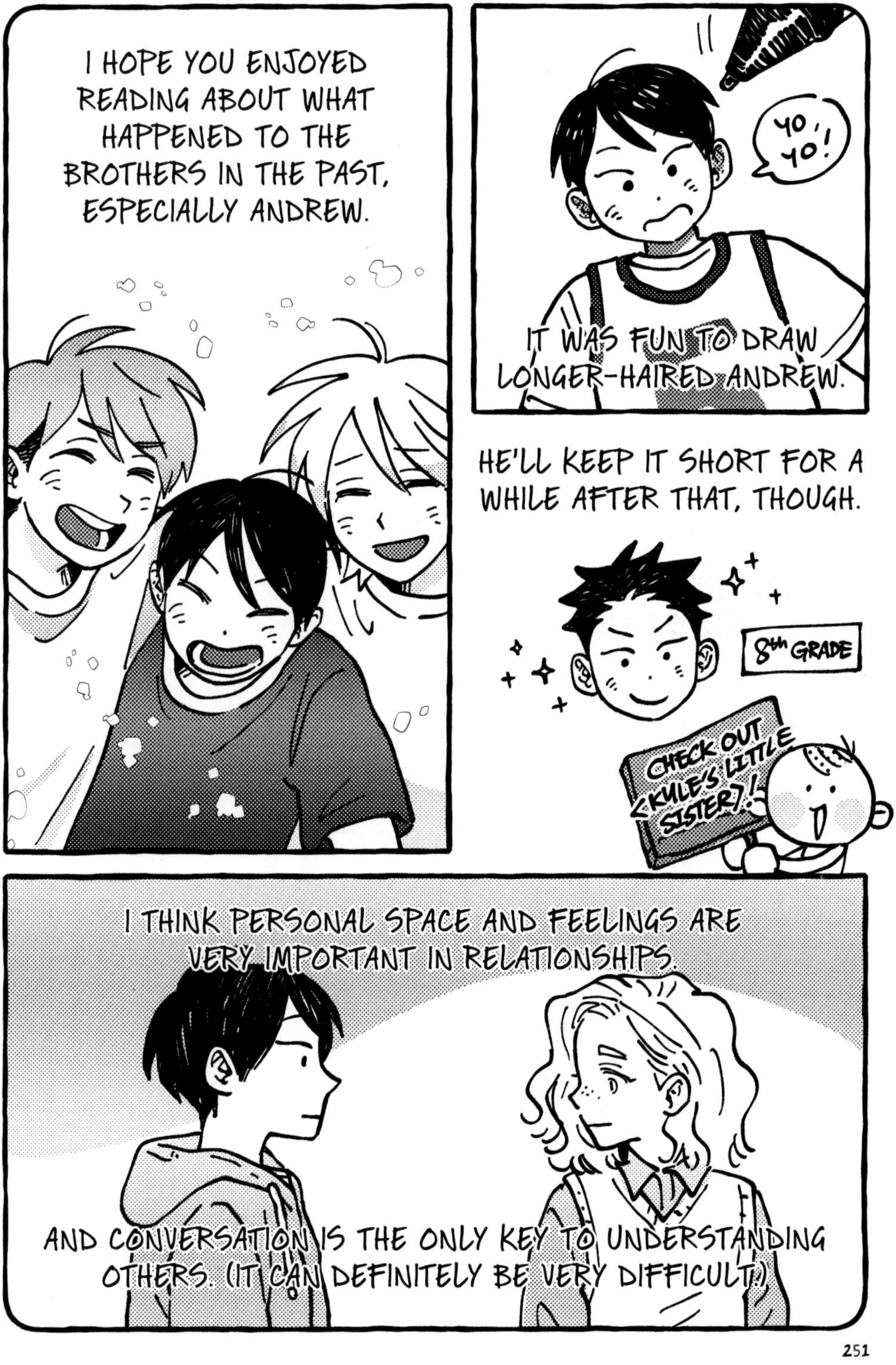
I HOPE YOU ENJOYED READING ABOUT WHAT HAPPENED TO THE BROTHERS IN THE PAST, ESPECIALLY ANDREW.
YO, YO!
IT WAS FUN TO DRAW LONGER-HAIRED ANDREW.
HE'LL KEEP IT SHORT FOR A WHILE AFTER THAT, THOUGH.
8th GRADE
CHECK OUT <KYLE'S LITTLE SISTER>!
I THINK PERSONAL SPACE AND FEELINGS ARE VERY IMPORTANT IN RELATIONSHIPS.
AND CONVERSATION IS THE ONLY KEY TO UNDERSTANDING OTHERS. (IT CAN DEFINITELY BE VERY DIFFICULT.)

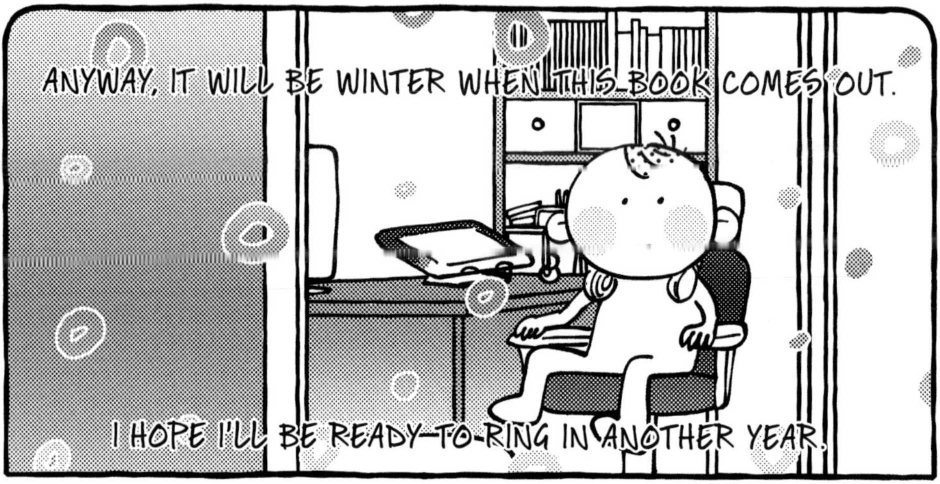
ANYWAY, IT WILL BE WINTER WHEN THIS BOOK COMES OUT.
I HOPE I'LL BE READY-TO-RING IN ANOTHER YEAR.

AND I HOPE YOU GUYS ARE TOO!

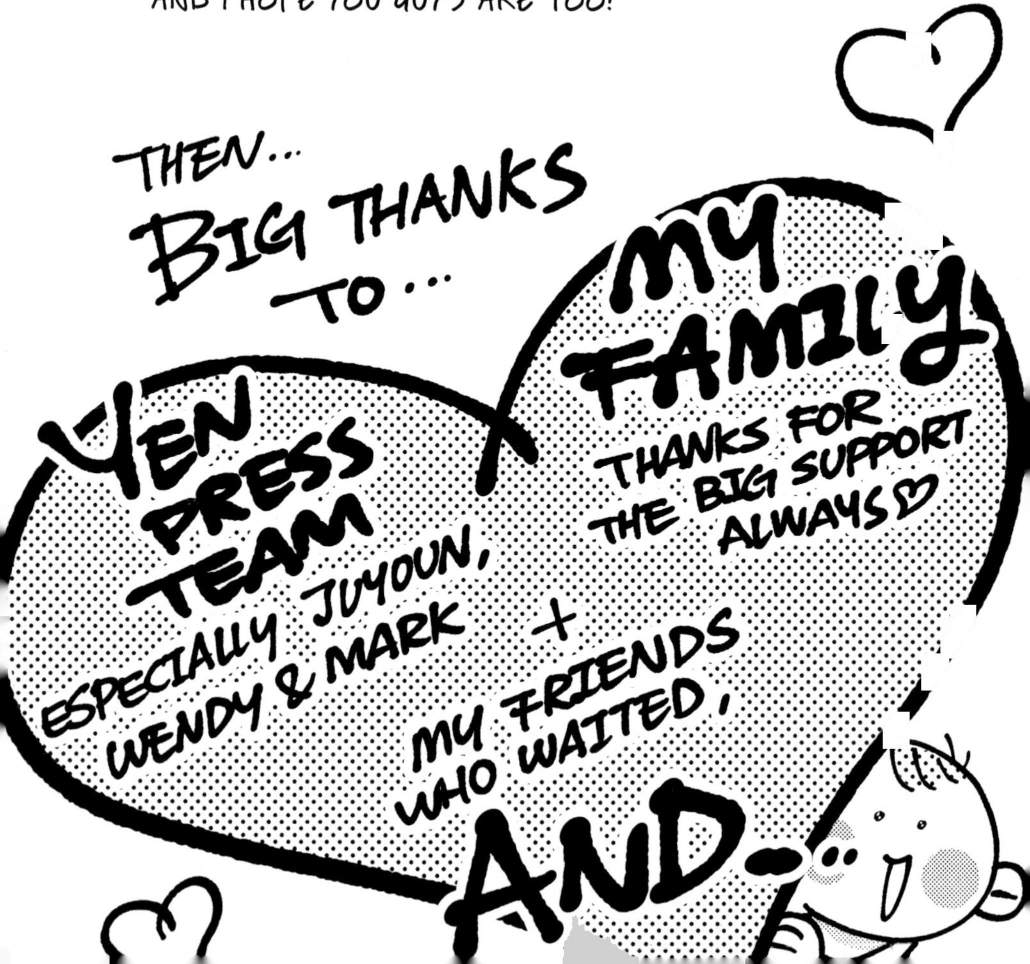
THEN...
BIG THANKS
TO...
MY FAMILY
THANKS FOR THE BIG SUPPORT ALWAYS
YEN PRESS TEAM
ESPECIALLY JUYOUN, WENDY & MARK
+
MY FRIENDS WHO WAITED,
AND-

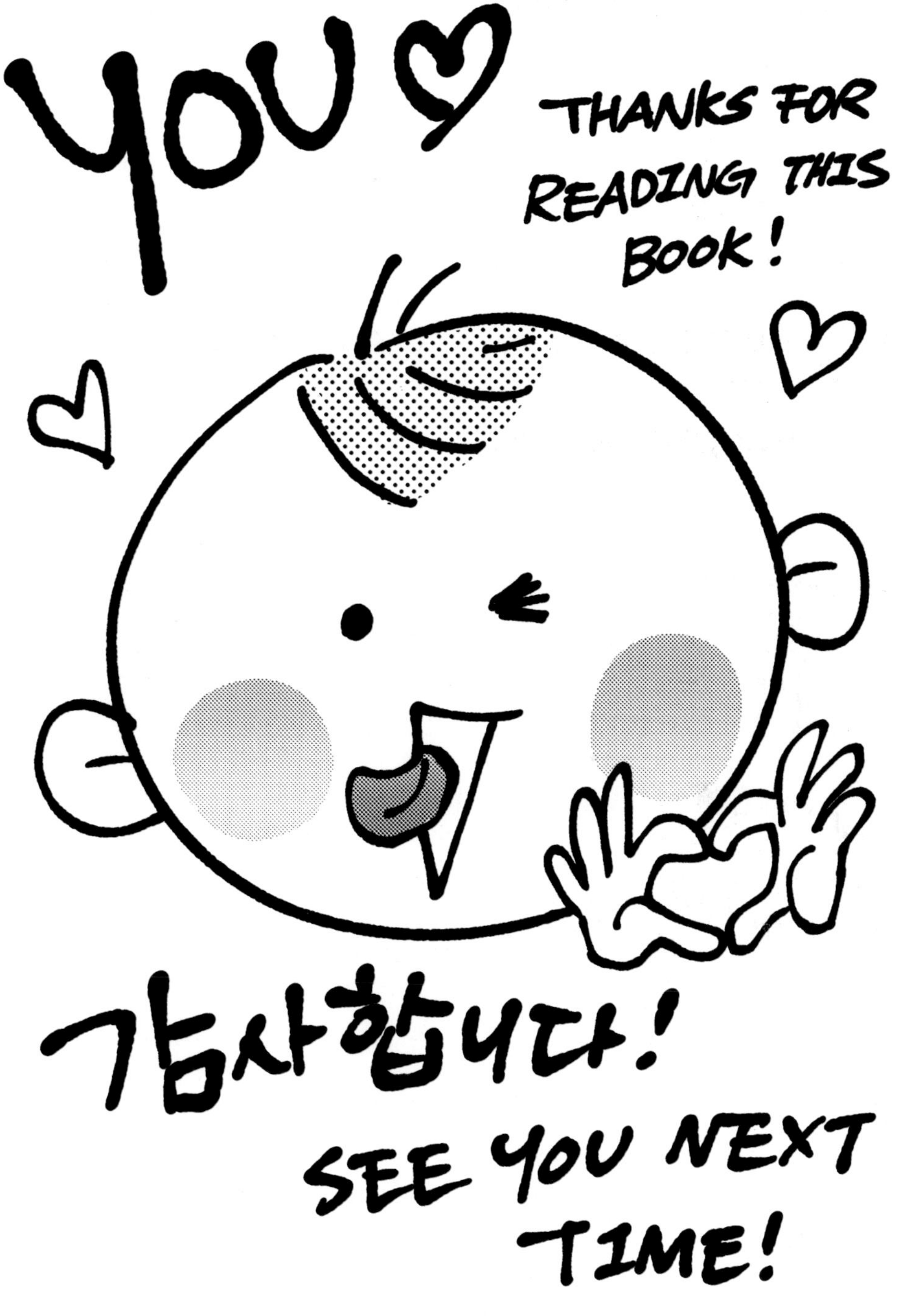

YOU
THANKS FOR READING THIS BOOK!
감사합니다!
SEE YOU NEXT TIME!

AMY'S BiG BROTHER